Whispers in the Wind
(Dead Men Lie)

DAVID T PROCTER

©2016

Copyright © 2016 David T Procter

The rights of David T Procter to be identified as the author of the work have been asserted and established by him in accordance with the copyright, design and patents Act 1988 all rights reserved. Apart from any use permitted under UK copyright law, this publication may only be reproduced, stored or transmitted in any form or by any means, electronic, photocopying or otherwise with prior permission in writing of the publisher, author or copyright holder.

This is a work of fiction, therefore all characters in this publication are the product of the author's imagination. Any resemblance to any person, either living or dead, is purely coincidental and no disrespect, or harm was ever envisaged. Though certain mention is made to historical groups, the necessary permissions, where needed, have been obtained. The author thanks those involved.

Printed and Bound in England by
Biddles Commercial Printing
Castle House
East Winch Road
Blackborough End
King's Lynn
Norfolk PE32 1SF   01553 842477
email: enquiries@biddles.co.uk
http://www.biddles.co.uk

Cover illustration by David Clarke
Edited by Lisa Chester-Hanna
ISBN 97809562056-0-5

Published by
Kentsman Publications,
21 Ingoldsby Road, Canterbury, Kent CT1 3UD
E-mail davidtprocter@mail.com
www.davidtprocterbooks.co.uk
First published by Kentsman publications 2012 ISBN9780956205629
1 **(2)** 3 4 5 6 7 8 9

Part One

The Colonies

January 1770

Acknowledgements

There are many to whom I owe a debt of gratitude. First and foremost I must congratulate my wife Josephine and daughter Halley for putting up with my intolerable moods. Without their constant guidance and motivation I would have faltered long ago. They endured the extremes of this creative process; therefore deserve my undying admiration, respect and deepest gratitude.

My family past and present are my guiding influence; my personality is derived from them. While the family history supplies an unending source of material from which I build my characters and stories. I use their adventures to keep their memories alive.

Colonel Michael Ball of the Princess of Wales Royal Regiment, Regimental Headquarters, Howe Barracks, Canterbury was kind enough to grant permission for the use of the name of the 3rd Regiment of Foot, 'The Buffs', and for assisting me in all things military. To the men of the 3rd Regiment, past and present and in memory of all they achieved, I extend a huge expression of thanks. My respect for them is profound; I trust I have used their name wisely.

One last mention goes to a very special little lady, my dearest granddaughter Alexis Elizabeth Mae Procter. She brightens my every day and is the family's future.

Chapter One
A journey of a thousand miles begins with a single step
Lao-Tzu, Chinese philosopher, 604 BC-531 BC

He was determined not to show emotion, not before such a seething mass of humanity, but he failed. Cuffing a tear aside, he turned away, unable to witness any more of this abomination. Was it only he, who found the hanging of a youth distasteful? Or did the crowd, who watched in sullen, silent anticipation, feel the same? More likely they waited, hoping to witness, even at this late moment, some form of clemency, a reprieve for the boy who was about to die.

Any such hope was dashed, as the hangman slapped the mare's rump. Unseated, Jeremiah dangled, twitching and thrashing as the noose tightened about his neck. A collective gasp rose in protest, as he kicked and fought against his imminent demise. The crowd bayed, voicing their disapproval with threats and accusations directed at the hangman, but intended for the governor ears as well. Few but the closest heard the boy's last muffled sobs.

Stunned at such disregard for the sanctity of life, Samuel could do no more than whisper a silent prayer. He begged God, to end his clients suffering as swiftly, painlessly, and with as much dignity, as was possible. He had no problem with the rope, the act of legalised execution, though unpleasant, had its place. It was a deterrent, the ultimate punishment, it could, however, be administered with a modicum of dignity, if the hangman was experienced and skilled at his trade. Alas, Jeremiah was to be denied even that crumb of human kindness. God, and man, had apparently abandoned him, for the hangman was a cretin, a bumptious fool. The noose, poorly placed, had failed to fracture the neck cleanly, meaning Jeremiah, swung back and forth in excruciating pain, gurgling and gasping for breath as he had slowly strangled. Such entertainment might be enjoyed and exploited, if the felon was of note. Jeremiah was not such worthy entertainment. He was a local lad, known to the crowd, and they disliked his treatment. Seeing the anger, the hangman stepped forward, intending to add his weight to the boy's legs and finish him quickly. He stopped mid stride, as a gasp of horror came from the crowd.

"Look at him," A man shouted, "shite himself."

"Cut him down. Let him live," More voices joined in as they watched a boy disgraced. They grew angry, shouted threats and a barrage of over ripe vegetables were thrown in the direction of the hangman. Apparently unconcerned, he looked at Jones, sniffed the vileness that trickled down the boys legs to puddle upon the ground. It was a normal reaction, the bowels had released their contents, but while the hangman was used to the stench, Samuel felt the bile rise in his throat. He wanted to wretch, but what good would that do. He was helpless, and along with the rest, he watched his client's final, precious moments.

For agonising minutes, Jeremiah choked. Samuel sensed that as his life ebbed away, he wanted them to bear witness to his suffering, to accuse, or at best plead for his lawyer to end his agony. Shamefully, he looked away. He had done all he could, he was unable to help the boy further. The seconds, seemed like hours, an eternity, until mercifully his client, finally expired. Killed by the establishment who cared little for his pain. Jeremiah's, final journey, his last great adventure, had begun.

"May God have mercy upon you and may you find eternal peace," Samuel whispered. He felt ashamed, annoyed, desperate and more importantly angry. Of all the hangings he had witnessed, none had affected him as this one had. *Mindless fools. Wouldn't recognise the truth if it bit them on their fat rumps.*
The law was an unrepentant mistress, rules had to be obeyed. The hangman was a necessity; the guilty, had to pay for their indiscretions. However, this vileness wasn't justice, it was nothing less than legalised murder. True the evidence had been substantial, everything pointed to his guilt and the boy had not aided his cause by remaining steadfastly silent throughout. Not until the final hours had he spoken out and blamed others.

All the while Samuel had tried, in vain to save his life, Jerimiah had stood silent, listening to the evidence, refusing to utter a single word. The case could only have gone one way. The facts were plain, a soldier had been killed, and three witnesses had identified Jeremiah as the culprit. If true, then death was the only punishment. Yet, Samuel, now knew the truth, and still wondered why the boy had declined to refute the allegations. With no option, the court had passed sentence. Jeremiah Jones's silence, had ultimately led to this travesty of justice. The Angel of Death had a new disciple. "Ignorant fools." Samuel cursed. The experience left him drained, devoid of any good intentions towards his fellow man. Breathing deeply, he turned his collar up as protection from the chill wind, and began his journey home.

"Are you proud of your day's work lawyer?" Samuel turned, and saw a man whose face bore pure hatred. His accuser was tall, well built, scarred with tar spots, and wore the coat of a rope maker. In his left hand he carried a wooden stave which, Samuel knew, was used in their work. Rope making was an essential, yet dirty, and dangerous job, carried out on the long straight quays.

"Out of my way sir, I answer not to you, but to a higher authority," The disagreement drew a crowd of angry townsfolk, eager to vent their anger upon anyone,

They had animosity in their eyes, but towards whom? Him, the verdict, the punishment, or did their hatred go far deeper? Only fools were unaware of the rumours and disquiet which plagued the colonies. So far Samuel had avoided openly expressing an opinion, but he could avoid the question no longer. *Was this*, he wondered, *the first flush of civil unrest.*

"Answer to God himself, won't do no good, nor make what append ere any less disgusting." Tar-face stood, intimidatingly, close and held the stave menacingly. He spoke with a passion Samuel had rarely witnessed, these people were known to him, he lived among them, respected them, and was, he hoped respected back. Here though, he was being threatened in the street, for no more than doing his job. Samuel, wasn't particularly brave, but he held his nerve, and forced his way through the gathering throng. Men so enthused with anger, were capable of making rash decisions and terrible errors of judgement. If their anger turned to violence, he wanted to be as far away from this place as possible.

"Scared to reply lawyer...well we are not! You wait; we will seek to redress this ignominy." Tar-face taunted him, while he, bravely resisted the urge to look back. He had expected some sort of reaction, mainly because Jones had acquired a certain notoriety, but had assumed if anything were to happen it would manifest itself before sentence. "See the sort of man entrusted with procuring Jones liberty. Not worth a salt lawyer, useless sop."

Passions were aroused, not only here in Boston, but throughout the thirteen colonies. It was such passions which had drawn excited women to the courtroom. They waited, all day just to catch a glimpse, or to toss food to the youth. His supporters had shouted his innocence, calling for his release. They expected justice, hoped their demands would convince those in power that the real culprits should be punished. That was never going to happen, not without a confession from those involved, and that was as likely as God, appearing before the Judge.

Samuel, was betwixt and befuddled, caught up in the politics of the colony he was confounded by laws issued in London, which required complete obedience. Such laws were implemented by a small minority who had little time for ideals and enforced, rigorously by the hangman and soldiers loyal to the crown. Soldiers whose word was accepted as fact, no matter what the truth was. Was it, any wonder, the Judge had been unsympathetic, unwilling to amend his verdict?

"Shame on yeez!" a woman's voice, instantly joined by others, made Samuel flinch. He expected Tar-face, or one of his followers, to attack him, but they seemed more concerned with inciting the crowd into directing their anger towards those in authority.

"Faking cullies," another voice shouted, reinforcing their displeasure with a barrage of ripe fruit, which splattered among the assembled dignitaries. Sensing this growing anger, Samuel feared for what might occur, their emotions were running high, which, if left unchecked, might turn deadly. All this because of one boy's silence.

"Damn his stupidity." Samuel cursed. He thought himself an excellent orator, a capable lawyer, well versed in court room decorum and master at discovering truth, even when overshadowed by deception. In the past he had rescued victory from the very jaws of legal defeat. Yet this judgment would taint his name for years to come. It would affect his reputation, and turn many from his door. As he moved cautiously through the crowd, such thoughts, made him doubt his abilities, yet he had done all that was humanly possible. Without Jones's testimony he was confounded, befuddled and betwixt. He had tried, had sought clemency, but as the judge had said in his summing up.

"Your client, sir, admits the charge. What is there to delay punishment?"

"Extenuating and mitigating circumstances must be accepted as a reason for clemency my Lord."

"Which must be disregarded due to your client's sullen silence." Those words would haunt Samuel for years to come. It sealed his fate, convinced the Judge of his guilt. Whatever Samuel did after that was doomed to failure, made worse by the Judge's next statement, "Soldiers, even drunken ones, are Crown servants. They operate under the auspices of the King, as such, they must be believed and obeyed."

Such reasoning was, illogical, even illegal but there was nothing he could do, or say to change what had been said. Boston was shrouded in fear, animosity, and politics alive with suspicion and illogical inconsistencies. Jeremiah, through no fault of his own, had become a pawn in the greater reasoning and that was what hurt most. The crux of the matter, the very point he had attempted to make, was that politics were not more important than justice. His arguments had failed, so despite his reputation as a gallows thief, the hangman had claimed another victim and the crowd grew ever more resentful.

"Horse turds," Tar-face shouted. "Scared to take on those able to fight. Instead, these brave men choose children to persecute."

Those dignitaries, who had come to see punishment carried out, wilted under a further barrage of fruit and vegetables. If this disturbance was to be quelled, action must be taken and swiftly. Samuel dreaded what might happen and was appalled to see an Alderman falter, wipe his brow then call out,

"Clear the square! Move them away." The bespattered Alderman reacted in the only way he knew how. He had summoned the only force available to him, the army. It was the worst thing he could have done. Many Bostonians were openly hostile to the soldiers, reluctant to accept that the military were there to protect, not suppress them. Samuel knew that the fear of rioting, civil unrest, perhaps looting and murder made the man act irrationally. Such fear, if not stopped, would see bloodshed, and Jeremiahs death would be forgotten.

"Make ready!" The young officer was young, no more than a child himself, yet he was prepared to commit a heinous crime. "Present!" The situation was desperate; soldiers in ranks aimed loaded muskets at unarmed townsfolk. All that separated them from disaster was a single command. Worthington, stood transfixed as the scene unfolded before him.

Not again, not here, Samuel prayed for sanity as a scene, similar to the one he had read about in a broadsheet, weeks out of date unfolded. That report had detailed in graphic detail, how soldiers had quelled a bread riot in a northern British town. By days end fifteen women, men and children lay dead in a town square. If he didn't act, the same would befall his neighbours. Fear, was the precursor to evilness; it made men act unpredictably.

"No!" he commanded, stepping into their line of fire. "What you intend is wrong. Must force be the only solution? Are we not intelligent enough to put aside such things, to come together and discuss our differences as intelligent beings? Can we not find alternatives to force, to achieve what we all desire, Peace?" His voice, though strong, hid a fear that made his legs quiver within his breeches. Twenty muskets remained aimed at him. The officer was torn as to what to do. He had his orders, lawfully issued, he was on the brink of greatness, one man would not detract him from his duty. "Bad laws, enforced by use of arms, are an abomination in the face of God. I beg of you, think sir, take your men back to their billets and I will speak with these good people. No one desires to see a violation, nor do mothers wish to bury their children. There is no need for such ill feeling to occur, not today, not ever."

His words, though compelling, had, it seemed, little effect. The muskets remained aimed, and cocked. The officer drew his sword and Samuel gulped in trepidation, bloodshed, it seemed was not to be averted. Samuel desired nothing more than to run and hide. He wanted to live, to tell of what occurred in this square. The silence was overpowering, sweat ran down his back, while the soldier, directly to his front, blinked, and mouthed the word 'sorry'. These were by all accounts the dregs of British society, guttersnipes and criminals, enlisted into the army rather than serve their sentence. Yet here was a man, willing to accept, that what he was about to do was wrong. Ignoring the threat, the mob were incensed, they continued to shout abuse; death was but a heartbeat away. All that was required was one word of command and a volley of lead would rip into flesh and bone.

Thankfully that command never came. Common sense, in the shape of the Town Sergeant, prevailed. He spoke to the officer, who paused, then commanded his men to stand down. A moment of panic had been averted, but feelings were so raised that such good fortune could not continue.

"Barbarians," Samuel whispered. The British had not changed, nor most likely ever would. Twenty-odd years ago, he had arrived with the hopes and dreams for a new life. But the old ways had followed, and his world was changing again. Sighing deeply, he realised that it wasn't the place, nor the British, but he that, had changed. His dream had died along with his wife and, strangely, Jeremiah Jones. Disease had taken her, while politics the other. That was proof of the pointlessness of it all. He saw it in the faces around him; fear and persecution were becoming commonplace and Samuel despised it

Chapter Two

"I must congratulate you sir." Drawn from his remorse, Worthington turned to face the man who continued speaking, albeit guardedly. "You are a man of many talents. A tragedy averted, the British humbled. A pity, poor Jones could not be so fortunate. Some might express the opinion that he was much maligned, treated, how shall I say… unfavourably."

"Indeed!" The lawyer remained disturbed by his closeness to death. His demeanour and manners as yet, unrestored to their normal polite disposition. "I fear; I do not share your thoughts concerning my talents, sir. I failed my client, and damned near got myself killed as well. Is that the talents of a sane man?" Worthington enquired as Elijah Forest, a merchant of repute, fell in step alongside him.

"I would disagree, I would say you were both, courageous and honest. You spoke with justification, as you did in court, where your oratory was a wonder to behold."

"Your words, sir, flatter, but would best be used, among those ladies, who seek such adulation." Samuel felt indisposed to engage with anyone, let alone a man such as Forrest. His heart still raced, while his closeness to death made him shake in fear. "Truth is, I failed the boy when he needed my aid. His death could…no should have been avoided. His innocence was obvious to all but a fool…or so I believe."

"I flatter not, but I do concur. I witnessed your persuasive closing statement. It was a veritable masterpiece of passion and common sense, if I may be so bold to say."

Worthington stared at the man in wonderment. Forrest was known throughout Boston, and beyond, as a wealthy, prominent merchant. Of aging years, he epitomised what this burgeoning county had to offer to those courageous enough to grab their chance. He was a philanthropic man, not afraid to show off what he'd achieved, nor, unafraid to speak out, when required.

"You were present; you saw the inequality…the way he was dealt with?" Samuel asked incredulously, for he found it difficult to image any man less likely to attend a trial than Forest. Yet, it was possible, the court had been packed, filled with tobacco smoke, so thick, the judge had ordered all pipes be extinguished, and Forest was a prodigious smoker. If he had witnessed the injustices, he was gratified. "The boy deserved far better than I was able to give. The odds were against him, you saw the way the soldiers bandied together, how they lied. Any right minded soul could see they had been schooled. Yet I could have broken them if only…"

"They were a trifle orchestrated." Forest stated, nodding politely to someone in the crowd.

"Then perhaps you would lend your voice to my own. Together, we may, even now, overturn that travesty and obtain justice. Too late to save the boy, but we might, at least, have his good name restored." The rot that existed within the judiciary had to be exposed, and he would seek aid from wherever it could be found to achieve it.

"I would willingly if I thought it would help."

"Of course it will help, but only if likeminded men like ourselves speak out." Samuel's voice rose, drawing the attention of two women who passed by. Forest drew him close and whispered.

"I caution prudence. Ask yourself if this is a worthy battleground, a suitable time to seek change? Or should you await a better opportunity, when your talents could do more good, on a...broader stage?"

"You speak in riddles sir, I am a lawyer, not a dandy. What care I for posturing and prevarication? My clients ask for nothing more than justice and we, I included, fail them at every turn. The hierarchy is rotten to the core, it has been defiled and corrupted and in so doing, has corrupted the very idea which our fore fathers brought to this new world. No longer can men find security, or prosper through honest endevours. Common sense and right of law have, all but disappeared, it seems, all we have done, is to import the same mistakes that forced those brave souls to leave Britain not that long ago."

"Have a care sir, your honesty might lead you to your own court, not as a lawyer but as a prisoner."

"I sir, care not who hears. Sometimes, I relish the idea of my time in court, to speak openly, and deride those who have brought us to this sorry state."

Forrest, grasped Samuels arm, and raised a finger to his lips,

"Sir, I do beg caution. There are those among us, who would take delight in informing the Governor of your words. In truth, I believe you are too harsh upon yourself. I witnessed an honest, God-fearing soul destroyed through no fault of his...or yours, for that matter." The merchant added solemnly.

"You are too kind, however, we are both aware that Jones was convicted, long before he stood in the dock. The trial was a travesty, a sham, a lie. Such matters make me ashamed of my profession. Justice is mocked sir, my defense was hamstrung, confounded at every turn. A child could see the lies that were told, yet, not one person spoke out, not even my client and that was what hampered me, despite my best efforts." Worthington sighed and shook his head in sorrow. Forest had instigated an outpouring of frustration which once begun could not be stopped. "Soldiers are the scum of the earth, thieves, drunken rogues, liars, the dregs of society. Yet, because they wear the red uniform, they are accepted as reliable witnesses and given immunity from reproach or punishment by a distant King."

"Have a care sir, the King has ears everywhere." Forest cautioned the lawyer when in truth, he wished to hear more.

"I care not who hears. I said much the same in court and was not sanctioned. Nor do I care who hears that Jeremiah's silence convicted him as much as any testimony. Why he did so still flummoxes me as I am flummoxed on many matters pertaining to this case. At least I praise God his mother was spared witnessing that…abomination." Worthington turned and pointed to where the boy still swayed on the rope.

"Indeed." Forest, had no wish to force his hand, but he was aware that the lawyer harboured much resentment and anger. If he could, nudge him a little further, his trap would be sprung. For the moment, patience was required, but if he planted the seed of doubt, then in time a new recruit would either emerge or wither and die.

"Indeed…Indeed sir. Jones was no more capable of committing that act then I am of speaking to the King. Rot his cold black, German heart!" Worthington spat and grimaced at the very thought of being anywhere near the King of England.

"Be careful, my friend, many would consider your tone traitorous." Forest warned, grabbing his arm in alarm, as a squad of soldiers marched towards them.

"Rot his heart as well, Forest…as God is my witness, I have lived by the word of the law; it has been my mistress for more years than I care to remember, yet today, I curse its name." Samuel, paused and Forest saw the man physically sag before he continued. "Not many know that my dear wife died, while I was before the bench in Philadelphia. I was saving a woman from the same fate as Jones. I won that case because I tore the witnesses apart and discovered the truth, yet here, I lost because of lies and politics."

"Have you evidence for such accusations? For as you well know, to accuse without unequivocal proof, is a dangerous course to take…do you have such evidence?" Forest asked.

"What is the use of proof, when it can be ignored as it was in there?" Worthington stated angrily, pointing vaguely in the direction of the town courthouse. "That boy worked his fingers to the bone providing for his elderly mother and his siblings. His diligence was what convinced me to take his case. His silence though…My God, if only he had spoken out I could have acted. Instead, he says nothing, until last evening when it was too late.

"He spoke? Jones told you what occurred. Why then was it not presented?" Forest demanded. This was going far better than he could have imagined.

"Do you think I did not try? I sent a note, begging...begging for clemency, but was ignored. MacTavish had retired, sentence had been passed."

"What did Jones speak of?" Forest asked.

"Of many things, he spoke so eloquently I cried. He told me of how he was protecting his mother and siblings from drunken louts, men so vile they behaved like animals."

"Why did he not speak, are these swine still among us, should the populace not be warned?" Forrest looked around as if expecting to be attacked himself.

"Be afraid Forrest. For even if warning was sent, nothing would be done. The reason being they are among us, they reside in our homes and wear the red coat. They are foisted upon us under this infernal Quartering Act. Men so vile, and evil, Jones thought the devil himself lived with them. He was forced to watch as his mother was ill-treated, and assaulted,"

"Did he not think to speak with the quartering sergeant? They could have been removed?"

"He did. He went to the office constantly, but was ignored. Seems the army does not care what sort of men they foist upon those who must house, feed, and care for them. A disgrace Forrest, that's what it is and for what reward? One penny a month."

"It is. What then occurred to make Jones turn violent?"

"A son's worst nightmare. Returning home that fateful night, he found his siblings cowering beneath the table, while his mother, lay upon the floor battered and bleeding. Two of the soldiers stood above her, one had his belt held in his hand, the reason plain to imagine. Anger, and shame, made him act, his temper flared and he attacked. Why only Corporal White was killed remains a mystery, but his predicament raises the question, how many others suffer in silence, and verge on such behaviour?"

"Too many I would guess. It is indeed a most disagreeable Act. The question I ask, is why could you not get a stay of execution? Surely once the boy spoke, there were grounds to have the sentence delayed, perhaps overturned."

"My sentiments precisely, unfortunately MacTavish denied me even a common acknowledgement of my note. Without his approval, or retraction of sentence, Jones's fate was sealed. It seems that our sainted and venerated Judge, believed the statements of those other soldiers, took their word as Gospel, and sentence was ratified. You were there, you heard what was said. 'An acquittal, might, under certain circumstances, be seen by those who defy the King and cause a soldiers death, as a means of securing their innocence,' Worthington had found the words derisory then, and still did.

"I am not surprised. I doubt MacTavish had any intention of listening to your plea, he is noted for his... inflexibility. Though I was surprised he did not heed your impassioned plea about the marks about the mother's body. Why?"

"A pity you did not sit in Judgement, for it would seem, you, were the only person present paying heed of my defense." Worthington sniffed and wiped his nose on his kerchief. "The marks were deemed of no consequence. I though, believe they were significant, and should have been taken into account. Unlike the prosecutor, I do not believe she harmed herself, for her bruises were distinct, consistent with the shape of a man's hand. My belief is that someone, more than likely, this Corporal White, held her tightly, while engaging in carnal lust. Be the act premeditated, or accidental, like as not White killed the mother, and his friends compounded his lies with their own. I said as much in court and was rebuked, while they stated she was simply clumsy."

"A clumsy cow, if memory serves," Forest added helpfully, "and that she had made those marks herself while gathering water."

"Hummmph!" The sound was derogatory, a guttural contempt from deep within Samuel's throat. "That was when I knew I was beat. It repulsed me to see the army closing ranks; protecting their own and sacrificing the boy. I would even dare to suggest that members of the jury were bought, and that too repulsed me."

"That would not surprise me at all. Too many seek a life of quiet existence without the army disturbing their solitude. It is a dangerous path they take, for some see such allegiances as questionable."

"Aye, tis an ill wind that begins to blow." Samuel mused, while Forest pressed him further.

"Jones's silence still begs many questions, surely you advised him to speak out, to tell his story?" Forest asked. Worthington, shook his head in mystified dismay.

"That was his choice, and I had to respect his direction. Though, I believe, the inexplicable death of his mother, finally made him speak, but by then it were too late. Megaw's statement that she died of some 'miasma' was also too...convenient. What would he know? He's pickled more often than not, wouldn't know miasma from measles. Oh, I know, the superstitious amongst our brethren think it comes in on the ships; 'The Devils Kiss' they call it, but are we really to believe that?"

"We must. Megaw is a respected surgeon." Forest stated pompously

"Respected by whom, the innkeepers?" Worthington's anger was such that he sought to lay the blame at anyone's door, and the doctor, was as good as anyone. "She never died from some foul invisible air, but at the hands of a killer. Her death occurred because of the injuries inflicted upon her by White. Jones knew this, yet chose not to speak of it until it was too late. Personally I believe he wished to protect others, but condemned himself in the process. Without one of the dead speaking, we will never know."

"That is the end then, add Master Jones's name to the ever increasing number of innocents indicted, and convicted, in the name of justice." Forest spoke sadly as he turned to walk away. The crowd was dispersing, the spectacle completed. Jones would hang for perhaps a week as an example to anyone who defied the King's laws. Importantly, Forest had information to pass on to those that mattered. Worthington had confirmed to being disillusioned, a man his group desired.

"I could have saved him, but he was more scared of them, than he was of death." Forest stopped, Worthington it seemed, was a man tormented by his failings, a man who had accusations and recriminations to make against those who had failed his client. If that was the case, then maybe the solicitor was closer to turning than he had envisaged.

"Could you? I doubt that, not here, not in this climate of foulness?" Forest waited for Worthington's reply. Depending upon what he said, would confirm if Worthington was a disciple ready to be inducted, or simply a man, frustrated by what had occurred. A man who spoke in anger at a case lost, not a radical who desired change.

"Is there not? Do you truly believe that? For if that is so, why do we bother? Surely that was why our forefathers came here. Were they not seeking a better life, free from persecution and tyranny, to build a life that would benefit those who followed them? Mark my words, if we do not force change, then more will perish before we see freedom." Worthington's voice rose to such a level that Forest was forced to act. Taking hold of him, he led the lawyer towards an alleyway between a smithy and a laundry house. Two men of influence, hid in the shadows and spoke of things that could land them upon the gibbet as sure as night followed day. Never had Forrest imagined such humble beginnings for insurrection

"I urge prudence sir, such matters spoken too loudly have a habit of reaching the wrong ears." Forrest cautioned.

"I say nothing that can be interpreted as treasonable." Worthington stated, as Forrest paused, considering his reply carefully. When he spoke, his words were whispered.

"If only that were true...Samuel, I ask, do you know of those who would advocate the need for change in the accepted order. If so, would you agree to such a statement?" It was time for Worthington, to think carefully before replying.

"I might, though I would urge caution, for such a statement, if overheard, would endanger that person, and any that listened." Worthington admitted candidly.

"Of course it would, but have you never considered, albeit when alone and in the privacy of your own counsel, how better off this land would be under self-governance?"

"I have pondered the possibility." Worthington confessed. In fact he had considered such events on more than one occasion. Until now he had kept silent, but a man had to be blind, or insane, not to have seen the leaflets distributed by the separatists. The King was draining the enterprise from the colonies. Each year brought a new Bill, a new Act, which took money back to England, restricting growth within the colonies.

"You are not alone. There are many prominent people who ask the same questions. Some are prepared to speak out, others seek more progressive methods. All, though, are united in the same cause." Forest paused and inhaled deeply. This was when he would discover if he had chosen well. "Would you be prepared to join their struggle?" There, the invitation had been made. Now he must wait, would Worthington be tempted, or would he call out for the soldiers? Might the merchant's next meal be his last, exposed as the traitor he was?

"What you speak of is treason, the punishment for which is death. I should summon the guard, have you arrested. However...I am mindful of what you have proposed" Worthington paused, reflecting on what to say next. "Your words are intriguing enough to make me curious to hear more. If I were to show interest, I would need to know who, these so called idealists are. I would wish to meet and discuss our mutual thoughts."

"That could be arranged...though they would seek to know in advance what your response might be if such a thing was to happen?" Forest enquired anxiously.

"It is too early to say, but certainly I would hear their arguments both for and against. More importantly, my discretion would be guaranteed"

"Mutual trust is the life blood of our cause. Of course, I have to discuss this with others who will decide. You will be contacted when their decision is made. For now, return home, await our word and I implore you Samuel, remain vigilant. There are those who would desire nothing less than to discover our group." Forest nodded politely, turned and walked away. His heart soared, he had another recruit. Samuel remained a while longer wondering what he had got himself into, nor could he be sure but as Forrest turned the corner he thought he heard a faint tune drifting upon the winter wind. Samuel had made a pact; he hoped he would live to see its outcome.

Chapter Three

The days that followed were fraught with anguish and indecision. He spent his time wandering the streets, invariably drawn to where Jeremiah still swayed upon his rope. Often, he simply stood, and reflected upon what had occurred, before returning home, where invariably, he slept fitfully, pondering his response, in case Forest summoned him. Four days after the hanging, Samuel was accosted by a man who appeared vaguely familiar.

"Aint pretty is he, will get worse 'afore he's cut down. Bastards want us all to learn from his mistakes." Samuel remembered him, he was the rope maker, Tar-face, only he appeared calmer, more rational, but no less frightening.

"What! Yes. A terrible outcome, I did all I could. I could do no more."

"So you say." Tar-face frowned, and shook his head. "I reckon, many would follow an educated man like you. No disrespect meant, sir, but there's much more you could do, if you listened to your heart, not your head."

"Perhaps?" Samuel whispered as he experienced such clarity of thought, he was left breathless. It was as if, God himself had lifted the veil of denial from his eyes, as if, the blight which had overshadowed him since Jones's death had been removed, and he knew what he must do. Fate had shown him which path to take, it might be dangerous, it might be adventurous, but he knew his life would never be the same again.

One week later, Samuel, sat beside a roaring log fire, in a secluded tavern. He was still unsure whether he were a fool or not, but he had done as commanded in the briefest of notes, delivered to his home under cover of darkness. Who made the delivery was unknown, but he suspected Forest had a hand in its conception, if not the delivery. The words had been simple and precise, *'Be at the Woodsman Tavern at seven, of the evening of the fourteenth of this month.'* During the past seven days, he had pondered the wisdom of his actions, but finally, he'd acquiesced.

The journey had taken longer than imagined; he had walked, for reasons, which remained lost, even to him, but he was glad he had done so. Self-consciously he waited. An hour later, he contemplated leaving, no one had approached, and he tired of their games. .

"Your name Worthington?" the tavern keeper whispered, placing a glass of ale before him

"It is," Samuel replied.

"This is for you," a scrap of paper was passed, which Samuel, held below the edge of the table, and read, while drinking his ale.

"Go to the crossroads on the high road." He paused as a drinker passed, *"Take the left fork and three miles further on you will come to a gnarled*

oak tree. Your destination will be the house in the valley below. Be there 'afore nine. You will be expected."

"Is it far to the crossroads on the high road?" He asked.

"An hour, less if you have a horse," Samuel thanked him, drank his drink and left almost immediately, arriving a little before the allotted hour. Pausing within the tree line, he considered his options once again. To continue, meant he was more than interested, to falter, and return, would mean he was no better than the cowards that had hung his client. Decision made, that first faltering step set him apart from many others. Despite the fact that fear made his heart race, he had a fire in his belly which needed quenching.

Brookside House, was a fine building, more ornate than he had imagined from where he had first seen it. Built in the Queen Ann style, it was more suited to the Shires of England, than the colonies. Ornate gates separated the house from the countryside, giving the impression of both strength and isolation. Torches illuminated the driveway, while candle-lit windows sparkled like fireflies in the gloom. Pushing one squeaky gate open, he entered the grounds and walked cautiously up the drive. His progress was hampered by lingering doubts, he still had time to turn, run, and never speak of this again. That was what the lawyer in him advised, his heart, though, forced him on, to discover if he were man, or coward.

Standing upon the top step, in front of a pair of oak doors, it was obvious Forest had wealthy friends. It was a known fact that many an intrigue had been born in such places, paradoxically, many a treasonable plan had also been discovered, simply because the establishment looked upon landed gentry as constantly at odds with those in power. Breathing deeply, he wondered which would occur here. Finally, he knocked and waited, moments passed, time in which he felt his legs quiver in anticipation, until finally, the bolts inside were drawn, the doors opened, to reveal a bewigged and liveried servant. Samuel swallowed deeply and stated,

"My name is Worthington, I am expected,"

"Sir." The servant was polite, not the least surprised by his late arrival. "Might I assist you with you topcoat?" He asked after closing the door, he bowed graciously, took Samuel's hat and coat and placed them upon a hall table. "The other guests await you in the white drawing room, if you would follow me." Only then did the small sword, worn about the man's waist become apparent. Decoration, or defense was yet another question Samuel hoped would be answered soon.

"My Lords, Gentleman, Mister Forest's guest, Mister Samuel Worthington, begs your indulgence, and seeks an audience." Samuel desired to laugh; the servant would have not been out of place in some European grand house or palace. Here, his manner seemed, ostentatious.

"Samuel, my friend," Elijah Forest said pleasantly, stepping forward to greet his friend. "I was wondering if I had made a mistake."

"No. It was I who had misgivings," Samuel replied truthfully.

"A wise man always questions his motives yet you decided to come. I am glad." Forest led Samuel towards the group. "Allow me to introduce you to the others." It was not unusual for Worthington to meet influential clients, or to stand in rooms which exuded opulence, but even he was in awe of the grandness of his surroundings. Portraits and landscapes adorned the walls, along with rich tapestries. Delicate tables, with fine filigree legs, supported silver candelabra; beneath his feet, was a rug of such richness, he thought it would swallow him to his knees. Brookside House was clearly the home of a man who liked, and appreciated, the finer things that life offered.

"Gentlemen, may I name my particular friend, Mister Samuel Worthington." Forest smiled broadly, as he proffered his guest to the assembled guests. Such an outward show of exuberance, was what drew Samuel back to the reality of his situation. He was, it seemed an adornment, a gift, to be preened over, and examined, he was not overly happy to be the centre of such attention. Twelve men acknowledged his arrival, some enthusiastically, some with muted reservation. Samuel accepted their uncertainties with due reverence and the merest of bows.

"Sir, you are most welcome. Forest has spoken well of you," a particularly elegant gentleman said, greeting him warmly. "He informs us you are sympathetic to our cause."

"Perhaps, perhaps not. I have reservations and require those to be quashed before I commit fully. However, if you ask, am I disgruntled by the manner in which the King treats these colonies, then yes, I do agree?"

"Disgruntled? A strange choice of words, sir, one that portrays annoyance and nothing more," another guest stated solemnly.

"My dear Otis, words can be so…arbitrary. What you perceive as paltry, to another borders upon a sense of outrage. My apologies, Mister Worthington, may I name our punctilious friend, Mister James Otis." Samuel inclined his head in greeting. The man Otis, was known to him by reputation, they both practised law, but Otis, was better known for his outspoken articles in the broadsheets.

"A pleasure, sir, it was with a sense of alacrity that I read of your speech in Boston. The words, No taxation without representation, were inspirational, exactly what I have thought myself."

"I was particularly pleased with that, though, I fear, it has become something of a rallying cry." The man Otis, answered. Samuel sensed unease, akin to shame, that his words had become to mean so much.

"No, it was exactly what needed to be said. The King assumes we are fools, assumes he can continue fleecing us of all we have, yet allows us not a word in our defence. It requires men of standing, men like your good self to speak out, to inform His Majesty that we are close to penury that, enough is enough." Perhaps it was the ambience, which made Samuel feel at ease and able to speak of matters he would normally remain silent about.

"Forest, where have you been hiding your friend, for he is both wise and knowledgeable. Have we not said as much, have we not attempted to make our views known?" Otis appeared overjoyed to have a new convert to speak with. "We tried, the Boston merchants, attempted to boycott English goods which attracted ludicrous levies. We are all aware of the results." The group nodded, as if it had been a personal attack upon each of them.

"Forgive our friend; he is never short of things to say," injected the elegant man who was obviously homeowner and host.

"Is that not our reasons for being here?" Otis asked fervently. "To think radically about what we have endured, and contemplate what can be done? My God, sir, as you well know we are being swamped with new Acts and Bills. This latest Stamp Act, brought in without consultation, will ruin a good many. It has doubled the cost of everything, yet we can do nothing about it. Our governor, is nothing more than the King's lackey, who implements each new idea without a word of complaint. For pity's sake, are we to do nothing while we are bled white? Mark my words it will only become worse!"

"Take care, my friend," their host warned. "We are aware of your feelings. But I implore you; allow our guest at least a moment to get comfortable 'afore you abuse his senses with your views. Gentleman, as time, I fear, is our enemy and as we have much to discuss, I suggest we begin." Gesturing towards the large mahogany table, around which were fourteen chairs, they took their places, Samuel sat opposite his host and accepted both cigar and wine when offered. Once all were ready, their host spoke. "Gentlemen, I name Samuel Worthington of Concorde. I am told that our guest is a notable lawyer of like mind."

"You agree the British should be disposed from these shores once and for all?" Samuel turned, noticing that the speaker was far younger and, if his clothing were anything to go by, of lesser financial standing than the others of the group. Something about him reminded Samuel of himself as Jones had swung on his rope. This youth was full of passion and believed that wrongs were to be righted. "Mark my words gentlemen, Britain will deal with insurrection in the only way she knows how, force of arms. We see it even now; the slightest murmurings of discontent, bring redcoats to quell our words and deeds. Why are there more than eight thousand troops on our shore if the King is not concerned? I will tell you, they fear losing the wealth we generate, more importantly, they fear losing this land to a more powerful adversary. I hear Britain is close to war with France, if that occurs we will be drawn into their fight. They will expect us to join them, despite how they treat us. We should deal with them now, while we can. Rise up I say, throw them out and keep them out."

"Mister Penn, I do so urge caution. Your words will surely upset our guest." He spoke with a hint of joviality, but Samuel sensed mild irritation, "I fear, sir, some of our members are a trifle spurious of the King's reasoning for sending us so many troopers. What we seek, what we hope to achieve, is a peaceful means of convincing the King that he must treat us with the respect we deserve."

"With the deepest respect, My Lord, you are a fool." Penn stood and for a moment Samuel wondered what their host's response would be. In this brief exchange he had learnt much, that there were issues to be resolved, that not all shared the same goal, and that his host was of noble birth, all very revealing.

"I concur with Penn, Kenardington. What you desire will never happen" Samuel baulked. He couldn't be sure, whether he was merely in the presence of a group of likeminded men who feared for their livelihoods, or as he supposed, members of the group known throughout the colonies as 'The Sons of Liberty'.If the latter, and if this man was truly the Earl, then he was in the presence of a very select group. Their name was spoken in hushed tones, no one admitted to being of, or knowing anything of their existence, yet they grew bolder every month. Word was, they sought to break away from England, form a new, self-sufficient and independent country. Samuel knew he would be asked searching questions before this evening ended and as yet he wasn't sure as to how he would respond.

"It must," the Earl countered. "Our future lies with, but not enslaved by Britain. The King must be convinced to relinquish his stranglehold on our economy. Without that freedom and the ability to govern ourselves, we will forever be paying vast amounts into the English coffers and receiving little in return."

"You speak of mutiny at best, rebellion and treason at worst, sir." Samuel spoke with trepidation which made his voice tremble. "I must caution against such action, for to continue, might see you all face the hangman."

"Your concerns are justified Mister Worthington. Treason is indeed an ugly word, yet sometimes, it is all that man has left. Throughout our history, men have strived for change against tyrannical regimes. Such men, have risked all in their efforts to gain, for others, the liberties we have come to expect. Such actions, such personal resolve, are now defined in our very being. We cannot impose our will upon you, for that would make us no better than those we wish to quell. Only you can do, as each of us has already done, examine your conscience and decide, if it is treasonable to want to live without fear of reproach or exorbitant taxation. Is it treasonable to want the freedoms those intrepid pilgrims sought when they arrived in this land, seeking freedom from persecution? When I was granted this office, I swore an allegiance to our King; yet, even I, am prepared to consider the unthinkable. The King restrains us with unfair laws and taxes, we are governed by fools, who are blind to what is amiss. Worse still, we are shackled by an army, which acts more like they, not our elected representatives are in control. No, sir, what I speak of is not treason, but liberty, a freedom to speak openly and not in secret, a freedom from oppression, the ability to think for ourselves, while enjoying the protection the King offers." The assembled men listened intently, nodding in agreement as the Earl finished.

"Well said, my Lord, but such wonderful words mean nothing, unless we have the strength of will, the desire, to proceed with what has been previously discussed." The speaker, Samuel noticed, was a stylish man whom he recognised immediately. The colonies were small, and talented silversmiths were few and far between. "The flow of money from our purses to the King's coffers must slow. Each month my position becomes more untenable; commissions are decreasing to the point where it will not be worth working. I say the time has come; we should proceed with separation, issue our declaration, and tell the fat German where to go."

"My friend, we have broached this question more than once, each time our deliberations end the same; with no firm decisions," the Earl spoke as if he grew tired of this subject. Yet Samuel sensed something had changed. Was it the sideways glances in his direction, the way such men spoke without fear in his presence? Whatever the reason, he listened intently as these men openly spoke of matters, most, would never dream of saying within their own families. "We are not in a position to rise in open rebellion. To do so would invoke severe repercussions. My God, sir, militarily we are at a disadvantage. Our forces, comprise militiamen, farm boys and tailors. Stout hearted and committed for sure, but how long would they survive against seasoned troops; days, weeks, one battle? The British are everywhere, they can reinforce from north and south, they count their cannon in scores. While, not a day's walk away, is a powder store, so large, it could keep those cannon fed for a week and make the ground shake in trepidation. What could we do against such power except grovel in the soil for protection?"

"Destroy it, blow the damn thing apart. A few dedicated men could remove it forever and leave the garrison almost useless."

"What if we did, what would the British do? I'll tell you sir they would move heaven and earth to find those responsible and not care who they hanged in the process. Would you desire to see your wives and children strung up? Of course not, which is why we must restrain ourselves until we are better prepared, or see our brave men slaughtered, wasted, to lie and rot, and feed next year's crops on their blood. I say no, no blood shed until we have no other option. In its stead, we should use our intelligence, not our resources. Mister Worthington maybe our best, possibly only chance of success."

"Me? What, pray, can I do?" He had not expected to become the object of sudden notoriety. To be spoken of, so candidly, implied he had been discussed long before his invitation had been issued.

"Travel, sir. You alone can move without raising suspicion. Upon your shoulders, you must carry our hopes, our aspirations. Take our dreams abroad, discover, and recruit, those who share our commitment to a new beginning," Kenardington said easily.

"I...I can not..." Samuel stammered. It was ludicrous to ask, how could he leave Boston, for countries he hardly knew? It was a strange conception for he had assumed he would never leave these shores.

"You can, and you must, sir," Kenardington insisted. "You see, you are unknown, you would be ignored, able to travel wherever you desired. We on the other hand would be watched, questions would be asked, our plans possibly discovered, or betrayed. You see sir, unwittingly, one tragic death may save countless others. We are entrusting our future into your capable hands. We implore you, sir, to carry our message to others, take our message of hope to those that matter and bring them to us, so that we may, by Gods virtue remove this intolerable yoke from around our necks."

"You ask much," Samuel replied. "The enormity of what you desire is mind staggering. If I were discovered, I could disclose your names, to save my own, is that the risk you are prepared to take?"

"Grant us the intelligence to judge character Samuel. From the moment Forest, mentioned your name. We have watched, and asked about you, we have delved into your past. We know more of your character, than perhaps you do yourself. Of all we have discovered, one trait is spoken of more than any other. That is loyalty, which is why we are safe in the knowledge that, should you accept our ordinance, you would do all in your power to protect those here. No man can have such faith, as from those, whom, he holds so dear, which is why you were invited here. Of course, in accepting this assignment you will be well rewarded. However, if you accept, there are certain arrangements that must be made."

"What arrangements?" It felt as if he were upon a slippery slope, from which there was no escape and must be ridden until a conclusion was reached.

"If you accept, Samuel Worthington dies this night." The statement left him gasping for breath. Kenardington saw his concern and reassured him,

"Have no fear, no harm will befall you. Forest will orchestrate some plausible explanation for your disappearance, while you will be hidden until your travel arrangements can be made. As for your name, that dies also, you must travel under a nom de plume. What would be a suitable name? That is for you to decide, for you will become that name, live with it, breath it. Upstairs, you will find suitable attire, and a loyal servant to assist you. When you are ready, you will be taken to a woodsman's shed where you will remain while arrangements for your journey are made. When we deem it safe, you will join a ship, and sail for England. Hopefully, you will be enroute in less than a week."

Samuel, was befuddled by the speed in which events were moving. Until a few hours ago he had been nothing but a provincial lawyer, now he was to become a spy, and spies, he knew were hanged.

"I see your concerns Samuel, but do not worry, you will be assisted every step of the way. Meanwhile, take this." The Earl handed him a sealed note. "Inside are instructions for my agents in London. That document will allow you to draw cash which you will use to further our cause, use it wisely. Meanwhile during your wait for transport, learn these names," he was handed a sheet of parchment, "They are friends, willing to assist our cause. Consign those names to memory; do not speak them again, for they will be of interest to the British and could see you hanged."

"Who are these people?" Samuel asked

"Men who will guide you to others, equally so disposed. Nurture such men, recruit others, and obtain what we desire, men, weapons, money. For if we do rise, we will need all you can obtain and more."

"Is that what you desire? Open rebellion?"Worthington asked. "For if that is your quest…I would have to relinquish my desire to assist you. I am a man of the law, yet you openly ask me to contravene those principles I have sworn to protect. I cannot condone treason, if that is your calling, then, I fear you have approached the wrong man. I am sorry..." Samuel rose, prepared to leave, but hesitated as Forest implored him to remain. The merchant's words were passionate, calm, each chosen for their impact. Elijah reminded him of why he had come, and what had prompted his disgust.

"None, would wish you to contravene your principles, yet each of us has had to look deep into our souls, to justify our presence. Be it our overburdened businesses, or, more personal reasons. Whatever the reason, each one of us is present because we feel we can do more, for our fellow colonists, than by doing nothing. Take yourself Samuel, only last week, I witnessed in you a struggle as that youth, Jones, was hanged. His crime, nothing more than defending his family. You felt his pain, and did all you could to aid him, I ask you, can you not feel the pain of those you live amongst? Are we not attempting to aid, not only ourselves, but our neighbours, are they not our family? More to the point, do you believe that boy was convicted in the name of justice? If so, then I want no part in legalised murder. Our King is supposed to be our protector, yet he is squeezing the very life out of us. He sees the colonies as a lucrative sponge which can be wrung out, sucked dry, then discarded. You said yourself that Jones had been dealt an unfair hand, that his fate was decreed long before sentence was passed."

"I did, and still believe so. But I fail to see what that has to do with this?" Worthington asked.

"Everything, Samuel, that boy was fighting for his liberty as much as we are. We are being suffocated beneath myriad laws and legislation. Perhaps, we will suffer the same fate, but know this my friend, our deaths will fuel another's sense of injustice. From our ashes, will spring hope for a better future." Forest's words brought a burst of applause from those gathered. Samuel was never more confused, but had to be sure before deciding.

"You truly seek a peaceful resolution...not conflict?"

"My dear fellow," Kenardington replied, "we do not desire any form of confrontation with our King. He is our Lord, or protector, but he must be made to understand exactly how we feel. With your able assistance, we will seek to rectify our differences by diplomacy, but we would be fools not to be prepared for the worst. If diplomacy fails, and a struggle ensues, then so be it. We must be ready for all eventualities."

"I'm sorry," Worthington interrupted, "how can you say that the King is to be respected, yet concede that conflict is inevitable."

"Look to your own misery, Samuel. You have seen how our people suffer and will continue so to do if change is not forthcoming. It is time King George, heard our cries." Forest implored, his passion was such that Samuel knew he had no recourse, no doubt as to where his loyalties lie.

"I truly hope the King is guided in our favour," the Earl stated. "But should events overtake us, if the King refuses to hear our pleas for clemency, what would you rather us do? Lie down and accept our fate? Or be prepared to fight for what we consider to be our birthright?" The Earl waited, head inclined in question as Samuel deliberated. There were so many questions that needed answering. Questions, which Samuel had considered, but always while alone. Now he was being asked to choose, and they sought his answer immediately. Was he being irrational? He knew what these men were saying was precisely what he had thought himself. They were just more willing to speak out whereas, he had not, as yet.

"Fight, of course," Samuel finally replied. The die was cast; he had joined them.

"Good man. Bravo!" Kenardington was enthusiastic. "I knew you were right for this, the moment I first saw you. If we have to fight, we must win, or die. The King will offer us no quarter, will not seek to parley. Our one chance is to take him to task, grab his manhood and squeeze until he cries out in fear at our capabilities. There will be many problems to overcome, the first of which is our army or lack thereof. While the British are strong, we are weak. Nor can we rely totally upon our fellow citizens, some will surely side with the King. Add such sympathisers to the army already here, and we will be hard pressed to win anything, without further assistance. Which is why Samuel, we need your strength, your forthrightness, your honesty. We must seek allies from beyond our borders, even those, we have fought against. You must go into the world, find like-minded souls willing to render assistance; that is your task." There, the offer had been made, and the Earl's question hung unanswered while Samuel considered his reply. The silence was almost palatable. One route would condemn him as a traitor, the other a coward. Which could he best live with? Finally, he looked at the assembled men and said clearly…"You can and I will."

"Then pour the wine. We have much to discuss before the night is out. Personally, I dislike seeking aid from the French, but France would be a useful place to begin. They will side with anyone against England, as will the likes of Spain. Look also to the Dutch, the Scots, and Irish, all have been persecuted. If they believe our cause just, if that is to be our destiny, they will join us and we will need all the friends you can find."

* * *

One week later a ship sailed from Boston harbour. Samuel Worthington was no more, the man he had become travelled under a new identity and carried the aspirations of men, eager to discover an identity and freedom for a young embryonic nation.

However, unknown to him, or the Earl, his departure wasn't the secret he would have liked. He had been identified; messages about his departure were carried swiftly to the offices of the Governor of the Colonies. Who added his name to a secret dispatch which was sent, via a naval Frigate, to England.

Samuels's task, would be allowed to proceed, but he would be watched. Wherever he went, agents would make note of who he met, such meetings would be investigated and reported on. The plan, instigated in Brookside House, was already doomed. The 'Sons of Liberty' had underestimated the British, something, they would never do again.

Part Two

Stormouth England

Jan 1773- March 1773

Chapter Four
*The only thing necessary for the triumph of
evil is for good men to do nothing*
Edmund Burke 1727 -1797

The woman shuddered beneath her cloak, not because of the cold wind that blew in off a slate grey sea, or the snow, which refused to yield its grip on the town, but through trepidation. She feared the imminent arrival of a man she loathed and despised. Behind the cotton kerchief, hid a smile, but now wasn't the time to display such relief. Lowering her head, in feigned respect, she tried to look suitably remorseful. Her devil would soon be gone, she would be free, while his time in purgatory would begin with the insects of the ground feasting upon his vile, putrid, rotting flesh. Her heart soared, she was rid of him, but her happiness was interrupted by a voice which drew her back to reality.

"Sorry for your loss, ma'am," Edwin Shawcross stated, knuckling his forelock in a mark of respect.

"Thank you. Pray, inform your wife I will call upon her, to thank her, for her kindness."

"I will, ma'am," Shawcross smiled as she clasped his hand, and surreptitiously slipped a coin into it. Times were hard, yet the priest had added to the man's hardship by imposing a penury fine upon him. His crime, to defy the priests, demand that everyone should remain indoors until the cortege had passed. Shawcross had opened his door, to allow smoke, from a choked flue, to escape. Her small token would pay for a sweep, a mere gesture, but it would annoy the priest, nor was it something either he, or the deceased would have ever contemplated.

High above her head, the tolling bell sounded. Its solemn note, reminded her of others she needed to reward. Confined in that eyrie, men would sound the death bell, from dawn, til dusk. For their service, the family, via the priest, were being charged six pennies. She neither trusted, nor liked the Reverend Bayles, she was sure he would deny them their wage, and pocket the lion's share. Which was why, like Shawcross, she had added the bell ringers to her increasing list of people to reimburse and reward. The town, was unfortunate to have two mean-minded souls residing among them. Neither rector, nor deceased, would have thought twice about men like Edwin, or the poor souls who slaved away high above them.

"My condolences, ma'am. My thoughts are with you all on this sad day."

"Indeed..." She smiled graciously, but the sight of Ida Furnell filled her with an all-consuming hatred. Overdressed in mourning garb, the woman appeared distressed behind her black veil. But, Funnell's intentions, like her own were she guessed less inclined towards respect or reverence. Some, a rare few, would attend to pay their respects, while most would be present to gloat, to make sure, he was really dead. Ida Furnell, if the rumours were to be believed, came for both duties. It was said, she and the deceased had shared more than tea and cake, that she paid her rent in kind, not cash. On the other hand, as the best seamstress in town, she had cause to be cheerful. With the town cut off by heavy snow, she had surpassed herself, making a tidy penny from the mourners who needed her skills. "Thank you for your diligence. My father-in-law would have been pleased."

"My pleasure ma'am, Mister Wood was a fine gentleman," the seamstress stated, bobbing in a curtsey, so exaggerated, the woman desired to laugh at Ida's obvious discomfort. But she restrained herself, placing her kerchief across her face to conceal her mirth. As wife of the deceased's eldest son, she had position and status. Yet was a curiosity, attracting both jealousy and curiosity, from the wives of other leading residents. Her every move, every word, was anaylsed, pulled apart, and vilified by the likes of Ida Furnell and her female customers. Yet they all came to see him buried.

"Indeed, he was. His passing will be difficult, but we will give praise for his life." It was an act, played out, not on a stage, but in the street, before an audience who, watched and waited for the moment a polite comment, turned to barbed contempt. Few, of them really, knew the deceased, for Joseph Wood was two men within one skin. Outwardly, he was known as a difficult, but decisive man. Staid and solemn, but ruthless in business, and harsh with those who betrayed him, yet given to unbelievable acts of generosity to those who he loved. She, and his sons, knew a different side to him, a cold-hearted devil who would do anything to get what he considered his by right. The woman beneath the mourning dress, had attracted his attention, which was why she despised and hatred him. One day, she would expose him for what he was, but not today, for the moment, she would remain silent, bide her time until she could destroy his name forever. Once the swine was buried and he could harm her no longer, the town would learn of his immorality.

"If I be so bold, ma'am you look well, radiant in fact." The seamstress glanced at her curiously, as if seeking some…hidden titbit of information.

Not for the first time, Abigail was thankful for the quality of the seamstresses work, for not only did it keep the chill from her bones, but also disguised her hopes…and fears. Despite her problems she had to retain her poise, elegance and compassion for everyone she met. She dispensed kindness in both words and deeds to rich and poor alike. Her beauty outshone, even that of the squire's wife, Lady Caroline, which, she knew, had caused more than one wife to chastise her husband for looking longing at her as she passed. If her tormentor had been here, he would have admired her, despite the sombre colour, but he was dead, cold, and soon to be forgotten.

"Not sickening I trust, ma'am?" Ida Furnell's qualities far exceeded her skills with needle and thread. Her abilities with the first, meant her work was as good as that found in London or Barminster. However, her gift for extracting information, meant her shop was where the ladies congregated, and where the price of taffeta, was interspersed with the latest scandal. *It was good someone had profited from such a day. But I will not become their next prized talking point,* Abigail thought while smiling graciously. The secret she carried, if revealed, would keep Ida, and her gossip mongering friends happy until next Christmas. In that respect they were no different, information was important, it fuelled their narrow-minded lives, while she desired to know what made Stormouth so intriguing.

"I am well, thank you, though I will be glad to see the end of this terrible day, and this infernal winter. Each day feels colder than the last." The mention of the snow, which had blanketed the town since before Christmas last, would, she hoped, do much to explain her healthy glow. There would come a time when she would no longer be able to conceal her condition. Until then, she was determined to keep her own counsel.

"I said to Mrs. Jones, only the other day, that you were blooming…When is Master Nathaniel due home?" The question made her shudder. Outwardly, she appeared the dutiful daughter-in-law, but as she pulled her coat tighter, she knew women, like Furnell, would soon realise. She wasn't naïve, her youthful years, were not an obstacle to understanding how the world operated. She knew of many families destroyed, because a secret which should have remained concealed became common knowledge. Such destruction, she was determined, would not afflict them. Her secret must remain just that, to fail would see their good name ridiculed and pawed over in the taverns of the 'Butts'. Dabbing away a tear, she wanted this day done. When she saw the casket descend into the grave, she would be pleased, for then, only she would know, and she would make sure, it died, also.

"His homecoming is expected this summer, though much will depend upon his ability in locating a suitable cargo and the predisposition of the tides."
Abigail doubted if that homecoming would be as pleasant as most might predict. It wasn't because people wanted to cause trouble, but that within this small town, everyone, either knew, or were related in some way, which made secrets very difficult to keep. Any husband, would find it difficult to imagine their wife had not been a willing partner in the crime. Why then would

Nathaniel, as Wood's son, not believe she had aided her predicament? That was far easier to accept than the truth. No, son, no matter how loyal, would comprehend a father's indiscretion. Which meant, Nathaniel's homecoming would, to say the least, be difficult. Which posed the question, *how had Joseph managed to keep his traits secret?* Abigail had spent many a night seeking an answer to that question. Surely, Joseph's status, would have invited gossip, but Furnell, had remained uncommonly silent on the matter.

"Then we must pray for fair weather and a swift return."

"Indeed we must. His safe return is what we all desire." Abigail, smiled but sensed that the woman knew more than she revealed. Had Joseph spoken of her predicament during their nights together? Or was it simply that women sensed such things? Now was not the time to ask, but to simply endure. "We would deem it an honour if you returned to the house afterwards." Abigail hated herself for what she was forced to do. The funeral was a duty, which, she would reluctantly, the gathering afterwards, was what she dreaded. Would she be able to conceal what that old goat had left her with, would those who knew him best recognise her condition once her coat was discarded?

Some, those who disliked her, would say she had brought this upon herself but truth be told she had become a victim of Stormouth's isolation. Family and town, were equal partners in the same dilemma, wealth, and poverty, existed side by side separated by one steep hill and a set of strict and well-defined rules. The wealthy, like Wood, Columbine and Richardson, lived in grandeur around the church, atop the hill. Those, further down, in both position, and status, like Ida, resided upon the steep streets leading down to the harbour. Together, merchants and traders, controlled the majority, the workers and the destitute. Those unfortunates were crammed into a rotting shambles around the docks known, collectively, as the 'Butts'. She had never visited, nor had any desire to, but if Ida, or any other realised what she hid, her life would be ruined. She would be shunned, by those who came to pay court to her today.

To avoid the ignominy of that vile place, she desired, craved, prayed for her husband's speedy return. Only he could give her condition credence.

"Please accept our condolences, my dear a sad day for us all." Her recollections were interrupted by the appearance of a couple who deserved, and expected, her undivided attention. Sir Stanley Cobb was both the local squire and largest landowner, but it was his wife, who wielded the most influence among Stormouth's society.

"You're too kind, Sir Stanley." She curtsied formally, only for Lady Caroline to reach out and assist her back to her feet.

"Not today, my dear. Formalities seem inappropriate; however, we will speak, anon."

Abigail, bowed her head, and inwardly sighed as they moved away. This day was difficult in many ways. She was required to grief for the loss of an animal, yet retain her dignity, while hiding the exuberance she felt. She wanted, nay, desired to climb the bell tower and scream her delight to the world that Wood was dead. That would have been pointless, she would be carried away, committed to some asylum as a lunatic, and Wood, would have gained his victory. That was something she would fight to deny him.

"Madam, I must offer you my condolences, but beg leave to speak with you before day's end."

Once again Abigail's thoughts were interrupted, this time by the appearance of an odious man named Edwards.

"Indeed," Abigail replied. "I am touched by your courtesy Mr Edwards." She accepted his proffered hand, with reluctance, for the butcher, even when dressed in his finest clothes, had the smell of death about him. Why such men as Edwards attended, was perhaps, the measure of Joseph's influence, or more likely, the power of the priest to cajole and persuade, those who would rather have remained at home. For if truth be told, Joseph and Edwards would have had little in common. One was trade, while the other, held sway over the merchants with his influence. Normally, Edwards would have drawn neither, a second glance, nor a single word, from Wood. Today though, the man was brazen in his approach and his request.

"Distressing that he passed away so quickly, distressing for you, his family, and for those with accounts unpaid. I assume you will be dealing with such matters in due course?" Abigail looked him in the eye shocked by his audacity. Summoning her last vestiges of dignity, she spoke with the contempt he deserved.

"Your impertinence is uncalled for, sir, especially at such a time. I would have expected more...respect. If you have outstanding business with the family, then present your bill. We will deal with it...but at a more appropriate time. For now we have a father to lay to rest. Good day, sir." Abigail, seethed, at his impertinence, but also because, she guessed, he would be the first of many who would demand payment from her. Wood was renowned for his lateness at settling his debts. If she was to retain any credibility, she had to appear defiant in dealing with this...upstart. Sarah, would have verbally abused him, or struck out, daring him to ask again, for such was her manner. Abigail could not, for she had to remain serene and dignified. Instead she turned away, cutting the loathsome creature dead. Public humiliation was sufficient, to do more, risked questions being asked, questions she had no wish to answer.

"The cortege has begun, ma'am." A youth, no more than fourteen stated, knuckling his forehead. His appearance and breathlessness, reminded her of why they were here. *The devil approaches.*

"Thank you boy, here a penny for your time." She handed him the coin and felt her heart leap. Now was not the time to show the joy she felt, but within the hour, perhaps three at most, all would be done.

"A cold day, madam, more snow in the offing." She recoiled in horror as Bayles spoke. The parish cleric was an odious toad like man, who haunted, repulsed and frightened her, he was the embodiment of all that was unholy ...yet, could also be charming, in a sly like manner. "Be gone boy you're not needed."

The youth backed away, and Bayles remained impassive. His face revealed nothing of his thoughts, he was, apparently devoid of emotion. But, his eyes were the mirror into his cold black soul, and they revealed that Reverend Bayles felt what...fear, revulsion, retribution? She would need to tread carefully when dealing with him for he was a man who played a mischievous game.

"A Godly presence, Joseph would have been well pleased." Bayles smiled for he had been specific upon every aspect of the day, to the point where, Abigail had wondered if he, and not the family, were in command. Stormouth, had heeded his words, save for the tolling bell, and those attending the internment, the town was silent. No one walked the snow-covered streets. Not a single child giggled in joyful amusement. Even the fishing boats remained tied to the quays. They did so, through fear of a man in black, a man who held their souls within his grasp. They did as he commanded, or risked his justice.

"Indeed, he would, Reverend." Abigail replied. She didn't feel like speaking, certainly not to him, but niceties had to be observed, while above them, the bell tolled on.

Chapter Five

"Damn them once......"
"Damn them twice...."
"Damn them thrice." High above the town, two men in their small, dusty eyrie, set the rhythm of the day. Their task, for which they were to be paid one penny each, was to ring the tolling bell. To sound its mournful note across, both town and nearby marsh, at a precise measured interval, from dawn til dusk.

"I see 'em!" The ringers, foul assistant shouted. "Coffin must have left. It will take some time 'afore it arrives, but the priest and the missus await it in the gateway. Shame ain't it? Mrs. Wood's, too young to wear mourning garb."

With a lecherous smirk, he bit into a soft-boiled egg, his third of the day. Runny yolk dribbled from his mouth, to join that which had already found a home in his grey beard. He coughed, then farted, expelling a cloud of noxious odour. He then cackled manically as his friend grimaced in annoyance

"I curse them once…"
"I curse you twice…"
"I curse your foul arse thrice…" After each cadence, the bell ringer laughed demonically, as the weight of the bell lifted him from his feet. But that was their only merriment, their task was to remind everyone why today was so solemn.

"Aye Mathew, but think. The swine will stench far worse in a week or so. The worms will feast on his vile flesh, and you will finally be rid of him."
The bell ringer grimaced, eight hours of such noxiousness, would, he was sure, see him on a gallows, for throwing his foul friend from the window.

"Broke many a man once…"
"Flogged a good few twice…"
"Rot in hell thrice…" Mathew chanted but felt elated and for good reason. Joseph Wood, worked his men til their bones ached, then drove them on til they dropped. Mathew spat as he remembered the merchant as a cruel, vicious employer who delay paying his workers. It was how he operated, and nothing could be done, except pray that other merchants found them work next day. Not that it ever changed, men like Richardson and Columbine, dealt with Wood, so no matter who paid, the wages, invariably Wood had a hand in who got what, and when. Today though, while the town waited his final journey, Mathew smiled as he rang the death bell which sounded across the rooftops until carried away on the chill breeze.

* * *

"A fine attendance, no less than we would have expected." The vicar's voice made her shudder. Dressed entirely in black from wide brimmed hat to shoes, Bayles was, in her opinion, an odious, sinister man, the apparition of death, yet, he would lead the coffin, from gate to church. "His final resting place has been prepared within the chancel." His voice was little more than a whispered sneer, as if he considered everyone to be beneath him. The sort of voice that implied much, be it contempt, disapproval, or perhaps, that he knew more than he desired to reveal. It was such implications that made him so dangerous.

"Thank you, a most fitting location." Abigail replied.

"It is the least we can do for someone as revered as Mister Wood." She shuddered at the mention of that name, and the close proximity of another man she mistrusted and despised. But decorum decreed that they waited beneath the lych-gate together. Two people, who outwardly mourned a man's passing, but who, in fact, held vastly differing opinions of the man they were to bury.

"Our thanks must go to the sexton. Pray, pass this on and express our gratitude." Abigail pressed a guinea into his palm.

"Most kind, madam, I will make sure Cole, receives it as soon as we conclude our duties here." Abigail smiled and thought, *No you will not you sanctimonious old goat. Master Cole, and his men, will never see any of the coin. It would be added to your purse without a second thought. That is why a joint of beef will be sent to the sexton, as a reward for burying Wood nice and deep.* As they waited, lost in the solemnity of the day, a chill winter wind whipped across the town, bringing with it a fresh flurry of powdery snow. Despite her clothing, she shuddered as her problems were reawakened in stark clarity. The kiss of the snowflakes, reminiscent of the tears she had shed in her room.

"May I comment on how well you appear, positively blooming, in fact, a picture of health." His words, so similar to those used by Ida Furnell, caused her to shiver in nervous anticipation of what he might say next. Was this co-incidence, or were the gossips already at work? Only now, on this most wondrous, yet distressing of days, did she notice how he resembled the name the children had given him. Behind his back, out of earshot, they referred to him as 'Raven' apt really, considering his beady, black eyes, and hooked nose and like a Raven, Bayles was almost malevolently intelligent. Though, she had spied him, on more than one occasion, leaving Joseph's home the worse for drink.

"I fear it is naught but the chill wind that flushes my cheeks." She declared, not wishing to give him anything with which he could use against her. The rector was known for his ability to gain information, from those he thought held secrets. His use of guile in discovering what others wished concealed, was why his sermons attracted such large attendances. His parishioners came, not because of some pious need for spiritual fulfillment, but to witness who Bayles had chosen to castigate from his pulpit.

"More an inner warmth, Madam, a glow which God, has so rightly bestowed upon you. One can, but hope that in the fullness of time, our community will celebrate more cheerful news." The Reverend Bayles smiled graciously, but the implications of his statement were not lost upon her. The Devil, was sly like a fox, while it was known throughout the family that he and the deceased spent many a night alone together, doing what though? Both were so different…yet so similar. She was unable to comprehend why such men were attracted to each other, nor could she work out why they enjoyed their friendship. In her opinion though, neither could, or should, ever be trusted.

Dabbing away a tear, not of sorrow, but of anger, she tried to appear as calm as possible. The family, was to whom she would seek comfort in the coming months, for only they could protect her from the vilification which would envelop her, when, no if, her horror was revealed. Her course was uncharted, Wood, had been a man most feared, including his remaining sons. If she spoke too soon, she would be denied, castigated and ridiculed. Fear of losing their inheritance would keep them silent, until that was theirs, they would deny knowledge of their father's deviant ways. Could she pass judgment? The simple answer was, no.

"Is it not gratifying to see so many eager to wish our friend well as he makes his final journey?" Her head snapped round, the priest stood, fingers interlaced, staring at the assembled gathering, apparently, unconcerned that his implied accusations had caused her to react. "We can, but hope, that his memory lives on. That an issue, is forthcoming sooner…rather than later."

"Indeed." She could say no more. Her heart beat faster, she perspired, felt the onset of the vapors. In that instance, she realised that Bayles knew. Her confidence drained away, as all hope died within her.

"Indeed. I shall miss him, for he was a good friend. A godly man, incapable of doing harm to anyone. Would you not agree, madam?" There it was, the implied accusation, delivered with a sly, inquisitive glance, and a smile. This day was becoming a travesty, yet it must continue. Bayles, she guessed, knew, but would he make it known to others? Or would he keep it hidden, to use against her when he deemed the time right?

"The family will certainly feel the loss of his presence, but will others? Pray forgive my insolence, Reverend." She saw his disapproving glance, and hastened to make amends. "I simply mean there may be those among the other merchants, who will see his demise as a means of expanding their own businesses. Mr Columbine, for example, has, from what I understand, always coveted the family's position. I doubt if he will mourn father's death for too long."

It was an unnatural conversation to be having, especially while surrounded by mourners, who dressed in their finery, heads, respectfully bowed waited in the bitter cold, for a coffin to pass. Was it right that they sparred like this, neither willing to disclose what the other knew, or suspected. In the week's preceding Josephs death, Bayles had visited the house often. Ample time in which the old goat could have condemned her, while purging his guilt before his friend and confident. If so, he would have embellished his version, while belittling her character.

"Men will always covet that which is denied them." Bayles stated solemnly, "But with Gods, guidance, most rarely stray from their rightful path. Those who seek to acquire what was his, will find the family reluctant to relinquish that which is theirs." Bayles frowned, while Abigail wondered if that was correct. The town was present, but was that simply because the cleric had demanded it? Most would have been ignored by Wood, he had lived among them, but had not been of them. He had been baptised, married, and was now to be buried within this same church. He had served on the town council, had brought wages and shelter to the town, yet he had also kept them where he wanted them, under his control. Most would swear, had been both pious and good, a few though, like Abigail knew him to be a monster, capable of deeds too dark to speak of.

"He was a man of many talents, Reverend, as well you know." She could be as devious as the priest and waited to see if he would take the bait. Not many had witnessed Joseph's evil side, she had, and so had his sons. They knew him as a bully, a tyrant, a man who ruled with a discipline that often boiled over into anger. Away from the respectability he nurtured, in the confines of his home, his true colours were revealed. He thrashed with a vigour that was awesome to behold. His sons, two of whom now carried his coffin apparently so lovingly, carried the scars of such beatings.

"Indeed he was, madam. A man of considerable astuteness to whom many looked to for guidance. I will forever be in his debt, will cherish his memory until God relieves me of life. No man will ever speak ill of Mr Wood, not in my presence." The passion with which he spoke, was such that Abigail turned to examine his face. Was that an admission that he possessed knowledge of matters which he had so far kept hidden? Unintentionally, she pulled her cloak around her, it appeared natural, but it drew his attention. Swallowing the acid taste that rose within her throat, she breathed deeply. To swoon now, would mean physicians and her deception would be revealed. Covering her face with a silken kerchief she fought nature, and tried to calm her beating heart. Those who witnessed her gesture would assume she was mourning the man they awaited, but Bayles saw her discomfort, and smiled discreetly.

"We owe him much, Reverend, some, more than most."

"Indeed we do madam, myself included. Which was why I was so distressed to hear of the manner of his passing. Taken so suddenly... consumption I was told, is that correct?"

"It was, sir, a tragedy which could not be prevented." Another lie, she had wanted to scream in exultation when the news had been delivered to her. Her maid had come to her, and stammered the fact that he was dead.

"Dead! How?" She had demanded, she had to be sure

"I fear so, ma'am. The surgeon has been summoned, but Cook says he's long gone." Her nemesis had died while she slept, not a few rooms away. Was she wrong to feel such happiness? Of course not. Wood should have eternity to wallow in the fires of hell, to feel as his victims had felt. Truth be told, he possessed not a single compassionate bone in his body. When she had confronted him with her dilemma, he had laughed, and spoken words, not normally heard within respectable homes. He had besmirched her name, vilified, and castigated her while she'd sobbed. She had shed tears before him, but never again, he didn't deserve tears, not then, not now, not until hell froze.

"An unpleasant demise, madam." Reverend Bayles spoke with a subdued tone but Abigail sensed he had more to say. "A death, any death is unpleasant, especially in one...apparently so...enthused with life. May I be so bold as to ask, why he was alone during his last moments?" Bayles, she sensed, wasn't prepared to openly accuse her, yet, but in some warped way he, she suspected, thought her responsible in ending Joseph's life?

"The family, sir, were either asleep, or absent. As for swift demise, the surgeon assured us that occasionally the patient simply tires of life, senses the miasma and breathes their last. That is what he succumbed to reverend, nothing more sinister than a terrible disease which, as you know, is rife within the town. There is no cure, but we prayed for God to look after him."

Truth was, she had heard him gasping in his room, had heard the rattling of his death throes and had ignored them. His grunting and wheezing, she had assumed, were simply due to an over indulgence of rum. Which, like so many other vices, Joseph indulged in with an enthusiastic fervor. Perhaps if Nathaniel, had been at home to assist, Joseph might have lived longer. If wishes were jewels, she would be encrusted in gems, for she had wished so often for a change in fortune. The devil, was the reason she had come to this putrid town, and now it seemed, she was fated to remain here.

Her hatred for the man would remain until she too died. She had watched and listened, but the reason as to how Wood had amassed his fortune still alluded her. Certainly he did not waste money on trifles. Unlike other merchants who paid urchins to sweep, and shovel, the night soil away, he invested his time and energy in acquiring influence and power. From without, Abigail had seen, a man who could be charming when it suited, but from within, he was a harsh and cunning devil. He would delay payment, as he had to Edwards, to gain another penny interest, yet expected his bills to be cleared promptly. "A farthing profit is a farthing nearer a penny and closer to a shilling," he extolled when questioned about his accountancy skills. There was also the side no one saw, the one only the family witnessed when the front door was locked and barred. She had seen it soon after her marriage, one morning at breakfast. Innocently, she had mentioned she wished to send a note by that day's coach. A trivial matter, but Joseph had rounded on her viciously, demanding that any letters had to be vetted and approved before being dispatched. Her husband's brothers, and their wives, had remained silent as Joseph had berated her further about her allegiance to the family and her apparent failings. By the time he had concluded she had felt violated, none more so than when Joseph had concluded with the words that still haunted her,

"Madam, I am entitled to read, know, and approve everything that occurs within these walls. Your soul belongs to me, and you will submit to my ruling. If you cannot, than I am sure, my son will find where you reside when he returns." She had mumbled an apology, but that had been an insight into his ways, an insight she despised. Was it any wonder she felt empty and devoid? Or that she felt nothing but contempt for Wood and that her words were empty and contrite? She was free, her nightmare ended, but could she ever feel happy? When, or if, her secret was revealed, she would become the talking point of the town. But wishes never came true, all she could do was wait, bible clasped to her heart in silent prayer.

I will take the truth to my grave. No one need know that he has left me carrying his bastard child. If I can conceal its presence until Nathaniel returns I might be able to pass it off as his. If not, then I must leave, with my work uncompleted. That is beyond contemplation, those who command have need of my skills, the quest must continue.

"Welcome, old friend. It is time to begin." The Reverend spoke softly, touching the coffin with due deference, while above them the bells tolled on.

Chapter Six

"The coffins 'ere," His voice was tinged with excitement as he leant from the belfry window. Cramming another egg into an already stained mouth, he expelled another cloud of noxious odour, and giggled.

"Damn the priest…once…"

"Damn the bastard…twice…"

"May he rot in hell…thrice…?" Mathew cursed, with each pull of the rope. Finally the town was witnessing the departure of an evil minded swine, who, many thought should never have been sulked from his mother's tit.

"Careful my friend, that bastard has ears everywhere, it will be you he damns if he gets word of what you think."

"Can't hear us here…once…"

"If you says what you hear…twice…"

"I'll throw you out that window…thrice…"

"What is said here, will remain here my friend, for like you, I have no love for either priest or deceased. Both should rot in hell for eternity. Aaah they be beneath the lych-gate. Bayles, is fawning over the Mrs, he'll be telling her how kind and good Wood was. Only we know differently don't we Mathew?"

The egg eating, bell ringer, chuckled demonically and leaned further from the window.

"Man was a tyrant…once…"

"Deserved all he got…twice…"

"Good riddance I say…thrice…" Even in death, Joseph Wood, continued to cause consternation among those, he had once controlled.

"True, my friend, but I wonder if this is the last we hear of him." That question would remain unanswered; and the bell tolled on.

* * *

Despite his outward calm, the Reverend Edward Bayles was a seething mass of indecision. A state of mind which, until recently, he had been quite unaccustomed to. The cause, a letter, entrusted to him by his recently departed friend. Three months before, Joseph had arrived at the rectory, just before midnight. His mood had been darker than the night, so black it had taken three glasses of best smuggled brandy, to quell his anger. Finally, he had removed a parchment from an inner pocket, placed the document upon a side table and stated,

"I entrust this to your safe keeping rector. Read it when alone, commit its contents to memory then place it somewhere safe. At some future date, we will have need to implement what you read, but for now, it must remain, our secret."

Josephs, sudden demise meant that last night, he had retrieved the document from its hiding place, where in the solitude of his study, had read and re-read it while supping a quantity of claret. More than once he had wondered as to Joseph's sanity. He had found his friend's words, difficult to believe. But having seen her, this day, his accusations appeared totally believable. *Jezebel, witch, daughter of the devil,* He wanted to confront her, but this wasn't the time, or the place. This was a day to bury a friend, not expose her for what she was, but he could begin the process. If Joseph had lived, he would have exposed her for what she was, but now it fell to him, to curtail her demonstrative ways. He was pledged to ruin her, to sever her from those she had duped. His method would, he was sure, end her days in this town. He would vilify her more effectively than by mere words, he would expose her vileness, but only when his actions would destroy her totally. As if seeking affirmation of intent, he laid his hand gently upon the casket and prayed for guidance.

"Have a care, my sons," he intoned to the four pallbearers, "Make sure he is well secure, as the path is deeply rutted." The casket lay upon a simple wooden hand cart, bedecked in winter foliage gathered that morning by girls sent, at his command, to the woods. They had, as yet, not received their payment, but they would, once this day was done.

"All is well Reverend,"

"Then we should proceed." His compassion hid the affection he felt for the deceased. Not affection lovers felt, but an affection born from a kindred spirit. Despite them being as different as any two men could be, a bond had existed between them, a friendship which had grown from their first introduction. They were as one, in both thought and deed, which made their…desires the more agreeable.

"Madam, pray assume your position behind the cart." He spoke as if offering advice, but she had affronted him by assuming the position reserved for the deceased's widow. Had he known, Joseph would have felt reviled, for no man despised two women as much as he had his wife and this upstart? *Enjoy your last hours in command, for I will destroy you before the month is out.* The strumpet looked at him and stepped away from the casket. She could act as temporary head of the family, while he would, for the moment, pay her due homage. But in due course, she would be exposed as the liar she truly was for he hated her, despised and detested her, even the air she breathed was tainted by her corruption. No man had ever hated a woman as much as he did her, yet she might have been his if events had taken a different course.

"I am the resurrection and the life, saith the Lord: he that believeth in me, though he were dead, yet shall he live: and whosoever liveth and believeth in me shall never die." Bayles had spoken those words more times than he cared to remember, today, they were a little more personal, more poignant. "Man that is born of a woman hath but a short time to live and is full of misery…"

Bayles glanced at the casket and felt his heart flutter in sadness. He would have carried it alone, if asked, for Joseph deserved to be revered. That was why his final resting place, within the chancel had been chosen so carefully. There he would be able to keep an eye on him, until his own life ended.

"He cometh up and is cut down like a flower, he flieth as it were a shadow, and never continueth in one stay." The words, so well-known, were contrite, even sanctimonious. Joseph should be here to witness her downfall, but his life had been curtailed, not by God's hand, but by that of a woman. Abigail Wood may not have thrust a knife into his body, but she had been instrumental in his end, of that he was certain. How, was the question that required answering? In an attempt to discover the truth, he had sought out the surgeon. Bailey's answer had been unacceptable, he had assured him that Joseph's death had been by God's hand, than no venom, or other method, had hastened his demise. Disappointed, that she was innocent in the eyes of the law, that she had not orchestrated his murder, it fell to him to end her evilness.

Whore! Devious strumpet! Such acrimony spoke volumes for the cleric's morality. He was set upon a path of condemnation, based purely upon what Joseph had stated in that document. Without further evidence it would have been insufficient to condemn, but she concealed the proof within her and that was what he would use to destroy her. Once presented, none within this poxed ridden town would see her for anything less than corrupted. *See the way she weeps for my friend, how she weeps tears for what she has lost. You fool me not, madam, for within your breast beats the heart of a corrupt and repugnant women.* The short journey from Lynch-gate, to church door, was long enough for him to reconsider his feelings. He had not always been so…malevolent. Two years before, when the town had been lawless and controlled by elements more interested in personal gain than moral righteousness. He had looked upon her in a far different light.

He had arrived, unknown and penniless, sent to administer to a lawless town where morals had all but disappeared. In those friendless days, he had been like Jesus, in the wilderness, tempted by the devilment that existed and seeking succour from those willing to help him. Instead he had discovered a town where, even, he had been viewed with suspicion and doubt. Questioned by the revenue who sought an individual known only as, 'The Chamberlin'. He had finally been released, but it was during that time he had gained his reputation. To this day, there were those who suspected him of having knowledge, as to where the looted goods were concealed. *I wish I did, for then I would be gone from this place.*

Joseph had befriended him, taken him under his wing, shown him what was what, who was who, and what could be achieved, if he was willing to throw off his cloak of piety. The merchant had become his saviour, tutor, and guide while Edward had been a perfect pupil, listening intently as Joseph had explained how Stormouth offered much to those willing to embrace what was on offer.

"Blend in, listen to those with something to say, ignore the fools, of whom there are many. Do this, and you will be shown the road to riches beyond your wildest dreams." He had done so, and they had formed an unlikely association, one that, even in death, the priest was determined to protect.

Today, he would bury a friend, and lead the town in a celebration of a life well lived, he would also begin the process of ridding the town of a heretic, a woman Joseph, had mistrusted from those first days. She had too much to say for herself, asked too many questions, sought that which all woman should be denied, knowledge. Nathaniel, Joseph's eldest son, had found the bitch alluring. Despite his father's warnings, and threats of damnation, the fool had married her and brought a devil into their midst. "Foolish youth," Joseph had stated. He had tried to curtail her, but despite his attempts to bring her to heel, she had refused his demands.

"Madam, Josiah and his brother must lead us into God's house." He saw her demeanour, the way she nodded slightly, and stepped aside allowing Josiah and Adam to lead the casket into the church. She could act as pious as she wished, very soon the seeds of doubt would flourish within the gullible minds of those who once thought her so perfect. She would be the perfect sacrificial lamb, a woman to whom few owed any loyalty. A few short steps away the great and the good, more importantly women like Ida Furnell waited. By the time he had presented his evidence, she would be ostracised.

"My sons, remember, dignity at all times. It is what your father would have expected of you."

"That, and a bottle of claret to toast his passing priest, remember that of him." Adam stated and Bayles nodded graciously, for what he said was true. Joseph was indeed a man with an insatiable thirst. They had shared many a glass, before engaging in their other shared passions. That, secret was their reason as to why Abigail Wood must perish. She had veiled her true self behind misrepresentations and falsehoods. She was a witch, had beguiled Nathaniel, and having done so, had married into a family who controlled much of the town. Some had even asked whether her arrival and subsequent marriage had been preplanned. Was she, as Joseph had questioned, an agent provocateur? If so, today would prove unsettling for her, while he would watch her every expression and wait for her to make an error.

"As we are in life, so we are in death, blessed are those who enter the Kingdom of God without sin, for they are few." His voice rang out so that those within the church, would know of the imminent arrival.

All this could have been avoided, if only she had acquiesced. Having arrived at almost the same time, they had become inexplicably linked. Both had ingratiated themselves into Stormouth society, but there the similarity ceased. While Abigail had been liked, Bayles was loathed, and feared in equal measure. Only Joseph had shown him friendship, had introduced him to a small but select group and in so doing, had allowed him into his confidence. Was it then, any surprise that, during the troubles, he and Joseph had been suspected equally of being the 'Chamberlin' In fact, he had, for a time, been convinced of his friend's guilt. But such accusations had come to naught.

Now, priest and fornicator, stood close to each other. They both knew of her guilt, both knew she had committed the ultimate sin, both were well aware her crime must be exposed. That was his commitment, to Joseph, to destroy her, and the bastard she carried. *You act so demure, yet there is a presence about you. You hide, not only that which Joseph spoke of, but another secret. What is it whore?* She would pay a heavy price, just as another father and daughter had paid the last time his licentiousness had raised its unwelcome head, but not yet. Today, his friend would be buried with dignity, while above them, two men toiled on a bell.

Chapter Seven

"Abigail," Josiah said softly. Torn from her thoughts, she nodded in mute acceptance that her job was done. Henceforth, she would become, simply, another mourner, while the sons would lead them into the church. Despite the chill wind, she couldn't help but notice the sweat-stained collars of the four pall bearers. Joseph was still exerting his influence upon those he had left behind. His sons had had to work hard bringing him up the hill to the church. She wanted to smile, but the priest's voice took on a more zealot manner as he entered the echoing church. Evidence she was sure that he wanted to be heard by one and all.

"Blessed is the Lord who calls the sinners to His house. For it is truth that only He can take away the sins of the living. On Judgment day the godly will sit upon the right hand of the Lord, while the fornicators and undeserving will seek solace in his benevolence..."

She flinched in trepidation. Was she being stupid, or was Bayles confirming her worst fears? If he indeed knew her pain, would he confront her privately to demand payment for his silence? *No, he will want to make me squirm, to intimidate, but what will he demand? Money was the obvious incentive though he would demand much for his silence. Or would he taunt her further and demand something far worse?* For the moment, she could only speculate upon his intentions, the time, would arrive, when she would have to face him and that she dreaded.

"Oh for the love of God." Ida Furnell's distinctive voice cried out in shock, before she collapsed to the floor, where she lay gasping for breath. The casket had barely entered the church, the congregation awaited, but Ida had stolen the priest's moment. From her position, Abigail strained to see what caused such consternation, then smiled behind her veil, for Ida had collapsed with an attack of the vapours. The cause, Joseph's body juices were seeping from the casket. *Suffer you swine,* she cursed silently. Despite the cold, and the ice packed around him, Joseph Wood, it seemed was reluctant to leave the town without one last show of defiance.

You will have to keep your sermon short, or suffer the indignity of seeing your friend dripping across the chancel floor. Were her thoughts inappropriate? Possibly in the eyes of God, but they reflected just how much she despised Wood for what he had done. As for Bayles, begrudgingly she admired his fortitude under such trying circumstances. Regaining his composure, he hastened the casket forward, made sure it was placed upon the trestles and swiftly covered it with the alter cloth. Then summoning a choirboy forward, he commanded,

"Go to the Donkey yard, fetch fresh straw! Be quick!" The funeral risked becoming embarrassing, as Joseph slowly leaked out to form a puddle of putrid liquid upon the stone floor beneath the casket. From her position, Abigail watched the cleric's laudable determination to conceal his friend's leakage. Stifling her mirth, she watched as the choirboy returned. Snatching the straw from him, Bayles spread it beneath the offending drip then called his congregation to prayer. The congregation were to be distracted, while Bayles and Furnell, both regained their composure.

Despite his confident manner, Abigail suspected that, while they stood heads bowed and eyes closed, he would be fortifying himself from a flask of spirits he kept hidden in his pulpit. She smiled as indeed he did drink heartily from a silver flask. *You swine, no better than the rest of us, yet you hold these poor fools to account for any minor lapse.* If he could, then she would also use this time to reflect upon her time in Stormouth. Much had occurred, some unpleasant, like the purges that had so nearly torn the town apart in violence. Orchestrated by Pope, the revenue officer, he had searched for the man he considered to be at the heart of all that occurred upon the marsh. Popes methods were harsh, anyone he suspected was persecuted horribly as he searched for the goods, suspected of coming ashore and which, to this day, it was said, remained hidden within the town. Despite his best efforts, nothing had been found, but many, including Bayles, had been suspected. He and Wood made an unlikely pairing. While Wood was the aging merchant, Bayles was far younger, some said early thirties, while others swore him to be of middling years. Certainly, he was far more astute than Wood ever could be. It was said the Cleric was, well versed in reading, and astronomical measuring, spending many a night atop the bell tower studying the heavens and making notes. Joseph would have found such matters impossible to comprehend. The only reading Wood did, was of his account books, while stars held little interest to him. Wood was, in her humble opinion, no more than a brutish lout who, through deviousness, had climbed from the mire to become the misanthrope she had known. While he may have taken his secrets to his grave, Bayles remained. If she could understand their friendship, she might understand what confidences they shared. Certainly, she suspected, it exceeded that of clergy and parishioner. It was such intrigue she found fascinating. The secrets which remained undisclosed, unspoken, were a measure of the loyalty few outside of the town could ever understand. Despite all that was inflicted upon them, none disclosed anything incriminating.

"Dearly beloved. We gather today, in the presence of God, to perform the saddest of tasks..." Bayles had recovered his composure, albeit with the aid of his drink. Suddenly she flinched as a hand touched hers, turning towards Josiah, she saw him smile, weakly. He was so different to Nathaniel, weaker, not so forthright, but they shared the knowledge of what Joseph had been capable of.

"To mourn the loss of a dear friend. Joseph Septimus Wood, was a God fearing, loving father, who daily mourned the loss of his dear wife, Charlotte, taken so cruelly, many years past."

Loving? She wanted to scream in indignity, the old goat had driven all, but his sons away, which was why the family were so few in number. Two sons and their wives, plus her, made up the entire Wood dynasty. Nathaniel should have been present, but he was abroad, seeking that which fed the coffers of the firm and kept them in the manner they were accustomed to. As the wife of the eldest son, she, for the moment, she was the guardian of the family. Not that their lineage concerned her greatly, her marriage had been formed from passion, not duty. Such a union had never been part of the plan, though it did allow her to watch her subjects closely.

"Our Lord called and His disciple Joseph, answered." Bayles raised his hands, to give greater credence to his words. "Our Saviour has need of strong souls to continue His fight against Satan and his licentiousness', souls that are not corrupted by man's impurities. Our friend, was such a soul, he will ably assist in those efforts. Therefore, do not feel saddened that we have lost a friend. Instead, rejoice in the fact that he goes about Gods work and that in time we will meet again. He will be there to greet us when our time arrives. Until then, he will fight the good fight along with the other souls called to struggle with Lucifer, and assist our Lord in the eternal fight against the evils of avarice…debauchery…and…lustfulness."

Bayles leant upon the ancient wood and staring down at her. 'The Ravens' eyes were cold, and menacing, they chilled her soul, making her head swoon. It was a look of contempt, which made her question whether she had unwittingly, revealed what that devil had done? Beneath such scrutiny, she turned towards the coffin, in an attempt to block Bayles from her mind. He was all powerful, he ruled these simple souls through fear, and if he so desired, could disclose her condition. *If you suspect me, this is the perfect time to cause mischief.*

She desired to denounce the cleric's words, to scream her defiance. Wood had been devoid of feelings, and kept his excesses hidden from those outside the home. His sons knew, they had seen him, when his temper had risen, and the devil had possessed him. Yet Bayles, she knew, would never mention them, if indeed he knew.

"Heed my words well, for debauchery is by far the worst of the devil's incarnations!" She jumped as he slammed his hand onto the leather-bound bible. "Satan works his evil, by luring you with the sins of the flesh. You were washed in the waters shed as tears by our Lord and yet…when the need arrives you debase yourselves! You lie down and fornicate! When your day of judgment arrives, you will be forced to kneel at the feet of our Lord and explain yourselves. Woe betide anyone who speaks falsely, because our friend will be there to make sure you speak truthfully."

Was he attempting to incite a response from her? If so, he would fail. She had no intention of falling for his tricks. If she could get through today, then maybe, hopefully, she would be able to make plans to conceal her impending confinement.

"Today we put aside our earthly sins as we perform an odious duty. We are charged with sending our neighbour, Joseph, gentleman and friend, on his final journey. We give thanks for his life and hope that he finds peace in a more enlightened place. I ask you to join with me, speak and affirm your faith by saying our Lord's Prayer."

Closing her eyes, the prayer allowed her further time to consider the Rectors next move. Without mentioning her by name, Bayles had revealed that Wood had made him privy to what had occurred. Now, would be the perfect time to berate her, for she would be forced to endure, while he berated her mercilessly. Bayles had chosen his time well, while Wood continued to leak upon the floor, she could not leave, but would be forced to listen while he condemned her. As the prayer ended, Bayles took his position for what would be, she was sure, an agonising sermon.

"Be seated my children." Collectively they did so and stared towards their vicar. His sermons were legendary, he would speak of God and his commandments as if he had been present that day when God had laid down his rules for life. God, wasn't the reason most attended. Most came to hear who Edward Bayles had chosen to be his latest victim. Each week some unfortunate, would be castigated for some minor misdemenours. Bayles did this exceedingly well, few present would forget the manner in which Mr Finch had been destroyed by the priest. The accusation was meaningless, something that should have been dealt with, then forgotten. Yet, by the time Bayles had concluded his character assassination, all that remained of Finch had been a gibbering wreck of a man. Frail, and aging, Finch had been forced to leave, simply because, Bayles, controlled the gossips, the rumour mongers. Fearfully she waited, if he knew, this was his time, for unlike Mr Finch, she had transgressed in the eyes of the church.

"Who can count themselves pure of heart and soul? Not you Columbine or you squire Cobb. Can I say I am as pure as our Lord intended? No, I cannot, I am beguiled and corrupted as we all are. Nor was our friend…Joseph was fallible, he made mistakes. He was both liked and mistrusted by those he dealt with in equal measure. Yet, he was in essence a Godly man who desired nothing more than to do what was best for those he called friends. I know I counted him as a friend. He took me under his wing when I was a lost soul, and showed me a path to lead. I would like to say more but there is need for haste, I fear. I ask that we spend time in silent reflection, to pray for our departed friend and to reflect on our own mortal sins. Dig deep into your souls, examine in minute detail all you have done and consider if you could live your lives any differently. None of us are without sin. Our moral duty, though, is to renounce such evil and pray for forgiveness, as is it to assist those that fall by the way side. When we find those lost souls, we should do all we can to help them back onto the road of righteousness. So as we commit Joseph to his maker, I say to those that seek a place in heaven, look within yourselves, no one is without sin. Any man that says differently is a liar. We shall now intern our friend, if the family would step closer."

Bayles was the conductor of this farce, while she had little suspicion and could not conceive how her life was about to change, or in what direction it would lead her.

Chapter Eight

Abigail, sighed in relief, Bayles had remained silent, why, she did not know, but she was gratified. Her deliberations were interrupted by Josiah who beckoned her towards him.

"Abigail, we wait upon you," She was required, but she knew she could not be present.

"I cannot, Josiah; I fear the vapours have affected me. I beg your indulgence to allow me a moment of quiet reflection. Continue with your task…I will join you when I have recovered."

"We would rather you were with us but, if you are unwell, I will instruct Martha to remain with you?"

"No, her place is at your side, leading the family, as your father would have wished."

"We are family, but I will allow this, if that is what is required." Josiah frowned as yet another of their small party fell by the wayside. He'd known this would be difficult but he had hoped for a more united presence on this unpleasant of days. Abigail remained seated while Josiah led the mourner's outside. The church, suddenly felt very safe, she would have some time alone without Bayles examining her. Clasping a hand to her face, she sighed in relief, but felt the tears well up inside her, so much had happened that she needed this time to reflect on happier times.

Her arrival had occurred as the town was tearing itself apart. Factions loyal to the Crown vied for superiority against those who supported a person known as 'The Chamberlin'. Outwardly, the majority supported the customs officers but secretly, most residents secretly aided and supported the smugglers. The situation was akin to a powder keg waiting to explode, and so it had. A duel, and a death, had led to the destruction of a family and the birth of such malevolence that to this day no one was sure who supported who. Unwittingly, she had arrived at the very height of the troubles, sent to discover the secrets of the Wood wealth. Essentially unrelated, she had been foolish not to have seen the relevance of both matters, or to suspect, one was not linked to the other.

As the last of the congregation left the building, she spent a moment, once again mulling over what she knew and what she suspected. None, were totally innocent. From the squire to the lowest street urchin, they all shared in Joseph's guilt. No man, could engage in a life as he had without his indiscretions being aided and concealed by those, as guilty as he. That was her task; to uncover that guilt, and inform others of it. But she did so alone, her letters to and from her father had ceased, and would not begin again until the road was clear of this infernal snow. Until then she was trapped, not only by nature, but also with the knowledge of what he had done to her.

Why, then, has the priest remained silent? That was a puzzle, to which there were varying options. One was that Wood, had indeed died without imparting his involvement in her predicament to anyone. The other, was that Bayles delayed, waiting for a more opportune moment to confront her. *If that be so, then I must be on my guard for longer than I dared hope.* There was a third, crucial element to take into consideration…the family. The manner in which they treated her, suggested they knew nothing of what Joseph had done, or that Bayles had spoken of it to them. She had asked herself more than once why that might be, or was she, seeing duplicity and deviousness where none existed? She cautioned herself to tread carefully, if she were reckless in thought or deed, she may condemn herself unintentionally.

Since first encountering this damnable family she had watched them closely. All were somewhat odd, Josiah tried, but failed continuously to live up to his father's expectations. Adam, the youngest son, was as cruel and evil as his father, a spendthrift who concealed something, which the other members of the family were not privy to. Adams wife, Sarah, was as bad as her husband, she liked what life, and Josephs money offered, and wasn't afraid to use her wiles to further her ambitious ways. Martha on the other hand was as good as the rest were bad. If any knew of what Joseph capable of, none spoke of it, or not to her at any rate.

During the service, she had glanced at all four, and all appeared devoid of emotion, all the time staring ahead in sullen silence, not once glancing at the coffin. Surely they knew of what their father had been capable of, or were they so dependent upon him, they accepted his nefariousness as the norm? If so, such acceptance would be unusual to say the least, as would be the ability for the likes of Sarah to remain silent without…some collective acquiescence.

If so, if they had agreed to remain silent the question was why? She could think of but one reason, and it appalled her. Could it be possible that Joseph had dallied with them as well as her? It would certainly explain their apparent sobriety. Were the tears they shed of joy, were her sisters-in-law as happy to be released from his unholy grasp as she? Such an improbability was unthinkable, or was it? Such a secret, would explain others peculiarities.

Wealth and its acquisition, was the motivation for every move that was made within the town. That being the case could any man, including Josiah and Adam, not deliberate upon seeking revenge upon the one person who had shamed them? In a normal family that would have been so, yet they were present mourning his loss, why? There could be but one reason, Joseph's wealth. As middle and youngest sons, neither had much to look forward to. The norm was for the eldest, in this case her husband, to inherit. The middle son, usually went into a profession, while the youngest was expected to seek their own way in life. Not so in the Wood family, Joseph's intention, had always been, to keep a tight rein on those close to him. That had changed with his sudden demise; their futures now depended upon how Joseph had worded his will, which perhaps explained why they appeared so dutiful, they desired to know how much they had been left.

None of this would have occupied their small brains, if Nathaniel had been present. But he was abroad, and so the burden of holding them together fell to her. If only she had listened to her father, if only she had heeded his words, perhaps she would have managed her task with more diligence. But if wishes were stars, she'd own the heavens. For Nathaniel had betwixt her, captivated her and won her heart.

Arriving in the town, under the guise of a woman of substance, she had taken lodgings at the fashionable 'George Hotel'. Her instructions were to watch, learn, and relay her information to those who knew far more than she ever would. Of course, word had spread swiftly about the wealthy, elegant lady who had arrived. The town, hierarchy, had come to her door, to pay court and discover her intentions, one had been Nathaniel. Their first meeting had been enlightening and fortuitous. She had been in the hotel parlour, reading when she had noticed him. Tall, dark well built, polite and more importantly armed, no sooner had he arrived, than a group men had burst into the hotel intent on causing mayhem. Nathaniel had stood before them, sword unsheathed, defying them to pass with words of such lewdness, she had stared in horror, his bravery had won the day and they had left with but a few broken glasses to mark their presence.

"Madam," Nathaniel had approached. "I trust that was not too distressing. I fear we are plagued with such fools."

"I am far from distressed, sir, in fact, I felt more than safe with you to guard me."

That was their first meeting; more were to follow in the coming weeks. Despite her instructions, to observe only she had begun a liaison with the very family she was watching. She should have denied his advances, love, though, knew no boundaries nor could it be confined by protocol. So she was to discover, her arrival could have been better timed. Stormouth was apparently locked in a desperate struggle. Every night she heard shots fired in the dark streets; every day, Pope, the revenue officer had another apparent smuggler, hanged. Apparently Pope sought, the men who had stolen and then hidden a vast fortune, taken from a ship, which had been lured onto shore and wrecked. Word was that Pope, desired that fortune for his own, which was why he was so ruthless in his efforts to discover its hiding place. Whatever the reason, she had written to her father seeking permission to leave. Fearing his wrath, that he would castigate her for not heeding his words earlier, she despised having to admit failure. But the situation had changed, the town had become, she considered, too dangerous to remain,

* * *

Long before her arrival, she and her father had met in a room, close to St James's Palace. It had been a cordial, if strained conversation, but it had been then she had received her instructions.

"That blasted family is like the wind, impossible to tie down. Now we are told the revenue are stirring the place up, which will make them even more difficult to infiltrate. My God, we have been given some tasks, but this may well be the one to defeat us."

"How so father?"

"It pains me to say, but they confound us at every turn. Each man sent find's it impossible to gain their trust. The patriarch, Joseph, is suspicious of anyone outside his own family. What, then, are we to do?"

"Something surely, for we have yet to be defeated."

"You are very perceptive daughter, yes we are to do something. Our masters have deliberated and decided. I have stated, I think them ill-advised and voiced my objection, but they insist that you have the last word. The plan, which I say is ridiculous, is to send you into their lair, alone and unsupported."

"I...How do I achieve, that which others have failed to do?"

"You will use those feminine wiles, which your mother used so successfully upon me, to gain their trust. I fear we are sending a lamb to the slaughter, but what can I do? Our masters speak, and we must obey. Your only advantage is your obvious attribute's which, if employed correctly, can defeat even the strongest of hearts."

She had sensed her father's concerns, but as he had said, what could he do? Neither of them were in a position to refuse, for how did one refuse their employer?

"I detest placing you in such a predicament, but you are the only, nay best, person who may discover what it is they conceal. You are commanded to do whatever is required, to gain their trust. Disarm them by flattery, and guile, but always keep your wits about you. Joseph Wood is a canny, wily old bird, he trusts no one, not even, apparently, his own children."

"He has sons?"

"Three, but do not draw too close .They are a family of criminals, no different to any we deal with. As far as we know, they have never murdered, or inflicted violence unto another, but you must tread carefully. They are suspected of transgressions concerning trade, offences to which we are no strangers. Their Lordships desire explanation as to why their business expands far swifter than would be expected for such a small, isolated town. Moreover we wish to know if they pay the correct amount of revenue, that they do not flitch some for themselves. You are to find the answers to those questions, send your reports by coach to this office. If that route becomes compromised, then as a last resort, use this man. He is loyal and can be trusted and will be aware that I propose to take up residence in the old family house in Barminster. That way my presence will not be seen as unusual. If you need me, do your best to get word to me and I will come as quickly as possible."

Her father had passed her a piece of paper. She read it, then threw it upon the fire and watched until it burnt completely.

"Only he can assist you, do not use his abilities lightly. While you are within that town, you are alone. No swift rescue will be forthcoming if you are endangered. Here is all we know or suspect, read it, then burn it."

That file was long gone, but what it had told her had proved beneficial.

"I fear I harboured grave misgivings about your suitability, but I believe you have the abilities to succeed. In truth, there is no one I trust more to go there and unearth their secrets. Do you consider yourself suitably confident to achieve our aims, my dear?"

"Yes," she had replied. There had been much more, details of what the men in London suspected, background to the family, and a carefully constructed lie that would hopefully deceive them long enough for her to gain their trust. It had sounded so easy, subterfuge and lies, but no one had anticipated the lure of a far stronger instinct. Love knows no boundaries; it weaves its magic. Months of careful preparations had fallen apart when Nathaniel had proposed marriage. Left with but one option, she had travelled to Barminster, there his anger had been frightening to behold, perhaps hurt, was more appropriate. Perhaps he thought she was abandoning him after they had enuded so much together.

"No! That was never to be a part of what we planned and will not occur! Your task was simple; at no time was such a liaison envisaged, or agreed. My God, but this will throw a spoke in what they had planned. You do realise they will demand your immediate removal. For what? A man, some callow swine who will end his days imprisoned for his part in his families deception. You disappoint me and leave me no alternative but to inform those who control our destiny. I foresee much grief for they will not look favourably upon this, my girl."

She had understood, of course, but had argued her case long and hard. Even now, she remembered her words as being defiant, almost insulting. He had not deserved her reproach; after all, she had been trusted to do as she was commanded.

"Why? Surely what I am doing is no more than was demanded of me, to infiltrate and learn their secrets. Perhaps I am wrong, but the opportunities a marriage presents are worth more than a thousand years listening at keyholes. In one year within their presence, I will learn more than we could ever have envisaged. I know this isn't what you hoped for, but it could be just what we need to bring us swift and conclusive answers. Besides, he isn't that hideous, one day you may actually come to like him."

"I will not allow it. You cannot place yourself in such a heinous and hideous position. My God, this should not have happened! How could you allow yourself to become infatuated? They are rogues and villains; I will not see you married into that family, not even if the King asked me personally!"

Defeated, she had returned to Stormouth, with the intention of declining his proposal. His presence, though, once again charmed her, the infatuation grew stronger, they explored the town and marriage became unavoidable.

Less than a week later a uniformed footman approached her during dinner. Upon his silver tray she saw a sealed notelet. Instantly recognising the impression, she had demanded a coach and driver to be summoned. Protocol had, it seemed, been abandoned; her presence was demanded at a very special meeting. Her imminent marriage had, she guessed, thrown their plans into disarray.

Suddenly she was brought back to reality; those events had to be placed aside, for the priest's voice had risen to a crescendo.

Chapter Nine

"Madam, we are about to commit the body of our friend into God's protection…"

Wood, had been interned, and four burly men, stood ready to begin levering the stone lid back into place.

"Madam, please, your place is beside the family." Bayles, glared at her, his nostrils flared. She expected him to say more, but instead, he simply indicated that she should resume her place beside the others.

"My apologies reverend." Dabbing her face with her lace kerchief, Abigail meekly resumed her position among the family. Joseph could rot to his foul, blackened heart's content. To feed the insects of his tomb was a fitting end to a truly despicable man. *Rot in hell! Enjoy everlasting misery and think of the torment you put your family through.* She was finally free; he could harm her no more.

She felt at ease as the stone lid slid into place, there were those who sobbed for him, she never would. Her task was finished once the final task of the day was completed. The gathering, at the church gate must be endured, she would be required to stand alongside the others and accept the platitudes of those who had attended. Some, not many, shed tears, while she wished this pretence to end.

"A fine service, he would have expected nothing less." His voice made Abigail turn sharply.

"Indeed. Please accept our thanks for attending." Abigail smiled politely, recognising the man as Mr Turnbottle, a ship owner and merchant, a man she knew as a rival to Joseph. Until now, though, a man she had been advised not to speak to.

"I consider it an honour, madam…May I beg your indulgence a moment, sir. Might I speak to Mrs Wood alone, so I might impart my condolences privately?" Turnbottle and Josiah viewed each other with suspicion; finally Josiah relented, but wondered what was important enough to be discussed so secretively?

"You may so do, sir, but do not stray far Abigail, we have other guests to speak with." Josiah viewed the man with annoyance, Abigail wasn't the chief mourner, yet he had separated her from her family why? Abigail paused, as Turnbottle spoke softly, just out of hearing of the others.

"Thank you, madam, for trusting me."

"That trust may be short lived, sir, all I need do is beckon, and your time will be terminated."

"Then I shall be swift" Turnbottle turned, as if checking they were indeed alone, then, very quietly, said. "This is not the appropriate time but…and perhaps this will come as somewhat of a surprise…I feel it is incumbent upon me, to inform you, there will be those present, who will be less than honourable. In fact, I might go so far as to say, some might find Joseph's demise amusing."

"Sir, your tone is both, offensive and inappropriate, for such a solemn occasion. Is this the manner you treat a family in mourning? Our father is not cold in his grave, yet you dare heap insult upon injury."

"Madam," Turnbottle leant closer, his tone subdued and refrained, but his intention was far from respectful. "I mean no disrespect, but you are still new to the ways of the town. Oh, I know you have resided here sometime and endured all that we have suffered." He paused as if considering his words carefully. "That will pale into insignificance in the coming weeks. I may speak out of turn, but you must be made aware that your position has altered somewhat, since Wood's demise. You should also be aware that many attend, simply to assure themselves that he is indeed dead and buried. Fact is, many won't be sorry to see the back of him."

"You dare to utter such words in our time of distress." She had to react, not to do so would have appeared disloyal, but Turnbottle spoke what she too thought. Moreover, she had to present a dispassionate and calm face before the other merchants, for if they sensed any sort of indecision, they could, if so desired, ruin the family within a month. Dignity and the family name was everything, it was what the business community relied and prospered upon. If that were lost, then penury and ruination must surely follow. She had no desire to witness the inside of a debtors gaol, or see bailiffs breaking their doors in.

Despite her personal feelings for the man, Joseph had commanded, if not admiration, then at least respect. That respect had to be maintained, if the business was to continue. Until Nathaniel returned and assumed command, she, as the natural successor's wife, had to nurture the confidence of such men as Turnbottle. To antagonise them, would possibly prove detrimental to their future dealings with them. Unwillingly, she would have to moderate her tone with Turnbottle. Immediately she offered a muted apology. "Please disregard my outburst, sir, I meant no disrespect. It has been a stressful day, and a woman is surely allowed a moment's lapse at such a time."

"We will speak of it no further, dear lady. I fully understand your grief, however, I must urge caution. Your father-in-law annoyed and upset many in the town, myself included…"

He was the first to speak openly about how Joseph had been perceived. To do so, begged the question, 'Was he the ally she sought?' She looked at him, evaluating his potential. Certainly he had the right attributes; Joseph had disliked and mistrusted him, had spoken only with anger and hatred when his name was ever mentioned, which was rarely. They had obviously despised each other, why that was, she was not sure, but if Joseph had felt so inclined then Turnbottle was a man she should speak with in greater detail. Like her husband, the merchant was tall, handsome and had deep, dark eyes, the sort any women could fall in love with instantly. A man who might have protected her, had he known Joseph's ways. He was also successful and understood the business community, something the remaining sons lacked in abundance.

"I should also warn you, that many will seek recompense from you for Joseph's…frugalness."

"Frugalness what say you sir?"

"I do not seek to offend madam but your late father-in-law was known to withhold both payment, and delivery. Many of your competitors will have goods in storage, they will demand their retrieval immediately. While there will be others who will demand instant fulfilment of their outstanding accounts. I would recommend caution until you are certain of both rightful ownership and accountability. I am truly sorry if I have caused consternation of any sort, madam but thought it best you knew the truth about old Joseph."

"I thank you sir, for your concern, but I believe we are best suited to know the failings of our late father.Perhaps, if that is how you saw him, it would be best that you leave, and take your cynicism with you." Abigail's anger was real, unlike her tears.

"Maybe I should. Though, I fear, if all those who felt so inclined, did so, the church would have been very silent." He paused, rubbed his face with his hand before continuing. "Forgive my impertinence, but I am told your husband is away."

"That is correct; he is due back in the autumn."

"In that case, may I be the first to extend the hand of friendship and assistance to you."

"Most kind, sir, but pray, why would we need your assistance?

"Madam, I deplore having to speak thus, but I implore you to take heed. There will be a backlash to what has occurred. No, please hear me out, Joseph controlled, he held sway over everything he did. His influence was everywhere from council to dock. As such, his death will leave a void, there will be consternation and confusion until that void is filled. The merchants and their backers will sense indecisiveness; that his business is not controlled by a steady hand. That will become your concern. We all know the younger sons are ne'er-do-wells, fools who could not control their own bladders let alone a business such as yours. If they took control, the bankers will become nervous and concerned, neither of which is conducive to stability." He saw her indecision, instinctively he reached out; his hand, momentarily brushed hers, before she drew it away sharply.

"Why?" She demanded.

"To explain that will take longer than we have, but I will endevour to offer you my advice. I may sound condescending, that is not my intention, but you must learn swiftly. Everything in this port comes in on ships, trade is our lifeblood. The men who control that trade are nervous madam, the markets are…fickle beasts one day's profit, can become destitution the next. Trade, like those that serve it, requires stability. Much like sailing a ship, trade needs a steady hand on the tiller, with such confidence we can negotiate any storm God or man throws our way. Put a fool on that same tiller, and hesitation occurs when you least wish it to. Our little town would suffer thus if you falter. Almost every businessman within the district will have money invested in your enterprises. Joseph's death will make them uneasy. Business people like consistency, they dislike change for change breeds mistrust. They will be afraid that their investments are no longer viable. Superstitious nonsense perhaps, but that is the nature of our world. I can see I have caused you some apprehension; that was not my intention, madam. However, I will make you a proposition. If you ever find yourself in need of advice, then do not hesitate to seek me out. I will offer all the help I can. Even so, I fear your husband may find a much reduced business upon his return, unless the unease of the town can be quelled…swiftly…I trust I have made the position understandable to you, madam?"

"I believe so, and many thanks for your concern, sir. Although, I would hope Adam and Josiah, know what has to be done."

"One would hope so, of course, but please remember my offer." She watched as he bowed, how he held her in his stare for just a little too long, then, with the merest of polite smiles, he was gone, back into the crowd. For a moment she was bemused, before a wave of relief swept over her. Turnbottle had, as good as said, he knew her secret and he could help if she needed it. For the first time in weeks she felt as if she was no longer alone, that she had friends after all; maybe she wouldn't be cast aside when the truth became common knowledge.

Above them, Mathew the bell ringer continued his chant, though not as spritely as he had at first. The bell continued to toll, its mournful lament to the deceased all the while Mathew's egg loving friend stared down at what was happening. Releasing a foul noxious odour, the man chuckled and proclaimed,

"The stags circle the doe. She attracts them like bees to the honey pot. Turnbottle's been given short measure now Columbine approaches, love to hear what dandy-legs has to say; trouble no doubt.

The man he spoke of was indeed a dandy, rich, well dressed, and unreserved in his opinion of others.

"My condolences madam, Joseph will be sorely missed." Columbine bowed daintily, one leg extended forward while the other bent slightly backwards. His hat, removed by his right hand brushed the ground briefly. She could do little but admire his pomposity and exaggerated elegance. "I realise that this is neither the time nor the place, but I have matters that need to be urgently discussed."

"Can it not wait until we conclude our mourning period?"

"Alas, madam, it cannot. I have goods in storage, bought and paid for but locked in your warehouses. I need assurances that you will be honouring the arrangements made with your late in-law. If not, I will be forced to seek reimbursement, or face penury." His attitude was harsh, but he was unprepared for her reaction. He stood aghast as tears began to fall from her eyes. "Madam, I will not be brushed aside with such a display of feminine emotions. I expect no more than what I am due."

Abigail, broke, she wept, sinking to her knees. Was this, what Turnbottle spoke of; were the vultures circling already? Her situation was unenviable, with Joseph dead, and Nathaniel absent, the question of inheritance arose. Someone had to lead, until the will was read, and the situation resolved. By rights, Josiah should assume control, but he, like Adam, was ill prepared to deal with men like Columbine. Such men would devour the sons like apples ripe on the tree. The business had to continue, and with no one else the responsibility rested upon her shoulders. How, though, would they react when the question arose of her condition? Would they believe her? Moreover, she had her own task to perform. She needed to get word to her father, but until the snow abated, that was impossible.

"You will mind your manners, sir!" Josiah stepped forward to confront Columbine. "You see what your tone does; it causes distress. Forty days is the usual mourning period as you well know. While we contemplate our loss, our clerk will answer any questions you have. Until we have grieved and examined the ledgers, we will not be releasing anything."

"That, sir, is unreasonable. I demand…"

"Demand all you like, that is our position." Josiah glared at the merchant, then took Abigail's arm and led her away. "Come Abigail, allow me to escort you away from this… gentleman."

Josiah had proven his worth; the family was, it seemed, important to him, which gave her encouragement. Her condition could only be disguised for so long, when the time came, when she was forced to explain the extremes their father had resorted to she would need men like Josiah on her side. Such a revelation would be distressing, they may find it difficult to comprehend, but hopefully both sons would have knowledge of what their father had been capable of. She had concerns of course, but Nathaniel was respected by Josiah and Martha, with their support, she might survive until her husband's return. Adam and Sarah were entirely different, they could be manipulated, bought, he would support anyone who supplied him with his life blood. Together they would control the business; she needed them, as much as they needed her. If Bayles did cause trouble, she would need the brothers on her side to protect and shelter her if his lies proved damaging. Certainly she would need their help until her father could arrive and save her from further embarrassment.

So engrossed in their grief, not one of the family saw the dirt-stained man appear from the opposite corner of the church yard. Only those near the lych-gate saw him arrive, and stared at him disapprovingly. He was disheveled and stank of horse sweat, yet he moved with a sense of great purpose. When he spoke it was with a loud and commanding voice, one that made Abigail turn in fear.

"Make way! Make way! I seek Mister Wood."

"Which do you seek? There are a number present!" Adam answered, chuckling at his own self-importance.

"Who dares disturb such a solemn occurrence?" Bayles demanded, staring at the man with obvious disgust.

"I carry an urgent message for Mister Joseph Wood from the Board of Insurers in the City of London." The mention of such an illustrious company caused those who heard, to gasp in astonishment. Many craned to see the document he held aloft complete with the great waxen seal. Those who witnessed its presence could not doubt it must certainly be important.

"You can carry a message from our Lord, himself. It will do no good. Mister Wood isn't accepting messages today. We have just committed him into the hands of our Lord."

The man looked confused as to what he should do. Abigail stepped forward, curtsied and asked.

"If acceptable, perhaps as the wife of his eldest son, I could accept it on his behalf, if there are no objections?" Abigail said looking sideways, seeking confirmation from Josiah as the next eldest.

"I am not sure but this document must be delivered…Please accept this with my condolences, ma'am." The man bowed elegantly and proffered the parchment. Abigail took it; using her thumbnail she scored the sealing wax and broke it apart. She read swiftly, gasped, and dropped the document before collapsing. Fate, it seemed, was dealing with her sharply.

Chapter Ten
Two Weeks Later

"Good day, Reverend."

"Good day, Mrs Jones," Bayles replied and cursed silently, for this was certainly not a good day. Winter refused to release the town of its icy grip, while the men sent to check, had returned earlier informing the Jurats that snow still blocked the top roads. *At least another month unless it rains,* they had gloomily reported and that was as likely as him forsaking beef for Sunday lunch.

"Be glad when spring comes, maybe then we can forget all this unpleasantness.... don't suppose you have seen the missus yet?" Mrs Jones indicated towards the Wood household.

He shook his head in feigned concern, aware that the events of the funeral were still the topic of conversation, from sewing circle, to tavern taproom.

"Unfortunately not, I daresay she remains indisposed. We must pray for her, Mrs. Jones, pray for her return to good fortune." He certainly didn't wish her well, but he had wondered when the harlot would reappear. Since the funeral he had pondered as to how he could impose himself upon her, how best to make her suffer as Joseph had suffered. But then, when he was berating himself for a lost opportunity, the lawyer Pawell, had sent joyous news. His opportunity to finish her was not lost, but simply delayed for a few more days.

"When I next speak to her I will inform her that you asked after her health." He would do no such thing, she deserved no one's attention but his. Bowing politely, he glanced, once more towards the house, and walked away. Edward Bayles, rector, keeper of the faith, and man of letters, had more than just a wayward woman to deal with. He had matters of such grave concern to resolve, that he needed time, and silence, to ruminate and consider his next move. That he could only do in the solitude of his rectory. Stormouth was tiny, a man of reasonable health could walk the length and breadth without breaking sweat. As such his walk home took but a few moments, no time to allow his mood to lessen. His coat, and tricorn hat were discarded upon the settle, the hallway gave him access to his study, where in the foulest of moods, he sat at his desk, brooding, seething, and scheming, until finally he called out,

"Bring me wine, a decanter, and a glass, girl." He barely noticed his housemaid, as she placed the tray before him. She was a comely wench, and under normal circumstances, she would have calmed his troubled mind. Today, her attributes were not what was required, he needed to think, and wine aided his mental vitality. Joseph had taught him that, as he had many other things, he had become his teacher, in what could be achieved if one strived hard enough. *Why did you leave me, why have you cast me into this role from which I will forever be called villain?* Memories of Joseph, only served to fuel his melancholy, he remembered the day when, in his darkest times, the Bishop had appointed him to this, his parish. Stormouth was as unknown, perhaps some mystical island in a tropical sea, he had soon learnt the error of such thoughts. The moment he walked through the crumbling gateway, he had seen the filth and deprivation. The town was a squalid, rat infested place, populated by lewd, foul beings, one step separated from animals. Beings so corruptible, so odious, and capable of such depravity, he thought himself at the gates of Hades itself.

More accustomed to rural life, Bayles had entered a cacophony of noise, where every other building appeared to be a tavern, filled to overflowing with the vilest customers imaginable. Fornication abounded, openly and unheeded; those not so absorbed, amused themselves with firing pistols at the unwary. Sodom and Gomorrah could never have been worse than what he witnessed.

Unwittingly, he had arrived during the town's darkest period, it was at odds with itself, and the outside world. Was that why the Bishop had sent him, to find good among so much bad, or to place him where he could do no harm? He knew not which, but the town would test him in those first weeks.

The church was poorly attended, God, had become lost, while the devil roamed unheeded. Criminals were in control and were themselves, controlled by a man known only as the 'The Chamberlin'. He was an enigma, his identity unknown, causing suspicion and accusation to abound. Such secrecy, condemned the influential residents, almost all were suspected; even Joseph's name had been mentioned as being the elusive smuggling master. When eventually, Pope, had revealed the man's identity, few could believe his guilt. Pope, was not to be denied, after disposing of the man he destroyed his family, but he never did find the goods, supposedly concealed somewhere within the district.

Despite all its horrors, good existed. Away from the depravity of the lower town, Stormouth's rich and influential families lived in splendour upon the hill. Isolated and cossetted, they attended church, socialised excessively, and lived well upon the good things of life. Wealth bought their safety and influence, those same families made up his congregation, along with their servants. One man, had introduced himself after that first Sunday service from that first encounter a friendship had developed, a friendship that became more than simply two men who shared a common interest. Soon, Joseph was teaching him that not all business was conducted in Pettit's coffee house, or on the quays, but secretly between like-minded men.

Joseph had been good to him, kind, generous, but that had changed, and he remembered that day as his 'Damascus Moment'. It was while walking along the quays that Joseph had spoken. All day he had been quiet, as if contemplating some weighty issue. Finally, as they had stood before the 'Butts' he had made his proposition.

"Behold our open wound, our sewer of depravity. More evil resides within that place, than in hell itself. The dregs, the dross, the vermin never sleep. They are active all hours and it is said Rector, that more goods are carried ashore on their backs, than arrive by ships into our harbour. Every tavern holds barrels of brandy brought ashore by them. Smugglers, Tubmen, Owlers, call them what you want; you will find their kind in there. Ask, though, and they will lie with the ability of a snake, they will deny any wrong doing, and swear on the Bible, as to their piety. They are scum but what can we do? We need them to work the ships, to haul the cargo. Oh, I know what you are thinking, priest, your piousness thinks me wrong perhaps you even desire to tell Pope all that I have spoken of. Laudable, but consider this question, what is your remuneration for being parish priest? I'll tell you; two pounds, five shillings a year and the use of the rectory. From that you must pay for kindling and a servant and your own food; not a fortune is it? What if I said I could show you how to double, triple, quadruple your stipend without fear of retribution; what would you say to that, my friend?"

Bayles remembered his response very well. He'd laughed at the apparent jest before realising the man had been deadly serious.

"I would ask you how such a means could be achieved...legally." Joseph had smiled, clasped his arm and guided him to a quiet alleyway, where he had been taught a valuable lesson.

"Wealth, and those who make it, drives our economy, Reverend. Despite our resident revenue officer, there is more than enough to be made. I can show you ways in which you could grow rich while avoiding the grubby fingers of our lords and masters. So I ask the question again, do you desire wealth, or, do you desire to remain a simple parish priest, and die impoverished like your previous incumbent?

His answer had come naturally, without thought or hesitation. For Edward Bayles desired all that life could offer and here was a man offering it to him willingly.

"A difficult question for a man such as I, to answer truthfully, though I would like to sample the finer things, if only once, before I die."

"If that be true, then you have reached your own crossroads of life, like Saint Paul you must choose which road to take. One will take you back to your church to continue ministering to the many; the other will deliver the better things of life. The choice is yours, but choose well for this will never be offered again."

"You ask a lot...my calling is to assist the weak, the infirm, am I to be seduced for a few gold coins?"

"Baaah, I waste my time if you believe such poppycock. The man I seek would know that such blather is spread by fools for the obedience of idiots. That such beliefs do not feed a hungry belly, nor do they provide comfort when the cold wind blows. I ask you again, sir, what is it to be?"

Sipping his wine, Bayles remembered the look that had crossed Joseph's face that day. He had insulted him and his offer, and was on the point of losing what he truly desired. Hurriedly he had spoken, hoping to stave off any misunderstanding,

"Comfort, of course," he had stated without further hesitation.

"Good, but be sure, for once indoctrinated there will be no return, you will be as guilty as I, and those I represent will deal with any indiscretion severely and without mercy, so be warned and take heed."

"I understand, Mister Wood, I understand completely." If Joseph had ignored his apology that day, he and Wood, would never have shared so much, but Joseph had been magnanimous and welcomed him into his heart. He had stepped across the line, joined Joseph, and in the fullness of time had discovered the extent of the dark underbelly of the town and entered Joseph's dark secret. Part of which had been that woman who had come to blight their lives. He wished now he had acted as Pilate had and washed his hands of her. But he could still right that wrong for he had Josephs confession and that was worth all the pain she had created.

That pleasure was for the future, for now he reconciled himself with more pleasant memories of that day with Joseph when he had been indoctrinated into a select group. Pupil and master had walked along the quayside, ignoring those who doffed their caps, or knuckled their forelock to them. Joseph's words had opened his eyes to what went on, and who really mattered within the town.

"Ignore the revenue, for they are but fools led by an imbecile. Pope believes he caught the Chamberlin, when in fact, it was we who gave him up to preserve our own necks. We needed to survive, to continue profiting from the ships which bring goods into our port and warehouses. Upon each load we pay the King's blood money, taxes which keeps his spies from looking too closely at what we do here. Do not mistake me, we pay our share, but far more goes undeclared, that profit flows into our coffers, not the King's."

"Do you not fear discovery?" he had asked innocently. His question had been met with the booming laugh that Joseph was renowned for.

"By whom, no one bothers. So long as the fat German gets what he suspects we should be paying everyone is happy. Perhaps we shouldn't bemoan our penury, for each pound won we lose five shillings, which is used to arm his troops and navy. They are a means by which our own trade routes are protected. In addition, it keeps his armies occupied abroad, while we do as we wish." At this point Joseph had shown a rare display of affection, he had put his arm around Edward's shoulder and smiled benignly.

"I think I understand."Bayles had stated, although he didn't as yet, but he would, Joseph had made sure of that.

"Wealth also gives us what you cannot. You, sir, give us impunity, you soothe our souls and redeem us with God, himself. We are but a small group, but we can aid you in what you desire most, serve us well and you will be a part of our family. A family to whom you will swear undying love, a family you will protect from those who seek to do us harm, for is that not what families do?

"I assume so." Bayles had been unsure at the time as to what he had agreed to, but certain it would be better than if he refused.

"Excellent, then we must show you what we do with our wealth and what could be yours."

Unsure of what to expect, Joseph had led him once again to the 'Butts' there he had stood, immaculate before such poverty, and said.

"A cesspit Reverent." Ignoring two children, who stood, arms outstretched seeking alms. Joseph had spoken with clarity of thought, and conviction. "The entire putrid hellhole should be raised to the ground. Never happen, or so some say, because there are those who state we need to keep the curs to off load the ships, I disagree. We are two separate entities with entirely differing economies, but each, apparently relies upon the other to survive. One is ordered and supreme, the other, this hovel, where they would slit your throat for a fresh cod, is putrid and rotten. Their only redeeming feature is that they deal with their own problems. They rarely disturb either magistrates or Jurats, dealing with most petty criminal acts themselves. Of course sometimes they over reach themselves and need our common sense to intervene. When such matters occur we deal with them swiftly and harshly. We transport a few; hang one or two, most we introduce to the lash. God knows they have to be controlled, left to their own devises they breed like rats.They are a necessity, they live, they die and they breed. However they take up land; land which we need to expand. I intend to clear them from this place, and build, but if my plans become known, those that have tenure will demand more for this hovel. Therefore, I must be circumspect, obtain each property by stealth and guile. For that I need men who will bid on my behalf. I pay such men well, in both coin and favour, and you, my clerical friend, would command little opposition if you did this for me as well. For your services you would find us very accommodating. Well, what say you?"

"God said that man must be accountable for his own actions. I myself have demonstrated that on numerous occasions." Joseph had nodded, but remained silent. "The fishermen, though, bring wealth to the town and much needed food, theirs is an honourable profession, for was that not our Lord a fisher of men?"

"You are a cully, sir, so I will impart some advice." Joseph had grasped the priest by the shoulder; and watched a boat unloading its catch. "If you aspire to more, listen well, sir…See what they land?"

He had stared down into the boat and listened intently as Joseph Wood had explained.

"They live off their catch of cod and crab. Not bad, but meager and hardly worthwhile. He'll feed his family today, but what of tomorrow? He will starve. What we need is commerce, Reverend, and with God's help and a fair wind, that is what I will bring to this carbuncle."

"I fail to see what poor fishermen have to do with what you foresee; can they not exist side by side?" Bayles had listened, but had not fully understood what Joseph desired.

"In part, but the dock is our future, our very existence relies upon its growth. These fools are stuck in the past, doing what their fathers did and failing to comprehend that we need to move on. Most of their catch will lay here and rot, then come winter, when the storms keep them in harbour, they will come; cap in hand to us merchants. Time has run out, we need to cast aside convention, bring down that abomination and build our future. More importantly, our commerce is hamstrung by that one road, down which everything must arrive and depart. A road which, becomes impassable by mud or snow during winter. My vision will see a new, flatter road through the 'Butts', a road, lined by warehouses and new docks, we must sweep aside the old ways and bring in new opportunities. Build our future on commerce, not fish. Imagine instead of that hovel, docks and quays filled with ships unloading into our warehouses. When I have finished the scum will live on the hill."

"While we live…where?" he had asked. At the time it had been an innocent question, the answer, though, had surprised him.

"Anywhere we damn well like." Then Joseph's words had seemed impossible. Now, as a respected member of the town, he knew Joseph's vision was possible.

"Until then, take what is on offer. Add it to the tithe your position affords you. Be patient and wealth will come as sure as night follows day."

Edward Bayles had relented and joined Joseph and his select group, whose actions while not always legal, opened opportunities to him to gain wealth he had never envisaged. No more was he simply the parish priest, a man who was to be pitied. From that day, his purse grew larger, with each service performed, be it marriage, christenings or burials. Cash was acceptable, but those who had little, paid in kind. His richer parishioners invited him to dinner; their pampered wives supplied him with interesting teas, where gossip came as second nature. Before long, not only was he living very comfortably, but he was also learning much about their private lives. Such information meant he could persuade them to do him the occasional service, in exchange for his knowledge not being made public.

Joseph, and the friendship they had forged was worthy of protection, as was Joseph's last, and greatest secret, a secret, so vile, it was not spoken of outside their group. It had, however, brought Abigail Wood to their attention and interest, especially when she was offered as payment for his continuing loyalty. Disappointingly, Joseph had died before the arrangement could be satisfied. Annoyance had turned to lust, which had become a brooding morass of stifled irrational resentment. His unfulfilled dreams were re-awakened in the silence of his study where, he had re-read his friends confessional letter.

Chapter Eleven

"Scheming Bitch." His anger made him throw the glass against the wall, whereupon he heard his maid behind the door and shouted, "Go away, be gone." She would have to go, for she had a loose tongue, and he could ill afford his private anger to be known throughout the town. Abigail had become, his festering boil which would not heal, or the stone in his shoe which, no matter how often you looked, failed to be rid of or forgotten. Deliberately he had kept his distance from her, and the family, since the funeral. He could have called, offered his hand in friendship, but that would have been hypocritical, for he loathed the very ground she walked upon.

Since first appearing at the 'George' where she had taken up residence, and from where she proceeded to hold court, much like the Queen of Sheba, she had haunted him. Her pretense was that of a woman of means, painting her way around the country, when in fact he knew her game immediately. She was a predator seeking a husband. As he had warned Joseph on more than one occasion

"She seeks a rich suitor, or a rich family. Nathaniel will be in her eye, for he is eligible."

"I'll see the bitch run out of town first, for she'll get neither, not if I have anything to say on the matter." Joseph had failed in stopping the marriage, but he might still succeed in discrediting the whore. From the time Nathaniel had brought her to this very house to formally introduce his intended to him, Bayles had sworn to do all he could to end their dalliance. It was what his friend had demanded and he would do anything for Joseph. The manner of her destruction was one he could not condone, but he could not doubt its effectiveness. Joseph had promised her to him, yet twice she had escaped their clutches, by fair means or foul, she would not escape again.

"My God, we could have ended this so easily." He cursed her name, the very ground upon which she walked, the very air she breathed. He despised her and wished Pope had dealt with her, but instead, that fool had condemned an entire family for no other reason than he had no one else to blame. Not one hundred yards from where he sat, the evidence of that stupidity, remained to be seen. Beach House, the Boatman Tavern, The church and the town square, had all played their part, and resonated with the memories of those horrors. The smugglers were finished, replaced with greed and avarice, and Bayles had often wondered, if what they had now, was worse than anything the 'Chamberlin' had ever done. Despite Pope's blood lust, the town had survived virtually intact. Allegations were made, but such matters were soon forgotten and the town had returned to doing what it did best, minding everyone else's business. She remained, and all the while she did, his lust for her grew, but now it had intensified into utter contempt, due in no small part by her deviousness, and the manner in which she had dismissed him so painfully. His shame was irreparable and made him determined to ruin her once and for all.

"The whore will pay for what she did!"His voice echoed around the silent study, his rage so severe, he slammed his fist onto the desk top. No woman would be allowed to discredit either him, or the memory of his friend. He would do all he could to prevent further insolence. It was an insult to Joseph's memory that she remained in his house. The moment wasn't right, but it soon would be for unknown to anyone, Bayles was a man, to whom death mattered little. He had killed before and had contemplated her demise more than once. He could have done it, throttled her with his bare hands while she slept, but what would that have achieved? A moment of pleasure, followed by the possibility of his own exposure and committal. No, if Joseph's plan was to be implemented, it would require guile and cunning, not outright murder. Pawell, Joseph's lawyer, would work his magic, and he would watch as the law destroyed her far more effectively than he ever could. She would be eradicated, snuffed out like the evilness she was, with not the slightest suspicion falling upon him, or Joseph's memory. The sands of time were running out, very soon, she would suffer far more in life than she ever would in death. With that thought, he summoned his maid, he desired her presence, for tomorrow, would bring much elation.

* * *

Dawn the next day brought little in the way of relief. The women he detested, she sat alone in her room, hurting within. Like her heart, the room was as cold as ice, but it was the overwhelming grief for her husband, snuffed out like a candle which left her so bereft. Staring forlornly through the frost etched window she shivered, the shawl and feeble fire unable to bring warmth to neither room nor soul. She was a prisoner, not through fear, but choice. Two weeks since the funeral and the town was no longer shrouded in winter's cloak. Mud strewn slush had replaced the pristine whiteness, purity replaced by filth. Tracing a tear stained finger across the windowpane, the crystalline patterns smudged and smeared, but like her hopelessness she knew that they would return.

"Am I to blame, is this why God has deserted me? Am I not pure of thought, if not mind, am I to be punished for rebuking his advances?" First Joseph and her shame, then Nathaniel, was there anything else she must endure before God allowed her to find sanity once again? "I am not guilty; I am the sinned against, not the sinner, dear God, open your eyes and see a helpless lamb seeking guidance from the evils that have befallen her."

The cause of her pain lay upon her dresser, crumpled, tear stained and discarded. The document, dropped in grief, had been retrieved by no less than Bayles, who had made great play of handing it to her. If he had realised how those words had made her feel he hadn't shown it. He had remained, cold and uncompromising, perhaps he had realised that, with such a declaration, any hope she had of escaping this desolation had ended. Each word had leapt from the page, slowing her world and ripping her heart asunder.

"We, the Board of Insurers, regret to inform you, the owners of the ship 'The Swallow', that said ship is reported lost with all hands south of the lands known as Honduras."

"Why...why you my love, why now?" The question, of course, was rhetorical; there was no logical reason why she had been selected to bear this pain. The news, and the way it had been delivered, were forever etched into her memory like those delicate filigree patterns etched by the frost. Unlike those, her pain would not melt with the warmth of a rising sun. Her life, already so complicated, had descended into a dark, despondent place from where escape appeared impossible.

Closing her eyes, the memories of that terrible encounter returned to haunt her, as it had, every hour, of every night, since Joseph had attacked her. When the truth was revealed, she would find a few who would believe her, but would those include his family and close friends? Would she be shown Christian Charity, or would they swear Joseph was not so inclined? Why Joseph, was, by character capable of much duplicity. Did he not tell everyone he despised strong liquor, while, in the privacy of his home, he indulged wholeheartedly on Rum, sometimes, as he had been that night, to the point of inebriation. That night he had been drunk and came to her room with evil intent. Innocently, she had opened the door, to find him leaning upon the doorframe, red faced, wheezing heavily. Spittle had dribbled onto his shirt, tinged with rum, it looked like blood. Initially, he had appeared calm, but that had changed swiftly. She had tried to close the door, but he had placed a foot in the gap, preventing her. Forcing himself into the room she had...no, the memory was too disgusting to remember. Unconsciously, she moved her hands so they caressed her belly; so far she had concealed her ailment. When the time came, she could feign illness, move back to Barminster until after the event and then return, cured; such things occurred all the time. *May he rot in hell* for that was her fate?

* * *

She still remembered little after reading the message, vague images of her heart pounding within her, then chilling like ice. She remembered swooning and of being carried, she assumed, to this room, where she had slept fitfully, tossing and turning, remembering.

"Dear God, guide me, I beseech thee." Her words, though profound were cut short by a loud voice demanding to be heard outside in the street.

"Be gone you scum, return to whence you belong...my God, to behave like beasts of the field is an abomination...be gone I say!" Normality existed outside her room and to hear it was something she desired to witness. Rubbing away a patch of ice, she searched for Bayles, for his voice was unmistakable, it echoed about the town as it did every Sunday from his pulpit. Someone had upset him, which was not difficult.

"There you are!" She whispered, as two figures retreated towards the harbour area. A sailor and a girl, the girl laughing, the sailor raising two fingers to the priest. For the first time in weeks she chuckled at his bravery. Such activities were becoming common place, apparently more ships than normal were in harbour, forcing such men to seek, what shelter they could find in the alleyways of the upper town. Her maid spoke of such things while combing her hair, she spoke of blood being seen upon the streets, evidence of the violence such activity brought to their doors. Not that she let it be known that she knew of such things; decorum had to be maintained. Maybe that was what Bayles was doing, attempting to keep order in a town that was becoming trapped by nature.

The road remained closed, and until reopened, the town remained isolated. Starved of information, everyone awaited the first coach, for only then would the residents have something other than her to gossip about. Until the weather abated, she was trapped, not by chains but by nature, along with the letters destined for her father which she kept secreted in her embroidery box. That sailor and his whore, were the lucky ones, they could run and laugh, disregard the 'Ravens' remonstrations and live a life she could but dream of. All she had was a view of the sea, a sea that had taken her only love and her memories. Though sometimes when the night was dark and the silence, perfect, she would shudder, as if he had stroked her shoulder with a ghostly caress.

"Good morning, to you sir, damned whores become bolder bringing their trade to our very doors, I shall speak to the squire, something must be done." Whoever, Bayles spoke to was hidden, but he looked foolish, hitching his cloak from the mud. She lent closer to the glass and saw him look up, stare directly at her, and she winced in alarm. Her heart quickened, as the reality of his destination struck her. He approached this house, her home, he was about to confront her of that she was sure. She relaxed, for he was gone, but shortly afterwards, a knock at her door made her wince in alarm.

"Sister dear...Reverend Bayles has asked if he might call upon you. If you agree, he asks to meet with you at your convenience." Abigail was torn; her sister-in-law Sarah was friendly enough, but the very mention of his name made Abigail shudder. She was trapped, with no escape, what could she do? She had known this day would arrive; it was only natural that she would have to confront, not only Bayles, but life in general. To remain hidden, like a frightened child, could not continue; there were important issues to be confronted. Joseph's will, must be read; merchants would be clamouring for their goods, the warehouses must be reopened. More importantly, Nathaniel's affairs needed to be resolved. It was only natural that Bayles would desire to meet with her, so why was she being so cautious? *Because, such matters pale into insignificance, whenever our venerated friend becomes involved,* Was she being fair, was it right to delay any longer?

"Fairness... has anyone been fair to me?" she whispered.

"Abigail...what say you?" Sarah asked from beyond the door.

"God save me." She had not meant to speak aloud, now her options were limited. "Tomorrow, sister...tomorrow afternoon, ask him to return then."

"Mr Pawell also?" Sarah enquired.

"Yes...I will see them both." It was done, her fate sealed, there was to be no escape. She was trapped, her life was now dependent upon the whims of the Wood family, while her father, had no knowledge of her perilous situation. *May God protect me because I doubt anyone else will?*

Chapter Twelve
February 1773. The morning

After a night of despair, Abigail woke to a winter sun sparkling through frosted windows. Despite her misgivings she felt relaxed, less perturbed than she had for many days. The reason for her euphoria was the realisation that before too long she would no longer be alone. With Bayles bent on her demise, she had taken steps to ensure her safety. She had contacted the name she had been given, and passed a message. With that done, she felt able to face her demons and end this heinous association with the past.
Unbeknown to everyone, this would be the precursor to whatever fate lay in store.

"A fine day, ma'am, the snow has stopped and Mr Weaver says the top road should be open soon."

"Then we must pray Mr Weaver is correct." Abigail sat up and smiled, though the mention of Weaver, the local vintner, caused her heart to miss numerous beats. Her maid, appeared happy that the veil of sadness had lifted from her mistress, while in truth, Abigail hoped for salvation very soon. Weaver called each week, he was pleasant enough, they exchanged the odd meaningless word, but he was also her contact, the name, she had been entrusted with. Upon his last visit, she had slipped a note to him along with his payment. That seemingly unimportant message about the road, was confirmation that there was hope. Her father would send assistance, end her torment.

"Will you be taking breakfast downstairs, or should I bring a tray?"

"Neither, I will eat later; for the moment, I wish to be alone with my thoughts." This day would prove disturbing, for she suspected Bayles could remain silent no longer. If so she needed to be prepared. "Ask Mistress Martha what time Mister Pawell is due to arrive, and then lay out my mourning dress. I shall not require you until one hour before our guests arrive, when I will need assistance to dress."

"As you wish, ma'am." Her maid was pleased that Abigail appeared brighter, more like her old self. There had been times when she and the staff thought she might fade away locked in her room. However, if she was taking an interest in the day-to-day affairs, that must mean she was coming to terms with her tribulations. As cook had said,

"It is the task of women to carry the burden of woes this life presents upon our shoulders." If that was true, then Mistress Abigail had borne her fair share. Two tragic events, so close to each other, had begged the question, would she ever recover? Perhaps now was the time, while she was happy, to

Ask about a subject that was causing the staff so much concern.

"Beg pardon, Ma'am… But Cook says there is to be a meal…she says there is much for the family to discuss."

"There is, it is a most worrying time, but what concerns you most?"

"We was wondering like…what with Master Joseph and all…well…will we keep our place here?"

Immersed in her own problems and fears, Abigail had forgotten that others were affected. A host of staff, mainly young girls, might be thrown aside without reference or prospect if the will was contested by anyone. Honestly, she replied…

"I fear…I cannot answer that…I do not, as yet, possess such knowledge. But I promise that if the reading goes the way I trust it will, I will do all I can for them."

"Thank you, ma'am," Maud curtsied and hurried from the room leaving Abigail to smile, at least she had made one person in this foul abode happy, if only for a short period. Once alone Abigail sat and with a renewed focus drew paper and quill towards her. *No longer will others determine what I do,* she thought. *I have been naive for too long.* If she were to fall, the truth must be known. She began to write, to place the events into a logical and forthright manner. The afternoon meeting would, she was sure, be the priest's chance. With the family gathered, he would have his audience, while she would be isolated and friendless, the perfect opportunity for him to disclose what, if anything, he knew. *I must remain resolute; whatever occurs, my defence must be denial. All they have is one man's word against mine. Without further proof they are powerless to act. If I can delay, convince them he lies, then even now I may be able to survive until father arrives, and I can escape relatively unscathed.*

She shuddered in apprehension but this was the life she had chosen, they were experts at what they did, but this time, Bayles and the Wood family had proven worthy adversaries. If she had heeded her father, remained at home all this could have been avoided. But that wasn't her way; she had been brought up to do what was right even if that included placing herself in harm's way.

Perhaps her arrogance had become her Achilles heel. Her predicament was of her own making, she alone had convinced those who had wavered of her ability. Despite her best efforts she remained no closer to discovering what secrets the Wood family concealed. Her only true evidence was the character of a dead man, Joseph was a sadistic bully, who cared not a jot for anyone and hid a secret so vile, that even she, had difficulty in believing him capable of such things. Why, if his traits were known, did so many admire him? That appeared to be a question she would never answer. Nor, if she was exposed by Bayles, would she have the opportunity to explore the town for further evidence. Her thoughts were disturbed by the sound of knocking upon her door and a voice asking…

"Abigail, may I disturb you?" Flinching in alarm, she tensed as she recognised the voice of her sister-in-law Martha. Of the four, she was the one she admired and feared most. As Josiah's wife, it was she who knew most of what occurred within the house, and who had assumed the mantle of hostess immediately following the death of Joseph's wife. Abigail had usurped her position after marrying Nathaniel but now it seemed she once again, desired to hold sway over them, at least until the will had determined who was to lead the family out of this quagmire.

"Of course," The door opened, and Abigail rose. Martha's presence made her feel apprehensive. She was a determined woman, not harsh, but not the sort to suffer fools gladly. She stood before Abigail, and said,

"We, your family, cannot comprehend how you feel or how we would deal with such news, but we fear for you, sister dear, alone in this room. You have not attended downstairs these past few weeks and we grow concerned as to your wellbeing. To that end, Josiah has asked that you join us for a small meal we have arranged for Mister Pawell. We thought it best to feed him, nothing grand, just a simple repast to ease what will, undoubtedly be a difficult time for us all.

"You are too kind, I will do so with pleasure. Pray, tell what time is he expected?"

"A little after noon, he has sent word as to who is to attend." Martha stated, glancing at a half-finished tapestry. Mention of others made Abigail inhale sharply.

"Is it not to be just family?" Martha remained ominously silent, as if she sought the right words. Such reticence was unlike her. Abigail and Martha would never be friends but there was a bond, an affiliation. Josiah's wife, had offered nothing but kindness and support. Unlike Sarah, Martha could, she thought, be trusted, she had remained silent throughout the past few weeks neither asking, nor demanding explanations, nor adding to her misery. Adam's wife, Sarah, was totally different. She was contrite, difficult…spoilt, a woman who loved anything that did not involve hard work, the family or running a house. She was hostile, for no apparent reason, rose late every day, placing great strain on both family and staff with her demands. She was in essence a wastrel, more suited to the life of society in London, or Bath, than the small town of Stormouth. Neither was she overstretched in matters surrounding the business; unlike Martha, her position was safe, she had few responsibilities and too much time to fill on nonsensical matters. Despite her faults, Sarah, was a fascinating person, who hid behind a façade of mayhem and intrigue. Was it any wonder that with three, such women beneath one roof, friction sometimes occurred?

"No. We of course are to attend, you would imagine nothing less. But the household staff are also commanded to be there. I cannot imagine why, father hated their presence, he viewed servants as unproductive, an unnecessary expense." Joseph had indeed been vocal about such matters, which had puzzled her as to why if he hated those who added nothing to his wealth did he allow both Adam and Sarah to live as they did? Adam, like his wife, was little more than a spoilt child who had much to say but contributed little. Only one explanation came to mind, they provided something the old goat had needed. What that was, Abigail had so far failed to uncover, but it had to be something, far more valuable than mere coinage. For they appeared able to manipulate him because of what they shared. Martha fingered a loose thread and sighed, as if remembering something, but wasn't sure whether to speak of it, or remain silent.

"Status, I imagine." Abigail paused. Behind Martha, Stormouth retained the snow that had, all but, closed the town, for so long. "Servants prove to those he needed to impress that he had the wherewithal to afford such things." For a rare moment she smiled, something she had done little of since the funeral. Like any woman entering a family, Abigail had, at first, been viewed with suspicion, perhaps still was by those who feared her. Such mistrust had allowed her to observe them closely, what she saw had finally made sense. Joseph was not the sort to allow anyone to live off him without contributing. To ignore his son's idleness, must mean there was a trust that existed between them. She thought she had worked out the reason, it pained her to believe such vileness, but Sarah must have been satisfying the old goat.

"As you say, he worked very diligently at presenting an acceptable face to the world. Despite what we knew…" Martha stopped, and Abigail saw the tear in the corner of the woman's eye. Suddenly it all made sense; it wasn't just Sarah that he had debased, but Martha as well. If that were the case, than she was no longer alone. Her heart soared in relief, together they would expose what he had done. But was this the time to ask for assistance? No, for to do so might force her to withdraw, and refuse to speak further of her shame. But Abigail needed to know, which was why she chose her words carefully, hoping Martha would recognise their meaning and feel safe to come to her at some later date.

"Indeed he did. I wonder if our lives will ever be the same again. Can his memory ever be erased, or indeed his deeds, more importantly, should they? Is it not our duty to tell the world what kind of man he was, or should we simply continue his work and draw a line under the past? Personally, I would wish to shout his deeds from the church tower, so all would know what gifts he left this world. Then when that is done, we can close this chapter and begin anew. The house has been maudlin for too long, it will be good to have such matters finalised."

"During father's funeral, Reverend Bayles spoke of fidelity and trust..." Martha paused, and Abigail sensed an inclination that she wished to speak but wasn't certain as to how to explain what troubled her. She turned and stared out the window, pausing before speaking again, but lost as if the moment had passed. Perhaps she had decided that with Wood gone, she could deal with whatever troubled her alone. "It is time we became a family again, sister ...time we settled any differences we may have."

"Differences; do we have any?" Abigail asked, wishing Martha would speak further, give her the evidence she desired.

"I trust not...however, your absence, causes consternation. We fear for your continued good health."

"I thank you for your concerns but they are unfounded. I ail not, but simply wished to console my loss alone. Is that not acceptable?"

"Indeed, I have stated this on numerous occasions, which is why we trust that this afternoon will see an end to any further misapprehension. That we can, as you said, put aside the past and move on."

"My wish as well, sister." Abigail agreed. "Please inform the family that I will attend shortly."

"Thank you. We look forward to your return."

"No need for thanks, Martha dear. As you rightly say, we have to learn from our misfortunes. We must reacquire the ability to trust each other, to work together for the greater good. It is what my husband would have desired."

After Martha had curtsied and left the room, Abigail sat and contemplated what had, and more importantly, what had not been said. They were concerned and she understood those fears. Joseph had been the driving force in both business and family, without his presence, would either survive? Hence Martha's visit, she was to gauge her demeanour. Downstairs, the family would have been contemplating their options. Who would lead the family, who would receive this, and how much. Greed would have raised its ugly head, more importantly they would desire to know how she would react at the reading of the will. More importantly, knowing his liking for young flesh, they would be concerned as to whether Joseph succumbed, and removed them all from his estate. Their other concern would be her, what role would she take in the coming months. As the eldest son, Nathaniel should have inherited, what now though? Had Joseph made provisions, would she by default take command? So much would depend on the specific wording of the document and that was why Martha had visited. They were worried, even the curtsey Martha had performed showed her much of their thinking; they were preparing to offer her homage, to form an alliance, if she took control.

What will they do when I reveal my news? Will they accept a bastard child into the line of inheritance? She was well aware of the laws concerning such matters. Whoever took control, would find the sons difficult. Neither had taken any form of interest in the business, which was why she envisaged Joseph discounting their involvement, which left just her, perhaps in conjuncture with Pawell, to take control. If that were the case, then she would finally gain sight of the firm's records, details which Joseph had concealed would become knowledge and that would aid her own cause, something that had stalled while Joseph had lived. In a few short hours, and with the aid of a document, life would never be the same. For the moment, she would remember a lost love.

Chapter Thirteen

"She agrees." Martha stated breathlessly entering the room where three expectant figures waited this news.

"Really, she agrees to relinquish all claims and give us control, without question?" Josiah stood before the open fire, foot tapping nervously against the fender, hands clasped behind his back. His voice, barely able to disguise the amazement he felt. They had gathered in the drawing room, the shutters were open allowing flecks of floating dust to be seen as they swirled and dipped within the reflected beams of winter sunlight before alighting on the old furniture. Like the family, the house could be said to be past its best and in decline. Yet here were three anxious people, who suddenly felt relieved by her words.

"Thank God, Pawell can now ignore her ridiculous claims and distribute what we are due," Adam Wood was far more elaborate than his brother. His face, powdered and rouged, was embellished with a black beauty spot affixed to his left cheek. Its presence, gave him the appearance of a dandy, which of course was what he aspired to. His periwig, brash and coiffured with care, appeared too large for his face and far too large to be accommodated within the deep upholstered chair where he lounged wearily.

"That is not what she agrees to," Martha stated. "She agrees to join us for luncheon. However, I believe she has sought guidance and reached a decision."

"It is a start," Josiah added. "What of her demeanour? Will she? Can she be manipulated?"

"Damn the bitch!" Adam exclaimed, striking the panelled wall with the head of his walking stick. His anger just as volatile as it had been since the funeral.

"Am I to assume, that your friend Irons, requires yet another payment?" This was a statement from an elder brother to an erstwhile younger sibling who spent money as if it were water. The death of their father created opportunities for them both, but neither expected, nor desired the responsibilities the business offered. Adam saw this as a heaven sent opportunity to escape, to take what was on offer and leave behind a waste land of bad debts and unpaid bills. As different as chalk and cheese, Josiah at least knew what had to be done,

"No more than I can deal with, brother dear," Adam sneered, removing a pinch of snuff from a small engraved gold box. Sniffing elegantly he inhaled the mixture and fought the desire to sneeze, to do so was considered humiliating. "Damn Nathaniel. How dare he be so…inconsiderate and die on us like that?"

"Have a care, she will hear." Josiah cautioned his brother. Adam had been coddled from life's tribulations, protected by a father who cared more about the family's good name, than the debts accrued by a young fool who had no idea of money or its worth.

"Do I care what the bitch hears? No, I do not. Admit it brother, even you found it difficult to contain your feelings of joy as he was buried." Adam brushed an imaginary fleck of dust from the cuff of his coat, a coat which was far finer, far better made and of such quality that Josiah marvelled at its cost.

"I admit nothing, though I would question how you came by your apparent good fortune." Josiah knew there were but two ways for a man, such as his brother, to acquire such finery. One was to garner credit in lieu of his inheritance, very feasible. The other was to have had the cloth imported by means of the Owlers. Smuggled goods was by far the more credible option. However the coat had been obtained, the cost far exceeded his monthly allowance.

"That, dear brother, is for me to know and you to ponder. I will admit though, it is a goodly coat, one I am most pleased to own."

"I would urge caution, consider your situation with your creditors. Ask yourself how long they will wait if she gains control of both business and your purse string. Not long I would think nor will you garner favour with her if she hears your comments. A lifetime of purgatory waits if you continue in that vein this afternoon, not only is your future at risk, but ours as well. Treat her unjustly and we might find ourselves on the street by nightfall." Josiah's words were harsh but true. Collectively they awaited a woman, who by rights should not be in such a position.

"By rights there should be no controversy. With Nathaniel gone, you as next eldest should take it all. That is what we should say if Pawell reveals anything to the contrary." Martha held her husband's hand and smiled sweetly. Abigail had misread the woman. Martha was a woman who wanted what she considered hers by right.

"Hush, wife, such matters are not to be spoken about aloud. Certainly not by you, such matters are for men to discuss rationally."

"Stuff and nonsense, have we not all conjectured as to how this absurdity will be resolved. Have not Adam and Sarah deliberated as to their position if that bitch steals what is rightfully ours? I have. With Nathaniel dead, we risk ruination. Consider this; we await the word of a dead man, a man who despised each and every one of us. Should I remind you, husband, that he called you a leech and you, Adam, as unworthy to bear his name?"

"I care little for what that old man said. His words count for little any longer, though in truth I fear his demise may have left certain aspects unfulfilled. What if he failed to make proper recommendations, if he did not then as Josiah states, we could find ourselves dependent upon Nathaniel's widow for everything down to how much we pay for firewood. Not a situation any of us would chose, especially to be beholden to a woman who you must admit, has been distressed and incoherent with grief. I sense the next few hours will be filled with trepidation, trepidation and grief. Mark my words."

"We do not often agree, but on this I must recognise your apprehensions and concerns, brother," Josiah concurred. "But I would still urge caution. We must cosset her, keep her safe, pander to her wiles and yes, if necessary, worship the ground she walks upon, just in case the old goat did leave her control of the business"

"Damn him, and the business. What of our home, our status, our position? I tell you truly, if he wasn't rotting in the ground, I would kill him. The man is a swine in death, as he was in life!" Adam wasn't the sort to stay silent. Those who knew him, would vouch that he had few desires in life save cards, women, wine and clothes, all of which required money. Coin and credit were his lifeblood, his air, his reason to live and the business gave him the means to live very well indeed. Work, of any sort, was unpalatable; he was a fop, a dandy, brash and loud. He rarely paid for any of his pleasures, such debts, as were accrued at Mr Iron's establishment, were settled from a secret account controlled by Pawell, serviced by Joseph. Why that occurred, was known to one man alone, and he had taken that secret to his grave.

"Will you be so vociferous when the money ceases? Of course not! For if that occurs brother dear, you will have to work for a living, not a subject either of you are acquainted with." Josiah was the sort of man, who rarely lost their temper, but Martha knew this was something that concerned him terribly. Even so, the thought of Sarah and her foppish husband sweeping streets or scrubbing steps made her chuckle inwardly. Both were more used to polite, genteel events such as taking tea and discussing matters at some house party. Most probably, when the money ran out so would Sarah. "I would suggest we do all we can to prevent such a tragedy befalling us. Our method…convince her that we should not be overlooked, that we should share control alongside her. To that end, we have but a scant few hours to convince her. I suggest we do not waste this last opportunity by upsetting her in any way."

"That is your plan, your master stroke? Your only idea is to…plead with her…to follow her like some lap dog awaiting her pleasure?" Adam sneered, this argument had simmered since they had been informed of their father's death. Both were rivals for the same position yet neither desired to reveal to the other, the hatred their father had shown towards them.

"Sneer all you wish, but I will do whatever needs to be done to keep this family together, and the firm successful. Perhaps, you are too…self-obsessed to hear the rumours that abound about our situation. Not a month since we buried him and already there is talk of our imminent downfall. Yet you speak of separating us from the one person, who might, just might, be instrumental in our salvation. You, sir, are a fool if you fail to acknowledge the fact that if we do not resolve this…improbable, our customers will look elsewhere. While those we upset will eventually send the bailiffs to regain their stock. To avoid such a travesty is why, I would toady to her, and I would urge you to do likewise."

"You're limp ways make me sick," Adam sneered, "father would not have conceded so easily. He would not have allowed this…to occur. Kick her out I say, take what is ours and damn the consequences." Brothers glared at each other, the younger sibling, shook with anger. They were different from their father, but also similar. While Joseph wouldn't have allowed such a thing to occur, they, by breeding, were already hatching plans as to how best to deal with the problem they had inherited. Adam, though, had more pressing reasons to inherit. Mister Irons was not his only debtor. There were others, less patient men, men who shared his intimacy and therefore could harm him far more than Irons ever could.

"So speaks the voice of experience…" Josiah, wasn't able or accomplished at negotiations. He'd tried, since hearing of his father's death, to contain so many factions. While Adam plied the gaming tables and Abigail sat morosely in her room, he had been left to deal with ever more belligerent customers. Each day another damning note arrived demanding the release of some item of goods. Meanwhile the family bickered and snarled at each other like a pack of rabid dogs. "…the man, to whom life means so little. If only you had paid heed to what was happening within this house you would know the secrets that must be protected. Yes, brother dear, I have known for some time your…traits. Mother confided in me, Nathaniel was also privy to your sordid ways, but she swore us to secrecy. Do you think that, she…will guard you as well? No, if pushed your vile peculiarities will become common knowledge, then what will you do? I will tell you, you will be devoured, then sat out once your bones have been picked clean left to rot on the street. But we, your family, your blood, can protect what you desire to keep contained. So you see, we are caught between the devil and this woman. She could hold our future, not to mention our fortune, in her grubby hands."

Martha and Sarah, waited. This was an argument only brothers could resolve. Neither would concede, to do so would mean a loss of face, destitution, perhaps death, the question was, which would occur first.

"You know…?" Adam asked.

"Of course. Did you believe he would not use your…ways to rip our mother's heart asunder? He used you against her at every opportunity, why do you believe he spared you, while I, and she took the worst of his temper. She protected you as best she could, but there was only so much she could do. But brother there came a time when…to protect her…and sickened by what he did, I followed him. God knows what I expected, I was barely fourteen, yet even then I knew you had to be spared his abuse…God knows why I tried, you never appreciated my efforts."

"I never knew"

"I know that was our pledge, but I conspired to harm my father. The Bible calls it a sin, but what he did was more of a sin and no one stopped him. I took a wooden stave, hid and waited for him to pass, then I attacked, I failed, he was wounded but alive. Returning home bloodied but sound of mind and arm, he sought retribution. While mother dressed his wounds, he stared at me, he knew, he may not have witnessed me during the attack, but he knew. With Nathaniel away, there was no one to protect us; he laid into me with renewed vigour. Mother nursed me, told me, he would never harm any of us again, yet, a year later she was dead. My God even then he did not change or waste time mourning his loss. Barely a month after her death, I caught him fornicating with a scullery maid. She was not the first, nor the last, our sainted father took anyone he desired, the younger the better. I confronted him and what did he do? He laughed at me." Josiah paused, looked at Martha, sighed then continued. "There is much that was kept from you, knowledge which, those privy to such knowledge swore to keep secret. But I swear, on all that is Holy, while carrying that coffin, I felt soiled, hypocritical. If I could, I would have left his corpse to bloat and rot on the marsh, allow the carrion to peck at his black heart, and I would have laughed, laughed at his demise, for that man was dead to me long before we buried him. So do not lecture me of suffering, My God sir, you are but the erstwhile son, who only appeared long enough to take what was on offer before returning to the tables? I had to deal with him, suffer his tempers, smooth his ego, and calm the staff. If anyone should inherit it should be me. But instead, I have to wait upon that woman and to hear what the will decrees. Until then, everything else is simply conjecture."

Josiah slumped into a chair and sighed heavily, his words left him feeling drained of emotion. He had said what should have been said long ago.

"A fine speech, but to use your own word Josiah, all that is…conjecture. My God, do you not realise that I knew what he was capable of, but your speech was more for your own benefit, to ease your own conscience? You may construe all you like but I tell you now, no matter what secrets you think need be to be kept hidden, that whore will, if she gains control, expose them to the world. She will hang our soiled linen out to be aired and viewed by all and sundry and not care one iota for our feelings. Moreover brother dear, if, as I sense, you hold out some forlorn hope that Nathaniel will re-appear, you will be sorely mistaken, for such a miracle would be as likely as asking that sickly priest to take snuff with the Devil. You were there, you heard, he is dead, feeding the fish. Salvation will not come from that quarter we are on our own now so I repeat my previous thought. Kick her out; retrieve what is ours, in doing so, you will recover your own self-respect. By God, sir, father would never have allowed it to come to this."

Adam saw his brother faltering, he was willing to whore himself before that woman in an attempt to keep what was theirs. While Josiah sighed heavily; perhaps his brother was correct, perhaps he clung to the forlorn hope that Nathaniel would return. Perhaps it was time to grasp the situation and act.

"The town is watching husband, they will expect to see us united in our grief," Martha stated, as Josiah wrestled with his conscience. "Not to do so will show weakness, such weakness will harm our business. I would counsel you both, keep your feelings concealed, at least until after the reading of his will. Once we know what is ours, I will gladly accompany you to piss on his grave."

Chapter Fourteen
The afternoon

Edward Bayles would, forever be grateful for Joseph's foresight, and his choice of friends. Pawell, was another, who was intimate with their plan. Joseph had chosen him well, had more filth upon the lawyer than most, for Pawell was a man who had...enjoyed the delights, offered by Joseph. He was as corrupt as any, had aided and assisted both in their acquisition of both property and wealth. The lawyer's hands were stained with what they had done, he had dipped his soul into the vat of corruption and profited from such, which was why, Joseph had gone to him to draw up the document which would finish her totally. Pawell would execute their plan legally, without any blame falling upon anyone but the bitch herself. She had annoyed him, and worst of all fallen foul. For such vexation, he would have pursued her to eternity, had he not died.

The time drew nearer, the moment when finally they would be rid of her but there remained a moment or two to read his friends final note once again. Some thought Joseph a bullish brute of a man, but in this document, he had shown his more subtle yet devious manner. He was indeed fortunate to have called Wood his friend for it was as if fate had drawn them, step by faltering step, to this precise moment in time, his destiny. He was fortunate, for he, knew, to the second when his journey began, not many could say as much. In saving a girl from a farmer's deviant ways, he had killed for the first time. Others had followed, another girl and her offish father, yet he remained as free as a bird, able to manipulate those who could be useful to his enrichment. *Fools; blind to what they fail to see. But soon I shall reap my reward. Take what was promised, or destroy them in the process.* The raven was intelligent, but also the messenger of death.

* * *

Ignatius Pawell smiled, then belched in grateful appreciation. The meal had been suburb, the meat and vegetables cooked to perfection, the apple pie and milk custard exquisite, while the claret had been excellent. It was rare for his clients to feed him, even rarer for the Wood family to exhibit such civility.

"My compliments for such a feast," Pawell remarked, delicately fingering the deep grooves in the oak chair, unaware of their significance, "however, the time fast approaches when we must begin this day's work." Withdrawing a gold hunter pocket watch from his waistcoat, he examined it closely, and noticed the hands had not quite reached the allotted time. "As you may be aware my client Mister Joseph Wood, gentleman of this parish, left meticulous instructions pertaining to the exact moment we should begin. Therefore I fear, we must wait a moment or two longer."

"While your bill increases exponentially, no doubt, damned lawyers," Adam, never one to be backward when money was involved, stared at Pawell testily.

"Be quiet. My apologies, sir, but as you can image we are all eager to hear our late father's wishes." Josiah glared at his brother and hoped the youth would remain silent for the remainder of this meeting. It would have been easier to stop the sun from rising, Adam had been drinking heavily and his disposition was one of annoyance. Pawell wasn't concerned, the family's problems were of no interest, he had a duty to perform, and do it he would.

"No need for apologies master Josiah, I have witnessed such eagerness before." Pawell smiled graciously at those who were seated around the table. Opposite him, Reverend Bayles was a picture of doom and despondency, dressed as always in his customary black, his face devoid of any apparent feelings. Between them sat the Wood family, while gathered around the room the house servants stood against the wooden paneling. "However, I am constrained by protocol, your father laid out specifically how this reading was to be conducted." Meticulously arranging his papers, he glanced, again at his pocket watch. The hour had not quite arrived, leaving him to stare at the expectant faces and recollect the strained meal they had just endured. "While we wait the allotted hour, perhaps you might like to hear of the interesting, yet disturbing, discussion I and Reverend Bayles had with our friend from London."

"Blast your insensitivity sir, now is not the time if what you speak of concerns the demise of my brother." Josiah glared at the solicitor. *How dare he raise this subject after eating so heartily from our table?*

"No, please, I would like to hear what he said, unfortunately I missed most of the detail due to my..."

"Vapours, madam," Abigail nodded politely, while the lawyer feared for what she had, and what she would have to endure.

"Damn you, Pawell, you are like a washer woman, full of useless gossip. What our learned friend attempts to relate, is that we took the damned man to the 'Boatman', where, over a pot of mussels, he told us what his employers knew of the loss. There done, simple, now get on with it." Bayles stated contemptuously.

"Mussels, a quart no doubt and wine as well, all added to our bill. We should express our thanks but I fear our pockets are not deep enough." Adam glared at the priest, eager to get this added tomfoolery done with so they could proceed to the real reason for their attendance.

"Master Adam, we meant no disrespect. Pawell and I assumed you would like to know all of what he knew, but if not, then I will foot the bill and remain silent." Bayles could be a pompous priest when it suited him, and Josiah had no intention of annoying anyone today, if it could be avoided.

"I am sure no disrespect was intended, please continue, tell us what you learnt?"

"There is not that much to add Master Josiah, the man simply reiterated what was written and what he had been told to relate to Mister Joseph…if he had had the opportunity."

"Which was sir?" Josiah demanded because he, as yet, had heard none of this…additional information."

"It would appear a slaver, discovered the wreckage some days after a storm had passed through that region bound for the Indies. The captain reported wreckage and, I fear, bodies. Among the wreckage were certain items which upon examination in Kingston, was proved to have come from your ship. They were the ship's figurehead, a winged Angel carrying a trident, and more importantly a chest bearing the Wood family cypher. By the way, Madam, I retrieved the note from the ground and asked Reverend Bayles to return it to you; I trust it gives you some solace?"

"Thank you, he did and I look at it every day."

"I am glad.

"Then it is still possible that our brother was not aboard at the time?" Josiah questioned.

"Possible, but unlikely, upon further investigations, and this was what took the time, it seems Mister Wood and the captain were seen boarding the ship in Boston. A town, I fear plagued by insurrection and traitorous intent. From what we know we must assume they, and other captains, deemed their safety compromised, and left with their holds largely unfilled. The messenger could only assume that they sailed south to find another suitable cargo."

"Damned rebels. I read of this problem. Ne'er-do-wells who think themselves above the law and speak of rebellion. The King will deal with them. Such intent must, if needs be, be quelled by force of arms, and so be it I say."

"You are, as ever, magnanimous to a fault Adam. If trouble did indeed occur, we should ask why and deal with those issues openly. Whatever their concerns, the colonists are kindred spirits. Whatever occurs in that troubled land, we will have to trade with them in the future, no matter what the King does? Or have you forgotten that the majority of our trade comes through Boston?

"Damn you, Josiah, and damn the colonies." Adam rose as if to leave, or worst still, strike Josiah. A moment of malice hung in the air as brother glared at brother. The tension ended by Pawell who, glancing at his watch, announced.

"I see the hour has arrived, I think we should begin." Smiling politely, Pawell waited while Adam retook his seat. The tension remained, but Pawell wanted this done, withdrawing the document with great pomp and diligence, he slit the seal, opened it fully and adjusted his glasses. "I state that the document remains sealed, that it has not been tampered with. Reverend Bayles, as witness to Mister Wood's instructions, do you concur that all is well?

"I do, Pawell, get on with it."

"I hereby testify, that in accordance to my instructions, the good reverend is also present to clarify that I conduct this reading in accordance to the terms as stated by the deceased. Should I deviate, then there would be grounds for a third party to challenge the legal validity of this document. With all the associated problems such a challenge would create."

"Meaning your fee would increase again, aye Pawell?" Adam sneered, but Pawell ignored the insinuation, today was difficult enough without being drawn into a families disputes.During luncheon he had observed them carefully, while appearing tolerant; they had fidgeted, continuously steering the conversation in one direction. Josiah, especially spoke constantly about the financial implications to both family and business, while Adam was more forthright. The boy's debtors were well known to Pawell, on more than one occasion he had delivered notes to some scurrilous individuals. Notes drawn upon the business, a father's attempt of concealing his youngest son's deviant like needs. Joseph had, for reasons known only to him, been prepared to do all that was required to hide the boy's problems. Strangely, those least concerned were Sarah and Martha, the son's wives. They said little but he did notice how they all avoided eye contact with the final guest, Mrs Abigail Wood. She appeared calm, hardly speaking, keeping her own counsel, yet it was obvious, she was the reason for the nervousness which existed between them.

"Meaning, sir, I do my client's bidding for which I have already received my stipend. Only if there are objections will that increase, the bill will then be shared equally among those named within this document. It would benefit all if there were no objections."

Pawell waited but none spoke, too ashamed, or too eager to get their hands on what they wanted.

"With that issue dealt with, I must firstly thank you for agreeing to attend. As you know, we are gathered to witness the reading of the last will and testament of Mister Joseph Wood, Gentleman of this parish."

"Is the document excessively long?" The Rector's voice was, polite but tinged with annoyance, "Only I do have parishioners to visit."

"I am afraid so, Reverend. Mr Wood made specific stipulations, insisting that the complete document had to be read in its entirety before all the concerned parties, I cannot stress that any stronger, if you are unable to spare the time I can…postpone until say…Wednesday week."

"No, carry on, let's see it through." Bayles sighed loudly and sat back. Unbeknown to those present he had no other business apart from a meeting with a very nice bottle of claret and the warmth of his housekeeper.

"Very well, if there are no further objections I seek your collective permission to take as read the numerous preambles, the minor points of law and legalities that are attached to all such documents. Or would you prefer me read them?"

"Oh do get on, man," Bayles said impatiently, "I for one tire of your blathering."

Pawell sighed. He and Bayles met often. Not only Joseph but death drew them together. To his eternal shame, they had, on occasions, aided those close to death to amend their thoughts. He had, with the priests backing and occasional encouragement, forged signatures upon documents, stealing from those unable to comprehend and without family to leave their wealth. Only rarely did they join forces, but Pawell knew Bayles as a less than honorable man.

"With your acquiescence established, I therefore have to inform you that Mister Wood attended my office a few weeks before his death. During that meeting various topics were discussed, one such matter was his reluctance to alter his will. Therefore, this is the document that was written long before the marriage between Master Nathaniel and his now wife… beg pardon ma'am his widow. To my knowledge no other exists, which is why the later codicil takes on a greater significance. This will become clearer as we discuss the legalities, but I stress, that codicil has gone before the Prerogative Courts and been proven. We are now at liberty to disclose what he desired."

Pausing momentarily, he sipped at a glass of red wine Sarah had thoughtfully placed in front of him. It was well known that he was a lover of fine wine, which the family were using to their advantage. It was common knowledge that he could be relied upon, when the need arose, to stretch a point of law if well fed. Delicately, he dabbed his mouth with a silken kerchief before continuing.

"This is the last will and testament of Joseph Wood, businessman and gentleman of Stormouth in the County of... Well we know where he lived, do we not? Good...good." Sipping the wine again, he indicated his appreciation with a satisfied smack of his lips, staring at the now empty glass in a way that indicated he wouldn't be adverse to a refill. A maid graciously obliged, dribbling a little on the table cloth which spread like a blood stain, something the family had seen at this table often.

"With that matter clarified we should progress to the important parts of the document. I Joseph Wood, dictated my wishes on this the twelfth day of September in the year of our Lord One Thousand Seven Hundred and Sixty Eight. I hereby affirm and bear witness before my solicitor and my God that I am of sound mind and body."

"Bloody old goat was inebriated and soft in the head," Adam said aloud, resulting in a stare of indignity from Bayles and Josiah.

"Is that an objection to the will, sir? Are you disputing your father's ability of soundness and clarity? If so, I shall duly note your objection, cease the reading, and instruct council to make representations."

"He means nothing of the sort, do you Adam?" Josiah demanded.

"No, get on with it, the old goat was sound in both mind and body to the best of my knowledge."

"Very well, but please do be aware that such terminology could be construed an objection, I do urge restraint." Pawell glared at them, before resuming reading from where he had stopped. "To that end, I do hereby bequeath and bestow upon my blood children, certain bequests as listed herein. To Nathaniel, my eldest son, I bestow as my legitimate heir, complete control of my business interests wheresoever and whatsoever there are at the time of my death."

"My God, he failed to make provisions. How are we supposed to do that ...Nathaniel is dead?" Adam demanded.

"Master Adam, I urge patience," Pawell insisted. "In the fullness of time you will understand why your father was so punctilious, also why his intentions were laid out so meticulously."

Pawell swallowed the lump that formed in his throat. If he had been one of them, he would be just as eager. Having written the document, he knew better than most what was approaching. He was of course studious, and when the need arose, of impeccable character and when allowed, executed his duties with compassion, humility and by the rule of law. However, Bayles had corrupted him, during the purges, the Priest, had come to him and suggested how best to survive all that Pope brought to the town. Before that meeting, Pawell had tried to tread a narrow path of righteousness, when most of his clients were known villains and the town was descending into lawlessness. He had tried to remain anonymous, but when he had discovered information pertaining to a heinous crime, he had taken that information to Pope. His actions had constrained a man to death. To this day he despised himself for what he had done, but until recently he had thought his actions worthy, now he knew differently. Bayles had used that incident, to blackmail him force him to do what the vicar required and he hated himself for what he had become. But that paled into insignificance compared to what he was to do. He had counselled Wood against such actions, pleaded that the wording be modified. To no avail, he had even thought about demanding Wood take his work elsewhere, but Wood had sneered at his words and countered his thoughts with veiled threats. As a mere functionary, he was innocent of wrong doing, he was simply complying with a client's wishes, no matter how much he detested it. He could delay no longer, they waited to hear what Wood had left them.

"As I explained, Mr Wood drafted his will some time ago. As such, much of what is written can no longer be held accountable in their singular context. However, taken as a whole, and read in conjunction with what comes later, much of what he desired becomes understandable."

The solicitor paused to find where he had stopped before continuing.

"What follows are bequests to certain members of the family. I must stress again that he was, in my opinion, of sound mind when he issued his instructions. Therefore, to Nathaniel, my eldest son, I decree and declare that as well as my business matters already mentioned, I leave my messauge and land in Stormouth. I also bequeath my warehouses and chattels, goods in storage, and business dealings. These are his to continue with as discussed during my life." Pausing once again, he glanced up from the papers and smiled weakly in Abigail's direction. "Your husband, madam, would have been a very wealthy man, as it is…well we must continue."

"A poisoned chalice, I fear, sir." Abigail stated. She witnessed the furrowed brow and wondered if his kindness was tainted with a degree of sorrow. Or was it simply her imagination running wild yet again? So far nothing that warranted concern had occurred. Perhaps she was to be spared after all. Clearing his throat, Pawell wiped his forehead, sipped his wine and continued.

"Your opinion my dear, my only concern is to what is written. To that effect Mister Wood continues. To Josiah, my middle son, I bequeath a one hundredth share of the family business. He is not a businessman, does not have the attributes, or the wisdom to know a balance sheet from a balance arm, but perhaps under his brother's guidance they will learn to work together and build on what I have begun. To Adam, my youngest son, I leave my plate, silver, furniture, and the sum of two hundred pounds per annum. Be it known that he will have nothing else. Once he has gambled, and whored his way to destitution, he will know the meaning of poverty. Perhaps he will learn a lesson when he has to work for a living; something which until now he has avoided with alacrity."

"Snot nosed bastard. I will contest, God damn it, contest it, I will!" Adam stood and stared at his brother with anger and hatred.

"If that is you're want, sir, then there is nothing more to say for I have no other recourse than to suspend these matters and refer them to another. Is that what you require?" Pawell asked

"No, God damn it, but really, a few plates and two hundred pounds is barely enough to…"

"To what Adam, clear your debts?" Josiah had problems of his own, a mere one hundredth share was nothing, and with Nathaniel gone who gained control?

"Am I to assume that you desire me to continue?" Pawell asked, receiving a collective nod from all but Bayles. "Very well then." He sipped once more at the wine, wiped his moistened brow and read on.

"To Sarah, wife of my youngest son, she has proved herself a most dutiful, accommodating and beguiling woman. For her understanding and assistance I leave her the sum of forty pounds per annum from the rental of my properties in Lower Ashbone. These properties are hers for the remainder of her life, to give her an income, to maintain her lifestyle. She is far too frail to suffer the indignity of ruination, which her irksome husband will no doubt bring upon them in the fullness of time. I also command my lawyer to make sure these properties are never sold out of the family, but to remain in trust in perpetuity. Sarah has been a joy to call my own, as has Martha, wife of my son Josiah. She likewise will be protected from the mishaps life can bestow upon the unwary. Therefore I do hereby bequeath the messauge and land in the village of Plymoil as hers in perpetuity to do with as she wishes. I trust she has the foresight to retain it as her right."

There was more, much more. Pawell continued reading, pausing continually to sip from his glass. Joseph Wood had been more generous in death than he had ever been in life, dividing his wealth between them comparatively equally. Surprisingly he even left bequests to members of his staff, items of clothing and so forth. One maid, Jane, barely seventeen was bequeathed an expensive gold locket.

"He wished it to be known that she was there when he needed solace from the tribulations of the world." Pawell remained stalwartly unconcerned, but all knew those words spoke volumes, certainly they were not the actions of the man most knew. Two people had apparently been overlooked; Abigail and Bayles. She noticed a bead of perspiration form on the solicitor's forehead. Pawell was feeling uncomfortable as he tugged at his neckerchief continuously. Then, avoiding their looks and with obvious reluctance, the solicitor read from the document.

"I leave those who mean more to me than anyone, until last for reason that will become clear. My good friend Edward Bayles has shared much with me in his time here. Together we have seen great change within our small community, have witnessed evil beyond credibility and have seen what avarice and greed has done to corrupt those who appeared incorruptible. More importantly, certain matters remain unresolved. Those matters have betwixt and beguiled so many over the years, which is why, I leave him, the painting he so admired from my parlour, the sum of twenty pound for the church fund and my most treasured possession."

Pawell stopped and retrieved a small key from his bag. Handing it to the priest he continued.

"My personal chest, which is secreted within my study, is opened by this key. Use the contents wisely my friend, for I have added to it often and wisely, enjoy the fruits of what was once our darkest night. However, if you have passed before me, then I will make this a gift to another of equal measure. Our secrets, and that which has confounded us, will pass to whomsoever I deem worthy of completing my work. Certainly, there are those, most able and willing who would wish to examine what we both shared."

As one, the family stared at the key and its apparent insignificance. The chest had never been seen or spoken of, yet it obviously gave the priest great satisfaction to have it within his possession.

"Do you know what it contains, Reverend?" Martha inquired.

"Indeed I do, madam," he replied lovingly. "Your father once said that this was his greatest gift, a gift only the church could comprehend. He once spoke of its significance before swearing me to secrecy. Within an insignificant casket, are memories that I will cherish forever, memories which are an honour to own."

"The old goat has taken you for a fool, Reverend. He has played you like he did everyone. If there is anything of value inside, the reason you have it is simple. He imagined he could find refuge for his soul by buying his way into heaven. Well, make the most of what he left you, because I guarantee whatever it is will not be worth the trouble he caused."

"We shall see, Master Adam, we shall see," Bayles whispered beguilingly. Pawell neither knew nor cared who got what; his task was to apply the letter of the law, no matter, who it upset.

"That concludes the reading of the main part of the will. Now I arrive at the codicil that Mister Wood added."

Abigail waited, unsure what to expect. So far she hadn't been mentioned and that was disconcerting. Surely if Joseph wished to denounce her, this was a God given opportunity. Pawell drank the remaining wine, wiped his mouth, and swallowed deeply before resuming.

"As I explained, I was commanded to draw up this document some weeks before your father's demise. He summoned me to this house…we sat in this very room, and spoke in great depth. Never have I seen a man so troubled and…angry."

"Are you suggesting he had some form of premonition? That he, and perhaps Nathaniel were to suffer tragic deaths?" Martha asked, clasping her hands together in silent prayer.

"No…I doubt that was his reasoning. My supposition was that he felt that…certain aspects of his wealth had to be clarified…yes, clarified, hence his additions. Certainly he was concerned, which was why I took great pains to complete the document as he requested. I must state to you all that never has a task been so…odious. I should also state that I neither condone nor condemn his wishes, but I was, simply his humble servant." This was proving difficult, which was why he removed beads of perspiration from his top lip with his tongue

"Your words may be wrapped up in legal double speech, but I see the way this is going. She gets control, does she not?" Adam added, pointing deliberately at Abigail.

"Be quiet or leave!" Josiah demanded. "My apologies for my brother's behaviour, Mister Pawell, I fear he is distraught."

"I need no one to apologise for me. I simply say what others are thinking. She is the only one not mentioned. It is obvious that our father suspected Nathaniel might suffer some disaster and placed her in command. We are overlooked, treated as imbeciles while she steps in and takes everything. Well, I will never bow to her, not while I still draw breath."

Beads of perspiration ploughed furrows through Adam's extensively powdered face. Those present sat, silently, waiting what would happen next.

Abigail had expected some sort of reaction, no matter what their legacies were. Adam would never be satisfied, he needed all he could get, to achieve that he would cause disquiet and discord among the family, no matter what was said in the will.

"It matters not, Josiah. Adam is correct in many ways and these proceedings were bound to raise such passions. Let us have this done as quickly as possible and put any bad blood behind us."

"Most gracious of you Abigail, pray continue Mister Pawell." Josiah bowed his head very slightly indicating to the solicitor that it was time to continue.

"As I stated your father was insistent that this was added, the document was drawn up without duress, and while he was lucid and coherent. I and my clerk witnessed his hand, making it therefore legal and part of the greater document. It now becomes and must be read in conjuncture with that document."

The solicitor mopped his brow, swallowed, and licked his lips before commencing.

"That being the case, and to complete my task, I now read the words of Joseph Wood of Stormouth dictated to me on the Sixth of December in the year of our Lord One Thousand Seven Hundred and Seventy." Pawell paused, closed his eyes momentarily, breathed deeply then continued. "If this document is being heard, then my worst fears have been realised and I am no more. In which case I am free to speak of events which have bothered me for some time, but about which I kept silent, until now. I fear it is with a heavy heart that I find need to add and amend this document, but deal with this I must. It has come to my notice, and I find no reason to dispute the validity of the informer, that there has been mischief perpetrated by one of my own. As such, I have no recourse but to act. This document will bear witness to their behaviour and dishonour. If these matters were not resolved, they would fester and cause much anxiety long after my death. I have consulted and considered the best course of action, these are my conclusions. By rights, my son Nathaniel should inherit all business and family dealings. To him would fall the burden of continuing what I have striven to achieve. To him would come all property and monetary wealth, he would, in essence, become wealthy beyond comparison. What I am now compelled to do, I do out of loyalty. The bequests made to others will remain unsullied and complete. These should be theirs by right...however; I have no recourse but to amend Nathaniel's inheritance, I do this in order to protect my family and wealth. I have instructed my solicitor to renounce and refuse Nathaniel's rights to any such inheritance."

Chapter Fifteen

The silence was palatable; collectively, they turned towards Abigail. The world paused for an instant, until Adam demanded,
"What does this mean?"
"He's destroyed her!" Sarah said with a sense of astonishment.
"Abigail? What say you?" Martha asked, her voice tinged with dismay as the enormity of what had been stated slowly became obvious.
"My God, Abigail, what have you done?" Josiah demanded.
"Mister Josiah, if I may continue, my client's instructions do unfortunately become clear." Pawell wanted this concluded as quickly as possible so he might leave this unhappy house. Dreading what he was about to do, he glanced across the top of his glasses at the woman, swallowed deeply and forced himself to speak.
"Your father, it would seem, was privy to certain knowledge, knowledge that he dealt with in this...document. As I said, I pleaded with him to moderate but he refused, which is why I will read verbatim what he said.
"Oh do get on; the suspense is interminable." Bayles, it seemed, was the only one who relished what was to occur.
"I instruct my lawyer, or his appointed representative, to make it known that the harlot who purports to be my son's wife, Abigail Wood, is to be henceforth and permanently excluded from both family and fortune. No one is to acknowledge her presence, give succour or aid to her. To do so will result in the relinquishment of their own inheritance. Her very name is to be expunged and eradicated; by her unnatural actions, she is to be denounced and denied any bequests that should be hers by right of marriage."
"Abigail?" Martha asked. She alone, it seemed, had grasped the significance of what was written. All Abigail could do was sit in abject desolation and silence as the enormity of what Joseph had done, became clear. He had ruined her, as surely as if he stood before her. All these weeks waiting for the priest to denounce her, and a dead man, had ruined her from beyond the grave. She glanced at the family and the household staff who all looked at her as if she had suddenly grown an extra head. All had questions, all were eager to hear her speak. All she could do was deny and hope this would disappear like some horrid nightmare.
"Mister Pawell I...I do not understand...how could he?" Her words were inadequate, but they were all she could speak, so shocked was she.
"I am deeply sorry but I am a mere functionary, employed to carry out the deceased's wishes. Though I do so trust you will believe me when I say, I did plead on your behalf. I beseeched and implored him to reconsider. I asked him

to resist and decline from putting such spurious words into print, but he insisted. I was compelled in doing what he commanded."

In this moment, he hated Wood, hated him for what he was forced to do. He was uncomfortable in the silence, the family, appeared shocked, the staff intrigued. Bayles though, appeared relaxed, smiling discreetly, as if enjoying the spectacle.

"I fear there is more, which will go some way towards explaining his feelings, though I should warn you it will not be pleasant." Seeing the servants fidgeting uncomfortably, he added "I am sorry, but your father, decreed no one was to leave until the will is read in its entirety, that includes his staff."

"I should think not." Bayles alone had an idea as to what to expect next. "Obviously he saw this as his last opportunity to speak out about that which concerned him. We should hear what was so important; pray continue."

"Mrs. Wood, I should warn you what follows will be painful, but he was most insistent that if needs be you were to be restrained, forced to listen to this as he intended. I apologise but I can do nothing to aid you at this time." Swallowing the lump, he felt in his throat, the solicitor began reading again.

"I have it on good authority, and have no reason to disbelieve my information, that Abigail Wood was ploughed by another, that the child she either carries, or which would have become her first born, is not that of her husband. Death is a commodity no man can purchase in advance, which is why I am forced to make assumptions as to the age and health of her bastard."

A gasp of disbelief from the sons and their wives was followed by silence and accusing glances towards the woman in question. Pawell glanced at Abigail across the top of his glasses, sighed deeply and continued.

"At the time of her seeding, my son, Nathaniel, her loyal and trusting husband was overseas, doing all he could to further our wealth. His absence at the time proves that it was inconceivable the child could be his. Therefore, we must rightly assume, she did lay with another, fornicated and was found out. By that nature, her child was born as a bastard. I also believe she performed this abomination willingly, acted no better than a common whore and assumed that she could pass the child off as her husband's. Such reprehensible, disgraceful, behaviour deserves our utmost disgust and retribution. However much time has passed her act of debauchery remains and must be exposed.

Therefore, I command her to be questioned, before those gathered at this time, as to the validity of this claim. Let my family discover the truth; let them see her for what she is. I defy her to deny this accusation before you, her witnesses, and before God, himself. She will fail, for my source is beyond reproach, the truth is undeniable, the evidence compelling. The proof, if so desired is lodged with my solicitor and affirmed by the hand of the priest, Edward Bayles. No matter how established, how influential she has become, Abigail Wood must be exposed as the woman of low morals I always thought her to be. Her act of treachery has despoiled our good name. As such she is to inherit nothing save my total and absolute disgust. I refuse to allow a whore, a strumpet to hold control, no matter how slightly, over that which I have built. Be the child born, or not, she will forfeit her rights to any part of my estate, as will my son, Nathaniel. So bewitched by her lies is he, that until he disowns this harridan, this shrew, he will relinquish all control and income from any of those assets he might have accrued through inheritance. Neither will he have any say in the running of the business. That onerous duty will fall upon my other sons, Josiah and Adam Wood. They, and their assigns, will retain those rights for perpetuity or until, Nathanial recovers his good sense. As for the bitch, I command you to cast her out, expunge her from the family with neither clothing nor monies. Her name is to be reviled by all, and I beg my friend, the good Reverend Bales to make this his personal mission. To facilitate this request I leave him the sum of five hundred pounds to be spent however he sees fit in purging her name from our memory. You have brought this upon yourself woman, I abhor the name you were given and will see you ruined for what you have done. Nor will I allow our good name to be dragged into disparity by her, or her bastard child."

Pawell stopped, removed his glasses and closed the paper. His movements sounded thunderous within the silence of the room. Abigail stared into nothingness, her worst fears had been realised. From the moment the solicitor had begun, she knew the outcome. Unable to speak, she had listened, powerless to halt this travesty as the enormity of what Joseph was doing struck her. Her chest tightened, her breathing quickened and the child, the spawn of his lustfulness, moved. It was the first time she had felt it. It was as if he had returned, to haunt her indefinitely.

"Is this true?" Martha gasped. She had always been the brightest of the group.

"Course it is, look at the bitch...!" Bayles screamed, lost in anger, he rose from his seat.

"How did father know?" Josiah demanded.

"I have no inclination, I am merely a functionary," the solicitor replied; his duty done, he desired to leave before this degenerated into further recriminations.

"Whore, observe her treachery! Who is the father? Tell us! Is it some labourer, a servant? Did you grovel on your knees like the gutter snipe you are?" Adam pointed an accusing finger and grinned devilishly. This was his chance; with her ruined the wealth which had been destined for Nathaniel would be shared equally between him and Josiah. No longer would he be beholden to anyone, his debts would at long last be repaid and he could start again. "Name the wretch and I will deal with him." He demanded rising from his seat.

"When did this happen?" Sarah asked, flummoxed by the revelation.

"Who cares? Simply thank God, Nathaniel isn't here to witness her demise," her husband retorted pacing the room like a caged animal while the others sat in stunned silence. "Our path has been shown; we must comply with father's wishes. The whore must be thrown out, cast aside; do it now and be done with it."

"How could you?" Martha said solemnly. She, like the others, had expected some sort of disagreement, some argument. But this…this was beyond belief.

Only Josiah remained silent. He recognised what their father had achieved. Any one of them could have suffered a similar fate. It was unfortunate that Abigail was to be the victim of his savagery.

"Speak, Abigail, deny such accusations." Josiah waited, the accused sat bewildered and silent, lost, unable to comprehend what had happened to her. The family demanded answers yet all she did was finger the tablecloth. Then very calmly and sedately she replied,

"I am perplexed by such a wild accusation. I do not understand from whence he acquired such mischief…he is mistaken for…I have been with no one apart from my husband. I repeat, he is mistaken, surely even he cannot mean to do this…he wouldn't be so inhuman."

"I am afraid my client was clear and concise with his instructions." Pawell said solemnly. "However, there is still time to prove your innocence and have the codicil rescinded."

"How, what must I do?" Abigail demanded, thankful but unsure if anything she did would convince them of her innocence.

"Undergo a simple examination, my dear," Pawell said wistfully. He hated Wood for placing him in such an odious position. Unfortunately, now the journey had begun, this path must be travelled until the final destination was reached, however difficult that path proved to be. "At my behest I have the power to overturn this abomination. All we need do is summon a surgeon, then, if he confirms it a lie…all this will be forgotten. Before we seek such an examination, I have to request a simple answer to a delicate question…Are you with child?" He peered at her, and for the first time he witnessed her wilt, she knew she was finished, and he felt for her shame. "I advise you not to lie, admit any indiscretions, for an examination will discover the truth easily"

"Are we to continue hearing this strumpet's lies?" Reverend Bayles demanded, slamming his fist onto the oak table with such force that the pewter plates jumped and clanged loudly. "Your client was convinced of her adultery, is that not sufficient? Besides, she will not tell the truth, look at her! Women such as she do not know the meaning of decency." His anger was awesome to see, his eyes blazed with cold, vicious animosity, his nostrils flared and his mouth formed a malevolent smirk from which dribbled white spittle.

"Reverend, I will not have such words spoken in the presence of our wives, pray desist." Josiah stepped between him and Abigail. He had seen the priest stand and feared he was about to strike her. Never again would any woman suffer such an attack, not in this house, not while he was in command. "Mrs Barnes?" Josiah looked round for the elderly cook who stood with the other servants fascinated by what was happening.

"Ere sir," the elderly woman answered, eager to witness what more was to be revelled.

"Remove the staff, this isn't for their ears."

"Straight away, sir." Ushering the younger staff from the room, Mrs Barnes turned one last time and cursed her lost opportunity to garner scandal. Once the door closed Josiah spun around and faced Abigail, grasping her shoulders he demanded,

"Is the accusation true?" He struggled to keep his voice calm, choosing his words with care, while the anger bubbled and welled inside his chest. He had no prior knowledge of the accusation and was therefore unprepared for the direction this meeting was taking; but he was torn. He may not have liked Abigail, may have been concerned that she would take what was theirs. Could he though, find it in his heart to believe the accusation? Was she capable of stooping so low, more importantly, did she believe she could conceal such a thing indefinitely? "Are you with child?"

"I refuse to answer such a delicate question in the presence of such animosity," Abigail whispered. She stared at the floor unable to face her accusers. Joseph's intentions were now clear, as was the reason Bayles had said nothing in Church. He had bided his time until now, when he could inflict most harm.

"There, the bitch neither refutes, nor confirms the allegations, proof enough I say." Bayles stood before her, while the family stared at her with a mixture of contempt, disgust, and sadness. Grimacing wildly Bayles sneered, "Do you believe, your father, my friend, would have embarked on this course of action had he not the proof to substantiate his claims? No, I suspect he witnessed her fornicating ways and realised her intentions were to rob his family. I cannot imagine the anguish your father must have gone through before coming to this unsavoury decision. His lost opportunity to admonish her is yours now, Josiah. As head of the family, you must take up the cudgel and finish his work, act; throw her into the gutter like the night soil she obviously is. Send the devils spawn back to purgatory." Lavishly he signed himself with the cross, as if Abigail truly was the devil incarnate. His vexation made Josiah gasp in horror; it was as if the priest had discovered the devil himself within this unfortunate woman.

"Can we be sure?" Josiah asked. "Our only evidence is what Pawell was directed to write. Can we condemn her with nothing more than a dead man's suppositions? I for one do not think we can, moreover I will not destroy her on that alone. I need substantive proof."

"Thank you, Josiah." She wanted to say more but the tears were close and she didn't want to embarrass herself.

"You're a damn fool!" Bayles rounded on Josiah, his face, so close the son smelt the wine upon his breath. "You doubt your father's word against that of a penny whore? What loyalty from a son. If you do not have the stomach, then I will cast her out and enjoy the experience." The priest glared at Josiah, willing him to rise against him so that he could swat him aside like an irritating fly. All the while Adam remained silent, enjoying the entertainment his father's twisted mind had orchestrated.

"For the love of God, show some humanity," Martha implored. "She is our sister; you cannot do what he asks. Tell them they are wrong, Abigail. Refute his lies! Tell them and be done with this now."

"Your loyalty is admirable but she cannot defend the indefensible," Bayles stated maliciously. "For her guilt is beyond doubt."

"You appear well informed Reverend, why is that?" Josiah tired of claim and counterclaim, required evidence and Bayles, it seemed, had that.

"Your father and I spoke of this some time ago, he came to me with his suspicions and concerns. He sought my advice as to what he could do both spiritually and morally. I saw a man distraught, devastated, and unable to believe what he had discovered."

"And what pray, was that advice, Reverend?" Adam demanded.

"To seek legal advice naturally, the accusations and repercussions were too severe. His only recourse was to speak with his solicitor."

"I concur, that is what your father told me when he arrived in my office," Pawell added. "He was in a state of agitation and distress and told me of his concerns. That was why, after due consideration, I concurred with the codicil.

What I said then, and reiterate now, was that I disagreed with the wording and the implications. I cautioned him to err on the side of prudence."

"I assume he refused to sanction such advice?" Josiah asked, looking at the solicitor. "More importantly, why were we not forewarned of any of this?"

"I fear your father was a man of considerable…inner strength. He ignored my advice, commanded me not to write you in advance. He said he was concerned with the ramifications towards the business and financial situation and the legitimacy of a bastard's future claim. He wanted the family interests protected from…scandal." It was not Pawell's place to discuss the merits of his client's thinking to anyone without permission. .

"Then the question remains. Is the accusation founded or not?" The room hushed, Bayles more than anyone waited her reply. Whatever it was, he had discovered the subject for a most enlightening sermon. He would use his position to tell one and all of her lecherous ways. In time she would realise that he wasn't a man who took rejection lightly. It was becoming a far better day than he could have imagined.

As for his victim, all Abigail could do was sit and stare in bewilderment. She was trapped, her secret was revealed but not in the way she had planned. All those hours fabricating a convincing lie had been for naught. Maybe, if time allowed, she might have been able to convince them that she was totally innocent, but they expected an immediate answer and she didn't know what to do. Like a frightened beast she looked around the room for an escape route and sighed. There was no escape; Joseph Wood had sealed her fate as surely as if he had reached out to her from beyond his grave. She had but one chance, to prostrate herself upon their mercy and forgiveness. Taking a deep breath, she spoke….

Chapter Sixteen

"Yes...I am with child." The disgusted gasp was immediately followed by questions, accusations and retribution. The family tore at her like a pack of dogs.

"Trollop!"

"Filthy courtesan!"

"You dare to foul our father's memory by revealing you brought your lover into this house? Have you no shame?"

"Women like her know not shame! Such whores reveal in their debauchery. What was it, the thrill of clean sheets? The fact he bedded someone of standing? Who was it? Tell us his name!" Never had she imagined such vileness, that they would hold her in such contempt. She had hoped for understanding, perhaps compassion, certainly not this vilification. The depths of their distain, was demonstrated by Adam, who lunged forward, threatening to grab her about the throat. Only the quickness of Josiah prevented her demise. Adam, though, wasn't to be denied. Abuse and accusations flowed like water from the town pump. His intentions, it seemed, was to pounce on her words and to complete what his father had begun.

"I said the bitch wasn't good enough for the family! Nathaniel should have taken what he wanted and discarded her like the tramp she so obviously is."

Beneath such pressure she wilted, felt the fight drain from her soul. Fear raced through her body as those she had once seen as family closed in upon her. In short, breathless gasps her words, made little sense, she stared, doe like, and struggled to be heard, her head swam as a faint drew close. Finally Pawell, in an act of humility, called for silence. Abigail waited, before glancing up to witness the anger and hurt they felt. Even Martha, the one person she hoped would understand, stared at her with contempt. Trapped by her condition, she had no recourse but to explain what had happened

"Call me what you wish...but in God's name try to understand that I am truly sorry. Not for loving Nathaniel, which will remain paramount and undying, but for becoming trapped within this house. I speak truly when I say I invited no one into this home. The criminal was here all the time, and came to my room soon after Nathaniel sailed." Abigail wept, after living with the strain for so long she had finally been broken.

"Do not be fooled by this Jezebel's act, she sheds tears, not of sorrow, but of guilt. Her lies are unconvincing, do not be fooled into believing anything of what she says." Adam slammed his hand onto the table, dislodging two glasses which fell and smashed upon the floor. "She has admitted to fornicating beneath our roof. That she and her lover committed an act of vile proportions, yet denies bringing him here. How can this be? What do you take us for…fools? Would you have us believe some thief entered both you and this house, that they defiled you while you slept, and that you knew nought of what occurred? I think not. There are many whores who could teach us all a trick or two, but what you suggest is implausible, if not illogical. Admit that you brought this…concubine here secretively…took him to your room to lie like the sow you are." He laughed and pointed at her as if she counted for very little. "I accuse you, madam, of lying, but those lies will not save you from the truth. I believe you wish us to feel sorry for you…to believe you are the injured party. I for one see you, madam, for what you are, a penny whore, intent on saving her rotten soul."

"I…I am not…I am the…" Abigail began, only to have her words cut short by Adam, who, relishing his chance to destroy her, shouted with such venom that spittle flew with every word.

"What…the innocent? That, madam, is something you have never been. Even your tears are a masquerade, tears of reproach as you attempt to once again shift the blame. Perhaps my family are naive of such matters but I have met your sort before, demimondaines who use their bodies for their own means, who lie through their teeth until they know neither truth, nor the meaning, of regret."

Flushed and excited, Adam dismissed her with a wave of his hand. This was a side of him, the family had rarely seen. Usually he was a schemer, who dealt with problems with cunning, not confrontation. His anger appeared abated, but he turned once more, as if refreshed and reinvigorated. "I will tell you what occurred here. Your lover satisfied you, like the dog you are. Then to avoid being compromised, I suspect he left before the house awoke, smuggled out the rear door no doubt like a thief in the night. But he left you seeded, and with a problem, made worse when father sent Nathaniel away. You saw your hope disappear along with your husband. But then, like the devious courtesan you are, you saw hope. Nathaniel's absence gave you time…time for you to hatch this abomination of deceit. Having fallen foul and without the means to destroy what you carried, you felt trapped. Knowing your condition would soon be noticed, you hoped that we might accept the child as Nathaniel's, give it a home. Your evil charade failed, father discovered the truth and decided to ruin you no matter how long it took. He would never have allowed a bastard child to inherit what a bastard had built."

"Enough! I command you to desist, now is not the time."Josiah demanded. He was uncomfortable having this conversation, like Adam he avoided confrontation as much as possible, which made him confused as to why his brother had chosen this particular battle, in which to reveal this demonstrative side to his character. Why was he so determined to reveal in her condition and destroy her reputation? Or…was it possible that he…the waspish one, had committed the unholy deed?

"Now is exactly the moment to expose her for what she is. What was it, bitch, did my father discover you? Did he catch you in the act of carnal lust? Was that what caused his malady? Were you responsible for killing him?" Adam lunged once more at the hapless woman; this time it took both Pawell and Josiah to restrain him. "Murderess! Is that the truth? Did he die witnessing your depravity? Did you not expect him to have the foresight to leave this testimonial to decry you for what you are and reveal your putrid secret?"

"No…No. You are so far from the truth, it might be construed as laughable was it not so terrible. I doubt, though, if you would believe me if I told you the truth."

Abigail knew she was being destroyed. Joseph had reached out from beyond death and had ended her life as effectively as if he had wielded a knife and plunged it into her heart. All she could do was beg for mercy and gain something from this terrible wrong.

"Enough…enough I say." Josiah, while wishing to know what had occurred also appeared to have retained a sense of dignity. He alone had remained calm. Kneeling beside her he took her hands, clasping them gently within his own, he asked,

"Tell us, sister; tell us who the perpetrator of this heinous crime was. Maybe then we can recover some dignity."

Looking at him from tear-reddened eyes, it would have been so easy to accuse some poor hapless soul. To pluck a name from the depths of her memory and accuse them of defiling her. But how could she? How could she accuse anyone for what Joseph had done? Certainly she could not stand by and see an innocent expunged from the town, chastised and denounced. He would protest his innocence, but the Wood family, desperate to erase this as best they could. What better method to kill a rumour than to see a body hanging from the crosstrees. That was something she could not contemplate. Josiah appeared to understand, to comprehend what it was she was going through, maybe he suspected the truth, but to be sure she had to name the person and that might be one step too far for them all at this time. However, her existence depended on the truth being known. Between frantic sobs she began,

"I beg you to understand. What I say will be difficult for you to understand but I swear I do not lie…The truth is you all knew my attacker; you all knew what he was like, how evil he was and what he was capable of."

"Who is she describing?" Pawell asked.
"Hush!" Josiah commanded.
"I demand you draw a halt to this absurdity! We have determined this wretch lies for her own sake, therefore how can you believe any of what she says as truth?" Bayles demanded. They had discussed this very event to the minutest detail, more times than he cared to remember. Their words had been spoken during nights of drunken splendour when man's mortality was not in question. It was stuff of nonsense, something neither had assumed would occur. That had changed with his untimely death, their plan, spoken of so glibly, was to be implemented sooner than they had envisaged. He was, though, satisfied with the outcome. With her downfall on the brink of completion, he was enjoying every last salutary moment. Pointing a boney finger, he sneered.

"She is a proven liar, admitting as much with her own words. I doubt if she could name but a few of her many conquests. Trollops like her do not keep balance sheets and ledgers, more likely the perpetrator of this…conception was but one of many such clients she serviced beneath this roof. A roof, I may add, given to her out of kindness by a man, I knew as a loyal and trusted friend…Shame on you, you strumpet! Your abuse of his memory is compounded by your inability to admit your failings. Evil does as evil is and you are evil indeed. Mark my words well, Jezebel, I will take delight in telling my flock what you have done, and what you are capable of. I will see you unwelcome in every house in this town."

The Rector was in his element, he stood hands raised to heaven, eyes closed, relishing his mission. He had a victim he could focus on, someone he could ridicule and destroy.

"I do not speak his name, sir, because I fear what the truth will do to so many. However, I have been ridiculed and insulted this day, now, perhaps it is time to speak out."

"Listen well for the harlot utters more falsehoods." Bayles turned and with a flourish dismissed her as insignificant. "We should draw an end to this immediately."

"I know him…as do you…we all knew him!" Abigail shouted. She had realised that there was no escape, rage at that made her scream in defiance. Bayles had slammed the door on her last hope of salvation, and suddenly she knew why. She had unintentionally ridiculed him, at the time she had dismissed it as nothing but insignificant. But the reverend had obviously seen it differently, and had carried that shame within him until now. Could he really be so shallow as to feel slighted by a girl, and carry that, as a burning ember within him, until he could convince and manipulate these gullible people, so they no longer believed her?

"I do not need to name him. However, I will say how I regret joining this accursed family, I should have remained..." Her anger had almost made her reveal her secret, that part of her life which must remain concealed until rescue arrived.

"But my love for Nathaniel blinded me into mistakenly believing I could overcome the purgatory that he might inflict. I should have realised that he was far stronger than I ever could be."

"Who do you describe? Tell us a name!" Josiah demanded.

"Come, Josiah, you are no fool, surely you have realised of whom I speak. He was present at my marriage and when you were sent to London." Abigail saw Martha, suddenly realise, saw the truth reveal itself and she held a hand to her mouth in horror. "I see at least one remembers that moment when you were sent to deliver papers to his London agent. Why do you think he entrusted that task to you while he remained here? The answer is that while you lived once again upon his wealth, he came to my room. My defiler forced himself upon me and laughed at my grief. He was a man who enjoyed the flesh of young serving girls, who used them, then disposed of them like others dispose of rubbish. Joseph Wood, was a man who thrashed his sons and treated their wives as playthings. He was also a molester of innocents. He raped me and I am glad he is dead."Abigail stated clearly and concisely.

Chapter Seventeen

Stunned silence, was broken only by Martha whimpering and Sarah's intake of breath. Moments, which seemed to stretch into an eternity, ended finally when Bayles, exploded in anger.

"Silence bitch! Silence or I will do so permanently!"

"Reverend, calm yourself." Josiah, it seemed was the only one present who had the intelligence to recognise the enormity of the accusation.

"Are you to do nothing? Will you allow her to speak thus of your father, to besmirch his good name?"

"I will do nothing hastily, and neither will you."

"Then you are a fool, Josiah. Can you not realise she lies, lies so easily that she is no longer aware of what the truth is. Remember that I cautioned her suitability as a wife, I told your father as much, it would seem my fears have been realised." Bayles shrugged as if the family's problems were of no concern to him. In fact, the opposite was the case, he had beguiled and deceived them until they believed him totally. They were like innocents, unaware that he had waited for this chance and was fully prepared for such revelations. He and Joseph had two issues to deal with during that night in his study. The first was how best to deal with a Bastard issue. The second was its erstwhile mother, both had to be silenced and their plan was simple but cruel.
If the mother, Abigail could not be forced to rid herself of it, then its parentage must be discredited. Joseph had wanted her dead, but Bayles had drawn him back from such a drastic course of action. "Use her condition against her," he had suggested, "cast her as the provocateur, condemn her as a whore, and seal her end with guile old friend not violence. Use this against her, have her and her brat cast out, vilified, thrown to the wolves without a penny or name." Only he and Pawell knew why Joseph hated her, she had not succumbed as others had, she had fought, and threatened and that he would not allow. While Bayles detested her because she had not been given to him as promised. He and Pawell were both complicit, as guilty as the other. Both had taken Joseph's money and instigated a course of action, which the sons knew nothing of. In return for burying his secret, Bayles had asked for little, a simple casket; small price most would assume, but that box contained a secret worth far more than anyone could imagine, and now it was his to exploit. Bayles stared at his victim with wild demonic eyes, apparently as demented as Adam and equally dangerous. Without warning his voice rose in volume, he berated them as he would have berated a victim in his church, mercilessly.

"Your father would have been so proud to see you afeared and speechless, unwilling to defend his name before such contemptible lies. Will not one of you speak out and complete that which he commands? I knew your father like a brother; if he were here, he would be done with this trash forever."

Silence greeted his outburst. Rarely did he perform as eloquently out of the pulpit but this would prove decisive in the butchery of a woman's good name.

"Do as you wish...but I will say this priest; if I am, as you accuse me of being, a prostitute, then, I am in good company. Like Rahab I shall be raised to high office in this, or the next life, for then I can be harmed no more. The truth will become known; word of what has occurred here will spread. Even you Reverend cannot silence everyone. Eventually I will be vindicated."

Abigail sat a little more upright, no longer was she the hapless victim, an inner strength coursed through her body as she glared at her persecutor. Inhaling deeply, she composed herself. If she was to be destroyed, they would know what Joseph had really been like. Once started there would be no return, so they also had to know she would not simply lie down and remain silent,

"You should be aware that I have made allowances should anything happen to me. I have sent a detailed note of what has gone on here, once examined, the recipient will bring down retribution upon you all. Like avenging angels my friends will seek you out, and do unto you, what you will do unto me."

Compassion for these people had gone. They were willing to accept these lies, so why should she feel anything towards them? Pawell appeared pious and reticent to assist her, perhaps he needed a lesson in reality.

"Examine the chair you sit upon, Mister Pawell, observe the grooves cut into the wood. Deep are they not? They were caused by the man that attacked me and left me with child. Joseph Wood embraced a lust for harshness and bloodletting; he abused anyone who defied him. I therefore name him for what he was, a vile vindictive man. Joseph Wood took me, sir, cocked me up, left me as I am and I despise him for it. I also accuse him of the untimely death of his wife, by fair means or foul, he drove his own wife to an early grave?" Pawell, she saw, fingered the grooves; felt them as if feeling the pain they had invoked, yet the lawyer remained resolute and unbending. In that moment she knew no matter what she said she was alone.

The family remained silent, their heads lowered in what? Shame or something else, she knew not which. Certainly she had become the focus for the Rectors vilification. He had set upon her with a degree of vexation which apparently had still to peak, as once again Bayles turned on her.

"You daughter of the devil...has Satan sent you here to do his bidding, is that why you speak such lies about a man we hold in such exaltation? You are an abomination. You belittle his memory and make his family sick at heart. To prove you speak untruths, I ask, neigh command honesty. Is there an ounce of truth, the merest morsel of validity in her statement? Speak or, as sure as I bear witness, God will punish you when he reads from the great book of knowledge. Does this...thing, speak any truth? Speak I command, for only you can save this...witch."

Bayles glared at the family, and heard their collective gasp of shock; none had suspected he would make such an accusation. Witchcraft was both a terrible and damning indictment. Few, so accused, survived the trial, even fewer survived the ordeals. Witchcraft was a sin against God, a crime for which only the church could convict or acquit. Abigail gasped in shock, knowing Bayles would be, both her accuser and judge. He would investigate, but, finding neither evidence, nor obtaining her confession he would, nonetheless, find her guilty by virtue of accusation. That was apparent by his manner, he would not acquit, nor would he absolve, or offer redemption. Her only hope for absolution was for the family to speak out, but if they remained silent, she would be tested, by fire or water. Such trials were old fashioned, rarely used, and never effective, but the accused suffered horribly until they confessed and were then punished regardless of their guilt or innocence

Never witnessing such an ordeal, she had though, heard tell of one such trial. The accused was made to walk the length of the church aisle, clasping a heated iron. The wound would then be bound for seven days, when the covering would be removed. If, the wound was healed, the accused was found guilty; similarly if the wound remained open and puss-filled they were accused as being in league with the devil and also found guilty.

"I...I" Abigail stammered, such words left her shocked, unable to speak; all she could do was glance towards those who could save her with just a few words of truth. None, it seemed, wished to do so, for they all remained silent, condemning her, as sure as his poisoned words had. Bayles had won, he would see her burnt alive upon the town green as a public exhibit. While Abigail sobbed uncontrollably, the family turned their backs on her, collectively succumbing to the priest's withering and vicious oratory. Jointly they had realised that, to defy him, would condemn them to a similar accusation. That they could not allow, their secretive glances and subtle affirmations condemned her. Better to see one naïve girl suffer than to become involved and risk losing all.

"None, she is touched by madness." Josiah could no longer look at her.

"Lies from a liar," Adam growled, his words evil, yet hiding a hint of happiness.

"Father was a...inspiration," Martha mumbled. Her words were most hurtful to Abigail.

"Exactly," Sarah concurred. Her denial was no surprise. The woman knew not how to speak the truth, or how to live a modest chaste life. Abigail knew what she was capable of and expected nothing less from her.

"A shame, madam, I expected more of you. To lie and expect others to assist you in that lie is...Reprehensible," Pawell added.

"You, sir, are as much a pawn in this game as I, and I pity you."

"Ignore her lies, Pawell. She deserves no pity, nor is she so placed to offer the same. Madam, by your own words and the confirmation from these, your family, you have been found guilty of lewdness and fornication outside of marriage. Those who acknowledge the difference between right and wrong have the right to ask for forgiveness and to rid their shame in penitence. You though, know not the meaning of shame, because you knew what you did. Consciously and deliberately, you lay with another. How often, we will never know, more than once certainly, you sicken me by what you have done. You have strayed from God's chosen path, you have beguiled and bewitched those who offered you succour. I can do no more than offer the Lord's hand as you suffer your fate."

Bayles paused, he had won, and he had his sacrifice. She had been a challenge, but that was what he enjoyed most of all, his verbal assault had ruined her as he knew it would. More used to condemning simple souls, who had transgressed, from the pulpit, she had proven a worthy opponent. But he had been more astute, he and Joseph had plotted, had foreseen what might occur, and planned well. She had failed, condemning herself by her own admissions and he had simply had to follow what Joseph had asked of them. It had cost him nothing, now it fell to the family to finish her.

"I will take my leave," Pawell muttered, desiring to be rid of this travesty as quickly as possible. He had no desire to witness her final demise; it would be undignified and not his concern.

"I think not, lawyer, your commitment to that document, is to see that we do not exceed our authority, is it not?" Bayles suddenly appeared concerned that events were done according to law.

"If you insist, but I reiterate, I do not condone what is proposed, nor do I approve. But, reluctantly, I will stay to make sure no law is breached."

Ignatious Pawell, had no ability to protect her, the law was his master and as such he could not interfere, unless the law was breached. Even then, and despite his considerable knowledge, he doubted, in this instance, she could be saved. The church, therefore Bayles, was more powerful than even the magistrates. Her case would be heard before the parochial court. They understood, what devilment could be caused by witchcraft and therefore they were more suited to understand the workings of the soul. However, he wasn't so naïve, to not realise that such judgements were more to do with which camp had significant money to offer the church in way of bribes. He knew that, if enough stones were turned, Bayles would find sufficient narrow minded snakes, willing to find Abigail guilty of anything. The church was a closed society; Bayles would have his supporters, men with like-minded sympathies who were able to understand the priest's accusations. The church had ignored many a fabricated death before, and would do so again. More than one unfaithful wife had suffered for less than what Abigail was being accused of. In his opinion, she was nothing more than a misguided fool, who had fallen foul of a loathsome, wealthy man. A man who, so troubled in mind, expected and received, all he demanded without any hint of recourse or punishment. Before any trial began, she was already ruined; the best she could expect was to retain her life.

"God bless you for what you must endure," Pawell whispered.

"I beg you brother, sisters, speak out and defend me...I am neither witch, nor any guiltier than you...we have all suffered at the hands of a man who should have been our protector."

Abigail had but one last chance; she could give in, or ask the family to show clemency. The first was not worthy of consideration, she would not accept her fate quietly. Her world might be falling apart, yet she stood before them with a sense of dignity and defiance. Bayles might have brought her to her knees, yet the family could defeat him, if they so wished.

"Josiah, ask you own wife...she will confirm what he was like...For God's sake, Martha, I implore you, tell them how he treated you, how he abused us all."

Not that long ago, she had expected to be leading them. Now, by the hands of fate and the lies of a monster, she was fighting for her life, prepared to throw herself at their mercy, and grovel for clemency. She waited, and felt sickened by their silence, all hope was gone, or was it? Josiah stepped forward, he alone, it seemed, had the good grace to assist her, but even he it seemed was beguiled and confused by the rectors accusations. Grabbing her arm and glaring at her with an anger she had never witnessed before, he spoke with calm, frightening clarity.

"How could you?"

"Josiah?" she questioned.

"How could you perpetrate such lies, about our father who, is not yet cold in his grave? I am only glad my brother was spared this debacle, for it would have torn his heart asunder. You have made your bed; you must now accept your punishment and God have mercy upon your soul."

Despite the furrowed brow, and latent anger, Josiah expunged the last hope she had. If she had expected sympathy that had disappeared as a snow flake would upon a fire…instantly.

"I do not lie!" she wailed, the emotion of the moment, making her cry, not for herself, but for the lies the family believed about her.

"See a conniving, devious lying whore, condemned by her own tongue." Bayles declared triumphantly, his booming voice resonating around the room.

"Desist, I beseech you, Reverend, I demand you refrain from further unpleasantness. I would have expected you, of all people, to show some Christian charity." Josiah stared reproachfully at the priest.

"Charity is a dish served to those who desire and need it, she does not." Bayles hadn't expected to be liked for what he had done, nor did he expect to be questioned. Josiah was irking him somewhat and the boy had best be careful.

"I have listened to your evidence and rhetoric, Reverend. I have weighed my response with consideration, while attempting to lay to one side the emotions we all feel. This is the hardest, most disdainful task any man should be asked to perform, but I shall not shirk from my duty. I believe, sir that as the wronged party, we, collectively, have the final say in her punishment, and I, as pro tempore and de facto, head of that family will decide her fate. Having listened to the evidence, and knowing a little more about the main witness than either you, or Mister Pawell. I cannot believe there to be any truth in the accusation of witchcraft, nor, in fact, do I believe her to be anything more than a deluded and naive girl who, through no fault of her own, has been debased by another. I believe, and here you will confirm or deny, that as the wronged party we have a right under common law to pursue a course of action. Our condemnation is required before anyone can prosecute her, even you."

He paused; he hadn't meant to speak out but had done so involuntarily. Committed to this course of action, he had no option but to continue.

"I do not believe her to be guilty of any criminal act…nor, do I believe her to be innocent of any crime save, for being puerile of mind and immature. Can we condemn her for such? No, we cannot, in which case I beg you on behalf of the family not to persecute her further. Allow us to carry out our father's wishes, to banish her from our house, to disown her forever. She will suffer enough in the knowledge that her disgrace is compounded by the bastard child she carries. I hope and pray that she looks upon it daily and ponders what her future could have been, had she not opened her legs for pleasure."

"Noooo! You lie; all of you…please tell them the truth."

"Be quiet, girl!" Pawell demanded. He had envisaged trouble, but this was becoming intolerable. Bayles it seemed had taken her condemnation to heart, was bent on some holy crusade. He, though, had the last word as to what happened, he alone was empowered to enforce the terms of the will despite what the priest thought."I will hear no more. By your own tongue you have admitted your crime and leave me with no options but to uphold the conditions my client laid down. However, before I close this sorry affair I have to speak. I knew Mister Wood, knew him perhaps longer than most including you master Josiah." The eldest son nodded but didn't reply. "I saw the good in the man; his charitable donations, his love of the church. Did he not sing each Sunday in your choir, Reverend?"

"He did, with a tone that only compared to angel song," Bayles replied, nodding solemnly

"Then played the fiddle straight after in the Cock and Hen Tavern," Abigail whimpered.

"Be quiet, only speak when commanded, or by God on His cross your tongue will be your downfall," Pawell commanded.

Abigail wept inconsolably, her life hung by a thread, and Bayles was the knife by which she would plummet. Confrontation between her and priest had always been possible. As far back as her first appearance in Stormouth they had been at odds. During the purge he had remained silent as men were persecuted and killed. He had said little as mothers had been hung for little more than doing their best for their families. While she had watched, the priest had grown stronger, all the time following his master, Joseph Wood. Then at the funeral, when the man had arrived with that dreaded news, Bayles had been the first she saw when recovering from her faint. He had appeared genuinely concerned, but she had mistrusted him then, and that feeling had not deserted her. Even now she was unsure if he had suspected or known of her condition. How she wished she had that letter now, for it would have brought Nathaniel close to her. *I pray I need you now, my love, for what is about to happen.*

"It is true," Pawell stated. "He did like a drink, but then again, who doesn't? Joseph was at best misunderstood, and despite what we have heard here today I believe he would be acquiescent to allow this wretch to be punished in accordance to his original decree. Therefore, as executor of his will, I command that no further action be taken against this tortured soul." Pawell turned to face Abigail and continued. "Madam, you will be taken to the door and cast out with nothing apart from what you now wear. The family disowns you and from henceforth will never speak or look upon you."

"I swear I tell the truth…Josiah…Martha…Sarah please, I implore you to tell him…I beseech you! Help me!" She pleaded with them. Four faces as one turned away from her, they had made their decision.

"You have brought this upon yourself; I can do no more…Reverend, your assistance please."

Aided by the priest, they took an arm each, Bayles twisting his harshly, making the woman squeal in agony. Dragging her to her feet, they half carried her from the room; all the while Abigail cried and pleaded for mercy. The distance was no more than a few feet, yet it seemed like a mile, then just before being thrown unceremoniously into the street, her final plea for clemency was rewarded with a harsh slap across the face from the priest.

"May God have mercy upon you," Pawell stated, before turning his back.

"If God shows mercy, I trust the town will not. Grovel, you harlot." Then, standing upon the step, Bayles called out in his loudest pulpit voice. "See before you a whore who has debased herself. Let no one give her succour!" With a final satanic like sneer, he slammed the door shut, leaving Abigail sitting amongst the dung and snow. She had been disowned, ruined, and she wept.

Part Three

Stormouth

March - April 1773

Chapter Eighteen

And I looked, and behold a pale horse, and the name that sat upon him was Death and Hell followed with him. And power was given unto them over the fourth part of the earth, to kill with sword, and with hunger, and with death, and with the beasts of the earth.
Revelations Chapter 6 Verse 8

A night of solitude, with nothing but a solitary candle, quill and ink for company had left him feeling jaded, but he was proud of what he had done. The events of that day were consigned to memory, but he would re-awaken them. Today promised further exciting opportunities to sully her name and remind those who attended of their duties to him, and the church? Sundays were his day, a time for preaching and sermonising, a day when he laid whatever ailed him to rest, or shamed a member of his congregation. One service today promised to be better attended than most. He had made sure the gossips knew that he had a treat in store for them.

His diatribe, the product of so much thought, lay before him ready to be delivered in his indomitable fashion. Those who chose to ignore his authority would soon learn that Edward Bayles, was not one to be annoyed, not if you wished to live a long and healthy life. Ever since that day, he had contemplated how best to deal with her. Should he attack her, deride and renounce her immieditatly or, draw them in with kindness then deliver his damning indictment to her wantonness? That was what had kept him awake, but now, after hours of careful and measured deliberation, of writing, discarding and amending, he had achieved what he desired. He would speak of what happens to fornicators who, like animals, lay with others, of the ramifications and consequences. Then, he would name the bitch and expose her for what she was. He relished the coming service, it would prove a heaven-sent opportunity to complete her degradation. From his pulpit he would tell her neighbours what happened to those that deviated from the path he had set out for them. The sermon, like the hymns, had been chosen for their meaning, perhaps such trivialities would be wasted on many but he would know, as would those with a modicum of intelligence and that was enough satisfaction. As the sun began to rise, heralding the dawn of a new day, he paused to reflect on what had brought him to this delightful moment.

We are almost done, my friend. Today we will rid ourselves of her forever. These fools, with narrow minds and little backbone will hear my words and bear witness to her licentiousness. I missed a trick with my accusation of witchcraft, I should have pursued it to the inevitable conclusion but Pawell meddled and your family lost heart. I, though, will conclude what you began.

His thoughts, so delicious in their simplicity, were disturbed by the infernal girl who acted as both bed warmer and housemaid.

"Well, speak girl, or be gone and allow those who know more than you ever will to be about their odious duties."

"It be Master Sprigg sir, wanting to see you on a matter he says is..."

"Damned important Reverend, and I'll not be kept waiting." A man, dressed for work, not church, entered the room without awaiting a summons. He was a large, red faced man, who, Bayles knew was used to getting his own way much like Joseph, but with less charisma and intellect.

"Sir I am about to deliver my service, can this intolerable intervention not await my return?"

"No sir it cannot." Sprigg was a bumptious, but wealthy fool, who had purchased Mullion House, and was determined to open and operate a brew house. Though Bayles doubted such an enterprise would ever work efficiently. "I would wish this conversation be heard in private reverend, not by your house staff?" Sprigg inclined his head in question and waited until the maid was dismissed only then did he feel confident to continue. "Have you done as I demanded. Will, Horn, relinquish that land?"

"May all this is holy, sir, but I have had rather a lot on my mind of late. Be that as it may, I have in fact spoken to Ezra Horn, and he states quiet categorically that you are to boil your head.

"What!"

"I agree, not the response we wanted, but I feel sure I can convince him of the errors of his ways."

"You must, it is imperative he rids that land of his sows. I mean their waste pollutes the harbour, while I can make far better use of it. Remember sir, I have endorsed you're efforts with a substantial endowment, yet I see no movement to justify my investment. It would be a sad day indeed if, by your laxity, the Bishop should become aware of our arrangement. He might see that jewel as an enticement, perhaps wonder as to why such a large donation was not passed on but retained, by you."

"Do not sir, attempt to threaten me? For you have no idea as to how far my reach is. For your information, I accepted your inducement as a gift for the church repairs, but rest assured, I will deliver as promised. Now be gone sir, afore I become more agitated than I would like."

"Agitated or not, I expect to see those pigs removed within the next week. Otherwise I shall return, and demand movement sir, definitely movement."

With that veiled threat, Sprigg glared at Bayles maliciously, then left the room.

Edwards Bayles, sat silently, outwardly he appeared calm, but that illusion was destroyed instantly as his anger was released as with a vicious swipe of an arm, he cleared his desk of papers and accoutrements, swore to God that no one would ever again treat him thus and cursed everyone within the town who threatened to cause him problems. His immediate problem was one Abigail Wood, who until a moment ago, had consumed his every waking moment. Sprigg's visit, reminded him of another family he had to deal with, another property to add to his increasing fortune. The land Sprigg so desired, was a substantial plot, ripe for development something Joseph would have agreed with had he lived. Now he would play one against the other while Pawell, under his instructions, would purchase it for his own needs. Both, Horn and Sprigg, would be encouraged to think one had cheated the other, while he would wait until the time was right to sell it on for a substantial profit. His one concern was Sprigg and his accusation, but he had dealt with such fools before. An accident could be arranged, after all there were still enough men of ill repute, living within the town, who would do as he demanded for a shilling or two or the threat of him disclosing some secret they wished kept hidden. Oh yes Sprigg could threaten all he liked but the raven was an intelligent bird and they came no less intelligent or evil than Edward Bayles.

"Anything amiss sir?"

"What, no, go, do something useful like getting another bottle from the cellar? Make sure it comes from the box beneath the canvas," his confidence had been shaken, but with just his maid, his malevolent self, returned. Later when he had dealt with the whore he would return home and she would comfort him, then he would partake of the excellent brandy his night visitors brought. Pope had thought the smugglers defeated but they still came with their goods, offering him a tithe for his silence. Oh yes he was well placed, and later after he had ruined the one who had denied him, his position would be far stronger.

The accusation of witchcraft, had been a spur of the moment decision, perilous, and not certain of success, he might have pursued it further had not the family lost heart, and closed ranks in fear of losing face. However, he was content with what he had achieved, Stormouth had suffered much and needed to cleanse itself, they would have something to focus upon, and with her demise he would be free. Like the cloudless sky, of a summer's day, his conscious was clear.

"What other course had we? None, if you had not spurned me, or threatened Joseph we would have paid handsomely for your silence. But you were too proud, and your continued presence would have been too uncomfortable to live with. Even your death was no guarantee to your silence, our only recourse was to besmirch your name so that no one would believe anything you said."

He felt safe in speaking aloud, his housemaid feared him as much as most, that arrogance had become the reason for their demise. He, Joseph, and the other members of their group, used fear to protect themselves. They had presumed themselves able to do whatever they desired, free from accusation. Certainly those they used would never be believed, who would listen to lies spread by whores? However, they had made an error of judgement in thinking she was no different.

The bitch had proven too independent, too eager to a show her mistrust and contempt for their authority. That had caused Joseph to react violently. Alone in the house and fortified with spirits, he had resorted to taking her by force. *Why old friend, why had you succumbed?* He knew why, but that didn't help their cause. To make matters worse, she had then presented herself to him proclaiming her condition, threatening to expose him for the devil she saw in him. Not many dared to cross Wood, but she had. Expecting sympathy, or for him to support her in some gentlemanly manner, Joseph had reacted, as any man would. He had sought the guidance of his friends. In this very room, he had told his priest of his problem.

"Speak with Pawell, if the time is right, if the quickening hasn't yet begun, there is still time to be done with it. Only when the thing moves does it become unlawful to destroy. Has such a moment arrived…has the quickening begun?"

"How the hell would I know? God sake man, do I look like the sort who desires to ask such things?" He had offered support, but doubted if his friend had ever been asked such a question. Three sons did not make him knowledgeable in such matters. Joseph had taken his advice, returning later to tell him what Pawell had recommended, and to issue his clear edict.

"I rely on you, old friend, to destroy her. With Pawell's guidance I have rendered her impoverished, now you must ruin her reputation. Tell the world of her filthy secret, make sure she is vilified, that no one offers her succour or sanctuary. I know you will not fail me, for we are alike you, and I more over you know I shall also keep your secrets safe long after we are both gone from this unkind world. No matter how long it takes, I command you to make sure no one believes her. The consequences are dire if we should fail, you and I, will be exposed, she will see our heads on the block while she escapes. I for will be exposed, she will see our heads on the block while she escapes. I for one have no intention of that happening, not for the likes of her."

The die had been cast, a pact had been sealed. What recourse was there in such a situation? Joseph's untimely demise, had caused some consternation but now his path was set he relished in the task. He had performed well before the family, had convinced them that it was she, not their father, who was the guilty party, now he had to end her before the town and that was what he relished.

"Have no fear; she will be vilified by one and all before the sun sets." His glorious thoughts were interrupted by a knock on his door.

"Come." His housemaid enter the room and he felt the yearning rise once again.

"Your bottle, Reverend." She turned to leave, but he demanded she stayed,

"A moment, my child, I have need of your services. My shoe buckle needs tying, do so for me."

Nervously she approached, head bowed in servitude, avoiding his eyes as best she could, but he knew she was aware of where he looked. Kneeling before him the view she offered was magnificent, voluptuous, and inviting. Her ample charms would wait, for within this house his word was law. He knew they saw him as heinous but he could live with that, he commanded and girls like Ruby obeyed. Her task completed, she stood before him, and felt his hand slipped beneath her skirt. He smiled lecherously, as he felt her shiver in expectant excitement; in truth, she shivered in disgust and fear.

"We have much to do today, child, unfortunately that means our own pleasures must take second place. Return to me later and we will repent together."

"Yes, sir," she replied, thankful that she was to be spared this time. Ruby despised the rector, but with nowhere to run, was forced to remain, and suffer. Bayles smiled as the door closed, Ruby was his. She stayed, and did as she was told, through fear of him and his power. It was what made her perform as she did, and she was but one of many he and Joseph had shared. It was that secret, which he was determined to protect no matter who he ruined in the process. Sprigg. Turnbottle all the pious righteous residents knew nothing and neither would they. Joseph would spend eternity safe in the knowledge that his reputation would remain, unsullied.

Fitting was it not that her ruination occurred within that room. He thought and smiled at the implication. As Pawell had sat in that chair, the image of its last incumbent had made him smile, for that had been their last meeting place. Somehow it was fitting that he had destroyed her in the very room where so many others had been humiliated. The chair where Pawell had sat was indeed a part of their torment, as the bitch had so fittingly commented upon. Many a young nymph had sobbed in that room, begging him to admonish them, to rid them of their sin. Coinage had worked far better than simple prayers. Many had left that room far richer than when they had entered. Such actions appealed to him, the needs of the flesh were satisfied, while his good name was maintained in the eyes of his parishioners.

All that had been threatened by one woman determined to speak out simply because she had fallen foul. Her allegations might have caused the ruination of many a prudent man, perhaps even the down fall of certain businesses. None of that could be allowed which made it more poignant, that her downfall had taken place where it did. He had wondered, while Pawell had driveled on about tin, copper, firewood and linen, if the lawyer had gone soft in the head. He had wanted to scream out in desperation but he had forced himself to remain silent, while his feigned indifference had disguised his devilish thoughts.

She had been Josephs one failing, he had promised her to him, but still he was denied the pleasure of seeing her humbled. Since their first meeting, she had invaded his waking thoughts, and bedazzled his dreams. He was in love with the woman. She was bewitching, beguiling and beautiful, young and innocent, with a face, so delicate, it reminded him of the new porcelain that Mr Wedgwood was selling. Joseph had seen the lust, and had sympathised; it had been discussed but once, behind bolted doors. Joseph had offered a way by which he could taste such forbidden fruit. How an innocent could be dragged into their sordid world.

Their deviousness had never born fruit, instead Nathaniel had married her, and he had been forced to watch her from afar. His lust had turned to envy and he had been forced to watch her grow from young woman to beautiful wife, but he shared her at night, when she came to his dreams. That was the secret Joseph had promised to guard, yet it continued to gnawed at him, chewed him up and infected his soul, feeding on him like a beast within. But now with her ruined she could be his any time he chose, for she was nothing more than a common whore.

Joseph's bastard was his means of control, she was thrown from the family and after today, after he'd spoken, she would be friendless. She would come to him eventually, on her knees, seeking redemption and salvation and she would pay for that in his bed. Woe betides anyone who dared to interfere with his plans. If they did, they would feel his anger, they would quake in fear as he brought the wrath of the church down upon them.

"Bitch." In a moment of weakness he forgot himself and uttered the blasphemy. Anxiously he turned, expecting Ruby to be listening as she so often did. He must be cautious, for rumour and accusation would be rife once word got out. A girl with a loose tongue could spoil it even at this late stage. He did not need, or desire, another Ida Furnell spreading rumour about town. Not that he expected that to occur; the majority was too naïve to imagine what went on behind the closed doors of these smart houses upon the hill. As he had said when the group had last met,

"I will drive the fear of God into them. By the time I am done, no one will have any lingering doubts as to her heinous crimes, nor will they believe her if she contemplates exposing us."

Today he would use God to do his work, work that would finish her, and slam that particular door closed forever.

Chapter Nineteen

Glancing inside, he was pleased to see that Ida and her gossiping women had weaved their magic. The church was packed, many standing along the sides, the masses ready and eager to hear what he knew.

"Ready?" he demanded. His lay preacher nodded, while the choir lined up behind the verger who stood with the cross.

"Reverend...Reverend! Mrs. Weaver has sent a note." A woman approached, breathlessly and handed him a crumpled piece of paper. Reading it quickly he said no more before leading the Laity into the church, where he longed to commence his work. Walking between his flock, he saw their nervous expressions, their glances that said so much about their sad lives. They had come today despite the cold not to hear what God said, but who it was, their priest had humbled. He paused, as the fidgeting ceased, raised his hand and stated solemnly.

"Blessed be those who come to this house seeking divine guidance and solace. God is merciful, God is good, but God is all powerful and demands obedience. In our darkest of hours God seeks those who can serve his greater good alongside him not here earthbound with so many sinners. It is therefore with sadness of heart, I must report the death of our friend, Horace Weaver. God, summoned him while on a journey to London to join Him and his Hosts in the fight against Satan and his followers. Rejoice in the fact that another sainted soul is with our father while, offering comfort to his widow and four sons, who we will pray for."

He did not care that Weaver had died, though he did wonder why he was enroute to London. There seemed no apparent reason, the vintner's trade was among the local residents and businessmen. Not only did his goods arrive at the quayside but were stored in the Wood's warehouses, so why the urgent need to travel? He had found the vintner an affable sort, ready with wit and certainly knew his stock. No doubt the reason for his journey would eventually come to light, until then, it would remain an interesting riddle. Consulting his notes, there was another small matter to be dealt with before he could begin. The needs of his parishioners were tiresome, but had to take precedence, announcements like these were but an example.

"We also read the banns of marriage for Ebenezer Crew and Dorcus Fairlight, both of this parish. This is the second time of asking and if any man knows why they should not marry then they are to speak now or forever hold their peace. Your silence is a blessing, now we shall sing a hymn you all know, and I expect everyone to sing, which includes you, Noah Wiles."

Bayles stared intently at a man who sat four rows back, drawing a few staid smiles from those who knew his reluctance to sing. As for Bayles, he sang with enthusiasm, for in a few moments, he would end her forever with his oratory. As the last echoes of their song faded and his congregation lapsed into silence, he made his way to the pulpit. He appeared subdued, solemn, dignified, but inside his heart raced. His sermon awaited, all he had to do was deliver it in his own indomitable fashion. Taking his place, he carefully laid his bible aside and looked at their expectant faces. This was why they were here, not to find peace and absolution, but to discover who was to be berated. The sight of so many expectant faces convinced him that his path was true, right and proper. Inhaling deeply, he began.

"God be with you and bless you all…may I say how pleased I am to see so many gathered in this sacred place. The sins must be mighty, why else would so many attend seeking absolution."

He paused while his quip sank into their tiny minds; a few smiled, some looked away, most waited in expectation. Rumour had swept through town swifter than an outbreak of the plague that he was intent of denouncing someone, but none knew who.Glancing at their faces, he sought out those who were missing, the usual faces were all present. Ida Furnell and her group of faithful gossipmongers, the Wood family proud but subdued, while directly in front of him was the local squire. Sir Stanley, dressed in his finery, sat beside his wife Lady Caroline, both apparently listening intently. Why the squire had returned was unknown. It was inconceivable he was present, simply because of this, more likely, it concerned the four red coated army officers that sat beside him. Soldiers meant change, but Sir Stanley was an approachable squire, he would inform the Town council and therefore Bayles, if significant changes were being considered. Apart from these notables, the congregation was comprised of the usual mix of merchants, shopkeepers, their wives and families, while to the back were the servants, gardeners and workers, forced to attend to retain their jobs. All, though, were mindful that today's sermon promised to be memorable, he would not disappoint them.

"It is with sadness and deep regret that I have to impart some dreadful news. Some will have heard rumours of what has befallen one of our own."

Pausing for effect, he heard the rustling of nervous expectation. He had almost choked on those words as he wrote them. That spawn of the devil wasn't local; she came from Barminster, a large town about eight miles away. Arriving in a blaze of flummery, she had held court at the finest hotel in town during the ver pinnacle of the troubles. Obviously, even then, she had been nothing more than a petty whore, who had married above her station.

"For those who remain ignorant of what has occurred, I suggest you listen well, for this is a tale, that could befall any one of you. Satan resides within each of you. Yes, even I have to fight his evilness on a daily basis. Sin is a master that seeks little provocation, anyone of us can be beguiled by its influence, and to defeat it we must be strong. We have all been washed in the blood of Christ, all have accepted His teachings and we all bow before Him seeking His blessing, yet none are innocent. You all commit grievous sin, as the one we are to reproach today has sinned. You sin now, at this very moment by waiting, piously, to hear the latest scandal. You wish me to condemn while you are no better than she, none are above reproach, none are above the laws of God, all of you expect to take your place within His kingdom when the time comes, yet you stand idly by and do nothing when a sister strays from the path of righteousness…DO NOT seek favour with your friends!"

He commanded pointing at those of his flock he had seen exchanging guilty looks.

"I take no comfort in revealing the heinous depths to which one of our own has sunk. Her sin is so foul, I have difficulty in speaking of it, but I must…I fear, my friends, we discovered among us a married woman, a woman who was blessed with wealth and privilege yet who, even so, defiled her vows and slept with another. If such a sin was not ungodly enough, she then has the audacity to carry a bastard child within her, contrary to God's laws, the sanctity of marriage, and common decency."

The collective gasp made him nod in pleasure. He saw Ida Furnell hold a kerchief to her mouth and steal a glance at Cooper the grocer. He had noted their secret, had consign it to memory where it would await a suitable time to be used against them. He had seen them steal moments of pleasure and exchange furtive touches during his sermons. Much had been speculated about their assignations, after all, with their shops adjoining, was it unimaginable that they slipped between each other's beds secretly, via the back yards? While morally wrong, he had often wondered whether, one day, they would come to see him, and make it legal. While not willing to condone or commend their liaison, it was nowhere near as bad as that which she had done. Her crime was despicable, lewd and betrayed the memory of a good man. Besides, if he were to banish all who sinned, himself included, his flock would be small indeed. Did that make him a hypocrite? Possibly, but he cleared his conscience by the reconciliation of what good he did.

Their innocent faces belied the fact that after attending church, after taking the sacraments and praying for forgiveness, they were no better than anyone else. Coinage absolved them of their sins. Husbands paid him handsomely for God to turn a blind eye to their indiscretions, while their wives knelt and prayed diligently, before going home and spreading themselves for their lovers. He absolved himself of their sins by syphoning a little from the collection plate, purely to ease his own needs. If only she had been more amenable, Joseph would have organised everything for her. Within the town there were those who knew of such matters, failing that an arranged confinement and a discreet birth could have seen the brat hidden and never spoken of again. But she was too contrite, too feisty, therefore she would pay the ultimate price.

"That woman is...Abigail Wood." He was good, had played his part well. His shame was, it appeared, heartfelt. He convinced them that he felt abject sorrow for her, which of course he didn't.

"No!"

"Shame!"

He listened and inwardly grinned. He had them under his control. They would do whatever he commanded. On days like this it was a pleasure to do God's work.

"It is shocking and we should pray for her and her family. For they are about to embark on the most fearful of times, a period of mourning, of inward looking, as they attempt to find God once again."

"Bullshit." a lone voice echoed from the side transept.

"Who speaks thus? Do you speak for yourself or the witch?" Bayles demanded. The outburst had caused him concern. Was there someone who knew that he lied? "Show yourself, explain that outburst...no, as I thought, you are a coward, your silence says more for you than your words ever could. Remain secreted in the shadows like the contemptuous villains they are. Ignorant fools remain silent, ignored by God fearing believers. My friends perhaps we should add another wretched soul to her list of concubines? I say a coward resides within our midst, we should pray for them and the family this loathsome creature has usurped. We should ask that she rediscovers her faith, that in time she realises the errors of her ways. I have seen the hurt her family is enduring, a family which took her in, cherished her, nurtured her and were thus rewarded. She has betrayed their good name, besmirched and vilified them in the face of God. I argued that they show mercy, but eventually had to agree that the treachery she had shown was heinous. Her family was left with only one course of action...they disown her, as we must. She had brought shame on us, her crime taints each and every one of us. Her family is saddened, but what more could they have done? Nothing, they tried to appease her tried to aid and comfort her but their assistance was rejected, by the harlot she is. We must rise above that, we must show clemency and aid the family through their troubled times. We must show them clemency, not shun them but approach them and give thanks that they are able to rejoice in their tribulations and seek succour from each other. We must help them through this terrible time; support them in their hour of need."

His words were having the desired effect. By the time he was finished a mob would make her life a misery. They would ignore her, until finally she would leave, never to be seen again. This had been a masterpiece of rhetoric. The reason he loved being a part of the church, his words could influence ignorant fools, while even intelligent men could be made to feel ashamed of what he saw as, frailties. Rich and poor, intelligent and fools, would complete the work he had begun. As for the family, well, they had done what was required, they had thrown her to the wolves, turned their backs on her when she needed them most. Assuming they did so to save their inheritance, they had condemned her. Wiping his forehead with his handkerchief, he licked his lips and continued.

"Only the devil or his disciple could take such kindness and treat them with such distain. Only Satan himself could do such a thing and expect to go unpunished. I prayed for guidance, I suffered the anguish and pain on your behalf as I considered our course of action. I asked if such a fallen soul should be denied our charity and received an answer.Our Lord God came to me and He cried...cried my children, for what we must do."

Pausing once again, Bayles was twisting and contriving these narrow minded bigots to believe that his Godly wisdom was the truth, that he alone knew what was right.

"God wept when he told me she must be cast out, that she was to be ignored. None must assist her, or offer her any form of gainful employment. When she cries for alms you must pass her by. If this foul and deceitful soul dies in destitution, then that is the Lord's will and we cannot interfere with what He has ordained."

Sir Stanley Cobb nodded in agreement, momentarily squire and priest locked eyes. It was a brave man who dare to reproach their priest, to do so risked eternal damnation. Wise man were advised to do as their priest suggested, for only they could guarantee eternal salvation. Men like Bayles were constant, they saw life begin and end, they held immortality in their grubby hands. To aid and garner favour for eternal peace, all that was required was to sweeten their cup, but fail to do so, and hell and damnation would be your eternal hereafter. It was that fear which convinced him Abigail would soon be gone. The town would turn upon her, no one would risk going against him. Her only chance, should she remain, would be to seek succour within the

'Butts' where the poor, the ne'er-do-wells and scum lived. That was his next point of call. For the moment, he had these, his wealthier congregation to convince. The merchants, the ship owners the shop keepers would be whipped into a zealot frenzy. By the time they left his church they would hate the very name of Abigail Wood.

"This woman has aggrieved our Lord, taken His name in vain, and hell and damnation is her reward for such action. Purgatory awaits her as it does anyone who shelters her or her bastard child. Go about your work, ignore the harlot and with God's blessing we will be rid of her one way or the other very shortly."

He saw fear in their faces, fear of him and what he could do should they fail in his command.

"Amen," a lone voice said, echoed immediately as others followed their lead. He had them convinced, they would shun her, make her life intolerable until she either died in poverty or moved away. Either solution was acceptable. But he also had to convince those within the hovels to do the same. The witch should not have insulted, either him, or his friend, by doing so, she had chosen her road, now she must be made to travel it wisely. If she failed to do so willing, then he would make further false indictments which would further harm her. His position on the council meant, that should she remain, he could influence and maneuver the Jurats towards his way of thinking. He would bring charges of drunkenness, theft, even of being a scold. Anything would do so long as he backed his accusations with witnesses, and they came at a price he could well afford. At worst, she might find herself jailed, at best, sent abroad to one of the penal colonies. He wasn't adverse to such action, Nelda Nichols sprang to mind. She had also crossed him and had paid a high price for her defiance. Having refused to do what he asked, he had laid false charges of witchcraft before the Jurats, convincing them, she had conjured up the devil. Utter lies of course, but he had stood impassively as the screaming hag had burnt. The smell of burning flesh had reminded him of the roast pork they had consumed while waiting her pyre to be built. One irrelevant, unresponsive girl was not much of a loss, there would be others who would accommodate him. Failing that the whorehouses were always a source of entertainment, but there he had to be careful. It wouldn't do to be seen around such places after taking such a high moral stance.

"Amen indeed, my children. May God have mercy on your souls and keep you safe until our next meeting." *Blessed was the word of God and make the next girl more amenable,* he thought, as he made his way to the door to greet his parishioners, servants of his lies.

Chapter Twenty

Today was a good day, his heart soared like a lark in flight, all that remained was to greet his parishioners at the church door, and gage their feeling. First out, Sir Stanley, would be the sample by which the others would be set against.

"A sad day; makes one wonder how a family can suffer, yet remain so steadfast." He shook the Clerics hand and glanced to where the Wood family waited. "I find it difficult to comprehend how she expected to hide such an assignation. A family such as that does not deserve such irreparable humiliation of their name. Your words, though, will give them strength, no more can be asked."

Sir Stanley was the sort of man who chose his words carefully. In fact, it was said he did everything carefully, hence the reason a son and heir had not been forthcoming. Certainly, he had to be prudent; his power depended on maintaining the goodwill of not only the town's ruling classes, but also the workers. Upset either, and he could suffer financially.

"I am sure the town is beholden to you for the good work you have done in seeing this trollop sent forth into the wilderness. Not the sort of person we need here, not at all."

"My thanks for your approval, sir, though I only do what God bids of me." Bayles bowed deeply like a lap dog that sought approval from its master.

"Indeed...however, we have more immediate matters to concern us. As you know, we live in difficult times."

"Indeed we do," Bayles agreed readily. The squire had the capability of making or breaking any man with the flick of a quill, or the lash of a whip. Neither was conducive to the rector's ideals, whatever Sir Stanley required, as the parish priest, he was only too willing to acquiesce.

"Glad you agree, Reverend. You may be aware that troubled times approach. We will be expected to do all we can to aid in any way we can. For that reason, our small community has been chosen to play our part in matters far larger than we can imagine. To that end, may I have the honour to introduce Colonel Sir Percival Fitzwilliam, commander of His Majesties Regiment of Militia."

"Colonel," Bayles nodded to the soldier. Such men held no interest to him, his brother served in the army and that was as much as he needed to know. Fitzwilliam was slim, well built, dare he admit, a good looking man of perhaps fifty. His uniform was expensive, well cut and embellished with so much gold braid it could have fed a family for many a week. He suspected, any man who could garner such wealth gained such luxuries from means other than soldiering.

"An interesting sermon," the Colonel replied courteously, when in truth both eyed the other suspiciously. "Trouble with your women...well, I fear your seclusion and genteel charm is about to worsen. You should prepare your parishioners for an incursion, the likes of which they may not be prepared for."

"Oh, how pray is that to happen? Surely we are not to be attacked by your men?"

"Attacked, no...overrun perhaps." The Colonel and the Squire chortled with laughter at some private joke.

"Forgive our joyful merriment. Fact is, the Colonel's men are to be camped nearby for a few weeks, while they await the arrival of ships to carry them to the Americas," Sir Stanley added helpfully.

"The militia to serve abroad, I understood that could never happen."

His voice disclosed his vexation. The militia was raised by shires or counties as a means of defending property from rioters, and as a final defence, should an invasion materialise from across the Channel. Why then, had the Government relaxed their own ruling in favour of this dandy? That was a question to which Bayles would seek an answer to, though not he doubted from the colonels own lips. He liked to think himself a relatively good judge of character, he saw, what men attempted to conceal. His talent, made him what he was, artful and he had already judged Sir Percival to be a wealthy fool, who used his wealth for his own means. The country was full of those who flaunted their wealth, while doing little. This man was different, he had done something few were able to do. He had raised a regiment, the cost of which was considerable. Why then had he spent his money on militia and not a line regiment? The answer, Bayles guessed was evident in his appearance. Sir Percival was slightly rouged in the face, caused by either his fondness for food or wine. Bayles surmised, Sir Percival, liked the prestige, the pomp, the ceremony, but not the brutality of war. He used his men as a weapon to get what he desired. He played at soldiering, and while wanting to be seen doing his duty he had no wish for his regiment to be wasted in the shires where they would be employed breaking bread strikes. Nor did he desire them to face the real horrors of a battlefield, where his toy soldiers would be broken and bled. The colonies offered a safe harbour, where he could flaunt his talents on a dance floor, not a battlefield. More importantly, he would be able to boast of his service to the crown, while not revealing the truth.

"Sir Percival approached the war department with a full regiment. What could they do but acquiesce to his request for an overseas posting? A full regiment at no cost to the Privy Purse, they would have been fools to refuse," Sir Stanley stated.

"And the government has enough fools to deal with at present," Sir Percival added as he and Sir Stanley chortled at their private joke, while the Rector seethe inwardly. Saul, his brother was ill served if he were commanded by men like this militia colonel. He felt his heart miss a beat, as for the first time in months, he thought of his brother. Was he alive, where was he, or had he died and been buried, forgotten by friends, family and country. Given the chance, Saul would have joined a militia detachment readily. Old soldiers were drawn to them because of the safety they offered. The wounded, discharged to find work, returned to the militia colours because of the stability, regular food, and safety they offered. Everyone knew that the militia never faced cannon, or the line of battle. They would never fear the writhing agony of lead ball in the gut, or the surgeon's table. That knowledge drew to their ranks, men and boys desperate to avoid being recruited into the regular army. The same could be said for their officers, safety and security bred arrogance. When the militia grew rowdy on cheap ale and caused trouble, the officers would be of little assistance. Many would be the young sons of wealthy families, happy to serve their time close to home and the attractions they craved, like hunting and whoring without the spectre of almost certain death that awaited them from disease or bullet.

"My apologies, Reverend, I am remiss. May I name my good friend, Mister Truman," Sir Percival stepped aside, allowing a serious looking man to step forward. "Mister Truman, may I name the Reverend?"

"Bayles…Edward Bayles."

"Yes, of course…my apologies. Mister Truman is one of lives oddities, he is from the colonies.

Apparently he dislikes the climate and so has returned to Gods home, to endure the rain and this infernal chill. Though I do admit he keeps us warm with his amusing anecdotes of the wilderness and the heathens that reside there, and that is just the colonists." Sir Percival laughed heartily while Truman, Bayles noticed, remained stony faced. "You will dine with us, Reverend, and he will regale you with his stories."

"It would be a pleasure, sir," Bayles replied graciously. "The son of a friend of mine was in the colonies recently."

"A successful trip I trust. Trade is our life blood we must nurture every ship load."

Truman appeared affable enough, but something in his manner alerted Bayles to something unsaid. It wasn't uncommon for traders from the colonies to arrive seeking goods to take back, but this man appeared uncomfortable. He suffered from excessive body leakage. Despite the chill of the day, his neck cravat was soiled and his lips and cheeks damp with sweat. Illness, fear, expectation? Bayles needed to discover which Truman was, certainly a trader that travelled with the militia was an enigma, one that Bayles was determined to uncover.

"Alas, no, he died. His ship was wrecked off the coast, lost with all aboard."

"A tragedy," Truman appeared genuinely saddened.

"Indeed it was. His family is, I fear, those the Reverend was speaking of during his sermon," Sir Stanley offered in way of explanation.

"Oh, the family with the…" Sir Percival exclaimed excitedly.

"Whore, sir, no other name will suffice." Bayles spat the word like serpents spat venom.

"Seems your womenfolk are more adventurous than I expected, we'll have to keep an eye on them otherwise my lads will be blowing off many a loose corn. The tents will be awash with your fillies all night long, while you will be up for a spate of hastily arranged marriages, aye!"

Sir Percival slapped Bayles, heartily on the shoulder, immediately he was alarmed. The military was a harsh place for any woman, how would his flock deal with an influx of roguish men? Saul, in one of his few letters, had told of many an officer who was ignorant of who commanded, or of where their orders came from. If true of regular troops, then the militia might be the same. How might such men react when word got out they were to be sent abroad? The reaction wasn't difficult to imagine, service abroad was worse than the safety of a camp in England, far from a bullet and death. Desertion was to be expected, one man who decided to run could be the start of their problems. He had seen summary punishment for himself, the military were strong on showing their wrath. The punishment for desertion was harsh, barbaric, but also exciting in a strange way. Times, he suspected, had not changed and Sir Percival looked like a man who instilled discipline swiftly and mercilessly. That might garner further problems. A deserter, recaptured, could expect to be tied to a wheel and lashed in front of military and townsfolk alike. Just one such act was bad enough in a regular regiment in a militia regiment it would breed hatred, a hatred that could bring desertions and whoa-be-tide anyone who offered such men sanctuary.

"It is indeed a rarity for such an occurrence, but we face turbulent times and must trust those who know best." Sir Stanley Cobb was not only squire, but local Member of Parliament, therefore knew far more that what Bayles knew from reading the broadsheets. When he spoke the town listened, not so Sir

Percival.

"Not sure about best, sir. Most senior officers, in my opinion, are too busy bedding their mistresses to worry about the colonies. Like Nero, they fiddle, while a tinderbox smoulders, which is why I lobbied and persuaded, until eventually I managed to convince certain influential people to listened, and recognise that what I proposed had legitimate advantages."

"You see trouble approaching there, sir? Bayles asked.

"I do, which is why we need men like Truman, to advise and inform on those who need watching. Though in truth I doubt too many of them will cause too much trouble after all the days are too cold. They spend most of their time bedding their women to worry about what is happening elsewhere." Sir Percival replied. Bayles remained silent as the colonel launched into what must have been his two favourite subject's women and the colonies. Bayles wondered if the two might be linked somehow, but that appeared unrealistic. From what he had gleaned, the man was a filibuster, a dandy he could be more harmful to his own men than any enemy.

"We need Truman's expertise if we are to prevail against his continental friends. There are reports from Boston of riots, bread shortages in Yorktown, and a sense of general disobedience. My God, sir, they openly refuse to pay duty on goods entering and leaving the ports. General Gage appears to be ineffectual and may have to be replaced. The Navy does what it can, but cannot control the settlements inland. That is why we go, and by God we will do our best to add to the rebel's defeat."

"Then we must pray you are successful in your tasks. Though, I fail to understand for what reason you have chosen our small community?" Bayles nodded to passing parishioners who slowed, to hear what was being said between squire, priest and soldier. Gossip like this would keep Ida Furnell happy for days.

"Training, and God knows they need it…we are also to await a regiment who will accompany us in our quest. Ain't that right Truman, are we not on a quest to liberate those fools, who stray from the righteous path. Apt is it not, Reverend? "

"Indeed. We can only wish you well in your endeavours." Bayles bowed his head and knew there was something else. He knew when men lied and this Sir Percival was lying through his teeth. His problems, though, were compounded by Sir Stanley's next statement, which left the parish priest reeling.

"Do you forget our friends, the Navy? We are to host a small armada Reverend. Sir Percival's men need to be transported and who better than our own jack tar? A feather in our cap, the navy have been absent from Stormouth for more years than I care to remember. Now we shall have a small fleet and one of his Majesties vaulted ships of the line in harbour."

Shivering nervously, the priest feared such a combination in the town. Sailors and militia were an explosive mixture, one was bad enough, but both at the same time, had the potential for disaster. During his tenure, the whores within the 'Butts' had been content with the crews of merchant ships, but to have men from the Kings navy among them could be disastrous. So many deprived men, all in one place, was stuff of nightmares. Seeking out those women of easy virtue would result in violence, drunkenness, damage to lives and property, and the prospect of the 'press'. He feared many a local would be taken to serve his Majesties navy; that would wreak havoc among the local families who would expect him to sort it all out.

"Ah yes, the Navy." Sir Percival brushed an imaginary fly from his scarlet and gold encrusted jacket and spoke sneeringly. "We are informed that even though our men are needed overseas; we have to wait until ships are available. Truth be told gentlemen, we may be here sometime, if fate and weather interfere."

"Come, come Colonel, you said yourself that tide and time are the one thing man cannot command. The ships, we are reliably informed, are even now racing back from the colonies," Sir Stanley stated proudly. He saw the look of despair on the rector's face and added. "Though, Sir Percival is correct. He and his men might be here some time; ships are like women, they need maintenance and restocking. But we can cope, can we not?"

"If we must then we will. Certainly the merchants will appreciate a lucrative period, while we will do all we can to make you and your men welcome." Bayles masked his insincerity with a weak smile. In truth, he was none too pleased that temptation would be placed in the way of every single woman in the district. Next week's sermon would be used to discourage the women of the 'Butts' from over indulgence. They would be eager to share their beds, and would need to be discouraged the most.

"My feelings precisely, which is why Lady Caroline has arranged a small reception for Sir Percival and his officers. I trust you will join us, Reverend?"

"I would deem it an honour, sir, to once again be in her presence." Sir Stanley smiled in undisguised pleasure.

"Splendid idea, but we need something grander...something by which we can show our collaboration and support for his Majesties men and his citizens. Might I suggest a ball, to be held on his birthday on June 4th?" Sir Percival smiled beguilingly, as Sir Stanley paused, mulling over what that would entail. Certainly Lady Caroline would enjoy the opportunity to display her charms and abilities. Bayles sighed, a party on top of all the provocations involved with the impending arrival of so many was not what he desired, but Sir Stanley was renowned for hosting lavish parties; maybe it was what was required.

"Then it is arranged. We will celebrate his Majesty's birthday and your forthcoming engagement with the rebels in style. We must have a parade, and fireworks! We will give your troops something to remember this town by," Sir Stanley enthused.

"As I said, I fear the dogs will leave you with more tangible evidence of their time here."Sir Percival saw their confusion and added helpfully. "Brats, Reverend, scrawny brats, it is a sad fact that more women are left with child by soldiers than any other group of worthless dogs. Mark my words, by the time we leave, your register will be filled with women giving birth to children spawned by my men."

"Then we must do what we can to discourage such fraternisation," Edward Bayles replied, in a feigned tone of concern. Though, in truth, he guessed that no matter what he did or said, there would be many only too eager to spend time with the troops.

"Never happen, try as you might, men will be men.Oh, we'll discourage them... give a number the taste of the lash, but it will not stop them. No, I fear by the time we leave, your Miss Wood...will not be the only one carrying a bastard child. Fact of life I'm afraid, fact of life."

With that, the two Knights bade him farewell. All Bayles could do was watch them leave and wonder what ungodliness was about to be unleashed upon his parish. Soldiers did indeed bring problems, boredom and beer were an ungodly mixture, mix in the arrival of sailors vying for the best girls in the whorehouses and he foresaw trouble, far worse than what Abigail Wood had caused him.

"A very good morning to you, Thomas, and how are you now Mrs..." he said politely as the last of the parishioners left the church. For the moment he had to complete his work, only then would he have time to think of soldiers.

Chapter Twenty One

Cursing his stupidity, the man who had dared to interrupt the vicar's tirade, slipped away unnoticed. He had erred, allowed emotion to rule his heart and for that he chastised himself. Subterfuge sat uneasily upon his shoulders, but like Bayles, he too had fears to contend with. Which was why, forsaking his usual position among the gentry, he had stood among the unwashed masses in the North transept. From there, he had listened to the rector's lies, until finally, unable to control his anger any longer, he had spoken out. He had been stupid, luckily those around him had not disclosed his presence, but how Bayles had react, was edifying to witness. Why the bastard had not demanded his accuser to be made known, why he had simply dismissed his outburst? Were questions he could not, as yet, answer, but he would.

The past week had turned the town into a rumour pit. He usually dismissed such things, but these rumours concerned a man he had despised, and another he hated. Wood had done all he could to ruin him, while Bayles had earned his displeasure since the first moment he had encountered the mealy mouthed weasel. That encounter was forever etched into his memory, this debacle proved his intuition had been correct. Why had they appointed him to the position? The answer was simple, his friends had looked after him even then.

He was no better than the others, he should have spoken out, voiced his concerns more forcefully. It was too late now, he had been out voted. The question was, what qualities had Bayles brought to the position? As far as he was concerned, the answer was nothing. Bayles had produced excellent credentials, appeared competent, and the letter from the Bishop was exemplary. Why then, if he was so good, had he been sent to Stormouth, a relative backwater? That was what irked him then, and still did. The other members of the council had ignored his concerns. The likes of Wood and Sir Stanley appeared to like the man, maybe they knew more about Reverend Bayles than they chose to reveal. Certainly in the intervening period the new incumbent had wormed his way into almost every aspect of the town and its hierarchy.

But slowly, his true self had been revealed, Bayles was a tyrant, and a liar. His sermons were full of hell and damnation, he used the bible as a staff to beat those who questioned his views. He was arrogant and wicked and more than capable of making all this up just to suit his own ends. *What is your part in this?* If, as he assumed Bayles and Wood were in some way connected to this travesty, the rector would use every devious means at his disposal to finish his victim, for he was dangerous; a zealot, full of fire and brimstone in the pulpit and a man capable of treachery and deviousness. There had to be more to this than simply a bastard child, for Stormouth had more of them than anything else. Whatever the reason, Bayles was more than capable of such trickery if it furthered his standing within the town.

"Damnation." He cursed, seeing Sir Stanley and his group. Eager to avoid being seen, he hurried away in the opposite direction. Was he being childish, or was it natural for a grown man to fear their priest?

"This one, yes," he muttered, for Bayles ruled by fear, unlike the old parish vicar, under whose auspices he had attended church regularly, and felt part of a family. That had changed with the arrival of Bayles and his moralistic teachings. Ever since he had preferred to read and pray in private, until one night a note had been delivered. The person had completed their task furtively like a thief in the night, afraid to be seen or confronted. At first he had tossed the offending letter aside, innuendos were for women, but then he discovered such notes had gone to every man of standing with the town. They were asked, no commanded, to attend this service. It stank of deception, the cleric must have had a hand in its inception, but he was no man's puppet and had attend to discover the truth for himself. After that service, he was glad he had, for at least he had confirmation of the rumours, first heard in a chandlery shop on South Quay. Normally he turned a deaf ear to sailor's talk, tolerating their crudities, because of his trade, but paying little heed to their tittle-tattle. That day, their tone and manner made him pause and listen as three foul mouthed men spoke of what they had heard.

"Thrown into the street, stark naked she were, and the cleric pointed at her bubbies and spilling his viciousness."

"Liked to have seen that, a rich whore with her bubbies on show." Raucous laughter was an indication that some obscene gesture had been made.

"He's nothing but a bastard....It was his poxy lying tongue that got young Winnie sentenced."

"Aye, he's a slippery one, I grant you but she must have really annoyed the lying cully, normally he would have shifted the blame onto some poor feckless sod like us."

"What was his excuse this time?"

"What I heard..."

"Who told you, some horse turd?"

"No, heard it from Wiklows, the groom, who heard it from the house cook."

"First hand then, is it?" The way they had laughed indicated that they no longer cared who heard.

"Scoff all you like, but I tells the truth. They say is she was cocked up, said the old man had ploughed her furrow good and straight."

"Maybe that's true...We all knows Wood was a treacherous, sniveling swine, wouldn't put anything past him. Glad the old goat turned his toes, no loss to anyone"

"Only his crews, they'll suffer."

"Aye, like as not they will, some trips will be lost 'afore the sons take over.

"What's the word on them, heard one's a buffoon, the other a pixie?"

"What I heard tell is that they have more important things to concern them at the moment."

"Aye, bad times ahead."

"What happened after they threw her out?"

"Heard she just sat in the snow, naked as the day she were born and stared at the door. Silly bitch must have thought they would open it to her. Not that they would, too damn careful they are. She must have really upset them to be treated like that."

He had been at a loss to believe such things, even of the Wood family. To turn upon one of their own, to cast anyone, let alone a woman, into the cold was despicable even for them. The question he wanted answered was why? Only two people knew the truth; her and Bayles. The cleric would lie through his teeth if it suited him, therefore he must find Mrs. Wood. She was adrift, friendless, would be easily cajoled and manipulated, eager to discover a friend and relate her tale. He would become that friend, but where to begin his hunt for her? He had an idea, but couldn't simply enter and demand answers, for then he himself would become the object of curiosity. He had to be discreet and that meant becoming as devious as Bayles. This was a heaven sent opportunity, if that accused family were truly falling on each other like rabid dogs, he could prosper from their misfortune. For that to occur he needed information, which, in his world, gave the possessor of such information power and control, and he wanted control of what the Wood's had.

Hurrying away his mind was a turmoil of ideas of what had to be done, and what might go wrong. He might already be too late, she might have crawled away cold and desolate, to die in some corner, unknown and unwanted. If she had survived, and he did so hope that was the case, he must chose his friends carefully. Certainly he couldn't ask Bayles or the Wood family, they alone knew what had happened, but their silence was their best protection. Nor could he speak to any of her so called friends, for they would have been poisoned by what Bayles had said. *He has completed a perfect assassination of her good name, no one will dare to speak out not know that the cleric had threatened them with eternal damnation. He would have to employ subterfuge and guile, if he were to discover her whereabouts...*Or, perhaps if all else failed, catch him one dark night in some alley way and beat the truth from his rancid body. No that would simply mean his friends, like Sir Stanley would order a hue and cry until the perpetrator was found and punished no matter who they deemed guilty. He would not have that on his conscience.

"God save us all," he whispered as he made his way through the churchyard, and down a narrow lane. He became aware of the noise his shoes created. They clicked noisily upon the cobbles but it could not be avoided. A plan was forming in his head, a plan so ingenious and cunning it made him laugh out loud. *Tyrants need to be controlled or destroyed.* So consumed with his ideas that he almost stumbled into a well loaded washer woman as he turned into one of the narrow lanes. Mumbling his apologies, he rushed on. He needed to make haste, there was only one he trusted to answer his questions without demanding answers, and she resided in his own home.

"Good morning to you, sir." His thoughts were suddenly interrupted by a small woman, who breathlessly approached him.

"Good morning to you as well, Mrs. Turk. You must excuse me, things to do, tide and time…" he had little intention of being waylaid by one of Furnell's band, but to ignore her totally would raise questions as to why he hurried away from the service so quickly. Bayles himself might learn of his presence and that he wished to remain a secret for as long as possible. Much easier to speak politely and trust in her saying no more of their meeting.

"Oh…of course, I too have things to do, the ovens you understand. Pray, were you there? Did you hear what the Reverend said? For sure her indiscretions will fuel the need for bread; her misfortune bodes well for us."

He smiled graciously and hurried away, muttering an obscenity as he did so. Thomas Turk the baker was unfortunate to have married a woman equal to, if not better than, Ida Furnell. In his befuddled state, he had simply forgotten that their shop was always busy after a service. Husband and wife never attended together, they alternated, one praying while the other baked. Desperate to avoid their shop and the gossips, he turned into a small alleyway between a donkey yard and a smithy. This was a longer route home, via South Row and Tan Yard, but meant he would avoid further contact with any of the congregation.

"Damn them, damn every last bigoted fool," he whispered as he hurried down the lane. He was still annoyed when, finally, he entered his home. Only after closing and bolting the door did he lean against it and catch his breath. His mind was whirling; he wished to vomit but heard at the back of the house the gentle sound of his housekeeper, Mrs Jones, practicing her hymns. Removing his coat, he ran his fingers through his hair, breathed deeply then made his way down the dark corridor to the second door on the right where he paused, just briefly, before entering his dining room.

"Ah, Mrs Jones, luncheon smells delightful."

"And so it should, only the best for you, sir. Nice piece of beef today, roasted veg and all the trimmings; just whats you needs 'afer a dose of the priest."

"Now, now, my dear, tetchiness isn't called for, or needed, not today of all days. As for your meal, it all sounds truly delightful." Pouring himself a glass of claret, he waited; his housekeeper was predictable and methodical, qualities he respected.

"As you wish, sir…meat prices are up again, you should really take that butcher to task."

"I will consider it…however; do we really wish to upset Mr Edwards and perchance, get a terrible cut next week?"

"I suppose not, sir, but he is terrible with his prices." He smiled while examining his table. Like his meal would be, it was perfect, two candelabra with ten lit candles, four place settings of the finest white china and silver cutlery, three empty crystal glasses, turned upside down, one filled with port. Mrs Jones was precise in the attention she lavished upon her employer even though he would dine alone, as always. She fussed about the room, disappearing into the kitchen occasionally, to bring steaming plates of vegetables, which she placed just so, until finally his meal was laid before him. He ate alone and in silence until she appeared with a rather nice sherry trifle; that was his moment to casually ask.

"Tell me, Mrs Jones, where would someone go if they had suffered the indignity of eviction?" He waited, sipped his wine and felt his heart beat loudly in his chest.

"Beg pardon, sir?" She stopped, turned to stare at her employer, confused and surprised at such a statement on a Sunday.

"Where would such a person go to find shelter and assistance?"

"Well…hard to say, sir. I mean you hear stories but…"

"Try! Please try," he implored.

"Without knowing…forgive me for asking, but is this person of quality or a lower order?"

"Quality," he replied carefully.

"Ah, I see…" The elderly woman wiped her hands on her pinafore and stared around the room. Something about her manner made him ask.

"What is it, madam?" he questioned.

"Just making sure we're alone, sir…I assume this person suffered just recently?"

"No name, a simple enquiry, nothing less." He knew she realised about whom he was asking, but so as not to incriminate her further, Abigail's name would never be mentioned.

"Well, sir, not that I know of course but…if I was to hazard a guess I would start with Maggie."

"Maggie, Maggie who?" He demanded.

Mrs Jones wavered; her employer was a Godly man, often seen on the wharf discussing loads and hiring staff. He was known throughout the town, had been present when Pope had arrived and like so many others had been questioned. But he was not the sort to know of the likes of Maggie or her trade, or so she assumed.

"Maggie owns and runs the Mariners Arms within the 'Butts'…If the woman you seek were in trouble, it's more than possible she would end up there."

"I mentioned not a woman, but should anyone ask, you know nothing."

"About what, sir?"

"Thank you, I trust I am not too late." Placing a silver coin on the table, he hurried from the room, collected his coat and hat and left. Abigail needed assistance and he hoped he wasn't too late.

"May God be with you," Mrs Jones mumbled after he'd left. It was common knowledge among the servants as to what had happened at the Wood house that day. The way Mistress Wood had been treated was, some said, disgusting. No matter what her employer desired, her name would be spoken of, it would be cause of scurrilous comments within the ale houses and alleyways of the 'Butts', in the fish markets, on the quays, and in dark corners. Until some other unfortunate became the next topic of rumour. Her fall from grace was on everyone's lips, which was why she had known immediately who her employer referred to. Her employer risked everything, his reputation and his standing if he aided her. The Reverend would make it his task to ruin him, if he became aware that he sought her out. Agnes Jones stared at the coin and decided to leave it where it was.

"Keep your coin, but I'll take a glass of wine and a plate of food from you," she muttered. Not for the first time would she dine alone at a fine table and in splendid surroundings. "Your, very good health, sir,"

Chapter Twenty Two

A cripple could walk from one side of Stormouth to the other in less than half an hour. In less than ten minutes, he had descended into darkness and despair, from social politeness, to the very edge of depravity. The 'Butts' was like an open door, through which, hell could be seen.

"Looking for someone, dearie?" He turned away as the woman exposed herself and laughed at his embarrassment. In a few short minutes he had entered a world most, from the hill, chose to ignore. Stormouth existed alongside this rag-tag, cesspit of humanity, where the streets were clogged with night soil, festering and putrid, the smell viler than anything Bayles could invent. Children were born, and died, without ever seeing what the likes of Bayles accepted as their right; clean water, good food and sunlight. While the rich, in their nice houses, expected to be waited upon, their servants, those who didn't live in, lived here, as did those who worked the docks. Within these dim, filth strewn lanes, lived the men who loaded the ships, the sailors who risked their lives every day to put beef on the fine plates of the wealthy. It was where the town had first been founded, when the fashionable hill, now inhabited by the rich, had been used for grazing. *Not much has changed; the rich are now the fattened cows who live off the poor.*

"Don't be shy, dearie, Nellie will see you right." A wizened old hag smiled showing a mouth full of blackened, rotting teeth. No man could be that desperate, or so he thought, until another voice called out,

"If you're free, come here."

"You'll pay like the rest, you swab," Toothless replied and spat onto the ground.

He was drawing attention to himself. Yet again he had allowed his heart to rule his head he had not thought this through, he had come to this place still dressed for church, as such, he stood out in this depravity. Word of his presence would spread, drawing to him the cut-purses and dippers eager to take what he had. He had been foolish, blundering into this place without thought or plan. Bayles would have eyes here, those he paid for information. If word of his presence were to be told, the cleric would want to know why a man such as he was doing in the putrid place. He might even put two and two together and work out that Abigail Wood was being sought within the town.

"Alms Mister, spare a penny for bread?" A boy, no more than six or seven and dressed in filthy rags, stood before him hands outstretched. Turnbottle should have dealt with him with a swift kick, instead he paid a penny and saw the youth run down the lane and out of sight.

"Damn..." He swore. He had been stupid, beyond comprehension. Turning away he hurried back the way he'd come, to remain risked injury or death; neither was conducive to his plan. If he were to find Mrs Wood, he must be more circumspect, more cautious. He would bide his time, in one of the taverns upon the hill and return under cover of darkness, where hopefully his appearance would raise less interest.

Stormouth had always been a town of ill repute, a place more noted for what was smuggled in, than for its legitimate trade. Under 'The Chamberlin' many, including himself, had made a goodly profit. But with such trade had come the ruffians, the villains. The arrival of Pope, and his purge, had achieved one thing at least. The smugglers had retreated, fled the town and left the residents feeling a little safer. If he had sat where he was a year ago, he would have feared for his life. The tavern would have been full of rowdiness, of men swearing and firing pistols. The streets had been alive with those transferring barrels of smuggled wine or brandy, openly up the streets between hiding place and customer. Death was a daily occurrence, more often than not, a body of some unfortunate would simply be tossed into the street to await someone, anyone to clear it away. While Bayles would have been struggling to deal with the amount of fornication that occurred around every corner or alleyway. The town had been dying, only the illicit trade kept it going until Pope's arrival and his terror.

Sipping his ale he stared through the dirt streaked window and shuddered. The world was changing, and Stormouth, had changed quicker than some could accept. The problems in the colonies were, he was sure, a precursor to war with France. If that occurred, Stormouth would once again be called upon to play its part. Throughout time the town had been used as a staging post for men going to war. From Agincourt to Flanders, men had sailed from this harbour, and so they would again. Even the place he must visit soon had been used for war. In the distant past, men had honed their skills upon open fields precisely where the 'Butts' now stood. Every Sunday, immediately, after church, they would have practiced their skills with the longbow. The skills learnt and practiced here, and in other towns, had produced the archers with the ability to kill Frenchmen at a hundred paces, to fire a dozen arrows in the time it took to count to ten six times. Skills that had once been essential to win wars for the King were now long forgotten, as were the targets.

As darkness fell, he drank some inferior ale and read a discarded broadsheet, while considering the options available to anyone residing within that squalor. They were trapped, the rich upon the hill, kept them half-starved by paying inferior wages. Underfed and underpaid, it was inevitable they fell into crime, and crime foiled any attempt to better themselves. Only once a week did the rich relent and allow them access to the church and that was simply so they might see how well their masters lived. The innkeeper lit some reed torches, and he knew his moment had arrived. Would she allow him to aid her if he ever discovered her whereabouts? His destiny, if that was what should transpire, lay within that cesspit of humanity.

"Halfpenny to look, penny a feel," he looked at the ugly scowl who suggestively flaunted herself while feeding her child, while between her knees was a flagon of ale. Overcrowded and oppressive, the lane was perfect for those awaiting the opportunity to attack. The woman wasn't simply being suggestive, she was used to lure unsuspecting fools into traps. They sought those who appeared different, like the visitor who wore a nosegay to erase the stench, or the fop who thought it hilarious to mix with such depravity. Such people were idiots, he was not, which was why he remained vigilant and walked in the middle of the lane.

"Lost, sir?" a youth asked, wiping away a sort of green puss from an open sore.

"Fake the way off," he growled angrily. The boy was another lure, another criminal's bait, sent to delay him while his accomplice robbed him. Children grew up fast within this place, no sooner were they able to walk than they began thieving, used by the real villains, men who used their brains to further their enterprises.

"Hope you catch somert and die, pig breath!" The boy ran off empty handed, no doubt is search of another, less volatile, victim. It was the men who controlled such boys he needed to speak to, to convince them he had something to offer in exchange for information. Despite the impression he had given, he did, in fact, know the name of Maggie. His workers spoke of her as the keeper of a clean brothel, but that was the extent of his knowledge. To know more, he needed an introduction, which came from an unexpected quarter.

"Spare a coin for an old soldier, sir?" It was not unusual, old soldiers were discarded to become a burden on any parish that allowed them access. Like all such men, he appeared dirty, tired of life, but his eyes were alive.

"What do you need, friend?" pausing, he reached, apparently, for his purse. Yet again the thieves in this hell hole had taken him for a fool. Like the women, and the sickly youth, this beggar wanted him to show where his purse was. Then an accomplice, watching from further down the alley, would strike. It was a common ploy, made easier by the gullibility of their victims. He though, wasn't without guile; his apparent kindness disguised his own actions. Discreetly he withdrew a knife and held it, threateningly against the man's throat. Smiling pleasantly, he whispered in a manner the man could not mistake,

"You chose badly my friend…now you have a choice…tell me what I want or never breathe again. No…don't look for aid; you will be dead afore your friend gets here. I would advise you to answer a few simple questions and we can both part amicably. Will you so do, or do I fillet you like a fish and seek my answers elsewhere?"

The old soldier flinched, the knife rested upon his throat and barely wavered. Johno should have been here, that was his job, to protect and assist if anyone tried this sort of thing, so where was he?

"Depends on what you want." Fear made him stammer, his words.

"That's much better. Now, we shall conclude this conversation and you and your friend can get on with what you do best. I desire to know if you have seen anyone acting strangely or asking about a woman."

Until now fear had worked to his advantage, suddenly, this piece of gutter shite, laughed at him.

"God help us, sir, that question gets asked every day, only reason such men as yourself comes here is to find a tuppenny whore."

"Do not treat me as a fool my friend. I seek a specific type, someone who perhaps shouldn't be here. I would recommend you think well and fast." The knife bit just a little deeper, causing a dribble of blood to trickle down the soldier's neck. Realisation that his attacker would slit him without a second thought focused his mind.

"Only one person fits that bill and that's the vicar." His fears confirmed, he sighed and grimaced, Bayles was seeking her.

"He was here?"

"Came day 'afore yesterday. Told everyone he was seeking lost souls who needed saving. Got short shift, I can tell you, not many need his sort of help."

It was the answer he desired but it still came as a shock. They had openly lied to a man who threatened to bring down divine retribution upon anyone who defied him.

"Did he go anywhere… anywhere in particular?"

"No, just wandered around, like he was looking for something."

"Thanks, friend, take this and share it." He handed him a coin.

"There is no other."

"Then keep this for yourself, though I doubt your friend that stands in the doorway will be best pleased." Calmly he walked away. There was still danger, but he doubted they would try anything. Despite the cruelty, there existed a code of sorts; they had been found out, yet had received a coin, that was all they desired, or so he hoped. Now he needed to speak with Maggie before Bayles discovered the same information, Maggie the brothel owner; he was sure, knew the whereabouts of Mrs Wood.

* * *

"Best behaviour lads, we have gentry in the house."

"Hotels are up the hill, sir."

"Aye safer up there, the beds be cleaner to."

"Now't wrong with our beds, cleaned once a month they be." Ignoring their lewd comments and inquisitive stares, he strode between them. He was risking everything by being here but what else could he do? The Mariners Arms was an old depressing hovel, its timbers blackened with tobacco and wood smoke, which, even at this hour, hung like a blue fog throughout the room. He did not speak, but listened to the sneered comments and laughter, for this place was well known for drunkenness and debauchery. Many a time it had been spoken of in council, never had he expected to visit this damned place?

"Fake off." A lone voice stated nastily, while others watched him suspiciously. Having entered this den of devilment, he stood out from the other patrons, who in the main, were sailors, dockers or those who it was best not to ask what their jobs were. His tri-corn hat, white stockings and leather shoes were at odds with their rough working clothes, while his neatly cut suit and white cravat marked him as a merchant of quality. Two further items marked him as wealthy; the finely decorated buckles upon his shoes and the elegant white powdered and neatly trimmed wig he wore.

"You're not wanted here; merchant…you'll find no one willing to work, not today." His face was a curse, in such a small town it was unreasonable to imagine he would not be unrecognised, he, Wood and the other merchants were all known. Nor was it surprising that these poor souls suspected him of looking for workers. But he felt gladdened by the fact if that was all they suspected, then his task might still pass without undue fuss. In amongst this filth, anyone with breeding or money was viewed with distain. For good reason these poor souls were worked half to death by him and his kind, yet, were ignored when there were no ships to work. Ducking below a low beam, he moved further into the building, he was intruding, but refused to be intimidated; there was one thing guaranteed to cease their belly aching and that was the lure of coinage.

"I will leave shortly, but before I do I have a guinea, awaiting anyone who will aid my investigations." He held the gold coin in the air so they could all see it clearly.

"For a guinea I'll sell you whatever you want," a voice shouted from the rear of the room.

"For that I'll sell you my entire family and my sow."

"No way to speak about your missus, Alfie." Instantly the tavern shook with laughter and shouted insults. He paused until, finally tired of the fact no one was taking him seriously, he slammed the coin onto the roughhewn wooden top

"For the last time, who will pick this up?"

"Pick it up yourself...then leave while you can." A woman had entered the tavern from beyond a curtain. Like a ship in full sail, she was beautiful, yet time worn, her face was lined with the scars of age. Her hair was lank and scraggily, but her bust was magnificent, full bodied and firm. Without asking, he knew immediately this was the woman he sought.

"Maggie, I presume?"

"Depends who's asking," she sneered. Then, as quick as you like, she stood upon the bar and shouted,

"Drinks all round. Fill those tankards, no charge."

"Are you Maggie?" He demanded again.

"As I said, depends, but you...must be touched. Flashing gold around as if it were lead could get you skewered." The woman walked away, collected a pair of pewter pots, spat in them and wiped them clean. Bravery overcame foolhardiness and he followed her, it wasn't the most salubrious of places to speak, but speak they must.

"Well?" The question hung in the air unanswered. The woman eyed him carefully, as she pondered if this gent posed a threat or not.

"Bloody fool, that's what you are, and I don't deal with bloody fools. Seen enough in here to worry about another, so tell me what you want. If I likes what you say, I'll tell you me name." She might be brash and wild, but she had spirit and determination. To have run a business in this morass of turpitude meant she had strength of purpose. She was likeable, in a strange, off hand way, more importantly, she wasn't afraid of him and that boded well.

"I seek a friend who might have come to you for shelter." He did not wish to say too much, not in such a public place where any bilge rat might be listening. The women, for as yet he still wasn't sure to whom he spoke, remained silent, deliberating as to whether he could be trusted. Anyone who entered her tavern and flashed gold around was either foolish, or desperate. As yet, she wasn't sure which he was.

"Friends today, become enemies tomorrow. My friends, don't necessarily become yours, simply because of how much coin you have. Best you go 'afore one of these good gentlemen takes a dislike to you."

She turned away, dismissing him instantly, but he wasn't to be defeated. He tired of her games and pressed on regardless.

"Madam, if I am correct, you have concealed, within these premises a young lady…"

"More than one, ducky, all available and good clean girls they be too." Her voice boomed out raising laughter from those, nearest them. Her laughter made his blood boil, causing him to wonder if he were wrong. If Mrs. Wood was here, she had chosen badly, the sniveling dross within this place would sell their mother for a few coins, none would think twice about selling information about her presence to the likes of Bayles. If he were to aid Mrs Wood, he had to convince this woman to take him to her. He had to spirit the woman away from this cesspit, where there were too many eyes, and too many loose tongues. Placing the coin on the counter, he whispered menacingly,

"I'm sure you have, and I will pay for an hour with a girl who neither farts nor belches. Money, madam, coinage for an hour of her time, if such a women resides within; tell her a friend requests to speak with her." Once again he pushed the coin forward. She was, he saw, torn between indecision and loyalty; she stood hands on hips, ruminating as to what to do.

"My God, you are a fool; for the love of God, remove that coin. Any of this scum would slit you for the price of a pot of ale." Knocking the coin aside she stared at her clientele. "You best be speaking the truth, because if you don't I will release them upon you, you will not leave alive. Wait there."

Compassion had won the day; the woman had taken the coin and retreated Through the filthy curtain. Alone, he felt desperately vulnerable, more accustomed to the quiet, genteel surroundings of coffee house or hotel; this was a desperate place, though perhaps, in some ways, no different. In his world, a simple nod or a wink, said more than words. Fortunes were made on a handshake, or lost with a turn of a head. But within his world, just as many rogues existed. Crimes were committed, but were concealed behind manners, politeness and refinement, using lawyers and priests. Maybe life within this place was simpler. Murder, and theft, while committed openly and with little compunction, was in some ways more honourable. They faced their adversary, fought it out, until one emerged victorious.

"A brandy if you please." Begrudgingly a wretch of a man served him; the drink, gave him time to orientate himself to the building. The public area was separated from the living area by that curtain. While a door, a few steps away, was in constant use. A steady stream of men confused him momentarily, until he reasoned, that was where Maggie's other trade was carried out. He may have given the impression of an affluent businessman, out of his depth, but he wasn't that naïve. He had attended council meetings where this place had been discussed. He had listened to Eli Porter demanding its closure on more than one occasion, had heard him describe it as a den of iniquity, while Bayles complained that Sodom and Gomorrah had been less an affront to man's dignity than Maggie's den, that it should be burnt to the ground. Yet it remained, why, he neither knew nor cared. He might disagree with its presence, but every man was entitled to come or go as he pleased, none were forced to enter. His only concern was the safety of a young woman, apparently forced by circumstances, to seek safe harbour in such a building.

"Come!" The woman whispered and gestured for him to follow. This he did, and for the first time he entered a house of ill repute, a dwelling of fornication and pleasure. It would, he was sure, be an experience he would long remember.

"Thank you, I feared I would be forced to leave, if I had remained any longer."

"Nah you'd be safe enough. Though, one of those toads, will be dining on this for many a long day."

"Just what I desire, my name bandied about town."

"Does it matter; will it hurt your reputation to be seen in here? Might even do you some good, Mister Turnbottle, sir." He smiled, Maggie, for he was sure that was who he spoke to knew him.

"Not really." He replied, while behind him, in a corner of the tavern, eager eyes watched him disappear. Tom Gasson, the rat catcher, finished his pot of ale, collected his bag and slipped out unseen. Already he was adding up what this information would be worth to the right person.

Chapter Twenty Three

The excitement of being in such a place made him feel like a young buck. His heart pounded within his chest causing him to reach out and grasp the woman's arm. Immediately, he felt her tense. She turned, shook herself free and rounded upon him viciously.

"Fake off you cully. Touch me again and I'll slit you, have no fear," her anger was unlike anything he had witnessed before in a lady though this woman was no lady.

"Madam, I meant no harm, I apologise if..."

"To hell with your words..." Without apology, or warning, he was bodily pushed into a small, dark storeroom filled with barrels. "Never touch me, least, not where we can be seen." Fingering her forehead, she paused, as if deliberating some improbable. "You're not that good at this, are yous?" Not many who came to her were so...innocent. She wanted to laugh but the situation was too dire for such hilarity.

"No, I suppose not, but give me a ledger and a balance sheet and I know what to do. This...this is as strange as it can get. I implore you madam, tell me, is she well?" She wanted to believe him, he had a look about him she hadn't witnessed in years...compassion.

"She is as well as could be."

"Then her good health wasn't always the case?" he asked.

"It were not. Fact is I thought she would be dead by morning. When she were brought here, she were cold, frozen. Fact is if those sailors had ignored her plight, she would have become, simply, another who died without friends or family."

"Sailors...they didn't?" His worst fears were aroused, he shivered at the thought of her suffering, not only at the hands of her family, but by local matelots as well.

"No, they did not. God save us from fools. They saw her hidden behind some barrels. Thought she might be one of mine, mistreated by a customer so brought her to me. Thank God they did. I recognised her immediately, said to myself 'why is a woman such as she doing down here?' What else could I do but bring her in." She was angry, and Turnbottle sensed he was close to alienating her.

"I am sorry. If you shelter the one I seek, I can but stress, I mean her no harm. My one wish is to aid her in her time of concern, for she is the embodiment of all that is wrong within this sorry town. I implore you, aid my quest or I shall seek assistance elsewhere."

"Talk's cheap merchant. Before I says anything else, you should know you were seen. Even now 'Ratty' Gasson, will be seeking a buyer for his news. Your name, and where you visit, will fill his pockets with coin. Which is why we must work quickly, for that sod of a priest will soon hear of this and hasten to find her." The woman stated examining his eyes for signs of betrayal, there were none, and she felt relieved, but not safe.

"Then, madam, we should press on, get her out of here as quickly as we can."

"She be in no state to be moved. She's barely alive, her body will take weeks to recover." Maggie declared.

"Move her we must for here she will be found. I on the other hand have places where she can be secreted, long enough for her to heal. Do this for her madam or see Bayles remove her and complete his devilish deed. What is it to be?" The woman paused before shaking her head, in reluctant agreement.

"Very well, but we may not have time, she be weak, you have been seen won't take long for him to put two and two together and come alooking."

"Then allow me to speak to her, for only she can decide her state of health. Or has she already spoken to you?"

"She has spoken a little. At first she rambled, made no sense at all, but later she told me some of what she endured."

"Of what did she speak? I must know otherwise how can I assist her?"

"That's for her to say…if she wants to. What I heard would curl your toes but that will go with me to my grave. For the moment, I will say she is who you seek, and has agreed to see you though God knows why." Maggie, had one rule in life, she lived by how others treated her. She was brash, brusque and unforgiving, she had survived and prospered, no mean feat in a town like this, where men ruled, and women seen as mere chattels. In this, her domain, she was queen, she would never be ruled by a man, any man, nor would anyone take what she considered hers by right, not without a fight anyway.

"Of that I am glad, though, I am at a loss as to how one speaks to those who have undergone such events. You, madam, have witnessed her demeanour, tell me what I should say, and do, tell me something, anything so that I might understand. What can I say to convince her, that my intentions are honourable? How can I explain that I merely see a disservice and wish to assist?"

"You're a strange one and no mistake. Don't get your sort in here too often." Thus far the conversation had been conducted in riddles and suspicion. Maggie appeared at odds with her own conscience, as if she struggled to decide whether he could be trusted and if she could begin to speaking honestly. "I tell you this, when you first entered, I saw a man full of pig swill, your position comes by money and that Guinea you flashed, proved you were not right in the head. I wondered if I should allow them out there, to tear you limb from limb. They would you know, do it in a trice, for less than a golden coin. But when I told her of your presence, I saw her eyes light up, not seen many men do that not in this place. You're different, yet even you thought, when I told you sailors found her, that they had interfered with her. That's what separates us from your kind. We're rough and loud but we have standards. Those sailors didn't so much as lay a finger upon her, save to keep her alive. Unlike your precious kind, we did not leave her to die; we aided her, yet you still assume that we would take advantage. Sometimes I wish to purge my stomach, rid myself of the evil that is shown to those in need. However, she says she would trust you, so I must allow you access, but I will tell you now, and I advise you to hear me, harm one hair on her head and I will come a looking for yous. I'll seek you out, and when yous least expect it, I'll take a knife to you, as cleanly as any castrator. Heed me well, sir, I neither forgive nor forget, unlike those that harmed her."

"You can trust me, I have but her safety upon my mind."

"We'll see, come we must not dally any longer, it will not take Gasson, too long to find those willing to learn of your presence."

"I doubt too many would be interested in my visit, what possible use would such news be to anyone?"

"You see, you prove my point that brains and common sense aint usually found in the same body. Neither would I have thought that the great Benjamin Turnbottle was so uncommonly stupid. You're important, any information about you is wanted by some. They feed on what the likes of Gasson bring them, it's like food and drink hereabouts, this aint some genteel parlour, this is my domain and I know what goes on. To those scum out there, information is something to stave off starvation, they will kill each other to tell what they have witnessed here this night."

"So my name is sold; my question, madam, is to whom?"

"To those that seek her." The brothel keeper pointed towards the wall, where he assumed the girl was. "You were stupid. Those that did that to her, will be wondering why your frequenting my house. Which is why we must now deceive them."

"How madam? For I certainly didn't think to jeopardise her safety?"

"If that means what I finks, then yes, you have harmed her badly. If we are to assume the priest planned this, then he wished her dead. Within twenty paces of us now, there are at least four, who would do the deed without blinking. So you see you have brought trouble upon this place."

"I still fail to comprehend, why should I draw attention to her and you?"

"Gawd love us! Think! Your sort don't come to me, I send girls to them, secret like. Your very presence here is trouble, therefore to protect us all, there is but one course of action, we must make them believe you are seeking my favours, blowing off your loose corn." She saw his look of total bewilderment turn to sudden shock.

"Madam, I cannot. It would be...intolerable," Turnbottle stated, angry at what she suggested. As she feared, his conviction was in doubt, she had said as much to the woman earlier.

"You can and must, you are known for your honesty, trustfulness, and piousness. You treat your workers fairly, pay the going rate without flinching so long as the work is done on time and correctly. Which is why if we present you as a man with....yearning, most will believe it. What we need is that golden coin you bandy about so willingly."

"A coin, why?" The question, was bemusing but he complied. Holding the coin out, he saw her eyes gleam in excitement.

"With that, you will gain a reputation. Wait here, I think we can save you both." Maggie disappeared, leaving a very bewildered man standing alone in a store room. His mind raced as he wondered what she intended. He didn't have to wait long, within moments she was back, in company with a gaudily dressed and made up young girl.

"This is Mary-Ann," Maggie announced. Turnbottle guessed the girl to be about twelve or fourteen, certainly no more. "Give her the coin...Go on, hurry up!" He hesitated; the girl stank of body odour and stale cologne. "She hasn't learnt the finer art of washing yet, but she's clean, if yous gets me drift. More importantly, them out there knows it." Maggie flicked a thumb towards the bar area and smiled. "Drink this 'Black Strap' then go out there, and tell them that Mister Turnbottle, just paid a golden Guinea for your services."

"Madam, I must question whether that is truly necessary?" He was aghast; his reputation, already sullied, was about to be besmirched even further but the girl swigged heartily at the bottle of strong Jamaican Rum, belched and smiled at him.

"If you want her to remain concealed, then, it is. Besides, do you not relish the idea of being seen as a dog? Come morning everyone will see you in a far more enlightened way." Shaking his head in dismay, Turnbottle nodded in agreement. Maggie smiled, her idea was simple and would be effective of that he was sure. "Worry not, she will lie like a toad, and convince those with loose tongues that you were here for one thing only. Now do as you're told lass, string them your tale then take the remainder of the night off."

"I drinks this rum, then tells them how good he was." Mary-Ann replied, giggling mischievously at her instructions.

"That's right; tell 'um he was a lion, powerful and strong, yet kind and considerate. Tell um, he were the best you'd ever had. Tell them well child, or instead of the coin I'll thrash your behind so hard you won't sit for a week. Shock turned to admiration as the girl and her madam shared mischievous smiles. It was a game they played, one, no man would ever understand but they did. Mary-Ann did this out of loyalty and to prove that loyalty she dutifully swigged heartily at the Rum bottle.

"Will she be believed?" he asked, as they left the child alone and moved back into the corridor.

"Of course, she's the best. More importantly, will your friends believe it of you?"

"Possibly...probably... some will find it improbable; others will laugh and slap me upon the back. My housekeeper will be shocked and will, most likely, leave me in disgust. Whatever occurs, I will accept their taunts just so long as we secure her safety. That is more important than my reputation."

Maggie remained silent; her charge deemed him her best chance of refuting their scurrilous claims. Yet they would have to remain vigilant.

"Words are easy; deeds are what count...I put her in the back room. It has a big fire that's been roaring ever since that day; even so, she can't get warm."

"How close?" he asked, his voice quivering in anger.

"Hard to say, seen men far colder after being fished out the water. But a woman dressed like that, and with child...possibly an hour, maybe less. What I do know is that whoever did that to her should be horse whipped. If she had died it would have been nothing less than murder."

"I agree...but we would fail in any attempt at bringing charges against them. Those involved would never see the inside of a Court."

Two people, so far apart in most things, nodded in silent agreement on this.

"Course not. Gentlemen did that, and begging your pardon, sir, but gentlemen stick together."

She was right; it was a sad indictment of their times that if you were born with enough money and status, it was possible to get away with murder so long as it was seen, in the eyes of the law and your peers, to be legal.

"The sorry state of our world, my dear," he agreed.

"Aye...It's just us you hang without fair trial. The poor go to their deaths while your sort watch, then toast each other as upholders of our moral wellbeing."

"You would do well to keep such thoughts to yourself. Some would say that's treason talk," Turnbottle cautioned.

"Oh, I know who to speak thus and who not. I am privy to too much, there are those who would rather see me dead than in a court room. Either way I knows too much and could ruin a fair few so called refined gentlemen."

It was best not to question her further, but one day, when the time was right, he would seek her out and take what she knew, for even he knew the importance of information.

"Here we are. I'll leave you alone...If anything untoward happens go through that door; it takes you into a donkey yard. There's a gate that leads to an alleyway, then down into Water Lane. Once there you should be able to evade anyone long enough to be gone. Be careful, she's not fully recovered, weepy like, but well you know."

He nodded, paused, steeling himself as to what lay behind this cracked and fragile door. Then taking hold of the latch, he pushed it slightly, wincing as the hinges squeaked alarmingly. The room beyond was dark; one cracked and filthy window allowed a feeble light to enter. As Maggie had said, a fire roared in the grate, warming the room wonderfully. Even so, he shivered in suppressed shock. The squalor took his breath away; her world had been of elegance, now it consisted of a single bed and one well-padded but ancient chair in which a bundled shape sat.

Chapter Twenty Four

Very slowly, she turned and he gasped. Within the period between the funeral and this moment, she appeared ten years older. Her face, once so fresh and young was now pallid and drawn. Her eyes, once bright and alive were sunken pits of despair. Holding his emotions in check he felt sickened by what had happened to her, and knew that if she began to weep he would join in willingly. *What have they done? If it takes the rest of my days Bayles and his kind will pay for this.* She had fallen from grace and he felt angry.

"Forgive me for not rising, sir, but Maggie insists I remain well wrapped."

"You have no need to apologise…madam, you must excuse the frailties of an old man."

"It matters not, sir. I am past caring about social niceties…please sit, but I urge not too close to the fire. Maggie keeps it so well stocked I fear one day I shall find myself slowly roasting in front of it." She smiled weakly, making him hate those who had done this even more. Seeing a small stool he drew it closer and sat beside her. Despite her predicament she appeared remarkably resilient.

"You posed me a problem; I found it difficult to locate you." In reality, thanks to Mrs Jones, she had been remarkably easy to find and that along with what Maggie had said, caused him grave concerns.

"Maggie…did that. She has been so good to me. Not many will be now that…well you must be aware of what is being said."

She was down, hurt, but he sensed not defeated. Deep within her was a spark of defiance which he hoped to rekindle and fan back into life. Time was their enemy, it dripped away, never to be reclaimed, at any moment Maggie might appear and tell them to leave, but Abigail needed to feel safe, to speak without fear. She was tired, that was obvious, worn out and weak, betrayed and castigated she needed to be nurtured into explaining what she had gone through. He had heard Bayles' version; hers, he was sure, would be far different.

"Tell me what was said. I surmise that black hearted demon is spreading his scurrilous lies about me?"

"I will not lie. He painted you as the fallen woman, a Jezebel, far worse than any of Maggie's girls, who I must say have proven to be both delightful and resourceful. I am not privy to what happened to you, but would surmise that both Wood and Bayles, had a hand in it."

"I have tried to obliterate that from my memory." Her eyes glazed, and he knew that both men had made mischief. Far more than he had first suspected.

"Then madam, I would remind you of what I said that day at the church, I told you then, that many of us were simply present, to make sure the old goat was truly dead."

"I remember...I thought you very rude and dishonourable..." Her voice trailed away at some hidden memory.

"Yes...I was rude, but I spoke the truth. You are not alone, there are many within the town that despised Joseph Wood, many who were glad to see him dead and buried. Some, myself, included spoke to him out of necessity, nothing more.

"You all seemed so..."

"Friendly...? A sham, a front, a masquerade; something we indulged in to preserve our businesses. There is much you need to know, much that he and others kept from you and the town, things that will shock you but which you must hear so that you may trust me, but not here not now. This place is compromised If you believe in me, you will entrust yourself upon my services once more. Gather what you need and prepare yourself for a journey into, hopefully, safety."

"Surely I am safe here, sir." He saw her indecision as she glanced around what had become her refuge from the world.

"I fear not, madam. My stupidity has endangered you once again. As we speak, the sham that Maggie prepared risks being exposed. Even now those that did this may be approaching. Bayles in particular is intelligent, but also sly, like a fox. He will not be slow in realising why I am here. He will arrive demanding that you be thrown into the street. Maggie will be implicated, her trade and name compromised, if we remain, and that I would not like to witness. She has been a good friend, but we must now take our leave and allow her to deny any knowledge with a clear conscience."

"Where, pray, is safe for me any longer?"

"Within the town."

"You jest. Surely, if this place be compromised, they will turn the town upside down seeking me...us." Abigail's surprise was duly noted by her new friend.

"They will, but we will pit our intelligence against theirs. They will think you have run instead we will hide within the town, where, I assure you, you will remain undiscovered. First though, we must leave this place, so I would urge you make haste." Slowly, hesitantly, she rose and began packing, she had precious little, supplied, no doubt, by the women of the house. As she made ready, Turnbottle asked,

"May I be so bold as to ask why the family turned; I would have expected the business community to make life difficult, but the family had no reason to turn as they undoubtedly did."

"Life is, as I have discovered, a fickle beast. The priest was prepared; he and the lawyer had information supplied by Joseph which implicated me. With such information, the sons were left with no alternative but to act. Do I blame them? Not entirely, but I had hoped for a little empathy."

"Why, both are toads. Neither, knew how to piss straight unless told how to by Joseph."

"They aren't that bad sir, oh true they are beholden upon his wealth, but I expected clemency simply because, they were aware of his…traits. Not many know, but their own wives had been dealt a similar hand in the past."

"What! Both, my God, Wood was indeed a swine. Speak no further of this until we are safe. When that is done, I would implore you to trust me fully and describe in minute detail what they accused you of and what was said. Only then can I know how to react." She stared at him and in the dim shadows of a dank and dingy room she smiled. She was weak, tired and battered by life, but in that instant he saw defiance. In the brief time since hearing Bayles spout his venom, Turnbottle surmised the truth. This poor, defenseless soul was no more capable of lying, than he was of sleeping with one of Maggie's girls.

In this sorry story she was the key. If he could win her over, convince her that he, and no one else, had her best intentions in mind, then, eventually, he would unlock their secrets and bring the Wood family to their knees. Until then he must continue to reassure her that he had her best interest at heart, while manipulating her to his thinking.

He couldn't achieve what he desired in this hellhole of fornication, she had to be placed where only he could influence her, control her every thought and deed. His plan, which still formed within his head, would need assistance and he knew just who to call upon. His man resided abroad, France in fact, where he lived upon the stipend he provided. Now was time to summon him home to complete that which he was good at. Death.

"Are you well, madam?" He had seen her hesitation and feared she was experiencing some sort of doubt.

"I am," she replied, and he heard her pain. "I simply do not understand how we, two strangers, can beat such a family. They are strong, they command, while we are…like the leaves on the trees come autumn; fragile and insignificant."

"Believe that and we are ruined before we begin. I pledge this to you; there are ways in which, even the mightiest oak can be felled by small men. We will become those men, we will bring down the Wood family, and any other who dared to accuse one as fragile as you. Now, while you complete your preparations I will speak with your saviour and tell her what I propose."

For a moment he had sensed her wavering, however she appeared to accept that he represented her best chance of salvation and that from a low point of near death, she had a growing band of friends who believed in her. *If only Turnbottle had made himself known before Nathaniel my life might have been very different.* The sudden memory of her husband made her shudder in wonderful anticipation.

* * *

"Where are you taking her?" Maggie asked, as Mary-Ann kissed her friend on the cheek.

"Better you don't know. Safe to say, she will be best served in my protection, rather than here, if they come looking." Their preparations had taken time, time in which Turnbottle, had expected the rap of urgency upon the door.

"Take my advice, get her away from here and travel as far as possible. Too many peepers in this hellhole, best she forgets and starts again." He smiled and nodded, Maggie's words were wise, spoken in genuine concern, but he desired her close by, how else could he weave his magic upon her?

"Rest assured, I will keep her safe. More importantly, if all goes well she will recover all she has lost." That was, perhaps, his first truthful statement. She was the key which might unlock a fortune and rid the town of that family forever. What he had to do was remain steadfast, if he began to doubt himself, it would result in a calamitous disintegration, of an already fragile idea.

"We'll see.God speed, my child, remember where we are. If ever you need any help." Despite the obvious pleasure he had brought, Maggie remained unconvinced of his sincerity. As the two women embraced she whispered,

"Stay safe,"

"I will, my dear Maggie." Abigail wiped a tear from Maggie's cheek. The woman was not known for outward signs of affection, what she thought would have been a better gauge of her feelings. As Abigail turned to wish Mary-Ann well, Maggie stared at Turnbottle and thought, *I'll carve yous face if yous hurts her.* "Thank you both." Her face lit up, Maggie had seen it only once before, in recognition of his unexpected arrival. *Serve her well, for I can be your kindest of friends, or your worst nightmare.* Her charge was being removed, going God knows where and she was concerned. Too much was changing and she didn't like change, however, Abigail appeared genuinely happy and that was what mattered most.

"We should leave; we have some distance to go before we can feel safe." Taking Abigail by the arm he led her into the donkey yard. Waving once more to the madam, they picked their way through the manure until finally they stood in the lane. Abigail wore an old, mud splattered cloak, its best feature a full hood which concealed not only her face but also the damask dress she had worn since that fateful day. Maggie had given her the cloak, "so you can become just another faceless figure" she had explained. Turnbottle hurried her through a maze of lanes, houses and alleyways leading her further away from Maggie and, what she thought of as safety.

"In there!" He forced her beneath a brick archway and stood before her. Clinging to him, she hid her face in his shoulder as a group of men laughed at them, assuming he was her client. Such was this place that whores and their clients drew little attention. The destitute, were more concerned about finding money, food or drink, than what a filly and her rider got up to. It was this acceptance, he was relying upon. Once they had passed, they continued, he knew they had to pass taverns and gin houses, and each one needed to be passed quickly and unobtrusively. He knew what those who lived here were capable of, and shielded his ward from the worst, the 'Butts' had to offer. Even so, she shivered nervously as she witnessed each new sensation this place presented.

"Almost there." He said softly as she saw the body of a dead child, abandoned and forgotten like so much waste. The first rays of a new dawn flickered the sky, yet it would take time for light and warmth to find its way into this labyrinth. She had to be concealed before daylight ruined any last hope of avoiding detection. Each delay reinforced the fact that he had mistakenly taken a wrong turn, imperiling them further and taking her further away from a life she had known.

"Pray, tell where we go?"

"I own a small residence where you will be safe. More importantly no one will think to look for you here. Trust me a little longer, will you do that?"

She clutched his arm, her grip telling him that despite having come so far, she grew anxious. To have gone through so much virtually silent was testament to her fortitude and their unimaginable luck. Any one of those who had seen them could have been their enemy, yet she hadn't flinched as yet, even so he wished to get her undercover as soon as possible.

"Of course Mr Tur…"

"Hush, madam! Walls have ears; we do not wish to give anyone as much as a sniff of our intentions. Not yet, anyway." He was pleasant, but his words were more like a command than a request, by his tone she sensed that even he was feeling the unease of their situation.

"Sorry," she whispered. Her eyes were wide but defiant looking, she was confused and could he blame her?

"That's alright; once we are safely inside, we will have time to discuss what each of us has endured and what we can expect next. Until then, simply walk swiftly and silently. If I tell you to stop, then stop. If I tell you to run then run like the wind and don't look back. Most importantly, never, ever speak my name. Until this venture is completed, call me…Tanner."

"Tanner?" Abigail queried. This was another strange occurrence on top of so much she had been forced to suffer since being thrown from the house.

"That name will keep you safe…Now, come." He had not meant to be so course or demanding, but safety was paramount, more so than her feelings. Taking her arm he led her further into the winding alleyways which stank of raw sewage and rotting food. A place where rats chewed at undisturbed bodies, be they either asleep or dead, she knew not which, nor cared. Bayles had once described hell as being a dark, foul, fearsome place which stank of brimstone, where the damned screamed for eternity. What she was witnessing was hell on earth, where the cries of women and children punctuated the darkness. Maybe that had been the most fear provoking, imagining what devilment caused such pain. That thought stayed with her, fuelling her imagination, until finally they entered a house in some God forsaken alley.

"No candles. Only whores and pin makers use them and you do not want unwelcome callers. Light a fire, there is ample firewood. I will come to you later with food and clothes."

She could not say how pitiful a place it was, he had been good to her, saved her when she might have been caught, but her descent into depravity had taken yet another step, simply by entering this…desperate hovel.

"It is not what you are used to, but it will suffice until we can redeem your rightful position." He appeared reticent, awkward, and she knew why. He had questions to ask, but knew not how to broach them; she saved his embarrassment.

"You spoke of Bayles venting his anger upon me in Church, yet you never spoke of what he said. Now would seem as good a time as any to tell me more. What, apart from the fact I was some loathsome fornicator, did he tell them, more importantly, how many believed him?"

"Almost all believed him I fear. As you know if he told them Satan sat in the bell tower they would believe his words totally. In truth he squeezed every last drop of viciousness out of your name. He spoke of you lying with another, defiling your husband's name while he was away. He said you took a lover into your marital home, where you performed lewd and crude acts. More importantly, he told them you were with child, and that it wasn't your husband's. That is what sealed your fate."

"And you, Mr Tanner…require me to refute and deny such claims…well I can't. I am with child; I was…well the act happened in that house but not by a lover, nor by my husband. The truth, sir, is I was taken by a man who was supposed to be my protector. Joseph Wood, defiled me and when I confronted him, he did this to me. Does that make me a bad person? Some would say so, but I do not. I believe I am innocent."

It was the proof he wanted, the reason so much had happened, yet he knew there was still more to discover about that wretched family. Now was too soon; she was distraught, he would allow her to rest. Tomorrow when he had food and wine to bring, he would question her further, tell her of his plans and recruit her into doing his bidding.

Chapter Twenty Five

Leaving the tavern, Gasson, like the rodents he caught, used the darkened streets to slip away unseen. Like them, Tom Gasson was, silent, nasty and sought those of similar traits. Scurrying through the alley ways, he made his way to the upper town, to a man who would pay handsomely for his information. As the church bell tolled the hour, he hid in the shadows, waiting until only one candle lit window showed where his master was. Even then he waited further, making sure the man was a lone, and not in counsel. The half hour chimed before he approached and tapped lightly upon the mottled glass window pane. Fidgeting anxiously, he waited until a face, all would have recognised appeared.

"What?" the 'Raven' demanded after slipping the sash and examining the darkness cautiously.

"Have news, sir," Gasson hissed in his nasally, rattish voice.

"Had better be worth it. Enter quickly." Like those he caught, Gasson climbed effortlessly through the window. Bayles wrinkled his nose at his visitor's stench and decided it prudent to allow some air to enter, so left the window open, just a little.

"Well what do you have?" Bayles reclined in a well upholstered armchair, and listened, apparently more concerned with the wine that filled the long stemmed glass, than with what Gasson said. In fact his heart leapt in unbridled joy. Now wasn't the moment for hysterics or anger, now was the time for careful deliberation.

"Are you certain...this wasn't some drunken apparition?"

"As God is my witness, he was there, talking to Maggie herself and getting pleasured by one of her whores."

"No...not Turnbottle, such an event is...implausible. You lie, you rat featured guttersnipe." Bayles knew the man, he wasn't the sort to indulge in what others saw as...their right. Why then had he been there, for Gasson was not known for bad eyesight.

"I do not sir. He were there, I saw him and why else would such a man be there but for the pleasures Maggie's girls offer?"

"Why indeed?" While Bayles ruminated on this good fortune, Gasson, awaited the reward, he was sure he was due while staring in awe at the riches the man surrounded himself with. The fire, flickering in the grate, reflected on gold and silver plate, danced in the reflection of fine cut crystal. Such affluence was rarely seen by men like Gasson.

"If you lie, I will see you roasted upon the fires of hell."

"On my old mother's life I do not lie." The ratter sneered, while fearing the man could, and would, carry out his threat.

"I doubt you know the difference between truth or lie, nor who spat you out and gave you life. However what you say has merit and is worth a small reward. Take this, but be warned, if you have deceived me then your sins will be judged by a higher authority than I. Come judgement day your deceit will be called into question and you my friend will have to explain yourself before God himself..."

"Thank you, sir." Gasson spat on the coin and placed it into his coat pocket. The penny would buy ale, and if God asked, he would lie to him as he lied to most, purgatory wasn't to be waited upon, it existed every day for men like Gasson. Bayles despised such men, but he used them when he had to. If correct, this titbit of information was an incredible stroke of good fortune and money well spent. Not only did it give him leverage against that pious pain in the rear, but also posed numerous interesting questions.

"Mean, not right is it, sir? Gentleman likes him should find their pleasures with their own kind, if yous knows what I means, sir..."

"Shut up! Your voice annoys me...go, and trust me when I say I will remove your tongue with a blunt knife should you ever speak of this meeting."

Dismissing Gasson, like master would a disobedient dog, Bayles waited while the rogue left the same way he had entered, leaving, as his only evidence of his presence, a nasty stench. He was an odious creature, avoided by most, he was ripe from unwashed, filthy, clothes and body. He was small and wizen, had teeth like discoloured tombstones and crept about town, always lurking in dark corners, waiting, and listening. That was his craft, he was ignored by most, and used their carelessness to garner information. Their secrets were sold to men like Bayles who had need of such information. Such titbits added to the cleric's knowledge of his parishioners. It allowed him to barter and blackmail those who could add to his wealth, both financially and influentially. Those who failed to comply, were dealt with much as he had dealt with that Wood's woman. He used God's name to accuse and ridicule them, he threaten them with a lifetime of purgatory and used the malevolence of his flock, with simple words like 'heretic' and 'non-believer's' to invoke their displeasure. His pulpit was his stage, from where he instigated retributions, far worse than anything he could have done alone

"Stupid fools cannot see what is in front of their naive eyes. Well that is their problem. It is not my concern that their wits are addled and they fail to understand what is happening. One day they will, and then I will be long gone, enjoying what they so graciously supplied."

He smiled a devilish smile and drank. The wine came from that idiot

Sprigg, despite that it was good, as good as any the squire served, and it quelled the rage he felt inside. Anger was his constant companion, but he had learnt to control and channel his enemy, though occasionally it arose to consume and haunt him when he least expected it. The last time had been when Joseph had come to him, the wine stain upon the wall remained as evidence of their argument. He had promised the woman to him, had said it would be as easy as all the others. They would have their way with her then dispose of her, never to be heard of again. Drink had befuddled his brain, Joseph had become greedy, had reneged on their agreement and taken her himself. Worse, he had left evidence of his indiscretion. Despite their best attempts to silence her, she had threatened to expose them, to shout her accusations from the bell tower if needs be.

"Stupid man, I told him what needed to be done, a few coins and a friendly physician and she would expire in her sleep. No one would have questioned it, so many died in the town every year, another would have roused little interest." Bayles spoke as if he were present, as if, like his anger, Joseph remained an entity to torment or guide him. "The lingering death of consumption did not take you old friend. Your demise was too swift, someone had a hand in your ending. Is that why you came to me? Did you have forewarning, a vision, what other reason could there have been for your foresight?" This question had confounded him since first hearing of his death. Joseph was clever, few would have thought to have provided and contrived such evidence as to condemn her through a death bed accusation. Nor would many have used their own seeding to end her so completely. It was the work of a genius to condemn her, by exposing her condition as proof of her infidelity and compound her culpability.

"Why, Joseph, is Turnbottle frequenting Maggie's den? He is not the sort to do so...or have we been misled?" Perhaps he had misjudged the merchant, perhaps the esteemed and respectable Turnbottle had a seamier side. Was he susceptible? Could his weaknesses be exploited? Such questions needed investigated, as did the one concerning the witch. Apparently she had disappeared not to be seen or heard of since that meeting. He wanted her destroyed, humiliated, but to do so he needed to find who was harboring her and where. Pouring another large glass of wine, he contemplated this puzzle.

"Is it possible that Turnbottle and this Wood woman were as one? Could they be colluding together?" An hour ago such a question would have seemed implausible, but now... who knew what was possible. "What to do with this titbit? Should we tell the town or should we remain silent?"

The possibilities were endless. If, as he liked to think, he was intelligent, he must use his brain to resolve this improbable. Turnbottle had been an irritating sore for too long, it was time he was reined in somewhat. Slipping his shoes, he toasted his feet before the fire. The assumption that Turnbottle and the woman were colluding was preposterous, inconceivable, and stupid. He had enquired and no one had seen her since that day, more importantly, Turnbottle had no reason to search for her.

"Therefore, my friend, we are left with one inference…despite your piety, you are nothing more than a lecherous old man. Next time you sit in judgment, I will remind you of your visits…oh yes, I will make you suffer for this night's work." Smiling at this conclusion, Bayles stored this interesting titbit away for future use. He used what he learnt against those that annoyed him, or as a means of blackmailing those with secrets to be kept hidden. Such arrangements had worked perfectly well until she had entered his life. Her demise would allow him to resume, unhindered with his work and build on what he had salted away.

The heat of the fire felt good, warmed his blood, making him tingle in anticipation. Fire, as the good book said, was God's cleanser. It rid the world of women like Mrs. Wood and made liars speak the truth. Yet it was controllable and Edward Bayles liked being in control. With glass in hand and toes toasting, he settled back and contemplated what he had achieved since arriving in Stormouth. He thought not of the 'Butts' or of Turnbottle losing whatever dignity he might have left, but of what he had achieved since first arriving. From near poverty, he had amassed a veritable fortune. Most from eager parishioners who were as gullible as innocents. Even the wealthy, Passionate and devote, had insisted on bestowing gifts upon him to ease both their conscience and to facilitate their journey into Heaven. Exploiting their fears, he had discovered that a sermon delivered on Sunday, containing sufficient hell and damnation, brought forth rewards on Monday. The more affluent, came bearing wine, food, jewels, silver plate and sometimes gold coins, while those from the more sordid underbelly of the town arrived with bread, chicken or a pig. No matter what they brought he accepted their gifts with a degree of servitude and reluctance, but then either consumed or secreted their gifts for future use. Those who had nothing, occasionally offered their wives or daughters. More often than not he refused, but, like Turnbottle, he occasionally needed to feel the touch of a woman.

"Destiny chose me, and who am I to deny her choice?" He chuckled, staring lovingly at the wine. As the youngest son of a tenant farmer, his life was destined to be one of difficulty. While his eldest brother got the farm, the next eldest had taken articles, and was now a mealy mouthed solicitor like Pawell.

Poor Saul, had tired of working the soil, taking the King's shilling at a market one summer's day. Last he heard he was somewhere in the Fever Islands, no doubt dead by now, but he would never know for sure. Destiny had played her part, and much to his disgust, he'd found himself accepting a post with a local cleric. Funnily he'd enjoyed his life, it had been simple and he'd risen to the officer of verger, until fate had once again stepped in. The Bishop had granted him this appointment, thus bring him into association with Joseph Wood, whereupon his outlook on life had changed forever.

"Poor Joseph, so many indiscretions, so much pain. How had we avoided detection?" It was Wood who had introduced him to the group, shown him what could be obtained. After an initial reluctance he had become the thirteenth member, apt considering his profession, but unlike Judas he would not reveal that they shared a liking for both carnal pleasure and the acquisition of wealth. Pleasures which, normally occurred between husband and wife, he first found repulsive and contrary to his teachings, but which he had come to accept. The heat of the fire and the excellence of the wine, were making him melancholic. Exhaling slowly, he stared into the flames and saw…demons from his past, images of his misdemenours and crimes, of shame and annoyance, and a more profound feeling of disappointment. Their group had disbanded while Joseph's dilemma was dealt with.

"Should have kept his breeches well buttoned." He chuckled for while his friend was considered a bore by some, certainly, that wasn't his worst foible. Joseph enjoyed the thrill of the chase and the exultation of the capture. Many a wench had been brought before them, used then discarded. While he, in his guise of minister, had admonished them of their sins. With him in attendance, the group had unleashed their wildest desires without fear of heavenly chastisement. For that service, he was rewarded with coin, friendship and impunity.

"What became of her? Damn her bones! She waits somewhere, like a leech waiting to suck our blood." The threat of a witness to their crimes, loose within the district, was not conducive to his well-being. Until she were discovered or her death confirmed, she remained a threat. That was his fault, he had not pressed them to finish her when they had the chance. Heretics should be burnt, if he had succeeded she would be nothing more than ashes and a memory instead she had simply vanished.

"Do they defy me? Do the fools lie about her whereabouts?" It was why he had ventured into the 'Butts' to ask, to seek answers to this problem but he had come away empty handed. Each person asked had denied any knowledge of her, which pleased, but also confused him. The agony of not knowing was a pain he could not disregard. He owed it to his friend, to discover her fate.

"Poor Joseph." Bayles remembered that night when his friend had arrived in an agitated state demanding retribution for her sins. He should not have agreed, but Joseph was persuasive, and when it had been explained that she was with child, his assistance had been assured. In this very room they had concocted their plan, a notion which would have remained simply that, a notion, but Joseph had died and their plan had been implemented far sooner than anyone had imagined. Her admission, and confirmation that Joseph was the father had left him dazed. He had expected lies and denial, but the silly bitch had, by admitting her guilt, hung herself with her own words. More strange, was that she expected his sons to believe, and forgive her. As if they would, money, status, power, were their reward for disinheriting her.

"So she be gone, dead more than like and no irate father has appeared seeking some form of retribution." He belched loudly, the wine was good, while the silence surrounding her was as good as any confession. With each passing day, he felt safer, "Crawled into some hell hole and expired, best thing that she could do, makes everyone's lives that much easier." The weather was improving, but dressed as she had been, she most likely froze to death that first night. He would perform at her funeral if her body were ever discovered, he would lie convincingly, telling anyone who asked that she had perished through no fault of his. Releasing a satisfied sigh, he loosened his jacket buttons, poured yet another glass of wine and sipped contentedly. His ruminations were disturbed by a discreet knock upon the door.

"Come!" he commanded.

"Beg pardon Reverend but I was wondering if you needed anything else 'afore I lock up for the night." His annoyance was tempered by the timely arrival of his housemaid, Ruby, a girl who shared youth with a freshness he so admired. Her voice was that of a temptress, instantly he felt the tingle of excitement.

"Come closer, my child, so I can see you." The flicker of the fire enhanced her voluptuousness and reminded him as to why he had employed her. She had many redeeming qualities; none of which involved her abilities with mop and bucket. Her family were from the very edge of the parish, were devote and would accept what he told them. While her most admirable qualities were the ability to remain silent, do as she was told without question, her freshness of face, and delicateness of skin. Tonight he would reacquaint her to the ways of this terrible world. The surge of excitement made him twitch in nervous anticipation. *Who needed the group when he had such wonders to hand?*

"Tell me child, are you, eager to learn, willing to do as required?" Like a nervous filly that needed breaking, he saw her hesitate. He had won; she would become the latest in his string of conquests that had been taught what they must do. She would act as he commanded, and be sworn to secrecy, or risk eternal damnation.

* * *

While Bayles introduced his servant to his varied and unspeakable tastes, others were fighting their own demons. Josephs remaining family, sat sullen faced and silent. Since the reading, they had alternated between silence and raging confrontation. This evening, was of the latter, tempers were raised, accusations abounded, and blame was to be laid at the door of anyone stupid enough to allow it.

"Has anyone seen her?" Sarah demanded, her question drawing villainous glares and venomous words.

"Hold your tongue, woman. How many more times must you be told?" Josiah replied harshly. Sarah turned away, she had discovered the best way to calm his anger was to ignore it when it flared, though this evening Josiah appeared tetchier than normal. "That woman is dead, her name will not be mentioned. We have to forget her, and the shame she brought upon us, and rebuilt both our lives and reputation." Josiah was finding the task of head of the family difficult to deal with.

"Must we claw at each other in this manner Can we not simply answer a question calmly?" Martha added her voice to that of her husband's, for even she tired of the constant arguments.

"What do you expect, joy and happiness after what she did? Do you expect us to apologise and to welcome her back into the arms of this family which she so nearly destroyed?" Usually as silly and self-centered as her husband Adam, Sarah suddenly found a voice and it was not something they wished to hear.

"Over my dead body. That harlot will never set foot in this house again, not while I have breath to denounce her." Adam added. He, more than most was most pleased to see Abigail gone.

"You presume she has gone?" Martha demanded.

"I do so presume, no one has seen or heard of her since she was thrown from this house. My assumption is that she has either, walked away, or lies dead in some gutter, either way we are rid of her."

"I am glad one of us is so assured," Josiah replied harshly.

"I have no desire to set eyes upon her ugly face ever again. Nor am I worried if no one looks for her. I mean, why should they? We all heard what father said," Adam added.

"Oh yes, and we all know how gracious he was, we all took what was on offer and paid him service." Martha, as Abigail had guessed, was the one with a conscience. The sons, though, silenced her; they did not require to be reminded of what their father had used to buy their silence.

"Hush your mouth. That is our father you speak of," Adam spat venomously.

"It is, and a more vicious person I wish never to meet. However, the deed is done; we must look to the future. We have customers who will be expecting us to provide a service that we cannot do until we cease this constant warring."

Josiah banged the wooden table with his fist causing pewter plate and cups to fall to the stone floor with a noisy crash. As head of the house, it was he who, now, determined how both it and the business were run. They had expected disruption when their father had died, what none of them had expected was the animosity that would be caused by Abigail's eviction.

"So, is that the end of the matter?" Martha asked

"I believe so, yes. Even if we wanted to help her, there is nothing we can do now."

A dreadful silence followed the statement, a silence that couldn't last long and Martha was the one to break it.

"Who pray, will tell Nathaniel that, when he returns?"

"If, wife, if. You were there, you heard what was said. It would take a miracle for him to have survived. I do not fear his return but if by some miracle he did what could he do? All we did, was follow what was, after all, father's decision." Josiah feared Nathaniel's return more than anything else. If God, was merciful and Nathaniel discovered what they had done, his response would be unthinkable, which was why Josiah dwelt on it rarely.

"A coward's answer, but one that might have to be faced. If he were to be resurrected, and God rest his soul if he is not, one of you will have to explain, not only her absence, but also why neither of you stood up for her before Pawell and Bayles. Personally I am glad that task will fall to you and not I, for I vouch, neither of you, will explain why you allowed those vile personages to do what they did, and why you did nothing to find her."

"A fine speech; one you will never have to deliver because, he's dead, she's gone, and we need to think of the business," Josiah stated flatly

"What have you in mind?" Adam queried.

"Simple. We have space on ships to acquire and cargo to arrange. I suggest we concentrate on that, not what might happen sometime in the future."

"I still say you're cowards," Martha added

"That's as may be, but I for one can live with that accusation." Josiah brought the conversation to an end, but they knew that, come the morrow, when the doors were barred and the family gathered, the same argument would reignite. Tomorrow, though, was hours away; before then the brothers had work to do, which meant different things to them both.

Chapter Twenty Six

Benjamin Turnbottle slept fitfully, his mind a torment of questions. Breakfasting at three in the post noon, he spent some time alone in his study supposedly working on his ledgers. Mrs Jones, had remained silent about the day previous, and he had no intention of speaking of it unless requested to do so by those with more authority than his housekeeper. As dusk drew in and the house candles lit, he put away his ledgers, collected the bag he had requested from the kitchen, and left for what would, he was sure be an eventful night.

Once more he went to the 'Butts', where, concealing himself he waited in an alleyway opposite the house. He was pleased to see his guest was being circumspect, the windows were draped, and she had heeded his advice about candles, only a flickering fire lit the room. He was a prudent man, his authority within the town was of someone who could be trusted, yet he waited upon someone who was so unlike him it was laughable.

"This it?"

"It is." Turnbottle had been so lost in thought, that the man's arrival startled him, despite having summoned him here. "I require that house watched; no one is to enter or leave without my permission, or being informed of where they go and whom they meet. Here is one shilling; more will follow if you do your work well." He trusted him to do as he was told. She must be watched, not only for her own safety, but his as well. If Bayles came sniffing he wanted to be aware of it first.

* * *

He found in her a despondent, shrunken husk of her former self. A sallow creature who stared at the burning embers with eyes that lacked the spirit she had once shown. She was defeated, brought down by lies and innuendos, if he were to encourage her to speak of what she knew she must be reinvigorated. He must instill within her, some hatred, make her loathe those who had castigated her and make her fight back. Maybe she needed time to recover but that was a luxury he did not have. Time was his enemy, she was with child and that would arrive sooner rather than later. She had to be ready before then. Despite his misgivings, she had to be convinced of this trustworthiness, which would mean revealing much of his past to her. Not to do so might mean his grand scheme faltered at the first hurdle.

"I brought bread and a cheese, not a feast but sufficient. I will arrange more for you along with extra firewood."

"My thanks, sir, but I cannot remain here."

"You must, for out there you will be in danger. Do not imagine Bayles will not be looking for you. The road will be watched while the harbour, a possible escape route, is controlled by him as well. Every fisherman pays him a tithe, many supply him with information as well. I fear, madam, you are trapped until such time as we can show the town what evil those people did to you."

"How...how can I fight the likes of them? One woman, guilty apparently, of a deed so vile she will never be heard."

"You fight, madam; you kick, scratch, and claw until someone believes your tale. You have made a start, you have recruited your first soldier. From such humble beginnings, we can but only grow. Though in truth, we need to be open and honest with each other. You have no reason to trust me, for we know little of each other's past, so I will tell you a tale, so terrible you will understand why I hate the very name of Joseph Wood."

"I guessed you despised him, but not why? He could be cantankerous, condescending, manipulative and deceitful, but what did he do to earn your displeasure?"

"I did hate him, madam, as I told you that day, many of the merchants despised him. My hatred though went deeper than most. It had been my misfortune to know Joseph Wood for many a long year. We had many an altercation, both personal and business wise."

"I never knew?" She stated solemnly.

"Not many did, I certainly never spoke of the reason nor surprisingly did Wood. We crossed swords many times but the worst occurrence was during the time of the 'Chamberlin'. You remember our smuggling friend?"

"I do. In fact, I had reservations about Joseph's involvement. I had wondered if he...well safe to say when the true identity was revealed I was disturbed."

"I can understand your problem, the town so very nearly tore itself apart with claim and counterclaim. I began to doubt my own sanity as each new revelation came to light."

"Terribly dark times, sir, terrible." He watched as she frowned at the memory of those days. Was it fair to involve her in this? But why not, she had lived through that nightmare, as they all had. More importantly she had seen and heard things which he now needed to know. It was not his fault that she had become a pawn in a much larger game? Nor was it his fault they had dismissed her and he had rescued her. The blame lay four square at the feet of Bayles and those who were, once again, driving the town into deprivation. He would tell her what she needed to know in an attempt to glean the knowledge she had within that pretty head.

"In business, Joseph was a giant. He saw the opportunities offered by the town's unique position. But in private I have it on good authority he was a devil madam who ruled his house with a rod of iron. I would imagine you know better than I about such matters. I will not ask you to speak of such malevolence, but you must be enlightened into what he has been involved in since the demise of 'The Chamberlin', and the arrival of Pope.

"I fear sir, I know little of what that swine did outside of the house. But will perhaps one day enlighten you into how he behaved when the family were alone with him."

"When you are ready my dear I would find such evidence enlightening, but in your own time there is no rush." Oh sweat Jesus, she would not need much persuasion to tell all, but until she was ready, he would continue his tale. "Through fair means or foul, your father-in-law acquired the position of comptroller, with which he controlled the majority of trade within Stormouth. Nothing moved without his say so, his influence controlled shipping, chandlery and storage. He set wages, prices and the cost of storage. He was madam a devil, a devil with deep pockets. My God, he even imposed a levy on every ship that arrived, or left, harbour. Unless we paid, our ships were not allowed to berth, stranding our cargos on board, leaving us unable to fulfill our obligations. He forced us to show him servility, made us grovel to him for the right to land our goods in our home port. Perhaps you understand a little better as to why he was so despised and where his wealth came from. His influence was...is still hurting."

He paused, wondering if she was strong enough to hear anymore. It was imperative she did, because he wanted to help her and ultimately she could assist him.

"You may not be aware but there are plans to break that monopoly. Those ideas were beginning to work."

"I heard nothing of such ideas," she stated turning towards her benefactor, who saw a steely determination appear in her eyes. Something he'd said was having an effect, or so he thought. Truth was she was playing him for a fool, getting information from him with which she could ruin the family

"I doubt if you would. Wood might have shared his thoughts with your husband, his priest, or perhaps his lawyer, but never with a woman. I apologise, madam, but we all knew he thought women good for one thing only. Your predicament is testimony to that." He saw her gasp and wondered if he should continue but to stop now would mean he would have to return to this at a later date, better to get it done and out of the way. "His wife's demise is, I fear testament to his true self."

"Meaning sir?"

"Meaning madam, I doubt if she went to her grave willingly but such matters are for later. For the moment, I wish to explain who we, a small group of merchants were beginning to hurt him. Wood controlled through fear and keeping his workers beholden to him, we on the other hand, had begun paying above the general rate, forcing Wood to follow suit. It was a dangerous game of cat and mouse to see who would break first. He had deep pockets, but no one, not even he had unlimited funds, we were causing him pain, and we wished to increase that pain.

"I heard nothing of this?"

"Why should you madam, he would assume such matters beyond your intelligence. Nor would he speak of the land we had purchased near Dartington. For that is where we envisage building a new dock. We have secured finances and an engineer, the work will take years to complete, but eventually we would be able to take trade away from Stormouth and Wood. Until then he would retain his monopoly and continue to make a fortune. Imagine, though, the long term benefits in we succeeded. Well paid workers mean better turn round times for ships, better warehousing and transport mean our goods will not be stranded in warehouses controlled by that family. Every day our ships lay idle, we lose money, we need them in, unloaded, and out again, not stranded as they are at the moment while Wood benefits at our expense. My apologies, madam, no doubt you do not wish to listen to business details, but I believe you have been dealt with harshly and I truly wish to assist you."

"My thanks, sir; your detailed description is well formed, concise and enlightening." Abigail stood and cut a section of cheese. It was the first time Turnbottle had seen her eat, it was a start.

"Of course such an enterprise could not remain secret forever; Wood discovered our plan and obviously wished it halted. A war of attrition began. After all, he didn't wish to lose his hold over the docks, they were his money base. The future looked uncertain, the side that could hold out longest would win. Then, in the space of a few months everything changed with two untimely deaths. My apologies if this is distressing, I meant no harm."

"None taken, I do not understand the technicalities of your proposal, though; I do see that with the family in disarray, you have an opportunity to destroy their business completely."

"Not our intention, I would like nothing more than to negotiate with the sons. If they agree to our proposals, this stupidity could end, we could all earn an honest living without any further disagreement. I fear though that will never happen. They rudderless, without purpose, neither son knows what trade is about…They are children lost in a void which, if not filled, could ruin everyone from the squire to the lowest mud lark."

Turnbottle was into his stride, spinning his tale with such ease, even he, began to believe the possibilities of his grand scheme. Seeing the woman stare at him questioningly, he continued.

"Joseph's death, while unfortunate, wasn't a major problem. In normal circumstances, after a brief period, a natural successor would have taken over. Such is the law of inheritance. Nathaniel, was his successor, we could have negotiated with him. The transition of power would not have been so damaging."

"Damaging to whom, sir?"

"Too many, madam, the world of commerce is like a spider's web; we are all reliant upon each other. Ruin one business, and the ripples spread through the entire community, other's, worthy businessmen, could be ruined also. We are too closely involved for that to happen. Nathaniel would have been the steadying hand upon the rudder, he might have steered the company in a different route to that of his father. With his death…" He stopped as he saw her gasp, as a surge of grief welled within her.

"Ignore my frailties…you were about to add that with Nathaniel gone his brothers will inherit, is that correct?"

"I was, and that is our problem. Without the determination of your husband, his brothers may flounder. Neither can be called businessmen, Josiah is an amiable fool, while Adam is nothing more than a fopdoodle. Either of them could ruin the company within a year, and bring many of us down as well. That we cannot allow, which is why we require your assistance."

"I, what is it you expect me to do? I am ruined, destroyed, exiled. I am expunged as far as they are concerned."

"That is where you are wrong. While you still breathe you are a worry to them, you know too much to be allowed to speak out, which is why I fear they will continue to seek a way to silence you forever. The process began in Church, by besmirching your name and character, Bayles assumes that when your body is discovered, no one will ask why, who, or how you died. You will simply be interned and your name forgotten. I apologise for being so brusque but he wants to be certain of your absolute silence. You however have usurped him, you escaped and are no longer beholden to them. Join our crusade madam, together our knowledge and insight will firstly prove your innocence, then reinstate you as head of the firm and return what is rightfully yours. That done, we can improve the lot of everyone in this town."

"A noble sentiment and a just cause but, impossible they have what they want, why would anyone listen to me?" Christ on his cross, was she so naïve not to understand, was it possible he had been mistaken and she was not the woman he assumed her to be?

"They will, one day they will kneel before you and share their allegiance before the next snow falls. Would you not like to see Bayles kneel before you and plead your forgiveness?" He paused, and witnessed her temptation. What he proposed could bring about their downfall and give her what she needed. Could he achieve what he said, or was it some wild dream?

"I would adore to witness such a sight, but even with Joseph gone they still command respect, too many see them as the law, whatever they demand occurs." She was wavering, while his plan, conceived in haste and littered with unimaginable variables continued to form and change. He needed her agreement, more importantly he required her to reveal all she knew about that misanthropic family. For the moment they were leaderless and vulnerable, now was the time to deal them a killing blow and take what he desired before they regrouped around the priest or one of the brothers.

"No one is above the law madam. Any criminal can be beaten, look at what happened to the 'Chamberlin'; destroyed by his ego more than anything else. So we can do to the Wood family, we use their ego against them."

"Can we? I do so long to see that but I have seen what they have achieved with their lies. With me gone, there is no one to question what they do. I cannot confront them; no court would listen to the words of a harlot. Our army comprises what, we two and nothing more? I believe you wish to assist, but in reality, what can we achieve? I fear our quest, though brave, is lost before it begins. Bayles and his friends will always win."

Abigail was faltering, but he had one last card left to play and he played it well.

"No! They haven't, we can still succeed." Holding her hand and looking into her deep blue eyes, he felt as Nathaniel had felt, enraptured by her.

"Succeed. How? I face penury, I have naught but what I wear and that is precious little. Fact is, I can neither remain nor return home, for Bayles will not rest until he has driven me to ground. Even now I would surmise he will have a note written ready for dispatch on the first coach out. A note to my parish cleric in which he will describe my indiscretions. Can I see a goodly man drawn into this intrigue? No I cannot, which leaves me one further option and that is to seek passage to one of our colonies, to lose myself in the wilderness and die an old woman with just my memories. Without money or patronage, that is not a viable option."

"Do not give up hope, all the while you draw breath, there will come the opportunity to make them suffer." Charm and gallantry were as dangerous as the sword or pistol and he was apt at the use of charm. He had to convince her, he was her salvation.

"You are too kind; even though we have just met, we are so akin in thought. It feels as if we have been friends for years but what can I do?"

"There is another way!" He stated solemnly,

"What pray?" This was his moment, she was finally asking his opinion and if he timed his reply correctly, she would, he hoped, do as he suggested. Clasping her hand, he spoke softly.

"Challenge their lies, change the thoughts of those that have persecuted you, claim back what is yours. But to aid your cause, you must tell me everything of what happened inside that house, from first meeting Nathaniel, til the moment you were expelled. Are you brave enough to speak of such things?"

"I can, if I must, though it will be painful for you as well as I."

"I have no wish to add to your despondency, but I have listened to what Bayles said, surely it is only right and proper to hear your version of events, so I know how best to proceed." He needed to know, but saw her bite her bottom lip, a sure indication of the pain this would cause. Choosing her words with great care, she spoke slowly and carefully.

Chapter Twenty Seven

"Earlier, you asked what the reaction would be to your plans. I can see him, here in my mind, launching into a screaming tirade, demanding something be done. Wood had, many traits, many desires, but only one true passion. Money, the acquisition and possession of as much as possible, to force him to part with but a penny, would have caused him palpitations. That though isn't what you desire to hear, for you are fully aware of his mannerisms, what you desire is an inner knowledge of the man. I fear I discovered his evilness far too late to disentangle myself from his clutches.

I will not embarrass you by glorifying the terrible sins he committed, or how he subjected women of his household, but it is with deep regret I ever laid eyes upon him. In hindsight I should have heeded the wise words I was given and distanced myself from that nest of vipers, but love is found in many a strange corner, even in that place, but I grew to loathe Joseph Wood and all he stood for.

"You might have been indeed wise not to have come to Stormouth madam, At the time many thought you either touched, or mislead as to what you expected to find here."

"I soon realised that myself sir. I heard the name mentioned at a dinner and was so intrigued I found myself desiring to discover if any town so tainted could be half as bad as Stormouth was reputed to be. Alas I soon discovered it was, but by then it was far too late to escape. It was my fault, I became smitten, and chose to ignore the advice given to me. How was I to know what I was entering into? Was it to be expected that while finding happiness I should also encounter an animal the like of which I had no knowledge. Nathaniel was a kind loving man who softened my heart, we shared a love which made me blind to whatever else lay veiled in secrecy."

"I remember that day of your arrival, I should have spoken out, warned you to reenter the coach and ride on, but like everyone else, I remained silent. For that lapse, I beg your forgiveness." He stated solemnly.

"There is no need, if you had spoken thus, I should no doubt have ignored your sage like advice. I was at the time headstrong and intent on completing my art. In hindsight though, perhaps you were right, maybe I should have continued and found a happier town. But in truth, because of remaining, I came into contact with a gentleman, then an animal. Unfortunately one lived with the other. My ignominious decline in fortune began on what should have been my happiest of days, the day I married Nathaniel."

"Terrible, I cannot imagine how you felt but if it aids you please feel at ease to speak of it."

"No, sir. I will not speak of that day, the humiliation is still too great. What I will say is that what occurred then, had a direct bearing on the events that transpired to bring me to this sorry place."

Turnbottle remained silent as she gathered her thoughts. Unsure of the workings of a woman's mind, he surmised it best to remain silent while she rid herself of her supposed guilt.

"If only I had looked beyond my own problems, perhaps spoken to someone like yourself, then maybe, we would not be here now. As it is, what started with a meal, ended with me thrown into the street? Their reason…fear sir, they feared me, Bayles, the wrath of God, but more importantly they feared losing their inheritance if they opposed what that swine had written."

"Knew there must be far more than what that dog spoke of. He portrayed you as the offender, but I sensed he hid something far worse that what he condemned you of." Turnbottle wasn't known for hysterics, but at that moment, if Bayles had been present, he would have attacked the man, "We must end his tyranny, and I shall aid you madam. Explain though if you will why the sons were so afraid of losing what they desired?"

"With the revelation of my husband's demise, they saw their grasp upon the business slipping away. I, and I assume they, assumed that I, as Nathaniel widow, would have control of the business bestowed upon me. Perhaps with Josiah and Adam to assist in the day-to-day running of the firm. That devil, though, had other ideas."

"Madam, you are an intelligent woman why then did you assume thus? It is inconceivable to imagine anyone, no matter how naïve, would grant such rights to any woman, even one as pretty as you. You are wise enough to know that women have no voice, can own no property or possessions save those granted to her by her husband. I may not endorse such sentiment, but it is the law; a woman lives by virtue of a man's good nature. Why did you imagine that Wood would pass his sons over for you? That was folly indeed, to contemplate such an ideal."

"That was my error. No one could imagine both passing so quickly. I assumed that Nathaniel would inherit, as was written, and we would control as husband and wife. That will though displayed the extent of that man's vileness. Upon his death I thought, wrongly, he would, firstly acknowledge his responsibilities, and secondly, treat me with respect. To my distress I discovered he cared for no one save himself and his reputation. He despised everyone, including his own children, why would he treat me any differently? His disregard was made plain during that infernal reading, he showed us all that, even from his grave he could still manipulate and control those he left behind."

"You knew, you were with child, and that Wood was the father?"

"I did sir, but do not think badly of me. I was prepared to tell the family beg their forgiveness and make the best of a terrible situation. But Bayles got to them first, he used what he knew with great persuasion. While I may not have understood his motives at the time, his reasoning became very clear."

"He protected a friend?"

"He did. The old man's traits had come to fruition too close to home. It was my misfortune to have been caught and he had to disguise his malevolence by deriding my good name. I am sure I was not his first; such a man commits such crimes more than once. If that be true, then some, if not all, who resided within that house were his retinue. Joseph Wood was reprehensible, with yearnings, I guess he released upon the women of his house. No one speaks, but it is an assumption, that every girl who ever worked there were his property, to do with as he wished."

"Then we should find those wretches and demand they lay testimony against him. They will aid your cause, confirm what you state is true."

"If you find them, how will you convince them to open old wounds and speak of that which they most likely wish kept secret. Joseph will have done all he could to keep his evilness hidden money or threats he will have used whatever bought their silence."

"We can try, we can but try. Do you have names, of those poor souls?"

"There was a parlour maid named Jane who fled in the night but where she went in unknown. I doubt she was the only one, the number of staff he went through was curious, to say the least. I believe also, that he jollied himself with both Sarah and Martha as well. Unfortunately, I have no proof of this, they denied me when I asked, and the sons will remain silent until they are forced to speak the truth. You see that is why he wanted my silence, I am the only evidence, the only one who could denounce him for what he was. No though, with my name besmirched, I will not be believed. But I speak the truth...Joseph Wood...raped me, not once, but on a number of occasions."

Drained by her admission, Abigail sobbed inconsolably. At last he had confirmation of what occurred within that damnable house, the reason for her demise and why she had been mistreated. Like most men, Turnbottle was unwise in such matters. Lost as to what to do, he waited, hoping she would regain her composure. He could only imagine what her statement had cost her, yet inside, he desired to scream in exultation. Her words had done more than simply confirm Bayles' words. She was ripe for plucking and he wanted every, nasty bit of information she had about the workings of that family. Only then, could he take what he wanted and leave them destitute. Hesitantly, he took her hands and whispered,

"Forgive the foolishness of an old man. The last thing I intend is to add to your worries, but if we are to prove your innocence, we need evidence. Do you have anything which might incriminate them?"

"Evidence; I have but this." She gently touched her stomach and he saw her frailty. "And some letters written to my father and...another. Within those notes might be the means of incriminating the family. They are, or were, secreted within a sewing box in my room. My maid, Maud, might help you retrieve them but I pray do so secretly."

"I will do my best. They are yours; no other should read what they contain. Besides, they might assist us if we are to take legal steps to recover what they have stolen. One last thing, and then I shall leave you alone, for I am not as young as I once was. You spoke of that day when the will was read, pray, tell what occurred in detail if you can."

"I will try, though, it is painful, every moment will remain etched into my memory. As I said, I expected no more than general gifts and some legality regarding the business. Instead of admitting his guilt, Wood laid the blame full square upon me, accusing me, knowing I would be powerless to refute his accusations. I tried, God did I try, but no other would speak the truth, I was isolated and that was when Bayles and the solicitor took over. Forced to listen to their lies, I was subjected to a verbal flaying by men who I assumed only ever spoke the truth. Pawell even insisted a surgeon was called to examine me. Can you imagine the indignity, the shame I would have felt? Bayles then demanded I be burnt as a witch; what was I to do? Perhaps I should not have been so stubborn, for he took that as a sign of impertinence. I remember him looking at the ceiling, hands held aloft as if calling to our Saviour. His words though, came from Lucifer himself, words which will forever be etched into my memory...*Be gone you harlot...take your snivelling hide away from these God fearing people. You are finished here...return to the cesspit of your birth for we have no further need for your kind.... not here.* All the while he stared at me with his holier than thou cursory stares. I have seen hatred before, but he looked as if I was beyond anger. His expression was one of...renunciation, the expression of utter distain. He looked at me like a pile of fresh dung that blocks the road. It is there, it smells, but you have to pass. I felt utterly humiliated." Abigail stopped, he thought she was about to cry, instead she smiled weakly.

"I have heard many acts of cruelty, but this beggars belief, it is they who should be ashamed, damn their hides." He wanted to find those involved, such was his fury, he would have attacked them all. But good sense prevailed, he sensed something else, for any man to go to such lengths as they had must mean they had greater secrets to conceal than simply one bastard child. Stormouth was full of such brats, so now his mission was to discover what they feared, then exploit them for his own benefit. "Was that when they....?"

"Yes. Bayles and Pawell took me to the door. I was screaming, calling for someone to help but the family turned their backs on me. I hoped a Christian man might see the injustice, feel some sort of remorse and halt that sorry episode."

"Obviously, Bayles did no such thing."

"No. There was a moment's silence where I wondered if he was going to show some degree of kindness. I should have known better, he and Joseph had been close and I thought then and do so now, that our pious cleric was doing his bidding. Joseph was extracting vengeance, and Bayles, was his voice. I was ignored totally, instead he stood, bible in hand, shouting out in his best sermon voice that I was a whore. Is that how I am perceived?"

"Not by I, and most likely not by half the town. But as you well know, he commands and only a brave man will speak against him."

"After being so wrongly accused and so badly treated I can believe that of him, for God and the town deserted me that day. If I expected clemency I soon discovered how powerful that most reverend swine was. No one in the upper town showed me any clemency, doors, once opened to allow admittance, were slammed in my face. My humiliation was to continue, I spied faces, of those once considered friends, shy away and saw shutters barred so no one could look upon me. It was humiliating, I called out, I pleaded, but there I was, cast into the snow, with just a housedress to cover me. All the while Bayles preached his lies and grinned demonically. Was it the cold, or the anger that made me shiver? I cannot answer, but he was determined to finish what he had begun He told all that could hear that no one was to render me assistance, and with that he closed the door."

"He did this without thought for your safety?"

"Indeed, in fact, he appeared to delight in my discomfort. I suspect he realised others would finish what he had started. It was then, that I heard them; neighbours, people I knew began their condemnation and it were terrible. Why did they believe him and decry me so unjustly?"

"Fear, Miss Abigail, old fashioned fear. Bayles is a powerful man, he controls and manipulates. While people, even you're so called educated neighbours are gullible. They pay him well to ensure they gain entrance to

Heaven. As such, they are obliged to do as he says. Very few would risk an eternity of damnation by upsetting him."

"I suppose you are correct...So that is my tale, accused by a dead rapist, condemned by a priest, cast out by a family, sheltered by a common brothel owner, saved by a gentleman. If such a tale was not so strange it would be laughable, but I lived it, sir, and hated it all. I can tell you, there is no sound more frightening than that of a door slamming shut, and locking bars falling into place. Society has accused and convicted me without either trial or evidence. I learnt how lonely and silent Stormouth could be sitting in that street. I thought I would die, such was my melancholy. The cold began to eat its way through my dress, I felt death's fingers grip my heart, and I began to feel as if it was the right course of action. But then, something told me that it was not my time, some instinct told me to move, to seek shelter, or die, the question was, where? Certainly not among those I had once called friends. It was with a heavy heart that I gathered my thin dress about my body, glanced once more at the house and moved away."

He had heard a story that defied belief. Did he doubt her, not at all? Even the most proficient of London actresses could not have performed with any more conviction, passion, or honesty. Never having been blessed with marriage or children, he had, once, felt the joy and pain of unobtainable love. He saw in this woman his duty in life, to protect her and destroy those who had impeached her name.

"Did you have any idea as to where you were going?" he asked softly.

"I did not. My one thought was to escape the cold...my God; I have never felt so cold; even now I cannot get my bones warm. I fear I must have appeared a pathetic creature, dressed as I was, yet I knew, somehow, that to live I must go where I least expected to find shelter."

"You came to the Butts and Maggie?"

"Not intentionally. I cannot explain why I just stumbled into a void behind some barrels and that was where I expected to die. It was a miracle when I awoke and found myself safe and warm. Now sir, I must make preparations. I should contact my family; ask that they come to my aid. I fear my father will be not be best pleased to hear of my situation. He will, no doubt, take delight in telling me I was stupid in becoming involved with that family."

"Then in the absence of your father look to me to become your sanctuary, your shoulder, upon which you can rely upon. But if we are to succeed in our quest, we must tread carefully for we are but two against a town. Secrecy must be our watchword until we have the evidence to condemn them, for what they have done."

Inwardly Abigail smiled, she trusted this man, but not sufficiently to tell him the entire truth. How would he react if he knew who her employer was and what command he wielded? Since arriving in this…hovel she had ruminated just how she could tell those she worked for about her situation. Charged with collecting evidence, children were not expected nor indeed envisaged. Nor was it conducive that now she was more alone than ever. Her letters, if they could be recovered might bring assistance but until then, she was at the mercy of a man she barely knew.

"Help me, sir, and I make this vow. I will do all you ask, tell you what you require. Retrieve what is mine, help me regain my strength, and I will do all I can to assist you in bringing those who did this to me before the Courts." She shivered as the memory of that moment when death had approached her and her resolution stiffened. In her direst of times, Maggie had saved her, now Turnbottle offered her a chance to tell everyone the truth. "We must seek retribution; they are evil and tried to kill me, they must be punished."

Chapter Twenty Eight

The winter of 1773, clung on stubbornly until well into the month of March. The last vestiges of snow were still seen beneath the hedgerows and along the edges of fields, but a watery sun became more intense. The late winter storms failed to appear, and each passing week brought a sense of spring and what it had to offer. The third week, brought bird song and a sense that nothing, was going to disturb the tranquility that had settled upon the town. How wrong they were.

A rumble shook the earth, disturbing the town, and bringing panic to the anguished residents who appeared at windows seeking the cause. Mrs. Jarrett's behaviour was typical; she stood in her doorway screaming hysterically before fainting in fear. Bayles had manipulated them to such an extent that they saw devils in anything they didn't understand. Even those with intelligence, like Benjamin Turnbottle, were apprehensive and crossed themselves hastily, raised their eyes to heaven and prayed for deliverance. Mother's dashed into the street, to gather their children, to hide them beneath their skirts. While men, both brave and intrepid, grabbed cudgels and blades. They waited, scared but ready to protect their families, from the wrath of the Banshees which approached their small town. All the while, the bells of St Michaels, added to the general confusion. The sexton pulled on the rope for all he was worth ringing out a call to arms, not heard since the French had last visited the town.

"Drovers, wagons, oxen and mules all coming this way: come and look!" It took a small boy aged, no more than ten, to ease their fears. He ran through the streets ahead of the procession spreading news of what approached. Many, though, remained cautious, fidgeting with their crude weapons just in case the boy had been possessed by Satan himself. Very slowly their fears were allayed as the first, lumbering, screeching, well loaded waggon came into view. The boy had been correct; there was nothing to fear. Cudgels were discarded, excited children ran, skipped and, laughed at the strange sight forgetting the anxiety their mothers had just recently shown. While young women stared in awe at the tanned drovers, and were rewarded with lewd remarks and blown kisses.

"Damn them to hell and back." Turnbottle stared at their passing suspiciously. With the arrival of this, 'train' came the dread of soldiers arriving sooner than he had hoped. Brushing his thinning hair into place, he cursed silently, his time was fast running out. Not many saw him thus attired, dressed in his nightgown, nor would they have witness him dressed as he had been that night in the 'Butts'. Today, though, he had need of working clothes.

"Sir! Sir! Gawd help us, what do it mean?" His thoughts were harshly disturbed as, his housekeeper, burst into his room unannounced, clasping her apron to her face.

"Madam, what is the meaning of this outrage!" he demanded.

"My apologies, sir, but I was afeard."

"There is nothing to be afraid of. Go back to your duties I shall be down shortly." Mrs. Jones was, more like a family friend than a servant and he despised his tetchiness. She looked after him like the mother he had never known, but she was, like now, prone to taking minor liberties. "Wait...perhaps you would be kind enough to fetch a glass of milk from the kitchen." She said nothing, simply did as requested.

Clasping his hands behind his back, he looked down into the street and saw an abomination. These drovers and carters would be a distraction, the real menace would occur with the arrival of the soldiers. No longer could he dally and delay, he had to quicken his pace or...possibly use them to conceal his own deviousness. Perhaps their arrival would prove fortuitous as a means of instilling a sense of security within her, thus making her more amenable and willing to speak out. Something, he required more of if he were to accomplish his task.

Mrs Jones returned with a jug of warmish milk, which he placed upon his nightstand.

"Thank you...I shall be out for the remainder of the day, however, I am expecting a caller either today or tomorrow. Be so kind as to extend my apologies and inform him I will contact him as soon as possible; he will know of what you speak."

Mrs. Jones waited, but surprisingly her employer closed the door without further ado. His intention hadn't been to cause offence but he had much to do. Hurriedly he dressed, taking care with his attire of stockings, knee length breeches, white flannel shirt, black waistcoat, neckerchief, topcoat, hat and leather shoes with plain buckles. Across his front he attached a gold chain and fob watch, into his right coat pocket he placed his purse, in which, was the sum of five guineas. A veritable fortune but if he was to succeed he would need coinage to pay for what he required. Dressed and ready, he had one last thing to attend to, a task that he feared, but needed to do. A head cold had facilitated a visit to the apothecary, where he had acquired the phial from Nichols, the apothecary a few days previous.

"Guaranteed to ease what ails you, sir, though, I urge, do follow the instructions closely," he had been told, though in truth his pain was far overshadowed by his need of subterfuge and guile. His rudimentary knowledge of such matters meant he knew that one small application, mixed with milk would induce a feeling of melancholy, turn his face a shade ashen, and induce a mild sickness. None of which he relished, but an illness would invoke a feeling of pity, making her far more susceptible to his lies. He drank the liquid and grimaced, the infusion would quickly take effect meaning he had to act swiftly. Calmly, he left his home and made his way onto the street.

"Morning to you, sir, a grand day, is it not?" He turned and saw his neighbour, who along with his wife and eight children, now waved enthusiastically as Porter and Johnson, mayor and town clerk, hastily assembled a welcoming party upon the steps of the town hall. *Time you discovered the real meaning of fear*. He thought, it was such inane exhibitions of self-worth which annoyed him about so many, so called gentry.

"It is not, sir! Pray excuse me; I have matters to attend to." His anger was unlike him and he saw the look of disbelief upon his neighbours face.

"I am sorry, sir, but why are you so pensive? The arrival of the army will bring prosperity to our town. Extra mouths to feed will mean profit for us all. We should embrace their arrival and pray to God, they remain until we have taken all we can from them."

He glared at the man, a man he had considered an admirable and most responsible father, now he saw another fool. People were weird and the residents of Stormouth were weirder than most, in but a few short minutes they had gone from frightened children, to excited jackanapes crowding onto the muddied streets, making his journey far longer than normal, lessening the time he had remaining.

"Are you touched, sir? Have your senses become befuddled? Such people will bring nowt to our pockets, but will give us difficulties and problems. Their food and necessities come from Government stores, bought with the money you give in this new tax, so in fact, they have robbed you and you never even knew. More problematic than that is the thousand odd men who will be foisted upon us. Most of whom are thieves, laggards, drunkards and fornicators, but with luck they will not be allowed anywhere near our town. Those that do, will be seeking more than a loaf of bread. For that reason alone you would be best warned to lock your daughters indoors until these misfits have long gone, or tell your wife to start knitting swaddling clothes."

His neighbour stood opened mouthed as Turnbottle walked away. So stunned by his vilification he saw neither the mischievous grin nor the lecherous glance the merchant gave his eldest daughter.

"Damned fool, serve him right if she did fall foul of one of them." he chuckled because his neighbour's daughter was a delightful girl of thirteen, old enough for scum denied female attention for months on end. His thoughts were halted as yet more wagons came, smaller carts which weaved their way through the town. It was as he crossed the street that he spied a small group beaming in excitement from the town hall steps. While most had been caught unawares, Johnson, Porter and the rest of the council stood bedecked in their finery ready to wave as bullocks strode past.

Prior knowledge must have been given, because he knew most of these talented councilors never rose much before noon. One particular man caught his eye, and he wished he had a pistol to hand. Bayles fawned and preened, listening intently to what some colonel of Militia was telling him. Money would be made, those like Richardson and Columbine, would strike deals and Bayles would make it possible with kind words and inference. He wasn't bothered, he had far fatter fish to fry.

"Laugh while you can, Reverend, your time is fast ebbing away," he whispered before hurrying away towards the harbour. His day had started badly; he hoped it would change for the better.

* * *

"Magnificent. You do the town a great service in choosing us as your staging area." Johnson, the mayor, said as he held his hat on with one hand and attempted to clap with the other. Along with Sir Stanley Cobb, Sir Percival Fitzwilliam, they stood behind the town sergeant, who held the ceremonial sword aloft which glittered in the morning sun. Behind them in their customary black capes, were the town Jurats, who appeared dowdy before so much gold and silver brocade and gilt buttons.

"Only the first train, Mr Mayor, more will follow," Sir Percival said, acknowledging a lady he had seen smiling in his direction, with a wave.

"And your men, when can we expect them?" Bayles enquired. His sour expression was at odds with what the council wanted to portray. His world was changing and men like the good reverend disliked change, unless they were responsible

"My regiment will be here in a week. However, their Lordships have amended their orders."

"Amended, how so?" the mayor enquired, horrified that his town might not be as important as he desired.

"Fear not, sir, if anything our new orders will bring further wealth and distinction to you and the town. We are to be joined by a regular regiment, the 3rd of Foot. They are to assist in our training, then we shall both sally forth to engage the King's enemies."

"Then we must wish you well in your endeavours, Sir Percival."

"Most kind Reverend, our endevours will be nothing compared to what awaits those rebel scum. But there is time enough for such talk, tonight Sir Stanley and Lady Cobb have graciously arranged a small dinner of no more than five courses. You will join us. Of course you will." Sir Percival was full of bonhomie, his enthusiasm affected those close to him. All except Sir Stanley, who eyed him maliciously? None present knew that he had not been Consulted about these arrangements. He had supposed the meal would be for a discreet number, not half the town. Nor could they have known that Sir Stanley grew tired of his guest already, Sir Percival, had turned into a bore who courted favour from those he saw as useful, and ignored men like Josiah Wood. On the outer fringes of the group, all Josiah could do was watch as the wagons continued towards their final destination.

"A moment, if I may, Josiah," Bayles asked. The man appeared morose, not invited onto the steps, he, was part of, but not included in, the official party. It had been some weeks since that fateful day and Bayles had avoided them deliberately. His reason, like all he did, was selfish.

"Reverend," Josiah bowed respectfully in greeting. "Busy times."

"Indeed, though that isn't why I sought you out. Tell me, how are your family?" Bayles was, as Josiah knew, a man who did or said nothing without a prior motive. A man, even the squire bowed to in acknowledgment.

"Well, thank you, we are doing well." Bayles smiled, but knew differently. He had heard talk about the brothers and what he heard distressed him greatly.

"Good. Your father would be proud of you, though, if I might be so bold, I have been approached by some of the merchants. They have asked me to make representations to you."

"Representations? Why? They know my door is always open should they wish to speak to me." Bayles said nothing, but it was becoming common knowledge that Josiah was struggling. Each day he opened their warehouses and each day, it was said, another, old, established customer was seen stalking away, muttering obscenities about their inadequacies and inabilities. As feared, Josiah was failing miserably, while Adam was nowhere to be seen. Rumour had it that both Adam and his wife were intent upon spending their inheritance as quickly as possible. He at the gaming tables, she at the dress shops. Both Irons and Furnell had been heard boasting of the amount they were spending. The younger brother wasn't his concern, he could sink for all he cared, his friend's business was far more important.

"I know, Josiah. I have told them that on more than one occasion, but they remain concerned...They have asked me to intercede on their behalf, to ascertain if you might be able to increase the speed in which you dispatch their goods."

There it was the hint of displeasure. He was becoming a fixture in their lives, acting as their moral guardians, watching what they did, always ready with a comment or a criticism. Why what motive did he have surely he hadn't forgotten what the bitch had done. Was it any wonder they were in such a mess? Many a time he had wanted to remind him of his part in her downfall, and how far his own morals had sunk. There were rumours concerning the cleric, rumours of strange men at the rectory and of bags being exchanged. The implication was that Bayles had failed to pay for some service and the man had arrived seeking payment. If true, than Bayles was not so high minded as he portrayed himself to be, that he swam with the rest, in the cesspit of depravity, that he had the same moral codes as any others. Smiling graciously, Josiah added.

"Perhaps you would be kind enough to extend my apologies. Explain to them that my father left his ledgers in disarray and that it has taken longer than we had hoped to ascertain who is owed what. Could you inform those who are concerned, that we hope to have some semblance of order shortly?"

"That's good, I will inform them. On to more glad tidings, I am informed the first stagecoach is due in later today. Normality returns at long last. Good day Josiah."

"Good day, Reverend." Josiah walked away wondering why the merchants went to the priest instead of dealing directly with him. More importantly, why had he mentioned the stage? No matter, he had work to attend to and a clerk to admonish, for he was sure his woes were of Mickelwhite's makings.

* * *

While the great and the good fated each other at the town hall, on South quay, two differing people were also meeting. A sickly looking man stood beside a fish stall and grabbed his victims arm as she passed by. Guiding her into hiding he pressed a hand about her mouth and hissed,

"Be quiet; I mean you no harm save to deliver a message from a person you once served. Be silent and I will release you, shout and I will silence you." He had sensed her body tense, before relaxing, then she had nodded in obedience. He breathed deeply and released his hold on her.

"Do you speak of Mistress Abi...?"

"Be silent. All I say is that a person seeks your assistance, are you prepared to help one in distress?" Maud nodded enthusiastically "Good, listen carefully, there are papers secreted." He saw the look she gave and explained. "Hidden, child, they are hidden in her old room. She needs them; can you be trusted to find them for her?"

"I can, sir, but what happens if the masters discover me looking?"

"Make sure they don't. If discovery is close, destroy them, for they must never be seen by them. When you have them, bring them here, I will wait every morning until the bell rings matins. Mark my words well, if I see anyone but you, I will seek you out, as I will, should you betray either her, or I. If I sense anything untoward, I will see you whipped and do nothing to aid you, do you understand?"

"Yes, sir," Maud whimpered

"Do not fret, child, I am not ungenerous. Get what we want and we will reward you handsomely. Now go about your business."

Without a backward glance she ran from the grey man. He had struggled to refrain from retching and now staggered towards another meeting, coughing alarmingly. The potion was working quicker than he had hoped and still he had much to do.

Maud did not stop until she reached her room. Then behind a closed and wedged door she retrieved the sewing box from its hiding place. She had saved it from the family, kept it as a token of her love for the women they said had been so evil. The contents meant nothing to her, a few scraps of paper with funny wiggles upon them. Now it seemed others wanted them, but not him, he had scared her. He had, though, revealed that her lady still lived. If Mistress Abigail needed help, Maud would do it her way, return the box to her without using a dying man. To do so, she needed to speak to a friend,

* * *

The first mail coach since the beginning of winter arrived a little after noon Four bags were passed down to the town clerk whose job it was to sort and arrange delivery. He was proficient, delivering the last note before six pm. One such note was addressed to Mrs Abigail Wood and delivered, unintentionally, to the Wood household. Adam was the first to see it when he prepared to leave for his night's entertainment. The sight of it on the table near the door made him draw breath, her name had been expunged, forgotten and belittled. With no intention of anyone speaking her name again, he burnt it. His actions meant no one would know that Abigail's father was concerned, that he was prepared to act.

Chapter Twenty Nine

Leaning against a wall, Turnbottle breathed heavily. The apothecary had either lied or given him a stronger solution, either way the elixir was working. The sickness had almost overtaken him while speaking to that wretched maid, now his legs buckled and he slid to the ground vomiting unceremoniously. Clasping his chest he suddenly wondered if this was how she had felt that night; cold, alone and without hope. *If so he knew how she must have desired to live.* Crawling to the doorway of a candle maker, he rested and remembered...

* * *

"Why, of all that is Holy, did you enter that brothel? You should have delayed, sought her out via another way." Castigating himself, he grimaced at the memory and the gut wrenching pain. He had acted unwisely, like a befuddled fool, his naïve stupidity of that night could so easily have destroyed any hope he might have had. Dressed as he had been, was beyond comprehension, as was his lack of tact by speaking to all and sundry. "You utter fool." He whispered as the pain returned. "If you desired discretion and why did you flaunt your presence by displaying a golden guinea. Who in their right mind displays such wealth in a den of debauchery? A demented fool, that's who,"

Yet, amazingly, and despite their superstitious stares, that was what he had done. Despite his own feelings of guilt and stupidity, it appeared his secret had remained untold. Even so he waited nervously, for the derision to begin, to be lambasted and exposed by his peers. While every Sunday, Mrs. Jones returned from church and she said nothing. Bayles remained silent, and he praised God that none of the dross, who witnessed his stupidity, had sold his name to the likes of Bayles. His excursion into that den of iniquity had, apparently, passed unnoticed or was it that the town had other things to concern itself about?

Over the weeks, life continued, children were born, they died, and business was done in either tavern or workplace. The road was open again, and the harbour was busy with each tide. Each morning Benjamin Turnbottle made his way from house to workplace to warehouses, ledger book in hand. No one commented upon his trip to Maggie's, nor did his fellow merchants speak of his enhanced reputation. Either they didn't believe what the girl had said, or they simply weren't bothered. But he was, every waking moment, what he had done, plagued his mind.

His plan, so hastily constructed and badly executed, had surprisingly worked. He and the girl had escape unseen but they had been strangely fortuitous. The donkey yard, normally used more for rutting than donkeys, had been empty and silent, while the numerous drunkards which gathered upon darkened corners were conspicuous by their absence. Maybe he had misread the situation, perhaps amongst so much depravation, Joseph's death, and her disgrace, wasn't as scandalous as he had imagined, perhaps her errors had been forgotten if not forgiven. Of course their journey had not been without difficulty, her feet stumbled on the uneven cobbles. More than once he had to support and aid her, but despite her condition, they had avoided the liberally spread dung uneven surface and reached sanctuary.

"By all the saints allow this to pass?" The pain dulled and he breathed a little easier, but he remained, incapacitated but not befuddled. It was a strange fact of life that when the body fails, the mind, becomes unhindered and surprisingly focused. Many upon their death bed experienced a final flush of sanity was that what he was experiencing, for his mind saw in perfect clarity what he had failed to do? If he had entered a trade arrangement, with as little foresight as he had employed that night, he would be penniless within a week. He had not planned, nor foreseen potential pitfalls. His mind was beset upon how, he could use her to further his ambitions and deal that family a killing blow.

"Once again you allowed yourself to be drawn into their scheming. That family is accursed." The truth was, he, like every male that witnessed her arrival, had been drawn to her. From the moment she had entered the hotel and their lives, he knew she would one day aid him. The reason was simple, Abigail Swann, as she was then known, bore a striking resemblance of a lost love. Her beauty and confidence reminded him of Charlotte, whom Joseph had so utterly destroyed. But unknowingly, that family had provided him with the means of repaying the debt. Abigail Wood had become an innocent pawn in a deadly game of bitter rivalry. He would use her to attack them, right a wrong, and finally control what Stormouth had to offer…wealth.

Of course in any game there were winners and losers. The Wood family for too long had assumed themselves impervious, but they had lost two players in quick succession, they were vulnerable and he would use their vulnerability to his advantage. When Nathaniel had seduced then married the woman, despite Joseph's obvious objections, he had thought his cause lost. But then …something had occurred, something which, until now had remain unspoken, but now he knew Joseph had taken her for his own and he could imagine the bastards reaction. In Joseph's eyes, women were supposed to remain silent, and simply accept their fate. But like Charlotte before, Abigail must have spoken out and wrought his displeasure.

I will avenge you my love. He thought, though until recently he had assumed his quest would remain unfulfilled, that he would die long before he reeked his revenge. Their association had been doomed from the start, he and Charlotte had tried to be discreet, but Joseph had discovered their assignation and waged a war against him. Always the stronger Wood had tried shutting him out of almost all trade that came into Stormouth, but he had been far cleverer than Wood had imagined. He had continued to amass a fortune which now he would use against the family of the man who had denied him of a love for so long. *I will carry those scars until my own death when we will be reunited.* He smiled, if he could think such things, he wasn't as ill as he felt.

"Are you unwell?" A voice, entered his thoughts. Looking up he saw a woman staring down at him.

"Fine...just a little tired...I will be on my way shortly," he replied, struggling to rise.

"Best you do, sir, too many toads hereabouts willing to rob you blind." She scuttled away leaving him to his memories.

"You may be right," he muttered, more than aware of what happened in these stinking alleyways. He had seen it close up, had experienced every terrible aspect of what men like Wood were capable of. The story he had told her was pure fabrication, utter flimflam. Oh there were elements of truth, but his motives were purely personal, financial and selfish. His plan, which he had so delicately woven would benefit no one apart from himself. So far, it was working out nicely, it had involved him drinking that vile concoction which the apothecary had supplied, and which was rendering him almost incapable of reason. Struggling to his feet, Turnbottle knew that to remain any longer risked death, and he wasn't eager to meet his maker, nor experience this ...pain any longer.

With one hand against the wall for support, he made his way towards where she had been secreted. Just like that night, the journey seemed to take forever, but eventually the smell of effluent, stale bodies and damp told him where he was. He stopped, within moments a swarthy, vicious looking man appeared.

"Took yous time." The voice, like the man, was harsh and strong, unlike Turnbottle, whose pallor was that of wet clay.

"I have my reasons," the merchant replied, struggling for breath.

"Trust one wasn't seeing an undertaker, you look like death."

"Do not concern yourself on my behalf, your fee is safe. Now...what have you seen?"

This wasn't a random occurrence. In fact such meetings had occurred once or twice a week since he had lodged her within this cesspit of a place. Such meetings were, contrived so that information could be passed from one to the other. Each meeting had been fraught, but none as fraught as this.

"Done as you asked, watched her closely and kept an eye on anyone showing any interest," he replied, while Turnbottle tried to avoid smirking at his voice. The cause, a gap in the man's teeth, and the whistle it caused when he spoke.

"Anyone come calling?"

"Only the brothel owner and a sweet young girl, who, I assume is one of her whores." He smacked his lips lecherously. "Oh yeah, and a couple of gutter snipes, who came sniffing round one night. Best you remind her not to light candles, attracts the wrong sort, so it do."

The pain had eased, allowing him to wonder if he had added too much to the milk. If so, he had less time than he thought to finish this night's work.

"I will. Do we know what they wanted?"

"The men? What all men want in this place, but I didn't ask. Made sure they knew they shouldn't come back again." He held one fist in the palm of the other and grinned. Turnbottle knew him well enough to know that whoever they were, they had been taught a salutary lesson. Suddenly, another wave of pain wrenched through his gut. He must press on, and once again warn her about her use of candles.

"Be careful, my friend, I do not want questions asked."

"I knows what I has to do, who can enter and who can't. You're paying me to protect her and that's what I'll do, but for how long, that's what I wants to know."

"As long as it takes. I had hoped to keep her concealed until she gave birth, but I may have to reconsider that. You saw the wagons?" The thug nodded. "Soldiers next. I can't have anyone speaking of her being here. I can delay Bayles, but soldiers have connections and strange morals about women. She is the key which will unlock a veritable fortune, so just make sure no one lingers too long."

"Just soldiers and footpads?" the thug asked. They had already discussed this but he wished to be sure.

"For the moment."

"Still say it would be simpler to slit their throats, quick and clean, we could do it tonight."

Turnbottle had considered that option. As his friend said, it could be done easily. He could find at least four men within twenty feet who would do it for a guinea apiece.

"No, too dangerous, we'll do this my way. I will destroy them in court where law will do more than a knife ever could. Once that is done, we step in and take over where they left off. That is why I need her. By the time I have finished, that brat will be the only remaining blood relative to their fortune, and its mother will be so beholden to me she will sign anything I tell her to."

"Fair enough, you pays the scram."

"Yes, I do, so make sure no one interferes." With that, Turnbottle vomited hideously, spat, then wiped his mouth with a kerchief which he disposed of dismissively. Without a backward glance, he shuffled laboriously towards the house. All the thug heard was his footsteps and the faint sound of breathless whistling.

Chapter Thirty

"Am I to remain, forever locked away, like a bird in a not so gilded cage? Dear God, I will not...I am innocent, so why do I remain incarcerated while the guilty walk free. Do you hear what I say, or am I to be ignored?" While her anger was real and unswerving, her audience remained deaf to her desperation. Finally distraught that she would broker no argument, she sat and sighed. "Ignore me will you? Well my little friend, I need you less than you need me, for I have a brain."

She berated the rodent which had, over time become her confident, then laughed, as her friend scampered away with a morsel of her bread. With each passing day, she had become more depressed. Ensconced within this foul place, her mood had lurched between a dark foreboding, which she feared bordered upon lunacy and, inane nothingness. With just that mouse for company, her saviour had become noticeable by his absence, while regret, fear and a sense of utter defeat had slowly turned into anger at those who had caused her so much pain.

"Who will care? No one knows my whereabouts." She told her small friend, who stared back with pink eyes, while nibbling at the stale crust. Isolated as she was, she had become dependent upon those who fed her and kept her secret. They were a small, insignificant group, just the three, Maggie, Mary-Ann and Mister Tanner as he liked to be called. But he had explained on his last meeting. "We must be strong. We can defeat them much as Leonidas defeated the Persians at Thermopylae. Strength my dear isn't simply about numbers it is about courage."

"Can we, Can we stand against them?" She queried, and her mouse stared back, content to eat her food. Three loyal friends brought her not only food but news, when they visited. Neither were in great supply, but welcome none the less. It was the solitude she detested most, she was used to being in command of her own destiny. Having worked alongside her father, she was considered as competent as he? If those who controlled her had not thought so, they would never have trusted her to come here alone. "And see how I repaid that trust? I betrayed them, my small friend, betrayed them royally."

Solitude, had given her time to unpick her mistakes. Stupidly she had allowed herself to become enthralled by the very people she had been sent to examine. She had allowed herself to become infatuated, trapping her in a nightmare of her own making. But that isolation also gave her time to devise ways of inflicting retribution upon those who had harmed her.

"With or without assistance, I will deal with that family. How, though, that is the question? You see, you do not know the priest, if you did, you too would fear him, as I certainly do."

Unlike others, she would not allow herself to wallow in self-pity, though for the moment, even her small friend appeared to have deserted her. It had finished its feast and busily cleaned its whiskers. Soon it would disappear and she would have no one to ruminate with just a myriad of unanswered questions, such as why did Bayles despise her so strongly? Reveal that, and everything else, might fall into place.

"You see, it was the priest who was insistent on my expulsion. I might have convinced Mr Pawell and the family that I was the victim of Joseph's lecherous ways. Bayles, though, was insistent that Wood's wishes were complied with totally. He disposed of me as if I counted for nothing."

The mouse, it seemed, had heard enough; with one final glance it skipped away leaving her alone once again.

"Even you tire of my questions. Leave me then, and I will languish with my thoughts, while I await a visit which will perhaps never come." As if her desperation could get no worse, she felt the devils spawn kick for the first time. Clasping her stomach, she hated what it represented with all her heart. Hated its presence, her stupidity, and vulnerability. It was the consequence of his actions, the reason, but not the cause, of why the priest had been so vindictive. This wretched place was not where any child should be born, not even one conceived so cruelly. She should have rid herself of it, then, perhaps, what she endured might have been avoided. But it was, albeit distressingly so, a reminder of Nathaniel and what she had lost. In hindsight, and having witnessed the way the family had dealt with her admission, she wondered if that had been the right course to take.

"Why, if they knew of Wood's capabilities, had the family not warned me?" Was another puzzle she had pondered? Not one had approached her before her marriage and told her to run as fast as possible. Even Nathaniel had remained silent, broaching the subject only after the ceremony. By then it had been too late, she had been committed, unable to leave without a justifiable legal reason. "Were they too trapped in loveless marriages, or did Wood protect them for their services?" The more she thought about that question the more she became convinced Sarah and Martha, did indeed pleasure the old goat in return for his protection. Which would explain their silence, and why they never sided with her. If they had, she might have been able to leave that house, but a lone voice, accusing him of such depravity would have sounded feeble, as if she sought some financial reward from a bad marriage. No lawyer would have taken her case on, and even her patron might well have turned his back on her. The family's silence, condemned her long before the reading of the will. They had cast the die, and laid the foundation for her debasement, by virtue of their silence, they were as guilty as he, be it through culpability or fear. Such questions needed answers but they would not be answered by wallowing in self-pity. She needed to fight back.

"Who to trust?" Even that question was becoming more difficult to answer. Her patron spoke eloquently of what they might achieve, but could she totally trust him? Certainly he had aided her when she needed an ally, but was he totally honest in what he told her? Despite his reassurances, his visits had become more infrequent, each delay brought tales of unexplained difficulties, how he needed time to resolve them before confronting the family, perhaps he spoke the truth, but she wondered if he tired of his commitment? Her one measure by which she gauged his commitment was his promise to recover her letters. If he succeeded, she would look on him more kindly, if he failed, than she would reassess him, and make her way in the world alone. Her other visitors, Maggie and Mary-Ann, were reticent to speak of Turnbottle. They were sweet and kind, but they had little in common, save the man who had brought her here. She had broached them about him, but as soon as she asked, a silence fell, a silence she feared she would never break. One day that silence would end, One day those that harmed her, would stand before a court and answer for their crimes. Those who desired to ruin her would be reciprocated in kind, for she would show no mercy, nor indeed would the man she worked for.

The knock, when it came, caused her stomach knotted in fear. She waited, then another sequence came upon the frail wood, only then did she relax. The code, had been contrived as their way of communicating that friends were outside and it was safe to pull the bolts and allow them entrance.

"My God, sir, what is amiss?" she exclaimed in horror as she opened the outer door. Before her, stood her saviour, his face a deathly grey, his cheeks sallow and pinched. He appeared to be gripped in pain, his breathing difficult, coming in short gasps

"A drink, ma'am, and a chair will suffice." He groaned, as she allowed him inside.

"A surgeon is what you need, sir. I will send for one immediately."

"Do that and you are as good as dead." He clasped her hand and she saw fear in his eyes; he had saved her, now he needed her assistance.

"No surgeon, no lights! Told you, we must be careful. You have been seen using candles, they are expensive like surgeons and must be used sparingly only to use what light is available, even at night." He explained, as she shut and bolted the door.

"I am sorry," she said apologetically.

"You'll learn. Now, there should be some wine hereabouts." She heard him moving around, lost in the darkness, until she heard the chink of glass placed upon the table. "It will be sour but it's better than nothing." Turnbottle was, so she was discovering, a man of many talents. Talents which, if asked to explain, he would no doubt ignore, but answer them he would, one day.

"I have to thank you for what you have done for me. Without your intervention there is no telling where I would be today. But I believe we have reached that time when I must make arrangements regarding my future. However, I see by your demeanour that you are unwell, therefore I shall delay until you regain your strength."

"I assure you it is but a mild malady which will soon pass." In truth, he guessed he had overdosed upon the apothecary's elixir. Nichols had explained it would purge the gut, but the effects could be rectified by an infusion of nothing more than liberal amounts of milk. So long as Nichols had not lied, he would suffer the indignity a little longer.

"Just so long as you are sure." She rose and placed a log upon the fire, as the sap bubbled under the heat, she watched as he poured some wine, unaware that he was watching her also.

"I am madam but thank you for enquiring." Despite her surroundings she appeared healthier than when he had first seen her in Maggie's whore house. She had an inner glow, was no longer that pathetic creature, she was more like the woman in the churchyard; proud, strong, determined. Should he then take her into his confidence? Perhaps, but the risks far outweighed the possible benefits. He had sought her out with one intention, to alter his plan now, might see her turn on him, and take the prize for herself. She had been extracted from the den of debauchery before anyone had told Bayles of her presence. It was laughable that a Lady, had managed to hide there for so long without being commented upon. At least here, under his guidance, she was safe but mystified, and mystified was less dangerous than a lead ball or a knife, for Bayles would surely have sent men to eliminate her, just as he had men protecting her.

"You will think me terribly...ungrateful, and I do not wish to appear so, but you spoke of owning property...I have to ask...is that how you know this house so well?"

Turnbottle coughed raucously, the pain in his stomach worsened; time was running out. He had a few simple rules, one of which was to never reveal too much about your past, break that rule and your competitors had leverage which they could use against you. However, if he were to gain her trust totally he would have to reveal more about himself than he desired.

"A valid question madam, in fact I am, what is known within this place, as a bastard landlord. Some would say I am a rogue, who cares more for profit than for his tenants, but in fact such people would be wrong, for I do care, which is why I do what I do. Some like Joseph set their rents too high, squeezed too many into each of their hovels while I try to treat my tenants with a degree of consideration but I have to make a profit on each property. You are but one of many such tenants. There, now you see ill in me, and for that I will be eternally sorry."

The pain gripped his gut. Grimacing, he remained silent, but his discomfort brought a reaction from her.

"Sir I must insist you seek attention. Or at the very least allow me to administer to your needs."

This was why he had taken the potion, to garner sympathy, and while she did so, she would tell him all he wanted to know. When that was done, when she had been squeezed of everything she knew, he would pluck her like a goose at Christmastide,

Fear not madam, it will subside but I sense you wonder why I brought you to such desolation? I can answer that simply. None of your delicate friends will think to look for you amongst such depravity. They will think you gone from the town, that you have been driven away by shame. While they think that, while they deny knowledge of you, I will spread rumour and coin around and convince the scum hereabouts that you are but a lost soul, another worthless tenant."

"I trust you are correct. Nathaniel said this place was the lowest of the low, where only the most scurrilous knaves lived and where no man or woman could be trusted."

Turnbottle laughed, shook his head despondently, sipped his wine and scratched his nose before answering,

"A wise man, your husband. What he says is possibly true, but for the moment, it will be your home."

Abigail stood aghast at the revelation. It took her a few moments before she found her voice, then she demanded.

"I cannot, sir...remain among this squalor. I have to return, either to respectability, or to my father. Either must occur most quickly so I might clear my name." She waited, hoping she had not overplayed her part. To complete her tasks she could not remain hidden, nor could she upset her host; to do either would simply give the Wood family credence to their lies.

"Squalor, madam, is a putrid word, spoken by those who cannot see further than the end of their nose. This, madam, is what the likes of the Wood family have forced upon their neighbours." His anger was frightening, only once before had she witnessed such fury in a man and he now rotted in his grave. Immediately, she regretted her words, she had no need to see his face, his tone told her of his anger. "If this is evil…it is what the likes of Joseph Wood created. Perhaps it is time I educate you in the ways of that family." He drank and grimaced, the wine indeed was sour, but he needed to clear his mind before embarking upon his story

"Why, sir? What could they possibly have done to be part of this?" Her task, once thought lost, finally revealed someone prepare to speak the truth about that family. While he was in such discomfort, she must coax every juicy titbit from him.

"The truth would shock you madam," He knew he had allowed his anger to almost destroy his lie. He wanted to tell her, but he also had to keep so much secret. His only recourse was to choose his words with care, create another lie and hope she believed him. "To explain what that family is capable of would take too long, and quite frankly, we do not have the time. My condition worsens, meaning I have to be away from here before it becomes a matter of concern. It would not do for me to drop dead on this floor, not if you are to remain invisible. But I will tell you a little, if you agree to listen and not delay me with questions. I promise to explain in full at a later date, but not at the moment. Do you agree?"

"I have little choice, do I Mr Turn…. Tanner?" She corrected her mistake. He smiled, swallowed the wine before pouring another. "Though, I should warn you, I could be gone if I dislike what I hear."

He grimaced, but nodded in agreement. She was capable of destroying him if she so desired, his only hope was to convince her that his intentions were honourable. "Sour. It has been open too long. I will arrange fresh supplies brought tomorrow. As for the Wood family…there are few words suitable for any of them. Each is evil beyond comprehension." He paused and she saw in him pain, from his malady, or what he knew, she knew not which. "A long time ago, before you came to Stormouth, even before the Chamberlin, a family lived here, a family that worked hard and asked for little. Through hard work and constant diligence they scraped an honest but meagre living. Then, one day, a young man appeared buying up houses and land, said he had some grand scheme to make us all rich. Truth was, Joseph Wood wanted the old tenants removed so he could re let at a higher rent."

"Why is that so wrong?" Abigail asked. He heard her sip the wine and immediately spit it out.

"Terrible isn't it?" He chuckled.

"Yes, it is," she replied though he did wonder if she meant the wine or his explanation.

"We sit, you and I, among such squalor most of your friends could not conceive existed just a few short yards from their comfortable lives. Yet you ask what is so wrong…perhaps nothing…perhaps everything. Some say the entire place should be burnt to the ground, cleared away and replaced. Some would be right, but Joseph Wood didn't allow sentimentality get in the way of making money. He knew that his grand scheme would take time and while he waited he could clear the rabble from their homes then re let them at triple the rents. How he expected anyone to manage beggar's belief, most could hardly meet the old rate. They complained, begged, and pleaded for clemency, told him they had to live somewhere."

"What did he do? Give in?" Her question was not malicious; she could guess what Wood said, Turnbottle though surprised her.

"Apparently so, he offered those who wanted to remain a way out. They could pay the old rate, providing they worked for him. They were given no time for thought, Wood and his men, stood at each door waiting, either the tenants signed or left immediately. A lot signed, some like the family that lived here saw through his grand scheme and were forced out. This family ended up living in the woods in a makeshift shelter where one by one they died, apart from one son."

"Why didn't they simply do what the others did and work for the family? Would it have been that terrible?" She paused, wondering how he knew so much about such an unfortunate family.

"Pride, they saw what he wanted."

"What, pray, was that?"

"Slavery, madam, Wood was purchasing a work force, who were beholden to him. He forced his tenants to work from dawn to dusk loading and unloading ships at his wharf into his warehouses. For that he paid them a pittance and then deducted his rent and other incidental expenses. By the time he had finished, most found they owed him money. What could they do, who could they complain to? Wood owned them, and their homes. Upset him and they would be evicted. So his workforce suffered while he did very nicely. His ships brought him a handsome profit, trade was booming. He shipped goods to the Africa's, where he purchased slaves and took them to the colonies. His associates there, men like your husband, loaded his ships with rum, sugar, molasses, cotton and tobacco. He called it his Golden Triangle and he was becoming a very wealthy man"

"Surely that is the premise on what business is built upon, profit and loss? So far I see nothing that warrants such animosity towards them. Is it not what you, in fact, do yourself, Mr…Tanner?"

"No it is not, madam, I thought you were a victim of their warped minds, someone who I could assist while learning about that family. However, if you believe me to be no better than them, then maybe you are not worth my attempts of assistance."

She had spoken severely, if he was to be calmed he needed to be a little more…sensitive. She knew what he wanted and broached the subject.

"You need a spy, sir?"

"That is such a dirty word, madam, with hideous implications. I did not expect your undying love, but I did expect you of all people to understand. I need you to assist me, to assist those out there. When daylight comes, look to your neighbours. Not four doors down is a woman with six children. Her husband is dead, killed on North quay two years ago crushed, between ship and shore. She is forced to work twenty hours a day for pennies a week, while her eldest daughter will be one of Maggie's girls in a year or so. She is one of Wood's tenants, yet they pay her so little she cannot put bread on her table. While you lived high and mightily, people die here daily from lack of food and warmth. Is that Just?"

She was shocked; no one had spoken to her so directly not since she had seen a bread riot some years ago. Certainly she had known none of this, but it was exactly what she had hoped to discover.

"Of course not, it is far from just," she finally replied with a voice that was thick with emotion.

"Of course not, the lady sees the injustice. I beg your indulgence, madam, I am not at my best and I apologise. It is not just and that is why I do what I do. I have been fortunate; I began with nothing, but saw an opportunity and took it. I began to annoy Wood, began taking loads from him and selling them further afield, made money and with that started relieving Wood of his properties. It has taken time, I had to be subtle and patient, but as each hovel came vacant, my agents offered him a price which the greedy old goat couldn't resist accepting. Now, this area is divided; he owns some, I own most, and in a few years, when I have it all, I will show this town what could be done with proper housing for the poor. For that I need leverage, and you, unfortunately, are my lever."

"What can I do?" She sensed his anger and something else, something far more potent. She heard grief in his voice, but grief for what?

"You know what went on in that house. You know what he was involved in, and if you don't, then your husband certainly did."

"Nathaniel? What possible use can he be to you; he's dead as you well know."

"That is debatable."

"Debatable? You were there when the message was read out. Nathaniel is dead. I am a widow and penniless."

"I mean you no disrespect, but that message simply stated that the ship was lost. There might still be hope that he survived, even if he didn't, then he must have left papers, which legally, you as his widow, have by default, the right to see anything pertaining to the family's business dealings."

"There, I fear, you are wrong. Pawell declared me defunct, and expunged from any connection to the business. I am legally devoid of any rights. Even if I wished it, I am unable to hurt them in that way. That is why I asked you to acquire my letters by, how shall we say it, devious means. Have you been successful in that matter by the way?"

"I have laid the foundations for their return. Even now my agents are at work, I expect results shortly," he stated, and coughed noisily

"Sir, you weaken, is it not time you sought attention?"

"Not while there is still work to be done. As for the legalities, do you think I would have embarked upon this venture without consulting more proficient lawyers than Pawell? My advisors tell me there is a precedent in law that would allow you to regain control. They tell me that if the interested parties can be proven to have committed a criminal act, they can be deemed unfit to hold office. That way, the remaining sons can be forced out, and you, madam, will be free to assume control. Now, as we know, Joseph, and to a lesser extent, Nathaniel ran the business. I cannot speak for your husband, but I suspect, and you can confirm my suspicions, that family committed a multitude of illegal acts, so we have jurisprudence. Besides which, do you in all honesty believe that either of the sons are capable of running the company as it should?"

"Josiah, possibly...Adam, no he is...what was it I heard him called once? Oh yes, a fopdoodle; apt, really. He had leached off the old man's money for years. He likes cards, did you know that?" Abigail chuckled, Adam was far more than a fopdoodle she had heard the word pixie mentioned, but knew not the truth of that.

"I had heard cards, and women, apparently. My sources say they will be the poor boys downfall one day. What of Josiah, would he be capable? I do not wish to harm any of them, should they bow to my proposition to have either you, or your child, declared the rightful heir, then I will do all I can to assist them, and you."

"And assist yourself, no doubt, sir."

"You see, we understand each other perfectly. You give me access not only to their businesses but also to their personalities. Together we can destroy them and see you put in command. Maybe that is why they are scared of you. Perhaps that is why he defiled and corrupted you. Oh yes, madam, I believe you when you say Joseph raped you. From what I have heard, you were not the first." He saw her look of disbelief. "There have been rumours of girls leaving suddenly. Some of us have begun to wonder if Joseph and the priest were somehow in collusion. He was a devil, more than capable of such atrocities. Maybe you were to be his guarantee, he expected you to do as he wished, then, when you refused you had to be destroyed."

His words caused her to fall silent; she was young, but certainly not naive. What he said could well be the truth, or, an elaborate ruse to gain her sympathy. Certainly there were imponderables that could not be denied. One was that she was alone, needing assistance, and secondly, the family had treated her with ill will and inconsideration. Until she knew differently she would have to trust this man, who unlike others had shown her nothing but kindness and consideration.

"Very well Mr…Tanner. We have an alliance," Abigail conceded.

"Good. We have much to do, but for the time being you will remain here out of sight. Unfortunately, to complete your disguise it may well be best if you join in with the other women, do as they do, act as they do. Consider it another part of your education."

"I will, sir, and you?"

"I will be working behind the scenes, doing all I can to destroy them in the coffee houses and the town hall. Without Joseph to lead them it is possible that the sons…"

"The fool and the dandy," Abigail added helpfully.

"Apt, madam…may become befuddled and lose control. I can facilitate their downfall by 'persuading' some of the other leading businessmen to move their 'services' to another ship owner…"

"You?" she said, smiling

"If that is what they want, then of course I would be obliged to assist them. If we succeed, your time here will be short and your return to respectability swift."

"We shall see. In the meantime, I would be obliged to see those notes returned, do all you can, sir," Abigail asked, adding as an afterthought, "You never said how you knew so much about the people who lived here?" She sensed his uncertainty, he wavered and stood as if to leave.

"I knew them intimately. Only the eldest son survived. He returned, was taken in by a kindly soul and hidden from Wood's gaze. Over time, that boy grew into a man, but he retained and nurtured a passion to destroy the man who had killed his family."

"Oh my…the poor soul," Abigail whimpered.

"As you can imagine, a terrible incident, one I have carried with in me since that day. Now I intend to finish that family forever, no matter what needs to be done."

"That was you…you were…?"

"It was. I vowed that no one should wield such control, over another's life. We would never allow an animal to be treated thus. It was from that encounter that I made a pledge with God. A pledge I will see to a conclusion, or die in the process. The Wood family are deviants, heartless, they must be taught a lesson, and if I am to be that man, then so be it."

"God be with you, Mister…Tanner." Abigail answered.

"Thank you, madam. Now I have to leave, time and tide as they say. Until tomorrow night, I will bid you well. I will send someone to speak with you. They will explain how best you should merge with these good people. They will be your guards against discovery. Trust them and they will assist you."

"I will, sir, and thank you." Abigail reached up and kissed him lightly on the left cheek, a kiss of friendship and hope. He smiled, bowed politely, kissed her proffered hand gallantly, then wheezing gently, he left.

Chapter Thirty One

"My God, you appear behest with an infliction, sir, indeed an infliction." Bayles stared at the man's pallor and appeared shocked.

"Would shoot him if he was one of my hounds, his very appearance would scare the hinds away," Sir Percival added, laughing loudly.

"You do appear unwell, sir," another added.

Turnbottle's appearance had, it seemed, caused some consternation among both friends and adversary. He had hoped to avoid Bayles until later, but that, now, seemed unavoidable.

"A mild indisposition, nothing a good dose of Sir Stanley's hospitality will not remedy, but I thank you for your concern, sir."

In truth, his guts felt as if they were flayed, he felt bilious, and hoped not to disgrace himself in the priest's presence. Bayles remained silent, no doubt hoping to see his demise here, now, and in spectacular fashion.

"Think nothing of it, small wonder you are not sick more often considering the place you work and what you deal with." The town clerk stated solemnly, earning him knowing nods from the other assembled dignitaries. The docks were known to be an unpleasant and dangerous place, which most avoided as best they could.

The 'Raven' hid his pleasure behind a veiled smirk, Turnbottle's illness was enjoyable to witness while he could but hope that it progressed to his possible demise which would serve his cause admirably. More importantly, he had sowed the seed of doubt, the merchant would cogitate and consider as to whether the priest knew of his time spent in Maggie's den. Stormouth was changing, while Turnbottle's death would benefit him greatly, it would not ease the concern he had for his security.

Bidding the group good day, Bayles made his way home. He was lost in thought, considering the ramifications, which the arrival of two regiments would have upon the town and its residents. Militia were bearable regular troops were a different matter entirely. He and his group would have to be very circumspect. He could hide their activities from ignorant fools by the use of rhetoric and veiled threats, but officers weren't so easily scared off. The groups meetings, already significantly curtailed, would have to be concealed even further. Such caution would, invariably mean the loss of venues like Wynford House. Sir Stanley could not indulge both camps, under one roof.

So much to do so little time to act. He thought as he approached the rectory, *the bitch has gone, crawled beneath some stone to waste away we shall not be seeing her again. If only I can convince Horn to relinquish his hold upon that patch of ground then he and his damned pigs will be gone and Spriggs will reward me admirably.* Such were the complexity of his deliberations he failed to hear at first the voices which came from the kitchen. Only Ruby should have been present and he despised unannounced guests.

"Damn the girl!" he swore. His annoyance at such a disturbance, was nothing compared utter condemnation and shock at what he witnessed upon entering the room. His brain ceased to function properly, his mood, already morose became foulest black. The depravity of the vision before him left him unable to move. What he witnessed was no worse than what he and his group indulged in but it wasn't what he wanted to witness, not in his kitchen, this was his home, his sanctuary from such bestiality.

"You filthy, sallow, guttersnipe. You swine, you piece of shit!" he finally bellowed. Good and bad existed everywhere, occasionally they bumped together before parting and continuing on life's magical journey. But there before him, was a sight which even by his standards was obscene. A man, breeches around his ankles, held Ruby down with one hand, while the other groped at her clothes. Her thrashings had upset numerous utensils, while flour lay discarded and upset upon the floor. The priest rushed forward, his anger so raised he was like a madman. Grabbing her attacker by the collar, he pulled him backwards, swung him round, and clasped his hand around his throat. A rage, so malevolent, clouded his mind, all thought of God fearing atonement ceased, replaced by a purely human response; 'Revenge'. "You useless excuse for a man; leave her be!" With one hand digging into the soft flesh, he slapped the man with the other. "You enter my home...attack my servant...like the animal you are...I will teach you a lesson!" The second blow drew blood; only then, at the height of his anger, did he recognise the man. "You...I told you never to return...I purchased her legally, for a fair price!" Recognition made Bayles lash out even more, a third and fourth blow landed as his anger raged unabated. A fire burned within him, and no amount of blood would slake his thirst for revenge. Finally, his victim managed to speak, through swollen and bloodied lips he sneered lecherously,

"Why should you get the choicest wenches? If she be good enough for you, I should be able to sample her delights meself. Don't worry priest, yous can take a turn next."

Bayles, saw blood drip onto the stone floor, and knew the beast had returned to consume him. A beast, he thought tamed, a beast which only rarely returned to envelop and torment him. He loathed it, but once under its influence there was nothing he could do until it had run its course. The toothless fool before him was to witness the horror of Bayles' inner torture.

"Guttersnipe...swine." They were locked together, so close he could smell him, sense his fear. No longer was he a man of God, but a vengeance, sent to end this violation. The devil possessed him, with a rage, no man had witnessed since Bayles had been little more than a youth. Then as now, this man suffered. He was no longer a man, he was but filth which knew neither right nor wrong. He was vermin which Bayles needed to exterminate. He smelt his stench of decay and depravity, every essence of evilness assaulted his senses. The rage consumed his very soul, like a serpent, it poisoned his mind, clouded his eyes and befuddled his judgment. Locked together in a deadly dance they stumbled around the room, upsetting the vegetables Ruby had been preparing.

"Blackmailing bastard, you will see not a penny more!" Bayles screamed, while the man continued to leer at the priest. The crime was despicable, but one that occurred more often that most imagined. Having sold his daughter, he had returned for more. He wanted what he saw as his right, but to submit his own blood to such bestiality was abhorrent. What happened next was inevitable. Overcome with rage and animosity, Bayles, felt the knife in his hand. Unerringly it touched skin, then blood, warm and sticky, spurted from his throat, drenching priest, wall, and floor in a crimson cascade. He didn't waver; this wasn't the first blood he had seen, nor, he suspected, would it be the last. Like a spent lover, the man fell to the floor where he lay as the last of his life drained from him. Bayles breathed deeply, sweat dripped from his hooked nose, while spittle dripped from his lips. His hand held the knife and never flinched, he had murdered and felt no sense of recrimination.

Turning to his maid, Bayles was surprised to see her shedding tears for the man. Why? He was about to break one of God's most sacred laws, and yet she wept for the swine. However, she was something he could control, better a scared woman than a man's loose tongue.

"He can harm you no longer…forget him…he means nothing to you…not anymore."

The priest held her, felt her breath upon his cheeks, the firmness of her body, and the scent of wantonness. This was his second devil, less violent than the first, but the one he lived with most often. This second demon could be subdued, controlled, lust knew when to show its face and that wasn't now.

"Summon the sexton… we will arrange a burial for him…move." The girl ran, leaving him alone with the body, the blood, the squashed cabbage. The kitchen resembled a slaughter house, something he would deal with once the body was removed. Of the town's residents, only he, and the butchers could dispose of a body swiftly and forever. Butchers could feed their victims to their customers. It was said human and chicken liver tasted similar. He on the other hand had an entire graveyard to hide his evidence in and a willing helper. Cole, the sexton, was a man of guile, a man who knew when to remain silent. Used to burying paupers at night, he would, if asked, and for a generous reward, swear that was what he did this night.

It took until dawn to rid the house of the blood; it was a night's work the priest would never wish to repeat, but eventually, once again, his home was secure and silent. Pausing to reflect, he sipped a glass of smuggled brandy *What have I done to attract so many problems?* The girl was upstairs sobbing pitifully in her bed, a noise he found annoying, not because she felt upset but because she sobbed for a father who deserved no pity. *Times are changing, the scum are becoming bolder.* He mused; it was as if the old order were losing their grip. A year ago it would have been unthinkable for anyone to enter his home and do what that man had attempted. The scum had known their place, had feared him more than they feared anyone else.

"My God, even that popinjay of a soldier would have felt the rough end of someone's boot if he had spoken to me as he did earlier. Continue as we are and we'll find ourselves governed by some illiterate sailor." His speech made in anger to an empty room revealed much about the man. He desired, demanded stability, he liked what the town had offered when he had controlled what his miserable flock thought and did. He had grown fat on their ignorance, which was why he detested the present situation. Joseph's death had left a void which needed filling…the question was, by whom?

As it was, the town was in a perilous position, with the Wood family leaderless, there was a gap in the market ripe for plundering by any merchant willing to rise against them. Of course the brothers would resist, but were they powerful enough to stop such a threat? The answer to that was perilous to contemplate. Both, Adam and Josiah were fools, incapable of defending their own piss pot, from a worthy opponent. Should insurrection arise, the town could become embroiled in a struggle for supremacy. Sides would be taken, father against son. The harbour would run red with blood, there would be chaos and Sir Stanley would be forced to call on Sir Percival's soldiers to break such rebellion by force.

"How to avoid such an abomination?" he asked himself. There was an unpleasant alternative, some other must emerge and assume control. The idea appalled him, strangers would look at everything, ask questions demand answers, might even demand to know why the witch had been banished. They might even call him to account, something he wished to avoid at all costs. *No strangers were not to be accepted.* So he was left with, what? Riots, a war between the Wood's and an unknown personage. The army meddling in what they knew nothing off, possibly even commissioners being sent from London.

My God that would be a disaster and no mistake.
"Far better if they retained control. Then life can continued as it had always done." He whispered. Of course, such situations had occurred before, he was used to aiding the family in times of need. Many a time he had rescued Joseph, buried some moral indiscretion so that it would never harm the family. The most trying of which had been when Joseph's wife had died. Amidst the sorrow, accusations and questions had been asked. Only by his timely intervention had he, eventually laid those rumours to rest. He had spoken from his pulpit and thankfully his flock had listened and obeyed. Her death had passed unnoticed except for Turnbottle, who he surmised, knew more than he revealed.

"Have no fear my friend I shall aid them in their time of turmoil." Rather than wait for the Jurats and bailiffs to come knocking, he would prepare them for their task ahead. Josiah must be helped, he would assist him in the peaceful transition of a member of his flock into businessman, or die in the attempt. Who could have known that the town's ruination was almost in place, all that was required was a spark to light a fuse, which would set off the opening explosion. That spark had arrived on ox carts, and dressed in red.

* * *

Peterson's field, to the Northeast of town was nothing more than soggy mud at the bottom of a hill. Overlooking the main road, it flooded in winter, while in summer it baked like iron, but this was spring and the grass was lush and green. Sir Percival's men had pitched their tents, slung their washing lines, and the commissariat had cooking pots steaming. This field was now a tented encampment, home to the militia, a place to be inspected by an entourage of military and civilians mounted on horseback. The foppish, Sir Percival Fitzwilliam, led them in procession among the tents. His pristine uniform shone in the sunlight, the array of gold braid sparkled, proclaiming his wealth and status. Beside him, Sir Stanley Cobb dressed also in the uniform, was more pleased than proud. This was his field, by leasing it he had earned more than he would have trying to grow crops there. Next were Sir Percival's officers, a mixed bag of rich young men who clung to his every word because of duty and the need for his approval. The merchants came last, eager to exploit their new neighbours; unknowingly they would be disappointed; Sir Stanley had already secured contracts for food and other essentials.

"Soon have the place just as we like it," Sir Percival stated proudly to the mounted group of influential town gentry, who cooed in satisfaction before staring in disgust at the men in shirt-sleeves that worked to complete the tented encampment.

Mud will cause them problems. Bayles thought as his horse picked its way delicately between patches of nettles and gorse and slipped in patches of glutinous mud. Unlike his brother Saul, Edward was no military man but he recognised the stupidity in this choice of land. Come the first rain and this field would become a muddy hollow, everyone knew it but none spoke out. Despite what their colonel said, the militia would spend half their time cleaning kit and themselves. To his left he saw men swilling down their groundsheets, adding to the quagmire already forming, reminiscent of that night in the churchyard when Cole had stood on the corpse laughing inanely.

"Devil of a job, Reverend, soil's claggy, waterlogged, he kept swimming up, still, she'll weigh him down won't she?"

Cole had known that he was concealing a murder. The widow Meredith would share her grave till the end of time. Unsure whether Cole spoke the truth, Bayles had paid him for his efforts, forgetting the dead man immediately.

"I pay for them to sleep in comfort; even officers share the tent line. I expect my men to live, fight, and perhaps, even to die together. No officer is better than the newest recruit; I do not advocate comfortable billets for my officers. Tough that's what they are, tough. Aint that so, Mathews?"

The question brought amusement from a group of town ladies, and embarrassment to the young ensign who sat on a bay gelding just behind his colonel. A young man of sixteen, perhaps, who like his colonel was dressed in the finest uniform that money and Martingale's of Pall Mall could supply. Most likely some rich father's son, who to protect him from harm had not only purchased his uniform, horse and weapons but also his rank in a militia regiment to spare him from the rigours and harm of a line regiment. Safe in the knowledge that no militia regiment served abroad, the family had secured their linage by aligning him to a man like Fitzwilliam. Young Mathews had become a toy soldier, his only role in life, to amuse ladies and remain alive until he inherited.

I wonder how that young man's family will react to hear their future has been sacrificed to the Gods of War. That this whippersnapper has died a bloody death and their future and fortune is now in the hands of a younger son, until then denied and deprived because of this dandy.

It was unpleasant or unkind simply, fact, something, he had seen happen, all too often.

"Indeed so, sir, tents for everyone." Bayles sensed the youth wanted to add that their colonel would not sleep beneath canvas, not when Wynford house was nearby with all it had to offer.

"Tell me, Sir Percival, what pray are those?" Lady Caroline asked politely, pointing towards four wooden structures. She was a delightfully pleasant woman who laughed at the right time and knew much about any subject, intelligence and beauty an unusual mix many men had concluded. .

"Punishment stocks, ma'am." Mathews answered for his colonel.

"Dogs stray," the Colonel added, "they get drunk and do unmentionable things. When that happens, we give them a dose of the lash. Mandatory twenty strokes no matter what rank, more if the crime permits. "

Fitzwilliam shuddered with either, excitement, or fear, Bayles wasn't sure which. The lash had never solved anything, yet Fitzwilliam appeared dependent upon it.

"Is that often? I mean, regular troops need discipline but militia, well they are volunteers who, if the mood takes them, can leave any time they like," Johnson the mayor added.

"In theory that's correct, but not in my regiment; they are mine, sir, body and soul. Every last one remains until they have served at least three years. Only then are they allowed to resign, though not that many will of course."

"Pray tell, why not?" Johnson asked. Bayles saw the nerve tic in Fitzwilliam's neck. He tired of this questioning but answered nonetheless.

"Where would they go? I own every man jack of them, they worked on my estates. Their families remain there because of my good grace. If any run, I punish their families, I ruin them totally. I will not tolerate ingratitude. If they run I hunt them down and throw their families from their homes. Haven't lost more than ten since commissioning, and they were the runts of the litter anyway, best they are gone and forgotten. As for the remainder, they are with me until I decree it. Death is their only release and I do not expect too many to die. For their service I pay better than others, but I expect a good return on my investment, a very good return. "

The colonel grinned devilishly; Bayles didn't much like him, but sensed a kindred spirit. Maybe Cobb was thinking of enlisting him into their circle for the duration. That needed debating, but not here, not now.

"Surely you do not see them as a commodity?" Bayles was shocked at the man's statement.

"I do, sir, they are mine to do with as I see fit and no man will dictate to me how I control my regiment. My God, do you comprehend how much it cost to raise them? Equipment, uniforms and all the hundred and one other things cost a bloody fortune, sir."

Bayles knew that such expenditure would have kept half the town fed for a year.

"They are soldiers, Sir Percival, men who could all be killed in their first battle. Your investment, sir, is precarious, which makes me wonder as to why you would wish to see them placed in harm's way?"

"Duty to our Sovereign, sir, to that end we are obliged to go wherever we are needed. That need is abroad, to fight the King's enemies. It would be remiss if I retained them here instead of where they can do most good. Soldiers are bred to fight and that is what I told them at Horse Guard. Oh, they were reticent…told me, my men, would not be required but I can be forthright, sir, when needs be. Called in a few favours, so to speak. "

This, he whispered, while Bayles smiled and nodded politely. Men like, Sir Percival, were dangerous, they used their wealth to further, both, career and fortune. From what he had seen, Fitzwilliam saw his troops, as little more than toys, with which he would play.

Part Four

Stormouth

April - May 1773

Chapter Thirty Two

In the weeks since the Militia's arrival Lady Caroline had performed a minor miracle. No matter how large or intimate a gathering, the preparations usually took months to organise. Sir Percival's dinner was far less formal than the birthday ball, that would be gigantic in comparison, but each required meticulous preparation. As the last notes of the Sarabande drifted across the ballroom, dancers bowed and curtsied elegantly, applauded the quintet politely, while many examined the strange feeding arrangements.

Lady Caroline had first seen this over a year ago and had revived it here for her guests. Morsels, upon silver plate, were arranged upon the sideboards and the guests helped themselves.

"It is, entitled a 'Buffet', French don't you know, all the rage in London," she stated grandly to a group of elegant ladies, who smiled graciously, and reluctantly approached the table, not totally convinced by the change of traditional values. The musicians played, dancers whirled around the room, while the less energetic watched in amazement. Most were couples, the few single ladies promenaded in a pre-ordained dance, eager to be seen by the few eligible gentlemen. Lady Caroline would be hard pressed to keep such eagerness in check as the night wore on. Soldiers, her husband had reminded her, were notorious for the wild behaviour and that included officers.

"One thing on their minds, that's their problem. They hear wedding bells whenever a suitable male is in view," Sir Stanley had stated forlornly, only to be rebuked by his more flirtatious wife.

"Better wedding bells than tolling bells. They are young; allow them to live a little before they are forced to see what this world really offers."

Invariably the more distinguished gentlemen gathered in small groups, their whispered conversations discreet and varied. Wynford House was no stranger to intrigue; throughout its existence, it had witnessed assignations and talk of intrigue and business deals. Was it surprising then, that over drinks and pastries, curtsies and elegant bows, the small talk turned to the questions that occurred whenever titled moneyed men gathered?

"The Times reports Boston ablaze and riots, don't you know."

"Fear not, Mister Mayor, we shall restore order. Any damned rebel we meet will run when my men march into that troubled town." Sir Percival was a fool; Sir Stanley had said as much and been rebuffed by his wife. It seemed the house was once again witnessing yet another intrigue between owner and his wife. Talk was that Sir Percival had enlivened her Ladyship, that Sir Stanley was too weak to halt it, and like his father, was destined to become a mere bystander to his own down fall.

"I heard it was nothing of the sort," another added causing Sir Percival to glare at the man disdainfully. The problem was most had read the same report and now added their thoughts to the conversation.

"The report did imply that an officer, refusing to pay for a wig, caused the concern."

"I concur; it is said, the guard was summoned, shots were fired and a riot ensued. The report also stated that men were killed and an officer and his men are to stand trial. Disgrace, if you seek my opinion."

"I cannot believe such a thing could happen. Not in one of his Majesties colonies."

"Do you suggest that the Times would relay untruths?"

"Of course not, a fine publication, would only report with candour and integrity. The question we should ask is, why, if all is well, are we sending more troops to the colonies?"

"A question our illustrious colonel should answer…Sir Percival?" If he had hoped his guest to fail, to disclose his naivety, then Sir Stanley was to be disappointed. The militia commander was far too canny, to fall for such a trick. Basking in the moment, Sir Percival, pursed his lips, as if deliberating how best to reply. When he spoke it was with a candour that Sir Stanley had come to hate.

"The reason, gentlemen, his Majesty is forced to act is dreadful to admit. He sees a terrible plot, hatched by French led agitators, who crave the success we have obtained. Our wealth gentlemen is what these blasted agitators require, they desire what we have, they see our success and wish to have some of that themselves. The Jewel, the prize they desire are our territories, the colonies to be precise. They wish to stir the colonials, and while we are thus distracted they will strike, mark my words gentlemen they will strike and take what is ours. Therefore His majesty sends us, not to quell our neighbours, but to oust these French agents and calm the populace. You, who have been there, will know what a vast region we control. That is the reason we need a large force, not to intimidate but simply to be seen by as many of our brethren as possible."

There was much nodding of heads and muttered agreement by men who consumed copious amounts of Sir Stanley's wine. One listened intently but remained silent. Bayles was at ease, able to mix with the great and the good as easily as he spoke to the merchants who, summoned from the town, mingled pleasantly with the regiment's officers. Sir Stanley and his family were gracious hosts. He was about to speak when he heard a voice and was drawn like a moth to a flame by his words….

"Can we wonder why such men feel aggrieved when a '50' is dispatched to Boston harbour, simply to prop up a failing act?"

Bayles had heard the voice before and was drawn to Sir Percival's friend. Truman appeared pleasant enough, and was certainly well informed about the problems affecting the colonies. He appeared well educated and well versed in the use of words to prove his point; he and the priest might have been kindred spirits. The priests reply was halted, as one of Sir Percival's lieutenant's, a mere boy of perhaps eighteen spoke.

"Ah, a '50', a fearsomely devastating weapon, one I fear I have never seen fired. In truth, sir, I am astonished by what our armouries can produce these days. No doubt scared the rebels witless when it was brought to bear on them, what…aye?"

Truman turned and stared at the boy, who had the haughty manner of someone, who would have trouble finding the correct way to button his fly without a manservant's assistance. Very slowly Truman turned and stared in utter amazement at the youth who smiled and bobbed his head like a chicken with a bone stuck in its throat. He looked the officer up and down and sighed in utter incredulity.

"I trust sir, that when you encounter the rebels, you will excel in your duties with more alacrity than you display here. If not the rebels will have nothing to fear. For any man worthy of command would know a '74' is in fact one of His Majesties ships of the line." Truman, said no more but simply turned away, he found the youth's attitude disturbing, enlightening and laughable. The lieutenant, smiled awkwardly and sipped at his wine the reproachful glare from the reverend, enough to caution him from speaking again.

"Forgive my ignorance, but may I ask when did that…ship…arrive?" Bayles asked, emphasizing the word ship for the benefit of the soldier. Truman, bowed graciously in acknowledgement of someone appearing with more mental faculties than the seemingly ignorant soldier.

"She arrived in 68, to aid in the implementation of the Townsend Act. Though in truth, I wonder if her presence did more to inflame resentment. The presence of a man-o-war and marines was, to some, an incitement to cause trouble.Can we blame them too harshly, how would the good people of this town react if the same occurred here?"

"All true Mr Truman but we have suffered in a similar manner. Not so long ago, customs riders and smugglers were fighting in these very streets. No naval ships entered our harbour, but we do know what subjugation feels like."

"Then you understand what I mean, sir, when I speak of resentment towards our Government. I despair, sir, despair to the future stability of that great land...Forgive me, do you have connections in Boston?" The man had the merest hint of an accent, which made Truman fascinating.

"No, apart from one brother who serves King George, God knows where, we are all country people."

"You are blessed sir. I have been away from those shores some time, but from what I hear, I fear open rebellion is but a stone's throw away. What then? Colonists in armed revolt against soldiers, neighbour against neighbour, father against son. One step from civil war; no, sir, it is best not to have family there."

Bayles heard an accent, one he couldn't quiet place. It was perhaps, Irish, or West Country, but his rumination was interrupted by Sir Percival's raucous voice demanding.

"Blood and fire Truman, have I not told you afore to stop spreading your damned rebellious thoughts wherever we go? Gives the regiment a bad name so it do. Forgive my ungracious friend Reverend; he takes great delight in antagonising unsuspecting individuals with his rebellious views." Fitzwilliam stood alongside Sir Stanley, each held extra glasses of wine which they offered to Bayles and the man. "Reverend, I trust this old scoundrel has not shocked you too much?" Sir Percival's tone was pleasant enough but Bayles sensed an undercurrent between them.

"Not at all Sir Percival, Your guest is most enlightening."

"Not a word usually associated with the scoundrel but if that's your opinion so be it. However I have been remiss, allow me to name my good friend and associate, Mister Octavious Truman. It is my misfortune to have known him both as a friend and confident. Now, I employ the scoundrel as a...liaison officer, to teach my officers about the colonies, who is who, and how we can determine a rebel from a merchant, that sort of thing."

"You are a colonist Mister Truman?" Bayles asked, a little perplexed.

"I am, sir, and proud of that fact. Born of Christian parents who left these shores and chose to make their lives in the new world. My home, sir, is near Boston, a small hamlet we named Concord."

"Fascinating...then if what we read be true, you must fear for what is occurring in that troubled land, however might I suggest we moderate our conversation? This is no longer suitable, not with Mister Wood and his wife present."

They turned and saw Josiah and Martha waiting to be introduced. Bayles had assumed they had either not been invited or had chosen not to attend. Now they cast a shadow of what had been a pleasantry.

"Ahh, see what you mean. Of course, I fully concur." Cobb nodded thoughtfully as his wife was introduced to the new arrivals. Bayles took it upon himself to explain to Truman.

"My apologies, sir, allow me to elucidate. You observe the man now speaking to Lady Caroline. He is the son of a most prominent family. The second son…a terrible sequence of events of a few months back saw the father succumb and die rather suddenly. Terrible for any family, but their distress was compounded further, when unfortunately, during the funeral service they received news that the eldest son had been listed as lost in a storm off the Americas. Our conversation might be construed as impolite; as it is probable his ship was, for a time, in Boston securing a cargo. So you see, the family might be a little perturbed by talk of riots and such like. Their loss is still raw….raw indeed."

"Quite understand." Truman nodded, solemnly.

"I hear the price of corn has risen alarmingly. Word is that the defensible's were called out in some of the Northern towns." It was a feeble attempt to change the course of the conversation; one that Sir Percival had no intention of continuing.

"Bugger the price of corn. No matter what the excuse, rioters deserve all they get. Hang them all if they dare to stand against the rightful rule. No better than cowards, should be dealt with rigorously. I tell you, sir, we will not stand any truck with such cowards. While we are present, we are at the town's service, just point out those you desire to be subdued, and we will oblige post haste, ain't that right, Truman?"

Draining his glass and beckoning for a re-fill, the colonel forgot them immieditatly. Truman though continued to stare at Josiah and his family.

"Must be a terrible burden to endure, two losses in such a short time. You know them well, sir?"

"I do, a most Christian and convivial family, but now bereft, requiring guidance. I try my best but I am but one man."

"They are what sir, trade or gentry?" Truman asked as he drank his wine.

"Merchants, though the family need to put their difficulties behind them and look to the future. We enter testing times, will need men like them more than ever."

"Indeed we do, with so much unrest, all any merchant can ask for is a full order ledger and a fair wind to bring his cargo safe home. Perchance you might introduce me to them. We have need for certain commodities, which they might supply."

He had not intended to debate their problems, not here not now. What ailed them was their concern alone, a local disruption which he could deal with given time. However, if Truman could put trade their way, who was he to deny them that? Glancing towards Josiah, he saw the boy alone; Adam and their wives elsewhere. Times were indeed changing; rebellion was spoken of openly, not just in the Americas.

"They would be most willing I am sure, I will speak with Josiah before we leave." Their conversation concluded, Bayles moved away, listening eagerly to other conversations as he passed each small group. Drink loosened many a tongue, and no telling what titbits of information he might overhear as the evening continued. The quintet played their way through their repertoire, the guests danced to the Minuet, Bouree and Gavotte, and as the wine flowed in abundance, Sir Percival became ever more vocal. Towards midnight, he and Bayles once again stood together near the buffet table.

"Ready for my dogs, priest?"

"I'm sure we will accommodate them with absolute decorum and dignity."

"Not worried about all that flim-flam, more concerned about my black hearted heathens and your women. Would seem they are a sprightly lot and pretty too." Sir Percival leered lecherously at Joan, the daughter of a man, Bayles knew would not be inclined to have a soldier within his family. "Have you found the filly which caused you such consternation?" Loudly he proclaimed to his officers nearby, "They can't handle their stable, allowed one to run amok. Perhaps we should show them how we deal with wayward hinds, could organise a hunt, sir. Drive her from her lair like a fox...view Halloo gentlemen, view Halloo."

Sir Percival, laughing suggestively, was the center of attention, while Edward Bayles, master of sobriety, and keeper of morals, almost fainted. He stumbled awkwardly, steadying himself before he fell. The last thing he wanted was a search carried out by the military. The harlot had to be found and silenced quietly, not taken before some court where her lies could...might damage him.

"No need to trouble yourselves, gentlemen. I fear the female in question has already shown us a clean pair of heels. Most likely, returned to her family, and good riddance I say. Trade you see, can't make that step up to polite society. She was, nothing more than a schemer with ideas above her station; we will not see her again. "

He wiped a bead of perspiration from his forehead and prayed he was right, the question of her whereabouts still troubled him. Even when Ruby lay beneath him, screaming and crying, he wondered where the harlot was and why Turnbottle appeared so secretive. Could she have eluded his search, escaped from the town? Could she even now, while he retold his lies, be hurrying back with the authorities to confront him? Had she managed to convince someone in authority that her wild tale bore merit? If so there was nothing to be done until it happened. *Should have filleted her when I had the chance, filleted her and sent her to the fishes where she could spread her lies no longer.*

"Trade? Good God, man, what sort of turd bowl are you running here? You allowed trade to marry into gentry?" Sir Percival's howling tirade tore his thoughts back to the present.

"I trust when you have spent time with us sir, you will realise that we are no better, nor any worse than any other town. First impressions are nearly always an ineffectual means of gauging anyone's integrity." He tired of the militia colonel's sarcasm. He spoke slowly, so that each word, would be heard and not mistaken in any way by a man he now knew to be a bumptious, yet dangerous idiot. Not many managed to infuriate him as that popinjay of a soldier had. In fact, his anger was so intense he failed to see Josiah approaching and almost ignored the man totally.

"Can you spare a moment, Reverend?"

"My apologies, what can I do for you both?" He bowed to Martha, who dipped in a perfect curtsey.

"I…we," Josiah corrected, "are experiencing difficulties with our father's papers. We… wondered if you could recommend someone to assist us in our endeavours, on a temporary basis of course."

"Sorry, Josiah, you have me perplexed…if you need assistance with your business dealings, your solicitor is surely the best to ask."

"Normally I would agree. But you were my father's particular friend, and we feel that if anyone can guide us without personal gain it is you."

"I'm flattered of course, and if I can assist then I will. To clarify…what you seek is someone versed in business to guide you through his books?"

"Exactly," Josiah stated in relief.

"Humm… give me a few days and I will consider your request. Now, pray tell, how are you all?"

"Each day brings pain, of course, but we also remember our father with affection. Our grief will take time to dissipate but we will get through this…as a family." Piously, Bayles nodded in understanding; however, Josiah had revealed a weakness. His words revealed that they were struggling. Neither was capable of running a business of such size and complexity. Why else would they seek his advice in such matters? This might just be the opportunity he had been looking for. If the right man could be found, he could make himself invaluable to the family. Oh, indeed, this required careful consideration.

"I will pray for your continued strength and fortitude."

"Our thanks," Josiah replied, and paused.

"Is there another matter?"

"I do not know how to ask but I have promised my wife I would approach you."

"Speak my son," he encouraged.

"She asks if you have seen or heard anything of Abigail." Josiah physically cowed beneath the priests glare, while Martha stared at the floor, each remembered the last occasion he had spoken about their errant sister-in-law.

"Strike her from your thoughts, never speak of her again, do you hear?"

He had no intention of prolonging their embarrassment, nor did he wish anyone in the room to hear what had been said.

"I suggest you mingle, you have business links to re-establish. Speak openly, develop contacts. As for the other matter, I will give it some thought and be in touch when a name comes to me. In the meantime, it has been a long tiring day and I need to rest, so I will bid you a good night."

A name had already come to him, but it would do everyone good to wait on him for a change. Making his way around the room, he apologised for his early departure, most were friendly and polite, until he reached Sir Percival. He, it seemed, had decided that the priest was to be the victim of his very personal attacks.

"Good night, Reverend. While you pray for our souls we will enjoy a few hands of cards and Sir Stanley's excellent cellar. Sleep well, for tomorrow my men will bring life to your little back water. Life in more ways than one, aye gentlemen?"

Ignoring the man's salacious words and hand gestures, which were rude in any society. Edward smiled politely and thought. *You are here for a short while, you arrogant fop. One battle with the rebels will teach you not to underestimate anyone. If not, may you die swiftly and good riddance.*

The colonel had made an enemy this night, an enemy that would bide his time until there was something in the man's destruction that benefited him. With that in mind, Bayles left the room. He would wake Ruby and indulge in a little nocturnal sport before the foolery of the morrow. "Sod them all!" he swore softly. The coming days would be interesting for Stormouth, of that he was sure.

Chapter Thirty Three
*Every citizen should be a soldier, this was the case
with the Greeks and Romans, and must be that of every free state.*

Long after Bayles returned home, long after the Wood family had put aside their torment, a young man rode through a cloudless night, as if the devil himself pursued him. In truth he was free to do what he wished without the constant attention of men he thought of as fools. His task, was onerous, it embraced all he despised, deceit, dishonesty, but if successful, his task might rid the world of a man he despised while determining the fate of many.

He was lucky, the road was clear, just a few remnants of snow visible, and no ice to hinder his progress. He had time to neither, eat nor sleep, he must deliver what he knew, to the one man who could find his knowledge useful.

My God I loathe him. So pompous he can't see the truth even if it bit him on his ample rump, but he will eventually.

Ensign Sebastian Mathews, was a spy. His task, though not one a gentleman should indulge in, was somehow gratifying. He spied upon his colonel, Sir Percival, a man he loathed and wished to see exposed. Fitzwilliam was a sycophant, a tyrant, a two faced megalomaniac who could charm both merchants and councillors alike, while leering lecherously at their wives' and daughters. To rid the world of such a man, he would have done anything, short of murder. Fitzwilliam was the embodiment of all that was awful about the militia. Summed up, by his total lack of knowledge of his officers

Find a horse, and ride post-haste to our gallant comrades. Deliver these instructions personally to Colonel Maitland and no other. Find a horse indeed! Did he not know that he owned both horse, groom and the wealth, to keep both well fed and presentable? Such ignorance belittled his abilities and his families standing. Nor indeed had he been welcomed, Fitzwilliam had disliked him immieditatly. His career as a spy might have ended before it begun had Fitzwilliam refused to accept him. He wasn't one of Fitzwilliam's own, hadn't bought his commission, wasn't known to any of the other officers and was therefore ostracized in the mess. Instead, his appointment came from the horse guards, which made him, unworthy and unimportant. As such, Fitzwilliam had not bothered to discover that there was far more to his youngest ensign than he would ever realise. During his brief appointment, he had witnessed both stupidity and harshness from the colonel. Fitzwilliam dithered, issuing orders which he immieditatly retracted. He was ineffective, and dismissed anyone who dared to contradict him. He blamed others for his incompetence, when in truth, it was his failings and arrogance which made him dangerous. To rid him of office, was why, when the offer had been made, he'd agreed, albeit with a degree of reluctance, to spy upon him.

"Who be you then?" the sentry demanded, then seeing Mathew's uniform, he stood to attention, "Sorry, sir."

"I need to see the Colonel immediately," Mathews stated, proffering the rolled parchment as proof of his task. He'd ridden for two hours and had as dawn rose found an army, ready for any eventuality, encamped in an English meadow. Now he waited while the sentry fetched the officer of the guard, and waited again for that officer to authorise admittance to the camp.

"What is your business, Ensign?" a Lieutenant of the 3rd regiment asked.

"To deliver an urgent message sir, personally." The officer was not much older than Mathews, but was due the respect of rank. The 3rd formed the night guard and were taking their responsibilities seriously, even here.

"Follow me." Escorted through the camp, Mathews suddenly realised what he was involved in. A regiment on the march, was an inspirational sight, two regiments, encamped at night, was a terrifying encounter.

"Fitzwilliam's?" Mathews enquired, as they passed a sleeping group.

"Aye, poor wee things. Tired they be from all this soldiering." The Lieutenant chuckled sarcastically. Even at night, to an untutored eye the difference between the two regiments was obvious. The 3rd were alert, ready to move quickly. They slept beneath the stars fully dressed, their packs supported their heads while every man cradled their weapons as they would a lover. The militia were far different. Half trained, they were little more than a rabble who sat around camp fires drinking and gambling, both of which, if seen by officers, should have invoked severe punishment but which appeared to be accepted.

"An awesome sight, aint they, half trained farm hands, dressed up to look impressive. They will run at the first shot fired in anger."

"I pray Sir Percival will be suitably impressed for their sakes." Mathews sighed deeply, doubting if anything would impress the man apart from a glorious victory in some forthcoming engagement. That was for the future, his task was simply to contact the column and inform their colonel of Sir Percival's demands.

* * *

"Again…aaah… much better. Perhaps, sir, your colonel would be better off venting his spleen thus, rather than inflict his ideals upon me." Mathews stood to attention, as Colonel Archibald Maitland sighed contentedly. The regimental surgeon pressed harder upon the machine and a trickle of blood seeped down his patients forearm.

"I am vexed to offer an explanation, sir, save what he told me to tell you."

This was only the second time they had met and this meeting was as bad as the first. Apart from the surgeon and his vicious looking bleeding machine, one other officer was present. He bore the insignia of a major yet reclined in a canvas chair, neither concerned nor afraid to be thus disposed before a colonel.

"I should kick his arse from here to Whitsun Tide. I am a soldier, sir, not a damned dancing master, well aint that so Major? No need to agree, sir, this popinjay seeks our assistance; do we give it him or do we tell him to go to hell?" Maitland would need bleeding again if he continued blustering as he was. His uniform was awry, while on a table, awaited a half drunk glass of red wine and a cigar. Mathews wondered what potmess he had become embroiled with. The officers of the 3rd appeared as lax and inefficient as Sir Percival's entourage.

"That, sir, only you can determine. The major added, "Though, in my humble opinion you would be vexed indeed to do as he requests." Despite their appearance, and their seemingly barbed comments, Maitland and his Adjutant, Major Herbert Wright, knew each other extremely well, having served together for longer than either could remember. It was that closeness which made regiments useless or efficient. Maitland counted himself fortunate to be in command of the 3rd Regiment of Foot, known affectionately as the 'Buffs.' They were a proud and distinguished regiment with over a hundred years of tradition to call upon. A Regiment who traced their antecedents back to 1572. It had been General Howard who, in 1744, had given them their popular name, derived from their buff coloured facings as opposed to the other Howard Regiment, the Green Howards. The 3rd had been bloodied many times, from the Low Countries to Scotland. As such, Maitland was used to orders that at first appeared perplexing, if not bewildering. Had he not said as much all those weeks ago when he had first encountered Fitzwilliam, Colonel of Militia? It was at that meeting that He, Wright, and Mathews had first met.
They had formed a small select group, who knew the reason for their deployment. Why Mathews had been chosen to join the militia, and why Maitland disliked him so intensely, remained one of lives imponderables. All he had been told were the fundamentals, one of which was to relay information back, as and when he could, to this man.

"What are we to do, shall we dance to his tune or ignore him? Personally, I would prefer the latter, but I am constrained by orders to keep the man sweet. To hell with it; we shall give him what he wants, I will give the fool his parade, Mister Mathews." Maitland eyed the young man with a degree of discomfort. Theirs was an unlikely association, two men so different, but drawn together for this one mission.

"I shall inform Sir Percival, upon my return sir. Is there anything further I should know?" Mathews stood before Maitland; proud and erect, waiting for whatever task this man wished him to do. Until a few weeks before, neither had met, but their lives had become inexorably linked due to a meeting at the Horse Guards. Maitland was a professional, unlike the fool Fitzwilliam. Such professionalism had overawed the young man as he had been introduced to an elaborate and audacious proposition in a dust strewn room.

"You will introduce yourself to Sir Percival, and attach yourself to his command. By stealth and guile you will identify, locate then inform Colonel Maitland, of the whereabouts of a government agent secreted within the town." Mathews had baulked at his orders, but used to such illustrious company, he hadn't refused.

"What is there to know, sir, apart from have you been successful in your task?" Maitland was tetchy; the bleeding had not quelled his spleen.

"I fear not, sir. In the short time we have been established within the town, I have been kept close, sir, unable to have a root around, so to speak."

"I see, so, we are confounded until this tomfoolery is completed? Damn the man, told them he and his bloody silly ideas would see us flummoxed. Again Mister, free me from this puss."

Mathews, watched in fascination as the surgeon once again placed the machine upon the colonel's arm. He flinched as the machine's vicious teeth sprang closed and blood once again oozed forth.

"Man's a desperate fool, and desperation causes mistakes. We will indulge him a little longer, but I swear if he becomes too hot headed I will remove him."

Maitland's anger was awesome to behold. Major Wright shook his head and Mathews suspected there were more secrets involved than he was aware of. Certainly the safe removal of a government agent from an insignificant little town was important, but why were they so eager to retain and give credence to Fitzwilliam's stupidity?

"Issue your orders, Herbert, get both regiments clean and presentable, we have a parade to attend." This was the moment Sebastian had dreaded, the moment when the true extent of the militia colonel's pompousness would be revealed. Inhaling deeply he stated...

"Sir Percival will be proud to see your regiment marching alongside his own...however, I fear there is more to his plans than simply a parade."

"What's the fool agreed to? Does he desire to see us parade in the buff?" Maitland and Wright, chuckled at their deliberate use of their regimental title.

"I have known men like our colonel before, seen them at work, full of pomp and bluster, who allow their arrogance and conceit to rule their head. We must hope that his arrogance will be his downfall; perhaps then this pretense will be ended. Speak, boy, what has he promised?"

Mathews was insignificant, the lowest officer in any regiment, yet it fell to him to tell this colonel what another had demanded. Such matters should not be allowed, but until his situation changed, it was his lot to be the sacrificial lamb.

"Sir Percival… has become somewhat of an idol to the towns officials. As such he is fated by those in authority perhaps that is why he issued his order."

"Orders, what driffle do speak of?" Maitland commanded testily.

"Sir Percival has promised the town council a most impressive display. I fear he is…how shall, I put it…lording it, sir, making out you, and not he is the subordinate. He has become friends with the local squire, Sir Stanley Cobb, and no doubt wishes to be seen as important." Mathews stared at a point above Maitland's head and awaited the outburst he was sure was to follow. Maitland stood, knocking the surgeon to the floor where he sat as the colonel paced. Unlike Fitzwilliam, when Maitland spoke, others listened.

"WHAT! Lording it, is he? Damn the man and his friends. I want this tomfoolery ended. We must rein him in Major, hobble him before he causes any more trouble." Maitland's anger was terrible to behold and Mathews waited for the repercussions. "Did I not say this was a mistake, that this entire scheme was beset with problems, that there were too many uncertainties?"

"You did sir I remember you mentioning the fact most specifically." Wright continued to sit and nodded in apparent understanding. Of his colonels predicament

"I did sir, told them straight, that the entire thing was an absurdity. We must keep him, and his militia occupied until transport arrives. Yet he spends his days gallivanting all over the countryside? More importantly we have this…personage to locate and remove from whatever it is they had got themselves embroiled in. On top of all that there is this…well there is something else I must deal with. I am flummoxed at times as to what they expect of us."

Maitland had almost revealed his secret, a secret that even he was denied full access to, but which he would be told of, when the time was right. His only confidents were Wright and Mathews, an ensign he didn't like, nor trust fully. It was irrational, but Mathew's irked Maitland; he simply had to see the youth and he felt an irrational feeling of contempt. It wasn't the boy's fault; he was simply a product of a cossetted lifestyle. Maitland wasn't a pauper, his income was sufficient to live well, but he would have struggled to pay for a uniform of the excellence Mathews wore. His expenditure, Maitland calculated, could have fed his grenadier company for a year. His breeches were the finest, tightest whipcord, his boots the tallest and shiniest, his red coat, the brightest with as much gold braid that was allowed for an ensign. Only one firm supplied such quality, a firm in St James's

"Cobb? Never heard of him, have you Herbert?" Maitland turned to his Adjutant, seeking answers. Wright was an asset, a man who knew many people, both good and bad, a man who with time could discover another's deepest secrets.

"My great aunt married a man named Cobb, but he was a Northumbrian man. Is our Cobb from the North?"

"I...I don't think so, sir," Mathews replied.

"Then add him to our list. Have him watched, if they are close maybe they are in collusion. Do you see collusion, sir?" Maitland questioned. Secrecy and diplomacy were two vices that galled and annoyed him. Neither were conducive for a man's soul, however, his orders prohibited him from doing or saying anything that might jeopardise or provoke Sir Percival into doing something rash. Time was their's to control, the militia were trapped, under his care for however long they remained within Stormouth. Only he could supply their transport, he alone dictated the terms. So there was plenty of time for Fitzwilliam to make a mistake. Maitland's time would come, of that he was sure, and he waited for that expectantly.

"They appear close, sir, apart from that I haven't seen that much of the man."

"Ummph, get up Mister Reynolds, no time to be sitting around. I will call you when I need bleeding again." The surgeon collected his apparatus and left, knowing the colonel would require another bleeding before day's end. He had advised against such excessiveness, but Maitland ignored all such warnings; it was his one true vice. When, like now, he had much to deliberate, his blood boiled and festered meaning the machine was required regularly.

"What form is this parade to take? What have our esteemed Knights arranged?"

"They speak of an event, of both regiments marching through the town between excited onlookers. Sir Percival requests that you are to extend them full military honours, to include drums beating, flags flying and sword blades fixed. He also commands..."

"He what!!!" Maitland slammed his fist onto a travelling case and swore profusely. Mathews jumped in fear, his voice quivered as he continued with his information.

"Sir Percival commands…that you halt the parade in front of the council chambers, where you will honour the town with a Royal salute while your band plays the new national song."

"NEVER...not my regiment, sir! My God, the audacity of the man, his gall astounds me! Does he not realise that the Royal salute is only given when a member of the Royal family is present…are their Majesties to be there, sir? Well, speak…is our Sovereign in Stormouth?"

"No sir, not a one." Mathews shrank under the man's verbal assault. He had expected as much when he'd been told to convey the instructions. Sir Percival was indeed a fool if he had expected a man such a Maitland to acquiesce to such a thing.

"I thought not…you can tell that fool and God himself if needs be that the 3rd will salute the town, but they will not…repeat not, give him a Royal salute. The only salute that popinjay deserves is this…" Maitland grabbed his crotch and made an obscene gesture, drawing a smirk from Wright and a gasp from Mathews.

"I suggest, Mister Mathews, your time is done with that man. You will remain under temporary assignment to me. Question those who may have knowledge of our quarry, redouble your efforts, but no longer are you answerable to that man. Good night to you, sir."

"I am your servant, sir." Mathews doffed his hat to his superior before retiring. Outside he paused, thanked God for his deliverance, and wondered if all senior ranks were soft in the head. He was well aware of his duties; they had been explained in great detail in London. He knew all he needed to know, save one important fact, the agent's name. Why that was remained an imponderable and evaded him. Until he discovered the answer he was stuck betwixt and between two opposing camps. He had relayed instructions for a parade, while important information was kept from him. Was he not trusted, did someone assume he would sell information to Fitzwilliam to further his career? If so, they were very wrong for he would rather die than betray a trust.

Chapter Thirty Four

"Preposterous." Johnson the mayor sat impassively while Turnbottle spoke against the proposal. "Just because Josiah Wood is now head of that family does not give him a right to a seat on this council. He should stand and be elected as any other member would be."

"Mr Turnbottle, is it not incumbent upon us to show a modicum of leniency in this matter. Josiah Wood has just buried his father, his elder brother, by all accounts, is drowned in some unknown sea, while his sister-in-law has brought shame upon their house. Can we not agree to his election to his father's vacant seat?" Reverend Bayles spoke with a voice which had chilled many a bone. He was not a man to annoy, but Benjamin Turnbottle wasn't easily scared.

"I see no reason to grant him such leniency reverend, what would he bring to the chamber, except his name?"

"Mr Turnbottle, one's name, is sometimes all we have to offer. Josiah is no different to many who began their term of office without a background of civic duty. Certainly we would agree that the family name has been tarnished recently, but there again so have many of us been so touched."

There it was, Bayles, had laid his threat upon the table. Unless he received backing for Josiah's election to his father's seat, the priest would speak of what he knew of Turnbottle's visit to the brothel.

"Register my opposition to the proposal, Mister Town Clerk, but you will no doubt take this to the vote. Should that be the case, remember this, I vow that he will not only prove ineffective in council, but will also drive that company into receivership. For neither Josiah, nor his brother are politicians nor businessmen. I wash my hand of it, do as you will but heed my words."

Turnbottle sat back, he had lost he knew that. Joseph's reputation and influence within this room, and with these men, remained strong. They would cast their votes with Bayles because of misguided loyalty and the threat of retribution by the priest if they did not. He, on the other hand, wanted no part in it. Josiah was a fool and would prove himself an ineffectual idiot without any help from those who would elect him.

"The vote is that Mister Josiah Wood be elected to the office of town councilor and should sit as his father once sat alongside those who knew him as a friend. Those in favour aye…" It was as Turnbottle suspected, not a single person, except himself, voted against the proposal. Josiah would become one of them and he despised them all for their inadequacies. "The proposal is carried the invitation will be issued. Now we move to our next item to be discussed reverend as this is something you have had dealings with would you tell council what it is that is proposed."

Turnbottle sat back and waited, he would oppose anything Bayles wanted out of principal but he knew nothing of what was about to be spoken of. He cast his eyes to the ornate ceiling, down the wall and past the ornately carved screen in front of which sat the Jurats, mayor and before them the town clerk. The councilors, those who were merely functionaries to vote for or against each article of legislation, sat below the raised dais and were dressed unlike the more official members.

"Mister Mayor, learned members of the Jurat, councilors. It is my sainted duty to present before you a plea for the removal of an offensive and unsightly blot upon our town. One of our residents is the purveyor of an atrocious stench, a wretched odour which if not stopped will in due course render us all dead in our beds."

"To whom do you speak of reverend, who has fallen ill, who has died from this noxiousness you speak of?"

"I speak of the possibility if nothing is done to halt his offensiveness. Ezra Horn was granted by this council permission to breed swine above the cliffs to the south of the church. But now he allows an abomination to feaster and spill into homes of those who reside below his farm. I say the time has come to close this pestilence down, and have his swine removed to a more sensible location where their waste can harm no one."

"Has anyone specifically died from Horns swine?" Turnbottle added.

"Not to my knowledge sir but it is only a matter of time. I suggest we insist Horn moves to a field out of town where his foul animals can harm no one." Bayles added. "Certainly we cannot afford a pestilence, a miasma, to run rife through our town which it will, if we do nothing."

"One moment reverend, what you propose is the ruination of a man's livelihood. A man who, by your own volition, has done no wrong. I refuse to back this proposal, not because of our personal likes or dislikes but because Ezra Horn is the innocent party. We should not be debating ruining a career on the whim of what might or might not occur at some possible time in the future. More to the point reverend, why is he not hear to speak his case before us?"

"No one speaks of ruination. I simply suggest a move from where he is to a more…. judicious position."

"No reverend, what you ask is no more than the start of his decline. Where pray would he be put. Somewhere as convenient for the butchers, or would our meat have to be brought in beneath the heat of a summer sun where it would attract both flies and the very real risk of theft?"

"The proposed site for him is indeed outside the town walls, in fact a suitable location has been seen on the road north. Abraham Wright has kindly offered one of his fields on main road as a possible location."

"Let me surmise, the field wouldn't by chance be the one that lies in the hollow by the burnt ash tree?"

"As it happens it is, a most suitable field near water for the animals and with an abundance of green grass."

That field, as well you know, is unable to support anything except weeds and fever. The water is stale, the grass sour, his animals will be dead in a week and their meat worthless."

"Sir you speak as if you accuse me of something other than judicious use of our available land. Is there an accusation you wish to share with the other members?" Turnbottle paused, Bayles had trapped him between a lie and the truth. Either might see his association with Mistress Abigail revealed. Was this why the priest had remained silent about his visit to Maggie's? Was this his moment to reveal that and what else he had discovered about him? The merchant had to choose, either back down or confront him. Neither were pleasant options but he was being backed into a corner from which there was to be no escape.

"Reverend I am sure…as are the other members, that Mister Turnbottle makes no such accusation. However, I must ask, is there not another solution to this matter?"

"The solution is very simple. Horn occupies a valuable plot of land, land which if used more judiciously could benefit the town greatly. We have a gentleman willing to build homes, homes for the poor and vulnerable. Homes which will afford shelter against the harsh winters, a place to raise families. Can we deny our people less while accommodating Horn and his swine?"

"Who is this generous benefactor reverend, the church, the squire or someone who wishes to make money from what we might generously give him?"

"It is true Mister Turnbottle, that Mister Spriggs has indeed offered the town a generous donation if we can accommodate his interest. He has offered us a small dispensary for the poor and infirmed. A generous offer indeed for land which at the moment lies idle."

"No reverent not idle, Ezra Horn has been in ownership of that land for some considerable time, I fail to see how we, as a town can force him off his own property. Can we not accommodate both he and Mister Spriggs?" Johnson was a weak man, so much so that Bayles had often wondered why he was made mayor, year after year.

"Mister Mayor, we should consider this, if not for any other reason, than the poor souls who reside below this stinking putrid abomination. As you are more than aware, those who live below that field are some of the weakest and most diseased of our residents. I wonder if their ailments are not, in part, caused by the foulness that Horn allows to flow so indiscriminately down the rock face. Does it fester within those homes, spreading illness wherever it comes to rest? For that reason alone we should agree to have his swine removed, for then, if those residents health improves my point will have been made…"

"And if it does not Reverend, will you then allow Horn to take his animals back onto his own land once again or will you have sold it to those with deep pockets?"

"You see once again our learned friend accuses me of underhand dealings without a shred of evidence. Maybe it is he who should look to his own morals before accusing those who only have the welfare of the town in mind." Turnbottle stood ready to refute the scurrilous remark but Porter halted proceedings before he could do so.

"As much as I enjoy such wordplay, I do so fear this is descending into an argument best suited for elsewhere. We have much to discuss and I cannot have the two gentlemen making this a debating society of their own choosing. I therefore call a vote. Ayes state your vote now." Turnbottle watched as fourteen men agreed with Bayles. "Make the count known in the ledger mister clerk, nays please state your vote." Once again fourteen members voted with Turnbottle." That leaves the town clerk and myself," Johnson paused and received a nod from the clerk. "We vote against the motion, therefore reverend, your claim is defeated, Mister Horn remains in business."

"Then let us pray for salvation, for come summer, you will see plague and pestilence rise from that cesspit and consume you all. I shall remind you of this abomination whenever another body is laid to rest."

Bayles stood and with an impressive swirl of his cloak he left the room. For a moment or two silence hung within the room like the kiss of death,

"Our priest isn't best pleased. Hope none of us have call of his service in the coming weeks for he will be worse than ever with his damnation of our souls." Jarrett one of the council members stated.

"Who cares? His silence means that Horn can continue to supply meat and that is more beneficial than one priest feelings." Turnbottle added, though in truth he knew he had made an enemy, one that he would need to watch very carefully, or deal with, he wasn't sure yet which he preferred.

I will see you damned for that. Bayles thought as he made his way home. *You may have halted me for the moment, but Spriggs desires that field and I*

desire what is offered, so Horn, and his swine must go as must you and you interfering ways.

Not often did anyone defeat him, this time Turnbottle had made him look foolish, but he would laugh longest and dance on the merchant's grave before years end. So black was his mood, he failed to see Maggie slip silently through the darkened streets if he had he might have been a step closer to discovering another mystery.

Chapter Thirty Five

She had come to loath her hideaway, for it was indeed the back end of humanity. No one with any sanity would choose to live here for everything died and withered. She tired of skulking behind closed doors, speaking to mice, she desired to be dealing with those who had brought her to this, and seemingly went unpunished. Her only delight in those dark days were the visits by Maggie and Mary-Ann. The three women had become almost sisters, sharing a bond which, even her saviour appeared unconcerned about.
Mr Tanner had, in fact, been conspicuous by his absence. His visits were few and far between, nor had her letters arrived which concerned her greatly. Which was why when Maggie appeared, she cheered up considerably.

"We come at differing times, and unannounced, so as not to cause consternation, nor draw attention to you, my dear," Maggie had explained when asked. Abigail soon realised that their visits, while appreciated, didn't bring what she wanted to hear. Their laughter, and kind words, hid the fact that she was still hunted, that her name had not been vindicated, nor that she could return to normality. But they did bring hope, hope that one day she would once again see the world that existed beyond these damp walls.

"My friends, you are most welcome!" Abigail greeted the women warmly, embracing, kissing, eager to hear what news they brought.

"Hush, my dear," Maggie cautioned, "the walls are thin, and we don't wants any beaky busybodies to hear our talks do we?" All three women turned towards the door, then at each other, before nervously laughing. Abigail knew what this place offered, and it wasn't security. If she rid herself of her prison, her abiding memory, along with the pervading stench of depravity and destitution would be of its hellish nature.

"Indeed, soon after arriving. I awoke and heard a noise by the door. Thinking my position compromised, fear gripped my heart. I expected the door to be beaten asunder and the priest to appear. But then I heard muttered sounds, a laugh unlike any I had ever heard before, then the sound of a man, some wretch, using the doorway to relieve themselves. I have not heard him since so assume he found a new watering hole. So you see you are correct to be cautious and I accept your chastisement." In truth, she cared little if anyone heard her, she craved companionship and conversation. Night was when the memories returned, when she missed anyone to speak to, but she only had her rodent friend, and he, she knew, was a poor substitute. "I shall, one day stand before my accusers and confront them with what they did. Until then I must remain patient…"

"And careful my child, especially careful." Maggie added.

"How be you, Missy, I sees the pain in yous?" Mary-Ann, was a child, with childlike looks, but possessed worldly knowledge few her age were blessed with.

"The child is restless, it desires birth. I had hoped that it would be born in soft sheets and a clean bed, not on damp straw. Apart from that, I am well; wishing to be free of this place, but still no news comes to end my misery." Theirs was a friendship, spanning less than a heartbeat in the great circle of life. Despite the closeness, a few months ago, Abigail, would have crossed the street to avoid being near them but now, she realised she had been secular in her choice of friends, they were as one, as if they had known each other a lifetime. Brought half dead to Maggie, a bond, stronger than that of mother and daughter had been forged. Call it Christian charity, fate or some other cause, but a kindred spirit, forged out of adversity and so strong, only death would break it apart. It was this inner bond which made Abigail sense her friend's discomfort. Maggie, placed a large basket on the floor, sat on one of the rough chairs and removed her shawl. This had become a ritual, the clothes they brought needed repair and Abigail was proficient with needle and thread. As Maggie had said, she had to be seen doing something otherwise tongues would wag about the kept woman who was never seen.

"See what we bring?"

"Very nice, but what ails you?" Abigail asked. Maggie, usually so brash and full of confidence, appeared troubled. Only once before had she seen her friend so disturbed, that had been the night her benefactor had come to remove her from Maggie's house. Then, as now, she had voiced her suspicions, questioned his motives, and been concerned for her safety. Then, as now, the brothel keeper said little, but Abigail sensed her concern. Could she blame her? After all, she had taken her in, nursed her back to health, only to see her taken away without a by your leave. Abigail saw the same anxiety, as she had seen then.

"Have you heard from…him?" Maggie suddenly demanded.

"Not for some time. His last visit, gave me cause for concern for he looked unwell, yet despite his obvious discomfort he insisted on discussing my escape. Why do you ask?"

"I…" Maggie faltered; Abigail saw that hesitation and pressed her for an answer.

"Is he dead, is that what ails you? Tell me what has become of him for if he has died, then I am aggrieved, not only for him, but for myself. Selfishly, I would be stuck here with no means of escape. So please tell me my fate."

"He's not dead, not yet at least. Soon would be if I had any say in the matter, never trusted him, never will…there, I've said it." Maggie replied.

"Praise be…he is well." Abigail sighed but saw her friend's hesitation. Maggie mistrusted the man, but had mentioned it rarely, to do so now meant she was truly concerned. "Do not fret, he has promised to help me restore my good name. I must simply bide my time until he can do so."

"Bugger his promises." Maggie swore, "Out there, I see nothing of his endevours. You have been forgotten, your name is rarely mentioned, if he works so hard to restore your name, there is little to show for his efforts." Maggie spat upon the floor and cursed as only she could while Abigail stared in abject bewilderment,

"That cannot be, he promised to end this, to work on my behalf. I was to remain hidden until his plans were formed."

Maggie clasped Abigail's hands, holding them tightly in a gesture of friendship. Now was time for honesty, it would hurt, but only for a short while, then she could move on and deal with her problems herself.

"We be friends, as such we must be honest with each other. From that terrible day, I have looked out for you, and do so now. It gives me no satisfaction, it breaks me heart so it do, but I have to speak out. Your friend, your saviour, is nothing more than a poxed liar. No, it be true," She had seen her friend about to speak in his defense. "He has harmed you greatly, more perhaps than that pious scumbag Bayles ever could. I beg you, forget him and his promises. Instead, think as to why such men desire you as a friend? Think of what you possess, and why they desire it?"

She had expected, Abigail to be betrayed. Men wanted but two things from the likes of her. The first was obvious, the second was to further their position and fortunes at her expense. She had seen such betrayal too many times, since her first memories, Maggie Swann had been betrayed herself but no more. Men now cowered beneath her, she dominated them, ruling her world with an iron fist. She could deal with most, could throw drunks and troublemakers from her house with the ease of discarding a night bucket. Yet, here, she spoke softly, clasping another's hands with a tenderness that betrayed her image.

"Am I intelligent?" Abigail, asked, "If that was so, perhaps I might have avoided all this." Her reply came with a sob in her voice because in truth, she had asked her friend, the mouse, the self-same question many times.

"Think, child. Somewhere in that pretty head is the answer; somewhere you have heard, read, or seen something which has worried someone greatly. Remember that and by God, you will have the means to destroy them. Until then the likes of Bayles and Turnbottle will forever twist you to their tune."

"There is but one thing which may explain my predicament, but I would require you to hear me out, and confirm my suspicions. However to hear this will place you both in jeopardy. Are you prepared to suffer as I have suffered? Before you answer, I must ask, how am I portrayed, if as you say I am forgotten?" It required another to light the way through a forest of deception and confirm her own suspicions.

"We pledged our lives to you long ago. So neither of us need to answer that not now, not ever. As to your question, Bayles spoke of you during a sermon, he decreed you a harlot and banished you because of your wicked ways and devious thoughts and deeds. But then, some wouldn't believe that devious scroat if he said night followed day. He be dangerous child, he's who you should be careful of."

"I am friend, every day I think of him and why he treated me so. Now I believe I have the measure of the man." If as |Maggie said Turnbottle had deserted her, his motive must be because of some small titbit she had told him. Realisation came like an epiphany, anger returned, anger at her stupidity and inability to reason and evaluate. No longer was she the pathetic wretch they had saved that night, nor the frightened wisp of a girl Turnbottle sought to use for his own benefit. Once again she was the woman her father would have recognised; strong, resilient and ready for a fight. If, indeed, intelligence separated her from the majority, how had so many managed to manipulate her, destroy her, and cast her out so easily? Why had she allowed a man to control her and then abandon her when she needed their help most?

"The cleric spoke of a devil child you carry, told everyone that you were to be denied succour or assistance. Laid it on good and thick, he did, said anyone who helped would be sent to the fires of hell. Told us that God himself would send us there where we would spend eternity stoking those fires with our sins. However, he's said little about you since, it's as if, with your disappearance, he has lost interest in you."

"Mister Turnbottle told me something similar, the truth is very different and I desire you, my closest friends to know how my ruination began."

"One thing we can promise, is whatever you speak of will go no further unless you ask us to do so." Maggie confirmed while Mary-Ann nodded in childlike acceptance.

"I know I can trust you Maggie, which is why I will speak of my hatred and loathing for Joseph Wood and all he stood for. He ruined the one day I should have enjoyed, instead I desire to forget everything about my wedding day. I should have walked away, but instead I foolishly believed I could cope. I rued that decision every day since, until now."

"What was so terrible? I can understand your dislike for old man Wood, but what else 'appened?" Maggie asked, curious to know what had caused her friend such misery.

"It was the start of what became this nightmare. I had retired to my room, when, unannounced and without invite, Wood appeared at my door. Until that moment I had seen him as cold and distant, as if he disapproved of my presence. What evil he inflicted that day, were scant to what he wanted later."

"He…" Maggie gasped.

"Yes, he showed his true self and I should not have ignored his evil. Drink, it seemed, had relaxed him and he leaned against the door frame as if inspecting some merchandise he was about to purchase. His words were lewd, not what I would have expected, but I put his insolence down to his inebriation. He approached, despite my state of undress, and reached out with those gnarled old fingers to touch that which was his sons by right of marriage. Of course I recoiled, and was saved when he stubbed his toe upon the night bowl beneath the bed. His annoyance was profound to say the least."

"Sounds to me like, both he and the piss pot, were of similar persuasions. Both full of rancid waste."

"Oh, he was, Maggie, he was full of that and more, but I left him writhing in agony and went to my maid's room where behind a bolted door I calmed myself, finished dressing and eventually rejoined my guests downstairs."

"What did your maid say?" Maggie asked,

"Nothing, she was a trusted servant, a girl I wished to protect. I do so hope I have not harmed her by giving her name to Turnbottle?" Abigail paused and failed to see the look that Maggie and Mary–Ann shared. "How was I to know my problems were just beginning? For among the guests was Bayles, invited by Wood, not by us, Even then I found him treacherous and deceitful, his sincerity was like a river, it flowed each way, going where it suited him best. Any man, who can change allegiances as quickly as he did, was not a man I cared to know personally."

"Never did like him as a priest; too pious, and his sermons too filled with hell and damnation. Christ, if every man followed his teachings, my girls would starve through lack of work. But now we knows he's full of shit, a liar, cheat and philanderer. His many trips onto the marsh raised questions, often wondered what he got up to, aint that many sick out there nor too many who likes the scriptures."

"We can only surmise. Though many remember him in their wills, perhaps he seduces the dying, and they leave him a gratuity, maybe that is the basis of his wealth."

"Gawd help us if he attends my last days, all I'll leave him is a bucket of swill."

"Ever the pragmatist my dear friend, but you have to admit that Bayles and Wood were close. Perhaps they shared more than scriptures; certainly their friendship was such that he was invited to attend a family wedding breakfast as an equal, not just as the parish priest. Back to that day, Joseph re-appeared in a foul mood, no doubt his pride and not just his toe were injured. We avoided each other, as if engaged in some evil dance, but those two, Wood and Bayles were never far apart, often lost in heated and sometimes loud exchanges of views. That night, as Nathaniel and I prepared for bed, I broached the subject of his father"

"Bet he loved that," Maggie chided.

"Surprisingly, he was most eloquent, almost pleased to finally have another to speak to. He admitted that his father rarely drank, and that some of his enthusiasm must be attributed to that demon. He stated his father would apologise eventually, that despite the rumours of his father's cruelty and evil mindedness, he was still the largest employer in the district. *If he is so cruel why do so many work for him?* Which, was I admit, difficult to criticise. But then, like a dam breached, he revealed that Joseph had yearnings which he slaked by the use of the house servants. Torn by doubt and indecision, Nathaniel slowly revealed what occurred in that house when the doors were locked. Perhaps he had been tainted by his success in business, perhaps, because he got what he wanted there, that he used his wealth to get what he desired whenever he wanted it. It was that sense of power which possessed him, those that opposed him he ruined, he did it in business and assumed he could do it within his home. He used the servants as playthings, as chattels, used and then discarded which goes to explain why his staff was all of a certain age, young and innocent."

"It is a wonder he kept such matters secret so long."

"It is, indeed. But then, Nathaniel told me of his own childhood, it seemed that their mother had tired of her husband's excesses, had met someone who intended to take her and the children away from Wood's influences, but Joseph discovered her plan and stopped it dead. Nathaniel explained that, as children, they were never privy to the reasons, but the man must have been local because his father would never speak of him. Why she remained silent, Nathaniel could only surmise she did so for the sake of the children and her status, or, that Wood terrified her, either is possible. Personally, I would guess she was worried about her financial situation. Wood would have cut her off without a penny, she would have been alone in the world, or that Wood would have done to her what he did to me. Divorce was not an option, nor could

Nathaniel be sent away, either option would have resulted in further torture for them all. As he said that night, they were his future Wood was not going to lose that."

"As I said, fear drove her silence." Maggie added.

"Fear was indeed prevalent in that family; Nathaniel spoke long into that night, he wept at some of what he recalled, the beatings, the abuse. He wept most when he spoke of his mother who died, unable to protect her sons further. Or, as some imagine, did Wood dispose of her when he could stand her treachery no longer? Was her supposed assignation too much for him to bear? There was always speculation about her death, is it feasible that he did indeed kill his wife, and others concealed his crime."

"Men are devious; they tell us what we want to hear," Maggie said ruefully. Her experience had, Abigail wondered, bent her opinion of men in general. "My God, girl, have you never fallen under their spell, then, in the cold light of day cursed your stupidity, or is that something only we, your poorer cousins have experienced?"

"I am no innocent." Abigail began, only for her words to be halted as Mary-Ann said,

"Miss Maggie is right, Miss Abigail. Never trust them to speak the truth; only got one thing on their minds. The Reverend's powerful, but your man is a liar," Mary-Ann stated simply as she laid out the meagre food. Usually so innocent and childlike, her words chilled both women to the bone

"Why do you say that, why do you call my friend a liar, has someone spoken about me in front of you?" Abigail's heart sank, Maggie and Mary-Ann, understood the wiles of men, knew what had to be done to survive, but the young girl spoke in a manner which made Abigail fear she had been approached. If questions were still being asked, then it was as she feared, she was still hunted, and would provoke unguarded answers. Bayles was devious enough to initiate such methods, Mary-Ann innocent enough to fall into his trap. If she had spoken out of turn, then it was possible that all she had been through, had been for naught, and she would have to leave immediately without knowing what Mister Turnbottle lied about.

"Stupid, stupid girl, what do you know about life and men? Ignore her, she knows nothing, and I will beat her black and blue for her wicked lies." Maggie cuffed the girl about the ear, until now, Abigail had never seen her show fear, but now she did. Mary-Ann belonged to her, was her property and if she had been indiscreet, her actions could prove disastrous for all concerned. They had to be sure, but fear would not reveal what they needed to know.

"Cease, she's a child, no more. No one will beat anyone. Mary-Ann, listen, this is important, tell us what you know, what you have said, and who you said it to."

"I aint said nuffing, may I be struck down dead if I lie...I remembers what Miss Maggie told us, if anyone asks, I tell's 'um me glims don't see nothing, and my ears are deaf. Honest, they don't hear anything from me, ma'am." She sniffed, rubbed her eyes with the back of a dirty hand. Glancing at each other the two women had to know what had occurred.

"Speak, tell us who asked and what you told." Maggie demanded. They waited as the girl continued, she stopped continuously as if searching for the right words, but the meaning was real and terrible.

"I hears things, ma'am, got a friend...she's one of the Reverend's servants...she told me that...well...she's been...well used by the priest... every night. Ruby, says he's wild, at it every night, with someone or another...when there's no one else, he comes to her and his tastes are well...strange, miss, if yous gets my drift."

"Of this I can vouch," Maggie stated." I fear it is known. She speaks truthfully, of things, some would wish to remain unspoken, but I knows, ma'am, knows all about him."

"How do you know, Maggie, and will it compromise my position?" Abigail was stunned at what she was learning. She had suspected much and now she was, it seemed, about to learn the truth of what Stormouth held so secret.

"I fear he is a customer. Since he arrived, I have sent girls to him. It is true our good priest has tendencies which are...beyond normal. Strangely, he hasn't come near since all this began. Have no fear; my honour lays with you, my dear. If he came a visiting, I wouldn't speak of you, of that you has my word...However, what she speaks of confirms what I to have heard."

"What is it, what secrets am I am denied?" Abigail felt lost, as if suddenly even those she held dear, were betraying her. I have heard that your friend seeks certain items, I wasn't sure whether to speak of this or not, but the fact is he desires items connected to you but which I am convinced he seeks for himself."

"What are these items?" Abigail asked. "Need I be worried unduly?"

"Possibly. You will not like this but your friend, stopped your maid, Maud, in the fish market. Scared her witless demanding she finds something for him."

"Letters, I know, I asked him."

"Has he said anything since?" Maggie asked

"Only that his contacts work in finding them, but are experiencing difficulties."

"Do you believe him?" Maggie asked.

"Should I not?"

"No, I fear you should not. He demanded them, and thank God your maid was brave enough to ignore his threats." Maggie paused, reached into her apron pocket and withdrew a bundle of sealed notes. "Are these yours?"

"Yes, but I don't understand."

"It's simple. We have all been duped; all along he wanted to read them for himself before telling you some cocked up story about never finding them. Maud sensed their importance and came, via Mary-Ann to me. You now have the proof of his lies; I wonder what he will tell you next?

Chapter Thirty Six

Loyalties, that night, were stretched to breaking point. Differing factions were discovering details which concerned them greatly. Eventually such discoveries must reach a point where one, or the other, won or lost. Stormouth was about to become embroiled in a war.

Abigail gasped at what she heard, it was such intimidation and deceit which she despised. In moments like this she wished she had been born a male, for then she could face those she despised and denounce them for what they were. She felt drained; all this time she had waited upon one man, only to find he contrived against her. Surprisingly, she felt anger more than fear, she was more focused, stronger in both thought and deed, the mouse had turned.

"Time we thought of revenge, ladies. Will you assist me?"

"Of course, but I urge caution. If I have learnt one thing, it is that men are best led to the trough rather than allowing them to charge forth unrestrained. Patience, my dear, will bring forth far more reward than rushing headlong into anything."

"Your words are wise indeed, Maggie. I shall remain in hiding for the moment, but we must prepare for an urgent move if things go astray. One day, I promise we will denounce Bayles and the rest of his lying fraternity, we will see them face the full force of the law and smile as they go to the gallows. Until then, my good friends, tell me what occurs away from this house, is there any exciting news?"

"Not much. Now the cold is gone we got ships sailing normal like, which means we are busier than in winter. Oh…and there's a titled man staying with Squire Cobb; word is soldiers are coming." Maggie explained nonchalantly, biting into a slice of bread.

"This man…he's a soldier I take it?" Abigail asked excitedly.

"So they say. Eli Porter says the Mayor is fawning over him, says that he brings troops here for mustering 'afore they gets sent abroad."

"Troops…are you sure?"

"That's the rumour." Maggie had wrinkled her nose in disgust, adding, "Course not real soldiers, but militia."

"Oh." Abigail could not help but show her disappointment.

"What's wrong?" Mary-Ann asked. "Soldiers is soldiers, Miss Maggie says we will be busy once they arrive."

"No doubt you will, but militia are not real troops, they are worse."

"In what way, Miss?" Mary-Ann enquired.

"Now't wrong with soldiers, no matter what badge they wear, they'll have pennies in their pockets and no one but us to spend it on," Maggie stated pointedly.

Abigail remained silent; she was better educated then either of her new friends, but Maggie was more worldly wise. Could she tell them how much trouble militia could bring upon them without scaring either women?

"Certainly they will have coin but they are…how shall I say, immoral…yes immoral. They are rogues and ne'er-do-wells, unruly and undisciplined. They join the militia to avoid being sent abroad to fight, they are used to living well with food in their bellies and not too much to care about except quelling unrest at home by force. They are totally without honour. My father says…" She paused, mention of her father would, she was sure, bring further awkward questions. Questions she couldn't answer, nor wished to dwell upon.

"What does your father say, missy, and why do he leave you like this…?" Mary-Ann spoke with innocence but her question was heart-felt. Mistress Wood was like no other she had met, she was kind, considerate; always spoke of things that were beyond her limited knowledge. Though, this time she knew she had said too much, she saw the pain well up within her friend.

"Hush your mouth, you bad girl, such matters are not for the likes of you to know." Maggie cuffed the girl gently about the ears, bringing a mild rebuke from her friend.

"It's alright she has the right to ask. After all, have I not sat here asking why I have heard nothing from him? I feared I had been forgotten; now I know that without these letters he knew nothing of my plight." She held them, testament to her failure "Truth is, mention of such men, would invoke a great consternation from him.

"Aye?" Mary-Ann queried.

"He would become angry, my dear. Truth is he believes such regiments should be disbanded, sent abroad where the real men fought instead of persecuting loyal Englishmen."

Briefly, Abigail had forgotten where she was. Such conversation would be meaningless on these women; they were lovable and loyal but lacked the knowledge of what happened in the wider community. She noticed the glances and realised that they knew little of what militia were capable of.

"We were in Manchester on…business. Looking to buy machinery, we saw a riot by millworkers who asked for their wages to be increased to two pennies a week."

This was the first time she had lied to Maggie. How could she tell the truth and retain her anonymity? If the truth, behind their visit, was ever told it would be a tale of sinister and dreadful repercussions. They had been investigating a mill owner who, like Wood, thought the government stupid. He had tripled the price he charged for his wool. Her father had attended as a buyer, with his daughter in attendance to supply a suitable subterfuge. While the owner and her father had discussed terms, she had slipped away to discover evidence. Their journey had been successful and the mill owner now shared a cell with fellow criminals.

"Two pennies a week, are they rich in Man...?" Mary-Ann asked, her astonishment at such wealth obvious, but she stumbled over the long word.

"Manchester...no, they are not rich, in fact, you are richer than they."

"Gor'n," Mary-Ann scoffed, brushing at her crumpled skirt.

"It's true, you are beholden to only Maggie and she, I am sure, treats you as well as any daughter. In the great towns of the north, the mill owners own the workers. They tell them when to wake and when to work, when to pray and when to sleep. They own their cottages and deduct rent from their meagre wages, some men have but three farthings to feed their families. I saw mothers with six, eight or ten children, all starving because the parents had not enough money to feed them."

"Poor wee brats. What about the fields, or the sea? Could they not get food from there, like we sometimes do?"

"There are no fields, or sea, just tall chimneys and large factories which belch thick black smoke day and night. Your priest speaks of hell, well those people live there every day, for when the weather is still, that poison seeps into their hovels chocking and killing them silently."

The memory of that terrible time made her pause, they had closed one mill and ruined another owner but hundreds remained, all as bad, all as crucial. Had they made a difference, possibly?

"You think the 'Butts' is terrible, you should see how they live; it is much worse. They live in small houses built back to back, perhaps four or five families to a house, sometimes two families to a room. Every home is the same; there is no grass, just darkness and poverty. People die in Manchester. Men, women, children, they just give up and die, and no one does anything about it. I was pleased to leave, but they can't, they have to survive as best they can. Like Wood, the mill owners control everything from birth to death; everything comes from them at a price. I doubt if many have a brass farthing to live on most weeks."

Abigail paused; both women wiped tears from their eyes. The picture she had painted was bleak indeed, but far better than what actually existed in that far off place.

"Makes you pleased to live here, don't it?" Maggie said forlornly.

"It does, even with everything that has happened to us, Stormouth is indeed a place to enjoy." She paused, seemingly remembering a painful past then added. "If we have troops arriving, how'pray do I get to see them?"

The question was asked mischievously, the two whores had unknowingly become instruments in her devious plans. She wanted, no, needed to get out and see what was happening, and this, she considered, was her best chance of doing that.

"You can't be seen outside, Miss, It be too dangerous, if you were seen...he would be told." Mary-Ann turned and stared at Maggie despairingly. In one act of stupidity, Abigail, could ruin all they had achieved.

"Who, ladies, will recognise Miss Abigail Wood when she is dressed in this and smeared in mud and dirt?"

She reached for a bundle of rags, smiling devilishly she held it up proudly as they inspected her handiwork. The dress was one which they had brought, but it was barely recognisable. Abigail had worked long and hard at her disguise, she had patched and sewed until she had a new dress and hooded cape. She had intended to use it to hide her escape, but this opportunity was far superior to what she had planned. Using its dowdiness she would remain unidentified while seeing what her accusers were doing.

"It might work," Maggie conceded, "if you stand among us...yes, we'll do it, but I advise not saying anything to 'you know who."

"I have no intention of telling anyone. Now, tell me the town's plans for welcoming these troops."

* * *

The troops, Abigail so wished to see, remained encamped far away while their officers debated the merits of a dandy and a youth.

"Told them. Said that boy was a bumptious fool, a popinjay, who will prove a liability 'afore this is done." Maitland neither liked, nor admired, either Fitzwilliam, or the ensign Mathews, one he despised, the other he suffered for convenience sake. The argument had raged back and forth ever since Maitland had returned from a meeting at the Horse Guards. It had been repeated on their march south, and would no doubt continue until Mathews performed some stupid act of bravery that Maitland could not ignore, which would prove unlikely, knowing as he did, their orders.

"So you say, sir, but 'Their Lordships' must see some redeeming qualities. After all, he could have joined any militia regiment and remained safe and cossetted. Instead he purchases an ensignship in a most prestigious regiment, before volunteering for this absurdity. I mean, is that the actions of a sane man?"

Major Herbert Wright was the perfect foil to Maitland's warring disposition. He was an excellent organiser, superb diplomat; a man who saw beyond what was obvious. Qualities which Maitland was sure would be needed before their work here was completed. Inwardly, the adjutant smiled and waited for the next outburst, his colonel would require further bleeding after this meeting.

"Sanity! The only redeeming features he possesses, are his connections. The Duke said as much when I broached the subject in London. Told me they understood my reticence, but his family, were well known and liked, said he was an intelligent sort, and well versed in what they required."

Herbert Wright sipped his port. His colonel, had more spleen to purge, and he wasn't disappointed by a long wait.

"I swear there is foulness afoot. Those such as our exulted ensign, are liars and cheats, given half a chance they would sell their own mother if it advanced their cause. That boy, Herbert, will fail and I'll tell you why he will fail. He lacks discipline and experience, that's why. He joined the army before his mother had finished wet-nursing him, remove those pants and you will see stains where he cannot wipe his arse as yet. Moreover, he will run at the first volley from some damn Frenchie. Not that he will be alone, for every man jack of that regiment will shit themselves as well. But we have to rely upon a callow youth, deemed suitable to discover the man we seek, and what pray are his credentials...I'll tell you, their Lordships see not ability but, his family name and his wealth. Personally I doubt he could find a whore in a brothel, but I do as commanded because I am the King's servant."

Maitland shook his head, poured more port and stared at his friend. Both were well versed in such discourse. Having known each other for almost six years, they had seen much, and grown to like and respect each other. Both were of equal social standing, both had incomes that afforded them the finer things in life, yet had chosen the army to be their career. The militia was their one matter of discourse. Wright saw them as a means to an end, many of their number became bored with the soft life and transferred to a line regiment. Maitland viewed them entirely differently, seeing them as a drain on men and supplies.

"Why us. Why are we saddled with that popinjay and his troops? I'll tell you why. We are the sacrificial lambs, we nurse Fitzwilliam and wipe his arse, we pander to his stupidity. Then when he fails, as he assuredly will, we carry the responsibility. I tell you, Herbert, the sooner that man and his fools are loaded and dispatched the happier I shall be. Such an assignment is a slight, a slight to our men; for it is a well-known fact that militia brings down the regular soldier. God knows what they will make of him in the colonies, but at least we will be shot of him."

Wright waited, for he knew this was more complex than a simple dislike of an ensign and a militia colonel. Maitland drank his wine, wiped his mouth with a pure white kerchief and gathered his thoughts. Wright knew some of the burden he carried, knew they were disproportionate to the orders he had received that day in London. A subject they had been spoken of often, and which would be discussed again tonight.

"Indeed, sir, indeed." Wright appeared far more relaxed than he really was. Maitland had spoken often about how the militia were to be treated, how The Horse Guards had ordered him to be lenient upon them, such orders galled Maitland and had caused more than one disagreement between the 3rds two senior officers.

"Thank God and His Majesty, for common sense Herbert. Someone at least saw reason and gave us this." He held a parchment aloft, "this document tells me I must treat him with reluctant obedience. In truth I am told to allow Fitzwilliam free rein and trust he don't kill us all. If he do, then this is our authority, our release should our gallant 'friend' becomes too stupefied with his own grandeur. By God they expect him to fail, expect him to bring disgrace upon the army or their Majesties. I was told to use it well, told that it might be all that stops the fool doing something we will live to regret." Reluctantly Maitland passed the document to Wright. "Read it well Herbert and know what I am entrusted to do. It has taken us three months to march that rabble this far. They are worse than useless, yet I am to train them to fight as a line regiment would. Now, we stand upon a precipice, less than a day's march from that town and we are still none the wiser of what we are to expect. By God sir I shall not fail, but I am betwixt as to what my purpose is. Am I to accomplish one or all of my orders will we be made to look foolish if we fail at any part. No sir, I shall not inflict such a disapprobation upon this regiment. We shall do all in our power to succeed, to that end, you sir will be busy this night preparing both regiments for a parade. Can you do it in what is left of this night?"

"It will involve a few hours of extra writing but...yes it can be done. Our officers know what to do and the sergeants will enjoy driving the militia into line. I will inform the sergeant major immediately." Wright smiled devilishly for Patrickson was a hard but fair man. He drove the 3rd, made them into what they were. He was also proud of what the regiment had achieved, more importantly, they needed men like him now, for he knew about men like Mathews and Fitzwilliam. If Patrickson had been present, he would have explained Ensign Mathew's appearance in simple terms. *He knows as much about soldiering as his horse's left buttock.*

"Another?" Maitland asked, offering the decanter to his subordinate. "I need to wash this travesty from my palate." Maitland was prone to honesty, maybe that was why he languished in his current position and had not been elevated to the Horse Guards like some of his lesser contemporaries. Maybe, that was why he had been given this assignment, as a punishment for his outspokenness.

"Perhaps a small one sir, I do have a lot to do afore the morrow." Wright smiled and accepted the wine poured from a fine crystal decanter. Maitland's quarters were a reflection on his life. Unlike some regimental commanders, he travelled with the minimum of accoutrements. He had no hunting dogs, man servant, or that much silverware. His few possessions included a bed, feather pillows, and a set of fine leather travelling cases, into which he packed the things that made life in the field bearable. One such case contained his cellar of fine wines and port. Maitland had purloined some excellent rare vintages during his years with the colours.

"Is this what we are reduced to, pandering to militia idiots and their lapdogs?" Maitland queried.

"For the moment, I fear we are. No doubt our inconvenience will be rewarded when eventually we see the popinjay shot down and reduced to a quivering wreck." Wright had witnessed Maitland's competence at close quarters. The colonel could not be called impulsive, he would rather delay for a moment, rather than risk even one man unnecessarily because of poor intelligence, or over confidence. "We do have one advantage, time sir, is on our side. Sir Percival cannot act until we deliver his men to him, more than enough opportunity for him to make a mistake, and when he does…"

"We shall delight in his downfall Herbert."

"We will that sir." One of Herbert's duties was to curb Maitland's anger, keep his colonel in check. In the days to come he wished Sir Percival the same privilege.

"As always, your perception and common sense surpasses my own. Tell Patrickson to assign one officer to the front and rear of each company."

"Might I suggest captains to the front, lieutenants and ensigns to the rear, although, we will have to amend that slightly as we now have a colour party to form."

"Damn the man…yes. What of the sergeants?"

"I would suggest, senior sergeants to form to the rear of each company. Their task will be to welcome our guest, wherever they appear from."

"That concerns me, how will this spy know what to do if, as that pup

Mathews says, he hasn't made contact. My God, I detest such secrecy, how can we operate when even I do not know what they intend, or their identity. Damn conspirators, give me an enemy dressed in French blue and I'll march through shot and shell to the gates of Hades. But get involved with secrets and you end up chasing your own balls. Rescind the ensign's orders, he will remain with us indefinitely. If Fitzwilliam asks, tell him the boy is drunk or poxed. Maybe, just maybe, that youth will be useful to us."

Wright smiled and sipped his wine. The colonel was not a happy man, disliking his orders and eager to cover all eventualities. He had been entrusted with a most difficult assignment and with the finale about to commence, the responsibility weighed heavily on his conscience. For the moment, he was a troubled man.

"If, or when they decide to make contact, I am to be informed no matter where I am, or what I am doing. Understand? Anywhere."

"Fear not, everyone has been informed of your orders."

"Tell the bastards again. If anyone makes a mistake I'll flog them personally

Chapter Thirty Seven

Joseph Wood's funeral had been the last time the town had gathered in such numbers. Then, the mood had been somber and the weather putrid, now the crowd sang and danced beneath a warming sun. Pie sellers plied their wares, while children ran through the streets unhindered and women carried posies of spring flowers gathered from the fields. Stormouth waited expectantly for a parade to begin, while on the high road, two regiments of King George's army paused.

Neither regiment had slept, spending the night beneath a star encrusted sky, polishing and cleaning their uniform and equipment until it shone. While the 3rd did so with the acceptance of veterans, the militia were concerned only in avoiding further beatings and hardship from their colonel. Which was why, long before the sun had risen and harangued by officers who had schedules to keep, both regiments had been formed up, the militia to the fore, the 3rd to the rear. To the uninitiated, both regiments, appeared the same; both wore the same red tunics, crossed by white belts, both wore white breeches, gaiters and black boots. Each regiment wore tricorn hats while the 3rd had Buff coloured turn backs and cuffs, the militias were plain white. Each soldier carried packs, muskets, and a sword blade, fifteen inches of steal which could be attached to the barrel of their muskets, or used as a thrusting weapon in heat of battle. For the moment, these vicious blades hung from their belts in leather scabbards. The most striking difference though was at the front of the column, The 'Buffs' colours, drums and mitered caps of the grenadier company, carried the ancient badge of a green dragon, whereas the Militia's colours were, as yet unadorned. They were as perfect as their sergeants could get them, but to those who knew, there were subtle differences. The men of the 3rd regiment stood a little straighter, they moved with a swagger that only came from experience, while the militia looked around apprehensively. Though, each and every man thanked their God that He hadn't sent rain, for that would have made their hard work useless.

Major Wright, had performed a minor miracle. Working incessantly he had urged, encouraged, cajoled and sworn until finally he was able to present to Maitland a force as ready as he could get them in such a short time. The militia had proved the stumbling block. With no colonel to approve his orders, he had to work with a surly major and some worse than useless captains. Despite his best efforts, Wright had finally had to call upon Maitland to intervene. The colonel's authority had, eventually, brought order just as dawn broke when, despite the irregular's ineptitude, they were ready to proceed. Maitland commanded both regiments to come to attention, then, with drums beating and colours flying, they marched forward towards a parade.

Maitland waited, apparently unconcerned but he knew, as did those with a modicum of intelligence that something was amiss. Their formation was at odds, they were out of step and appeared at odds with each other. Such differences would cause Sir Percival palpitations, inducing in him an attack of the vapours, which in turn would bring about a verbal assault and possibly, depending upon the man's disposition, a number of his men being flogged mercilessly. Eager to avoid such treatment, Fitzwilliam's second in command, the pompous Major Entwhistle, did what no regular officer would dare contemplate. With the arrogance of financial security and a safe posting, he approached the senior officer on parade, saluted extravagantly, and asked…

"Beg pardon, sir, but may I enquire as to why your ranks are formed so differently to ours?"

"Good day Major Entwhistle," Maitland said happily. The question had come a lot quicker than he had thought. In fact, he now owed Wright a guinea in payment, small price to pay if it went some way to spoil Fitzwilliam's parade. "By God sir, is something amiss? Good of you to point it out to me." He rode on, smiling happily until finally, he asked, "I presume you are not aware of the orders issued by the Horse Guards pertaining to how a column of troops should approach an unknown objective?" He stood and glanced at the militia then frowned. "Oh dear…we do seem at odds, do we not? What pray, are we to do? Sir Percival, so wanted everything to be just right."

Unsure if he was being ridiculed, Entwhistle frowned. Unaware of any such new instructions, he was at a loss. The two regiments were out of step, their ranks unequal, the ordered drill which Sir Percival so adored appeared farcical and imbalanced. His colonel demanded perfection and this was not as it should be.

"I fear Sir Percival will dislike the appearance, he appreciates uniformity you see, sir. Might I be so bold as to request you reform?"

Wright inhaled sharply, expecting Maitland to explode at Entwhistle's audacity. Instead, Maitland appeared quite unperturbed.

"Can't sir, first lesson we old soldiers learn. Always obey the last order received by a senior officer. Ain't that so, Wright?"

"Indeed, in fact, if I might be so presumptuous to add. You, sir, are the senior officer on parade, therefore by seniority, and by virtue of the honours adorning the colours, your regiment takes precedence. Therefore, and I do beg the majors indulgence on this matter, I would suggest if anyone reforms it should be the militia. Just a minor matter of etiquette, nothing personal you understand."

Maitland remained stolidly somber, but loved every moment of Wright's eloquent put down. Where matters of etiquette and courtesy were concerned, Herbert Wright could be as prissy as any well born Prince.

"Hear that, Major, Wright reckons you should reform. Ever given that command to troops on the march, sir?"

"I have not, sir." Entwhistle replied curtly. He was a man who, if he could avoid giving orders of any sort, was quite happy to do so.

"Dogs bollocks, sir, that's what happens if you get it wrong, but pray feel free to try if you like." Maitland rode stiff backed at the head of his men and knew the major had but one course of action. It took a few moments, but eventually he asked,

"Might be better for all concerned, sir, if you would be so kind to issue those orders? You being the more senior and experienced officer on parade." Maitland remained silent, but stared at Entwhistle in disbelief. If so ordered by a senior officer he would have stormed an enemy breech or led them into the gates of hell, but to be asked by a mere militia officer to do anything was… incredible, boarding upon insulting. Sighing heavily, he turned his horse and broke rank. Wright followed his colonel and mouthed an insult in Entwhistle's direction.

"Man's a fool," Maitland stated when he and Wright were far enough away. "Like Fitzwilliam, neither sense nor sanity. We shall enjoy their gullibility a little longer Herbert, but God help me, if he steps out of line allow me to kill the bastard."

"With pleasure sir, with pleasure."

The 3rd could have carried out the manoeuvre easily enough. It was something they practiced for when the time came to perform any number of maneuvers quickly and without hesitation, as death thinned their ranks. The militia, unused to such orders would need to be coaxed led not harried. To aid the task he halted the column, something any good officer would have done. Something, even an officer of Entwhistle's limited experience should have known if he had any sense at all. After twenty minutes of order and counter order, and aided by those sergeants in the militia who had smelt the smoke of battle, both regiments were finally formed in a similar manner. Maitland smiled as twenty companies resumed their march. They made a marvelous sight, a red column snaking its way down the road towards a sleepy town. A light dust rose above their heads, making their uniforms appear dowdy. Out of earshot of their superiors, the men grumbled about the hours spent preparing for this parade, and the hours they would have to spend later on cleaning kit.

"Steady men, shoulders back, heads up, you'll soon be among them. Do us proud lads, more to the point, do yourselves proud. Show these good people what a real regiment can do."

Maitland gestured Wright to come closer. Quietly he said,

"Check everyone is ready, we'll be there in a few moments."

From his position, Maitland had seen the crowds lining their approach. His men knew what to do; Wright and the other regimental officers had made sure of that. From youngest drummer, to Patrickson, they knew what to expect. Even so, he was putting a lot of trust in men most officers despised and mistrusted. Worse, he was expecting a lot from this agent, a man no one knew and who would have to make his presence known. How he would do that was anyone's guess. All Maitland could hope was that their spy would choose correctly and make themselves known to a member of the 3rd. God knows what a pig's ear Entwhistle would make of it if the militia became involved.

"Smile, you heathen bastards, they are English women not French dragoons," Patrickson snarled.

"Do that mean we gets a night in town, s'arnt?"

"It means, Jones, if you don't shut up, and do as you're told, you'll feel my boot up your arse. So be quiet and look as if you're enjoying the day."

Discipline kept the 3rd under control, something they would need as the road narrowed and they passed the first houses. Immediately the first flowers were tossed into the ranks, no doubt the first wine bottle had also been passed. Wright and the other officers would be hard pressed to find all the contraband that would be concealed within their backpacks.

"Thank you, my dear," Wright said politely but solemnly as a young girl pressed a posy towards him. His task was that of office clerk, but he was a soldier and could sense trouble before it arrived. The crowd was gathering; growing larger by the minute, where they all came from was anyone's guess. Most likely Fitzwilliam had a hand in organising them. Whatever the reason, just ahead the road narrowed and the crowd spilled into the street.

Unknowingly, they approached the 'Butts', an area not designed for columns of men. Fitzwilliam, was responsible for the route, he had stated, demanded in fact that as many should witness the armies arrival as possible. A laudable idea, but totally impracticable, in his arrogance he had forgotten one tiny matter. A regiment marched eight abreast, far wider than the narrow streets into which they entered. Constrained by the narrowness, and the expectant crowds, the troops automatically compressed. The 3rd held their dressing, sergeants dealt with anyone who came too close swiftly and brutally.

It was the militia, the lead regiment that began to waver, pressed from both sides the inexperienced troops stepped inward. Once begun there was little to stop them save experience, and they lacked that in abundance. Chaos was but a heartbeat away when Wright rode his horse unceremoniously into the ranks of women and troops. Bellowing loudly, he shoved his way past women armed with flowers, wine, babies and bare breasts.

"Hold the line, damn you! I will shoot the next man who steps back...Patrickson take one man in ten from each company, form a barrier either side of the column...Damn your heathen eyes! Look to your front not hers!" He swore, forcing his horse into a group that appeared about to break "I swear I will fire!" To emphasize his validity he drew his pistol and cocked it deliberately.

It took time, but Wright's foresight saved the day, order was regained and the 'Butts' were negotiated without further incident. The crowd's cheered, old soldiers watched in envy, shaking their heads at how the army had become more ragged since they had served. Children ran alongside, earning further cuffs from sergeants when they approached too closely. Bottles of wine were passed and women smiled seductively. Eventually the column reappeared into the relative quiet of North and South quays to begin the long climb up the hill towards the church. Many furtively concealed bottles of wine from view or carried posies of flowers. The militia had almost broken, while the 3rd had stood solid. Regardless of their orders, despite the good intentions of the officers, many a woman managed to pass their tokens. RSM Patrickson walked the line removing those favours he could see. No civilian was going to make his men look like Fops, or God forbid, worse.

"Sarn't Major?" A voice called from the column.

"What!" Patrickson demanded. The man was the regimental malingerer, a waster, a trouble maker of the worst kind. A man he would gladly flog every day if he had thought it would do any good. "Speak you idol son of a bog whore. What is it? Whatever you want had better be good to makes you speak on parade."

"Found this Sarn't Major. Orders were to bring anything strange to your attention." The man held a scrap of paper which Patrickson snatched from him in disgust.

"Strange, he says! Whole bloody day's strange. Should be...give it here, I'll send it on."

Patrickson was a bull of a man who none would argue with. His face was emblazoned with both moustache and bushy sideburns. What skin could be seen was crisscrossed in thin red veins, testament to the amount of drink he consumed. For all that, he was the essence of a soldier, elegant in his pristine uniform, stiff backed; the very picture of all things military. Importantly he detested civilians, hated anything that detracted his men from what their true use was. *Killing Frenchies and rebels, not collecting flowers*, tucking the note inside his jacket. He kicked a child who had slipped among his carefully dressed ranks "Bugger off, turd." He swore then, with swagger stick tucked under his arm, he marched forward with a sense of pride and duty. If the day was all flim-flam for the officers and nobility, he, Sergeant Major Patrickson, a one-time pickpocket from St Giles's rookery in London, was not going to shirk his duty. The word from the officers was to expect anything and this could be it. Curiosity had made him look, but what he saw meant nothing. All he saw were meaningless scratches upon the paper. Reading was not for him; he could neither understand, nor did he wish to know what it said. Whatever it meant was for someone else, not him. The drums beat, the flags flew, the crowd cheered and Fitzwilliam waited his parade, oblivious to the fact that a message had been delivered.

Chapter Thirty Eight

Benjamin Turnbottle watched the parade and cursed. He despised the military especially here, now, in his town, more importantly months of careful manipulation and subterfuge were threatened by those he employed who were too stupid to comprehend simple instructions. Wiping his collar, he cursed at the ineptitude of those he employed. Only a few weeks ago, a ragged urchin had appeared at his door, demanding money for a message he had. Reluctantly he had paid the brat a half-penny and hurried towards the meeting. A meeting which had left him feeling melancholic and haunted by what had occurred.

"Why am I, thus summoned?" he had demanded. His anger lost on the fool he employed to keep undesirables from disturbing her. A simple enough job for anyone of limited imagination or intelligence, who's only attribute in life was quickness with both fists and knives. *Why then had he chosen that particular moment to act without direction and to do more than was expected of him?* Turnbottle had witnessed life's seamier side, but what he had been told made his blood run cold, and left him stunned, and concerned. "I told you to watch, nothing more. Did you have to cut him?"

"I were told to make sure no one disturbed her. He were about to...well he won't no more."

The oaf had killed, and tried justifying it as Turnbottle's instructions. He had been mortified, and tried desperately to control his anger. A man had died because he simply desired somewhere to piss in solitude and had chosen the wrong doorway. Was that justification? Certainly not in his mind, but he was ultimately to blame. The oaf had appeared unconcerned, the knife, evidence to his crime, had still rested in his bloodied hand. Even now, the memory of that blood red weapon made Turnbottle swoon in disgust, as did the stupidity of his actions which would haunt him perhaps forever, or at least until he had succeeded and put this period behind him.

"Get rid of that in there," Turnbottle had instructed, indicating first the knife and then a pile of manure. Anger and frustration had overwhelmed him. He had been about to lambaste his man when, realisation struck. He was as implicated as the killer; he knew about a murder and had helped conceal it from the authorities. A line, which as a gentleman should never be crossed had been. His knees had felt faint and he had leant against a wall as the killer had nonchalantly thrust the knife deep into the dun. "Who was he?" Turnbottle had demanded.

"No idea....some scum...don't care much...shouldn't have come around should he?"

"But death is ..." With that he retched, death was not for him and he knew he had crossed his own Rubicon. The deed was done, he was implicated.

"I was doing as you asked, watching out for her. This gutter snipe comes out the tavern, first he looks around like…as if checking for lookers…next he tries the door handle. I thought he were going to enter, to thief or…well you know what."

"I see your dilemma. You assumed he had evil intent in mind, would be best to keep such thoughts in mind. Should anyone ask your intention was to protect; we can use that as a defense, if needed. No one would fault you in your execution of my directive, but a death for using a door for…that, is excessive."

"Shame, but how was I to know all he wanted was a night bucket. Funny really, he'd just unbuttoned and was, well, just starting when I came upon him. Still won't get took short again, will he?"

"Suppose not, but it was a risk, which we cannot make any more. In future remain concealed, do nothing else to draw attention to our presence. I require her kept secreted, don't want questions about her or…this." He had, or so he assumed, told the oaf this more than once. His plan was complicated enough without boneheaded dolts like him complicating matters further. "Where is he now?"

"Best you don't know, all's I'll say is he'll not come back to you or me. Even his mother won't know him. As for your lady, she'll be safe, so everyone's sweet ain't they?" Since then, neither had met, or spoken of the death, nor had the body caused them any concern. As his man had stated, it was as if the dead man had simply disappeared, becoming someone else's problem.

That had been then, this was now and was why he hurried away from the parade, he had a number of problems to overcome. One had required an urgent message sent to a small town outside Paris, to a man who owed him a great debt of honour. The other was to a man whose skills had been honed here and would be waiting for him within the Butts. One further problem remained to be resolved, that silly maid had still not delivered those letters. Obviously she had not fully comprehended his threats. If she considered them important, than he must also read what was written, and to whom they were meant. Only then would he know how to proceed. He would have to emphasise his position more forcefully, convince her to do as he commanded, or suffer the consequences of ignoring him.

For now he had to attend a meeting, he had evil of his own in mind, it was why he hurried, he was eager to speak of another death, one he would enjoy, savour and inflict himself. Stormouth, like he, was changing, never would he have contemplated such an action had not events overtaken him. Life was becoming complicated. With hundreds of new faces descending upon the town he needed this man's skills now more than ever. His problem was, one of culpability, if he was caught he would be hanged for sure, but to achieve what he desired, murder had become a risk worth taking.

The plot was discussed and sealed not within the genteel surroundings of the town hall or coffee shop, but in a dark dank alleyway, beneath a hastily built stairway. It wasn't ideal, but was adequate, no one would hear or disturb them, even so their discussion was conducted in whispers and the bag of coins changed hands furtively. Two men, as opposed to each other's way of life as fire was to water, had reached an understanding

"Very fair, and that is all you want?"

"It is, I assume you saw their arrival?"

"I did, pretty ain't they?" The man tossed the small leather pouch, feeling its weight. Trust was all among thieves, if the amount was light, his patron would know about it one dark night with a knife to his throat.

"I need a uniform, clean, no holes, is that within your capabilities?" Why the merchant needed a uniform, was never asked, simply accepted.

"It can be done, though it will take time. Sure as night follows day, the lobsters will be kept in camp. Only when they are allowed out to discover the delights of the town will I have the chance. Be patient, you'll have it eventually."

"Fair enough, but do it as soon as possible, more importantly, do it quietly. I don't want the army scouring the town for a soldier's killer, nothing must come back to me, understand?"

He waited while the instructions sank into the man's less than intelligent brain. Simple instructions were all he understood; who to kill, when to kill and what it was worth. Eventually, he knuckled his forehead in thanks, turned to leave but was stopped abruptly. His employer grasped his forearm firmly; the strength of the seemingly mild mannered businessman was as strong as any man that worked the docks. Urgently he hissed,

"Remain vigilant. I cannot be discovered ...not yet."

* * *

Sir Percival Fitzwilliam had thoroughly enjoyed his day. He had stood upon the town hall steps, alongside his influential new friends and beamed in undisguised pride. His men had been immaculate, every inch the perfect soldier, clean, well-presented and impeccably led. The people had cheered and sang as his men had marched through. Women had thrown garlands of flowers and fated them as conquering heroes. However, he was also aware that troops were scum, the very worst this country bred, every one of them drunken louts. His own militia, hopefully were not so infected, but the 3rd had been bloodied and knew the ways of avoiding punishment. Beneath the joy and excitement, gifts would have been passed. Wine, the bane of the army, would be secreted in backpacks and despite his officers best efforts half the force seen on parade would be incapable. He would speak with Maitland, demand a search be made and any bottles found be confiscated.

"Search away, colonel." Maitland agreed readily when the question was presented. He knew far better than Fitzwilliam that his regiment would be well versed in concealment and subterfuge. A few bottles would be recovered, his officers would drink well for a day, but most would go undiscovered. It was this respect which existed within the regular troops which differentiated them from the militia.

The irregulars were, in essence, an under-trained, undisciplined rabble, whose loyalty came through fear of what their landlord, Fitzwilliam, could do to their families and the harshness of discipline he enforced via the lash which he used without hesitation. Maitland's troops had something else, they had discipline, knew how to obey orders, but also they relied and trusted each other. Of course they drank, but mostly they stayed just within the rules. It was that loyalty which had stopped the note from being discarded and why Maitland read what it said.

"Well, there's a to do and no mistake, what do you make of it Herbert?" Maitland had read the note three times since its delivery it, and still found the content staggering.

"It does seem a strange request, but one that fits with your orders, sir. If I may be so bold to suggest, you do as it requests. Then, at least if it is a sham, you have done all you were asked to do."

"You're right, of course…very well, summon Ensign Mathews…serves two purposes, gets him away from Fitzwilliam and gives him a real job"

"He will enjoy that, he's very keen and bright," Wright added.

"Is he, by God? Doubt Fitzwilliam liked that. Keenness and intelligence are attributes that he would never understand. Very well, arrange it, but inform him he is to keep out of trouble."

"I will inform him of your orders. However, are you aware that his father is eminent, very eminent? Has the ear of prominent people. He could be a valuable asset to the regiment."

"Could he…he endears himself to me with each revelation. Very well, instruct our young gentleman of what he must do. Meanwhile, I will draft a report."

Drawing ink and paper towards him, he began scribbling. By the time Wright reappeared with the young man, he had his dispatch ready.

"I am entrusting you with this document, Mathews. You are to deliver it personally, ignore any distraction until you have done so. Major Wright informs me you are an exceptional horseman, those skills will be tested. Take this dispatch and ride like the winds, but guard it with your very life…understand? Upon arrival at the Horse Guards you are to seek out Brigade Major Fisher. You will wait as long as it takes and ignore any request to deliver this elsewhere. You will hand this to him and no one else, not even the King himself, understand? If anyone deems to interfere this should facilitate entry, you recognise the seal I assume?"

Mathews nodded in eager anticipation, while Maitland was torn between what he must do and how to achieve it. He was placing his trust upon a youth he disliked and one who had barely discovered the use of a blade, the down still visible upon his chin. He could have sent Wright, his experience would have convinced them easily, but Wright was needed here. Needs must and Mathews was expendable; finally contact had been made and upon those instructions the Horse Guards had to be informed.

"I do, sir." A royal cipher was easily distinguished. Mathews straightened his back further, standing a little prouder, if he wondered why he had been given such strange instructions, he did not show it.

"Very well, once you have delivered this to the General's hand you will place yourself at his disposal. You will obey any instruction or order that he may issue, no matter how strange they may seem. Any questions?"

"None at all, sir"

"Then go and may God guide you and give your horse wings." Mathews saluted, and in a whirl of sword and gold braid, left to begin his mission. With his departure the tent seemed quieter, Maitland and Wright stared at the tent flap for a few moments, until the colonel stated quietly,

"I trust he will be in time. Lives are at stake, Herbert. I do so hope we are not the instigators of some heinous crime."

"Time is not our prime concern, surely? The message suggests that nothing will happen until the King's birthday, which gives us…"

"Three months…" Maitland interrupted. "Three months in which events can change in the wink of an eye. I dislike secrets Herbert, I find such matters dishonourable. Imagine if you will what could occur, our friend might be discovered, their identity and purpose revealed, then how would I be expected to react? I will tell you, we would be expected to perform a miracle. We now hold this emissary's life in our hands, upon our decisions rests success or failure. I foresee grave concerns and problems before this episode is completed, that is why as of now and until we are done, half the regiment will be kept on standby, see to it and pray we are in time."

Chapter Thirty Nine

"Damn your hides! I will flog the next man to fail. Do you hear? Flogged!" Sir Percival's annoyance was palatable. Eager to show the town how good his men were, he had paraded them every day but grew annoyed at their inefficiencies "I'll flay Styles alive if he can't master the simple art of walking in step."

"Oh dear, should we lend our assistance, sir?" Maitland and Wright stood to one side as the militia finally fired a ragged volley. Maitland turned as a nervous cry sounded from a group of ladies gathered around a carriage. To such female attention the militia appeared competent enough. Though in truth, those who cried out in wonderment at the copious noise and smoke came, not to see what his men could do rather to seek potential husbands among Sir Percival's officers.

"We should not, sir. Damned impolite to detract anyone from their enjoyment, and our friend there appears to be enjoying himself immensely." They watched and smiled as Sir Percival harried his officers mercilessly, ordering them to execute some elaborate manoeuvre to which his men were totally unsuited to perform.

"I feel a sense of sadness, I mean, look at them." Wright gestured towards the irregulars as, harassed by their sergeants, who in turn were harried by their officers, trudged back into line. "Give them the proper leadership and some adequate training and they could be more than capable of holding their own in any line. Instead they get worse, not better."

"Could not agree more, Herbert. They are but a half trained rabble who will falter in their first encounter with an enemy. It is beyond comprehension as to how our eminent colonel convinced anyone he was capable of leading troops." Both men turned towards Fitzwilliam, who sat upon his horse preening to his audience. The question as to Sir Percival's suitability had been raised more than once, as had the Horse Guards reasoning for sending him to join the Buffs. The answer still eluded them but they smiled graciously and whispered their well-rehearsed response as Sir Percival nodded in their direction.

"Ours is not to question, simply to do as ordered."

"What makes a man so willing to waste such an exorbitant amount of money on this…folly of a regiment?" Maitland asked.

"Pride, breeding. He considers it his destiny, sir. Men like Sir Percival, are born to lead."

"If that be so, then I despair, Herbert. Indeed, I do." Maitland knew how to command, had learnt his craft through experience not from books. More importantly, he had met officers like Sir Percival, arrogant fools who would kill more of his own than the enemy ever would. Pity was while their men died, they invariably survived, garnering favours until eventually gaining high office. "He will destroy them, Herbert, which is grossly unfair for they deserve better. But I am hamstrung, until the fool is seen to be idiotic, we cannot do a thing. We must pray that when that time comes, we are not too late."

His words earned a nod of approval from his adjutant. Maitland admired good officers and detested any who fell short of his standards. Fitzwilliam was such a man, a total incompetent, and that was why Maitland despised him. It was to his credit that, despite ample opportunity to rebuke and revile the man, he and Sir Percival had clashed but once. Fitzwilliam had demanded that the 3rd participate in some ridiculous posturing. Such was his audacity that Maitland had flown into a rage, which in turn had produced a strongly worded reminder that Militia officers would never command regular troops or their officers, and that he should look to his own command before interesting himself in matters that did not concern him.

Suitably chastised, Fitzwilliam had vented his spleen on his troops, purging his anger by constant practice of every manoeuvre he could think of, including some he took from a book of field craft written by some unknown author from the colonies. Such idiotic behaviour made troops wary of those who commanded them. It made the men sullen and ill-tempered, made them think of home and what they had left behind, made them suitable to abscond, to run or worse mutiny. Regular regiments knew what was expected of them, while some officers mistrusted and perhaps feared those they commanded, there was trust of sorts. They may be ordered to perform acts which at times appeared strange, but they remained silent and did what was required while doing just enough to avoid conflict from their officers. The militia was different, essentially tricked out civilians; they strove to find new ways to avoid all but the essential parts of their duties. Trouble makers mainly, who told anyone who asked they were present because of loyalty to their colonel and the cause. An obvious lie, Wright saw it in their faces; the insolence, the desire to be rid of their colonel and everything he stood for.

*

Peterson's Field, therefore, was essentially two differing camps, where each group eyed the other with suspicion. That tension grew during darkness, when apart from the night guard, the men were stood down. Confined to their tented areas, they spoke about dissatisfaction, about returning home, about mutiny. It was those treacherous thoughts that Maitland needed to hear, which was why his men were encouraged to mix with the militia, to share their wine and stories. Reluctantly, among the damp washing which hung from tent ropes, amid the cooking fire smoke which drifted across the field on a light breeze, two regiments shared their thoughts.

"Animals, sir, nothing more nothing less, not a one have a good word to say about anything. Most are here simply because they were told to be, most would run given half the chance," Patrickson reported next morning.

"Sir Percival?" Wright questioned.

"Aye, sir. When he formed his regiment, he sent word to all his tenants, told them any man that didn't join would find themselves and their kin on the street. From what's being said it's fear of him that keeps them 'ere and nothing else."Dismissing Patrickson, Maitland said thoughtfully,

"Trouble, that's what we have on our hands, trouble. I will not have it Herbert, not among my regiment. Keep a close eye on our lads if…no, when trouble begins I require it stopped. Inform the officers of our concerns. My God, I would gladly shoot the first mutineer myself."

Wright believed him, discipline was the age old problem. Mutiny was controlled by luck more than anything else, but when the infection surged it was a devil to eradicate. Maitland didn't need it to rear its ugly head, not around his men.

"Is this what the Horse Guard fear, the reason we have been placed in this odious position? Are we to quell any thought of rebellion before its poison spreads and destroys from within? Ironic if that be true." Maitland saw his companions look of bewilderment and added. "Fact is, Herbert, their Lordships have always assumed it would be the Irish who would be our undoing. Can we be so surprised when, we take them from their bogs and hovels, feed and train them, then send them back to quash their countrymen? My God, half the bloody army is Irish; if they rose in insurrection, we could be in the mire and no mistake."

* * *

Two soldiers, contemplating the uncertainties of an unsettled world was, in the context of the town, totally normal. Stormouth had shaken off the despair of a bleak winter and now basked beneath the warmth of early spring sunshine. The town was renewing itself; birds sang in the trees, flowers bloomed in the hedgerows, more importantly, it was once again at work. Gentlemen did business as if nothing had occurred, they promenaded between coffee and financial house, hurried to sell that last ounce of goods before they were beaten to a better price. Ships arrived and disgorged their goods into the safe keeping of the various warehouses along south quay. Normality resumed, for most, but not for all. For some, the town would never be the same again, Stormouth had been cossetted from the evils of what happened outside their town, that was about to change.

Those of influence and status saw the New Year as an opportunity. Abigail Wood and her indiscretions were consigned to history, she was but a distant memory, nor was anyone concerned about what happened deep within the 'Butts'. Sir Percival, it seemed, found a town that offered him all he desired. He dined at the squire's table while enjoying the pleasures Lady Caroline afforded to him. Wynford House had witnessed such assignations before, and would no doubt again, but Sir Percival appeared unworried about consequence. Or indeed did his officers who, taking their lead from their colonel wined, dined and romanced the eligible ladies. They used their wealth and positions to avoid the regular army, but such wealth was a lure to wealthy merchants. It wasn't long before liaisons were forged and dowries were being discussed.

Reverend Bayles remained as dangerous as ever, continuing to take innocent young girls to bed. Despite the murder of her father, Ruby had served him well. Even that night when her father had died, her distress had made her exciting. Reticent to perform, he had explained the consequences should she refuse to perform. Her tears had made him shake her vigorously and restrain her. Her hysteria had invigorated him, able to take her more than once, but, in the aftermath he knew he had lost her. He felt slighted, angry, but the devil had been contained, there were others he could influence. After all, what could she do? Speak out, decry him? Who would believe her, a girl whose only evidence was buried beneath the hag, Mother Cox? Poignant that finally that old witch would share eternity with a man at last. But Ruby had changed, she no longer feared him, instead, he sensed she now despised him and wished him dead. Perhaps she had learnt the meaning of revenge? If so a new recruit was demanded before the silly bitch did something stupid. He had a number of candidates to choose from but one, pleased him greatly. One such girl had grown into womanhood and was now ripe for plucking. His future bed partner was, but one problem he faced, his main concern, his overwhelming problem was the Wood brothers and they would need careful manipulation if he were to succeed in wresting control from them.

He had a plan, a subtle devious idea, but it would require the assistance of a man he despised and detested, Turnbottle. It grieved him to contemplate asking the swine to help especially after his comments during council but he was best placed to help and he did have certain knowledge which, if the need arose he could use against the pious merchant. *I shall use his own gullibility against him, speak of what might occur should the Wood brood destroy the company. Threaten him with the spectre of bankruptcy and ruination for him and his fellow merchants. That will make him consider my request. But I need to speak to him alone and in secret.* He had the perfect place for such a meeting, and wrote an invitation there and then. Turnbottle had two options, he was sure he would choose wisely.

As for his other concern, there was still no word of the trollop. No body had been found, nor had anyone appeared demanding answers to her disappearance. More importantly no proclamation had arrived demanding he appear before any sort of court, in fact, it was eerily silent. To be sure though, he had sent word to the priest at Barminster, an innocuous message asking after a family that lived there. Like everything else, no mention of her had been forthcoming. It was as if Abigail Wood had been expunged forever. With no hint of a hue and cry, he felt able to relax, safe in the knowledge that his secrets remained just that, secret. With a sense of serenity and composure that came from the security of control, his group began meeting again, albeit with more prudence. Their numbers were at first small, the group subdued. Without Joseph and other notable patrons, they had indulged in nothing more than a few hands of cards and some fine Claret. The next had improved and the third had been as if nothing untoward had ever occurred. The entertainment had been….fresh, young and he had indulged as had they all. Oh yes, as far as Edward Bayles was concerned, life once more was good and the fine things in life were his again.

As for Benjamin Turnbottle, he appeared more concerned with goods arriving than what had happened since Joseph Wood had passed away. Though, he watched the Wood brothers closely and marveled at their inaptitude. Bayles would have been surprised to learn the merchant actually admired the cleric in a strange, obtuse way, perhaps in differing times they might have proved worthy business partners, but at this moment in time he was content in the way his business grew. Unimpeded by Joseph Wood's interference, he and the other merchants were at last free to do what they had always wanted. The sons would remain unable to fill their father's shoes, while with Abigail hidden he still retained the means of bringing them down whenever he desired. If he succeeded in placing her back upon the throne, he would at last be able to examine the ledgers and learn firsthand what that family knew and did. *Far easier to learn what I want legally than creeping around like a thief in the night. But what to do with her once her usefulness was complete? Would he be able to order her demise? Oh yes after everything I have endured one more death was little to worry about.* .

Maybe all concerned should have been far more worried. Abigail was very much alive and planning her revenge. Always in the company of at least

Mary-Ann, she was leaving the house more frequently. Occasionally, Maggie joined them, and when she did, Abigail was happier than she had ever been. Her disguise, so good even her mother would have not recognised her, allowed three friends to finally enjoy the freedom of a town that had disowned her. Gone was the delicate waif-like woman who had sat in the snow. Now, her face and hands were blackened, and she smelt as everyone else. Her figure, enlarged by the child almost ready for birth, meant she shuffled through the alleyways, just another wretch with little money and even less hope. Appearances, though, were deceptive, beneath her disguise the heart of a lion beat strongly. Those who had hurt her, would, in turn, be hurt. Once the child was born, she would make her way to her father and bring the forces of law down upon them. That was her plan, but that changed when like a malevolent ghost a ship arrived in harbour. Not some small coaster but a goliath, a beast of war whose gun ports, for the moment remained closed, but pointed towards the town.

Chapter Forty

Curiosity drew them to the quayside. The town came to stare in awe at the stranger within their midst. A warship, one of England's feared wooden-walled gun platforms glistened in the morning sun's glow, and sat majestically at anchor on a gentle sea. While around it, and within its protection, were three less ornate merchant ships. England's superiority at sea, sat within touching distance of Stormouth and its people.

Distance hid much, no one smelt the stench of rot, mildew, decay and dampness, not to mention the putrid odour of three hundred and fifty souls crammed within its hull, which mercifully the morning breeze carried away. That noxious odour, clung to the ship, pervaded every inch but was contained, only evident to anyone venturing too close like the occupants of the long boat which left the quayside. It went unnoticed for some time, before finally those on shore saw it heading towards the warship. Few who watched knew how those intrepid visitors would suffer as they approached the 'Kentsman'

"My God," one gasped from behind a rolled up kerchief, as his nose wrinkled in protest.

"I fear it will only get worse," his companion uttered.

"Pray God, I am indebted to my parents for choosing the army for me."

"She does suffer from noxiousness, I fear. She's long overdue for a refit but needs must, so we persevere." The speaker was a midshipman, a youth, not yet into his teens, yet entrusted, with this, his first command. "Please take care as you rise, would hate for you to get drenched with...well suffice to say it would not be too pleasant." He nodded towards a plume of water that spilled from the ship's side, not three feet from the entry ladder.

"Hell's teeth, sir, but that's a climb," Maitland stated, staring upward at the wooden hull. It was precarious to say the least, made worse by the natural bulge of the ship's side.

"We could winch you aboard, sir. We have a device which allows the less able to board...however, I advise against it."

"Why?" the colonel asked haughtily.

"Not dignified, sir, if you gets my drift. Men will think you less than able if they see you using what we usually keep for women and the like."

"Thank you for the advice. We will climb." Maitland had no intention of showing his inabilities. Holding the side of the wildly pitching boat, he grabbed hold of the lower step and stepped into the unknown. He hated ships and sailors, thought them a drain on England's resources. He was often heard remonstrating that the navy did little but waste the King's money. Money which could be better spent on more soldiers, better equipment, and modern warfare methods. He would extol the virtue of anything new, would exclaim joyfully at any new weapon, *By God, sir, that scares me; let alone what it will do to our enemies.* However, we must utilize anything that gives us an advantage. The army, not the navy, will defeat the King's enemies, as they have done for as long as can be remembered. Mark my words ships cannot take land held by the French, ships cannot storm a breech, nor charge a square. The King's navy will rot on blockade duty, or will be confined to harbour being repaired. Why His Majesty wastes so much on them I cannot fathom, but he does, and we, the common soldier, suffer from lack of essential supplies. However, we must maintain a sense of decorum, and not upset our brave sailors. After all, while they sleep safe and sound in their confined worlds, we have the stars to keep us safe and not much else. His mood, this day, hadn't been helped by being roused from his bed so early, long before most sane men were awake. While the captain of this hulk slept, he and Wright had been summoned like insignificant pupils to a headmaster, an analogy which Colonel Maitland disliked as it brought back unpleasant memories.

"God save us if this is all we have left," Maitland whispered, as the boat bumped against the ship's side, threatening to upset his climb.

"Sorry, sir, did you say something?" Wright asked mischievously. He knew that despite his commander's bravery, Maitland suffered from the "mal-de-mere" and that he would be bilious until they were back upon terra firma. Nor would the smell assist his disposition. Close to, the very fabric of the ship appeared to be impregnated, the stench, like a miasma, oozed from its wood, to hang like a shroud about the ship, like the smell of death.

"Just surmising, Major, just surmising," Maitland replied. He would keep his thoughts to himself, for he had met the captain of this 'Armada' and knew Stilwell, thought only the Navy would finish England's enemies. Though if so these ships would need to work damned hard. England was perilously close to being overwhelmed, they fought the French across the globe, and now the treacherous scum who called themselves colonialists were becoming bolder. It was a worsening situation. Open warfare with them was becoming more likely as they sought to befriend France. Should that occur, Maitland doubted if England's armies and navy combined would be able to halt them from supplying the rebels with what they desired?

"Saints preserve us," Maitland whispered, as he approached the final few feet of his climb. Perspiring with exertion, he had not envisaged such application when this madness had been devised in London. Only he, Wright and Captain Stilwell knew that these ships were the final part of an intricate plan. *I trust he has been properly appraised as to what we have to do,* he thought, as the curve of the hull made the last few feet easier. Finally his head appeared above the deck. Relieved that his journey was all but concluded, he whispered a silent prayer. *Trust in God and all will be well.*

"God had better be on our side..." he whispered, though that was not a forgone conclusion. If all went well they would succeed without a shot being fired, though he would not hesitate to destroy anyone who stood against them no matter who they were.

"Welcome aboard, gentlemen." The naval officer doffed his hat in salute, but made no move to assist the colonel onto the deck. Maitland stepped from ladder to deck and returned the salute while fighting an impulse to gag. The noxious odours were almost thick enough to cut with a sword. Was it any wonder when beneath the main mast was a byre containing sheep, goats and a scraggly cow?

"Ah, you see them, a capital idea, what. We enjoy fresh milk daily, and then when the time is right a quick flick of a knife and we dine on fresh meat." The officer beamed with delight as he saw their bewilderment. This was what Maitland detested, the navy's supercilious attitude, cooped up inside these wooden walls men became impervious to what was happening in the wider world. Animals in the army were perfectly acceptable, but here, where their waste could only flow down into the bowels of the ship, it was ridiculous. Yet, despite the dismal appearance of crew and officers, and the stench, His Majesty's ship 'Kentsman' had to be relied upon to do what was asked.

"Capital, indeed," Maitland replied in feigned admiration. "We are expected, I believe?"

"Of course, please, follow me and I will take you to the captain, he is waiting in his cabin." The two men followed as he led them to a doorway below where the huge oak wheel stood.

"How many guns do you have?" Wright enquired.

"Seventy five, sir, we are but fourth rated, but are more than capable of looking after ourselves. The cannon are hidden away at present, but when needed they can be wheeled out and manned by men who are more than capable of destroying an enemy, quicker than they could harm this ship."

Wright smiled. It was this sense of invincibility which the navy had bred into their men over many years. They would need that self-confidence if they were to survive any future conflict.

"Do mind your heads, gentlemen," the youth stated, touching the low beam. "She was not designed for anyone taller than a midget." Hurrying forward, the officer eventually stopped before a door and knocked.

"Come!" a bullish voice demanded from within.

"Your guests, sir," the officer stated, after opening the door and stepping aside to allow entry. The room was huge, taking up the width of the ship. The rear wall was comprised entirely of glazed windows which offered a spectacular view of Stormouth. "Gentlemen, may I name Captain Stilwell, of His Majesty's Ship, 'Kentsman'."

"Welcome, gentlemen." The man unerringly mirrored his voice, large necked but not large in stature. Even so, his presence filled the room. "Maitland, pleasure to meet you again." He stated, stepping forward.

"Your servant, sir," Maitland could be gracious when the need arose now, seemed appropriate. Removing his hat, he bowed low and elegantly.

"Good, good, but please, do refrain from such earnestness…and you are, sir?"

"My apologies, may I name Major Herbert Wright, my adjutant and privy to our orders," Maitland said, introducing his companion.

"Good, at least we do not have to waste time explaining everything then." Stilwell indicated to chairs placed around a large mahogany table.The three men sat. "I have arranged a small breakfast, if that is acceptable? I fear it is a little too early for anything stronger than tea but…if you desire." Both soldiers heard the inference and took note, accepting the tea graciously. As he waited, Wright stared at his surroundings in awe. The cabin was sumptuous, but practical, an indictment of the man's personality, masculine, yet subtle, without any feminine frivolities or influences. Apart from the gentle sway, the creaks, groans, and slap of water against the timber sides, and of course the view, they could have been in a gentleman's study. Though, not many gentlemen would associate their studies with the final oddities that marked this as a warship. For, lashed to the deck and beams with ropes were two huge cannon. Belligerent weapons that were cold and silent now, but which when in use would fill this space with noise and smoke. The soldier within him knew the power of such devices, but he wondered how the captain lived with such things. Stilwell saw Wright's bemused expression and asked, "Your first time aboard a warship, Major?"

"First time in such a cabin, sir, I did not expect…" He looked at the cannon.

"Ahh, you wonder about my friends, Eliza and Emma." Stilwell sat back and smiled. "They and their sisters are our reason for existing; we are naught but for their presence. When the need arises I am forced to pander to their whims, they force me from my abode, and these gallant ladies takeover." Stilwell chuckled at Wright's incomprehension. "Allow me to explain, Major. Before we join in battle, all this disappears." He waved an arm to indicate his furniture. "Everything is either hoisted among the rigging, put into boats and trailed behind us, or stored in the holds. We strip for action; bulkheads, furniture, this table, my books, everything in fact, apart from my bed, is removed and this cabin becomes part of the fighting gun deck."

"Where do you go, sir?" Wright asked perplexed but politely.

"The quarterdeck, Major, I am expected to fight the ship in full view of my crew and enemy alike, to be seen and give what guidance is deemed necessary. In truth, once battle is joined I am no longer needed, the knaves know what to do without me hindering them. I simply become a figure head, a target for enemy snipers. By the time we are within cannon range, the gunners become the saviours of the ship."

"I think you do yourself an injustice, sir, for without their captain what would become of them if orders were needed?" Wright asked.

"Most kind, sir, but my officers know what to do without being chivvied by me, and should they all die, then the petty officers take over, and if we all die, I trust some lowly powder monkey will see sense and blow the magazine before the ship is taken." Stilwell paused and pondered that last statement. The reason he had accepted this assignment was because rebels had dared to attack this ship. He had almost lost a King's ship and he desired that memory erased. "Now, to business gentlemen, I assume those involved are still unaware of our actions, and that nothing has changed?"

"It is as before, though, I sent a message recently to the Horse Guards. As yet, I have not received a reply. I hoped you might bring further instructions," Maitland stated. If he expected confirmation, the captain's reaction was surprising. Stilwell said nothing, but rose, walked to the stern windows and looked towards the town.

"Instructions…oh yes, I have instructions, though, I find it difficult to believe such things." Stilwell never turned, hardly moved. All they saw was a slight twitch of the fingers, where the captain clasped his hands together. Maitland glanced at Wright and grimaced.

Unbeknown to the soldiers, Stilwell was recalling the meeting he had attended at the Admiralty. He had stood before the board of admirals, beneath the paintings of past battles and shivered in anticipation and trepidation. The room was dominated by a huge granite and marble fireplace above which was an engraved map of the world. Occasionally a 'tick' could be heard from a machine, which attached to a weather vane atop the roof, indicated the wind direction. That map, along with the instrument, allowed the admirals to imagine they were in control of their ships even though they were miles from the fleet.

Summoned upon the same day as Maitland, Stilwell had stood before fourteen aging Admirals and listened in horror, as a tale of depravity and treason was revealed. *Why me?* He had thought as his task was laid before him. It wasn't for him, a mere captain to question these venerated men, but he hadn't liked what he heard.

"A nest of vipers,"An admiral of the red had stated. "We have to act, or lose everything if this insidiousness succeeds. One single ember might, if not doused, flare into life and spread. If it does, nowhere will be safe. We will be so consumed; our forces will be spread thin, offering the French and Spanish a chance to come out and join. Then we will be humbugged….not enough ships, can't be everywhere…My God that is a frightening thought. We could suffer badly. Imagine for a moment that we should lose the Indies? No…well consider it, sir. It might happen if the French time their assault correctly. Which is why you must succeed, it has to be stopped. You hear, sir? You and this Maitland fellow must stop it afore this ember bursts into a conflagration which we will never extinguish. You will proceed to that place, and aid Maitland in eradicating this afore it takes holds do you hear eradicate it sir permanently."

Could it be true? Could such events really be occurring, if so it was more than possible that this poison could spread to Plymouth, Portsmouth, or any other town that rested beneath the care and diligence of their King? But like others he wasn't accustomed to the ways of was conducted by spies behind a veil of darkness. He rarely fought alone but in company alongside great floating walls of wood. It was then, he had realised, the meeting wasn't normal in anyway.

"Your old command is at Deptford awaiting dismantling, go there, bring her back into service, and cut out this canker before it can begin."

Go to Deptford, save a ship, and rid the country of a disease. During his carriage journey across London, Stilwell had wondered if they also expected him to part the Red Sea again. To assume command of the 'Kentsman' once again would be a joy so long as she was capable of saving. Earmarked for destruction, he could already be too late, if so this plan would die before it had lived.

Thankfully Deptford was not associated with speed, despite the ship being stripped of cannon, top masts, and rigging, she was still his ship. True she looked, like an aging aunt who, far too old for the ball, desired to attend one last time no matter what she looked like. Fortunately, the ship had not been beached, she was still afloat. He had a matter of weeks to get her back into service, not nearly enough time. It might take that long just to negotiate with the dockyard hierarchy. Corruption was the bane of the navy; stores were either delayed or disappeared and many a captain had been forced to smooth the actions of civilian administrators from their own purse. He was loathed to use bribes to oil the wheels, the dockyards were financed by the crown, the ships belonged to the crown, and he was a crown servant. Why, should he pay for what he was due?

Such principles were all well and good, but did not get their Lordship's orders carried out, only coinage did that. To complete his task he would have to pay, or so he thought. The admiralty must have wanted this to be done for within hours of arriving Marines from the local barracks arrived to seal the 'Kentsman' from the rest of the facility. By the following morning, a crew arrived instilling life into her once again. By week's end she was fully manned, stored, rigged and armed. Best of all, not once did he have to draw upon his own money. The Admiralty had used every ounce of its considerable muscle and persuasion to ease his task. Never before had he seen anything like it. His officers, men he knew and trusted, were back in command. Then, one early morning, a messenger had arrived with his final orders. He had stood in this very cabin and realised why so much effort had been put into getting his ship back into service, time was running out.

Finally aware he had been lost in thought, Captain Stilwell turned and looked at those, who along with himself, were charged with a terrible duty. For the next few minutes, he explained what he had been told, what his instructions were, and what the Admiralty expected. Only when he had finished did he ask,

"I assume my orders are comparable to what you were told?" Maitland nodded in agreement. "Then we have to assume that message you sent, that small piece of paper, will no doubt set the cat among the pigeons and stir the Horse Guards into action. Until someone orders differently I suggest we act independently as per our last instructions. Can't do harm by doing that can we gentlemen?"

"I concur Captain. Not many in London can act swiftly or courageously. Until they do, I suggest we play a little game, play them at their own game. I shall seek your guidance and thoughts." Maitland said calmly.

"A game? Nothing to adventurous I trust?" Stilwell questioned. He had been told to contain the situation, extradite the agent but above all, he was to apprehend and deal with those that wished to do damage to England.

"Not at all sir, besides we know...no, we suspect nothing will occur until after the tomfoolery Sir Percival has organised for the 4th. Why not wait, play along with their evilness and do as they wish?"

"Are you suggesting..." Stilwell stared aghast at the colonel, unable to believe he recommended such a course of action.

"Why not, they are contained; they cannot harm us, why not do what Sir Percival wants? We can prepare to transport him and his men, while putting them through their paces. We bide our time until our man reveals himself. Perchance, if we act unconcerned, they will make their own mistakes and we will have little to do."

"It might work," Stilwell mused, not entirely convinced.

"Be hell to pay if we fail, and what of the agent? How do we orchestrate his escape when we do not know who we are dealing with?" Wright conceded.

"Not my concern. He chose to work secretly; we must assume he will be well versed in survival. We must also assume he has put in place a means of escape. All we need do is be ready to facilitate him, when he deems it necessary," Stilwell answered. "Damn secrets, will be the death of us all in the end."

"If he is a man," Wright added, noticing the looks of horror that passed between the senior officers. Eager to press his point he continued, "I mean, we don't know, do we? He could literally be any one in Stormouth or the neighbouring villages. Might even be one of our own men."

"Thank you for your observations, Herbert. If we believe your theory, then it could just as easily be you, could it not?" Maitland added sarcastically.

"Should I send for the marine's colonel and arrest your major?" Stilwell added helpfully.

"No, I do not think that will be necessary," Maitland smiled in reply; a moment of hilarity did much to calm a tense situation. But Wright had illuminated a problem. "Gentlemen, in all probability he ...or she, will have to orchestrate his own escape. Unless he is fortuitous in his timing, I fear we will be far too busy with other matters."

"I assume Sir Percival isn't to be privy to any of this?" Stilwell asked.

"Not if I have anything to do with it, he will not," Maitland stated forcefully. Was it providence, coincidence, or pure bad luck, but no sooner had the words been uttered than there was a knock at the door.

"Come." Stilwell commanded. The same officer who had escorted Maitland to the cabin entered, touched his cap in salute, and said

"Gig coming alongside, sir, four passengers, all militia officers, they ask permission to come aboard."

"Sir Percival, no doubt? Well gentlemen, what's it to be?" Stilwell smiled "Come, come, do I grant his request or tell my men to repel borders?"

"Oh, what a desirable thought," Maitland mused. "If only we could rid ourselves of the man."

"As bad as that, aye...?" Stilwell chuckled. After hearing so much of the man, he was looking forward to meeting him personally. For no other reason than to see for himself why he was deemed such a menace to the nation. "However, gentlemen, protocol demands that I have no alternative. Permission granted, allow them to board and show them through

Chapter Forty One

Stilwell watched in annoyance as Sir Percival Fitzwilliam, without seeking his host's permission, poured himself another glass of brandy. He had foisted himself upon their hospitality, took what he deemed his to take, and now appeared set upon regaling them of his exploits.

"Cost a veritable fortune to equip and train. Keen though, very keen," Fitzwilliam stated then belched loudly. "Got a piss pot handy sir?"

"My personal toilette is through that door sir feel obliged to use it."

"My thanks sir. Wynford house has pots in every room don't you know, secreted in tiny cupboards for use at any time. The ladies have been known to use them while dancing, versatile creatures, and so comely."

Maitland groaned silently, if he had expected dignity and respect from this fool of a colonel, he had been sorely mistaken. Throughout their meal, they had been told how he would deal with the colonial problem and what was wrong with the present strategy. Stilwell, also appeared to tire of the man who appeared unwilling to leave.

Within an hour, Stilwell would have willingly tossed the popinjay overboard, four hours after boarding, the Captain would willingly have throttled him himself. Though, in truth, both admired him for raising a regiment. It was how he used them that worried the two professional men

"Nice view Stilwell, straight down into the sea, handy for unwanted guest what!"

"One should always be prepared Colonel."

"Quite right, always telling my men that, but will they listen, will they hell."

"I can imagine," Maitland had begrudgingly agreed. No matter how he felt about the man, he admired his enterprise. It was no mean feat to raise a regiment, albeit militia, nor did it come cheap. Like him or not, that wealth must have been stretched to the limits with such a venture. The Horse Guards would have done nothing to assist his enterprise, but would have accepted an extra regiment with gratitude. However, his opinion of the man altered not one iota. Fitzwilliam was a dangerous fool who used guile and pleasantries to achieve his aims. If that failed, his wealth was there to assist him.

"Money well spent if we assist in restoring calm within that troubled land," Fitzwilliam continued, pausing only briefly to fill his glass from the captain's decanter.

"Indeed, sir," Stilwell's annoyance at the man's lack of respect for his position was almost palatable. He was in his opinion, a pig, a disgrace, a guttersnipe, who lacked any respect, or indeed gentlemanly manners. Without seeking permission, he took what he wanted and damned the consequences.

However, to those gullible enough not to see him for what he was, he appeared amiable and charming, willing to using his wealth for the good of England. Why then had someone seen through his deception, had something been overheard, were spies involved, watching listening? It appeared conceivable because someone had decided that Sir Percival Fitzwilliam must be stopped at all costs. That was why, both Maitland and Stilwell wanted the man gone, they had much to discuss and could not do so with him sitting between them. Even when Stilwell had ordered his table laid for dinner, Fitzwilliam had failed to take the hint, instead he assumed the invitation extended to him and sat, apparently untroubled, regaling them with stories of his associates and conquests. If only half were true then the man had rodgered his way through half of London society. Perhaps some cuckolded husband was the reason he sought safety in the colonies. If so he played a dangerous game, one that could see him hanged in due course. With dinner completed and further wine bottles opened, Sir Percival asked,

"I assume you have been to the colonies, Captain?"

"I have, sir, was there in May 68, and again in 70. The stench of rebellion and treachery was worse then. You could smell the rebels, sense them spreading their poison."

"So you witnessed the troubles?" Fitzwilliam asked.

"Saw them, heard them and hated them. Tempted to send the Marines ashore and finish them there and then, but orders is orders. We had no option but to stay on board and witness the abomination of King's troops being terrorised by nothing more than rabble." Stilwell paused, as he remembered the inability to act. His temper was aroused as it had been then but he forced himself to remain calm. "Had the men stood too all night. We manned the guns and prepared for anything even to repel borders, that's how bad it was. Some of the moored merchant men had the right idea, saw two up anchor and leave. No place to be when blood was raised like that, I can tell you. Nor did I expect what happened next." Stilwell was reluctant to continue, for their spy could be any seated around this table. Fitzwilliam included, though Stilwell knew his crime was far worse. The admiralty had issued him with a final word of warning before he had sailed. Their words returned to warn him of the soldier's potential to cause trouble.

"Remain vigilant, whatever occurs, whatever he attempts, not one of his scum are to be allowed to board. They are to be kept ashore no matter what they do." Yet he had allowed him on board without a finger being raised. Aware that his guests watched him, Stilwell continued,

"Never did I consider that the day would arrive when colonialists, people we call brothers, would take up arms against His Majesty's forces, but they did. In front of the Customs House, Bostonians, Englishmen, forced the guard to form line and fire. Injuries were inflicted, gentlemen, and the next day British soldiers were arrested. ARRESTED!" His voice rose in obvious anger. "Not only that, but then they were put on trial. I ask you, is the world not mad?"

"Mad, indeed," Maitland added. Glancing at Fitzwilliam he saw not a flicker of anger or guilt. If he felt aggrieved at such talk, he simply, listened, nodded and drank. In fact in that instance Maitland wondered if the man was capable of the crime he would be charged with he appeared so incapable of such treachery. Unperturbed, Sir Percival leant forward to light a cigar from a candle, puffed gently, then stated,

"Fear not sir, when I and my loyal men arrive we shall show these rebels how British troops fight, if that is what they want.

"Then King George has little to fear, Sir Percival." Stilwell smiled courteously. "In fact, we were discussing that very matter prior to your arrival. Perhaps now is a good time to make our preparations."

"Good as any," Fitzwilliam said eagerly.

"Of course, whatever we propose will need to be ratified by the other masters, for they have the last word on their own ships and their safety. But they should be amicable to whatever I suggest." Stilwell, like Maitland, had the ability to be punctilious when needed, though Fitzwilliam failed to see the hint of sarcasm, as without a pause, Stilwell added "Do please help yourselves to more wine while I explain what I have in mind."

* * *

By the time Stilwell had finished, he despised Fitzwilliam as much as Maitland did. The fool argued every idea, rejected and debated them to the point of distraction. His voice, droned on incessantly, each word, each new idea more absurd than the last. He ranted about punishment and what should be done to combat the rebels. Once, he had almost betrayed his true self, during a particularly vivacious bout of rhetoric, Fitzwilliam, had stated,

"We shall be forward thinking. I see my troops, not skulking in some garrison on guard duties, but seeking the rebels out. For we are of kindred spirits, we know their thinking, we are as one with our friends."

Having learnt to ignore the man as much as possible, as most of his ideas bordering upon lunacy, Maitland had almost missed the inference. Maybe it was the wine but Fitzwilliam had become lax, explaining to Stilwell how he would win any encounter. Finally as he paused for breath, Wright had casually asked,

"I must compliment you sir on your perception of the difficulties that face our armies. However if I comprehend correctly, your intentions are, to lead our entire continental contingent into the interior. Draw the rebels out and, attack them at their heart, destroying them in a fatal and defining engagement."

"I do sir, for that is how battles should be fought. These rebels are merchant's farmers, not soldiers. We shall end this stupidity in one attack, much as a surgeon removes a leg, swiftly, decisively and with courage." Fitzwilliam smiled, pleased that his superior intellect had been recognised. Maitland though waited, he knew Wright wasn't the sort to allow stupidity to go unchallenged. He had witnessed his Adjutants sarcasm numerous times before and he was about to unleash it now upon an unsuspecting Fitzwilliam. Taking his time to glance through the glazed stern windows, he began to speak in a measured, calculated, purposeful tone.

"Forgive my stupidity but I am concerned…as a mere clerk, I am ignorant of such things as military strategy…"

"I would be pleased to educate you in the art of warfare, Major." Fitzwilliam was blind to what was about to come, and had relaxed in his chair while those who understood waited with anticipation.

"My thanks, sir, but allow me a moment to ascertain your intentions. As I see it, if we were to comply with your tactic, we would thrust our entire Continental army to one line of march. His Lordship would have what, eight thousand men, mules, wagons, cannon, strung out in a single column upon one road. To a clerk that appears to be a troublesome tactic, especially through, what is at best, hostile territory…no doubt you have given this much thought but I am concerned that such a manoeuvre would expose the entire force to attack. The column would be caught, with no hope of reinforcement or rescue, isolated and surrounded. We could lose the entire army, all its supplies, and the colonies in one encounter. Stranded miles from the sea, and out of reach of our navy, the King would be told of a terrible loss. I would surmise that not one tenth would be able to escape, those that did would be harried all the way back to whatever port they could reach. Your plan, if implemented, would see an army lost as easy as wiping away a tear from an eye. Faced with such casualties we would have no option but to surrender to the rebels; not the glorious victory any of us desire."

Wright wasn't the fool he liked to portray himself as being. In fact, his military mind was far superior to many, especially this fop before them. Maitland used his napkin to conceal a smile as Fitzwilliam blustered to form a response.

"An exaggeration, sir. Of course we would not simply allow ourselves to be cut off. We would fight, sir, and defeat the rebels where they stood." Smiling benignly Wright wondered if it would be better all round to allow this fool to leave unopposed. His naivety would cause the rebels more harm fighting with them, than against them. Instead he goaded the man further.

"We are speaking of a vast country, Sir Percival, vast and dangerous. Despite our army's endevours and even with all their resources, we would be desperately lucky to defeat a well-trained force there. However, we are not fighting a European war; we will be fighting rebels, farmers, people who know the land far better than we ever could. I fear your idea would destroy any hope of us retaining control of the colony in a matter of days."

Perhaps Maitland should have defended Fitzwilliam from Wright, but had enjoyed watching the unequal contest to much to do so. The consequences though of this encounter would haunt them he feared. Humiliated, Sir Percival would be eager to reciprocate at the earliest opportunity. For the moment, the militia colonel appeared unperturbed, continuing unabated, as if he had not heard Wright's words, such was the man's lack of humility.

"Luckily wiser heads than ours dictate strategy. Now as to our deployment and accommodation, my staff, dunnage and horses will be embarked upon the 'Empress' while the 'Enchantress' and 'Seaswift' will carry the men, one regiment aboard each. The 'Highland Spirit' will take all other accoutrements. I, and my senior staff will travel with you, if that is acceptable, Captain? That's settled then. No doubt, Maitland will join me aboard as well?" Fitzwilliam didn't pause, didn't hesitate, he had taken control of the accommodation and as a Knight of the realm, where he slept was all important.

"I assume by accoutrements you refer to those essentials needed by soldiers; bedding, packs, muskets, ammunition...food!" Maitland added sarcastically. Trouble was brewing and that wasn't what Stilwell wanted, not yet, not here, not now. Hurriedly, he added,

"Sir Percival, is it really necessary for your entire stables, including fox hounds, household staff and effects to accompany us on our journey?"

Stilwell had examined the list, supplied by Fitzwilliam, prior to this meeting, and was amazed by the quantity of what the militia deemed essential.

"Totally, as I informed the Horse Guards when they agreed to my request we do not know how long we will have to remain in the Americas. Pointless to arrive and find that some, crucial item has been forgotten.

"Like a nail file, perhaps," Wright whispered softly. Maitland heard, but now was neither the time nor the place to speak of such matters.

"Very well, in which case I must insist your men practice the art of embarkation...no, I will not be distracted, sir...it is not only their lives at stake, but the entire squadron. Imagine what their Lordships would say if we lost every ship because we got the balance wrong. Too much weight in one and not enough in another might render the ships to be off kilter and that would spell disaster if we encounter foul weather between here and our destination. Nor would I wish to explain to His Majesty why we had not taken sufficient precautions. It will also quell any fears the masters might possess as to where to put everyone."

Stilwell had seen Fitzwilliam about to remonstrate, to argue about the logistics of such an enterprise. While the captain of the 'Kentsman' had a myriad of problems to overcome, his first most pressing was to delay departure until after the 4th of July, time which he would utilise as best he could. Importantly the merchant captains weren't best disposed to taking orders, they could refuse to load the regiments especially if they considered such matters might jeopardise their ship. He should not have worried, Sir Percival, it seemed, was in no hurry to leave until then either.

"Of course, capital idea. I will assign two of my officers to assist and liaise. Unfortunately, I will be far too busy along with the town council with our preparations for the King's birthday celebrations. Once that has been dealt with, we can sally forth and do battle with His rebellious citizens."

Maitland sighed, apparently Fitzwilliam never had any intention of leaving before the ball while that message only indicated that the agent would not reveal themselves until at least that date. He could only hope Fitzwilliam remained suitably occupied until then.

"Tell me, sir, how is your relationship with the town at large?" Stilwell watched the fool's face with interest.

"My relationship...is cordial, distinctly cordial. We, by that I mean my officers, have courted them, and their daughters. We fit in nicely, are as one, so to speak."

Maitland stared towards the officers Sir Percival had with him. They remained silent but nodded politely. The man, it seemed, bred not only loyalty, but total subservience. Stilwell may have seen it as well, but he had more important matters in mind.

"Excellent, then you will know, who we should speak to about supplies? Our ships were victualed, far too quickly. We need to transfer certain items between vessels, while I and the other captains will have needs as well; cordage, wine, water, all manner of trivial, which keep us at sea." Stilwell had found another means for delay and was prepared to use it to his best advantage.

"Ahhh, I understand. " Fitzwilliam sat back and loosened a button on his under jacket. "Well, let me see...the local priest is one that I would recommend...He is, how shall I put this? A bit of a zealot, but he knows everyone who is anyone. I have heard his sermons and each is full of hellfire and damnation. Yet he lives well, enjoying the comforts his parishioners bestow upon him."

"So, he preaches one thing and does the opposite," Maitland added. "We all know such men, do we not?"

"Indeed we do," Stilwell agreed. "Any other person we should know about?"

"None that rapidly spring to mind, there are two families of merchants, well, one family and an individual. The Wood family was the leading traders until they suffered a number of unexpected demises. The father died of consumption, while the eldest son was killed while on a trading journey."

"Unfortunate," Stilwell stated. Fitzwilliam had drunk too much, making him liable to speak out of turn. He had almost revealed his deviousness once this evening maybe he could be courted to expand upon his indiscretions a little more. "And who is this other?"

"A man by the name of Turnbottle, difficult man to understand, but one I would recommend. He keeps very much to himself. Rarely attends gatherings, if he does, he rarely mixes with anyone he does not know. He is though, a man of great ability, who by all accounts is fair minded and honest."

"Honest? Not a word associated with merchants. Those I know are the opposite, why is this one different?" Stilwell was intrigued, there would have to be more investigations, more checks made, but he sensed a breakthrough. Turnbottle might be the one they sought.

"The man is perhaps too honest, mean to say, how many merchants can we name that would appear so reticent to fill a gap, left in the business community, by the death of another?"

"Few...none to my knowledge," Wright stated, "Those I have met would have killed each other in the rush to stake a claim. I assume this man...Turnbottle is right in the head, not befuddled or anything?"

"Man has a sharp mind from what I can ascertain," Fitzwilliam added. Pleased that his words were found to be so important. "Not addled at all, but mindful, definitely mindful of what occurs within the town."

"A man we should keep a close eye on, Maitland." Stilwell stated.

"I will, sir, I will." Maitland felt slightly aggrieved that Stilwell had extracted their first name so easily from Fitzwilliam. Perhaps that was the measure of this sailor, and why he had been sent here?

"Anything else, Sir Percival?" Stilwell prompted.

"Nothing which comes readily to mind...there was the woman who the Wood family cast out for an indiscretion...Oh, yes, and the local rabble made a farce of my punishment detail."

"No farce, sir. The man should never have been flogged for such a misdemeanour." Maitland stared at the colonel menacingly, he remembered that day and it still rankled.

"Explain," Stilwell demanded. "Why did a simple punishment end in a...debacle?"

"It should not have ended so, the dog found the local brothel, reported back drunk and out of uniform. A flogging offence as laid down in regulations. That should have been the end of the matter."

"Did he give a reason?" Stilwell asked

"He did, said he lost it by no fault of his own. Man lied, so I had him flogged in front of both regiments." Fitzwilliam sipped his wine, while those, who had witnessed the event, waited. "The townspeople heard about it and caused untold mayhem. What it had to do with them, I never did discover." Fitzwilliam still felt aggrieved that he had been slighted over something that should have been dealt with swiftly and without interruption.

"Perhaps they saw the punishment for what it was sir, excessive and harsh. Field punishment would have been acceptable, extra guard, not one hundred lashes." Maitland remembered how he had remonstrated about the excessive punishment, but had received naught more than a curt reply.

"My decision, Maitland my regiment, I give them everything, yet this is how the scum reward my expense. They fornicate and mislay articles of uniform. What should I do, reward their carelessness? No, his flogging will serve as a deterrent to others."

"That is your want, sir, why though, were we involved?" Maitland demanded. Stilwell looked on as the two men clashed figuratively, this was something that needed to be ended, lest it festered any longer.

"Solidarity, Maitland, the dogs now understand who their masters be."

"The townsfolk, then are rebellious, are they?" Stilwell asked. "Is that your opinion, Maitland? Should we be concerned by their actions or that of this woman the priest destroyed?"

"No, treated fairly, they will respond to the sound of coinage of which we will spend a vast amount. As for the woman, she is a petty distraction, not the first or last to fall foul of a lecherous man. Her predicament is an amusing aside, but not one to concern us. Personally, we should confine ourselves to our task rather than the tittle-tattle of a small town. Whatever happened to her was most likely deserved and certainly of no concern to us."

Fitzwilliam had proved that day just how malicious and dangerous he could be. The man had been like a rabid dog bent on destroying a man who thought he'd failed didn't deserve such a harsh punishment. If the townsfolk had not interfered, Fitzwilliam would have had him flayed alive. Before both regiments drawn up in a three sided square, he had faced a near riot. They had brayed each time the lash fell, inching forward with each lash of the whip. Blood had flicked backwards, warm red droplets which, the men tasted upon their lips and they silently cursed. A riot was a second from occurring when Fitzwilliam had turned his men around and levelled muskets at the citizens. He had been on the point of firing, when Maitland had step in and taken control of the parade. That was when the professional soldier realised how insane the militia colonel was. Money gave the fool power and position and allowed him to act as he did. Take that away and he was nothing more than a danger, a danger that could destroy them all *Thank God I will never have to fight alongside him!* Maitland had thought, pitying any man that relied upon the fool's judgment.

Sir Percival had found the episode amusing and brought it up whenever he could. Said it showed the mentality of the narrow minds that operated within confined communities. If only he knew that Abigail Wood still had an effect on the town that her presence still influenced what happened there.

Chapter Forty Two

The crenelated bell tower was his domain, it was where he came to watch those he controlled while remaining concealed from view. It had proved an ideal place to contemplate in solitude, to spy on his parishioners or, like tonight, a venue for discreet meetings. While he awaited his visitor, Stormouth's cleric spied those who hurried about their business. The merchants, some walking sullenly uphill, weighed down in anguish or debt, others rushing home, full of pleasure at some deed done, some deal sealed. A few ladies made their way back to their homes eager to be inside before nightfall when those ungodly souls, who frequented the night came out to play.

Another day drew to a close and he witnessed many of his flock making their way downhill towards the fleshpots of the 'Butts' where they sought solace, amorous liaisons, unabated and unashamed. Life was stretched below him and he marveled at the way they so easily forgot. Up here, he was like the malevolent name the children had given him. He was, a raven, watching for his next victim,

"There you are!" He breathed a sigh of relief to see him approach. God was in his Heaven and all was now right with the world, or so he hoped. From his eerie, his guest appeared older, less intimidating. But he knew what he had had to use to achieve this meeting. "Come into my web and tell me what I need to know," he whispered as the figure stopped appropriately beneath the lych-gate, for was that not where all this had begun? Sighing contentedly, Bayles, had used guile to attract him to this place, not blackmail that he would store away for future use, if so required.

Sighing contently, he was pleased with what he had achieved, 1773 was proving to be eventful for the entire town, but in the evening glow of a setting sun, Stormouth appeared to be at ease with its self. Until he saw two figures hurrying away from the upper town.

"Where pray have you been my pretty?" he whispered, recognising one of the many working girls as she hurried past the gate. He wasn't too concerned about a common whore, but to see one so early was a rarity. "A gentleman had needs no doubt, and you fulfilled them, but a word in Maggie's ear is called for, we have an understanding." He was close to fulfilling his greatest desire, but there were still those who could ruin everything. The man he awaited, and the answers he gave, would determine if his delicate plans were likely to succeed. Joseph had known the secrets he kept, had aided and conspired with him to keep his traits well concealed. His demise had forced him to rethink his life, with no one else to aid him Bayles had to rely on his own malevolence to achieve that which he desired, wealth. Once this task was done, once he had more wealth than he could ever imagine, he would leave this hellhole and seek a new life elsewhere. But if his intentions were revealed, those he sought to destroy and rob would turn upon him. That he could not allow, until he was done he must remain discreet, remain alert and keep his wits about him. Lost in such thought, he was about to turn away, when he saw a figure he recognised easily.

"And where pray, are you a going Master Adam?" Now wasn't the time to concern himself with the morals of that particular alley cat. He would deal with him once he knew what his guest had to say. This meeting would have far reaching effects, none more so, than for the Wood family. If this meeting went as he hoped, he would have power over them, and power meant wealth. The problem was, his guest still thought he, and not the priest, held the winning hand. "Foolish soul will soon learn the truth," he whispered as the sound of footsteps upon stone steps echoed up the tower staircase. His destiny was but a heartbeat away, but there was time to catch a fleeting glimpse of a woman who paused at the church gate. Nothing strange in that, but she was dressed in a hooded cape, despite the warmth of the evening. Her age, indeterminable certainly old judging by the stooped way she walked. *Another filthy whore from the 'Butts',* he mused, forgetting her immediately as his guest stepped onto the lead roof, perspiring slightly and breathing heavily. They bowed politely, acknowledging each other's position and status.

"Good of you to come; a pleasant evening is it not?" Bayles stated pleasantly.

"It is, Reverend, most pleasant. Though I doubt the outcome of this farce will be so pleasant." The man stood, silver topped cane in one hand, while, with the other, he wiped his forehead with a linen kerchief. "A most exhilarating meeting place. Dramatic, in fact, but we are not here to comment upon such matters. Best state your business so I can be gone." Bayles smiled, he had expected animosity, perhaps even outright hostility but he had him here and that was half the battle won.

"My eyrie is advantageous, it allows a solitude which I can employ when vexed and perturbed. I use the silence to commune and…seek guidance from one who is greater than any of us, or, as now, to speak without being overheard, unless we include the multitude of errant pigeons, though I doubt if they count do you?"

A priest was not supposed to gloat, but tonight he felt empowered. He laughed, a rarity which few had ever witnessed, like the man it was weird a sort of clacking sound from deep within the priests throat. Hearing the sound his guest moved uneasily away, as if deliberating his answer. Then, slowly he began what was a difficult response.

"I doubt if they do sir, but we are not here to discuss the merits of some rodent. So speak of what you desire and we may end this farce here and now."

"Oh my dear Turnbottle this is no farce. In fact you and I are one of the same we both require, nay desire, what the Wood family have to offer."

"In that you are mistaken sir, for I need nothing of that family." He'd lied, his every waking moment, and most of his dreams were consumed by nothing else.

"Really, am I so mistaken?" Bayles questioned.

"You are sir, which is why I shall bid you a good night and leave you to your....insane manifestations."

"You may not believe me but I have struggled with my intentions, asked God Himself to grant me guidance. I have searched my soul, spent many a sleepless night questioning myself as to whether you are the right man for the task Each time I come back to the question as to why our noble Mister Turnbottle would frequent a whore house. A question many would find disturbing if such a thing was made public. No say nothing sir for your secret is safe with me, however I do have a price and that price concerns the Wood family."

"Go to hell. I shall do nothing to aid those sons of bitches." Turnbottle snarled and walked towards the stairs. Bayles remained silent, then added

"Hell is what we make here on earth, and we may all encounter it shortly if we fail to aid the Wood brothers in this hour of need. You and I despise each other as Joseph despised you for what you did while his good lady wife was alive. For that betrayal you owe them this one chance to redeem yourself."

"As I said I owe them nothing nor do I know to what you refer."

"Really, then Joseph lied when he implicate you in the struggle his wife had before her demise. Do you deny the lust that existed between you, or how Joseph was befuddled by your deceitfulness?"

"That is old history, such lies cannot harm me, or her, not now." Turnbottle's anger rose but he knew Bayles had him cornered.

"No they cannot, but if such rumour was made public, the inference might harm far more." Bayles had myriad problems to deal with, this was but one.

"Consider the ramifications if such news was made public. Your trade and that of the brothers may suffer. You and they could face penury and with such demise others may well be drawn into the conflagration and perish alongside you. Could any of us survive such an event?"

"Impossible to say, but I fear your threats come too late priest, for they are already facing ruination. Word in 'Pettit's' is that the smaller merchants are tired of waiting, they contemplate their next step against them. Whilst I sympathise, I will shed not a tear at their demise, for they have brought it upon themselves. If the merchants move, there will be nothing you, or I, can do to save them. Perhaps, truth be told, it might be for the best. The longer this continues, the closer they come to total ruination. Bankruptcy will be messy, by the time the bankers and lawyers have finished, and no doubt some of our brethren will fail also, but at least it will be finished. We will be able to move forward from such despondency, free of any recrimination."

"No! That cannot be allowed, such an action would ruin the economy, place many in dire straits. My God, even I might suffer the misfortune of having my accounts examined! Not to mention the prospect of prominent townsfolk being taken before the bankruptcy courts. You have to act… I implore you aid them ….for all our sakes." This had not gone as he had hoped, Turnbottle was meant to acquiesce, through shame and guilt, agree to aid the boys in their everyday dealings with their customers. His voice rose, he spluttered, he felt faint, his alarm evident. This was terrible news; how could he protect his future wealth, if this man wasn't prepared to assist Josiah?

Sensing the man's discomfort, Turnbottle remained silent, removed his hat and wiped perspiration from his head with a silk kerchief. He marveled at his deception and performance. He had deliberately misled Bayles, allowing him to threaten then making out the situation was far worse than it really was. Now Bayles was confused and had shown his hand, Turnbottle had played him masterfully, like the gambler he was and Bayles had fallen into the trap nicely. The mere mention of bankruptcy was enough to make the Reverend react, all he needed to do was squeeze him a little further, and Bayles would beg him to aid the Wood family.

"Move swiftly, do what needs to be done to avoid such a debacle. Aid them and I shall relinquish everything I know of that visit and everything else. It will be as if nothing ever occurred."

"Everything, you will mention it no more…do I have your solemn word on that as a true Christian?"

"You do, as God is my witness."

"Then I shall endevour to aid them, but I shall need access to their books but that is something no merchant will allow another to do. You must convince them to allow it, can you so convince them, for nothing can be done unless I see everything pertaining to their firm."

"I will speak to Josiah tomorrow; inform him that you are to be allowed access to the records. But can you save them?"

"Possibly, we shall see." Bayles had failed, his scheme was rent asunder and he was begging for assistance. Turnbottle paused, making the priest suffer just a little longer. He had access to their business without the need of the woman after all. Very calmly, he replied. "Speak with Josiah. Tell him I will do what I can. In the meantime, I will attempt to alleviate some of the tensions within the trading community. Perhaps, with my hand upon the tiller the merchants will feel a little relaxed, though, in truth, they may require further assurances." Turnbottle had played the priest like a baited fish; made him wiggle, then had struck.

"Such as? Surely with you in command they will see the benefits of discretion?" The priest frowned, Turnbottle should have been the one under pressure, instead he was dictating terms.

"There…is your first problem, a pixie who agrees to nothing least it suits his needs. He must be shown the errors of his ways, forced, if need be, to agree to our terms." Turnbottle pointed towards Adam Wood who strolled nonchalantly towards the 'Crown Hotel'.

"He will!" Bayles exclaimed. "I will speak to him…and the family. Rest assured, they will come to see that what we propose will assist everyone, keep the priorities in balance. One man, no matter what his persuasion, can disrupt what has always been." Cursing Adam for the fool he was, Bayles wondered if the world would have been better suited if he and not Nathaniel had died. Turnbottle had thwarted his plan, he had emerged victorious, while Adam Wood walked away unconcerned that he was being discussed.

"No doubt you know them better than I… but perhaps if I spoke to the boy…I mean as an equal…as men of the world. I might convince him that we mean no harm and our suggestions might ultimately benefit everyone, including him and his expensive tastes. He might find my approach more …receptive." Turnbottle sounded convincing though in truth he wondered what hold Bayles exerted upon them. Certainly Abigail had told him much of the youngest son. How he leeched off the family spending their wealth on wine and clothes in which he promenaded like a well fed peacock. He had little stomach for business, enjoying instead gambling. Yet even a parasite like Adam had his uses, which was why he feigned emotion when he replied.

"Such an approach might work. He sees me as perhaps too alike his father, my words, no matter how well meant are seen as a rebuke, a slight on his attributes and abilities…Yes speak with him, inform him of our intentions."

"Then we are done, go about your work and I will mine. Speak to them and when they agree, I shall endevour to deal with their …inadequacies. Until then reverent I shall bid you good night."

With that he turned, leaving Bayles with his cogitations. He had turned the meeting around with ease. Bayles could think what he liked, this was far better than the original scheme, which, devised in haste, was now, thanks to the priests capitulation, all but defunct. All that energy wasted on finding, hiding, and keeping her safe was superfluous. The family had fallen apart, their trade waned, while his flourished as both army and navy came to him for stores. That trade, along with the customers, acquired from the Wood's by fair means or foul, meant he had little to be worried about. Though the added possibility of appearing to his enemies as their saviour, did appeal to his vanity.

To succeed, he had certain things to do. He needed to stir them a little more, create further agitation and ill will among the family and the business community, then he could put this elaborate hoax aside. How he had juggled so many differing people was beyond him. Bayles, Abigail, the Wood family, all believed his lies. Save for Mrs Wood, he felt little sorrow for any of them. He liked Abigail, had never meant to harm her, always intended to return her to the family, but as his puppet a mere figurehead to do as he wanted and commanded, she would become simply a pawn in his game. But now, after being handed all he wanted on a plate, she was a hindrance.

"Damnations." The word whispered in anger meant that once again he would have to go in search of the man he employed to keep her safe. The man who, if events altered significantly, would become her executioner. Without prior warning, Turnbottle had to enter the 'Butts' and ask for him by name, but when needs must the devil drove. Eventually, and much to his dislike Benjamin Turnbottle stood in a darkened alley. Sent there by a toothless man who promised he would get word to his quarry. He didn't have long to wait, jumping in surprise when a hand rested silently upon his shoulder from behind. The scum had approached via an occupied house, using it as if it were his own. Perhaps that was how, such men lived, but he found it disconcerting. He made to turn, to face him, but a voice, full of menace, stopped him.

"Weren't expecting you sir, but its best we're not seen together. Face forward and whisper your requirements, that ways we both stay safe."

"The girl…I need her protected until the 4th of June. By then I will know what is to be done. Whatever I decide, I trust you to deal with it effectively. As a token, here's a little extra for your troubles and diligence."

The purse dangled temptingly, before being taken from his hand.

"Appreciated, though you may be too late, her time draws close, might not reach June. What then?"

"Not what I have been told. My information is that she is fit and well," Benjamin Turnbottle added confidently.

"That's as may be, but whoever tells you that ain't heard he a moaning and a groaning? Don't know much about such things, but I reckons she's close."

"My thanks; I will investigate…if anything happens…."

"Aye, don't you fret, I'll send word immediately." The villain would do as asked so long as the coins kept coming.

"Good, our fate is in her hands, or, more precisely, her swollen belly. For now I need you to meet a man who will be approaching along the Barminster road. Meet him and give him this," Turnbottle handed the wretch a notelet, "make sure he knows who Adam Wood is then disappear. Do this and our association will soon end."

His feigned resignation to his situation was far removed from how he actually felt. He had become like Bayles, he now schemed and contemplated crimes which a few months before he would never have thought of. Adam Wood had a surprise coming to him, and his hands were clean of guilt, for Mrs Jones would vouch that he was enjoying an evening meal when the boy suffered his accident. *Life was good, or soon would be.*

Chapter Forty Three

Adam Wood paused briefly, turned, shook his head and continued upon his journey. Since his father's death, he had experienced such manifestations on more than one occasion. It was as if the old goat followed him from beyond the grave, watching him, disapproving of what he did, but it matter not he was dead, while he was alive.

"Good evening, Mr Wood, sir." The liveried doorman held the door open and bowed courteously. Not many attracted such attention but Adam did for Mister Irons, owner of the 'Crown Hotel' considered him a valued client. Considered to be a respectable establishment, guests were treated like royalty and in return were expected to behave accordingly. Irons, demanded decorum and a strict dress code, Elegance was foremost, to Gentlemen and ladies alike, something which Adam subscribed and adhered to impeccably. Clothes were one of his passions, they portrayed both his own and his families importance. Because of that, he had invested heavily in another new pair of shoes and exquisite buckles. They were an extravagance, one his father would have lambasted him about, as he had about frequenting this place, but Adam no longer cared about such criticism.

"Have my guests arrived?" Adam demanded as he entered the hotel in a flourish of powder and perfume. His father's demise had improved his status considerably. He now had a fortune in his pocket, and was free to do as he wished. No longer would that old goat tell him what he could, or could not, do, he could indulge in his passions without fear of reproach or the need to go cap in hand, begging for funds. More importantly, financial security allowed him to engage in his other passion, fine clothes. He had spent excessively, adorning himself in an ensemble of exquisiteness. His knitted stockings were of the finest quality, while his breeches were adorned with four silver buttons to each leg and were of the finest doe skin. A magnificently silk embroidered coat, was worn over a cream waistcoat, which was adorned with a gold chain.

Around his neck was a white cravat, and silver pin, the entire costume was topped with a tri-corn hat which he removed with panache. Beneath which was the most elegant of whitened wigs this side of Barminster. The entire ensemble was completed with a silver topped cane, a full four feet in length, which aided his gait most elegantly. He was a dandy and as such, he lounged in a sophisticated manner while awaiting a reply. Excitement was what he craved, and no one would halt his quest. He had avoided the horse dung which lay scattered across the street, for tonight he had no wish to stink of manure. All being well, he would be fortunate at cards and leave, not only with more than he entered with, but also perhaps a 'guest' with whom he would spend time in bed with before returning home.

"Your guests await you in the back room," the maître d'hôtel, replied. As a mere functionary, Williams, had no say in who entered, but secretly he disliked Wood intensely. In his opinion, he was the embodiment of all that remained immoral within the town. He was conceited and arrogant, now possessed more wealth than was good for him, and worse still, was of that persuasion which should have resulted in imprisonment and horse whipping.

"Excellent. I shall require a pot of coffee and at least six bottles of your best Claret. We shall have some sport this evening, I wager?"

Flouncing through the room with the grace of a cloud that drifted across a clear blue sky, Adam accepted the nods of approval from men he saw as friends, and women who he viewed as future conquests. Smiling arrogantly, he wallowed in their veneration, finally free of his father's overbearing influence, he searched for those he truly desired. With no one to rein in his exuberances, he was determined to make a name for himself. He had many vices, gambling was the worst, cards or dice, dogs or badgers, it mattered not, he would bet on anything the hotel was offering. He was good, but did not excel; his debts had nearly become his downfall. Before his legacy had materalised, Irons had pressed for payment. Irons still held those damned promissory notes, which until his inheritance was spent, would remain a discreet secret.

"Will you require a bill, sir, or should we charge it?" The question was rhetorical; Williams knew the answer before he had spoken. Since inheriting, his wagers had become larger; instead of a few guineas he spent a few hundred. As yet he wasn't a problem, winning as much as he lost, but the position could change in a trice.

"Charge it, add it to my account; do you expect me to carry cash?" Adam knew the room watched him, and the question irked. Did these fools think he was a risk? Men such as Irons should know that gentlemen sometimes languished in the doldrums, sometimes fate played an unkind hand which was what Adam had experienced. Even now, he won and lost, his debts were manageable and all being well, he would have an appointment with destiny. By tomorrow he would have regained some of what he had lost. It was what he relied upon and when the tide turned he had to be there ready to accept Lady Luck's good fortune.

"Of course sir, have a pleasant evening." The Hotel never expected the young Wood to actually have cash upon him. He was a fool, a dandy, a fopdoodle, who used his name and status to obtain what he wanted. Like all last born, he carried a fiend upon his shoulders. Considered unworthy by those born before them, they were never consulted about anything and struggled to find a position in life. Adam was the same he had meandered between home, hotel, and parties; he was a non-entity, a bored young man who had nothing to interest him. As he sauntered through the lobby, Williams wondered what Wood would do this evening. Would he be found next morning lying in his own vomit in some gutter, his fancy clothes soiled? Or would he take a room upstairs to 'entertain his friends'? If so, he, as the Hotels protector, would have to be aware of the constable's presence, otherwise their own name could be implicated in his sordid assignations. Sighing heavily, Williams beckoned a footman forward. "Add this to Mister Wood's account."

The young fool was trouble waiting to happen. Only recently he had narrowly avoided being challenged to a duel, for the non-payment of a debt. Before much longer, someone would do it again and this time Adam Wood did not have the protection of his father's wallet to keep him from debtor's prison.

"All quiet this evening?" Mister Irons asked. Normally, he remained discreetly in the background, but he was more than capable of protecting his investment when the needs required.

"So far, sir, Mister Wood has just entered." Williams gestured towards Adam who was speaking to a particularly attractive lady.

"Thought he would stay away a little longer. Watch him closely; allow him to play cards, nothing else. His luck might change and we might see a return on some of his debt. Keep him away from anything else; temporarily, I will set a house limit on him."

"Won't like that, sir, don't like being told how to spend his money."

Irons trusted Williams to run his hotel, but it was his and as such he set the rules. The added duties of nursemaid to that fop irked Williams, irked him mightily.

"I suppose not...inform me if he tries anything else."

"Very well, sir." Having watched Wood closely over a period of time, Williams knew it wasn't entirely the young man's fault. He had the extraordinary ability to count and remember cards, an insight few possessed, more importantly, he had possessed the rare ability to leave a card table ahead of the game. His problems stemmed from his other 'traits and tastes'. He was generous to those he called 'friends', buying friendships with money, which until recently he lacked. The manner in which he greeted his friends was proof, if proof was needed, that he intended tonight to be enjoyable, which meant he would have to have words with him before the night was out.

"Richardson, Saunders, good to see you again, ready for some sport?" Adam greeted his friends warmly as he entered the room

"Not if you intend that sport to include cards, lost too much to you already this month. However, I am told that Williams had procured dogs and fighting cocks in the cellar...that would be more of a challenge."

The laughter was genial, but Williams sensed the undertone of misgiving.

"Piffle, games for old women...Williams, why are there no pugilists? I am told that the brute, Meadows, is in Barminster. In fact, a friend lost a hundred guineas betting against him not three days ago."

Wood shouted towards Williams, beckoning him forward.

"That is correct, sir. Unfortunately we tried, but I fear our attempts came to naught. His man refused our purse, said he could get more at any travelling fair. So until next week, when our scheduled bout takes place, we cannot offer you that entertainment."

Adam sighed, his disappointment evident. He did so enjoy a hard fought bare knuckle boxing match between two equal men. It was, undoubtedly, far more entertaining than racing, which he found tiresome. He had said as much on more than one occasion, *See the damn things at the start, or the end, everything in between is totally wasted. My God, there is enough time in between to take one, if not two sprightly fillies to bed and still be in time to see the finish.* "So be it...Gentlemen, we shall play a few hands to amuse ourselves." Adam sighed in mock acceptance, while Williams hurried off to find his employer. Unaware of the trouble awaiting them, Adam and his friends settled at a card table.

"I assume we are all invited to the Mayor's tomfoolery on the 4th?" Saunders asked as he shuffled the cards and began dealing.

"I leave such things to my brother. He is more adept at such things, he and the women will no doubt attend; I on the other hand will find other amusement that night,"

Smirking nonchalantly, he looked disinterested as he spread his cards. It was common knowledge that he had been forced into a loveless marriage, while rumour had it that he was incapable of producing children due, in some part, to an affliction. His friends knew better than most that his only affliction was that he enjoyed the company of men to women, but that was a secret his friends would aid him in concealing as long as he had coinage, if that went, so might they.

"I sometimes wonder, gentlemen, if Josiah believes me when I inform him that day follows night." He spoke in jest, but that damned ball had caused more disagreement than that bitch ever had. Since its announcement, the brothers had argued morning, noon and night. Josiah was adamant, stating only this very evening that they should attend.

"We must dispel the innuendos that run riot among the business community. To that end we must attend and show a united face,"

"I will not!" Adam had petulantly exclaimed before storming from the house. He had remained agitated until he reached the Quayside, only then had he calmed sufficiently to make his way to this his spiritual home. He had sensed someone's presence near the church, and wondered if Josiah had come to apologise, but after turning, he had seen no one. There was a chasm between the brothers, a void made worse by the problems which afflicted them daily. Adams concerns were, he felt genuine, as he continuously asked, how could they attend such tomfoolery, when they were deadlocked in constant turmoil? More importantly neither brother knew what they were doing and had no one to whom they could ask for guidance.

"My father said just the other day that Josiah looks unwell. Is he ailing Adam?"

"Your father, Richardson should look at my constitution if he seeks anyone inflicted by what we must endure. My God sir, I am denied any word on how the business is run, I am ignored now more than when my own dear father was alive. Is that right sir is it right that I should be so denied?" He had assumed Josiah would seek his assistance, but it appeared not. Even the foul bitch who had scorned their name, appeared to have more sway in what happened than he. Was it any wonder he found solace among like-minded souls? All he ever wanted was respect, was that too much to ask? Or did others see him simply as the youngest son of an influential family?

"I do not believe anyone could ignore you Adam surely Josiah seeks your help?"

"You think? I'll tell you how he ignores me Columbine. I attended our counting house to finds Josiah studying the ledgers intently. True I was a little late in attending but was that cause to berate me so?"

"How late sir?"

"A little after noon, but there was no need for his tirade I was prepared to assist him, but no he began to castigate me then and it hasn't stopped since. The man is becoming tiresome very tiresome. Actually accused me…me of not caring about my wife nor my responsibilities. I mean, I do care, I care deeply, do I not?" Placing a card upon the table Adam knew the argument had been far worse than he made out, Josiah had vilified him murderously, his words sounded just as loud here as they had earlier in their offices.

"Why do you leave your wife at home all night and not contribute anything to solving our problems? You sir have influence in this town, yet still you waste your money at the gaming tables. I assume you imagine that throng outside are simply here to wish us well?" Josiah had pointed at the window, his anger such that spittle had dribbled down his chin, his hand trembling in fear or anger Adam knew not which.

"I have influence, do I? That is difficult to believe. I suspect I will never influence anyone or anything. As for that mob, I had wondered why we were attracting so much attention."

Adam had indeed wondered why the crowd that gathered outside on the street. Such insolence and his brother's continuing self-importance annoyed him. Yawning loudly, his feigned indifference caused Josiah's hackles to rise even more.

"Sneer all you want brother, but they gather to pick over the bones of our business. A business you seem incapable, or unwilling, to assist with. Perhaps our situation means nothing to a laggard like you, but we are floundering, the ledgers are written in a way I cannot decipher!"

Adam had waited then with a malevolence born out of frustration and animosity, he had checked to make sure they were alone. Only then had he turned on Josiah as he had never turned before.

"Surely you are not surprised? Father took great pains to make sure no one could read what he did here. Oh…am I to understand you know not of what I speak…you are, are you not? My God, I know more than you, then allow me to advance your education. Micklewhite told me that father was a cautious old goat who trusted no one, least of all us. For that reason, he never wrote anything down without first encoding it in his inimitable style. He said it was to confuse anyone wishing to steal what he knew. Surely, you knew of this, more to the point, with your vast knowledge of what father did, and didn't do, the encryption should not be beyond your capabilities?"

"What surprises me more than anything else is your knowledge of what he did, I cannot imagine him speaking of such things to you, therefore I can only assume that rogue Micklewhite enlightened you, and for that he will be spoken to most severely."

"You are the fool Josiah, you know the answer to your problems. Have I not offered to aid you more times than I can remember, but each time I am denied?" He had known his barbed comment would annoy his brother. Josiah had said more than once, that he neither needed, nor required, anyone to aid him in the business. That was the cause of the constant arguments, Josiah's pride prevented him from seeking help. He felt it his duty to deal with matters he had no knowledge of, such stupidity would be his undoing. Because in truth he could not fail, more importantly; he could not be seen to have failed.

"Despite all that you believe, do you imagine I have spent interminable hours simply staring into nothingness? No sir I have not, I have been here day in day out, trying desperately to find the damned key to his code. If I could do that I could solve all our problems in an instant, I unite customers with goods and rebuild our reputation."

"Then give me the opportunity to help. That obnoxious fool we buried, would have kept any code simple, beguiling perhaps but simple for he wasn't intelligent enough to have devised anything too complicated, more likely he used something known to us and no one else. Ask, Josiah, and I will assist. Certainly we cannot continue in this manner much longer."

Adam remembered his brother's response for it was no different to every other response they had ever shared. Josiah always saw him as the youngest without intelligence or credibility. Nor it seemed was he about to change his thinking. He had slammed his fist onto the desk and turned into a raging maniac, screaming defiance and abuse at him while Adam had stood and looked on contemptuously.

"You call me a fool! But I am not such a fool as to know what you would do. I will not allow you to remove these books to some back room of a tavern where your friends could gaze at them and laugh at our misfortune? I will not allow that. The truth of the matter is they were written for Nathaniel. Only he was destined to break the codes."

"Then you will never succeed…because Nathaniel is dead, and you are too pigheaded, too blind, to accept that fact. Once again you decry my offer; I shall not offer it again. But, I do implore you to seek help from someone, anyone. Do so quickly and end this torment you inflict upon yourself." Adam's words had been heart-felt but scathing, the disagreement had ended with Adam shaking his head and turning to leave. Josiah though had not finished, he had one last word of condemnation, he yelled at his brother furiously,

"The only torment I suffer is you…Now I understand why father despaired of you ever making anything of yourself!"

"Fake the way off! You imbecile…you are an oaf, a coward, certainly not fit to sit in that chair. Father, if he wasn't dead, would cringe at your stupidity." With that, Adam had stalked angrily from the warehouses and made his way home where, the argument had continued, until he had left to make his way here.

"I tell you gentlemen, if this ball isn't damned favourable, I will eat my hat. Not only is my brother a judicious fool, but he appears unconcerned that he will bring penury upon us by year's end. He needs help and will not accept it.

However, I will make up for his inadequacies; I will make a name for myself and grind his into the mud. Mark my words, the name Adam Wood will be spoken of for many years to come."

Unknowingly, Adam was being watched. From amidst the blue tobacco smoke of the grand salon of the Crown Hotel, his harbinger of doom awaited his chance.

* * *

The night was becoming tainted with the scent of death. Satisfied that Turnbottle would aid the Wood brothers, Bayles descended the stairs. He felt a mixture of emotions; elation and weariness, but primarily he felt a deep sense of pent up frustration which had to be released. With a sense of anticipation, he made his way home. He had almost fulfilled the promise made to his friend. He had destroyed the unfaithful wife, while the sons were finally to receive the guidance they needed

"With God's guiding light, we will emerge from the darkness into the brilliance of another day," he whispered, exiting the tower and making his way across the churchyard. Ruby would still be awake. She would be his reward for a satisfying days' work.

Chapter Forty Four

Beneath a swinging lantern, a small group discussed the memory of a debacle. Death was abroad in Stormouth but for the moment these men were unaware of its presence.

"Hells teeth, but they are the worst troops I have ever set eyes upon."

"It was not a pretty sight, I agree," Maitland replied. They were in Stilwell's day cabin discussing the latest attempt by Fitzwilliam's troops to enter long boats. The results were discouraging to say the least.

"Had to call a halt, had to send up the signal. Eight attempts, eight, and still the fools do not comprehend the fundamentals of getting from ship to shore without drowning either themselves, or my boat crews. By God, I fear they will kill someone afore they are finished. They are by far the worst led, most undisciplined rabble I have ever had the misfortune to see. Their officers have no comprehension of what they have to do, which in turn makes their men worse than useless. Every man jack of them from Fitzwilliam to the youngest lieutenant should be dismissed, but that isn't what their Lordships desire, is it? So, I suppose we will have to attempt it again?" Stilwell paused, astounded by what they had witnessed. "Of course we must, day after tomorrow, but how much longer, Maitland? How long must our sufferance continue before our man steps forward?"

"I cannot say, but like you Captain, I pray it ends soon." Maitland had watched the last debacle from quarterdeck of the 'Kentsman' and asked himself that same question. Amid a chorus of catcalls and abuse, he had watched the boat crews struggle with the soldiers as they splashed helplessly in the surf. Now, along with those who held the militia's future in their hands, he sat, glass of wine in hand and wondered how much longer the agent required.

"Then we must wait like old maids, until they condescend to show themselves. It irks me Maitland, irks me gravely."

"I agree, sir, but wait we must." They were both frustrated and confused. Stilwell had mentioned he wished to be rid of the town and all it represented many times, while Maitland was concerned that he had heard nothing from London, or their elusive friend since that note had been delivered. With each passing day, June 4th drew closer. If all else failed, he and Stilwell would be forced to begin loading the militia. What then? Do as Fitzwilliam required and hope the whole lot threw themselves overboard in some mass suicide pact before reaching the colonies?

"Our quandary remains, we are compelled to keep them active until either we load them, or this agent is exposed. Either way, this could become a farce if Fitzwilliam, or his officers, discover the truth. Should that occur our task will pale into insignificance for that man is conniving enough to deny all knowledge and escape. That, we cannot allow, no traitor escapes me, sir, none."

The hatred both felt for Fitzwilliam grew daily, The Naval captain was at least spared the man's constant belligerence, Maitland on the other hand was constantly reminded of the militia colonel's madness. He and his officers were the instigators of this travesty, the men, the ordinary soldier were mere pawns in their deceit. Yet they were leaderless, almost useless and afraid of what their colonel, come landlord, could inflict upon them at a whim. Fitzwilliam, conspicuous by his continuing absence, left the burden of their training to junior officers and sergeants. Maitland had tried, but there was only so much he could do. The militia was a travesty, idiots led by fools, but they could become a reasonably efficient force, if they had the right officers and training, but time was ebbing away.

"Admirable sentiments, but you saw them, nothing but drowned rats. We must hope that whatever enemies they encounter allow them sufficient time to unload their dunnage, wig boxes and silver. By God if they were regular troops, the principle would have been knocked into them from an early stage. By now they would be proficient in landing from boats and attacking from the sea. This menagerie could be suppressed by children and old men with nothing more than rocks to throw," Stilwell stated angrily, as those assembled nodded in agreement.

"Lucky for us that occurrence will never materialise, that all we do is keep them busy," Wright added helpfully.

"Just so, mister, just so. However, we must prepare for the worst." Stilwell beckoned them to join him around the table, where he had his maps and notes laid out in readiness. "On the assumption we have to leave, I suggest we begin loading on the morning of the 4th. I would have preferred to have had confirmation before continuing on that course of action, but with no instructions to the contrary we must assume we sail with our friends as arranged."

Maitland cursed inwardly and prayed that Mathews would return in time with some form of guidance. Since dispatching the ensign, he had heard nothing, not a note, not a whisper. Each morning he stood, watching and waiting for a horse bearing his errant messenger to come into view. So far his wait had been a forlorn one. For the moment, and not for the first time in his career, he must fight this battle alone, without orders from the Horse Guard.

"In that case, if there are no objections, I suggest we commence loading dunnage and supplies first. That will allow Colonel Maitland to retain the militia ashore for as long as possible. I would like to keep them busy until after dark, that way we might delay them a little longer assuming we have a tide the next day. I assume, all being well, you will be ready for them?"

"Oh, yes." Maitland replied. "We will care for them admirably." Unbeknown to Fitzwilliam and his men, this was but one of many conversations Maitland and Stillwell had had during which their plans had been discussed and ratified.

"Good. I will arrange for orders to be issued to the marines so that they may be distributed among our transports on the night of the 2nd. If all goes well, our deception will be completed before any of them are aware of it."

"Seems a shame," Wright said, glancing towards where the redcoats had floundered ashore.

"Shame, sir? The shame is theirs. Their officers brought them to this impasse. They implicated their men by their own duplicity. Do not waste pity on scum, sir. Thank God, their heinous scheme was discovered before we were implicated...with disastrous results."

"I apologise, unreservedly, sir." Wright stumbled. He hadn't meant any disrespect and explained hurriedly, "I only meant it's a shame that, in our time of need, we lose a regiment when they could be used in our forthcoming struggle."

"Harrumph." Stilwell cleared his throat. Those that knew the captain waited nervously, for he was not a man to cross, and Wright had come close to questioning his competence. "Apology accepted, sir, but you would do well to remember there is too much at stake. Mistakes, even at this late hour, could herald disaster. I for one will not rest until the 5th. Only then can we debate the rights and wrongs of this escapade."

"On behalf of my officer, sir, I can assure you no disrespect was intended."

"So be it, Maitland. Major Wright, my apologies, it is the good office of senior staff to appear correct at all times. However, these are unusual times and we are all afeared. I should not have been so vivacious, I suggest we put such petty differences aside and concentrate on what must be done?"

The moment had passed and in the way of gentry, words had been exchanged and apologies rendered, the matter was closed.

"What of their colonel?" Cross, Stilwell's first officer asked.

"Ah, the popinjay. He will get a ball, an evening he will remember long into his dotage." Stilwell's vilification of Fitzwilliam would be the one thing he would truly enjoy.

"If he keeps his head," Cross mumbled, barely audibly.

* * *

While military men spoke of tactics, the Reverent Edward Bayles felt justifiably pleased. Events, while not having gone exactly as he wished, were, he felt, still under control. Turnbottle would comply and in so doing allow Joseph's business to come under his control. When it was, he would sell it, take the profit and add it to the wealth he had already acquired then move to some quiet corner of Britain's expanding empire. Until that occurred, he was safe behind the ill-fitting front door of his rectory. Dominating the square, the building had become his place of refuge where he could, like the changing seasons, throw of the cloak of respectability and act however he desired, within reason.

"Ruby…blast your eyes girl, answer when I demand you!" he bellowed, he expected his maid to be present when he arrived home to aid him in divesting his cloak and offering him whatever he desired. Thankfully, the coming of spring had dispelled the frigid draughts that cut through the hallway. He despised winter's chill for not only did the freezing weather cause misery and hardship, but also made his favourite past time a veritable obstacle course of material. The warmer weather made his indulgences far easier for all concerned.

"Wine…now, girl!" The obvious absence of his maid annoyed him. Throwing open each door in turn, he searched in vain. "If I catch you with someone, I will punish you. You know that don't you? Damn your hide, your master awaits you, show yourself, you slovenly bitch."

Staring up the stairwell the house remained silent, Bayles wondered if she had finally summoned the courage to leave. She had been subdued since that night when death had come to his kitchen, subdued, but had resumed her duties with undisguised vigour, as if she had somehow felt obliged to offer herself in return for his protection. Whatever her thinking, he had delayed bringing the new girl in, until he tired of Ruby permanently.

"Where are you, you God forsaken wench?" His insult went unanswered, the house was empty and he must fend for himself. "You will pay, my girl, for this lack of diligence."

Annoyed, he entered the parlour, poured a glass of wine, and sat before the roaring fire. Life was good. His time as incumbent had been worthwhile and rewarding. He was fed, housed, and received a small stipend to which he added the gifts his wealthier parishioners bestowed upon him in return for ensuring their place in heaven when their judgment day dawned. *As if, he, Edward Bayles, would do such things, he would pray and say what they wanted to hear, but he was well aware that when his own time came he would share eternity with the devil. But by God he would enjoy his time here while he could,* he thought.

"Am I wrong in desiring a little comfort?" he asked the empty room. "No, I am not, nor am I concerned about my reputation. Show yourself, you daughter of the devil, answer me or I will beat you till your bones show white. Do as you are told, or I will inform everyone on Sunday of your sins."

He tired of her non-appearance. She was failing in her duties, and that could not be allowed to go unpunished. All he demanded was that she, cook, clean, and to be at his beck and call when he demanded. Tonight, she would suffer, such fools feared him, as they should fear their clergy, and he used that fear to achieve what he wanted. His parishioners believed all he said about hell and damnation, they quaked in fear of what awaited them for indulging in fornication, and pleasures of the flesh. Then, when he was done, after they had filed out suitably chastised, he returned to this house, where a penny whore usually awaited him and his pleasure.

Of course, if that wasn't enough, if he desired more…amenable company there was always his wealthy friends. Invitations to weddings, dinner or other acceptable gatherings had become a major part in his social calendar. While even his pastoral ministrations added to his comfort. The mortal coil ended for everyone, and many remembered him in their wills, adding to his wealth. He had witnessed deaths untimely attendance too many times, which was why he was determined to enjoy every opportunity, to taste every pleasant thrill life had to offer before his own demise?

"I smell your presence and 'bout time too." He turned and saw her standing behind him. She was all a man desired and he stared at her with lecherous eyes, noting the way her fingers, nervously, intertwined and how she stared at the floor. Licking his lips in anticipation, he imagined the touch of her skin and the sins that awaited him. She was young and ripe, just as he liked them.

"Very nice, my dear, very nice indeed. Pour wine for both of us and bring mine hither immediately." He watched as she poured the liquid into crystal glasses, before carrying them carefully to him. As she bent to place the glasses on the table he reached under her skirt and fondled her flesh. "Go and prepare, I fancy the Grecian Nymph this evening. I shall be Zeus or Apollo…and wash, you smell like an old sow."

The priest released his servant but not before one last squeeze of her rump. Unlike his previous servants, Ruby had never worked in the 'Butts', she had never been one of Maggie's girls. Despite that lapse in her education, he knew, she would be making obscene gestures towards him, not that that mattered, she was but a convenience, a plaything. He thought no more of her than he did the penny whores he purchased for his rich friends. Long ago, soon after their fateful meeting, Joseph had set him a task. *Find us an amicable madam, one who will furnish us with what we want and not ask too many damned questions.* He had visited them all in turn, and Maggie had proved most obliging.

"Make haste, or by God, I will teach you manners before throwing you back from whence you came." He smiled evilly. Like the ancient Gods he so admired, he held the power of life and death over these mindless fools, he instilled fear and his maid was no different. She would do as she was told or face the consequences. None, in this town, had a backbone, apart from one and he had ruined her.

"What takes you so long?" he shouted angrily, his eagerness was becoming unbearable.

"Nearly ready, sir," Ruby answered, her voice quivering in fear, or anticipation, he cared not which. Her nervousness made him smile. "It be the laces, sir. I cannot tie them."

"Leave them! I cannot be bothered to waste time."

That was what he liked about her, always eager to please and she kept her mouth firmly closed. Such virtues were not evident in all the girls he had been sent. One, her name escaped him, had screamed incessantly until he had silenced her. Like Ruby's father, that bitch would scream no more. Ruby, though, was worth a small gift, nothing excessive, simply a few extra shillings a year.

"For the love of God...appear or I shall lose interest." He tired of the delay, she was taking longer than that fool Porter took to read petitions in council. . The thought of the town clerk made him reach for his top coat where, in a pocket, was a delightful silver locket which shimmered and shone in the candle light. Stormouth had been a cesspit of depravity, and was becoming so once again. God, it seemed had deserted them when they needed him most. Joseph's death had left a gap, far larger than any man could fill successfully. It wasn't just in business, or within their secret group, but in council. The memory of that damned meeting haunted him, Turnbottle had made him look ineffective and that hurt as did the meeting upon the church tower. *He must pay for such insults.* This locket, a gift from Spriggs, was case in point, the man had paid him well to rid that land of Horn and his swine, yet Turnbottle had befuddled that, and now Spriggs desired recompense. "Should have delayed, waited until Josiah had been elected, then at least, I would have had one more councilor to do my bidding." He cursed his stupidity, Spriggs had insisted he act. He sat as an unelected advisor upon the council, but until now they had acted as he commanded. He had the power to influence, with a sigh, or an upraised eyebrow. His piety gave him power over lesser mortals and all for the added income of £5 per annum. It wasn't the money he sought, but power. Many a petitioner had failed simply because they had not sought him out first, and paid for his assistance. As for Spriggs he was a mean minded man who, unknown too many, had worked for 'The Chamberlin' at the height of his power. That was how the town had once been, only within the 'Butts' did the remnants of that past life remain, none more so than within Maggie's brothel. "Maggie…I do so believe you have betrayed our trust." He sighed as realisation slowly dawned upon him.

They had shared much, she had lain with him, in this very room where their association had been sealed in sweat and pleasure. Neither trusted the other, but the bond they shared, he thought to be unbreakable. Therefore it was logical that he had gone to her first when the witch had disappeared. What he had on the madam was such that he could ruin her with the merest click of his fingers. Despite this, he was sure she had brazenly lied, sworn ignorance about Abigail Wood. "She knew all along where that whore was. "I shall revisit her, make her speak the truth. If not we shall have another witch to rid ourselves of by weeks end." He had the power, many a girl had been shipped abroad by members of his group, just to make sure they could not speak of what they had endured. He smiled devilishly. The question remained, where was Abigail Wood? For the moment that must wait because he had more pressing needs,

"Dress as you are and attend me instantly." He demanded as he began to divest himself of his clothing. Excitement on his part, would be mirrored as nervous despair by his servant. He had not felt so exhilarated since the Bishop had given him this parish. If he stood before him now he would kiss his hand in gratitude for what he had bestowed on him. Nowhere else, and certainly without the friendship of Joseph, would he have excelled as he had in Stormouth. For that he would forever give thanks.

"For God's sake, am I to wait all night? Or are you here to do my biding?"

He grew tired of her apparent ingratitude, he risked having his nightly frolics becoming stalled and interrupted. Rising from his chair, he walked, as naked as the day he was born, across the bare wooden floor towards the room where the bed and Ruby awaited him. "I will have my way with you child; there is no good hiding from me, you bitch."

"No one is hiding; Reverend…we were simply awaiting your arrival."

Bayles stopped dead; it was not the voice of an innocent, but a deeper more menacing tone. Straining his eyes to see deeper into the darkened room, he stepped hesitantly inside.

"Who...?" He began, halting immediately as he saw visions of hell. Two red painted devilish faces with bright white teeth and blazing eyes glared at him. Whoever, had the audacity to act in such a manner, dressed in dark clothes, and carried a vicious looking, wide barreled pistol which were held, cocked and ready to use.

"Come to us priest, and allow us to explain." The invitation wasn't one he could ignore. While one apparition held his stare, the other moved behind him and pushed him violently into the room.

Men, Bayles thought, as he fell at the feet of Ruby who was dressed in her outdoor clothing, not the gossamer thin transparent dress he had expected.

"Anything you wish to say to your ex-employer?" The question sounded menacing, and he sweated in fear as Ruby crouched lower, touched his face, smiled sweetly and spat. For one so young she produced a copious amount of spittle. He winced as it clung, then dripped from his face.

"That wasn't too lady like, was it love? But well done." The red face came close and an open hand slashed across the priest's face with such force he almost lost his sanity. Bayles desired to cry out but stifled the feeling, instead he watched as the man, who had struck a priest, handed a golden coin to Ruby, and say, "Take this and go with our thanks. Forget what you have seen here."

They had paid her, more importantly, she appeared to, no longer be in awe, or dread him. A few hours ago and she would have done what he ordered, now her reaction was to spit in his face.

"Now, good reverend, we have been told to treat you with the respect and due consideration your position deserves, just like you showed poor old Jed."

The name Jed, struck a chord, which was when Bayles realised he was in trouble.

Chapter Forty Five

The darkened figure of death had been unleashed upon Stormouth. It rode upon the wind, breathing its foul breath upon those it sought. It could not be stopped, nor ignored, many would feel its wrath before its thirst was quenched. Those that tasted its vileness were consumed, and so it would continue until the reaper had completed its feasting.

* * *

While Reverend Bayles suffered indignity, heaped upon indignity, Adam Wood regaled his guests with quips and merriment, unaware of the evil which stalked the town. The night was theirs, and they intended to enjoy it. His small group were relaxed, unconcerned, they had played a few hands of cribbage and drank a bottle of claret. They were at ease with the world and each other, life was theirs to enjoy. Irons watched them, and indicated the harpsichord player to play a little louder. He knew how to manipulate the atmosphere for his clients, it was into this ambience that Adam made his move. Tired of gentlemanly games, he desired excitement.

"Shall we make the evening a, little more enjoyable, gentlemen? What say we play a few hands of Quadrille and raise the stakes to a guinea a hand?" Adam accepted a new deck of cards which Williams offered, and began dealing before anyone could protest. Cards was his forte, quadrille his favoured game, one he excelled at. "A few hands combined with a little gaming will serve us well, do you not think?"

"Not tonight, Wood." He turned to see that Saunders, a man he had known and played against for longer than he cared to recall, had stood, refusing to play.

"What ails you, my friend? I simply assumed we would partake of a few hands of friendly gamesmanship."

"I fear, my father threatens to curtail my account should I lose any more to you Wood. He sees in you the ruination of my credibility, and that I can ill afford to lose. I will watch, or ask Irons for a girl, but I will not play my friend."

"But my dear fellow, Quadrille is a four handed game. Without you this evening would be boring, to say the least."

"I would rather be drunk and bored, than poor and satisfied with merriment. You will have to find another." Saunders turned and left unwilling to risk all for Wood.

"How unfortunate, it appears our friend has lost more than money, his wits are addled as well." Adam smirked but felt slighted, without another to make up the table, the game could not begin. More irksome was the sight of his other friends standing, ready to leave also.

"I could take the empty seat…if there are no objections?" The man's voice came from the direction of a deep buttoned, high backed, leather winged chair. Wood sighed contentedly as the man leaned around the chair for not only did the stranger appear wealthy, but his exquisite appearance appealed to Wood. His apparel was certainly not cheap. From his shoes, to the wig upon his head, his elegance oozed sophistication. His one embellishment, the beauty spot on his left cheek marked him as a dandy, a wealthy fool who, hopefully, had more money than sense and knew nothing of Adam's abilities.

"You're welcome, sir, but be aware we play for high stakes; pounds not pennies," Adam replied, eyeing the man carefully. He was, he determined, someone of equal standing, certainly no one's fool, not that Adam cared one way or the other. He wished to discover this man's merits, while his money was as acceptable as anyone's.

"I heard Quadrille mentioned and was intrigued. I have not played since Paris. I trust this will sweeten the pot for all concerned." He placed a money bag upon the table, eased the bindings apart and allowed Adam to see gold within.

"Admirable, please join us." Lured by the coinage, Adam was enthralled; this could prove a profitable, and enjoyable evening, indeed.

"It will be a pleasant re-acquaintance with a lost art," the dandy stated pleasantly.

"You were in Paris?" Richardson asked. "I too was there last summer, spent the season edifying my knowledge of all things French. It is most gratifying to meet another who shares my fondness of that city. Pray where did you reside?" Always eager to discuss the merits of that city, he failed to see the look of irritation Adam gave him.

"Oh, a little place, more country really, but it served. I was there on business and my host kindly accommodated me. I am sure we never met."

"Your name, sir, you have not furnished a name," Adam asked, without looking up.

"Mister, Thomas Sudbury, at your service, gentlemen, as for my trade, I am but a humble merchant and man of the world." Sudbury bowed elegantly, nodding politely to each man in turn.

"A merchant, aye, perchance you might call on my family's establishment before you leave. My brother and I operate the largest, and oldest establishments within the town. Not much Wood Distributors and Warehousing, do not know about business, ain't that so…aye what?"

Adam preened in uncontrolled gratification, while shuffling the cards. What happened next surprised everyone. Sudbury appeared too foppish to be dangerous, but he moved with a speed which defied his apparent relaxed demeanour. In the blink of an eye his sword was drawn and the point rested gently against Adam's throat.

"One move, Wood, and I will slit you from ear to ear." Taken by surprise, Adam's friends demanded an explanation while Adam himself dared not move.

"What is the meaning of this undignified behavior, sir? Put away your sword immediately!" Richardson alone seemed to recover quicker than the rest.

"I will, sir, but only to challenge this fool to a duel," Sudbury replied. Not once did his sword quiver, nor did his eyes leave Adam. The skill and strength such discipline required was not wasted on anyone.

"A what? A duel? Why sir, for what reason? Surely my invitation to make up a fourth is not enough reason, if not that then what else can I have done to annoy and upset you?" Adam spoke softly and with apparent confidence which was surprising as thirty-nine inches of polished steel rested gently against his throat. His mind though, worked quickly, trying to place where he might have irked the man. No matter how well he tried, neither the place, nor the incident came to mind, he was flummoxed.

"I care not for the cards, nor your pride. I made a promise to seek out and deal with those that disgraced my family. In truth, I did not think my quest would be so easily discharged." Sudbury spoke evenly, but those who witnessed his demeanour saw, just a hint of anger.

"You leave me confused, sir. How pray, have I disgraced your family? We have only just met, and your name, I fear, means nothing to me." Adam was no fool; he knew that if he stalled long enough, someone would come to his aid before he was either forced to accept the challenge, or this madman could be convinced he had the wrong man.

"Adam Wood, I charge you with cowardice and dishonesty," Sudbury said calmly. The sword did not flinch or waver, nor did Sudbury perspire under the strain, such was his composure.

"I assure you, what you state cannot have any bearing upon this man. He is a model of discretion, a man who would never do anything to inflame the passions of one so accomplished," Richardson stated, in an attempt to calm the moment.

"How little you know of this piece of horse shit. This mealy mouthed wimp treated my sister as a common whore. Drove her to an early grave, upon which I pledged to rid the world of her accusers." Sudbury's eyes flicked between

Wood and Richardson, he allowed his accusation to linger a moment then continued with his indictment. "This...sniffling toad, this treacherous cur, is the first of that family I have met. Therefore, he will answer for their crimes here and now, or die like the coward he is. Which is it to be Wood?"

Sudbury's blue eye were dead, like cold pools of water. Adam saw controlled hatred and anger towards him, Sudbury wasn't to be placated Fear slowed his brain, it took a moment to realise what had been meant. Then, as reality struck him, he demanded,

"You are Abigail's brother? I did not know...you were not at the wedding," he stammered.

"Unfortunately, I missed that abomination, but I assure you, I am her brother. More to the point I seek retribution for her death. You, Wood, were one of her accusers, you sent her into exile without a chance of explanation or common assistance. You killed her as if you pulled a trigger yourself."

Sudbury's words infiltrate Adam's brain. His words came softly.

"Abigail is dead? I didn't know." He perspired profusely, and his nerves made his left leg quiver. "What do you intend to do?" It was a stupid question with a sword blade close to slicing his throat asunder, but he had to know.

"Do? Why, kill you of course, what else did you expect?" Sudbury replied.

"Is this true; are you truly the girl's brother bent on retribution, or a common murderer?" Richardson asked.

"I am, sir, as such I have right to seek retribution for what this toad and his family did to her."

Richardson paused, then spoke to his friends in hushed tones. Confused by their apparent lack of attention Adam watched in amazement. He had assumed his friends would rush to his aid, argue his cause, and overpower this upstart. Instead, it seemed there was doubt, as if they were concerned, perhaps even believed him. Which wasn't so far from the truth, Unknown to Adam, Abigail's fate had been the topic of many heated discussions. The consensus of opinion was that the Woods had been overzealous in their judgment, that she should have been given the opportunity to explain herself fully before being accused and punished so severely. Now, it seemed, retribution had arrived in the form of a dandy.

"I fear, Wood, Mister Sudbury has just cause in calling you out," Richardson finally said.

"No. He lies! Surely you can see that?" Adam pleaded.

"I see nothing of the sort. Our association requires me to ask if you will accept me as your second. If you do, I would suggest the pit as a suitable place, and it should take place immediately, if both gentlemen agree."

Richardson's manner had changed. Gone were the kind words of friendship, replaced instead by the formality of a duel.

"Agreed," Sudbury stated his blade still at his victim's throat.

"I...I should take counsel from my brother," Adam stammered, sweat dripping from his nose. Then, to his embarrassment, and the horror of his friends, a stain appeared on his breeches. Adam Wood had pissed himself in fear.

"You turd," Sudbury sneered. "Were you this cowardly when you threw a young girl into the night? No, sir, you will seek counsel from no one, we deal with this here and now, pistols or foil? The choice is yours."

"I...I," Adam stammered.

"Answer, you cowardly milksop, I give you the chance to die a man and still you whimper. Choose, or I swear I will run you through here and now." Sudbury twitched the blade and drew the faintest amount of blood from Wood's neck. It was no worse than what any man might suffer while shaving, but it made Adam whimper pathetically.

"F...foil," the young Wood stammered, as a tear rolled down his cheek, adding to his humiliation.

Satisfied that his victim was beaten, and offered little or no threat, Sudbury relaxed his position and turned away. In that instant, the youth acted. Reaching forward, Adam snatched Richardson's blade from its scabbard and attacked Sudbury while his back was turned. It was a futile attempt at murder; the youth never stood a chance. Sudbury, with the ease of a master swordsman, sensed the attack and stepped neatly aside. With infinite expertise, he cut through skin, sinew and muscle, severing a major blood vessel with consummate precision. Adam fell to the ground, his blade falling upon the stone floor as he clasped both hands to the wound. He lost colour, his eyes rolled within his head as he tried to keep his blood within his body but he bled to death swiftly. Sudbury remained in his killing pose, while his victim's friends gathered around the body. Finally, Richardson looked up, and said,

"He's dead...Have no fear, sir, we will testify as to what happened. It was provocation; if you had not reacted he would have murdered you. Self-defence is a valid reason for killing the idiot."

"My thanks, gentlemen, at least now my sister is partly avenged." Sudbury stared at the body before finally lowering his sword.

"We will have to inform the authorities, of course, but with our evidence there should be no problem. The constables will need to speak with you. Where shall we say you are residing?" Richardson stated calmly, as if such events happened daily within the town.

"I have rooms at the 'Star'. I can be found there."

"Very well, I will inform the relevant authorities of that. In the meantime, perhaps you should relinquish your sword until after the enquiry."

"Of course," Passively, he handed the blood stained blade to Richardson,

"He didn't deserve anything less, gentlemen; the man was a fool and a coward. The world is all the better for his demise."

"We cannot comment on his behaviour. He was, after all known to us, but his family did act abysmally, they did your sister no favours. Please accept our condolences on your loss. However, we must ask, do you intend seeking out Josiah Wood, his elder brother?"

"I do. No doubt you will feel justified in telling him what has occurred and why I seek him. If that is so, then inform him that, until his family has suffered as mine has, I will not rest. I fear, gentlemen, there will be more bloodshed before I conclude my business here. Now, I will bid you goodnight and my apologies for the disturbance."

Sudbury returned to his chair, finished a small glass of red wine, placed some coins on the table, and retired from the room leaving Adam's friends alone to explain the death to Mister Irons and the constables.

The 'Star' was down the hill and to the left. Sudbury turned right as he left the hotel and disappeared into one of the many back alleyways that crisscrossed the town. There, tethered to the rear fence of a darkened tailor's shop, he found a horse which he unfastened and mounted. Then, with an unhurried ease that belied his foppishness, he discarded his wig, removed the beauty spot, and tossed them aside. He had vanished into the night long before Richardson informed the constable about him. Stormouth was far behind, when finally, he reined his horse in below an oak tree on the main road. His meeting with the man that waited there was no accident.

"Is it done?"

"It is, and far easier than I imagined. The man was a simpleton," Sudbury replied. Gone was his genteel accent, in its place a far rougher tone.

"Good. Here is what I promised, plus a little extra." A small leather drawstring purse was passed, Sudbury, weighed it in his palm. Seemingly satisfied, he opened the neck, peered in and smiled.

"Gold; such a pleasant colour, my thanks," He paused then asked, "His friends mentioned a brother, do you…?

"No. I have other plans for that one, my thanks anyway. What of you, back to Paris?"

"I do not believe so. There is a husband that would like to…well, let's simply say I think it best if I stay away a while longer. London, I think, I haven't seen it for some years. About time I reacquainted myself with what it has to offer."

"Then I can do no more than wish you well in whatever you do next," his benefactor said pleasantly.

"Too kind...Mister?"

"You know better than that.No names. Best that way, do you not agree?"

"As you wish. I would, though, suggest caution, family feuds can turn nasty. I would hate anything to happen to you." With that, Sudbury, gathered the reins and rode off into the darkness. As he faded into the night the man watched him go and smiled

"One down, two to go. Then, my dear, you will give me what I want," he whispered to the night sky. His plan was coming together and no one was any the wiser. Whistling happily, he turned and walked towards the lower town where another awaited his attention this night.

Chapter Forty Six

Death had feasted, consumed its first victim and went in search of another. From the affluence of the Crown Hotel, the dark angel descended upon the hovels of the 'Butts'. Searching for those who had but a little time left, it paid little heed as to how they came to him. Some, those who had lived longer than most, caught its glare and sighed before slipping away peacefully, their time expended. Others, like the decrepit and wizened drunk who had lived but a short while, died in a stupor. The tally rose with each new disciple but still it desired more. With evil malevolence it searched every darkened corner taking those it wanted until finally, it came upon a hovel and watched as its next victim awaited his final agonies.

* * *

"I demand you release me!" Edward Bayles, priest and liar sat, upon a wooden chair, alone, naked and afraid. His voice echoed around the room and haunted him with its clarity. Time had lost its significance, darkness enveloped him, and like any man, faced with such trepidation his mind conjured up all manner of self-doubt. Whoever the painted demons were, had planned well. They might be roughnecks and scoundrels, but he could influence and recognise them, if and when they removed his blindfold. Until then, he had other senses with which to aid his deliberations. His voice echoed, meaning where he was, must be large, no one spoke but he sensed their presence. More used to inflicting fear, he found his situation, unnatural, something he was not used to.

"Release me...do so now and we will consider the matter ended." He knew his words were wasted, men who hid behind childlike masks were cowards. Eventually they would make their demands and when that occurred, he would discover their identities. This stupidity was simply their way of scaring him, if they meant real harm, he would be dead by now, slain as easily as a chicken was killed for the pot.

"Show yourselves you cowardly dogs!" His belligerence was deliberate, he would use his anger and intelligence to induce errors. When they revealed themselves, he would then make them suffer. "Let me see your faces...Speak, or has the devil got your tongues?" Tilting his head, he strained to hear any fleeting noise upon which he could cling to. "I hear you...I am your priest, I demand you release me or suffer eternal damnation!"

He heard movement and turned his head in that direction, but still no one spoke. Someone was present watching him, but they seemed intent of remaining hidden, why, he knew not, but it was annoying and...frightening. With sight and sound, two vital points of reference inhibited, he must rely on his other senses. The room smelt vaguely familiar, which he could not place, while he could taste something which eluded him for the moment.

"End this foolery, and I make this promise. I will speak in your favour, do all I can to ease your guilt. The alternative is dire, continue with this nonsense, and I will make sure you suffer unmentionable punishment...are you prepared for death, you cowards?" Nothing came, had they gone, had they ever been present? In desperation, he screamed, "Speak...for God's sake, answer me...are you there?" The silence continued, making him doubt his sanity. Desperate to escape, he wrestled with his bindings, shaking the chair and wrenching his arms as sweat formed beneath his blindfold. All the while that taste grew in intensity. *What was it?* Fear, took his brain in tormented directions, alternating between clarity and obscurity. Whoever they were had crossed a line, no one should have the audacity to raise a hand against God's representative. Had he not told them often enough what their punishment would be if they dared to question the judgment of their betters?

"Your silence confirms to me that you are indeed whelps, runts, the lowest of the low. Have you returned from whence you came? Have you crawled back to the bowels of purgatory, to the crevices of hell and damnation? You are naught but cowards, knaves, scurrilous toads...you are certainly not men. I fear not cowards, so do your worst. I shall seek retribution on you all, no matter what you plan." His tirade, appeared pointless, for no one answered, most likely no one heard. Bayles was startled by a voice which sounded so close, so calm, so terrifying.

"Brave words, whoremonger, but you must wait a little longer, for we are not yet ready to deal with you." He sighed in relief. Men were present, men who he could influence. But to do so first he must gain their trust, then discover their weaknesses, exploit them and only then could he destroy them.

"Call me what you will but I am your friend, only I can give you what you need. Release me and we can talk of this like men." He would offer them anything, compassion, redemption from prosecution, a gaggle of Maggie's girls, anything but once he had outwitted them, he would turn upon them, and wrench their black hearts from their bodies with his own hands. "Come, friends, tell me what concerns you... tell me what you want me to do, then we can cease this absurdity, go our separate ways with no harm done." He knew he must show fortitude and confidence, that they could not break him, while working his magic upon them. He must turn their fears against them and weaken their resolve. Only when they realised the stupidity of their actions would falter and release him. But he had to offer them something tangible, he must offer them a means of escaping his wrath. "I sense you mean me no harm that this was meant to scare me nothing more. Well friends you succeeded, your cleric has seen fear, and doesn't like its face. What say you shall we part this place on good terms?" He waited, but his words failed to garner a response. Tiring of pretense, Bayles finally sneered with the arrogance he was known for.

"You fools! I have offered you a way to avoid further unpleasantness, and you refuse. Therefore, I will inform you of your choices. I am not afeared of you or death, I have made my peace with god and as for you well, when you realise your stupidity, you will be forced to release me. Then we shall see who has the last laugh, for I shall enjoy your discomfort as you are dragged kicking and screaming before the magistrates and Jurats. I shall laugh as you cry out for mercy and redemption and when you finally ask God to release you from your pain, I will ignore you, as you ignore me."

His arrogance failed to get a response. Neither his lies about assistance, nor that of punishment, had brought a reaction, his situation was dire, without assistance, he had but his own wit and guile to aid him. Desperately, he sought clues about his prison. The chair was rough, not delicate like the parlour chairs he was more used to. It was well-used, crude and creaked beneath his weight, he felt gouges in the wood. It was, fit only for some peasant's hovel. He wriggled and sniffed, that wafting aroma came to him again. Still unable to place where he knew it from, he put it aside and focused on what he knew. The floor beneath his feet was dry dirt which his toes dug into it easily, importantly an earth floor indicated a poorly built house of perhaps timber and mud.

You would desire to remain concealed, couldn't be seen carrying me through the streets, so where? 'The Butts' that had to be where they would bring him, to hide him among the labyrinth of narrow streets where no one would speak of what they saw, or heard. He cringed at the thought; he avoided the area as much as possible, as he did those who lived here. *Rats* he hated rats, the way they stared with beady eyes and chewed on everything and anything. If he were in the Butts, then rats would come to feast on his perfect skin. That smell came again, stronger, accompanied by a feeling of heat behind him. He felt it burn his neck and he wanted to move. Too hot for a fire, it came in waves, more like…Suddenly he knew, he had unravelled the clues, he knew where he was. The heat, the small grains of grit he felt in the soil, they had made a mistake, he knew where he was.

"Fools that you are, you thought yourselves clever, but I have you. I am the master, my Intelligence has defeated your ignorance. I know this be a smithy, and that will be your downfall…I shall demand every smithy searched, and when we discover the owner, they will be…encouraged to reveal the names of those that do this."

"Very clever, we bow to your superior intelligence. However you assume too much, you speak as if you believe we should fear your intellect. Maybe in the past we might, but no longer. I suggest you reconsider your position and imagine what your fate to be, for you have missed one vital, element."The voice was soft, precise, and Bayles knew instantly that his captor had been present all along, watching, listening.

"What have I missed? I see nothing in your actions which I cannot counter. You have revealed much and when you release me, as you will, my intelligence will be your downfall. It is what separates you from your masters, for you have erred, your tactics have not worked, and now you are trapped by your own stupidity. You have but two choices, kill me, which would be an abomination in the eyes of God, something no sane man would contemplate, or set me free. My offer for clemency remains on offer even now at this late stage I am willing to show mercy but I will not be willing to help much longer. If you confine me then the town constable will become involved, I shall testify as to what you have done and there will be no recourse save to pursue you to a rightful punishment. You may wonder how I know this, I will tell you, my sad friends. I know, because I can foresee your futures, and it looks bleak, very bleak?" Bayles spoke with renewed certainty of his impending release.

"Brave words reverend, but we are not ignorant fools, we began this knowing our destiny, and aware of the consequences. You offer us nothing but a day before the beak and then a journey to the gallows, no matter which path we take. My question to you then is this, if death is our destiny, why should we not continue upon this road, for is it not better to die as free men, than serfs." Edward Bayles listened intently, the man was, intelligent, but also cold single minded, focused. His logic made him dangerous and Bayles shuddered in trepidation, for he knew this man was no fool. Controlling his words as best he could, Bayles replied,

"Murder is a hanging offence…So far, you have done nothing to warrant that charge, do not do so now. I sense your anger, but I also know that if murder was your intent you would have done so already. You hide in this hell hole because you are unsure, unsure of your next step. I say, remove this rag from my eyes, step into the light and face me like a man, not a coward together we can resolve what ails you."

"You sir have balls, and for that I commend you, but it is you that is the coward not us."

"Then why hide like rats in corners? Show yourselves like men not painted fools." Bayles heard footsteps, finally he had provoked a response, the man was moving approaching. Inwardly he smiled, It was the first step in winning; the man was doing as he wanted, as he commanded.

"We do not hide but have been waiting, now we are ready to proceed." Bayles turned to face the sound of a new voice, one that sounded far more dangerous than the first.

"How so?" the priest asked suspiciously.

"I fear for you sir …I truly do for your intelligence isn't as well-honed as you perceived…I would have thought even you would have realised by now we care not for your offers of clemency or for your threats. Maybe I should explain our plans for you in far easier terms. You are here to answer charges that have been levelled against you, charges of corruption, deceit, violation, degradation and fornication. You are on trial sir for which your life is at stake." Bayles felt the breath on his neck and shivered, not with fear but, with satisfaction. His accuser was educated, with knowledge of the law. It was possible he came from the upper town, might even be someone he had dined with now he must ascertain who that was.

"If I am to be accused and tried, you sir, cannot do so.To do me harm, your accusations must be presented before the magistrates. Which, if you had absolute proof, you would have done which means sir this …trial has no bearing in law. So do your worst, I confess…to everything. Take me before my peers, let them decide my guilt." He knew that he could admit to anything here and it had no place in law. He had friends who would dismiss such a conviction and release him before the sun rose. Without credible witnesses, a judge and jury, a confession gained under duress was without credence. "Do your worst, for you will soon realise your stupidity and end this farcical charade.

"Brave words, but your views matter not. Perhaps in more normal times such words would mean something, but we are not bound by convention. Unlike the manner in which you dispensed justice, we shall present evidence, hear testimony and then indict you for your crimes. We shall offer you the same rights you offered your victims. You may make your confession, plead your case but afterwards we shall wash our hands of you for you are already condemned."

"A travesty, you speak of murder nothing less. You are no better than a mob and I spit on your principle!" Bayles liked to control but here he was unable to do anything but listen as they mocked him and all he had achieved.

"Be that as it may, but after your guilt is proven, we shall meet one last time, when I shall reveal myself, for only then will I desire you to feast upon my face. I desire to see you broken, defeated, accused and convicted by those you have abused with your lies. You will see my face and beg me to forgive you, only I will not. I will turn my back as you turned yours on those who sought aid from you. We are your harbingers of death, your winged angels who will dispatch you back from whence you were spawned and may God have mercy upon your soul."

"WHAT!" The icy grip of fear gripped Bayles as the reality of his position finally struck home. "You cannot! It is not legal. Harm me and you will suffer the fires of damnation. You will be hunted, decried in both the eyes of man and God. Are you prepared to endure eternity pursued and persecuted by both God and Satan? You can end this foolishness and disappear without me ever knowing your faces, or continue and suffer, which is it to be?" He almost screamed in defiance. He had but one last chance to halt this madness or they would do as they said, he would be accused, condemned and possibly committed, without either trial or defense.

"Silence swine, prepare to meet your accusers." The voice was strangely familiar but had been muffled to make it hard to place. "But while you listen, be aware, my purpose here is but for one reason only…I am your executioner.

Chapter Forty Seven

Without warning the blindfold was removed leaving Bayles momentarily disorientated. After so long in the dark, his perception was slow to return but slowly, a room, lit by one flickering reed torch, became clear. His tormentor stood out of sight, behind him, only his breathing betrayed his presence. Then from the left, a wizen, old cripple, shuffled into view as if carrying a great load. Bayles smelt his arrival, the peasant stank as all such swine stank, but as this shriveled bag of bones stood in front of him he saw in his eyes, hatred and animosity.

"Do you see the criminal?" the voice demanded from the shadows.

"I do, sir, that's the bastard that murdered my son." For such a frail man, the force with which he slapped Bayles across the face was unexpectedly harsh.

"Bastard...how dare y…"

"Silence…the prisoner will not speak until told to do so," the voice demanded.

"But I never murdered anyone, nor have I ever seen this old goat afore." Bayles's indignation was pitiful, but it brought nothing but scorn from his accusers.

"The accused should remember he will be dealt with more speedily if he but acknowledged his crimes. To attempt to refute our accusations will simply delay the inevitable but…we can continue. You did know this man's son."

"How so?" Bayles demanded.

"Was it not you that dealt with Will Greenman, as if he was nothing more than night soil that stuck to your shoe?"

"Aaah, now I understand. You expect me to grief for a common thief? Well sir I will not for Greenman was a common thief and waster who was tried and found guilty in accordance with the law. Is this why you treat me thus? By God but if that is all you have then I have little to fear."

"You bastard, you knew the evidence was false, that your witnesses lied like dogs." The decrepit old man seemed to straighten, as if he had received some God given strength of purpose.

"Do I? From what I recall, Greenman was accused and convicted for the theft of eighty buttons from his employer. The magistrates heard the evidence, discussed the merits and decided his fate. As for my part in the trial, I do not remember saying anything, either in defence or condemnation. Oh, I admit, one hundred lashes did seem a trifle overzealous, but more than fitting for the crime. Am I to be condemned for that as well?"

"Didn't have to speak, did you? You had convinced them before he ever got into that court room." The wizen old man stared with defiance making Bayles cringe. He had indeed remained silent because sentence had indeed been agreed with Joseph and the others over a fine pot of hare stew before the day's proceedings had begun, that was how justice was done. With so many indictments each week, it was how justice was done in Stormouth. He now knew these fools were not only naïve, but more than likely common criminals with grudges to appease.

"Your arrogance astounds me Cleric," the voice added. "No Man could survive such a punishment but you said nothing. For all your sanctimonious words, you killed him as surely as if you had killed him yourself. More damning than that, you cared not for what happened to his family."

"Why should I concern myself with the plight of a thief's family? Obviously, though you are about to tell me."

"Oh, I will. Your punishment not only killed Will but condemned his wife and children to penury. Without his wage, they were forced from their home, to find sustenance where ever they could and come next winter they will all die unless his friends aid them. But you don't care, do you? I can see you don't, you're a killer, with blood on your hands."

"Sentimental piffle. Am I to be blamed for every thief and beggar that lives in the parish?" he sensed the flaw in their accusations, admittedly he was still in trouble, but if this was the best they had, he would defeat them in a trice then his friends would deal with them brutally. All he must do was survive a little longer. "I thought not. Men such as I carry a heavy burden, we must make difficult decisions, if the majority are to live in safety. We have to rise above personal feelings for the greater good. So if that is all you h....."

"We have other charges, more damning than just one poor soul. Bring in the next witness." Edward yawned in mock boredom, their puerile claims could be defeated with logic and intelligence. Greenman had been defeated he would deal as quickly with another they produced.

"Is this him?" the voice demanded as a young pretty girl appeared. A girl Bayles would, in more social situations, have gladly used for pleasure,

"It is, sir," she replied.

"Tell us what he did to you."

"Must I, sir?" she implored.

"If you wish to see his evilness punished, then you must. Speak the truth, girl, for you have nothing to fear from him....not anymore." His accuser sounded concerned, and so he should. Bayles recognised her, she was one of many whore he had used. Most, he forgot, but this one had been remembered for her exceptional abilities. Reticent at first she had blossomed after he had broken her in. That had truly been an enjoyable summer until she had gone, only to return now.

"Tell them, child, speak the truth for we are all eager to hear what I did which was so wrong." He sneered, craning his face forward. She would not speak out for he had taught her well. She feared him, more importantly she feared the will of God, which he could summon at any moment. They had lost ignorant peasants would never condemn him, for they still thought him capable of granting them eternal salvation. "Tell them that you came to me as a common whore, you took my money, yet I am now accused of what …debauchery? My God every man present has committed that crime. But speak child, tell them how I pleasured you, but be aware, any lies you utter will be recorded in the great book of truths. Then, on Judgement day, when you stand before St Peter he will recall every lie you have ever told, especially lies spoken about your priest. He will look upon you with dismay and have no hesitation in sending you to the fiery depths of hell to share eternity with all the other liars in Beelzebub's domain. Is that what you wish for yourself, Eternal unrest? If not, I suggest you consider your words with care." Safe in that knowledge that she was anxious, fearful and unwilling to condemn him he smiled devilishly. It was this misguided obedience, this innocence which made them easily manipulated and controlled. Another of their witnesses would fail, and he relaxed. His smirk sealed his fate, she saw it and shrank before him, her head bowed in apparent dismay. "Do not fret child your bravery is to be complimented but you have been misguided by fools. Now do what God demands, speak the truth and be free of lies and liars."

Unexpectedly, she struck, spitting and gouging at him. She swore, she cried, she screamed, every emotion was released in one great outpouring.

"You swine…I was only fourteen when he forced me, ordered me to fornicate with him. Then…he said, as a whore my only use in life was on me back, said that, then sold me to his friends for a silver shilling. Told me, if I did not obey, my Ma and Pa would be thrown from their home, said he would make them watch as he and his friends defiled me. I don't know what that means but, it don't sound good do it?" Her anger turned her into a wild cat, overpowering her awe of the priest. She clawed and spat, spittle mixed with his blood; she had to be pulled from him before she finished what they had begun.

"She lies! I said nothing of the sort," Bayles sneered. "She'll say anything to save herself." The muscles in his neck stretched as he stared intently at the girl, while blood trickled from a cut lip.

"She doesn't need saving, not by you," the voice said coldly. "We know what you are and what you do. You are vile, Bayles. Some of us knew that from the moment you first arrived, and since then many others have witnessed your depravity. They know only too well what you are capable of, none more so than your own housemaid who tells us you killed her father. Murdered him and disposed of the body in a grave meant for another. Not the actions of a Godly man, is it? I say, enough of this travesty"

"I agree," Bayles added. "As for my maid, did she not say that I saved her from being raped by him? Did she say that I, in fact, saved the ungracious bitches life? No, of course not, you hear what you wish and ignore the truth. I should have been thanked, not condemned. She has connived and twisted the truth into what she thinks you wish to hear. This mockery, of so called justice, has lost any credibility. You rely on unsubstantiated rumours. No court would believe any of this...lunacy. Now, let me go and I promise we will say no more about any of these events."

"Have you not comprehended any of what has been said here?" The voice was suddenly right behind him, so close that he could smell the coffee and tobacco on the man's breath. "You will never leave here alive." The sudden reality of his predicament made him whimper in fear. Until now he had clung to the hope that this was nothing more than an elaborate hoax, designed to scare him. Now his demise had become a reality and he was truly concerned. "Shut up, you lump of shit!" the man demanded, grabbing Bayles by the hair and pulling his head back violently. The priest closed his eyes; death, he was sure, was only moments away. "You will suffer as you made others suffer and endure that pain long enough to understand what your victims went through...Bring it in," the voice demanded, and Bayles waited. With his head firmly held, he could only stare, wide eyed, as two men carried something into view.

"NOOOOO!" the priest screamed as finally, he saw where the source of heat came from. The brazier, carried between two well soaked wooden poles, which steamed as the water evaporated, was carried by two men one of whom Bayles recognised instantly.

"Set it down and prepare him," the voice commanded.

"Why? What is the meaning of this?" Bayles asked of Spriggs.

"Do you think I would allow you to make a fool of me? I paid you handsomely to acquire that land and you failed me. This is no more than you deserve and I relish to be part of your demise."

"Demise, no, no this cannot be, what of my defense?" Bayles spluttered, his voice filled with fear. "Will you not allow me the opportunity to defend myself?"

"No!" The response was short and final. "You are found guilty by this court and committed to death. We are your executioners; you will never see the light of day again."

Bayles struggled pointlessly, Spriggs stood by as men appeared to lash a thick chain to his bindings. Harshly he was released from the chair and secured to the chain. Then when all was ready, he was hoisted to his feet.

"What...what are you doing?" Bayles whimpered as realisation that his trial and death had been pre-planned.

"I trust you appreciate our macabre sense of history and the nature of your death," his persecutor sneered. "Spriggs here suggested it as suitably fitting seeing as you like swine so much."

"I don't...tell them, it was you who wanted Horn and his swine removed, tell them...I beg of you."

"Tell them what priest...that you are a sniveling lump of mire, who has used his position and authority to steal, lie, and spread fear among these good people. Methods you used to fill your pockets, and to feed your depraved body and mind. No I'll not speak for you but I will watch as you finally suffer for all you have inflicted. Your punishment, while painful will be appropriate and fitting for your crimes."

Bayles screamed hysterically as the chain was pulled tighter. Pain, seared through him like branding irons. His muscles were torn and he screamed in agony as he was pulled higher. Terror, made his body react, and he soiled himself, the stench made them laugh, but not stop their work.

"See what he has done? Is this a man to be feared? No, he is not. Tonight, Bayles, you will experience what religious men have inflicted upon the innocent for centuries. You will suffer that fate, and no one will mourn your passing. Continue."

"Noo! Please, I beg you. I am not a harsh man; I only did what I did because others made me. I can change. Let me go and I will leave here chastened and repentant." He cried out as they began smearing his legs in a slippery substance. His cries were ignored, only the voice spoke malevolently.

"You will leave, but not alive...you have persecuted and terrified too many for too long. Your death will reflect the harshness meted out to many in the name of the Church...hoist him over."

The chain rattled above him, tears streamed from his eyes, as he was positioned above the fire. He sobbed, and whimpered as he saw a man pumping a set of bellows which fed the fire in the brazier, making it glow brighter.

"Lower him...slowly; he must feel the full effect. Fitting, isn't it priest?

That you now endure what your church once used to force confessions from their victims? You will be roasted, Bayles, the flames will sear the evil from your body. Like you, the church used this against innocent men, roasted them until the flesh fell away." His tormentor spoke softly, as the chain rattled and the priest dropped another few inches.

"You cannot…it's…nooooo." Bayles twisted and cried, tears fell as the heat caused the fat to catch. The stench of cooking flesh made many feel sick, but only Bayles felt the pain in his legs. He pleaded, he cried out, but no one attempted to move him.

"Spread more fat, add it thick. I want him to feel the pain as long as he can bear it," his torturer commanded.

"If…I…am to die…allow…me…to…see my executioner," Bayles whimpered. He was close to unconsciousness; the pain, unbearable to begin with, had all but gone as his flesh dripped to the floor. His blood was boiling, death hovered at his shoulder. His bones came into view, as the fat bubbled and cooked. One of his executioners vomited at their cruelty, only then, as Edward Bayles died, did his tormentor step into view. He leant forward, gagging at the smell, and forced open the priest's eyes.

"See who I am…witness your executioner."

Through lips drawn tight in pain, Bayles cried out in agony as he recognised his tormentor.

"Why…what have…I done…to you…I thought we…were…friends?"

"Never…you served my needs, nothing more. However, I will grant you a last service; a courtesy, something you never gave your victims." The blade slipped between the priest's ribs, severing the heart's main blood vessel. To make sure his death was final and complete; his killer twisted the blade back and forth. In those last moments of the devil's life, his killer saw the contempt and hollowness of the priest's existence.

"May you rot in eternal hell? Burn his clothes; destroy anything that links him to this place," His killer commanded. He felt a mixture of emotions; joy, redemption, satisfaction and a tinge of remorse. It was fitting that in his last seconds Bayles had seen his killer, it made his desecration more poignant, yet the swine had not sought redemption for his sins.

"Cut him down, brand him so no one will recognise the scum, then dress him in that redcoat's uniform. Once done, set him adrift in the harbour with a jug of brandy and a pipe of baccy. If he is ever discovered I want his discoverers to think him an ignorant soldier who got drunk and set fire to himself. Hopefully, he will be buried in an unmarked grave in some desolate graveyard and forgotten."

Chapter Forty Eight

Death had claimed its second victim, now only one remained. While the pure of heart slept, an entity, a Dark Angel, unseen but malevolent, visited the homes of those it wished to take. It went unheeded and unstoppable; no mortal could foretell its next victim. The spectre took young and old alike, the innocent and the infirmed. Life had a natural order, but this night death was aided by another. Men were killing as well as the ungodly. Adam Wood had died a coward's death, while Bayles had gone to his maker with angry words on his lips, screaming retribution.

The third would be more difficult, an innocent and its mother, were to become pawns in a morbid game. Death's cold, fingers paused, ready to touch each in turn and end their thread of life; eternity beckoned and she fought back. Unsure whether to accept their lives, the macabre being watched though soulless eyes and waited as she moaned and writhed in agony. Mortals might yet have a hand in her fate, though failure would mean their lives being forfeited.

* * *

"Bastard!" she screamed. "Sweet Jesus!" The pain was agonising, never had she endured anything like it. It came in waves, relentless and excruciating, sweat poured from her and she held the old woman's fingers in a vice-like grip. The child was due and she was scared.

"Swear all yous likes, my dear. Soon be over, dearie." The woman was ancient, her face haggard and hard and all the while she sucked upon a stubby clay pipe. The aroma of the baccy gave the room a comforting scent and she whispered soothingly in the ear of her charge, while wiping her forehead with a damp cloth. "That's right child, breathe deeply…this little bugger wants to make his appearance. No holding him, is there? Calm child…calm, soon be over."

Never a place of comfort or calm, the room had changed significantly, now it was a place of pain, blood and blasphemy. Mary-Ann had been there when the girl's labour had begun. Instinct, and remembering what Maggie had told her, she had summoned Ma Epps. The old midwife had brought nearly everyone in the 'Butts' into the world, she would do the same for Abigail.

"Bloody bastard, may he rot in hell." Rarely had she succumbed to the use of blasphemies, now it came naturally. Through tear reddened eyes she stared at the wizen old woman Maggie had employed to deliver her child into the world. From opposing ends of the social spectrum, for the moment, they were as one

"Aye, they all be bastards, but its God's will that we bear their pain. Breathe deeply my, dear, soon be over." Ma smiled a toothless smile, but knew that this would be neither easy nor painless.

"I will seek revenge! I would rip his throat out," The girl screamed, writhed in agony, then sank back onto the filthy bedding. She was becoming weaker, praying for the agony to end.

"Course you will, dearie…plenty of time for that…breathe deeply, my dear, just breathe," Ma soothed, sipping heavily from a stone bottle of ale. There was little to be done, she'd seen such things many times before. The girl would die, as would her child. For all her cursing and screaming, there was nothing to do but wait and pray.

"I will kill them all for what they have done to me," Wracked in pain, and with death awaiting her, Abigail, found the strength to curse Joseph Wood and those who lived in the style she deserved. For almost six months she had lived in destitution, hidden away, forgotten, yet Wood, once again made her cry out in pain. "Sweet Jesus!" The words died on her lips and Ma Epps looked aghast at her patient.

"She lives but not much longer," The old woman said shaking her head despairingly. "I needs another flask, for sure she'll need a tipple afore this is done, and so will I. Keep her calm, I'll be back." Ma Epps struggled to stand, her knees stiff with age. "Only be a moment, my dear." She was trying to be kind, not that Abigail heard her. She was adrift in a sea of pain, her mind lapsing between reality and what was her worst nightmare. She dreamt of being back among servants, fine wines and food, to sleep in beds with clean blankets. That was her destiny, but they had conspired to ruin her which was why she had murdered them many times in her dreams. Upon her nemesis Bayles, she had inflicted such humiliation, pain and depravity, he had screamed for mercy. Each dream had begun with him stuffing his ponderous jowls with food. Sometimes the dream had changed then, sometimes she had appeared from one of the dishes to either stab him with a silver fork or to remove his eyeballs with a blunt spoon. A more macabre vision saw her as a boatman, employed to take him to a ship at sea Lounging in the stern, Bayles regaled her with lurid stories of what he did to girls such as her. His vileness was such that only the appearance of dearest, sweetest, Nathaniel, descending like a vengeful angel had finished the priest by plunging him head first into the sea. All she had seen, as she rowed away, were his stick thin legs waving in the air. In another vision, Bayles laid upon a bed of nettles, his robes all gilded and heavy, open, revealing his nether regions bare and bloodied. That dream had woken her, because in her hands she held his manhood, which she had sliced from his body. Her visions came randomly; some were torrid, making her scream out as she did when the pain coursed through her body, while others were of happier times like those weeks when first Maggie, and then Mister Turnbottle had saved her. In the solitude of this place she had dreamt of revenge against those that had treated her with such contempt. Never would she grow fond of another living soul, no one would ever do such a thing to her again. But in her darkest hours, three women had grown close.

"Is she to die?" Mary-Ann asked, Ma Epps turned scornfully.

"Told yous to stay with her" Epps drank deeply from the bottle. Despite her reputation the aging midwife was a drunk, who lost as many new born's, as she delivered live. Now though wasn't the time, or the place, to say that. "It be unsure, medicine might help, for she's weak, but such things be only for the wealthy and this one'll never see a bedchamber with sheets and silks will she? Nah thought not, all we can do is aids her, and deal with the aftermath as best we can." They stood in what Abigail referred laughingly to as her living room. Despondently, they exchanged worried looks before Ma Epps held the girl's face and said,

"Should have dealt with this afore the quickening occurred. A tight corset or a dose of soapwort might have finished it, as it is she'll die afore this one's born. Seen it too many times afore, it's choked, yous see, needs a proper physician, she does. Can she afford one?"

"She ain't got any money," Mary-Ann added wistfully

"Pity...she's a pretty one...but such is life. Without proper care she's as good as dead," Ma whispered, and held the young girl close to her.

"No!" Mary-Ann screamed, before the old hag clasped a hand across the young girl's mouth silencing her instantly.

"Hush your row, you silly bint. There be nowt I can do. Her only hope is a doctor man, but yous said she aint got no scram, so we must keep her quiet until God takes her from us."

"No...what I means is she ain't got any coins...but she knows someone who does."

"Then I suggest, whoever that be gets her some proper help and quick." Mary-Ann was caught between loyalty to her friend and the need for secrecy. The women had shared many ordeals, and a few bottles of wine. Could she though, break a promise, more to the point, Miss Abigail's friend wouldn't be too happy if she was to die, or lose the child.

"I will send word, ask them to aid her but that will take time, time you said she don't have. I beg of you, is there nothing you can do for her? Do whatever needs doing, help her, but do it quick."

"I aids these girls best I can, but when the child is choked, even a doctor man would be hard pressed to aid them.

"Please, I beg you. Her friend will reward you handsomely." Mary-Ann wasn't sure if that was so but she had to offer the old hag something to aid her friend.

"There is something."

"What...what do you need?" Mary-Ann pleaded.

"There's an 'erb, it may aid her but I don't have any ere. Yous will have to get it. Can you do that, girl?" Ma didn't sound too hopeful but Mary-Ann knew they had to try.

"I will. Tell me what I needs to do."

"Alright, but listen good, yous has to find Nichols the Apothecary; he will have what I needs. You have to be quick, and quiet like. I'll watch over this one while you're gone."

"Where...where do I look?" the child demanded, pulling her shawl about her.

"His shop has been closed some months but...you'll find him plying his trade in the 'Lamb' or the 'Lion'. Tell him I needs two pinches of his special herb. Tell him not to sell me short then fetch it ere quick sharp. Only when you've done that can you look for her friend."

"What is it, Mother?" she asked, pausing at the door, hand on the latch.

"Never you's mind, girl, just pray its magical properties relax her enough to pass the child. Run like the wind, her life lies in the fleetness of your feet...oh, and tell Nichols I'll pays him 'amorrow."

Mary-Ann, young, but worldly wise ran as fast as she could, she had no intention of failing her friend. Ma's instructions were vague, and she neither wanted, nor needed to know any more. Ignorance in such matters was far safer for all concerned. Hurrying through the back alleyways, she avoided outstretched hands that clawed at her as she raced passed. She ran as if the devil was on her tail, until finally, she burst into the snug of the Lion tavern.

"Nichols the apothecary?" she called out breathlessly.

"Who wants to know?" the barman demanded.

"A friend," she replied.

"Not here. Haven't seen him in two days," she didn't wait to hear anymore, but turned and raced towards the Lamb Inn. Stormouth was no different from any other port town, taverns and ale houses were in abundance. Sometimes they stood side by side but not the Lion, nor the Lamb. They were either end of the quays. More than once she was forced to stop and breathe deeply before resuming her search, until once again she burst through the door of the tavern, the silence she caused allowed her ask her question without raising her voice.

"There," the landlord stated, sullenly pointing to a dark corner. Mr Nichols wasn't difficult to spot. He was a small, weasel like man who twitched nervously. A man who's eyes had a crazed, glazed, look about them as if he had all the worries of the world upon him. He spoke in short sentences, while sniffing loudly, a truly despicable looking man. Sideling up to him, she told him what Ma had said, then waited. He took his time, pondering if she could be trusted, before eventually taking her by the arm and leading her outside to the log store.

"Never, do that again, might have scared off my customers. You say Mother Epps sent you. Why?"

"A girl having difficulties with a birth, Ma wants your herbs to ease her suffering."

"Aaah I gets you…alright, I'll trade. Ma knows what to do, but tell her it's fresh. She should cut the dosage down a little," he explained, removing some leaves from a pouch. The smell was heady and overpowering, and for reasons unknown to her she suddenly felt very hungry. "Tell her its good stuff, straight off the boat. Tell her the cost has gone up, but I will trust her. Or you can pay me now in kind. Come on darling, how's about a little fumble on account?" Nichols grabbed Mary-Ann around the waist and squeezed lecherously.

"Sod off, you old goat, aint got the time, nor the inclination. Ma said you would get paid, so you'll have to wait like the rest of us." Taking the herbs, she placed them carefully into her apron pocket, and ran as fast as she could back to the tumble down shack. Even before she entered, she heard her friend scream in agony.

"Shut her up for the love of God." A disgruntled voice shouted angrily from a neighbouring property. "Spit it out, or die, but shut up!" It wasn't pleasant, nor was it compassionate but it was typical of the people who lived in the 'Butts.'

"I have it, he gave it to me," Mary-Ann cried out in relief as she entered the building.

"Let's pray we are in time. Bring it here and do as I say." Abigail was worse, bathed in sweat, and her face, contorted in agony.

"Should I find her friend and get him to fetch the doctor man?" Even for one so young, she knew that if Ma's potion didn't work, her friend would surely be dead before morning. If that happened, then all they had done for her would be for nothing.

"Give me a moment, to prepare this and infuse her, then we'll know." Ma took the herb, ripped the strangely shaped leaves apart and placed them into a bowl. Using a wooden spoon, she ground the leaves even finer until they were tiny particles. Eventually satisfied, Ma then took a pan of boiling water from above the fire, added the water, and mashed the leaves until they turned into an infusion. Satisfied, she poured the liquid into a mug and returned to the girl "Hold her down while I feed her this." Immediately, Mary-Ann smelt the fumes, the strong scent filled the room and she felt hungry again.

"What strange herb is that?" she enquired, innocently.

"You don't want to know, child, but those that use it turn into crazed knuckleheads. I have seen um do the wildest of things after inhaling the fumes, but it do have medicinal qualities, as we shall hopefully see. Now, cover your face otherwise the demons of hell will enter your brain and carry you off to damnation."

Mary-Ann was a naïve, God fearing girl, who had heard the priest talk of damnation and hell and believed that was the fate that awaited anyone who didn't do as they were told. She knew the word knucklehead, but as yet had never seen one. The way Ma described them; she had no wish to either. So, she clasped the bottom of her dress and held it across her mouth and nose as the old woman took the bowl of steaming liquid, and lifted Abigail from her filthy pillow.

"We will know shortly if this works, if it don't, her fate will be in God's hands, only he will be able to decide what becomes of her."

Gently the hag blew on the vapours which swirled before Abigail who inhaled the fumes. Mary-Ann gasped, even with her face covered she smelt the pungent sweet smell which made her swoon, her head was light and she saw stars.

"Get out, girl! Stupid sod, told yous not to breathe it," Ma Epps hissed in anger. She had enough to contend with without a knucklehead as well. The last sight Mary-Ann had was terrible. Her friend was thrashing about the bed in pain, inhaling a sweetly scented smoke.

"She's going to die and I will be blamed." With that dire thought to stir her, there was but one thing to do. While Ma looked after Mistress Abigail, she needed to fetch those that had been with Abigail since the beginning. With that thought, she ran unsteadily through the lanes.

Chapter Forty Nine

Despite her tender years, Mary-Ann knew Maggie had to be told. Her desperate race ended with her bursting into the brothel. Maggie, as hard as nails, was left stunned as the youth gasped out her story.

"Oh my gawd; run lass, fetch her man while I go to her, and pray God we're not too late." Grabbing her shawl, Maggie swore viciously and hurried to the girl she had come to love.

Maggie's day had become a nightmare, while Abigail's, was far worse. She was dying, and no one could halt the reapers arrival. Ma Epps had seen enough failed births to know the herb hadn't worked. The girl was still wracked in pain, the child stuck firm, she had but an hour at most left as her life ebbed away. The only Godsend was that she was delirious, mumbling nonsense to those only she could see. Clasping her hand, Ma kissed the girls forehead, it was done in kindness to ease her passing and the girl smiled briefly as if acknowledging the help the old woman offered.

"Those who have passed await you in God's kingdom child. Go to them, end this pain, and live forever in eternal peace."

To slip away would have been so easy, Abigail feared deaths gossamer kiss no longer. The herbs had eased the pain while her mind ran wild, visions, memories of who she loved and how she had suffered came to her in a weird sort of dance. The angels were with her; they took her hand and whispered to her.

"Nathaniel..." Her husband, not seen for so long appeared; standing beside her, hands outstretched beckoning for her to follow him. He was as she remembered him, young, handsome and alive, and she felt comforted in seeing him. "Are you my guide?" she whispered, but he faded before her. The herb was strong within her, taking her on a drug induced journey she could not control.

"Wait for me my love." Nathaniel smiled, whispered words she could not hear and then, he was gone, leaving her alone once again in a place as dark as night. She fought, she searched, but could not discover a way out, until, from the very edge of her consciousness a light, bright, warm, comforting, appeared and calmed her. She rose and moved towards it only once looking back to see herself upon her bed. She was alone as she had been that first night when rats had been her only companions as they had scurried about the hovel. That had been her lowest point, she had lain beneath filthy blankets which crawled with insects and vowed she would never fear anything again.

"Time to join me, my dear," the soothing voice was close, God, she assumed had come for her. Abigail wanted to follow, wanted to let go of life because, if this was dying, it wasn't that bad. But suddenly, the image changed, gone was the serene voice, replaced by visions of evil and hatred. From a heavenly mist, a face, she wished never to see again, appeared. Joseph had returned to torment her along with his friend, the vile priest, but how, Bayles was alive.

"Be gone!" she screamed at the hooked nosed priest who laughed and pranced before his friend as she suffered. "Nathaniel, aid me please." her life hung by a thread yet others came from the darkness to torment her further, Maggie, Mary-Ann and Turnbottle all came to her. Friends and enemies alike had all abandoned her and came to make sure she passed on. They stayed but a short while, until another haggard face appeared. This was dressed in rags and she held her, soothed her, and eventually the darkness returned and she was at peace.

"Hush, child, it's almost done, rest, dearie." Ma Epps sighed and swigged from her bottle. Smuggled brandy aided her in such situations. Death was never pretty, but in her time she had grown accustomed to it. This one was a pretty thing, but would never see another dawn, so she drank while the girl died. "Such is life," she muttered as the girl cried out once more.

"Spare me...help me." Abigail's voice was softer, more resigned she had little strength left to fight deaths approach. Ma spoke softly, soothingly, and it seemed to calm her a little.

"I see them, child...relax, let Ma help you," Abigail sensed more than heard the voice again, distant, soft, haunting. Was it, she wondered, the Virgin Mother who spoke? If it was, maybe she should tell her of the heinous crimes Bayles committed within the town under her name.

"He is ungodly, Mother!" she shouted, before once again hearing her mystical voice, close to her.

"Yes, my child, all men are ungodly. Which is why we woman must help each other," the image replied, before fading. More faces rushed forward to be seen and then were gone. So many faces she recognised, only to disappear, to be replaced by Alice, dear sweet Alice, Abigail was pleased to see, her childhood friend once again. Dead for so many years she was as she remembered her, young alive happy, had she arrived to lead her to her own death?

"Alice!" she cried out.

"Alice...is that its name?" the voice asked soothingly. Abigail was beyond comprehension, the pain and the drug had befuddled her brain. Nothing was making sense and she was getting weaker by the moment.

"Alice," she whispered one last time and reached out to touch her ghostly friend.

"I heard, my child, I heard," the voice said soothingly before the dreams ceased. Abigail slipped into a darkened silence. She was finally at peace.

*

Resigned to her friend's fate, Maggie looked into the room and knew there was little hope. It resembled a slaughter house, blood had soaked the bed and Maggie knew her friend would be lucky to survive.

"It's alive, very weak, but alive, for the moment." Ma Epps said gently as she handed the poor soul to Maggie.

"Abigail…what of her?" The question was asked more in hope than anything else. Ma looked forlorn, desperate, shaking her head sadly, she answered simply,

"She called the child's name…Just after it was born…She named it."

"What is it to be?" Maggie sniffed back a tear and wrapped the infant in a cloth.

"Alice. She were talking daft. Saying all manner of things, even said the Virgin Mother was with her. Sure sign I fear. But if that's God's will, then so be it. Don't matter much, the brat will die by morning, too weak and well without a mother it can't survive."

Slumping to the floor, Ma wept. This had been one of the worst she had attended. Death though hadn't finished with them, it watched as she drew her final breath, then descended, clasped her body within its claw like grasp before leaving with its newest disciple. Maggie was alone, and wept for her friend and child. She hated this place and what had happened and vowed revenge for what men had done here.

*

He wasn't the sort to be frightened, but the challenge, shouted at him as he left the smithy, scared him. Suspecting either arrest or treachery, he turned and saw Mary-Ann running towards him in a distressed state.

"Sir…Mr Turn…" she shouted.

"Shut up!" he demanded, dragging the wench round the corner and out of sight. Mary-Ann recoiled in fear. During his many visits to Miss Abigail and the house, never had she heard him speak with such venom. What she saw was what was common within the 'Butts' a man capable of murder. Recoiling in fear, she expected a slap at least, perhaps something worse but Miss Abigail needed her to be strong so summoning up her failing courage she delivered her message.

"It's Miss Abi…" she began.

"What of her, is she ill?" The mention of her name made the merchant recoil in apprehension.

"Not ill, sir…but, due and Ma Epps…well, she don't like the look of what's 'appening…Reckons we should get a…Doctor…course, we can't afford one…and well…we was…wondering if yous knew where to get one…at this time…us not aving any coins like, sir."

"What…?" he was slow to comprehend, the last thing he expected was this especially after what had occurred this night. "Are you telling me that her time is imminent…is she giving birth, girl, is that what you say?" Death walked these streets, yet, this whore, spoke of a birth. The incredulous timing made him think how fickle fate was. The girl stared, unable to comprehend what he said, then he remembered, she had the intelligence of a snail and the morals of an alley cat a perfect woman if he were so inclined.

"That's what Ma says, but she reckons they ain't going to survive. Said, that to save either, she needs a doctor fast like. You are her friend, sir; she needs you now more than ever."

"My God…why is she present?" he demanded, attempting to gain some control over this unexpected occurrence.

"She's delivering the child, only she don't fink they will survive, which is why I needs you to 'elp us like."

"Hells teeth, this cannot be." Caught between two very different events, Turnbottle paused. Not ten feet away, Bayles had slowly roasted to death, now this brat spoke of both, a birth and the possibility of more deaths. He needed to reassess his options.

"Does Epps assume they are both to…die imminently?" Turnbottle asked. The news placed him in a quandary, one that, if he was not careful, could trap him by his own deviousness. It would be fortuitous if they died, for it would save him soiling his own hands. If what Bayles had set in motion worked, he had no further use for child or mother, but he could not be so callous as to show his delight.   Neither could he do nothing, if he did her friends would say he had abandoned her when she needed him most. He could not allow that, such statements could harm him,

"Yes, sir… she does." Mary-Ann sobbed through tear filled eyes. The ability to react, separated men, from boys. He could have faltered and given up; instead, he saw an opportunity to end this sorry tale. Grabbing hold of the snivelling wench, he looked her in the eye and commanded.

"Do you know Castle Street?"

"Of course, one of my best cust…."

"I care not about your customers…make haste to Number 4 Castle Street; tell the mistress of the house that the doctor is required. Inform him that I will reimburse him any fee he requires, but he is to accompany you immediately. Do you understand?"

"Yes, sir," the frightened girl replied, thankful that her friend might still be saved.

"Good. Take him directly to where she is; tell him he is to do whatever he can. I will meet you there just as soon as I have…finished here. Go…her life depends upon your fleetness of foot." Nodding in understanding, she hitched up her skirt once more and ran. Turnbottle watched her disappear, swore loudly and returned to his work.

* * *

"Too late, dead before I arrived." Turnbottle slumped at the news. It had taken longer than expected to finish at the smithy. His haste, it seemed, was for nothing.

"You're sure?" he asked. He and the doctor had known each other for some time, not friends as such, but Stormouth was a small town. Men of profession occasionally needed friends of discretion, which meant Turnbottle believed him implicitly.

"Quite sure, I fear in my line of work I see far too many dead women. Nature, you see Benjamin, has a way of dealing with such things."

"I must see…express my grief and condolences." Turnbottle stepped forward to be stopped by the doctor who blocked the doorway. Shaking his head solemnly he advised,

"Best not, my friend…not pleasant, if you get my drift." Turnbottle stared, then nodded. Never having had children of his own, he could only imagine what had occurred within that room, and he had no desire to witness such things. Anger, though, forced him to seek answers, and these women were his only witnesses.

"Fools. I leave implicit instructions that she is to be protected and what occurs? She dies, that's what!" His anger was terrifying, his eyes blazed and his face reddened. Maggie and her young girl, as the closest, faced the full force of that anger.

"We tried, sir. Did all we could? Ma used all her skills, even used her special erbs, but nothing…'elped sir…nothing." Maggie added between sobs of grief.

Turnbottle, inwardly consoled himself, in how fortunate he had been. One by one those who knew what he had done were dying, only one remained, and Bayles had kindly arranged that introduction. However, this pretense must continue a little longer, these whores had been affected and must be dealt with. It would not do for them to speak ill of him in the coming days.

"Herbs...what manner of witchcraft did this woman use? Speak or I will tell the constables of your complicity in her death." His lie worked, he saw their looks and knew he had their silence.

"Special herbs, sir, sent me to the apothecary to gets them, she did. Said they held special powers and would calm her...didn't seem to work though...sent her into a sort of madness, kept calling out so she did," Mary-Ann added, before resuming her uncontrolled sobbing.

Turnbottle knew all about the poison Nichols sold for pennies around the inns and brothels. It was his trade that had eventually caused his wife's demise at the hands of Bayles. Normally his weeds caused nothing worse than a strange behaviour. Death was something new; Abigail was, perhaps, the first his concoctions had affected so drastically.

"Where is this woman now, aye? Where is the old sow?" Turnbottle demanded, grabbing hold of Maggie by the shoulders and shaking her violently.

"Gone, sir, left as soon as...well, when it was obvious she."

"Had killed her? Is that it?" He finished the sentence. Neither woman warranted his condemnation, but his reaction had to be what they expected. Never before had he done such a thing but, in frustration, he lashed out. One blow and he felt mortally guilty afterwards but, the damage was done. Never again would Maggie trust him.

"That's enough, Turnbottle; you overstep the bounds of propriety. A gentlemen does not sink to such levels, no matter what the provocation. I suggest you either leave or curtail your vindictiveness. After all, it is no secret what Nichols peddles, nor Ma Epps and her abilities."

The doctor detested violence as Mary-Ann knew. He was known among the girls, as someone who paid without fuss upon completion, and who was kind to those he bedded. But as he knelt to assist Maggie to her feet, she sensed Turnbottle had made an enemy.

"My apologies, Bailey, uncalled for but the lady was a particular friend of mine; her death has grieved me deeply."

"I can see your distress, Benjamin however a modicum of decorum in light of such grievous news is called for, especially with ladies present."

Turnbottle wanted to laugh at the thought of such women being entrusted with the title 'Lady' but he refrained from commenting. Instead he asked,

"You say she gave birth? What happened to the child? Where is it now?"

"Gone, died not long after the mother," Maggie replied sullenly, through bloodied lips, as Mary-Ann hid her face in the folds of her dress.

"I acquiesce to that hypothesis, judging by the quantity of blood within, I surmise a rupture of some major vessel. Certainly any birth so dramatic would prove fatal for both mother and child. I doubt even my experience could have saved either of them. Perhaps, old chap, it was for the best."

"Best, he says...oh no, doctor, this wasn't for the best," Turnbottle muttered, adding quietly, "Am I to assume then, that she what...bled to death?"

"Certainly, though I would surmise her heart simply gave up," the doctor replied solemnly.

"Did she speak...say anything...before her demise?" Turnbottle asked, he needed to know if their association remained a secret.

"Nothing that made much sense, called out for a Nathaniel, said the Virgin Mother had named the child," Mary-Ann whispered between tears.

"God damn it," Turnbottle swore.

"What do we do with...her, sir?" Mary-Ann asked. Maggie, it appeared, had decided she wanted nothing more to do with the man and remained sulkily silent.

"What? Oh yes....arrange her funeral and send the bill to me." He paused, staring at the closed door and realised he had but one opportunity left. "Hells teeth, I have work to do....but I can still do it." With those words and without saying anymore to the gathered group, a very angry man stalked from the house and disappeared. The house suddenly became very silent. Two women and one studious looking man waited, looking at each other until finally, Maggie regained her composure, speaking very calmly,

"Thank you, sir...I always said you were a good man. Here's your guinea and I'll send Mary-Ann to you free of charge for what...three nights?"

Maggie would nurse a bruised mouth for some weeks, but she had suffered worse. The doctor licked his lips and smiled lecherously before saying,

"Much obliged, my dear, pleasure doing business with you." Then, bidding them a sad farewell he departed, his night's work concluded.

Part Five

Stormouth

June 1st - June 4th 1773

Chapter Fifty

You have brought a child into this world against the commandment. Prayer is wasted on your sort. (Unattributed)

The night of Thursday, June 1st, had been both, advantageous and disappointing. Having eliminated two of his obstacles without endangering himself, Abigail had conveniently died, taking with her the bastard child she carried. While upsetting, it had eliminated a potential problem. With sleep eluding him, his brain calculated what remained to be completed because if he were not to be haunted by failure, he had to proceed without further disruption. Fail now, so close to success, and three, no, four deaths would be for nothing.

Which was why, the new dawn found him concealed within a doorway, watching his next victim arrive a little after six am. Josiah had changed; he appeared tired, walked slowly and without purpose as if burdened by a multitude of problems. The young man fiddled with the lock before entering a building upon which hung a sign proclaiming, 'Joseph Wood Shipping Agent' Moments later he spied him beside a high desk, conveniently placed in front of a dirt-streaked window. As he watched, Josiah opened, what had to be a book, before placing his head in his hands as if weighed down with tribulations.

Worry not, my friend, your problems are about to disappear. The merchant smiled, pleased with what he had achieved. Without risking himself he was about to wrest control away from that family and no one, not even the man he watched knew how or why. Taking one last look at what was about to become his, he walked away. He needed to speak to his fellow businessmen, and that was best done in the confines of the coffee house, where likeminded men met.

* * *

Josiah was indeed perplexed and befuddled. His problems mounted daily, the business confounded him, customers continuously demanded that which he had no knowledge of, while his wastrel of a brother and his extravagant wife did nothing to aid him. Despite his limited knowledge, he knew that expenditure far outstripped income. |The family and more importantly the business were floundering, as he struggled in a mire of uncertainty. He wasn't trained for this, Nathaniel and his father would have dealt with the constant problems in a trice, yet he was at a loss, evident by the constant haunted expression which marked his working day. Small matters, like the sign that hung above the main door, irked him and became matters of grave concern.

Five months had passed since he had asked Adam to have it changed, yet it still hung there, testament to his brother's inability to act responsibly.

"I suppose I shall have to add that to an increasing list of things to deal with," he snarled angrily before bellowing for the only other person to whom he could vent his anger. "Mickelwhite! You snivelling, dried prune of a dog...where are you?" His voice, echoing through the warehouse, mocked him before fading to nothing. Somewhere, amongst the bales and packages, his clerk would be skulking, ignoring his commands. "Show yourself or by God, I will come looking for you!"

Josiah was like a petulant child denied their favourite toy. He wanted to lash out and with no one else to chide, his clerk was a convenient victim. Mickelwhite had been his father's man, the two had spent long hours alone in these warehouses, yet Josiah found him incompetent, surly not to mention a total disregard for his authority.

"Damn your hide you scurvy fool show yourself immieditatly." Nothing, not so much as a curse came from the man. It was this, lack of respect, Josiah detested most. He had tried, and despite what was said about him and the family, he had begun full of enthusiasm for the task ahead. But untrained in the ways of business, he had little idea what to do and now wallowed in loneliness and frustration. Second sons, as he had discovered, were not expected to inherit anything worthwhile. Lost in a maelstrom of odious duties he required guidance, fate though had given him an idiot of a brother and a clerk who between them might have just raised enough intelligence to boil an egg.

"Damn them all...how can I be expected to make sense of this if only I do any work!" He spoke not only of Adam but of Martha and Sarah also. His wife was kept busy running a home, sewing and socialising, while Sarah was no better than Adam. Both were flibbertigibbets, neither knew, nor seemingly cared, about anything apart from their own pleasures. Only last evening, Adam had left the house after another disagreement and had not, as yet, returned home, no doubt wasting more of his inheritance at the tables. The firm, therefore, was his responsibility, and it was vexing him terribly. "I shall succumb beneath a mountain of paper, and no one will know of my demise." He had had enough, purgatory would have been more appealing than this. He was tired, and filled with a sense of dread that something terrible was about to happen. He had no explanation but he had been haunted all night, unable to sleep. "God damn it!" he exclaimed kicking a sack and sending the contents spilling across the floor. Hells teeth!" his anger made him slam his hand upon the desk sending an inkpot crashing to the ground and the ink to seep away through the floorboards. "Is this to be my lot in life, my punishment, to endlessly stare at these inane meaningless ledgers?" Clasping his head in his hands he slumped to the floor, where tears of frustration mingled with ancient dust. His desolation was compounded by a voice, which sounded far to calm,

"You called, sir?" Startled by his clerk's arrival, Josiah hastily cuffed the tears aside in both disgust and embarrassment. Rising to his feet he had no other recourse but to bluster and curse, or face condemnation from a man he both loathed and mistrusted.

"I did. I assume you were making lax with my time. I expect more Mickelwhite, far more."

"Sorry, sir, I were in number three warehouse and didn't hear you until I came out,"

Josiah suspected he lied, doubted if he would know the truth if it bit him on his arse. John Mickelwhite should have been dismissed long ago, certainly Josiah should have made that his first order of business, but he had failure in that as well. Truth was he despised the man, had done since his father had first brought him into the firm. But the three, father, Nathaniel, and Mickelwhite had been close, and truth be told, Josiah needed his knowledge.

"Why…what were you seeking, apart from somewhere to smoke your pipe?" He regretted his utterance immieditatly because it displayed his own failings. He had revealed a weakness which, if his father had taught him nothing else, it was never to show vulnerability to either staff or customers.

"No, sir, I were checking the inventory and seeking a misplaced order."

"Whose order, tell me you laggard?" Bluster was Josiah's means of disguising his failings. Mickelwhite stared at him strangely forcing him to look away. The man was undoubtedly intelligent, yet he also caused concern among some of the more …delicate clients. He was certainly strange, he took little pride in his appearance, his apparel was threadbare, he never wore shoes, stating when asked that he found it quicker and easier to get around. Josiah guessed it was more probable he simply didn't want to be heard. As for his age, Josiah had no idea, but from his thin build, bald pate but thick, unkempt beard and bushy sideburns, he could be any age between thirty and fifty. Rumour was, he had been found beneath this very building, more dead than alive. A survivor from a ship wrecked outside the harbour and that his father had taken pity on him. He had been here ever since, growing closer than brothers, yet arguing like cat and dog about matters he had not understood.

It was also said that Mickelwhite had sailed with pirates, a story his father had first told many years before, and he saw no reason to dispute it then, or now. He looked the sort, who could kill but that was something else Josiah wasn't about to ask. Preferring to believe what his father had told him that the ribbons the man wore in his beard, denoted the number of men he had slain.

"Mrs Furnell's." His expression remained stolidly nonplussed, he had not lied, nor had he told the entire truth. He had been doing both things, but he had also sat, staring out to sea wishing for the return of Master Nathaniel while smoking a plug of baccy.

"Well…did you discover her infernal order?" Josiah was nonplussed, the clerk's reply had been terse, sullen, but not sufficiently disrespectful to bring about reproach or dismissal. He suspected the clerk had been employed on matters of his own, as well as the firm's. *I will discover your secret and then I will finish you.* Josiah vowed.

"Not as yet," he stated solemnly. "I remember your father saying it had arrived, so it must be listed in the ledgers. Perhaps if you could tell me what it is she has ordered, it would aid my search?"

There it was, he was goading him, chiding him because he suspected he knew more than the master. The duties of clerk were to be responsible for entering everything into the ledgers, to know what came in, and what went out, but Mickelwhite had never once entered anything into the books.

"I would if I could, but…" Josiah had almost revealed the fact he could not make head or tail of the businesses books, not that John Mickelwhite would have been surprised. Mister Joseph had kept the ledgers up to date. The knowledge contained within, was the cause of the upstarts problems, whatever the old master had written had died with him, as had the cypher to break his code. The two leather books held myriad secrets which, only two men knew how to break, and both were dead.

"Shame, sir, for she be sure to come back wanting what we have of hers. What do I tell her?" The merest hint of a grin formed, as he eyed the books. The boy needed to know but there was no one to aid him. Mickelwhite might have helped but he only did as he were told. Until he was asked, politely, he would remain dumb. Truth was, his loyalty to Joseph Wood, was unshakable, they had shared much, which unless he so desired, he would be reluctant to share, least of all Josiah.

"Tell her she can't have what we can't find. Tell her God himself has stolen her damn goods, tell whatever you wish but keep her away from me."

Josiah did not have the luxury of time, he couldn't forge an alliance with the clerk as his father had. He needed answers now, not in years to come because the business was at risk of floundering. Mickelwhite must have knowledge he needed, after all he was entrusted with much of what the old master did, who he knew, and where the money came from. Why else would a servant have been present at his father's funeral? The simple truth was the clerk had to be encourage to speak out, or they would witness the demise of a business the clerk said he cared so much about.

Curse all yeez like little man, it will do no good not afore you make your peace. Mickelwhite watched a man, more a child, waver, and knew this milksop had no answer. It was just as he had predicted when the terrible news had broken. No one, apart from Master Nathaniel, could run this place in the master's stead. The future for him looked bleak, neither had any respect for the other in fact he saw Josiah as a pampered poodle, an idiot with less brains than a flea, nor would he have the stomach to what had to be done. Fact was he knew what went on, it was why he and the master had been so good together. Along with 'The Chamberlin' they had grown rich on profits from smuggled goods. At any time he and Mister Joseph knew what was in stock, where to find it, and who wanted it. More importantly they knew who to call upon when goods needed delivering, in all the years together not a single item had been lost, nor had any customer, legitimate or not, come seeking retribution. Now, thanks to this idiot who stood before him, it had all gone to cock.

"May the devil rot his devilish hide? Why was he so secretive? Why did he hide his thoughts in such gibberish? Tell me, you worked for him, surely you spoke of such matters?" Josiah slammed his fists onto the books but offered no apology for the anger he aimed at what he saw as his personal nemesis, the ledgers.

"Never spoke to me about them sire, I was just an 'umble worker who didn't ask questions." Mickelwhite shrugged indifferently. He knew the reason for the cryptic method of accounting, but that was now destined for someone who appreciated his worth. This business was doomed, the hawks were gathering. Not two days before, he had been approached in the 'Star' and offered employment by another merchant. All he wanted was information, but offered far more than the Woods paid him. Cautious he'd hadn't agreed…as yet, but seeing what depths Josiah had sunk to he saw no reason not to accept. They could drown in their own mire for all he was concerned, and the reason stood before him. A fool who would not ask for help, and who was disrespectful to those who knew all there was to know. "I just did as I was told."

Which wasn't strictly true. Mickelwhite had intimate knowledge of why the warehouses were full to bursting and why irate customers arrived each day demanding their goods. But he wasn't about to reveal that to a son barely old enough to wipe his own arse and another who flapped about town like a headless chicken. But he might have had they offered him an apology.

"Then why are you here? Bugger off, continue with your search...I shall require a complete inventory by close of business, otherwise how am I expected to furnish my clients? Go you laggard...wait, as clerk, you would know if there are any more papers secreted about the building; if so, tell me." Josiah stared demonically at his clerk, his father had taught him to treat menial staff no better than dogs. Customers and family members were due respect simply because of their status. Men like Mickelwhite should feel the lash occasionally, father would have done so had he behaved so in his presence.

"Not to my knowledge, sir, though your father liked to keep some of his ...transactions close...didn't like to disclose everything he did to those in authority." He could barely speak a civil word to the youth; such was his dislike for him.

"So be it... find what the Furnell woman needs. At least we might be able to fulfil one order."

Dismissed with as much regard as something one might tread in, Mickelwhite left the room. Once out of sight he spat viciously, made an obscene gesture and whispered, belligerently,

"And a good day to you too..." An enemy had been made, something many had died regretting.

Chapter Fifty One

Mickelwhite, was many things but he was no fool. If Josiah had been more …amicable, he would have done all in his power to aid him, for there was still a fortune waiting to be made. If he had quelled his stupidity, he might have discovered what really went on within these buildings, and why his father had employed an ex-privateer. Truth was Joseph Wood and 'The Chamberlin' had been close, so close in fact, that most of Josiah's inheritance had been accrued, not by legal trading, but in a manner so foul, the revenue may even now come knocking on his door.

Nor would they would not be the only visitors, men armed not with legal writs, but with knives, would come in the dead of night with knives. 'The Chamberlin' may be defeated, but the trade he'd begun continued. Goods still came and went under cover of darkness, goods which needed storing and moving in secret, and that was Mickelwhite real duty, to make sure such men were treated fairly. Joseph had been one of the best, the Chamberlin had entrusted his goods to him and he had served him well, while adding to his own wealth. Even the day before his death Joseph had swindled the revenue out of a fortune not that that mattered any longer. The man entrusted with his future lay dead in some distant sea but Joh Mickelwhite would not rest until he saw proof, until then, he would guard the secret well.

Josiah Wood stood alone and despondent as his clerk left the room.

"Damn you and damn my father," He stood alone, as his clerk left the room, he had dealt with him unjustly, despite his personal feelings towards the man he should have asked for his help instead of decrying his competence, but the man brought out the worst in him. This was his father's domain his counting house what could a clerk know of what went on here? *The truth lies within the ledgers all we need do is break the infernal code and we shall know what mysteries he held dear.* Succeed in this task and he would be able to reunite customers with goods, collect what was owed, and rebuild the lost confidence that leaked through his fingers like sand.

"How I wish you were here, Nathaniel."Despite what his clerk thought of him, Josiah was no fool. He realised his problems could be attributed to a sequence of events, which had begun the day his father died and ended here, though in truth that was too simplistic. There were numerous reasons he was failing, problems he wasn't equipped to deal with. His lack of skills, his brother, their grief, that witch, all added to his turmoil. While the family hid behind the requirements of protocol and observed a suitable period of mourning, the business languished behind closed doors. Nothing was sold; goods remained upon the docks unaccounted for, customers were demanding their goods, and unpaid bills began to mount. That was why, faced with imminent ruination the sons had been forced back to work earlier than they had wished. Only then had Josiah discovered the real reason they were failing John Mickelwhite had done nothing, his reason supposedly, was that he had received no orders. Under normal circumstances Nathaniel would have taken the reins and led them through this troubling period but he too was gone. Josiah untrained in stock control, invoicing, and the thousand and one other questions that flooded in every day floundered, while Adam had fled to the safety of the gaming tables.

"How I wish you were here, Nathaniel." There was no escape from his torment; he had no idea where to start. Instead of a natural transference of control, the business was in turmoil. Mickelwhite had thrust the books into his arms that first day as if offering some gift from God himself, and expected him to know what to do. He had endeavoured to make sense of them but the counting house had proved too distracting, so he had taken them home, to the privacy of his study. However, even there he had not found inspiration. Countless hours had been wasted trying to discover what remained concealed, all the while alienating his family.

Until he discovered what to do, this was Josiah's personal purgatory. What he needed was assistance, or time to find his feet, but he had neither. Questions came every day, questions to which he had only one response, and that was to hide. Apart from his clerk, who obstructed him at every turn, and a plethora of irate customers, he also had an irate comptroller of customs, who demanded notice of duty due. So far he had avoided that meeting, but after three visits, the man grew impatient. Nathaniel, gifted in such matters, would have smoothed the pompous dignitary's ruffled feathers, plied him with some stock, or drowned him in wine. Same with the customers, he would have fawned over them, made them smile, convinced them there was nothing to be concerned about. He would have immediately understood the ludicrous and inconceivable cipher and known what needed to be done. Instead Josiah languished in purgatory, completely lost. At his lowest point, Josiah had resorted to praying for help, he had knelt in silent prayer begging for guidance. *Forgive me Lord, I beseech you; help me your unworthy son. Tell me...tell me what I need to know! I am undeserving of your clemency, but if I fail in this task, I will be responsible for the loss of everything my father worked so hard to create. Lord, if I am found wanting in this task, there will be nothing left to save in a few weeks.*

Many had become similarly desperate, few though had been fortunate to have divine intervention. Josiah, if he had but recognised it at the time, had been offered a way out, now was time for him to seek out his saviour. He had not thought of Bayles since he had called a few weeks ago. Having dismissed the priests offer as an insult, he now wondered if he had been rash and if it might still be available.

"If he will assist, we might still retrieve some semblance of sanity from this nightmare." Stooping to retrieve the inkpot, he realised he had been naive, impetuous, stupid in fact. Bayles had stood in this very building with that fool Crowfold. A minor merchant who had continuously badgered him about some goods he supposedly waited for. Merchandise, which Josiah had no knowledge of, but which he insisted was stored with them.

"My presence is, simply to intercede, to arbitrate between the two of you and seek a resolution." God Bayles had sounded so piously condescending, it had galled Josiah but he had been forced to listen as Crowfold had whinged about some lost spices. Speaking as if they were the best of friends, the cleric's words, even now, resonated with a sense of rebuke and pity. Intercede? Josiah would have dealt with Crowfold, but instead, the idiot had gone whining to Bayles. The man was a dog, attempting to exert pressure upon him to act.

If your goods are here we shall find them, all we need is a modicum of patience and you shall have your order." Josiah had wanted to throttle the man but instead, with a few words, Bayles had dismissed Crowfold. When they were alone, Bayles had told him how others were feeling, said that more merchants were losing faith in his abilities, that while their goods rotted in his warehouses they lost money and credibility. It was then, quiet innocently, that the priest had made his proposal. So matter of fact had it been presented, that at first Josiah had mistaken it as another voice of disappointment. Actually, Bayles had offered his services, had suggested he knew someone who might be able to unravel the accursed cyphers and bring order to chaos. At the time, he had felt aggrieved at the slur on his abilities, assuring him that all was well and that there was no cause to be concerned. Now he wished he had succumbed to the priest's offer, more than anything, he wished whoever it was he had in mind, came immediately.

"I will speak with him this day. Discuss the need to seek assistance," Josiah stated glancing out of the office window and noticing the small group of men who gathered on the corner of Water Lane and Middle Street. He had witnessed mobs before, such gatherings meant trouble for someone. Then he saw one man point towards him. Fear made him rush to the main street door to throw the latch, and drop the bolts. If they meant him harm such measures would delay them for perhaps thirty seconds. Of course, he could be worried for nothing. Maybe their presence had nothing to do with him at all, but with Adam absent and only Mickelwhite and himself present, an old man and a dog could force their way in and take whatever they desired.

"Good news, sir. I believe I have discovered at least two deliveries. With confirmation from you, we can arrange to have them dispatched." Drawn from his concerns, Josiah took the sheaf of papers Mickelwhite handed him. One small piece of good news, did not alleviate their problems. Even with the goods found, there was still the matter of the gathering mob, and the fact that nothing could leave until all the invoices and documents had been located.

"It is a start, now we need to discover if the taxes have been paid and if the customs officer has authorised their release. Until then we are still flummoxed."

"There is another problem. Fact is, it's my fault, with everything that's been happening I clean forgot, sir."

"Forgot what? Not by any chance the reason for that gathering?" Josiah wondered if his clerk was being deliberately obstructive, doing all he could to hamper and destroy them from within.

"Partly, yes. Mister Joseph always said I knew more about his business than he did. He liked his jokes, did Mister Joseph." Micklewhite was stalling. He knew what he said next would bring about another argument. "Fact is, I never got any written words for when things were due in. Mister Joseph would simply leave me a code, like, upon the wall. Old fashioned perhaps, but it had worked very well, sir, allowed me to be aware when we need more men."

"For pities sake, get on with it, man!"

"Wasn't until I saw them out there, that, I remembered. Completely forgot, what with all the other jobs I have had to do."

"What are you blathering about?" Josiah glanced between his clerk and the door; he still expected the mob outside to break in at any moment.

"The men outside are here to unload the 'Penelope' when she arrives, all being well, on the high tide this afternoon and we have no storage available."

Josiah turned and relaxed, his fears dispelled. The men were workers, not a mob, but now he had far serious a problem.

"How...Where...We have no room, we cannot squeeze another bale in anywhere...Do we know what she is carrying, and who the customers are?"

"All I knows is that she has a load of barrels...molasses, sugar, rum, spirits, could be any, or all. Certain we'll need wagons and mules, drivers to take it to where it's got to go, and we'll need that lot out there."

"I assume you haven't organised such transportation?" Josiah feared the worst.

"I fear not. Mister Joseph only told me when the ships were due. I never got involved in any load from the Indies, your father dealt with them personally."

"Did he? Do we know why?"

"No, kept such things to himself, he did."

"Of course he did.... So we are bamboozled! Do we, perchance, have a name, an address for delivery; where do the wagons take the stuff after it's landed?"

"Aye, I know that," Mickelwhite replied.

"You do, do you? Well, pray tell, or must I drag it from your poxy throat myself?" Loyalty was earned, Mister Joseph had used such language, was expected, but this pup wasn't fit to sit in his father's seat.

"The contact's name is...was, the 'Chamberlin.' How you get payment from him, though, beggars belief."

"This day gets better by the hour. So, pray tell, what we do when the 'Penelope' docks?" Josiah was annoyed, and frustrated. Mickelwhite simply shrugged and stood indifferent to what happened next. "I will tell you...we have to store it until such times as we can move it on, though God knows where or how we do that. We have what...a day to make arrangements?"

"About that, yes." Mickelwhite appeared unperturbed, but secretly his heart leapt in joy to see this popinjay floundering helplessly.

"Do we know how much room we'll need?"

"No."

"Then I suggest, Mr Mickelwhite, we prepare for the worst. Those men, you say they are here to work?" Josiah, pointed at the mob opposite.

"That's right...but they will expect cash payment at close of business."

"I am sure they will. Tell them they will be paid. I personally will cover any cost involved. As for storage...we can take no more...so scour the town. Rent whatever space you can, use the old smugglers lairs if needs be; anywhere will do, but make sure the rents are kept low. Then, contact any wagon drivers you can find, have them put on standby."

"All that will cost, sir."

"Of that I have no doubt; nothing comes cheaply...tell them to send their bills to me personally. I will cover the cost, if needs be, from my own account. Go, I will attempt to discover what we are to expect."

Alone once again, Josiah wished for a miracle. He had money, but only what he had inherited. That would not last forever, and if they were to continue trading, he had to discover where the cash was secreted. There had to be some; even with the warehouses full his father must have had cash with which he paid those he dealt with. Until it came to light, his liquidity was going in one direction. Out.

"Oh and Mickelwhite…"

"Sir?" The clerk turned and stared malevolently knowing another job was about to be added to his already excessive list. Josiah pointed out the window and demanded,

"Get that bloody sign changed."

Chapter Fifty Two

Whistling merrily, the merchant returned to the quayside to examine the progress of his plotting. Having enjoyed an excellent cup of coffee, he was eager to see how the pup was coping. Less than two hours had elapsed, yet his mischievousness was bearing excellent results. The men, he had paid, appeared to be worse than useless, there was no cohesion, no reason as to why when, one man put a bale down, another moved, it while a third stood by laughing. As for Josiah, he was conspicuous by his absence, if Josiah was in command, he saw little evidence of such control. *Time I twisted the knife a little, and watch him squirm,* he thought, leaving his place of concealment he walked towards the warehouse.

"Morning John, is Wood available?" he asked politely as Mickelwhite appeared with a ladder and hammer

"Aye, he is, sir. In a foul mood though, best watch out," Mickelwhite replied grinning devilishly. "Up there sir. Looks like it might be a grand day, a very grand day."

"We can but hope…do be careful, do not want accidents, not today do we?" The man stated as Mickelwhite climbed the few feet and attacked the sign with uncontrolled venom. *The boy has finally made a decision,* he thought.

Entering the counting house, he stared forlornly at the mess it was in. No merchant liked a full warehouse, stored goods earnt little, perishables rotted, and until the customer took delivery, the liability for any loss remained the merchants. But he looked at the shambles with a degree of satisfaction, his money had been spent wisely, Josiah would be susceptible to any offer of assistance, or so he hoped. The test would be when he was confronted, only then would he discover if his work had undermined the man sufficiently.

Breathing deeply he stood momentarily on the bottom step, this was almost spiritual, he had entered the inner sanctum of a family he had for so long despised and been ridiculed by. His goal was within touching distance, but he paused a little longer as Josiah suddenly bellowed form above,

"What the hell were you hiding, you swine?" The visitor listened, was he berating someone up there for his tone was laced with anger and frustration. Knowledge was power and the boy was being indiscreet, revealing his vulnerability. "Your stupidity will see us ruined while our warehouses burst at the seams. We shall be the laughing stock of the town, yet all you do is frustrate and impede. Some help would not go amiss!"

Curious to see who Wood spoke to, the visitor called out pleasantly as he climbed the stairs,

"You there, Wood? Halloo," Immediately, Josiah ceased his tirade, exited his office, and peered down.

"You...how...yes...fine...I mean, what the devil do you require?" Never would such a visit have happened if his father still lived, Turnbottle would never have got past the front door. Joseph Wood, had been harsh in his opinion of the man, calling him a toad, a mealy mouthed cur, and other, more colourful names which were far too derogatory to mention. Both were merchants both vied for the same trade and dock space, but for such animosity to fester for so long meant the reason for their dislike went deep, very deep.
Yet now, he entered without invitation or trepidation.

"Require...nothing at all my boy, happened to be passing and heard your anguished cries. Must admit I perceived trouble, thought you were being attacked. You're not, are you? I mean, too many cutthroats about these days, a gentleman isn't safe to walk the town anymore."

Josiah, inclining his head quizzically, despite what he had heard about the man he had always found him likable. A man who dressed well, conducted himself admirably and apparently was honest and trustworthy, or so it was said.

"I am well; thank you...Though in truth my anguish is not of fear, but disillusionment."

"Oh dear, then I shall leave you to your deliberations good day sir." Turnbottle turned and was but one step down when...thankfully Josiah called him back,

"Pray sir if you have a moment you may be able to assist in a most perplexing problem."

Is it to be this easy? Turnbottle thought, as finally entered a place he never imagined visiting again. Once before he had come here, but then Wood had attacked him, thrown him down the stairs, and threatened to kill him if he ever returned. Now he was invited to enter by a son who was obviously befuddled.
For a family that controlled so much, and wished to encompass even more, the heart of their fortune was disappointing. Dust clung to every surface, papers stood piled high upon shelves that looked ready to collapse. The desk, the very center of their business was old, cracked and liable to fall into disrepair. For all the apparent disorder, one relic of a bygone era almost made him laugh. Above the desk, an old oak beam held an antiquated accounting system. Vicious looking hooks, held a veritable cornucopia of discoloured papers. It was perhaps the last vestige of a ancient past, one he had dispensed with years before, but which the Wood family retained, though why was hard to imagine.

"Sir I am at a loss, the ledgers are indecipherable and I am besieged with irate customers. I detest asking but reverend Bayles mentioned you might...."

"The bane of our trade...accounts. Our friends in Customs House get a little tetchy if we fail to pay what is required? Not having problems with our resident Comptroller are you?" Said in jest, Turnbottle was pleased to see how Josiah looked away, how he appeared distressed and reluctant to reply.

"I ...well...he has sent word more than once."

"Damn the man; doesn't know his Tun from his toe, but he can be discommodious. I would suggest you deal with him swiftly and harmoniously."

"I would like nothing less but these damned ledgers are proving troublesome. Fact is, I can't make head or tail of them. I flounder; while Mickelwhite and my brother offer no assistance."

Now was his opportunity to ingratiate himself, to conclude what Bayles had alluded to.

"I sense your pain, my boy...I...I might be in a position to offer you some assistance. As men of the world and fellow merchants, surely we can aid one another in time of difficulties."

"I don't know, sir...my father and yourself were never what could be called friends."

"Pah, disregard all that. A new day is dawning, your father...well, you command now, though I do comprehend your reluctance. As I said to Reverend Bayles, I will do whatever I can to alleviate your difficulties but only if desired."

Josiah sighed in relief, the priest had spoken about them to Turnbottle and despite all the animosity that had existed, he was still willing to assist. Obviously his father had been wrong about this man. It was time to accept help from any quarter, and Turnbottle was the first to offer any assistance. His arrival was, indeed fortuitous, much longer and there would be nothing left to salvage.

"My deepest apologies sir. It is I who is foolish. I did, speak to the Reverend about this matter, though I didn't expect him to approach you in particular. I doubt if you have either the time or the inclination, what with our past animosity and your many commitments. However...if there is a way in which you can aid us, it would be appreciated." He hated to admit defeat, but what other recourse was there? Businessmen, no matter who they were, disliked seeking help from anyone, be they bankers, money lenders or fellow merchants, but if he were to get out of this quandary he had to swallow his pride, and who better to help than a merchant who had nothing to gain?

"Quite understand, dear boy, would feel the same in your position." he scratched his nose, then added deliberately. "I must say I am glad you came to me. Fact is there have been mutterings among your fellow traders. They grow concerned, their anxieties, fueled by rumours and innuendos that you have creditors and customers all anxious as to what is occurring."

"I fear I have allowed matters to slip, but there is nothing that cannot be remedied. If you could reassure the other merchants, convey my regrets and apologise, I am sure your words would quell their anxieties." Josiah felt relieved to be free to speak to another about his worries.

"I am sure we can accommodate you, their leniency is no more than we would offer anyone in your position. What is it you are in urgent need of? Capital? Storage? Name it, my boy, and we will do all we can to aid your needs."

Turnbottle's flesh crawled as he pandered to a member of the family that had inflicted pain on so many, but to succeed, he was forced to fornicate himself to them. He waited, examining his fingernails in an attempt to remain calm. The youth was blissfully unaware that he was being robbed, the germ of an idea had been planted, all he had to do was wait, while the idea grew. Surprisingly, the answer came far quicker than he could have imagined.

"I fear my father left his ledgers in a terrible pickle. Wrote them in code for some reason, a code I have so far failed to breach. I am bereft of ideas, if you could hel...?" His voice trailed away, ashamed at having to admit defeat, while Turnbottle nodded comfortingly. Business could be so pleasant, the boy was bereft, and close to collapse, yet he felt neither pity nor concern. Their self-righteous and condescending attitude had brought them to this impasse, why should he not profit from their downfall? If the roles were reversed, they would be dancing on his grave. His last triumph was to slam the door firmly shut and claim his prize.

"Say no more, Wood, only too pleased to be of some help. You say the books are your prime concern? Alas, I know hardly a jot about such things; leave that to my accountant..." Turnbottle paused, touched his finger to the side of his nose as if deep in thought, then slowly stated, "Maybe if I brought him here, you would like him..." He saw the concern and hurried on, before Wood lost all his confidence. "Fear not, I mean nothing untoward. My man is a marvel with ledgers and the like, while I enjoy the art of codes and ciphers. You and your brother have no fear of me, I assure you. My one concern is that normal trading resumes. It is not conducive to see such a fine firm struggling, Rumours hurt us all."

"You are most kind, we have been remiss, and if Adam ever appears, I am sure he will agree." Josiah felt as if a great weight had lifted from his shoulders. Finally, someone who understood the workings of his father's mind was willing to assist. What could be so wrong in that?

"I'm sure of that as well. In the meantime I have some errands to run...what say we meet back here this afternoon? I am confident that between us, we will be able to circumvent your predicament." Turnbottle bowed and walked away, leaving Josiah alone, staring at the doorway.

Not since the day his father had died, had Josiah felt so relieved. There was finally someone willing to help, hopefully this purgatory was close to ending. Adam might prove difficult to convince, he would accuse him of giving in too easily, of taking too long to unravel the ledgers, of dithering about what they should do. Maybe he was right, perhaps they should have worked together and solved their problems themselves. But it would have proved difficult with a brother who rarely ever showed up for work. Even as a child Adam had been precocious, demanding, and difficult; his behaviour was not helped by a mother who did everything for him. Only after her disappearance had their father even spoken to them, by which time the damage had been done. Adam had become more fastidious, grown apart from his brothers, preferring the company of those at the various hotels which attracted him and his kind. Nothing had slowed his passions, not even the arranged marriage; his absence from his marriage bed was equaled by his wife's lust for life. Both trod separate paths, with Sarah enjoying a life without Adam but enjoying his money. Both had degraded themselves by not respecting a suitable period of mourning before resuming their unacceptable lives. Martha had spoken of a carriage that came to collect Sarah; where it took her neither Josiah nor his wife knew, but he would have to broach the subject soon. Social standing was a fickle beast. It might survive a financial crisis, but not a scandal as well. Sarah had to be told that she must show a modicum of decorum, to appear as if she was faithful to her husband even if, God forbid, she wasn't.

Could he really condemn, when his own marriage was undergoing turmoil and confusion? Could he expect Sarah to do as he asked when he was unable to stop his own wife from attending afternoon tea parties? Why Martha supported such idiotic events was a mystery. He hoped it was to ingratiate herself into polite society, to bolster their standing within the town, to impart stability and confidence in their business. Certainly it was where the ladies of great, and the good, gathered to tell each other how well their husbands were doing. Unfortunately, those gatherings had also been the source of yet another disagreement. He and Martha had argued about the amount of money she spent on dresses, when that money could be better spent in the business.

"Would you have me attend in rags, or to cease attending? To do so would reinforce the rumours of our demise," she had haughtily stated. "One word from their wives and your merchant friends would know the Wood family were cutting back. The gossip those delicate ladies impart would do more harm than a few late deliveries."

"Trapped by tea and cakes, and held to ransom by my own wife," he had replied, while knowing she was right. It hurt to be reminded that he was trapped in a circle of deceit, damned if he did nothing, and damned if they continued.

"What is that stench?" He suddenly recoiled as a pungent odour percolated through the building. Something was wrong; something smelt appallingly and it appeared to emanate from the warehouse next door.

"Mickelwhite...Mickel...white! God damn your eyes, where are you, you poxed wretch?" The smell was becoming stronger, wafting on the afternoon breeze that blew across the harbour. It carried a multitude of odours; rotting fish, seaweed, damp wood and salt water, but this obnoxiousness was far worse than any that existed on the quay.

"Sir?" his clerk asked, before recoiling from the stench. It was a miasma, an invisible stench that mixed with everything else. "By God in heaven, what is it?"

"That is what I want to know!" Josiah choked and gasped for air. The smell was stronger outside, more solid like, and it seemed to emanate from one of their buildings. "Where's the key to this building?" he demanded, pointing at the door that was chained shut.

"I'll find it immediately," Mickelwhite stated, disappearing back into the counting house. While his clerk searched, Josiah walked to the door and rattled the chains that held the doors closed.

"Make haste... hurry!" The warehouse was a three storey, timber built monstrosity. Double doors, one above the other, allowed access to each of the storage floors. A large copula on top concealed a wheel from which a rope was attached to a platform. That allowed goods to be hauled up the front of the building and in through whichever door was needed. Twenty years ago it had been the best in town, a pinnacle upon which his father lauded his wealth. Now though exposure to the sea air, and over use, it showed its age, it was leaky and decrepit, myriad gaps allowed the smell to leak out. Bending to the door, he sniffed deeply and recoiled in horror. *Why had no one else smelt it?* But this wasn't the time to ask such questions, the cause had to be discovered, rectified, and losses assessed.

"Open it immediately," he demanded, as the clerk arrived with a large bunch of keys. It took time, but finally, the door was unlocked. Heaving for all his worth, Mickelwhite struggled to open the huge, heavy built doors, which had been made from old ships timbers. Reluctantly, Josiah added his weight to the task until eventually the doors creaked open. Then the smell hit them; a sweet heady scent that was more pungent than anything they had ever smelt. Both men recoiled, clasping their hands to their mouths.

"By God, what is it?" Josiah gasped.

"No idea, sir," Mickelwhite choked. "But whatever it is, it's gone off."

Josiah stood back and stared ruination in the face. Whatever it had been, was no use to anyone. Worst still, as it was in his warehouse, he would be expected to carry the loss.

"By God, I will not allow this to finish me." His words were uttered out of frustration. Disaster was heaped upon disaster. No man could be expected to suffer such setbacks. "How much more do you expect of me?" he screamed to the wind, his despair carried away across the quay. He could have given up there and then, but adversity made him more determined to find a way out of his problems. Turnbottle would be of assistance, but more importantly, he needed to find Adam. Together they had much to achieve, now more than ever.

Chapter Fifty Three

"A very good day to you ma'am." Life was perfect, despite some hurried adjustments to his tenuous plan, he was almost ready to administer the *coup de grace*. Finally, he would end the Wood family, and rid them from the town. He, though, wouldn't wield the final blow, that honour was reserved for those wealthy men who resided within the upper town. Whistling happily, he left the squalor of the lower town behind and made his way towards where the men who would become the Wood's executioners awaited him.

This had proved to be a fortuitous few months, his wealth had brought him both success and revenge along with a modicum of regret but life was full of such tediousness and one had to be candid about such matters. Josiah, his final problem, was ready to be plucked, all it would take was another small confrontation. That would be provided by men who took their orders from Turnbottle and his agents. Men like the one who stood outside Edwards the butchers sniffing at a pig's head which hung from a billhook. His man wiped his nose, brushed away a fly and nodded at the merchant discreetly. No words were exchanged, but that almost imperceptible gesture set in motion yet another part of his plan. Josiah would never know why his workers were to prove so inept. By the time the *'Penelope'* arrived, Wood would be incapable of controlling the last of his failing business. By then, the gentlemen he was to meet in Pettit's Coffee House, would finish him

Pettits was a small shop, but within its smoke filled rooms, merchants discussed how their wealth would be increased, and it was where those who would finish Wood were to be found. Their cost, nothing save the information he was about to impart.

"Good morning, gentlemen," he said airily, as he entered the establishment. "A cup of your finest infusion if you would be so kind…Mr Booth, I need to arrange space on a ship to the Indies. We should speak when you have the time." He smiled mischievously; such news would cause a stir as the assembled merchants pondered what load he was transporting. More importantly they would see this as another indication that Josiah was failing forcing him deeper into trouble. *A good businessman must adapt or die,* he thought, and he had proved himself to be more than capable of adapting. Avarice, and the desire to have what they owned, had made him what he was. But no one remained wealthy by standing still. Each day presented opportunities to be grabbed before they were lost, something Josiah had failed to realise. For too long, he had lived in their shadow, watching them prosper while his achievements went unnoticed. No more; he was as good as they, in fact, he lived exceedingly well, but the Woods were always a little better.

"Morning, Turnbottle," a large rotund man replied from the confines of the window seat. "Have you heard the latest on the Wood saga?"

Immediately, the room stilled. Pettit's consisted of little more than two average sized domestic living rooms, which, eight years ago, was precisely what it had been. James Pettit had opened his shop during the conflicts; despite that his emporium had flourished. More business was done within this small place than in the more traditional trading houses on South Quay. Merchants gathered here every day to discuss prices and loads, while agents came seeking space on ships. By its very nature, influential people felt at ease here, which made it the ideal location for rumours to start. In fact, as he well knew, if you wanted a story to gain credence, all it needed was to be mentioned here and someone's livelihood could be made or destroyed before the sun set.

"No...What pray, have the fools done now?" Turnbottle smiled and appeared uninterested, but shivered in anticipation. Placing his hat upon a vacant peg, he sat and awaited his order to be placed in front of him before saying nonchalantly, "Nothing was said while I was there." This was where he had laid the foundations for his grand scheme. All good ideas were born of frustration, grew and gained maturity or withered and died. By virtue of exceptional circumstances, his scheme blossomed nicely. Opportunity had aligned nicely at Joseph's funeral. The Woods had become vulnerable, disjointed and dysfunctional, while Bayles, open to bribery, had played his part nicely, giving him access to the inner workings of the family.

"When was that?" another demanded.

"Not ten minutes ago. I came directly from their warehouses. Where, I admit, Josiah was in a most foul mood indeed," Turnbottle added nonchalantly though in truth his mind was continuously thinking about what he had done and what remained to do. Abigail's death still troubled him. Her insight into the family's innermost secrets had been enlightening. He had exploited her situation, and it had cost him what? A few kind words, a shoulder to cry upon. The idiots who had discarded her, needed their bumps felt, no one in their right mind would treat someone with such intimate knowledge as she possessed, in such, a manner. But she was gone, the moment had passed, but if she had survive, he would have presented her at a most opportune moment when she could have denounced those who had treated her so shamefully. Their culpability and guilt would have finished them. That moment had gone, he had rethought his plan. He could still succeed. With no other competition, he would command, set the prices, build the new port and rule as others had. He was a breath away from controlling all of Stormouth.

"Wonder the man is not laid low in remorse," the rotund man declared. "Mean to say, not natural what that family are capable of." Gazing at his acquaintances in feigned bemusement, Turnbottle never ceased to be amazed at how reliable the gossip mongers were at spreading titbits of news so swiftly. Which item was it? He mused, the priest or Adam? The brother was the most likely, his death had been witnessed, word of that would spread quicker than the disappearance of the priest. That might take days before it gained credence.

"I fear, gentlemen, you have me at a disadvantage. Has something occurred?" Turnbottle eyed the gathered men with interest.

"My God, sir, you must be the only one who remains unaware. Fact of the matter is, Adam Wood was killed last night."

"Killed! Surely not?" Turnbottle replied in astonishment. "What, pray, occurred?" He leaned forward and waited. Would the story resemble the facts, or would it be embellished? What did it matter? Adam would prove more beneficial to him dead than he ever would have done alive.

"Tale is he cheated at cards. Chose a fop to dupe and was discovered. The man called him out, proposed a duel like a gentleman, but Wood tried sticking him in the back. Word is this stranger skewered him like a kipper. Irons say's the bounder was dead before he hit the ground. Surprised his brother hasn't heard about it yet?"

"As I say, I have just returned from speaking to him and he said nothing, although his mind wasn't on what he was doing." Turnbottle sighed to disguise his pleasure. His devilish scheme was beginning to bear fruit.

"Man's ruining that business," stated a sallow faced man who sat near the open fire, shoes resting upon the fender, sucking lovingly on a churchwarden pipe. He only spoke when the pipe was burning nicely, which was not often. "Owes me a ruddy fortune, and can he find my goods? No, he cannot."

"That, gentlemen, is the reason I am here." Turnbottle paused. His timing had to be perfect otherwise his advantage might be lost. "It is time we discussed what to do about them."

"What's on your mind Turnbottle?" the portly man asked.

"Not sure," Turnbottle mused in feigned resignation. "Fact is, Josiah will destroy what is left of his business within a week…If we wait, we might all be impoverished. Therefore we have no other recourse but to demand he stand aside. I realise it isn't palatable, but if we convince him such actions were best for his family, we might yet salvage some respectability."

"He'll never agree. Like his father in that respect…stubborn." The portly man's words brought about a cacophony of sound. It seemed as if all present wished to speak at once. Turnbottle allowed them to grumble and complain for a few moments before slamming his cane upon a table. The silence was instantaneous. Shocked men stopped talking and turned to stare at him.

"Gentlemen, is this what we have become, a braying pack eager to taste blood? I don't believe so, for that would not be the behaviour of serious men? Of course I share your concerns... but there maybe a way out of this mess."

"How?" the assembled group demanded. This was it, his chance, and Turnbottle was not going to squander it. Carefully, he spoke his rehearsed lies.

"It will not be easy, but I believe if we present a united front, Josiah might be convinced to yield ground. He must, for the alternative is unpalatable. Should he refuse the repercussions on all of us are dire. Imagine the consequences should that firm fall into bankruptcy. Our own positions would be compromised; imagine the effect such a thing would have."

"It could ruin me. I have spices, cloth and...well, various other commodities in their warehouses. Lose all that to a firm of receivers, and I will be next in the debtor's prison," the portly merchant stated, as he rubbed his jowls in thought.

"I feel your pain, sir.Gentlemen, I believe, for the good of the community, we should act, demand access to their warehouses. Perhaps simply so we can retrieve what is rightfully ours? I dislike speaking badly of anyone, especially those who have undergone such tragedy, but I fear that family can no longer honour their debts, or fulfill their obligations."

"How are you so sure? What is it you know that we do not?" a voice came from the back of the room.

"A valid question, to which, I have no response. I know no more than any of you. I am simply surmising, but it does not take much intelligence to see what is happening. Why, only this morning I witnessed Josiah and his clerk, John Micklewhite..."

"Good man knows what he is talking about," the portly businessman interrupted.

"Aye, and fair," another added

"And honest," a third added, sincerely. Turnbottle inwardly smiled, as the compliments of his man continued. It had taken a great deal of time, money, and persuasion before certain people had done as he'd asked. Patience, though, was a virtue, and he had waited until his scheming and monetary outlay brought forth rewards.

"I concur. He is all of that and more, he knows his job inside and out, and is underused by Wood. However, I witnessed a sight only this morning, which filled me with dread."

"What was that?"

"I saw Josiah, distraught. He and Mickelwhite were searching one of the warehouses. Wood was yelling like some sort of maniac, then, as true as I sit before you, they began dragging bales and sacks out and disposing of them into the harbour…I ask, is that the actions of a firm that is in control of what they do?" He stopped, sipped his coffee and allowed the men to voice their concerns.

The event had not occurred, but Mickelwhite had done what he had paid him to do, cause trouble for Josiah. Having, 'innocently' met him in the 'Star' and having plied him with ale, the clerk had been turned far easier than expected. The man had poured his grievances out, like water from a pump. Tired of Josiah he was ready to leave, but Turnbottle had convinced him, eventually, that working for him would bring him greater enjoyment. Spying was a dirty word, procuring favours was far more pleasant, but the result was the same. Mickelwhite would provide him with information, and all it had cost, was the promise of a nonexistent opening in his own company. In fact Josiah's latest problem had been the old pirate's idea. "The more delicate will rot quicker if dampened with salt water. I knows what to do and when." The Wood family must have truly upset the clerk, for Turnbottle had smelt the stench and it was most foul, most foul indeed.

"No, it is not." The words drew him back to the present. The merchants, it seemed, had decided. One by one they nodded their acquiescence.

"Gentlemen, should they be permitted to treat fellow business people like they have? Of course not, nor do I wish them harm. Believe me, they have suffered enough. However, I ask, has anyone been paid or had goods delivered in the last few months?" Turnbottle could be charming when the need arose, and this was such a moment.

"I certainly haven't," the man with the pipe added. "Though, I admit I have allowed them a certain latitude, and clemency because of their tragic position. I mean the loss of old Joseph, his eldest son, then a daughter-in-law who brought shame and disrespect on their name is enough for any family to endure."

"True," another added. "I too have debts outstanding which…if they settled their account with me, I could clear."

"I say, hang the laggards. I have Ivory from Africa in storage, worth a veritable fortune." Turnbottle listened as each voiced their concerns.

"I have spices," another said.

"So, what are we to do?" yet another demanded

"I fear I did not realise the extent of the problem." Turnbottle feigned astonishment, his acting worthy of any stage. Shaking his head solemnly he continued, "I fear, gentlemen, we must act to save ourselves. The time is upon us to be bold. As I see it, we have but two options. We either wait, and in all probability flounder, or we confront him, present ourselves at his office this afternoon when, fortuitously, I have been invited to attend. I believe we should use that opportunity to demand satisfaction." He paused as the merchants considered their options; he saw a few wavering and so added to their concerns. "Believe me when I say I sympathise, truly I do, it is a situation that I dread. But...there comes a time when we must act."

"Must we? Must we act like a mob, force them to close their doors? Surely there is another way to deal with this problem?" The lone voice surprised Turnbottle; he thought he had convinced them to follow him. It appeared there were still those who harboured a certain amount of sympathy and loyalty. Should he have been surprised? After all, they had traded longer than most could remember. If he was to succeed, he must end such sympathy here and now. He did it with a tear in his eye and a knife in his hand. Shaking his head regretfully, Turnbottle ended all such feelings for the family.

"I fear we must. Sympathy does not feed your families, or those of your workers? If we starve does that aid those that rely on our wise endevours? I mean without trade, without the revenue raised, our troops, who are even now being attacked by rebels in the colonies may go hungry, or be denied the means to repel such insurrection. Does sympathy keep the bailiffs from our doors...? No, it does not. Only free trade, and the wealth such trade brings, does that. I, for one, have no desire to flounder while they hold goods which belong to us...I fear we must say, enough is enough...we should act, and act today."

He paused, he was playing on their fears. These, hard bitten merchants were scared, that fear made them act as he desired. Almost instantly he saw their agreement grow before him, what he desired was a consensus, a collective mandate to act on their behalf. With such an agreement, he would speak with Josiah this afternoon and achieve legally what he had wanted for so long; access to those ledgers.

"Aye."

"Well said."

"I said all along we should hang the dogs." The last comment, he hoped, was meant to shock, not to be taken seriously.

"A trifle harsh at this stage," Turnbottle said delicately at the less than gracious comment. "However, we must have agreement...do we have it?" He waited. This was a strange situation, never before had they worked together.

They made their fortunes by using their wits and skill, at out maneuvering each other, and living by the consequences. Now he was asking them to act together, to speak with one voice, against a common problem.

"Aye, there is no other option, when and where?" a tall, thin man, asked. Turnbottle sighed silently and smiled, replying sadly.

"I suggest a small deputation accompanies me when I meet Josiah. We can put our concerns to him then."

"Why not all of us? Show the little runt that enough is enough." The merchants were roused and smelt blood.

"I think a mob would do little good," Turnbottle stated solemnly. "The boy lives on his nerves, we do not want him to shut up shop and refuse to speak with us. No, a small, but eloquent deputation will achieve far more than an angry mob."

"Fair point, who then do we send, who speaks with him?" Victory made him humble, now was the time to appear compassionate and reserved. Sipping his coffee, he stated solemnly,

"If I might suggest, we should sent Columbine and Tremlett. Both are known to Josiah, he will feel less intimidated by them."

"And you, Turnbottle," the man Columbine added. "We may have position and status, but you have the man's ear. You have displayed the ability of both common sense and eloquence that might prevail." Amidst the shouted approval, applause and back slapping, Turnbottle mentally ticked off one last item that he had completed. His moment of triumph was but a few short hours away.

Chapter Fifty Four

Contentedly, Turnbottle, closed his eyes and allowed the excited chatter to wash over him. Pettit's was alive with the inane chatter of eminent men, but he allowed himself a moment to reminisce on all he had achieved.

In the darkness of the previous night he had become a murderer. The reason was easily justified, he felt no compunction for what he had done, each had been essential to his cause. Bayles had deserved all he got, his death had been …enjoyable, pure theater, retribution for all he had inflicted on so many. How a Godly man could ooze such vile evilness was difficult to comprehend but he had, his screams were small recompense for all those he had defiled, driven to their graves, ruined, or upon whom he had inflicted such pain. The vision of his death, had been pleasurable, no longer would he fornicate and steal, no longer would he berate those he saw as weaker than he. It was somehow poetic, seeing how he had died, that his disappearance had been announced by cries of anguish. Abigail's death however had been hard to accept. Her demise was unfortunate, but not unwelcomed. She was simply another victim caught up in things she didn't understand.

Death had come to Stormouth, but he had also used subtle guile to achieve the fear he wanted aroused. Long before dawn, before he had visited the warehouse, he had stood opposite the church, where, concealed among the market vendors he had watched his plan unfold. The Plunkett woman had arrived, to set out the bibles as she did every day .Discovering the church doors open, she had bent to retrieve a discarded shoe. Her consternation almost made him laugh, he'd stifled his joy with his hand as the old sow had cautiously entered. He waited for the havoc to sink into her puny brain, then with a howling scream she fled. The Alter cloth had been desecrated, the candlesticks, and cross, stolen also. He knew all this, because he had ordered it. The woman's one task was to raise the alarm, which she was doing perfectly. Howling and screaming, she rushed across Church Square to the rectory where, she found the house in much the same state, the door ajar and the priest nowhere to be seen. As was the way of elderly women, her concerns and distress were conveyed in the only way she knew, slumping to the ground, she continued her banshee like howling.

Leaving Church Square, he had wandered through the back alleys, contemplating Adam Wood. Like Bayles Adam lived a vile despicable life, unlike Bayles Wood's death hadn't been personal. Bayles had instigated a sequence of events which had aided his cause. Adam's death was no loss to the world, the insinuations, that he partook in unnatural and illegal activities had been rumoured about for some time. His father did much to suppress those rumours, but without that protection, they would reappear. The town would turn on him, damaging their reputation further, hastening their fall from favour, adding to the merchants mistrust. Far better his disgrace ended, saving further ignominy. But it had to be public, it wouldn't have sent the same message if he had died in some alleyway. Which was why he had sent for an old friend, a man capable of ending Wood swiftly, and with undue opposition. Josiah would be isolated, without Adam, there would be just two women to aid him and Sarah Adam's wife was little better than her husband. She was an embarrassment, apparently bent of self-destruction. Her blatant wantonness with the militia colonel wasn't even discreet. They flaunted their desire before everyone, being seen together openly in the squire's carriage, defiling her marriage vows without any recourse. Not that he cared that much, but their behaviour had influenced his decision as to which brother died.

* * *

"Are you well, Turnbottle?" the voice drew him out of his daydream and back to reality. "You appear lost in another world."

"I…I am sorry," the merchant replied. Pettit's appeared calmer and Columbine stared at him quizzically. "I simply reflect upon what has befallen us." He would have to be careful, laxness now could undo all he had achieved and possibly destroy him. Eli Porter, had almost caught him out earlier. Drawn by the commotion, he had rushed from the Town Hall towards the howling woman. Always a figure of mirth, he had appeared even more so in the half light of a new day. Clasping his wig to his head, and wrestling with his cloak, which flapped in the wind, he had nothing with which to hold his unbuttoned breeches which threatened to fall to the ground. Then, like now, he had to quell his mirth. Any form of slackness, could, inadvertently, expose him to awkward questioning. Columbine was no fool; his mind was razor sharp despite his foppish attitude. Importantly, he had succeeded despite Wood.

"No need to apologise, dear chap. Fact of the matter is we would all like to escape for a moment or two, especially with such weighty issues to deal with, what?" Columbine towered above Turnbottle, tall and extremely thin, with a sharp chin and long bushy sideburns. Turnbottle had always thought he resembled a heron; all he needed, was stand on one leg and the impression would be complete. "So, Wood cheats and is killed. Poetic really, considering his life."

"Yes… indeed. We live in strange times, do you not think…when one's fortunes and destinies can change so quickly. Do the Constables know where his killer might be?" Turnbottle asked warily. He was sure he had covered his tracks, but it would take but one misplaced word to expose his involvement.

"Yes and no; he told everyone his name, made no secret of the fact. Purported to be the brother of the woman they evicted. My son says, he was fop, back from that dog's underbelly named France, but skilled in sword play. Boy said the way he skewered Wood was a delight to observe...the action, not the result, if you get my meaning, bad luck really, on Wood's part." Columbine was the sort of man who kept his cards very much close to his chest, saying what needed to be said and no more, but this day he appeared blessed with an infection to speak.

"Man makes his own luck," Turnbottle stated. In truth, his connection with Sudbury went back many years, to a time and place best forgotten. Then a young man had recruited a soldier, discarded and forgotten, in one of the many taverns between London and the Channel ports. He had been paid, housed, given employment and allowed to make a new life for himself on the understanding that when he was called, he would serve his master in whatever task he desired. That engagement had ended; Adam had been his one and only task, servant and master would never again meet, nor would either speak the other's name again. "Fate plays a part, but it is our superior minds that separate us from the animals of the field. We live and die by the decisions we make...you of course allude to our forthcoming encounter with Josiah?"

"I do...I was contemplating how things have changed. Less than a year ago none would have contemplated such a situation; certainly none would have been discussing ruination or moving against them. I blame the military, we were far better off without their presence. It is a strange world, is it not?" Columbine appeared pensive, Turnbottle waited for what else he had to say. "I suppose we must make the best of what we have, and thank God we can enjoy it for as long as possible. Which brings me to my point, may I be the first to congratulate you."

"Me, sir, what have I done?" Turnbottle stared at the merchant in bewilderment; he had expected much, but not this.

"Modesty is a requisition you will need; it will aid you during your term of office. I am sorry, I have delayed long enough. Last evening, Benjamin, the town council met and your name was discussed. Barring any unfortunates, you will be named as next year's Mayor...May I humbly place my name forward as your assistant?" Turnbottle was stunned; could this day get any better? His enemies destroyed, his fortune made, and now honours bestowed upon him for doing what he enjoyed. It took him a moment before he could speak; when he did, it was with unforced humility.

"I...I am astonished, and not a little humble. I had no idea my name was being spoken of." He removed his kerchief and wiped his forehead. "Of course, if such an event should occur, if it becomes reality, I would be most pleased to have you beside me."

"Much obliged, I am sure." Columbine doffed his hat to his friend. "Now, when do you wish to leave?" He removed his pocket watch and tapped its glass. Why he did such a thing, Turnbottle had no idea, but it showed that the man was eager to proceed.

"An hour, maybe two," Turnbottle mumbled. "I have another appointment, someone I have to look in on. It should not take long, then I am at your disposal."

"Two hours, capital, time for a spot of luncheon then we sort these dogs once and for all."

"That we will, my dear Columbine that we will." The master of subterfuge left the coffee house floating on a tide of ecstasy. He had to focus, he had two hours before his final meeting, time in which he could savour this latest delight and view what his conniving had achieved.

* * *

The journey from coffee shop, to church, passed in a blur. By the time he arrived, the scene was still of confusion, Porter, in his position as Town Clerk, had assumed command. For that reason alone it was utter confusion, no one knew what had occurred, but he insisted on seeking everyone's opinion, no matter how fanciful their ideas, as to where the priest was. Men spoke their mind, while one adventurous landlord, plied all and sundry with ale, while his potboy followed behind collecting their pennies. Turnbottle though listened to the women. In small nervous groups, they pointed and whispered. The object of their discussion was not so much the cleric, but his housekeeper Ruby.

The more mature women like Mrs. Jones, Turk, Foulds, and Furnell cried, and spoke in hushed tones of elopement. Why, until Bayles was found he might simply have forgotten to lock the church, and thieves had walked in. There was no reason to suspect anything else, but these women suddenly assumed he, in some way, was the fountain of knowledge?

"Rum do, Mister Turnbottle, rum do, indeed," Mrs Furnell stated, as she caught sight of him approaching. "Mrs Puckett says the Reverend is missing along with Ruby. Word is they have run off together. I fear a scandal afore this is concluded."

"I doubt that is the case, my dear lady. Reverend Bayles is far too dignified to do anything so remiss." He smiled, and the women shook their heads in concern. Ignorance and rumour would weave their spells, while he maintained an air of detachment. Adam's death, he knew, would cause consternation, but was surprised that Bayles' disappearance was causing such profound concern.

"That's as may be," the woman had continued. "Why then, have they summoned the constables? Answer me that." Mrs Furnell inclined her head and waited an answer. "As I said, rum do indeed. I tell you, sir, they have absconded, gone to set up together and him a man of the cloth! Why else would they be sending out search parties?"

"A precaution I suspect nothing more. Our priest would not desert us. You wait; he will reappear long before dusk." His words appeared to calm them, eventually allowing him to leave their presence and make for the lych-gate. He was so enthused, that he almost missed seeing a woman hurrying away from the crowd. Despite being dressed for concealment in a long hooded cape, Sarah Wood was easily recognised. "Where have you been, as if we cannot guess? Fitzwilliam plays a dangerous game, as do you, but not for much longer."

Wynford House, had been her hunting ground; her illicit liaison no longer worthy of concealment. Though no doubt, the news that awaited her would cure her lust. No sooner had she fled the scene, than the fool she dallied with marched into view. Remarkably he and his men looked impressive as they took guard, preventing the masses from encroaching upon the investigations

"Good day, Turnbottle. No time for pleasantries, I fear, the council requires our services this day," Fitzwilliam stated importantly, brushing past the merchant. "Form up, form up, damn your eyes! I'll flog the next man that moves!"

"His blood is up, I fear," Sir Stanley Cobb stated flatly. Standing alongside Turnbottle, the squire appeared strained, he stooped as if weighed down with problems, and scowled at Fitzwilliam whenever the man spoke. "No good will come of this, mark my word, no good at all."

"You are well, I trust?" Turnbottle asked politely. The squire glared at the militia colonel, who barked orders to anyone who would listen. Trouble was Cobb had tired of his guest, had realised he was nowt more than a sham, an over- dressed, tricked up, unimportant actor.

"As well as can be expected," Cobb replied. He hesitated, then, drew closer and whispered, "I hear congratulations are in order. No...do not try to be modest, I ratified your appointment. As mayor, I fear you will be kept very busy...I sense we will need men of your caliber if we are to return the town to normality."

"You are too kind," the merchant replied in mock embarrassment. Before he was finished, there would be many queuing to pay their respects to him. "I must beg your indulgence Sir Stanley, but I have matters to attend to do and little enough time to complete them. I trust you will succeed in discovering our wayward priest." With that, two men parted, one whose heart soared on wings of joy, while the other glared at a militia colonel with hatred, and wondered why Porter called upon this idiot instead of the 3rd?

His time was almost done, Pettit's beckoned but he took a moment to walk past 'The Crown'. Unsurprisingly a crowd were gathered here also, eager to hear of the events that had led to a death. Unlike at the church, no women were drawn here, perhaps because of the violence involved, but that was conjecture on his part. These men, watched as Johnson the Mayor directed the investigations into Adam Wood's death. Turnbottle watched from the rear and was surprised that none of Wood's friends were present. He chuckled as he imagined the sons of rich merchants fleeing from this place, not through fear of being implicated, but because of being seen frequenting a gambling den. Death was nothing compared to having one's reputations sullied by such a thing.

Hearing the Church bell toll the quarter hour he hurried on towards his last but one destination. He walked casually passed Furnell's and the butcher's, until he stood before the entrance to the 'Butts'. Nothing appeared untoward, life continued, unaffected by the events of the day, death was something these wretches lived with. He passed by without a second glance. Only once did anyone look at him. Peter the blacksmith, nodded surreptitiously, it was almost unseen but Turnbottle nodded back, Bayles was gone, their nights work forgotten. Satisfied he was safe, he turned once again, to head back to his friends. He should have looked more closely for Maud had defied him. Finding her mistress's letters, she had given them to Ruby who had passed them onto Mary-Ann. Turnbottle remained a threat until he was dealt with she could still be harmed for her betrayal. Perhaps she would follow Ruby, who was, even now, aboard a ship bound for Canada. Come New Year, Stormouth would be a distant memory, as would a priest who liked dressing up.

Flushed, but invigorated, he perspired slightly. He heard the church bell toll the half hour and felt his first pangs of doubt as he entered the coffee house..

"Mr Turnbottle, sir." He turned to face the coffee shop owner." Your friends are to the rear, sir…making use of the privy, sir."

"Columbine and Tremlett are they ill?" he demanded. Surely something as trivial as an illness was not to thwart him at this late stage

"Ill? No…a trifle, how shall we say…"

"Intoxicated?" Turnbottle added helpfully. Mr Pettit smiled and nodded. "Better see them, hadn't I?" They were not difficult to discover. They lounged in their chairs, flushed and sweating profusely. The cause of their distress, evident on the table in front of them, which bore the remains of a chicken dinner, a gooseberry tart and a very fine looking syllabub. Not to mention three empty bottles of claret

"Are we ready, gentlemen?" he asked cordially. "Our duties await us."

"Unfortunately not, Turnbottle," Columbine belched loudly and attempted to loosen the bottom buttons on his waistcoat. "Damn lunch was rotten; appears my friend and I will be of little use to you on your quest." This was confirmed as Tremlett vomited onto the wooden floor. "See? My friend is expiring as we speak. I fear the worst. Best you deal with Wood alone; sure you are more than capable." If the food was off, then the wine certainly had not been, and that, he surmised, was what had caused their biliousness. Their drunkenness though, gave him what he wanted; the chance to do the merchants bidding, but unhindered by witnesses, just as he liked to work.

"Shame, sir, perhaps it is best that you rest awhile, and recover your abilities. As you say, I will attend Josiah and explain our concerns. Leave it with me, I will return with his answer."

"Good man, do that." Columbine belched, farted, coughed and dabbed some spittle away with a lace kerchief. Turnbottle feared for the man's constitution.

* * *

"Not here, sir," Mickelwhite explained to Turnbottle, who had entered the counting house unopposed and unafraid.

"Damn the man, John. I had an appointment, is he that obnoxious?" Turnbottle was annoyed, not just with Josiah, but with anyone who delayed him. Too much was at stake for idiots to act so sullenly.

"He knew, sir, but just after you left, we were disposing of some rotten goods into the harbour when a constable arrived. He and Mister Josiah spoke, then he ups and goes. Told me afore he went that you were expected and I was to allow you whatever you required. Do you know what 'appening, sir? Only, I saw 'Lobsters' on the quay."

The reference to soldiers confused the merchant momentarily. Eventually, he replied,

"I fear there has been some trouble…the town is in a state of confusion, which is why the soldiers are out, to calm and protect until all is well again."

"What's amiss?" Mickelwhite asked.

"It appears that Reverend Bayles is missing, run off into the night. While Josiah's hasty departure, I fear, is caused by more troubling news. It would seem that his brother suffered a fatal accident at the 'Crown'. They say a fop skewered him."

"What!" the clerk exclaimed. "How…why?"

"Brought it upon himself so they say. He were playing cards when a stranger called him out for cheating."

"Sounds right enough," The clerk stated.

"Well, we know what he was like. As it is, he lies dead while his killer remains at large." Turnbottle was at odds; was he dumfounded or could he still rescue this unholy mess? Carefully, he said, "These are trying times, John. We must pull together to make sure Mister Josiah has nothing to worry about. We must make sure he has a business to return to when this unpleasantness is concluded. Do you agree?" He paused, they looked at each other solemnly, then, very slowly, they grinned like the conspirators they were.

"Oh, indeed I do, sir. Mister Wood is indeed fortunate to have you to assist him." The clerk had waited many a month to witness the demise of these fools, while Mister Turnbottle had offered him a pretty sum for his assistance.

"Good man; best you continue as afore. While I examine his books, you should, keep guard for me and I shall see what mysteries they hide." Without further ado, the merchant entered the inner sanctum of the Wood Empire. "Best lock the outer doors John; we do not want to be disturbed by damned customers, do we?"

"How long will you need?" the clerk asked.

"As long as it takes, Wood has struggled for months; I have but a few hours. I will endevour to be as quick as possible."

Nodding thoughtfully, Mickelwhite left the merchant alone. Enthralled by his good fortune, Turnbottle stood silently, absorbing the significance of all he had done. The buildings were eerily silent, until the metallic clunk as the bolts were thrown on the main doors made him jump nervously. "Fool," he admonished himself. "Tell me you swine what it was you concealed all these years?" He shivered in nervous expectation as he climbed into the high backed chair and stroked the leather books lovingly. Breathing deeply, he opened the first book, sensing the same thrill as he had that first night when he had lovingly undressed her that first time. He closed his eyes and sighed, his hands shook, and his lips became dry. Excitement was tinged with a feeling of guilt and reluctance. Very slowly, almost seductively, he turned the first page and gazed upon the words. It was as Josiah had said; every word, every order was hidden by a code.

His sense of accomplishment made him waste valuable time. That first page was, as she had once been; exciting, absorbing and rewarding, but a little dangerous. Eventually he knew he had to continue but that first page would remain as a lasting impression. Reaching for quill and parchment, he breathed deeply and began. Over the next few hours, he tried every conventional code he knew. Substituting a letter for a number, reversing the alphabet so that Z became A, and so forth. Nothing he tried worked, the code refused to be broken. In desperation, he searched the room for a mirror hoping that Joseph hadn't been so crass as to waste their time with something so childlike. His search took time, until eventually; he found a very ornate gilt framed mirror in storage. Taking the ledger to the mirror, he held the book before it and stared intently. It would be a miracle if the solution was so easily discovered, that Joseph had used a child's trick to confuse his sons. He had not; the words were as confused as before, nothing he tried worked.

"Something more complicated, perhaps," he mused. "Maybe the old goat used the sons' names? Maybe they held the key, that and their birth dates." Cursing himself he knew that was pointless. Surely Josiah would have already tried something so simple. Nor did he have the luxury of time to ask for such information.

"Most codes are written to be read easily by those the information is meant for. In which case, the reader would have to have access to the means of deciphering it quickly and without causing any form of suspicion. Wood had been, for all his faults, an intelligent man. If I am to succeed I too must be as intelligent; think man, think!" he commanded himself.

Taking fresh paper, he began again with a simple transposition code, a method where letters were moved to random, but logical positions. After wasting more time, he realised that even that did not work. Wood, it seemed, had not used any known cipher.

"A key, maybe the old goat used a key word or symbol. If he had, it had to be something he knew, easily accessible, something here, within this room." He stopped and looked around. The room was a mess of piled papers, chairs, tables, books, slippers invoices; nothing appeared to be out of place. He grew concerned. His time was desperately short, but he couldn't give up, not yet. Clenching his fist he swore in anger, frustration was making him careless. Mistakes would hinder, if not defeat him, as it had done Josiah. Innocently, he walked the room and by chance retrieved a copy of the bible from a table. Thumbing its pages innocently, inspiration suddenly came to him as realisation dawned as to how stupid he had been.

Joseph Wood was a mean spirited, vicious man, with few redeeming qualities, but he had one passion in life and that was the Bible. He could quote chapter and verse as well as Bayles, while his sons were named after prominent characters. His one focus was his heir, Nathaniel, and that was Joseph's weakness and triumph. His ledgers, Josiah had said, had been written with one man in mind, Nathaniel. To that end, the boy would have been instructed in the ways of the books and taught the code which, in reality, Turnbottle now knew to be very simple. Desperately, he searched for the correct passage, eventually finding what he was looking for. Hidden among the pages was a marker, a pressed flower.

"You clever, clever, malicious old goat. Only those with specific knowledge would have seen the connection." Turnbottle sighed as realisation dawned. Wood had used his son's name as the key.

John 1:- 45-51 unlocked everything. In the past, Nathaniel had also been known as Bartholomew, *a man in whom there was no guile*.

Once realisation dawned, Nathaniel's name allowed him to unlock the remaining ciphers, of which there were three. The first was Latin; Wood had used that language as his source, not English, as Josiah and Adam had assumed. The second was a simple reversed code using the letters of that ancient language, while the third was a substitution code. With that elaborate combination finally unlocked, it took him less than an hour to unravel the first few pages. He would need further access to Wood's ledgers to discover the full extent of their devious trade. But he was sure the family would be grateful enough to grant him all the time he needed. After all, he was their friend and benefactor, intent on assisting them through their difficulties, and looking after their interests.

"Fools, I look after no one but myself."

Chapter Fifty Five

"A disgrace, sir, a debacle, total pig's ear." Captain Stilwell, RN, needed to vent his spleen, and the officers of Fitzwilliam's regiment were handy scapegoats. "That...travesty, was by far the worst demonstration it has been my misfortune to witness. Never, in all my days before the sail, have I seen such crass stupidity." Slamming his fist onto the oak desk, he disturbed various maps and made his guests jump in alarm. "Six times you have practiced that manoeuvre, six times you have failed, and this time your ineptitude leaves...that!" He pointed through the astern window at the harbour.

Stilwell wasn't tall, but, but his temper more than made up for his lack of stature. His tongue lashing was aimed at six redcoated officers, men he had come to despise, men who visibly wilted before him. As one, they stared in the direction of his outstretched arm and saw the reason for his vexation. The remains of six long boats littered the water, all upturned with men floundering, drowning or clinging to them awaiting rescue.

"I care not one iota for your men, if they wish to commit suicide then so be it, but your...ineptitude almost deprived this ship of a large number of trained sailors! That I will not abide. I assume one of you commanded, for I see no evidence of your colonel."

Two officers had been in each boat; twelve bedraggled men now stood dripping water onto Stilwell's sailcloth covered floor. If they had expected time to dry off, they had been disappointed. Stilwell believed in dealing with discipline instantly, not after officers had had the chance to compose themselves

"Sir Percival was in overall command, sir," the senior major present, added helpfully.

"Was he? From where did he command, for he failed to make his presence known to either myself, or my officers?" The captain's anger wasn't to be quenched that easily. The major wasn't to blame, but he was a part of the problem. He was not a soldier, but an over indulgent sop, an officer who spent more on a uniform than most of his men would see in a lifetime. Such men annoyed Stilwell to the point of exasperation. Mistakes in training were inevitable, but when such mistakes continued, day after day, that was inexcusable. Men, badly led, were not to be blamed entirely. The problem was exacerbated when basic fundamentals could not, or were incapable of being absorbed into a collective mind. Then, there was but one place for blame to lie, and that was with the officers who commanded, such men were, either incapable, or too lazy to teach and lead. Inhaling deeply Stilwell waited for the response, unsure to which group these officers alluded to.

"The Colonel has many onerous duties sir. He commands but leaves the mundane requirements to us. We have to accept responsibility," the Major stated solemnly.

"Not the answer I sought. From where did your Colonel command?" Stilwell tired of this foolery; he had more important duties to perform, duties which would prove most enjoyable. The Major, he saw, fidgeted, looking to his companions for assistance, before stating sadly,

"He commanded from the cliffs to the west of the town."

"From land... How pray, did he intend commanding from there?" It was beyond comprehension, never had he heard of such foolishness. His rage still burnt, and while it did, no man was safe from his castigations, yet he paused, as if contemplating his next cutting remark. He gazed through the great glazed windows of his cabin which gave him a view of the entire harbour and town. He found it incomprehensible that one small town could cause such tribulations. However, he to, was at odds with his own conscience, Like Maitland, he despised having to keep secrets. They were in essence, like a Trojan horse, unable to disclose what they knew, doing one thing while concealing their true objective which could tear this place apart. He was compelled to continue this charade for as long as Maitland needed. Closing his eyes in despair, he wondered what punishment the admiralty would impose upon him if he had these fools flung into the sea once again. It would most probably see the end of his career, but it would be so pleasurable. Shaking his head he rounded once again on his victims, castigating them further.

"If you were officers of mine, you would be hauled to the top gallants and left there until wind and rain had washed the lunacy from you." It wasn't the fact that these men were idiots, but that they failed to learn, that was what galled him. Thankfully, before long, they would no longer his responsibility. Arrangements had been made, decisions reached and he had news for them and Fitzwilliam.

"I should have you horse whipped and your Colonel flogged, but I can't." Stilwell ran his fingers through his receding hair and grimaced. "Why, you may wonder, am I so compassionate...God help us all, but you're to be released upon a real enemy? I have here, gentleman, your orders." He held aloft a piece of paper, which bore an impressive and ornate official seal. "You are to prepare for embarkation, we sail on the night of the 5th. You have been deemed ready, though; I doubt anyone took the time to examine my reports about your competence, certainly in view of that...debacle. God help us all, but I fear for your safety, not that of our rebel friends. Your men will begin boarding on the afternoon of the 4th. I suggest you use what little time you have left to finalise your preparations."

Stilwell paused as if considering further recriminations; instead, he addressed his First Lieutenant.

"Mister Cross, when our men are safe aboard, secure the longboats. I will not attempt another exercise today."

"What about the Lobsters we have aboard?"

"I should send them ashore to risk their necks once again, but we will keep them aboard. Those ashore can board on the 4th as arranged.Make the arrangements, if you please." Cross saluted and made to leave but stopped when he heard....

"You can't!" Cross bit his lip and whispered a silent prayer for the major's soul, which was about to be flayed by his captain. Stilwell stared in abhorrence at the major who waited in bewildered anguish. In his colonel's absence, he was in command. As such, he had experienced Stilwell's chastisement on more than one occasion. Reluctant as he was to repeat that experience he was obliged to question these orders; they were contrary to what Sir Percival would agree to. As a ship's Captain, Stilwell held a rank that was higher than that of a militia Colonel, even so, the Major felt sufficiently slighted to question his motives.

"You speak, sir?"

"I mean you no personal disrespect, sir, but I feel I must question your orders."

"You dare, sir, to question my authority? Dare to speak out when you should be apologising to men who risked their lives saving your scrawny hide? You, sir, are a wastrel turd, a ne'er-do-well who has no right to be before me."

"I...I..." the major stuttered.

Like his colonel, Stilwell found in the major, everything he abhorred about the irregulars. Both men were haughty, proud and incredibly vain; unable to accept neither advice nor criticism. Stilwell had witnessed such men before.
Too many good sailors and soldiers lay dead through incompetent officers. Most, like this one, failed to recognise their own inadequacies. This man still failed to understand why a sailor found constant fault with their ability to load men and materials aboard the ships. It was this ineptitude which caused him to launch into a stinging condemnation of their efforts.

"We have tried...my God have we tried to teach you a modicum of what you will need to know. His Majesty has shown fit to grant you the undoubted esteem of being the first regiment of irregulars to serve overseas. Yet you are found wanting in every manner...no, sir, I will not give ground, you will hear me out." Stilwell had seen the Major about to interrupt, but now wasn't the time, "By God sir but Colonel Maitland has endevoured to teach your men to shoot three, maybe four shots a minute. He has spoken often of the army's ability to do so and the advantage it brings to the field, yet despite his protracted efforts, none of your men can achieve anything like the standards of a line regiment. Your men, I fear, will do well to survive their first encounter with a determined enemy. That is, if they even get ashore."

His fury made him pause, to sip from a glass of Madeira, remembering the only time he had seen them in training. Maitland had invited him to watch as the regular troops of the 3rd had fired volley after volley in precise and even timing. It had been an exemplary example of well trained and disciplined troops. Then Fitzwilliam's men had tried to emulate them; it had been embarrassing and somewhat amusing. Their musketry was appalling to the point of being terrifying. Not one Company fired in time; there was no withering hail of ball, no wall of smoke, no regularity of shot. All he saw was a muted and ill-disciplined rag tag effort.

"That is why we practice, why my men have tried to teach you how to get from ship to shore, yet even at this late stage you fail to comprehend. The enemy has little to fear from you, because most of your regiment will be dead before you reach shore. That's right you...so called officers will have murdered your men as if you had shot them personally." He watched their faces and saw, finally, a little comprehension. The major finally found his voice and stated,

"I fail to see why the vagaries of tide fall upon our shoulders, sir. Surely the sailors sent to man the boats are more adept at seamanship than my men. It is to them you should direct your criticism, we have attempted to acquit ourselves with as much endevour as we can, but each time we are met with some new difficulty or rule. Our men are farmers and woodsmen, with little knowledge of the sea; they ask..."

Bravery had made him speak, but seeing that his words were having little effect, he stopped. The outcome would end the same way as the one they had indulged in less than three days ago. Then, as now, he and the captain had exchanged words when that embarkation had ended in a similar disaster. It wasn't his fault; a year ago he had been a farm manager on Sir Percival's estates.

Stilwell knew when discipline was needed and when to cease. It wasn't brave to continue lambasting a subordinate, no matter what the provocation, when the real culprit wasn't present. Fitzwilliam should have stood here, but he was elsewhere, as he was every time such meetings were called. Major Entwhistle was the sacrificial lamb, the scapegoat for a man too lazy to attend and hear of his failings. In truth, it wasn't just Stilwell and Maitland who grew tired of Fitzwilliam, Entwhistle himself was irked by the man's ability at deflecting criticism. Each disaster brought a summons to attend a meeting such as this, each time Fitzwilliam remained mute. Entwhistle had witnessed his stubbornness, despite the rebuttals and disapproval, nothing, it seemed, would detract the titled landowner from his schedule. Instead of answering for himself, he remained ashore, presiding over the King's forthcoming birthday celebrations which apparently took precedence over everything else.

An awkward silence descended on the room. Assuming Stilwell had finished, the militia began to prepare to leave. With as much pride as they could muster, and disregarding the sloshing sound from within their boots, they stood to attention and saluted.

"Major," Stilwell continued, "I have witnessed some fools in my time but you are the giddy limit...you have the audacity to imply the fiasco we witnessed today was the fault of anyone, apart from your total inadequacies? I would suggest you spend what time you may have left on this earth, teaching your men how to be the best they can...because when you arrive at your destination, those skills will be needed, by God, will they. Good officers adapt, they see a problem and amend their decisions to suit the situation...you must search your soul and determine truthfully if you are able to do that...if not, I will accept the resignation of any officer, yourself included, to me, here, before dawn. Colonel Maitland and I will see you replaced with men able to do the job. Can you do that, sir? Or are you inept and incompetent? Speak up or improve, the choice is yours."

He paused, his anger cold and calculated. He wished to continue, to flay them with what he knew, but stopped himself. His orders did not include Sir Percival Fitzwilliam; he was ostracised because of his ability to cause mischief. Even now, he deemed himself too self-important, isolating himself within Sir Stanley's home. He was a hermit, refusing to accept orders and information, Cross had been sent ashore on numerous occasions and been denied an audience with the man.

"Colonel Maitland and I have discussed this...problem, and have decided you need as much time to load as possible. We will endevour to get your regiment on board without loss of life, but I will not guarantee that as fact. You and I will be shipmates for many a long month, I suggest you learn our ways swiftly. For the moment return ashore, speak to your colonel and God help us all. Mister Cross, see these gentlemen over the side."

Contemptuously, he turned his back on them. His sanity had been tested ever since his first meeting with Fitzwilliam, and there was still the potential of a long voyage to look forward too. Days and weeks in the man's company would stretch him even further. This cabin had seen battle before; he himself had lain wounded here. Never though, had he approached a voyage with as much trepidation, dismay and a modicum of pleasure. He needed time alone, but Maitland was due for another meeting. The outcome of which, would determine his next move.

* * *

"Is this true?" Stilwell demanded staring at the paper in awe and disbelief.

"Apparently so, as you know I have been sending my RSM and a few trusted men into town on a fairly regular occurrence. It seems Patrickson has hidden talents concerning deviousness. I have no doubt that what he has discovered during his visits to the taverns and…whorehouses is close to the truth. Certainly it is revealing."

They had sat alone within Stilwell's cabin, discussing the latest intelligence on both the militia and the possible whereabouts of their elusive spy. Upon their shoulders rested the fate of their mission.

"If what is written here be true, then this little backwater is a hotbed of intrigue. Good God and 'HE' wishes to attend! Dare we risk it?" Stilwell had questioned.

"I do not see why…or how we can refuse. I have enough men to deal with most eventualities, could always do with more of course, but we have secrecy as our ally. No one will know about this until it occurs, that negates the risk somewhat."

"So be it. I wish we could share your finest hour, but when that occurs, we will be busy ourselves."

* * *

With much to discuss, not least Maitland's efforts at subterfuge, their meeting had gone on longer than anticipated. Finally alone, Stilwell had sat, cigar in hand, assessing each small detail, and putting them into perspective.

"Sanity, dear God, give me sanity, along with a fair wind and deep water." Like all sailors, he loved being at home with his family but despised what the land offered; disloyalty, secrets, deviousness, qualities which sailors could not abide. Even here, in this small town, he was witnessing more of the same. He stood, and unconsciously touched the barrel of one of his iron companions. Maitland's man, a mere ensign, had returned with sealed orders, they were authorised to do all that was necessary to complete their preparations with the utmost expediency.

The ramifications of such orders weren't lost on him, He was here while those with ultimate authority were in London. He and Maitland must make instant decisions. Fail and they would be judged harshly, succeed and their Lordships would reward them lavishly such was their life. Retrieving the document from his desk, Stilwell read the words once again

"To Captain Stilwell, commander of His Majesties Ship 'Kentsman' at present in the port of Stormouth.

Sir, be it known that you are ordered this day to remain in harbour until at least the night of the 4th inst. During this period you are to render any and all assistance to Colonel Maitland of His Majesties 3rd Regiment of Foot. Your task is to delay and then apprehend any and all personages who seek to make traitorous demands upon his Liege Lord King George, his subjects, lands or possessions. You are further commanded to take all necessary measures to protect the safety of His Majesties person. Further, you are to render to Colonel Maitland and all assistance as is deemed suitable in his endevours to reveal and apprehend a rebel agent. For means of expediency that individuals name will be conveyed by the bearer of this order, one Ensign Mathews of the 3rd regiment of foot. We find this officer to be a trustworthy and diligent individual. He will articulate a name to you and Maitland personally. No other is to know the identity of that name.

It was concise and to the point, just how he liked his orders to be. Such directness gave a man stability, allowed him to use his judgment when needed, but also told him exactly what he had to do. Mathew's had spoken the name, leaving Maitland and himself speechless. Neither had reason to suspect, nor indeed, would they have searched for them, such was their surprise. He simply hoped those who knew more than he, knew what they were doing. But that was an officer's lot in life, as he had told Maitland on numerous occasions

"Some damned fool had been convinced by Fitzwilliam that his regiment was fit to serve, how though defies belief. They are a disgrace, a liability, totally useless. Mark my words, Maitland, we will have trouble there afore too long."

Thankfully, some, more intelligent man, had recognised the problem. The militia's poor training, made them ineffective to become a part of the colonial army. Their presence would have been disruptive to good order while now it was known that Fitzwilliam and his...friend simply desired passage to the Americas where, Fitzwilliam would have presented a fully armed regiment to the rebels. Maitland had relished their departure, stating more than once,

'They will become a hindrance wherever they go, better the rebels have Sir Percival than our army."

"True and they may actually aid our own plans. If they cause too much disruption, the French may sail, they may be drawn out. Far from home, their fleet would be exposed, we might catch them napping and finish them in one grand battle. Without a safe harbour, the survivors would be harassed by our own Indies Squadron who, with God's grace, would chase them to hell and back."

The meeting had closed amicably with a glass of Claret. Maitland had been ferried ashore, where he had much to do before the King's Birthday Ball, While Stilwell was to embroil the militia in further mischief. The final part of their orders had summed up the feelings in London admirably.

"When such personage is apprehended you will be free to deal with the militia in a manner fitting their crime. Bear in mind that at no time are they to be given passage, do what needs to be done, but they must not leave England. We suggest you...."

* * *

"Come," he replied to the knock upon his cabin door. Hastily he placed the paper in his coat pocket. "Well, Cross, are they dealt with satisfactorily. Have you drowned their useless carcasses?"

"I did consider it, but thought it wasn't sporting. Nor, I fear, would such an occurrence aid us in any way except to make a tiresome task even more depressingly irksome."

"Pity, the best place for such scurvy sops is at the bottom of the sea. Very well Mister. Is all in place? May we continue unheeded?"

"We are, sir. I must say that last episode proved more troublesome than we had envisaged, almost cost us the bosun. A Lobster became deranged and almost drowned him. Harkness dealt with him... suitably"

"A tot of rum for Harkness. I trust Colonel Maitland will fare better in his endevours. I tell you, Cross, I will be glad to feel open water again. Hate the land; too many slimy people live ashore, people who have too much time to plot and scheme. Give me the oceans; there at least it is pure and simple, you work together or die together." Stilwell sighed; his time in this infernal port had not been pleasurable at all.

"True, very true, sir...I too will be glad to be under sail again. That Major...Entwhistle, is a bigger fool than his colonel. I mean, he doesn't even suspect that we have them so confused they do not know what day it is. We could tell them the world is square and some would believe us. All we need is your command, and we can have them aboard and stowed within a day."

"Then your prayers are answered, Mister. We sail, midnight on the 4th."

"You mean you intend…"

"Yes, Mister, they must all be aboard their designated transports before dark of that night. Begin loading as soon as you can, but do it surreptitiously. Use whatever means you see fit, but get them aboard including their food, tents, weapons, ammunition, uniforms, horses, dunnage everything mister including officers whores undergarments. Colonel Maitland though wishes every officer of captain rank and above, to remain ashore. Seems he wishes them to attend a ball while we ferry their men away. He will determine when he springs his trap. All being well this ends here permanently, and hopefully, if we do it right, we will snuff out any further like-minded individuals with similar ideas. We will not fail, certainly not because of Sir Bloody Percival and his cronies."

"Colonel Maitland has discovered his spy, then?" Cross asked.

"I cannot answer that, not yet. But suffice to say; if all goes well, Sir Percival is in for more surprises than he expects…I actually feel sorry for him. While he prances like the fool he is, we shall be mid-channel and no one will be able to question where we go. I do so wish we could attend his tomfoolery, but our duties are clear. Tell the men, Mister Cross, and prepare the ship."

Stilwell had discovered the perfect way to exert retribution against Fitzwilliam.

"A pity, I have a full card of dance promises…Oh well, such is life." Cross removed a paste card from within his jacket and laid it upon the captain's desk. "Seems I am to be otherwise engaged, and they were all most comely and engaging, very engaging indeed."

"My apologies, Mister, but a Royal Command overrides your carnal lusts. It will be a welcome change to feel the wind upon our faces once again; I sense we have become lax during our time here."

Cross smiled. He had but one duty, to present a fully manned and trained fighting machine, a ship the Captain could rely upon. He knew his job to the letter, could do it blindfolded, he wasn't concerned with the ship at all. What did cause him a modicum of concern was quartering. There was barely enough room for everyone onboard already. If as he suspected, they were to take on more, the ship might become dangerous in more ways than one.

"Beg pardon, sir, but I do wonder if our forces might be stretched mighty thin."

"Explain, Mister!" At such a late stage, Stilwell neither desired nor required further complications.

"As I see it we are to embark six hundred men and their equipment. Spread about the flotilla, each ship will carry an extra hundred or more, semi-trained, armed men. We can secure their officers, if that is what is planned, but what of the merchantmen? Their crews would be overwhelmed if that was the militias want. Even if we spread our marines thin we could not stop a determined attempt to take them. I know not what you and the colonel had planned, but we would be thin, sir dashed thin with a scant twenty five men to each ship. Not exactly an army, sir, unless you intend requisitioning some of Colonel Maitland's men?"

"I see. Indeed, I do thank you, Cross, for your thoughts. Inform Colonel Maitland, that I am amending the disposition of our forces. Damn the Horse Guards for their short sightedness. Maitland cannot afford to lose any men, so we have but one option. Tell the Lobsters some tale, make it official, but make sure their powder and ball, muskets and swords are sent to one ship while they are dispersed among the others." The captain paused. "I dislike the notion, but I see no other option. Once we have them aboard, we will lock them below until we reach our destinations. I was not supposed to become a jailor, but when the needs must, Cross, when the needs must."

"Is there anything else, sir?" It never failed to amaze the first officer how quickly men like Stilwell were able to react to given situations. He had spent his entire career at sea and still marvelled at that ability, and hoped one day to have the same confidence. Unknown to him, the same questions had been discussed earlier, during Maitland's visit.

"Yes, Cross, there is. Officers are to join me for dinner tonight; extend the invitation to Colonel Maitland and his senior officers."

"Shall I extend the same invitation to Sir Percival and Sir Stanley?"

"No, sir, you may not. If all goes well, those gentlemen will be enjoying a far different fare very soon...very different indeed."

His Captain was fair and even-tempered, but rile him and he could make any man suffer painfully. He actually felt sorry for Sir Percival, and looked forward to hearing all about his experiences very soon.

Chapter Fifty Six

With the information, denied him for so long, Maitland had two vital jobs to do before his plan could begin. He was a professional soldier, while also a spy master. On the one hand, he had to facilitate the safe return of the missing agent, while also delaying Fitzwilliam, until he either made his move, or hung himself in the process.

Ensign Mathews was crucial to his preparations, as was Patrickson. He and some trusted men, had been sent into town dressed as seamen. As he explained to Wright,

"No one speaks if they spy a redcoat. Seen it myself, the conversation ceases until our men are gone. Dressed like that, Patrickson and his men can move among them and hear what they speak of without hindrance. Any news will therefore be unearthed more swiftly."

The plan had worked far better than he had dared hope. Each morning Patrickson appeared with more tales of intrigue and duplicity. It amazed, Maitland that any man in Stormouth had the energy to work after their nighttime assignations.

"The sexton has been seen entering a house after dark, not his own. While here, two merchants accused the coffee shop owner of serving stale wine. Oh, and apparently, there was a commotion in the town which necessitated the calling out of Fitzwilliam's men." Explained Wright.

"Why was I not informed immediately?" Maitland demanded, "Everything that fool does causes me palpitations."

"You were aboard the 'Kentsman' at the time and we were not called out. Fitzwilliam, evidently, saw no need to inform us of his outing."

"Am I to assume the French landed, that they were assailing the town, laying it to waste?" Maitland grew more tired of the fool with each passing day.

"Unfortunately not, for that I could have dealt with. It would appear the town council got their breeches in a knot. Apparently the priest, Bayles, has gone missing," Wright stated, reading a badly written note. "It seems he has run off with his maid."

"Another one? My God, what is wrong with the women in this place? Wasn't there a similar report...?" Maitland thumbed through a pile of papers, withdrawing one he read and then said, "Here, Corporal Mead reports that a maid...booked passage on a merchantman which sailed not two nights ago."

"Two girls leaving in quick succession is...suspicious to say the least," Wright, saw his colonel's bemusement and added swiftly, "Course, might be completely innocent."

"Nothing in this town is innocent, Herbert. Maids are poorly paid, how then, do such people purchase passage? Certainly she couldn't have done so without assistance, discover who her benefactor is, get Mead to ask around the taverns, I want to know who she was close to, who she spoke to before sailing. Discover their identity and we at least will discover why she was dispatched so quickly. Damn this place and all who live here. I thought London had enough chiselers and thieves. This place is worse by a long chalk. Is there anything else to concern us?"

"Just vague mention about the Wood. If you remember sir, she caused some commotion some time back well apparently she has now died in some hovel while giving birth."

"And Herbert. I can see you have more out with it man."

"Disturbingly, we have also received reports, that a certain Adam Wood, apparently her brother-in-law, got himself skewered in a hotel at about the same time. It appears to me, a trifle co-incidental. I mean one gets accused of witchcraft, while he is accused of cheating at cards." Wright paused, he knew his colonel had a low opinion of the town, minor items, such as this added to the overall image he had of what secrets the town concealed. One thing was certain; no one spoke the truth, if a lie sufficed.

"I honestly do not know, Herbert. I thought I did, but no more. The entire place is riddled with lies, innuendos, and deceit, everyone, from poor to rich hid something. Our Lords and masters would have been better served sending someone who understands such matters. Instead, I have to deal with not only stopping Fitzwilliam from decamping to the colonies with a regiment who he intends to present to the rebels, a regiment which, may or may not be aware of his intentions. By God, sir, can you imagine what they could do if they are bamboozled as we are? No, well I will tell you, if they realise too soon, while still here, we might see mutiny on our hands. Something I would wish to prevent at all costs. Once they are gone, they become some others poor fools problem. As for ourselves, our major problem remains this government spy. I am commanded to facilitating their safe return from whatever clandestine mischief they have been embarked upon. We evidently are to render whatever means they require to facilitate their escape. I dread to think what their Lordships thought when they gave us this task, but it might possibly be the only thing we achieve without causing consternation. No we know who we deal with, we can make our plans, though, in truth, I could do without this flummery of a ball. I tell you, I will be glad when that is finished, and we can return to normality."

There followed a moment of silence, both men lost in thought before

Herbert said,

"Those engaged in such deviousness must be made of strength few can command. I mean, to bewitch and beguile so many, while remaining sane must require fortitude few possess. I swear, if I were asked to become embroiled in such things I would soon lose all reason and sanity. However it would make a damn good story to tell ones grandchildren."

"Such is their life, we should count ourselves fortunate that our opponents do not hide in the dark, but stand 'afore us in rank and file. For the moment we must play their game, but when this is done I shall be too pleased to go back to what we do best…soldering. Which brings me to this tomfoolery." Maitland held aloft a paste card delivered to him earlier in the day. "I have matters to attend to which means, we shall not meet again until the allotted time. I leave you in command Herbert, do all we discussed, deviate not, and with God's will, we will persevere."

"I shall sir. Good luck to you and have no fear we have right on our side."

"I do so hope you are correct. Remember Herbert ignore all other commands save mine. If we prevail, we shall end this once and for all."

Both men knew precisely what was at stake, taking his hat from a stool, Maitland left for a meeting with destiny.

* * *

Not since the witch-hunts, perpetrated by Pope, had Stormouth been so apprehensive. Few in town could deny knowledge of what had occurred, almost all had turned a blind eye and a deaf ear to the excesses they knew occurred, while those guilty few, men like Josiah Wood, desired their guilt to remain concealed. His guilt, was made worse by his silence, he had not interjected, as a woman had been pilloried and destroyed by evil men. His culpability allowed them to exist, allowed their evilness to fester and grow like a boil on the rump that was the town's guilt. Dead men lay within their graves, forever in silence, but their lies affected those left behind. The untruths his father, had spread, harmed them as much, if not more, than when they lived. Which was why, when the pounding upon the street door came, he jumped in fear, thinking a mob had truly come for him.

"Who…who goes there?" he had asked, anxiously.

"Town Constable I need to speak with you, Mister Wood." Josiah breathed a sigh of relief. He felt a little safer, a mob could string him up, while a constable could only take him before a judge.

"What do you require, do you come to arrest me?"

"Of course not, sir, Mister Porter sent me. I fear something amiss has occurred."

Josiah's heart slumped, in the space of a year his world had already fallen apart now, he feared this to be the precursor to more bad news.

"What is it?"Josiah, observed the constable's manner how he declined to look him in the eye. Could the family survive further bad news?

"It is my sad duty to inform you of an accident…Your brother Mister Adam sir, was it seems involved in a…. sword fight and suffered a grievous injury."

"Rubbish my brother was useless with a sword, he would be more suited to killing anyone with a deck of cards. You have the wrong man you bumbling fool, be gone, find the correct family, for you are not wanted here."
Josiah was relieved this fool had erred, but the Constable remained steadfast and stated solemnly.

"There is no mistake sir, we have witnesses. Mister Adam is grievously wounded. You should go to him sir afore it's too late."
Realisation was slow to dawn on him, finally it did, and all thought of meetings were forgotten. He needed to be with what remained of his family. Devoid of any sense, he walked home, unseeing, unfeeling, his world was devastated. His house was damned, cursed as if every brick of the building sought to bring him down. Such feelings were ridiculous, of course, bricks and wood could not control and influence such calamitous events? Built to impress by his father now death lurked in every room. Josiah had toyed with the idea of leaving; such thoughts now, seemed quiet appealing.

"Where is he?" he demanded entering his home which appeared darker, colder; even his wife, who stood in the hallway appeared to have changed. She looked like a ghost awaiting his appearance. "Well, where?"

"They took him to the surgeons…I fear there was no hope, husband…the constable said we can see him any time." Martha's tears fell uncontrollably, but, despite her pain, she took his arm and led him into a room where she closed the door.

"What the hell are you doing? I must go to him! Leave me alone, woman!"

"Hush, husband, Adam is not the problem…not immediately. I fear you have a visitor, he awaits you in the parlour. He insists you speak to him, said it was most important." Martha spoke in a whispered tone.

"Damn them, whoever they are! I have a brother to mourn and a family to comfort. Tell the swine to be gone; I will speak to no one, not until I have grieved yet again." At the best of times Josiah disliked unannounced visitors.

"I told him that, but still he awaits you. He will have heard your arrival, so time is of an essence. Tell me, husband, what is amiss? Why does a soldier, an officer want of us? Why does he demand to see you privately?" She whispered, while wiping her eyes. Her husband withheld something from her and she knew not what.

"A soldier? I have no idea why he should be disturbing us. Courtesy demands he explain his presence, go and demand that of him, or throw him out. I am too grieved stricken to speak of anything unless he knows who did this to us and why."

Josiah had assumed to be greeted by wailing women, perhaps the town clerk, but not a soldier demanding an audience. Bewildered and befuddled, he could only think to send his wife to quiz the man, to discover the reason for his presence, only then would he determine a response.

"He says Adam died last night, in a duel. That cannot be, we would have been informed earlier. Why leave it until now? What occurs, husband? Tell me, only then can I assist."

"What am I, an oracle? You know that Adam is…was a law unto himself."

"They both were husband, not a month ago I had cause to confront Sarah here in this very house about her own conduct."

"What has that hussy got to do with this?"

"I suspect much. I demanded she answered to allegations that she shared another's bed demanded she refuted or confirmed such allegations."

"And?"

"She confirmed, she was proud said little simply turned and left as if it mattered not a jot."

"Yet you said nothing to me why?" Josiah demanded his mind a morass of unasked questions.

"To protect you, and the family name. I said nothing through all the trials and tribulation that have beset this family. I said nothing during the reading of the will, and the aftermath, despite wishing to speak on Abigail's behalf. I hid what I suspected about the shenanigans Sarah was involved in and the assignations she attended. Now I believe…well, you knew his leanings as well as I. Perchance Adam dallied where it wasn't wanted, maybe his preference was discovered, perhaps he…and a soldier. No, it would have to be an officer, someone of position who wishes this swept away. Perhaps were caught, compromised and was killed by one of their number."

"No, absurd, I will not hear any more of your lies."

"There is an alternative," Martha continued, "That Adam was killed because of Sarah. Rumour is a carriage collects her, takes her to meet a man, a man of wealth, an officer. There is only one, capable of such demands, and we all know who that might be. If so this visit, may not be to confront Adam's traits, but his wife's. Does her lover have a wife, children, do they need protecting? This man may be here to make suitable arrangements, a payment, so she can take her leave. Or does her lover wish to deny their liaison, to deny he had cuckolded another man's wife? More importantly, does he seek recompense from the family? Is he here seeking a duel to satisfy some lost honour? Whatever the reason husband, no good will come of meeting him, but you must do so, for he will not leave otherwise."

"Ruination! We face ruination or possible retribution. Whichever I have no desire to meet the man nor indeed madam am I concerned with your wild accusations. Your job is to run my house and comfort me. You fail miserably in both." Immediately he knew he had said too much. Grief made him lash out, he was, hurt but Martha didn't deserve such degradation. "My apologies madam, tell the fool I will speak with him in perhaps a months' time. Tell him to arrange an appointment, perhaps in due course I might feel more amiable."

"I will, of course, do as you command, though, I fear he knows something terrible."

"Terrible...in what way? Surely the most obvious reason for his visit is that he has news of the man that murdered my brother, a coward that cut him down like a dog. If so, I will not rest until the perpetrator is hanged." Josiah's anger was such that he slumped exhausted into a chair and wept uncontrollably. Life was unfair, his family was rent asunder, yet the army expected to be received as if nothing had occurred.

"He knew about Adam, that is true, but I fear that is not his true reason for calling. He has the air of someone with much on his mind. He was insistent that he waited your arrival, would not leave until he saw you. Take care, husband, his visit could be innocent but I do not wish to wear mourning for you as well."

"Your wife speaks the truth, sir." Josiah turned, to see a soldier standing in the doorway. A soldier he knew by sight, but a man he had little in common with, more importantly, a soldier who had entered the room without invite. A man who was obviously no gentleman. "As inconvenient as this may be, I must insist on speaking to you." He spoke with an air of confidence Josiah had lacked all his life, a confidence men gained on battlefields, not board rooms.

"Who...who are you? What right do you come to my house, making demands, without so much as announcing yourself?" Brought up to abide by a set of rules, as well defined as any soldier's, Josiah demanded, decorum, etiquette. Yet here he was, being told what to do in his own home while mourning the loss of a brother, left him bewildered by the soldier's impertinences.

"I apologise for disturbing you at this time, but the situation that exists demands the utmost expediency."

"You speak eloquently, sir, but whatever you desire must wait. I must ask you to leave and return when the time is more...convenient." Josiah turned his back on the officer. He would not grant an audience to anyone, least of all someone who represented the elite. Who, he was sure, had a hand in his brother's death.

"Then we are at odds, sir, for you will hear me out or suffer the consequences."

"Consequences? What consequences, you speak in riddles, sir. I will have no truck with this. Bugger off! Go! Leave us to mourn 'afore I call the town constable to have you removed."

Martha saw her husband's anger and stepped between them, though she recognised that the soldier was calm, polite, yet resolute, not in the least worried by the discomfort he had caused.

"I believe, husband, we should hear him out."

"Et tu? My own wife rises against me?" Josiah stumbled as he saw Martha had resigned herself to whatever her fate was.

"I do nothing of the sort. But observe him, he is not scared, nor does he mock our suffering. I sense he has matters of some relevance to our pain. Surely if he has knowledge, which might relieve some of our agony, we should hear him?"

"Do as you please; I wash my hands of it all." Josiah wilted before them, his stamina all but gone.

"My thanks, ma'am," Maitland had known this would be difficult. There was no greater burden than to inform an already overburdened man with more injustice, but this family had brought a lot of their problems upon themselves. "We have, if you recall, already been introduced, though events of late may have clouded your memory. In which case, may I introduce myself? My name is Colonel Maitland of His Majesties 3rd Regiment of Foot." Maitland bowed courteously. Pleasantries and respect were emotions he did not feel at this moment, but he and Stilwell had agreed that if their plan was to succeed, they needed their own infiltrator. Wood was the perfect choice; a man, so distraught, he was susceptible, able to be manipulated. "As to why I intrude upon your grief.....Well, I would like to explain, but need your permission to include your wife."

"My wife...What the hell does she know about anything?" Josiah demanded.

"More than you think...it would benefit you both to listen to what I have to say, sir. Your position depends upon it, and if I may be so bold, your freedom." Maitland stood rigidly, waiting the man's response.

"What say you, sir? Do you not realise what has happened to this family?"

"I do. In fact, that is, in part, the reason for my presence. If you permit me to explain, I might alleviate your pain somewhat." Maitland had seen enough fools since arriving in this town. Josiah Wood had been mentioned as being one of the worst dunderheads, yet what he witnessed was a man drained, but who retained a modicum of clarity to understand his position. "Of course you could have me thrown into the street. You do have experience of such matters." He saw the light of understanding appear in the man's eye, the inference hadn't been lost on him, which at least showed some remorse for what they had done. Remaining impeccably polite, Maitland had continued with his rehearsed speech. "Of course, that is but one option open to you. Other options might include listening, and then denying all knowledge. To do so would mean I would have to approach one of my other witnesses…I should state, there will be a trial at some point. Your position, be it in either dock, or witness box, depends largely upon what is decided between us…in private. I would rather this was dealt with civilly, but I will implicate both of you if you remain resolutely indifferent to your crimes."

"Crimes…what does he mean? What have you done?" Martha demanded.

"You see what distress I can cause?" Maitland was enjoying himself. Patrickson had brought so many stories to his attention and most contained one name. Taken as individual events, they seemed uninteresting, just rumour touched with a modicum of malice, but looked at as a whole, they took on a completely different perspective. If correct, this apology of a man had his hand in so many sticky pies it was a wonder his hand wasn't permanently stuck up his arse. His confidence in the credibility of his evidence slowly dawned on Josiah. Despite his depression, he realised this soldier, could harm him, emphasised by the next statement. "Of course, if you wish to continue denying what you have done, then I shall leave and allow you to suffer further. But please, be aware that this is your only opportunity to escape with impunity. Once I depart, the next visit will be when charges are brought, if that occurs it will be too late for you. No one could halt the process. Convictions are a certainty, you and yours will, I fear, be called to answer for your crimes and suffer the full consequences. This is your last chance. Consider the ramifications. Answer my questions, tell me all you know and I will do all I can to assist you. Or suffer your inevitable fate. Which is it to be, sir?"

Josiah remained silent, beaten destroyed; Martha took up the cause and replied on his behalf,

"You seem well versed in our affairs Colonel."

"That, I fear, is a task imposed upon me, one which in truth I take no pleasure in. It is my job, nothing more."

Martha suspected the soldier had far more evidence than he had so far revealed. Evidence which could implicate them terribly, it was time to be prudent. They must either, comply or be damned, the latter wasn't a pleasant option.

"Mister Wood, sir, I need an answer." Maitland saw a man struggling with his conscience. Eventually, despite his trials and tribulations, common sense prevailed. Josiah Wood had no options remaining, but to listen to what this man wanted.

"Lock the outer door, wife, we will see no one else this day," he stated despondently. Neither knew what was about to happen. Only when the house was secure did the soldier begin to reveal his evidence. Josiah had suffered much, but now Martha heard how deeply he had become embroiled. Like a beast being led to the slaughter, she watched his final humiliation, and knew that if they were to escape, they must comply completely.

Chapter Fifty Seven
The King's Birthday
June 4th 1773

Sir Stanley Cobb's day had begun badly and had deteriorated even further. Having ridden his estate, he was returning home via the route the plethora of guests would approach from. He had little to worry about, Wynford House shone like a jewel in the early morning sun. Built of mellow, honey coloured stone, it was his crowning glory, akin only to his wife, Lady Caroline. This night, everything he had worked for was to take center stage. A veritable fortune had been spent in preparation for the forthcoming celebrations, and that was what hurt.

"Damn his hide!" the squire swore viciously. With just his horse for company, he was able to vent his anger at a man he had come to despise. He had been manipulated to such an extent, he saw no easy way of extraditing himself. He had been cuckolded, yet had done nothing about it, had been made to look dunderheaded yet had remained silent, which was why his anger rose at the thought. Kicking hard, his horse galloped across the wild flower meadow towards the ornamental lake, which would, after dark, take pride of place in the celebrations.

"Lady Caroline requires the lake to sparkle. Arrange more floating decorations immieditatly." Cowering beneath the Squires anger, the unfortunate gardeners knuckled their foreheads to the man they must obey, no matter how absurd his orders. "Damn the man, illuminate it, make it so."

Forced, by circumstances to play both genial host and dutiful husband, Sir Stanley secretly plotted the means of ousting his erstwhile guest. It was proving difficult, due to the fact that Lady Caroline appeared infatuated and would hear nothing bad about the man. There was the crux of his problem, she was beguiled, believed his every word, and swooned at each extravagant idea. The final account would be excessive, no expense, it seemed, to great. From the garland draped ornamental gates through which his guests would arrive, to the ornate flower and candle lit decorations that would float and sparkle upon the mirror like surface of the ornamental ponds, he convinced Lady Caroline it should be procured, despite his requests for prudence, a never ending stream of tradesman arrived with yet more flummery. By nights end he would be the poorer, money wasted at the behest of a dandy fool who strutted as if his purse paid. *If only that were so,* Sir Stanley mused for he knew the popinjay contributed nothing. Money best spent on the house and estate was being wasted on baubles by a dandy fool, named Fitzwilliam.

Sir Stanley had inherited his father's desire for prudency. Spending only when it was deemed essential for the upkeep of house, estate, or family. Such caution had allowed them to create all he saw before him. His father had purchased the site, demolished the decrepit farm and buildings, and built Wynford House on a perfect elevated site where it could be seen and admired, though only from a distance. Wool had been the means to their wealth, the house, an edifice to extravagance. The means by which workers and visitors alike could admire his wealth and wonder upon his good fortune. Though few guests had ever visited during his father's life for he had been a solitary man, unlike his daughter-in-law who thrived on entertaining.

Approaching his home along a long tree lined drive, Sir Stanley admired what they had achieved. In recent years he had lavished a vast fortune upon the house. The now mellowed stone gave the house a sense of belonging, while the deer park and gardens, had blended into the countryside perfectly. Trees, planted by his father, now fully grown, had been trimmed to form a tunnel through which the driveway passed. Where they were thickest, torches were being set, to be lit when the sun set. In the darkness they would flicker and give a magical illusion, just right for some subtle assignations in one of the numerous bowers. Yet, he saw as he reined his horse in and awaited a groom to take the head collar that builders still worked.

"Make sure she's well rubbed down Brown, and tell Prior, there will be explosions this evening he will want to make sure they are well settled." His stable manager would know without being told but Sir Stanley had an easy relationship with his staff. "Get this mess cleared. My God do you want carriages upended when they arrive?" His anger at a small piece of wood left on the drive was a reminder that the Portico and ornamental pond were brand new, barely finished. He had seen both while visiting an old friend, and had ordered them for his own home immieditatly. "Will these damn doors be dry by the time the first guests arrive?"

"They will sir, oh yes, just need a bit of air sir and the last coat will dry nicely."

"Better had or the bill for some stained dress will be sent to you by god it will sir."

The entrance hall would bedazzle his guests, its marble floors and gilded ornamentations, would sparkle when it became dusk. Lady Caroline had demanded that everything should sparkle and shine. Servants had struggled for two days lowering the crystal chandeliers, replacing the everyday tallow candles with pristine scented beeswax tapers. Their flickering light would cast a magical glow reflected from mirrors, crystal glassware, and marble. It had better be spectacular, or he would flay anyone who let him, or the estate, down.

To left and right, the reception rooms were veritable hives of activity. In the grand salon vast quantities of food and drink were arranged upon crisp, white linen covered tables. His home had been stripped in readiness. The best furniture had been removed to make room for their guests, though, Lady Caroline insisted the finest china, glassware and ornaments remain, to bedazzle and amaze their guests with their affluence. The salon was not large, but empty as it was, it should be sufficient. His guests would enter and be delighted with what they saw. The frivolities were still hours away, but already an elaborate display was taking shape, prepared by cooks and their assistants hidden in the kitchens somewhere beneath the house.

"Trust they have healthy appetites, otherwise the poor will sample my purse more than I," he mused, pondering the cost of such delicacies. One item, guarded by a liveried servant, took pride of place upon the first table. It was the first of Meredith's charges to bear fruit, and the head gardener waited for his master to pass judgment.

"Magnificent," Sir Stanley stated proudly. His man smiled and bowed, but remained silent. His job was complete; he had produced the fruit, now his master would take the praise. "The first of many, I trust, and before Lord Malvern. Well done, well worth the cost." If Cobb counted his coin on most things, this he did not. The pineapple would draw admiring glances from his guests, more importantly, it would draw society to his door and that was worth every penny it had cost to grow the damned thing.

Leaving the fruit, he walked on. The next table was being filled with cooked meats; pheasant, partridge, beef, lamb, pork, in fact everything that the heart desired was there for the taking. He had also heard that a monstrous dish was being prepared, a dish of such magnitude that it would surprise and delight the hundred or more guests. Lady Caroline had insisted no one spoke of its existence; she desired its arrival to be the "piece de la resistance."

The second table was to be used for the wonderful desserts; syllabubs, sugared sweets and the deliciously decedent chocolate. He paused and wished no one was about, so he could secretly indulge in some. The third table was his domain, the wine table. He and Stagg had spent days in the cellars choosing and tasting the very best he had. If he were to have any say in this, no one would leave feeling slighted by his choice of wine. Stagg had decanted the very best while arranging wine fountains, one red, one white. While champagne, waited to be served, chilled in ice, from his personal ice house.

If the salon was magnificent, the ballroom was utterly stunning. Here, Lady Caroline had worked her magic. Floral wreaths and swags hung from every available position. The wooden floor had been swept, cleaned, polished and dusted with French chalk. The piano bay was bedecked with flowers, amidst which a small string ensemble tuned their instruments upon a raised dais built especially for this evening. Outside, upon the lawn, awaited the grand finale; a display of fireworks was being prepared for later in the evening. By all accounts, it would be magnificent, a fitting end and celebration for the King's birthday. Cobb awaited it expectantly; it had better excel, considering the cost it had incurred.

Damn the fool, he cursed his stupidity. The absurdity that he, Sir Richard Cobb, squire, land owner, Member of Parliament and local Justice of the Peace, had been made to look foolish, hurt. Fitzwilliam was like the pox, unpleasant and impossible to remove. He resided in his rooms, rarely venturing downstairs, indulging in what could only be called flirtatious liaisons. Had it not been for the diligence of his Butler Stagg, might have remained oblivious to what went on beneath his own roof. Thankfully he had brought his doubts to his attention.

"Ordered your coach sir to be sent to town to collect…a lady."

"Devil he will. Order it stopped Stagg, and command Sir Percival, to meet me in the library." Never had he been so determined to oust an erstwhile guest, as he had been to see the back of Sir Percival. The fool had become, an inconvenience, the quintessential annoying house guest who everyone wished to leave, but who could not be persuaded to go. That confrontation though never came. Fitzwilliam had been summoned to the town, while Mrs Wood had been returned to her husband as swiftly and discreetly as possible.

Cobb cared little for the merchant's wife, indeed she could die of the pox and he wouldn't have cared. What did concern him was the scandal she might bring to his door. Fitzwilliam used his home and his wife, he dallied with her emotions, toyed with her vanity, caressed her ego like a master to get what he wanted, and when he grew tired, he would move on to his next conquest.
Sir Percival courted favour from Lady Caroline, yet blackmailed him, the position was becoming intolerable and untenable. The man had discovered secrets Cobb wanted left undiscovered. They had been disclosed during one of many conversation they had about Fitzwilliam's assignations.

"Sir I would appreciate if you dallied with your…guests in a more favourable location. Might I suggest somewhere more suited than my humble home…the local whorehouse perhaps?" Sir Percival's reply, his arrogance had left the squire deflated annoyed and a little scared.

"Oh I think not sir. Truth is, why take my pleasures elsewhere, when your home has seen far worse than I can ever indulge in. No sir you are not concerned about my foibles, you sir are concerned that your lovely wife will discover what you and your friends get up to during your…'meetings'.

"Damn you sir." Cobb had exclaimed in anger.

"More likely I shall be sir but until then it would be…unfortunate if such matters came to light…I mean, how, would the Lord Lieutenant view you're…peculiarities? Might even cause a scandal in London, force an election, might even wake the King from his slumbers not that he'd care to busy himself most days. Did I tell you he and I are on nodding terms? Could have a word if you like, or you could simply turn a blind eye. Be a good chap, allow me to do as I wish, and I will remain silent. After all, I shall be gone shortly and you and your…friends can continue unabated and undisclosed. I would suggest, sir, that before you make assumptions and accusations in the future, you make getting your own house in order your prime requisite. Cut along, sir, I have matters to attend to and they do not include you… but do involve your delectable Lady wife." Cobb had been beaten, his wife was payment for Fitzwilliam's silence. Perhaps some kindly sailor would toss the arrogant blackmailer overboard and rid the world of another wastrel.

"Stagg, make sure no one enters without an invitation, no one do you understand? I'll be damned, if I will feed the entire district."

"Of course sir." His butler acknowledge. His master had told him this perhaps four or five times in the past days testament to the squires apprehension.

Muttering to himself, Sir Stanley left the room. Those damned cards had been another bane of contention. More suited to a Royal event, they had become ever more elaborate. More annoying still they were Fitzwilliam's idea, then commanded that Sir Stanley's staff delivered them personally, while dressed in full livery. Stagg had baulked, but had remained steadfastly silent, like the loyal servant he was.

"A bottle and glass to the orangery, immieditatly." He needed time alone, away from the hubbub, to reflect on what had occurred in his little bit of England during a most tumultuous spring. Drawing a chair forward, he sat, propped his feet upon a terracotta pot, and unloosened his waistcoat. Stagg brought his wine and departed, allowing the squire to consider his options.

Fitzwilliam was a bore, a man who knew what he wanted and how to get it through fair means or foul. The saving grace as far as Cobb was concerned was that he and his men would soon be gone and normality might be restored. Caroline would be distraught, he knew he had been cuckolded, but would resort to any means, to keep such shame from ruining the family name. She wasn't entirely to blame, women desire excitement, and Fitzwilliam had brought that to her home in abundance. She must however be convinced to remain silent, for if her assignation became known he would have to deal with her harshly. *Stupid women* he mused but knew his problems were of his own making. He had neglected Caroline, allowed estate and political duty to keep him away from her, and Fitzwilliam had made his move. Before she had been more than happy overseeing the house, dealing with church flowers. She also had her other duties, the summer fete and entertaining dignitaries to dinner and supper. Would she ever be happy returning to such a tranquil existence? Possibly not, but he would try.

Unfortunately, Fitzwilliam had stumbled across Cobbs darkest secret, how it had been revealed he had no idea, but the devil now knew and that was the hold he had over him. Trips to Parliament, as the local MP, provided him with the opportunity to enjoy what London had to offer. It was there, in those homes in Pall Mall, where he had become embroiled in a small, likeminded group. Like brothers they shared matters which should have remained in the bed chamber. He had quelled his feelings of guilty by convincing himself that his licentiousness was nothing more than a means of releasing emotions that became restricted. No doubt Caroline thought much the same when she lay with Fitzwilliam.

You know of our group but will you speak or remain silent? That was his sword of Damocles which hung above him. Fitzwilliam had discovered the names of those Cobb had joined, here in Stormouth. Men like Wood and Bayles, men who had committed acts of debauchery, in this very house. Penny whores were procured, Joseph and the rector did that, and Bayles would forgive and expunge their guilt and admonish them severely if they lacked …enthusiasm. In fact on more than one occasion, the man had been heard administering to them in the privacy of his locked room. With Joseph's death, Bayles had insisted upon a halt to their meetings. Hence the reason Cobb was trapped, the third, silent partner in a marriage where love had all but disappeared. A marriage, where the lover gloated about what he did, and what he knew, while he was unable to evict him because of those threats. Maybe, possibly if tonight's frivolities went well, if Caroline enjoyed being the center of attention, if the ball was a success, he, and not Fitzwilliam, would see her later this night?

"Sir Stanley…" Drawn from his thoughts he turned to see his butler standing in the doorway.

"What is it, Stagg?"

"My apologies, sir, but your guests are arriving."

"Hell and damnation! What do they expect beds as well? Very well Stagg, announce them, then clear the rooms, what isn't done must remain undone. I shall retire as soon as possible to dress, best feed them as well Good God what is wrong with these people? Oh yes, send word to my wife, tell her she is required immieditatly."

He should have expected such inconsideration. There were a few among society who deemed it their right to intrude upon their hosts as early as possible, to feed from their table not their own. It was inconsiderate but entirely normal. They did however cause a degree of confusion, Stagg, loyal and true, cleared the rooms as if by magic. Four hours before the appointed time, Sir Stanley, unprepared, fastened his waistcoat, straightened his wig and walked to greet his guests. King George would have been well pleased with how they celebrated his birthday. Certainly, Sir Stanley and his Lady would have greeted him with suitable aplomb and dignity. Nothing could surprise the squire, nothing he could not deal with, or so he thought.

Chapter Fifty Eight

"Her Grace, the Duchess of Mabelthorpe and Lady Matilda Fitzgibbons," Two elegantly, dressed and bejeweled, women waited as Stagg announced them. They were the first of many, Cobb knew that apart from those who came because they wanted to be seen the ball would attract those who awaited each social event with the affection of hungry peasants. The Duchess was such a person. Known throughout the district as a woman who had all but lost her fortune to an idle son. Her house had gone, she now lived as a house guest with her niece and husband, but refused to hide away.

"Your Grace, you do my humble abode a service by attending our celebrations."

"You are too kind, Sir Stanley. I do so hope our attendance will not cause any inconvenience or consternation, but my niece was most insistent. It was she who enticed me to attend, told me most forcibly that you would do more for my constitution than any amount of fresh air."

"You are most welcome, Your Grace, as are you, Lady Fitzgibbons. May I say how delightful you look my dear, simply delightful?" Sir Stanley, smiled graciously and stared in awe at the vision that stood before him. The Lady Fitzgibbons surpassed anything Stagg had achieved, she was, a vision of delightfulness, dressed in a pale blue creation, full skirted and low cut, accentuating her small waist and full bosom. A delicate, pure white, powdered wig, sat upon a perfect head, which in turn was supported by an exquisite slim neck. She curtsied, allowing him a tantalising view of her curvaceous and powdered bosom which, while being magnificent, was eclipsed by the stone that shimmered and danced upon a delicate diamond and sapphire necklace and nestled between her ample assets. Taking her hand, he knew half the men present, would be thinking that she, or more likely a suitor, had spent a fortune on jewellery and dress. Certainly the expense was worth the effort, and the Lady Fitzgibbons smiled coyly at the attention, while Sir Stanley wished himself twenty years younger. Her name would be added to his dance card though he doubted he would have much time for dancing as the stream of early arrivals continued apace.

"Where is Lady Caroline?" Sir Stanley demanded, as a lull in the line of guests allowed him to speak freely to his butler.

"Word has been sent Sir. To the best of my knowledge, she is preparing herself upstairs," Stagg replied, though if the rumours were correct, her Ladyship was entertaining Sir Percival Fitzwilliam. The question he faced was, should he inform his master of the suspicion that a guest was cuckolding him in his own home? The answer was, no, it was not. Neither though would he lie to protect her, if Sir Stanley asked him outright. Stagg was loyal to the squire, would do anything to protect him and the family name. Fitzwilliam had upset many of the staff with his manner, too many had witnessed the way he behaved, how he made a mockery of his hosts' hospitality. All wanted him gone, so the house might return to normal. Perhaps after this tomfoolery it might, and her Ladyship might also make amends, though it would take much to avoid this scandal,

"Damn her! Inform Her Ladyship it is customary for the hostess to be present to greet her guests. Oh, and find Sir Percival, he should be here, after all, this is his doing."

"At once, sir," Stagg suspected, any servant sent to find one would discover both. For the moment only the house suspected a liaison, a servant finding both in a state of...indiscretion would release a hubbub of consternation which would be almost impossible to contain. The Colonel would be gone soon, saving Sir Stanley the indiscretion of having to confront him with his accusation. But were his efforts at avoiding such a scandal doomed? Was Sir Stanley's anger the precursor to exposure? Would the squire risk all in a confrontation before so many witnesses? Sir Stanley had always been a weak and ineffectual human being, who blustered but achieved little. Lady Caroline had changed him, would he risk all, would she be able to worm her way back into his favours, after the dog had bolted?

Stagg was right to be worried. Sir Stanley did indeed suspect the worst. What to do was the question. He could, as he had earlier surmised, remain silent and await the colonel's departure. Or, he could risk all by calling the man out, challenge him to a duel and be done with it one way or the other. That was risky, against a flock of fowl he was competent enough, but pistols, or foil, against another more skilled man, would he feared, be tantamount to suicide. Nor was he able to issue proceedings against Fitzwilliam through the courts. His imminent departure meant there simply wasn't time for solicitors to draw up papers and get such a case to court. Had the man remained, he might have considered such action, but his solicitors would surely attempt to dissuade him. Firstly, such a case would be time consuming and a drain on his purse. Secondly, win or lose, the ignominy of having his name dragged through the courts would certainly ruin him. The broadsheets would write about every sordid detail, it would be exceedingly unpleasant and he might be forced to conceal himself. He would become a pariah among society, until the humiliation were forgotten. There was a third option; one that the Reverend Bayles could assist him with. When Lady Caroline was alone, after the fool was gone, she could be sent away, to recuperate, in India perhaps, where the death rate among Europeans was exceedingly high. He would then be free of both scandal and a wife. Of course a fourth option did exist. If she came to her senses, fell at his feet and begged forgiveness, he might, even now, accept that as sufficient penance and forgive her. Such matters were for another day. Tonight they had to be united, but it didn't stop him brooding as to how he might deal with the cuckolding bastard. Twenty minutes later, Sir Stanley was joined by his wife,

"You are late, madam!" he snarled, as a lull in the arrivals once again allowed him to speak harshly to his wife.

"A woman's prerogative surely," she replied, as the first of the uniformed officers of the 3rd regiment appeared.

"No, madam, it is not!" her husband hissed. "You are required to attend on time. You have little else to fulfill yourself with, unless…"

"Unless what?" Lady Caroline turned, and asked serenely. Her face was a thing of beauty. Her looks were, after all, what had first attracted him to her, and he could, even at this late stage, forget everything, if she would just beg his forgiveness and denounce the swine that had seduced her.

"Unless, madam…your delay was unavoidable." Both knew that, given the chance, the secret could remain just that. Caroline might be forgiven but her lover would be banished from the house as soon as this evening concluded. He would become a pariah while she would have to choose where her allegiances lay. Not that there was too much to think about. Her husband might be staid and boring, but at least he kept her in the manner she had become accustomed to. Sir Percival was an amusement, nothing more, someone whom she enjoyed but could easily forget. After all, he would be gone very shortly, on a morning tide, never to be seen again. Could she jeopardise everything, her comfort and security, to become nothing more than a camp follower in some fly ridden backwater abroad?

"I apologise profusely for my delay."

"So you should Madam. Is the, matter resolved?"

"It is dear husband. A malady, a lapse nothing more, it meant nothing and will ever be repeated."

"Then we shall speak of it no further." The Squire had his answer. Caroline remained his, and Fitzwilliam was to be considered a non-entity. His name would never again be mentioned once this night was over. "Colonel Maitland Good of you to attend." He offered his hand to the officer. "Please take your staff through to the salon. We have music, dancing, food and wine in abundance; enjoy."

"May I say, sir, it was a pleasure to receive your gracious invitation. Your home sir, does you proud, while you, Lady Caroline, if I may be so bold, appear radiant." Their hostess flushed as she realised her boudoir antics had been more vigorous than she had realised. Maitland kissed her gloved hand elegantly, and smiled as he wondered if the stories were true. "I see the town is suitably represented."

"Oh yes, invites went to anyone of any note," their host replied. "Everyone wishes to celebrate our Majesties birthday; should be jolly, what?"

"We are to be entertained royally, for there are to be fireworks later," Lady Caroline added helpfully.

"Fireworks. How jolly. Nothing better to excite the blood than a few good bangs, is there Wright?" Maitland said jokingly. The officers smiled, expressed their appreciation to their hosts, bowed once again, and made their way into the hall. Once out of earshot the colonel turned to Wright and whispered, "Our hosts seem excited…So pleased he enjoys a good bang, gets the blood flowing."

"Indeed, sir," Herbert Wright replied. "Exceedingly exciting, I must admit to being a little enthralled at the prospect, of witnessing them later." Two men, not friends, but both who shared a mutual liking for each other, took glasses of champagne from a silver salver proffered by a waiter. Wright sipped the chilled liquid and smiled. "Indeed yes, fireworks are such fun, sir."

* * *

"My Lords, Ladies, and Gentlemen, pray welcome for your delight and edification Sir Stanley's gift to you all. Be upstanding for The Twelve Bird Love Roast."

Stagg moved aside to allow the chef and under-chef to enter. Between them, they struggled to carry the monstrous dish. Twelve birds, one inside another, had taken almost eighteen hours to prepare and cook, but the result was magnificent.

"Delightful!"

"Oh my!"

"Excellent!" were but a few of the statements made as the dish was carried triumphantly to the table. The outer skin was that of a monstrous swan, complete with head and neck stuffed and arranged as if the bird slept upon the salver. Within its skin, were hidden the delights of turkey, goose, chicken, duck, pheasant, partridge, pigeon, guinea fowl, woodcock, quail and Poisson. All garnished and filled with such delights as walnut and hazelnut, ginger and juniper, stuffing. Sage and onion, parsley, thyme and lemon and orange relish. It was truly a feast designed for the delight of royalty.

In the few hours since the Duchess and her niece had arrived, the house had filled until the rooms were crowded to capacity. A ball had a strict etiquette. While the dancing was in progress, those watching admired and were, themselves, admired by eligible partners. Young men, in a pre-ordained ritual, preened before eligible young ladies, introduced or were introduced and dance cards filled. Some, older and bolder, women gathered in groups to flirtatiously discuss the merits of particular gentlemen, their suitability in the art of dance and marriage. As the last notes of the Sarabande drifted across the ballroom, dancers bowed and curtsied elegantly before applauding the quintet politely. Some awaited the next dance, others dispersed to the adjoining salon, where their partners graciously collected food or wine, spoke politely, or whispered discreet words of temptation to each other. Sir Stanley's bowers would be used extensively this night. There were other assignations to be observed; those of older and wiser gentlemen who gathered to discuss the price of corn with other like-minded souls. Senior officers watched their younger subalterns and worried about how many fathers would arrive the next day complaining of some indiscretion. All the while the musicians played, ladies, both wives and daughters, danced before their proud but cautious husbands and fathers. A ball, it was fair to say, was an eclectic mix of all that was good and bad of eighteenth century society.

"Whip that fool in, Herbert," Maitland demanded, indicating a very junior lieutenant. "My God, did he not understand? I'll have his commission if not more, sir."

"I will deal with him immediately," Wright answered, spying the errant youth. "A spell with the RSM will cool his ardour." Wright hurried away, aware that his colonel had been tetchy ever since they had met in the receiving line. Obviously whoever he had met, the meeting had not been as conducive as Maitland would have desired. Or it was simply, this young fool had decided to ignore the orders Wright had read out earlier in the day.

"He can serve a week as officer of the day, and indulge Patrickson." Maitland was indeed tetchy, more because his clear and concise orders were being flaunted. *Officers will behave with the utmost grace and reverence to our host and his guests. They are to enjoy the evening's festivities, but must remain vigilant. No one is to stray from the room, nor are they to fall under the influence of drink, or the guile of some pretty girl.* Satisfied that Wright would deal with the young fool, Maitland accepted a glass of champagne and moved through the throng towards the orangery. He was concerned, the next few hours were the most difficult period. Only he and Herbert knew what was planned, yet the element of surprise could be lost, simply by an officer stepping out of line. Maitland felt tense as he did before battle, this was no different their task was both odious and exciting yet had demanded as much planning as an assault on a determined stronghold. The errant young man was forgotten, Herbert would deal with him. His task, was to concentrate on the more serious matters, which was why he viewed the crowd as if searching for an enemy. He sipped his drink and waited.

"All done, sir," Wright declared, resuming his position beside his colonel. "Patrickson will keep him busy." Maitland nodded; the matter had been resolved quickly, efficiently.

"I assume we are prepared?" Maitland eyed the opened doors that lined one wall of the building.

"As ordered. Come midnight all will be revealed. We are as prepared as can be, all we await is…well you know sir."

"Yes, I do. I also know whose head will be on the block if we fail…mine!" Maitland rubbed his chin in careful deliberation. The next few hours were to be the longest of his life, not that the last few had been a joy. His visit to the Wood household had proved tiresome and depressing. The family were bereft, unable, it seemed, to comprehend half of what he told them. Could he blame them? Even he found it confounding, and he had had time to examine it for flaws. So many elements, so many issues, any one of which could see them exposed and incriminated. Fitzwilliam and his militia could act, they could see through the deception and bring them down. That was why he had ordered Wright to bring the 3rd to readiness early. The 'Buffs' officers knew their duties while Entwhistle, of the Militia, had been ordered to commence another, so he assumed, practice loading. With luck, Stilwell had kept them entertained, and would, by 10 this evening, have them safely aboard their transports. If not, their presence might ruin everything. "Check Herbert, send one of the ensigns to the beach and make sure. Captain Stilwell will be obliged to know we worry about him."

Sensing his concern, Wright departed, Stilwell knew what had to be done, and wouldn't take kindly to being harangued by anyone, let alone an ensign. But Maitland was fraught, perhaps, a little fearful as to what was planned which might explain why, when he glanced back, his colonel was in conversation with their host. In fact, Maitland and Sir Stanley discussed nothing more sinister than the dancing. Usually, Maitland, enjoyed such things, but this was work, and it had been planned with military precision.

"Not dancing, Colonel?" Sir Stanley asked.

"Not tonight, sir, too many conundrums to deal with before the fleet sails."

"Quiet understand, Tell me…if you may…when exactly is their departure?" Maitland paused, so many lies abounded, that, for a moment, he was unsure who knew what.

"No secret, sir. Captain Stilwell desires to depart afore the next full moon, less than a week away. That is, evidently, the most suitable time to avoid the storms that lash the eastern seaboard of the colonies." Maitland lied convincingly. The squire was known to have fallen out with Sir Percival that he desired the man gone as quickly as possible. It wasn't in Maitland's power to tell Sir Stanley the exact date or time, not yet, not until this sorry process had been completed. "Of course, as a mere soldier I do not understand such things. All I desire once we sail is to feel solid earth once again," he added politely.

"We will be sorry to see you leave."Sir Stanley appeared genuinely disappointed, but Maitland knew he would be glad to see the back of the militia. "Oh dear, some fool has requested a Galliard; how tiresome." They turned to observe the more athletic dancers indulge in the, now, old fashioned, but vigorous dance which involved leaps and spins. "Not something to be attempted by men of our illustrious ages, aye Maitland?"

"Indeed not, sir. Good soldiers like to take our time and view the battlefield, not rush in as if there was no tomorrow." Maitland smiled as the squire moved away, and thought the conversation had been a little strange. Was the squire attempting to glean information about the erstwhile Sir Percival? More than likely for according to Wright, he and Entwhistle, had been less than enthusiastic to learn of more practice, and a delayed departure date. Wright had had to be particularly ambiguous and subtle to convince them that their men would learn quicker under the guiding hand of Stilwell and his sailors.

"A new broom so to speak Sir Percival let's see if the navy can teach them how to perform." Wright had enthused, eventually Sir Percival had concurred and the plan was set. Maitland feared that Stilwell would do well to contain those officers already aboard, but if all went well, this sorry episode would be concluded before daybreak. Dismissing his concerns, he watched the dancers, until their gaiety lessened and their whirling bodies finally slowed to a halt. He would have liked to indulge in the Minuet, a dance of elegance and one that did not expect too much. Tonight, however, he was in no mood, so he stood aside as others rose and fell gracefully to a fairly simple, symmetrical like pattern. *Enjoy yourselves while you can, for tonight holds far more importance than you imagine.*

"Patrickson assures me all is in readiness, sir," Wright surreptitiously whispered, disturbing his colonel's trail of thought. "Tells me a sergeant was dispatched to see what the militia were up to. By all accounts they fare well, have loaded all their officers' dunnage, and begin loading food and ammunition."

"Blast their hides, now they act like soldiers when it is far too late. Intend to dance, Mister?" Maitland observed Wright clasping a champagne glass in one hand and a dance card in the other.

"One never knows, and it is ill mannered to refuse, isn't it, sir?"

"Be careful Herbert." They were alike in many ways, but in affairs of the heart they were at odds. While Herbert held women in awe, and observed them recovering from their exertions as chaste young things. Maitland saw predatory beasts, spying the assembled young men to opportunities to further their social standing. Wynford House was not so much a dancing emporium, more a cattle market where liaisons were made, marriages were arranged and dowries discussed. No doubt, there were many fathers among the portly gentlemen who watched from the sides. A good marriage could make a family, while a bad one could bring penury and ruination upon them. As the ballroom became the focus of adventure, the orangery and salon had fallen from favour and emptied considerably. To ease the crush, Sir Stanley ordered every door and window opened, allowing a cooling breeze to waft through. Archibald Maitland shivered, from nerves or breeze he was unsure, but certainly there were gentlemen present who commanded more respect than he did. Nervously he spied them as they stood in little groups. Gentlemen bedecked in awards and ribbons, swords and sashes, men of standing, experience and power. Any one of them could overturn his command if they so dared. "Not many fathers wish their daughters married to a soldier."

"I will sir, but one must study form before placing ones wager mustn't one?" There was no Mrs Maitland, no family and Herbert had never asked why, he suspected some inner pain but good grace demanded the subject was never raised. For all the colonels' stiff backed obedience to orders, Maitland was a fair, compassionate officer. He demanded much, but punished only when the necessity demanded it and his men trusted him for that reason. That trust counted for much, especially tonight when his officers conduct was paramount. One hint of impropriety and these noble gentlemen would pounce upon him.

"I wonder if Captain Stilwell is enjoying his night's work?" the question wasn't something Wright had considered

"Captain Stilwell is, I believe, a man who knows his definition of duty, and will not allow anyone, especially militiamen, to ruin his carefully laid plans," Wright added helpfully

"I agree. He is more than capable, but Fitzwilliam could ruin it all if he decides to interfere. Perchance, have you seen our gallant colonel?"

"Not a sign, sir, not a sign. Holed up somewhere, no doubt."

"No doubt. Still, we will have to persevere and await his pleasure…By the by, any further information on that flare reported in the harbour?"Stormouth held many secrets, none stranger than the report, received earlier, of a flame being seen in the pre-dawn. None of the moored ships had been caused problems but Stilwell had asked him to enquire as to what it was. Come daylight, nothing had been found. Whatever it was, had gone, swallowed by the vast expanse of the ocean, and that was the end of the matter.

"None whatsoever. Strange that Captain Stilwell saw fit to tell us about it, don't you think, sir?"

"Not at all. We agreed to inform each other about anything that happened within the confines of the harbour. He was simply complying with that agreement," Maitland replied absently, his eyes drawn to the doorway where an excited crowd was gathering.

"I realise that, but a flare at sea is his responsibility, surely." Wright sipped his champagne and smirked. "It would seem this town has many events which can be construed as implausible. Speaking of which, I do believe our main event is about to begin."

"I see…My God, look at him! The rebels will find him a most tempting target if he ever sees battle."

Sir Percival had timed his entrance to perfection, entering like an actor onto a stage, just as a clock chimed the hour. Dressed in his finery, he glistened in gold braid, he was a veritable jewel among lesser men. He demanded attention, he preened; he swaggered, ensuring everyone knew he was in attendance. Accepting their applause he smiled at the shouted 'Hussars' from those that knew him.

"A fop, Herbert, a dandy, a fool. He is the sort of officer who unfortunately infects the entire army. Such attitudes endanger all those that become associated with them. Their stupidity usually results in their downfall, but they cause harm, sir, harm to all who stand alongside them. We would do well to remember that in the coming days."

Few noticed the delicate exchange that occurred between Fitzwilliam and Lady Caroline, the merest of smiles but it was enough for them both to know their liaison had ended. Lady Caroline had shared his bed had proven to be as tempestuous and exciting as Mrs Wood. Breeding though determined how she behaved in and out of the bedchamber which was why she returned to her husband and why he arrived long after her; decorum was, after all important. Shaking his head in disgust, Maitland knew nothing of what existed between these gentlemen of status what concerned him was Fitzwilliam's abilities as a soldier and they were lacking in abundance.

"He exerts his authority by flogging, but too much breeds contempt, not loyalty yet he fails to understand the difference. He thinks he can thrash discipline into his men when in fact the opposite is the case. His regiment will either run, or be decimated during their first encounter. Either way, he will show not an iota of regret. Too many die because of fools such as him. My God, we must not be found wanting this evening. We must do all we can to end his sorry enterprise, and save English blood from being spilled needlessly. Fail, Herbert, and we are no better than he."

Maitland prayed their task would succeed. Champagne flute in hand, he looked around the room and saw Ensign Mathews standing at a pair of open doors. "Good," he whispered, one further element was in place. The man he had dismissed as useless not that long ago, had returned to stand beside a sergeant. His appearance meant that, barring an act of God, nothing could halt his scheme. Maitland was ready, all he required was a few minor players to appear, and he could end this charade. Looking around the gathered mass of humanity, he saw the cast of his play taking their positions. Johnson the Mayor, along with Porter his Clerk, Pawell the solicitor and a strong contingent of town businessmen applauded the popinjay, who accepted their adulation until, like a withering fire that applause died slowly.

Rarely did Maitland show emotion, but what occurred in that room almost made, a 'hussar' escaped his lips. A miracle occurred as a small group, momentarily hidden behind Fitzwilliam, appeared. A stunned silence descended, broken by a murmour of recognition, as one by one the identity of the group was realised. Fitzwilliam finally acknowledged their presence, made to speak, thought better of it, and stepped aside. Very nervously, Josiah Wood and his family stepped into full view.

Chapter Fifty Nine

"They are the last people I expected to see."

"Did you hear? The sister-in-law is said to be sharing her affections with someone influential."

"Is that why her husband was murdered?"

"Possibly,"

"Shame," After such a stunned silence, the comments sounded extra loud. While for those who had drawn such attention, time seemed to stand still as they waited, self-consciously, before those they had thought of as friends, neighbours, fellow businessmen. Unsure as to how to proceed, they began to Wilt, beneath the interminable attention.

"Appears you are today's sacrifice," Sir Percival stated calmly. "I would suggest you show them you are beyond reproach. Not to will have them pounce upon you like wolves, and I do so hate the sight of blood before the syllabub…Ladies…Mrs Wood, my condolences, but a pleasure at seeing you so revived."

Josiah saw the way Fitzwilliam bowed to Sarah and lick his lips. To say nothing was to court further ridicule. Already, it seemed, many within this room had decided they were soiled would be pleased to see them falter and ceased trading. While he might have accepted their mistrust, he could, nor would, accept his own guilt and cowardice. Fitzwilliam was chiding and belittling him, he had neither remorse nor shame. He wanted the world to know that if he so desired he could have any woman he desired when and where he chose. Even now he smiling lecherously awaiting the crowd's adulation to begin again. Nor it seemed was he overly concerned to be confronted by Josiah and his family. Ridiculed, betrayed and damaged, Josiah was in all but name a beaten man but for one splendid moment in time he felt empowered. Stepped forward, so only Sir Percival heard, he whispered,

"You are a gutter snipe, sir, and I will see you in hell before you touch a member of my family again…do not speak, sir, because I am in no mood to deal with you at the moment. But be aware, your days are numbered, you have done your worst, but we survive, we will not regret your passing."

He looked into Sir Percival's eyes and saw nothing except sullen acceptance. Fitzwilliam was truly an obnoxious prig, not worthy of further attention, defiantly Josiah led his family away, leaving Fitzwilliam to stand alone, unable to reply in fear of recriminations. For the first time in many a long month, Josiah felt like a man again but he was not finished, he had further arduous duties to perform.

From his position, Maitland watched and smiled. Yet another small piece of the puzzle had been put in place. He had been concerned about that one moment more than any other part, Josiah was the unknown, he might have allowed his emotions to get the better of him and expose far more than he should, but he had performed admirably. It was no small feat to control ones emotions, especially when you faced the man who had seduced your sister-in-law while your brother was murdered. Maitland had had to warn Josiah from calling the colonel out by explaining,

"If another can live with being cuckolded, then what right have you to bemoan what your dead brother's wife does? Fitzwilliam will be gone shortly and you will never see him again, so best to remain mute."

Perhaps he might have succeeded if one other had not stepped forward. He too appeared unconcerned with what he had done, he smiled, spoke in a tone that disguised his crimes and offered his hand friendship.

"Josiah, ladies, a pleasure," Josiah grimaced, for in his mind's eye he saw a blood smeared hand. To know what this man had done, made his flesh creep. It was because of him, that soldier had stayed so long, it was the reason he was here, the reason he had to do what he must do, and for those reasons Josiah would never forgive the man.

"Sir you must excuse us, we have need to speak with Sir Stanley." Was it rude? Of course it was, but the truth was, he had no desire to be in the same county as his nemesis. He felt faint, the ballroom appeared to drift out of focus. He heard everything, saw everyone but his mind registered nothing.

What he had been told, how the indiscretions had been presented in such stark clarity, haunt him, and he hated, not only this man, but the soldier as well. The memory of that meeting would never leave him, he would never be free, and this was to be his punishment

* * *

Maitland had forced them to listen to matters which, at first he had been reticent to hear. Each revelation had left him a little more distraught, he heard things which concerned this very night, matters which his father had been associated with. Already battered by life, the soldier had torn Josiah's world apart with his revelations.

He remembered with a sense of horror the manner in which he had blustered in indignation, how he had dismissed the soldier's statements, unwilling to hear any more lies about the family. But, Josiah had fallen silent as each significant detail had been revealed. The soldier had humiliated him in front of his wife, within his own home. In a slow measured tone he had revealed what those he thought of as, not friends, but associates had done in his name. That betrayal hurt, so much so, he had slumped into a chair where, forced to hear such calculated deception, he had wondered why he had been so blind. Eventually Maitland had broached the subject of this ball, and Josiah had said,

"We shall not attend, we shall all remain ensconced within this house until my brother is buried and until his murderer is discovered."

"No sir you will not."

"Why sir would you imagine we would desire to attend that tomfoolery? I have a business to save, which cannot be achieved by attending the Birthday celebrations for some Hanoverian King. Good God sir, he will never know that such an occurrence took place, nor indeed who attended. No sir, we shall not go, I forbid it."

If Maitland had understood, he appeared not to care. He had listened then state,

"You sir, would be advised to attend. For you will discover the event most enlightening and …entertaining. In fact sir, I insist you attend as your options are limited."

"You insist, by God sir, by what right do you insist?" Josiah tired of being told what to do by all and sundry, but he sensed this soldier held a better hand of cards than he did, so it was proved.

"I stated your options were limited, and so they are sir. You can choose to decline, which is your God given right, but should you do so I would then need to inform you of the other recourses I can employ. I can summon the means by which you would attend, the manner though would not be conducive to your honour sir. In fact, if I were in your position, it might make matters worse, and bring about a situation from which, even I, could not aid you, once such methods had been deployed. Should you chose that option, the consequences will be your's and your's alone."

"Do you threaten me sir?" Josiah demanded, the soldier had paused, before stating solemnly,

"I do sir…I threaten you as you're family has threatened many in this town. You see sir, I can have you imprisoned this very night, have you taken away and incarcerated until you are dragged before a court at some future date. I can send your family abroad, I have the ships in harbour, they can be sent to one of our penal colonies where they will die, unloved and forgotten. Or you can listen and do exactly as I demand. Only with your full compliance can you avoid the punishment you so richly deserve."

He had expected much but not this, the reality of his situation shocked Josiah to the bone. A father dead, a brother lost, another murdered and now the threat of a trial, prison and transportation, was too much to bear.

"If I agree what guarantees can I expect?"

"None...I offer you nothing, except the chance to rid yourself of your guilt"

"What of my family, will they be spared if I do as you demand?"

"They will be spared prosecution, but they will attend. Mrs Sarah Wood in particular is expected. Her presence will be entertaining for all concerned."

Josiah doubted he was the culprit the soldier sought, but he would be used, to lure some bigger fish into his net. Despite that thought, Josiah still felt ill at ease as they had discussed what he was expected to do. Nor was his good temper revived as each devious accusation was revealed. He had been made a fool, treated like the imbecile he thought himself to be, his trust had been betrayed and that more than anything else hurt most, but aided his decision.

Dinner that night had been a fraught affair. He had to convince Sarah, as to why he had changed his mind, without disclosing the entire truth.

"I am at a loss brother. Only yesterday you spoke of it as a travesty, not worthy of our presence."

"I was wrong. We must show those who think us finished that we are, in fact, united. Only then will we defeat those who wish to see us ruined." The reply had been trite, but he had hoped it had been sufficiently plausible for Sarah to believe him. She was the fly by which they might be discovered, for this to succeed she must remain ignorant of the truth a little longer. He need not have worried, for unbeknown to anyone, and despite the loss of her husband, she was actually excited that Josiah had finally relented.

"I bless you and your foresight brother. Our attendance will indeed lay to rest the rumours which abound around town."

It was then Sarah retrieved the paste card from the mantle, and held it in excited hands. Such a small inconsequential thing had become the harbinger of such grief. It had mocked him every day since it had arrived causing consternation and argument and for what? The chance to be seen at the squires home nothing more.

"I shall dress in pink." She exclaimed.

"You will dress in black madam, for your husband is not yet in his grave. You will also remain by our side and not dance, nor engage in any conversation without my express permission. I will not condone any nonsense for our attendance mocks our grief but I am commanded to attend."

"Who by...The King?" Sarah had exclaimed.

"Your stupidity astounds me at time. The King has no interest in our town nor indeed would he have the inclination to grace Stormouth with his presence. Affairs of state concern him more than what we do in this forgotten backwater of his Kingdom. No madam he relies upon men like Sir Stanley to keep him informed which is why I am not a little surprised that he has time to waste on such nonsensical, and idiotic displays of outrageousness. Though how he wastes his money is of little concern to me. My one concern is this family and how we are perceived. That was why I was so reticent to attend, with all that has occurred at the warehouses with our clients and the tragic demise of my family. I feared madam that our creditors would perhaps set upon us take their chance to entrap us when we had no escape to press their claims. Ever since that damned invitation arrived I have dreamt of them confronting me with their demands. A veritable flood gate would have been opened, I would have been forced to explain myself. That madam is why I had no desire to attend, now however, circumstances force me to do what I have no desire to do."

Josiah's reasons were valid, in fact until a few hours ago, he had convinced himself of the validity of his arguments. Even his wife had citing rumours she had heard while taking tea with her meddling women friends,

"Every house of quality in both town and district has received such an invitation,"

"You take heed of those tea sipping; witches? Madam such groups are good for nothing else save spreading rumour and innuendos. No good has ever come from such a gathering and I shall not be direct by women's gossip." How he wished he had not been so harsh. For now he was having to make amends, he suspected Sarah, wondered why he had changed his mind but he could not tell her for that was part of his parole.

"Women speak of many things Brother, we may not have the diligence for business but we see how one effects the other. Within the home we see the passion the conviction which our husbands possess. It is also where we see the excess troubles you have to bear. That is why I believe we should attend this nonsense. To be absent, I think, would confirm the insinuation of our complicity in supposed malpractice. While to attend, would show those with too much to say and too few brains to think, our innocence. Guilt drives the shamed into hiding, while innocence should be displayed. Our presence will prove we have nothing to hide or fear, and that we are doing all we can to remedy the situation."

Sarah had then spoken eloquently, too eloquently for Martha. Never before had she shown such interest. It was as if Adams demise, had released some hidden sense of decorum. Her voice was calm, proficient, the one Martha had witnessed when Sarah had wanted to manipulate Adam, to achieve what she desired.

"My thanks, sister; I am pleased that you feel so inclined. We must shoulder our burden, present a unified presence. We shall attend, we shall be forthright and proud of our station, and no man shall speak ill of our losses or of what we have endured .Make your arrangements, we have forsaken too much, allowed others to control us, but no longer. My God, even I have bowed before them in appeasement. In my quest to appear innocent, I have almost destroyed what my father built.I have been remiss, have allowed myself to be manipulated, control. But no longer, I must correct my failings and face my accusers, or no doubt he that has brought us to this sorry state will further incriminate us. By God, he might, even as we speak, be regaling the merchants, with a story of financial ruination. If I do nothing, he will succeed, I will not see him win, nor suffer the injustice and indignity of eviction."

Martha knew of whom he spoke but Sarah looked at him in stunned silence. For any man to admit he was no longer the master of his own destiny took courage. But he had no alternative, if he were to save anything; he had to do as the soldier demanded. They would attend, more importantly; they would appear with heads held high and damn them all.

"You are not at fault, husband. Desperate times call for unusual demands." Martha knew how Josiah had been humbled. The soldier had explained in great detail how he had been duped. The name had left them stunned, now it was time the town knew the truth

"Who do you speak of…tell me?" Sarah demanded.

"His name is unimportant. Suffice to say he is known to those that count, and will be dealt with. I fear, dear wife, I have been neglectful in my dealings. I should have trusted you, told you what was occurring. Instead, I tried to maintain a façade of respectability. Maybe I was at fault, maybe, I should have told you and Adam long ago what was happening, but, I did not and that predicament is what irks me."

Finally Josiah was ready to reveal this last piece of information, though the doubts still existed. He had accepted the hand of friendship before and been duped, could he trust what the soldier had stated? Was the man, the villain, or were lies still manipulating those involved? Indecision whirled within him, duplicity could still be at work, maybe the soldier had a plan of his own and Josiah was yet again a mere pawn in that plan? But the soldier's threats echoed within him, and his indecisiveness faded away. He now understood what the priest wanted, why he was so insistent that he was unable to run the business. Why else had he offered him assistance from a man whom his father thought a charlatan? Nothing his so called benefactor offered was for the family's benefit, he wanted control. Had it not been for a stranger pointing out his untrustworthiness, his plan might have succeeded. Now Josiah was on the offensive, and his adversaries had better watch out.

* * *

"Pray sir, accept my hand in friendship and hospitality. Sir Stanley can wait a moment longer."

"Sorry?" Josiah's voice stumbled, he was back in the present, his thoughts fading like an autumn flower. While so called friends stood open mouthed, only he, the very essence of their problems had dared approach them.

"Forgive me, my moment of apprehension. Yes I agree Sir Stanley can wait awhile." Josiah stated solemnly.

"Give it no thought. Ignore these fools and allow me to show you some much needed hospitality." Led through the throng by their nemesis, Josiah and his family walked across the ballroom floor. Like Moses parting the oceans, the crowd allowed them through. Their journey began in terrible silence, both deafening and loathsome, until Columbine and Richardson began clapping, slowly followed by others until the entire room rang out with wild shouts of 'Hussar' and 'Hullo'. A crushed and defeated man suddenly realised he had little to fear, much to the annoyance of one Sir Percival Fitzwilliam. Josiah smiled uneasily, remaining steadfast for the sake of the family's name.

"Tell me, sir, did you have chance to peruse those dratted books? I fear I was remiss in not being there to greet you. I trust Mickelwhite did all that was required of him?"

"There were no problems at all. Your clerk did all I could wish for. As for your ledgers, they are dammed difficult to comprehend. I fear it will take longer than anticipated to unravel their secrets, but never fear, I will persevere. Enough of such talk tonight is for celebrating. Come; enjoy some of Sir Stanley's fine Champagne."

Josiah smiled politely and knew in that instance that the soldier had told the truth.

"Is the Reverend present?" Josiah asked, looking around the room. "I would like to extend my thanks to him." Turnbottle baulked, but chose to ignore the question. This wasn't the time to worry about scum like Bayles. But he did, just for a moment, think wistfully of a girl, a bright, delightful girl, who had died for no reason.

"I fear not. Ladies, might I tempt you to join me in a libation?" he asked politely, only to be denied an answer as a whirlwind tore the night asunder. Stormouth's isolation came to an end with a cry that echoed around the room......

"The King...The King is without!"

Chapter Sixty

Illuminated by the flickering torches, a line of exquisitely painted carriages waited outside Wynford House. Stagg and his footmen struggled to make sense of it for the King never travelled without an entourage of flunkeys, courtiers, hangers-on, wives and lovers.

"Is it Stagg?" Lady Caroline asked appearing upon the front steps.

"It is My Lady, it's him," Stagg stated as a receiving line of perplexed guests hastily formed behind them. Stagg's confirmation was unnecessary, despite the courtiers, bedecked in their finest jewellery, dresses and uniforms not many could confuse this carriage for anyone else's. It was magnificently presented, the paintwork gleamed, the gilding glistened, the postilion's and driver were all dressed in scarlet and braided livery and sat perfectly still despite a profusion of sweat which soaked their faces. Men who knew of such matters whispered to each other that the horses had been driven hard. Evident, to all but a fool, by the four, sweat streaked horses which stood before them, blowing hard, and pawing at the ground. If further evidence was required as to who sat within, all one need do was examine the Royal cypher upon the carriage doors. But the crowning glory was the mounted soldiers that stood guard front and rear, on pure black horses.

"Oh my," Johnson the Mayor said, brushing at an imaginary speck of dust while a throng of courtiers sprang from their own coaches to gather beside the black painted Barouche and the man inside

"Decorum Mister Mayor, you are to be presented." Fate had brought him alongside Lady Caroline, while other, more prominent but less fortunate guests were forced to wait, trapped inside. Sir Stanley and Sir Percival vied for position within the hallway, while others were forced into the orangery. Among those, was a man whose future hung by a thread and a soldier whose future rested upon his shoulders? Maitland chose the confusion to sidle alongside and whisper.....

"Ready?"

"As I will ever be." Beads of perspiration formed on Josiah's top lip. He had been forced into this position, and liked it, not one iota

"Make sure you do what is required...otherwise." Maitland held his arm and squeezed menacingly. "Only you can end this...remember what is at stake."

"I know...I am prepared." While conspirators spoke guardedly, the King remained in his carriage nodding seriously to what two men told him. One was an exquisitely dressed general, the other, an elegant but elderly gentleman, both had the Kings ear, sharing something important.

While they spoke, the excited crowd waited, wondered and whispered as to why King George III delayed. The reason would never be explained, but delay he did. Finally the King stood and accepted the adulation of his subjects.

"It appears he is ready...act wisely." Maitland breathed heavily before slipping away into the crowd. The scene was set; the final player was in position and the final act about to begin. Their futures rested upon the courage of a man who was scared witless. A surge of enthusiastic cheering erupted, the crowd parted allowing the King to walk unhindered towards Lady Caroline and her guests.

"A most edifying welcome thank you me dear." Lady Caroline curtsied, rose, and presented the mayor. All was going splendidly yet Maitland had cause for concern, glancing at the windows, he wondered if, come the morn, any of them would be the same, or would they be dancing to a very different tune? "Where is that rogue of a husband of yours?"

"He awaits you inside Sire, if you would allow me to welcome you to our humble abode."

"Humble she says, humble indeed madam most splendid in fact most splendid indeed." The king laughed, Maitland waited to be introduced while Lady Caroline led the King through the guests and into the house. Women curtsied and men bowed in silent acknowledgement, until finally, Sir Stanley, stepped forward, bowed graciously, and listened as his King spoke.

"We are pleased to be among friends, here in my favourite town of Stormouth." King George stopped mid-room and smiled as he accepted the gracious applause, while Sir Stanley accepted his Monarch's praise graciously "When we were informed that the good people of this most pleasant town had arranged a celebration for one's birthday, we decided to attend immediately. Such loyalty, we believe, is to be rewarded, and we decided to express our thanks personally. Lady Caroline tells me that fireworks are prepared....We do so love fireworks...when, perchance, may we expect them?"

"I fear, Your Majesty catches us unprepared, therefore there will be a slight delay while the preparations are completed, but soon Your Majesty, very soon."

"No matter, we are more than willing to be gracious...for the moment." The King smiled benevolently and waited.

"My thanks, Sire...I will send word for them to begin at once." Hastily, Sir Stanley turned and issued instructions to Stagg. "While we await their commencement, may I take the opportunity to say your presence turns our little gathering into a most auspicious occasion?"

"Damn your thanks, sir, where is your wine?" King George smiled, defusing what might have been construed as a rebuke. "Come, Sir Stanley, champagne for your Monarch, or am I to die of thirst?"

Those, nearest laughed nervously; that was conveyed to those in the other rooms, so that moments later, an echo was heard, causing the King to look around as if expecting some jolly jape to be occurring. His bewilderment ended with the arrival of a footman who presented him with a charged glass of chilled champagne.

"Our own ice Your Majesty," Lady Caroline added.

"From our new ice house, dashed expensive, but worth every penny." Sir Stanley added. Monarchs were a devilishly strange breed. King George was often referred to as 'Farmer George' but those close to him, knew he was passionate about many things, none more so than science and the arts. Unlike his grandfather who had alienated himself from his people by speaking only German and spending more time in Hanover than England. This King George understood his subjects, and they in turn liked him. To prove that point he had arrived dressed to impress, his uniform was of the highest, brightest quality, tight woven and cut impeccably. His awards and medals sparkled and shimmered in the flickering candle light. He was a man who adored admiration, and why not? He was a man who exuded wealth and statue, from the neat white powdered wig to his leather shoes.

"Fine champagne Cobb, is like a fine woman; a pleasure to hold…and consume.

"Indeed Sire." Cobb stated summoning more wine.

"But I was promised fireworks and I fail to see any! Surely you are not going to be precocious, and deny me an evening to remember? I say, is that Fitzwilliam I spy? Well, indeed it is. Bring him close." The King beckoned Sir Percival forward. Those closest heard the next remark waited nervously. "You sir are a rogue… He will Rodger anyone's wife, given half the chance, but a charming man for all of that." Sir Percival smiled at the Kings jest, his conceit and haughtiness evident as he was recognised and singled out. "You are well I trust Sir Percival?"

"Very well, Sire."

"Good, good. Stay close, sir, we are about to enjoy some fireworks. Or, I trust we are. Cobb appears to be having trouble getting his fuses lit. Powder a tad damp, Sir Stanley, perchance? " The King chuckled at his provocative insinuation. "Never had any trouble there have we Sir Percival? For sure I suspect you already have a conquest or two added to your growing list, or have you refrained? Doubt it, what! Madam, has he propositioned you as yet?" King George asked a particularly attractive courtier. "No? Well, give the rogue a chance, he will. Sir Percival, you displease me greatly."

"I, your Majesty? How?"

"I fear for your sanity. In your position, it must have been difficult to refrain with so many attractive ladies present...I say, is that Maitland I spy? I do believe it is." The King forgot Sir Percival, ignored those near him and beckoned the colonel to approach him. "Maitland, is that you? So many good fellows in one place, I am spoilt for friendship. What pray, are you doing in this backwater?"

Maitland stepped forward, bowed to his King and commander and felt nervous as the moment fast approached. Two men separated by so much greeted each other as old friends, none not even Sir Percival noticed the merest flicker of conspiratorial recognition.

"Your Majesty is too kind. It has indeed been some time since we last met."

"Windsor, I believe, the Queen's birthday last year, if we remember correctly."

"Which you do, Sire, a most pleasant day, if I may be so bold."

"Oh you may, Maitland, you may. We are proud to have an officer of such boldness as a friend," the King stated loudly, so that those nearest heard him. "Come, Sir Stanley, where are my fireworks? I tire of this flummery."

"I fear, Sire, our host has experienced some difficulty," Maitland offered. He sounded calm, but his heart was banging like a drum. He was about to do something which, would see him imprisoned for conspiracy if it failed. "With your permission, I will attempt to resolve the situation."

"Please do, Maitland, resolve away." Perspiring and quivering ever so slightly in fear, Maitland once again bowed, turned and walked between white powdered and rouged faces, towards the center of the room. The guests watched in amusement, grinning demonically as a soldier marched into battle. Pausing briefly, Maitland glanced around the room, checking that those who needed to be present were in place. They were, Sir Percival stood, before his King, preening like the peacock he was. Beside Lady Fitzgibbons, stood Lady Caroline, a woman who carried herself with such grace, he found it difficult to imagine her beneath that fop. The King had already stated that Sir Percival had a reputation, the room had heard it and Maitland hoped it was enough to end the man forever. He knew the ways of the world, was accustomed to being in a Royal presence. He had witnessed almost every wickedness man could inflict upon another, but this evening he felt truly sorry for Sir Stanley. *I hope they can absolve each other in the morning,* he thought. Then with a salacious smile he calmly pulled a silver whistle from his uniform, placed it to his lips and blew heartily.

The sound startled the guests, causing some to cover their ears, others to squeal in excitement and look on nervously. One man uttered a blasphemy usually unheard in Royal presence.

"At last the fireworks begin. Splendid!" King George shouted in jubilation. While those of senior rank froze in terror and turned towards the sound. Most had heard it before but never in such exulted surroundings. It was the call to advance, but who and why none knew, only Maitland and his officers were aware of what would happen next.

Outside, in the darkness Sergeant Major Patrickson shivered in apprehension. The sound of Maitland's whistle came as a blessed relief, the men of the 3rd had heard it many times before but tonight they were to commit treason. Seconds after hearing the sound, soldiers, armed with bayonet tipped muskets, stood at every window and doorway. Maitland's 3rd Regiment had surrounded, and imprisoned the King by force of arms. Confusion reigned as those guests nearest the doors pushed, shoved and screamed, until finally most realised no one was leaving the room, not until Maitland so ordered.

"Maitland what is the meaning of this?" The King bellowed, while Josiah and his family clasped hands one last time. His destiny awaited him and he was powerless to resist. Sweating profusely, he began to walk purposely through the crowd. Sensing something special was about to happen, the crowd once again parted. Staring in awe they did nothing as Josiah walked towards his King, in a daze. Forced to comply with Maitland's orders he eventually halted directly before the King, reaching into his coat he fumbled to find his weapon. An officer finally moved, to be halted by Wright, who drew his sword and held it against flabby flesh.

"Pray do not move sir, blood is a devil to remove from a wooden floor. Though it would give Sir Stanley a tale to tell his grandchildren."

Monarchy knew not to show fear, King George, stood motionless and dispassionate as Josiah, found what he wanted and withdrew his weapon of destruction. No one breathed, nor attempted to interfere instead, they watched and waited his next move.

"I assume sir, you must be Mister Wood? I have been told about you," King George stated, as Josiah stopped and bowed. "Come, stand beside me and enjoy the next few moments. Maitland…damn you, Maitland! Bring an end to this tomfoolery, I tire of it."

While, most had remained stupidly still, fearing for the King's life, Maitland appeared to be the calmest in the room, quite unconcerned. Soldiers had risen against their monarch, a potential assassin had strode forward to within arm's reach, yet no one had done anything to stop him. Why, was the question the more intelligent in the room began to wonder.

"QUIET!" In the confines of the room, Maitland's voice, more used to being heard amidst the sound of musketry, sounded deafening. Instantly conversations ceased, faces turned towards him and he had their attention. No one understood what was happening. It might have been troubling had it not been for the strangest of sights. King George stood, glass of champagne in hand, laughing so much tears rolled down his powdered face. He laughed not in fear, but in enjoyment. While outside, separated from the mischief inside the building, Sir Stanley's men heard the whistle and took it to be the signal to begin and finally set off the first firework.

"Oh my," the King declared. "Fireworks, I do so enjoy fireworks…" Josiah jumped in shock, as his King rested a hand upon his shoulder in friendly greeting and stated amiably, "My grandfather once had a man attend upon us who composed music. A tiresome man, but his 'Music for Fireworks' was enjoyable…Such a pity we do not have it played now. No matter, I am enjoying this immensely….Maitland, the floor is yours for the moment…carry on, but make haste my boy, make haste…Sir Stanley, do please join my good friend Mister Wood. You should find what is about to occur edifying….very edifying."

Confused and confounded Sir Stanley was stunned into action, the squire, joined Josiah, while the King, beckoned for chairs to be brought. Four servants rushed forward and placed chairs in a line across the ballroom floor.

"Remove one; three will be more than sufficient," King George ordered. "Do please sit Sir Stanley, Mister Wood, any one whom Maitland summons can stand, for I fear they may be…how shall we put it? Otherwise engaged…Gentlemen, I trust you will enjoy our production." The King sat and awaited the evening's main event. "A stool, if you please… gout, Sir Stanley, a martyr to it, I fear," the King explained, then chuckled as a stool was fetched. "Carry on, Maitland. Carry on."

"My thanks, Sire." Maitland paused as the audience stared at him; none knew what was to happen next. Every eye watched him, every ear strained to hear what would be said. This was his moment, when he would bring to an end Stormouth's torment. "If I may, could I ask Sir Percival Fitzwilliam and a Mister Truman join me."

The King nodded his approval and the room waited…waited, but neither man appeared.

"Gentleman please, your presence has been noted, do not force me to find you." Maitland asked politely. "Mister Truman, you are present for I have seen you, do not make this any more difficult that it need be. Your refusal will necessitate me ordering your immediate arrest and have soldiers drag you out. Surely you do not wish to be embarrassed, not in front of ladies."

Maitland, remained tense, but with each passing moment, began to relax a little. Their plans, devised aboard the 'Kentsman', and approved in London, were progressing better than he had dared hope. Sir Percival had been beckoned forward by the King, while Truman hid, but could not remain so indefinitely.

"No need, Maitland, he is here." Sir Percival indicated a man approaching from the direction of the salon, where he had stood beside one of Fitzwilliam's captains. "Your Majesty, I apologise for Colonel Maitland's absurdity. I can only ask you to forgive his discourteous behaviour. If you desire I shall have him removed immieditatly. My God sir what are you doing, The King must wonder what insanity runs through his realm." Fitzwilliam's bluster was his attempt, to disrupt whatever Maitland had instigated. He was to be made to regret his words.

"Have no fear Sir Percival. You would be surprised as to what we know, and how we keep track of what occurs. However, for the moment, I am but a mere spectator. Colonel Maitland is the master, so perhaps we should allow him to continue, there's a good chap."

"Your wish of course, is to be obeyed. Though, I fail to see what stupidity he is performing. I truly fail to comprehend what he hopes to achieve. As your Majesty knows, we are due to sail shortly. As comrades in arms, we are to sally forth to defeat your enemies. Perhaps we should suggest he puts an end to whatever is on his mind. Speak, Maitland, then we can regain our composure and our King may enjoy his birthday."

"Have no fear, Fitzwilliam…We have never enjoyed ourselves more…Haven't had so much fun since…well, enough said…Pray, continue Maitland."

"My thanks Sire." Maitland had feared this moment more than any enemy he had ever faced. Despite rehearsing this many times, he wanted to be sure before he spoke. "Sir Percival, you expressed a moment ago a desire to sail with your regiment."

"I did. As well you know." To emphasise his point, he turned and said proudly, "We have practiced nothing else these past weeks. My men, Sire, are ready to face those rebellious souls who dare to take up arms against your legal title. We shall do all we can in quelling their ardour and bringing them back into his Majesties fold. That is my task in life, to serve you to the best of my abilities, no more no less." Percival bowed to the King and received a polite nod in return.

"I am sure His Majesty is pleased to hear of your loyalty…of which we will return shortly," Maitland replied, unimpressed. "For now, there are matters of propriety to answer." Maitland had not desired to go down this route, but Wood had insisted. It had been a condition of his agreement, forged in his home. As such, he had to deal with this before going any further.

"Propriety? What foolishness do you speak of, man?" Sir Percival looked at the colonel and smiled. If he understood correctly, he desired confirmation of matters which were not suitable for such an audience. He suspected Maitland would not desire to reveal them. To do so would inconvenience more than just two officers. *Proceed; make a fool of yourself,* he thought.

"I trust you will agree, that gentlemen, sir, are charged by rank and honour to uphold their office with decorum and dignity."

"I do," Sir Percival agreed, nodding happily.

"Then I must ask sir, why is the town live with rumours of your myriad illicit affairs with married women of the town?"

"What a Gentleman does is none of your damned business Maitland. Sire, are we to subjected to such scurrilous remarks as this?"

"Well you do have reputation Sir Percival. I for one would like to know if the reputation is justified. Continue Maitland."

"Sir I ask again, either refute such accusations, or we will accept your silence as an implication of guilt?"

"Do as you please, sir," Fitzwilliam sneered. "I have no desire to explain myself to you." Fitzwilliam guessed Maitland had no desire to provoke him. To do so would expose the deception and lies, certain noble women had been hiding behind. Fitzwilliam, though, had misread the insinuation. Maitland had powerful allies who could, and would conceal much if the need arose. Fitzwilliam's credibility was about to be destroyed. The King waved a hand for silence, before asking him directly,

"Sir Percival, we are known to each other, is that not the case?" Fitzwilliam nodded uncertainly, as the King continued. "Of course we are. You attended us at Court for many years before your services were dispensed with. Remind me, why was that, Sir Percival?"

"I…I cannot remember, Sire."

"No, I suppose you cannot…perhaps, sir, I can aid your memory. The reason, I fear, was impropriety; the same accusation you now face. Tell me, have you seen the Lady in question since? No? Pity. She and her daughter are looked after by her husband very well indeed. It appears you are beset by the same problems yet again. Some would say your tailor should sew in stronger buttons, ones that remain fastened." The King smiled as a discrete ripple of amusement came from the enthralled audience. "We seem, yet again, to have the same questions being asked, and I, as your Liege Lord, demand an honest answer. Have you offended anyone in this town? Have you indulged in nocturnal exercises with other men's wives, sir?"

"I have not, Sire. I have not lain with any married women since our arrival."

"There," the King shouted in pleasure. "I told you as much Maitland. Told you no Knight of the Realm would do such a thing; utter nonsense! I have to believe the word of a man who carries the honour of such a position. Therefore, let it be known, there has been no impropriety carried out here. That there is no stain upon any person's honour. Let it be known that I have decreed this, and will be much annoyed if such rumours persist."

Maitland smiled. The King had circumvented a problem, had made a public proclamation that nothing untoward had occurred. No man could question such a statement without offending a King. Sir Stanley and Lady Caroline would be able to put her indiscretion behind them, be able to rebuild their lives without innuendo ruining their positions. It also meant that Adam Wood's memory would not be ruined by rumours of his wife sleeping with Sir Percival. All in all, it was a very simple solution to a possible debacle.

"I trust that concludes such sordid affairs...oh my, a slip of the tongue. Carry on Maitland, I assume you have further matters to disclose?"

"Thank you, Sire...I am sure there are those who are pleased that has been resolved. However, I do fear I must seek your indulgence a while longer while I ask Sir Percival about matters appertaining to his regiment."

"Do so but be quick, I spy a syllabub. I do so like syllabub, don't you Lady Caroline?" Ignoring the Kings gastronomic preferences Maitland went for Sir Percival's throat with a relish.

"Sir Percival, you express a desire to serve His Majesty abroad."

"That is correct," The militia colonel declared pompously

"Admirable! His Majesty must be pleased with your donation of an entire regiment free of charge. However, pray explain to us mere mortals, why it is you employ, as one of your advisers, a leading member of the rebellious cause?"

Sir Percival stared at Maitland in utter fear. He was forced to think quickly, not something he did often. He realised though, that to deny the allegation, would simply convince Maitland of his guilt and thereby the King also. .

"Well, sir, do you deny such knowledge? Do you wish it known that a colonial rebel foisted himself upon your kindness, and you knew nothing of his position, or reason for joining you?"

"Of course I..."

"You what sir, you knew that Mister Truman, is in fact one Samuel Worthington a rebel spy. That he was sent to Europe with orders from the rebel congress to seek out like-minded souls willing to raise insurrection and fight against their lawfully elected parliament and their King? Did you know that this same man has attended every royal court in Europe, has been in meaningful discussions with our enemies concerning the acquisition of arms munitions, and finances, with which he and his friends will continue their attacks against His Majesties loyal colonial subjects. Is that not the case?"

"Tch, Tch, Sir Percival, have you been dallying with politics? We find this difficult to stomach that you, a loyal, and tireless believer in our nobility...wish us harm? I fear we are ashamed at your deceit." The King could be sarcastic when the need arose, and this was such an occasion.

"I did no such thing, your Majesty! I am your servant! I could never do anything to harm you," Percival assured.

"Perhaps we should seek confirmation? We have the traitor with us this evening maybe he will bear witness as to your guilt or innocence especially when his neck is at risk. What say you Mister Worthington?"

Maitland knew all he needed to know about the lawyer turned spy. Agents had followed him extensively, had watched him tirelessly since he had arrived from the Americas. He didn't expect a confession, not in front of so many witnesses, so what occurred next stunned him totally.

"I fear Sir Percival we are undone. It is true Colonel, I do travel under the auspices of the Continental Congress, I am no spy more an ambassador seeking out what assistance I can muster against a puritanical Monarch who would see his subjects starved and subjugated rather than simply hear our cries for assistance and understanding."

"So, you be no spy. Would you then admit to being a damned weasel, sir?" the King demanded.

"Better a weasel than a toad. But I am neither sire, I am a free man, a solicitor who has seen persecution and abhorrent treatment by your servants against loyal subjects. Subjects, who I might add, have been crippled by exorbitant taxes, and insidious laws, imposed by a less than generous Monarch. I have witnessed firsthand the murder of your citizens, simply because they dared to speak out against what is happening in the colonies."

"Enough!" Maitland commanded.

"No, allow him to speak. Let him explain how dishonourable we are." The King stated.

"I never said your Highness was dishonourable," Worthington stated. "Ill-advised perhaps, misled certainly, your honesty though cannot be questioned."

But we hurt, Sire, each day your punitive laws impede our advancement. All we seek is the chance to have a say in our own government, to send representatives to Parliament. This is denied to us, which is why, I admit, I came to discover who might speak for us should the need arise, and who we could trust. In my mind, I have done nothing wrong, not in the eyes of the law as such; I demand to be returned unharmed to my home country."

"Is this not your country Mister? Are you not an Englishman destined to live under our protection and laws?" the King demanded, his anger rising.

"I am, Sire, as such I seek the protection of you, my King, and the laws of the land."

"Ha!" the King snorted. "I will show you justice, but not here, sir. We have reports of your travels." The King indicated towards a member of his entourage who held aloft a sheaf of papers. "They are reports of your scandalous meetings with representatives of both the Dutch and French governments, both of whom are enemies of your King. These are not the actions of an innocent man. No, you will not use your legal babble to escape; you will answer for your crimes. Colonel Maitland, there are troops outside, members of my bodyguard. Have this scum conveyed to London. Parliament and the courts will decide his fate."

Mister Worthington, or Truman, as most knew him, was a brave man. With his identity discovered he was led sedately away leaving Sir Percival standing alone in the center of a less than happy crowd.

"I assure you, Sire, I had no knowledge of his true identity," he pleaded.

"I do not believe you, and neither does the King," Maitland stated, beckoning two of his soldiers forward. "You, sir, wear the King's uniform, yet you devised treason…"

"I…I" Fitzwilliam stuttered.

"Treason, sir. You sought to manipulate the Horse Guards into providing transport for your regiment. In collusion with your adviser, you sought to lie and cheat, to scheme and manipulate everyone into delivering you and your men to the Americas where, no doubt, at the first chance you would have absconded to the rebels. You expected us, your countryman, to feed, supply, and ship you to your destination where in time you would then fight against us."

"No, Sire! This fool has got it all wrong! I beg you, do not believe him, he hates me, always has…"

"Shut up… you appall me." So far Maitland had restrained his anger, but the man's blatant denial brought that to the fore. "A man with your deviousness deserves everything he gets. Treason, while wearing the King's uniform, carries the ultimate price. If it fell to me, I would take you outside now and shoot you, but the King has decreed that you stand trial. Your fate will be determined by your peers and God have mercy upon your soul. Before that occurs and before you are removed, I have one last question." Sir Percival said nothing, but stared in bewilderment at the colonel. "Why, when all that has happened, do you not ask after your men? You whinge and whine and plead your innocence, but your silence shows the utter disregard in which you hold them. Do they mean so little to you?"

"I love my men, all of them are known to me personally."

"If that were true, why have you not asked what is to become of them? Is it because you only fear for your own skin?" Maitland hated the man, Fitzwilliam was a coward, such men were beyond contempt, and should never be allowed to command troops. Perhaps Fitzwilliam's fate would convince others not to be so ineffectual. "In case you really are concerned about your regiment, I should tell you that Captain Stilwell sailed an hour ago. On board his ships, are your men, they are under guard and stripped of their weapons. Their shame is yours Fitzwilliam, for what you attempted, they will be taken to every Crown colony from here to Australia. They will be released in small groups, to eke out a living for the remainder of their lives. No man will be allowed to carry arms ever again; we will make sure of that. Nor will any man be allowed back to England. Your shame has infected them, until they die, they will be watched. Any hint of rebellion and they will find themselves in prison. It is unfair that they must suffer for your stupidity, but perhaps, out of your clutches, they will once again become useful members of society. If not, well, their fate, as always, is in their hands. As for you, sir, you are ruined. Take the scum away."

"No, Sire, I beg you!" Percival fell to his knees begging for his life. Maitland, felt his victory was sullied by his pathetic groveling. His one satisfaction was that the main protagonists had been ensnared without a shot being fired. Victory and defeat were close bed fellows, either had been but a heart beat away. So much could have gone wrong, but he was happy their plan had succeeded without mishap. *I wish I had been aboard those ships when his men realised what was in store for them,* he thought. Captain Stilwell had done well dealing with his part of their subterfuge. He would have taken great delight in finally ending the charade he had been compelled to indulge in.

"The King has no wish to speak to you," Maitland commanded.

"Thank you, Maitland," the King said, as the crowd watched silently. None had envisaged such scenes, but it seemed there were still surprises to be revealed. "I suggest we continue. Don't you"

Chapter Sixty One

"I do, Your Majesty, and it is a sorry tale I have to tell indeed," Maitland replied, taking his cue from the King, who it appeared, was enjoying his birthday far more than he could ever have imagined. "Your Majesty, behind the façade of respectability, this town, apparently no different from any other in your realm, is a hot bed of lies, debauchery, evilness, wickedness and immorality. With your permission, Sire, I desire to expose those that have held the residents in fear for so long; they consider it impossible to rid themselves of their evilness."

So far this evening had progressed far better than he could have dreamt. The hardest part was done, he had brought armed men into a room, a room where the King was unguarded and vulnerable and had survived being shot as a traitor. More importantly he had exposed a spy and a liar, and protected at least two women's virtues. Now everyone watched him intently for his next revelation. None knew what to expect, but King George had commanded the soldier to continue.

While Fitzwilliam was a guttersnipe, who deserved all that came his way, and Worthington was nothing more than a callow spy who should be hanged for his evil, the real reason for him being here came next. He had already quashed one rumour, by using Fitzwilliam's pomposity against him. The King had mentioned his past indiscretions, and Maitland, with the speed of a snake, had realised he could trap the man into publically denying his licentious assignations. The King had tricked the fool into publically denying any such liaisons, Now by Royal consent, neither Sarah nor…the other lady would have a stain on their character. Rumours would be scotched and any further claims would be seen as ludicrous, simply because no man would be brave enough to implicate himself publically. Once their names were restored, Sarah would be free to find a new husband, while the squire would, at least in the eyes of the town, be a vindicated man. With that problem dealt with amicably Maitland was free to enjoy himself and rid the town of a problem that had beset it for so long.

"Sire, having exposed two criminals for what they are, I must now indulge your Highness while we deal with further matters of impropriety."

"By whom sir, name them!"

"I fear sire, we must look at the good citizens of this hellish place,

"You intrigue me; Maitland…Is it possible that such evilness exists in such a pleasant place? Is there anyone present who can shed light on, or deny our gallant colonel's claim?" The King waited but not one voice spoke out. "Your silence intrigues and concerns me. I am confronted with accusations which, while not so far proven, have not been denied. I give notice that if Maitland, can prove his case, then I will deal severely with those who hide behind silence, deal with them most severely indeed. Take heed, this is your final opportunity to save yourselves…Very well, those who are found wanting will plead their case before the Courts… Do not say you were not warned, woe betides any who are convicted." He waited a moment then added, "On your heads be it…continue Maitland."

"I am obliged, Sire. With your permission I shall expose the deviousness which goes far beyond simple intrigue. Lies, Sire, lies and dishonesty is rife within this place and must be evicted or the perpetrators must suffer the fires of damnation." Maitland was enjoying himself, his voice resembled that of the priest, and the townsfolk trembled. "I call my first witness, Mister Nichols to attend." A buzz of excitement echoed around the room, only silenced by the officer's voice. "Mister Nichols, Sire, is a local apothecary who has a sorry tale to tell." As one, every head turned toward the doors as they opened to reveal the man who now took centre stage. "State your name, and the reason you attend his Majesty." Maitland directed, after Nichols had bowed to King George.

"Nichols, sir, apothecary, I…am here…to denounce the Reverend Bayles as a lying cheating devil, Sire."

"My God, sir, that is serious indeed. You know the penalty in denouncing a priest? I cannot harm them, but your own soul will be questioned when that time comes."

"I know that, Sire, and still accuse him."

"So be it…where is the accused?" the King demanded.

"Absent, Sire, rumour has it he has absconded with his house maid." Maitland had heard the story, but like many he doubted its validity. He suspected the priest had heard what fate awaited him and had run. Where to, was the question?

"Absconded…run off with a wench…well many a priest has done that 'afore, aint they?" The King turned to Sir Stanley and laughed heartily. "Still, I assume you desire a warrant issued so he might answer your questions?"

"It would benefit our cause, Sire. I have searched the town best we can without raising alarm, but he is not to be found. He should be made to answer the charges against him."

"Will cause havoc with the Bishops, but very well." The King detested confrontation with the bishops, a pious lot if ever there were any. But if one of their own had erred, they must be brought to answer the accusations. Loudly, he proclaimed, so that none might misunderstand his words. "Make it known that this priest...Bayles, is to be brought before us, either here or in London at the earliest convenience. Inform every port to look out for him, every squire to tell their tenants, every sheriff to post notices. This priest is now wanted by the Crown; make it known. In the meantime, Mister Nichols, what is your story?"

Nichols visibly shook, it was not every day a King demanded answers so publically. Maitland had foreseen such an event and took a position close to the man, giving him the encouragement to continue.

"I, Sire, am a qualified apothecary, taught and examined in London. For many years I cared for the ailments of this place...I served the people well until, that is, I was beguiled by our priest. I fear, Sire, I have been misguided, forced to use my skills in an immoral manner." Nichols lowered his head in shame and wept. Maitland had worried about this man ever since he had uncovered his secret. Now was not the time to falter.

"Immoral manner? What does he speak of Maitland? What immoralities can an apothecary know of to bring on such a display?"

"Speak, sir. Tell your King what he made you do," Maitland urged.

"Like I said, Sire, before the priest arrived I were but a simple man. I aided those who needed my skills and was trusted by all. But then he came to my shop. He were kind like, Sire, kind, but with a menace which belied his true self. He were the devil, Sire, who cajoled and harassed me and my wife into doing what he demanded. Before I knew what I were doing, he had me producing potions and strange infusions from herbs Mister Joseph Wood supplied. Herbs, which I had never seen 'afore, but which had strange effects on men's mind and bodies."

"Two things, Nichols. Firstly who is this Wood fellow? Any relation to our friend here, and, is he to be brought before us, if not why not? Secondly what were these strange herbs?" the King demanded.

"Joseph Wood, Sire is...was the father of Mister Josiah. He be dead, these past nine months. As for the herbs, they were strange, indeed. Weeds, Sire, with a heady aroma that befuddled the brain, turned those who used them into what is commonly known as knuckleheads. Under such influence, the patient is unable to remember what they do, but their senses are heightened. The reverend said it increased a man's virility, made them more amorous. Problem was, it also caused some to act irrationally."

"In what manner was this irrationality witnessed?" Maitland demanded.

"All manner of ways, one man, while under its influence, climbed the bell tower and threw himself off. It were said he smiled all the way down, shouting he could fly. He did this on a Sunday, in front of the congregation. Bayles said he was touched, but he weren't. He were overjoyed, as if full of exuberance. It were then that I told the priest we would not supply him no more."

"He accepted that, I assume?" King George asked.

"Seemed to at first, Sire, but soon after, my wife was arrested and accused of witchcraft. The priest lied at her trial, told so many untruths that I knew he was punishing me. He was telling me to do as he said, or he could harm me in ways I could not imagine."

"Serious charges, yet the man is not here to answer the accusations. Your case is in peril, Maitland, unless you have other forms of evidence."

"I am aware of the peril involved, Sire, but I have further witnesses who will testify to his evil ways, if you so desire?"

"I do, Maitland, I do. Mister Nichols, we thank you for your diligence and extend our sorrow for your loss. Pray, remain while the Colonel continues with his evidence. I do so fear he will wish to consult you further." The King was enjoying his birthday, as he had been informed he would. "Bring forward your next witnesses, sir."

"With your permission, I ask Mister Josiah Wood to step forward. Mister Wood is a merchant within the town and now the head of a family which has suffered grievously during the past year. He is the son of Mister Joseph Wood, and has intimate knowledge of what this town has endured. Mister Wood has a document he has prepared, it details everything, known and suspected of events over some years. It is an intimate document, one he desires submitted as evidence. Now is not the time to examine its contents so with your permission sire, I would suggest I retain it, at least until more learned men can ascertain its legality."

. Maitland hoped Wood would remain steadfast, and that despite his appearance of total collapse, would complete what was expected of him. Josiah, handed the document to Maitland, who accepted it as if this was his first sight of such a damning document. In fact, he had dictated it, then coerced Josiah to sign it while effectively imprisoning the man within his own home. If challenged, the document could be deemed useless by the manner in which it had been procured, or Wood might, even now, falter and deny any part in this ...heinous debacle. However, if Wood remained silent, so would he and press on with this the most satisfying part of his plan.

"Thank you, Mister Wood." Maitland held the document aloft so everyone could see it, stating, "Sire, this document details every aspect of how criminals subjected loyal Englishman to such depravity it makes Sodom and Gomorrah appear to be blessed places of virtue. This document details the manner in which crime was committed in the name of greed. How taxes were withheld and disregarded. How land was stolen and procured, from those close to death by means of illegal wills and testaments. It also details, so I am informed, as to how, wages were denied, forcing many to live in penury. This document, freely written and properly witnessed also details so many crimes, you will wonder how people managed to survive. However, written words can be contradicted. Clever men can argue the rights and wrongs until the innocent are forced to give in. It is for that reason I would desire a witness to speak, here and now, to confirm what Mister Wood has committed to paper. With your permission, Sire, I would like to ask a young officer to attend us; he has, while under my command, held this witness safe until this time."

The King nodded, and Maitland beckoned to Herbert Wright. The adjutant disappeared, returning almost immediately in the company of a young well-dressed officer. Maitland acknowledged the nod from Wright and continued, knowing that his witness was safe and well.

"Sire, may I name Ensign Mathews, who until recently was in London. While there he was tasked with an assignment so secret, no one, apart from two officers and myself, knew of their content. Mister Mathews has travelled much, has spoken to many interested parties and gathered much evidence. More importantly, he has brought some of those discoveries with him this evening. With your permission, Sire, I would ask him to present his guests to your Majesty."

Maitland spoke well and eloquently. What none realised was just how close they had been to total disaster. But what the King did not know would not hurt him.

"If you must Maitland, continue, but hurry up." The King beckoned Stagg forward and said, "Another glass my man, a large glass mind."

Maitland gave the merest of nods to which Mathews snapped to attention, saluted his Colonel and retired from the room, leaving the Sergeant he stood beside isolated. This had proved, both the hardest, and most pleasant part of the evening to organise. To maintain their safety, and this illusion, they had been ensconced in a place no one would have dared to look. He smiled as he saw them appear, they entered the room as if they belonged, and certainly they appeared to show no fear of any sort. Theirs was true bravery, for Maitland had learnt much from his few meetings with them as to what they had gone through. No wonder they were petrified of what they must do.

"Delightful, and a pleasure to finally greet you my dears, one has heard so much about your experiences. We are pleased to see you looking so well refreshed." Unusually, he rose to greet the three, elegantly dressed women, who despite their fears curtsied to their King. For his part, the King could be gracious when the mood took him, and these women were visions of loveliness, which might have explained the way he smiled and spoke to them. "If I were but a little younger, I would deem it an honour to dance with each of you in turn, but Maitland, I fear, is taking so long we will be too old for such flummery afore he completes his work, what?"

They had beguiled him. Three provincial women had beguiled a Monarch, turning him into a love struck fool, but King George cared not. He was speaking to his people in utter honesty. His beguilement was halted as Maitland announced,

"Your Majesty, My Lords, Ladies, and Gentlemen, may I have the honour in naming Miss Margaret Swan, and Miss Mary-Annabel Barker."

Two of the women curtsied, while the third waited. Maitland was building the tension, waiting for the guests to turn to face her. Only when he was satisfied did he state,

"May I also have the pleasure of naming Miss Abigail Scott, better known to most here as Mrs Nathaniel Wood?"

He smiled in satisfaction as an audible gasp went around the room. Those nearest heard first, they whispered her name to those further back. Like wildfire, the names reached the ears of those that mattered, and his heart went cold as the implications of her attendance became clear.

Chapter Sixty Two

Until her name was mentioned, Turnbottle had not been concerned by what was happening. While Maitland, droned on about Fitzwilliam and Bayles he continued to dine from Sir Stanley's excellent table and cellar. Nor had he been concerned by the King's arrival after all such personage would not come to speak to him nor indeed any of the local dignitaries. Indeed after he had been lost in a mêlée of bodies, his presence had paled into insignificance. The announcement that Truman was some colonial spy had proved mildly interesting. Having met him, he had found him to be a paragon of politeness and interest, but one never knew about people, did one?

"No…she's dead." He dropped his glass, when her name was announced. He turned, and felt the colour drain from his face, he was in a dream, a nightmare. Shouldering his way through the throng, he felt weak at the knees as sure enough, beside the King, stood a woman, he had been assured was dead. "Treacherous swine," he whispered. *It cannot be, she is no Lazarus, someone has lied, but if not her, then who died in that hovel?*

Turnbottle felt drained, his world, once so assured was near collapse. Wood and Abigail in the same room was impossible, yet there, before him, was a nightmare of certainty? He stared in bewilderment, she was far different from when he had seen her destitute and impoverished. Once again she was, the picture of health, her beauty, accentuated by the fine dress she wore, made her appear radiant as she enjoyed the attention of a King.

"Damn them! Damn every last one of them!" he exclaimed. He was ruined, her appearance had sealed his fate there would be questions, recriminations, his word, would be examined and found wanting. He needed to get away, as quickly as possible, and with the minimum of fuss. But he stumbled, his intention of leaving like a thief in the night became a myriad of disasters. Blathering incoherent apologies, his eyes became misted, his blood ran cold and his mind whirled in confusion. Those, he encountered saw a madman, heard his mutterings and moved away leaving him exposed and vulnerable. "This cannot be!" he whimpered. "The bitch lied…said she was dead, as was her child…the whore duped me and found others to assist her."

Finally, reaching a doorway he found his way barred by two women, their dresses so large they seemed entwined. "Let me through, God Damn it, allow me to pass!" He demanded. One, a woman, possessed a magnificent set of lungs, screamed loudly arousing the attention of one of Maitland's officers. He was trapped, forced to remain, to be humiliated, perhaps, even brought before the King. Myriad thoughts flashed before him as he tried to comprehend what this meant. She lived and knew what he had planned for her. Such knowledge would see him imprisoned. How to escape, how could he turn this to his advantage?

Caught between soldiers and these women, he had nowhere to run. The world, he had created was about to fall upon him. *The bitch will seek retribution.* That must be why she was here, to see him ruined. *Think man, think! There must be a resolution, a way of avoiding the hangman.* Perhaps he could plead to her better nature, explain that what he did was all part of his grand scheme to put her back where she belonged, certainly she appeared to have the Kings ear, was comfortable in his presence. *She will never believe that.* Suddenly he remembered, *if she lives, did the child also survive? If so, she will seek justice for making her bastard suffer as well. What to do?* That was the question. Given time, he might have shifted the blame elsewhere, but time was something he did not have. Nor indeed could he depend on the whores who had worked so well for him. They now stood, cleaned and tidy, looking the very picture of respectability, no doubt ready to knife him as well.

"Turnbottle said she was dead!" Columbine, the merchant, muttered. His friends nodded thoughtfully as questions arose in their heads.

"Aye, he did. Told us, both she and her bastard child had gone. Man's an outright liar! What other falsehoods has he spread?" The mumbling grew, heads began turning seeking out the man who, it seemed, had duped them all.

"He told me she had returned to Barminster" Mrs Furnell exclaimed her presence was her fortune, tonight she would glean enough gossip to keep her ladies happy for months to come..

"Last I heard, the whore had been thrown out by Reverend Bayles," an unknown voice stated, just a little too loudly. Turnbottle heard it and winced, while a King declared an end to such hostility.

"Enough!" his voice bellowed. It wasn't polite, certainly not majestic, but, not for the first time this evening, he tired of the town's petty minded bigotry. "Any more talk of whores and I will see the orator incarcerated indefinitely. If you desire to join Fitzwilliam then speak once more...But should you value your liberty, take heed and remain silent. By doing so you might learn of the treachery that certain people have suffered. Mister Wood, I assume you have something to add?"

"I...I" Josiah began, but faltered badly.

"Get on with it, man, the night is short and my temper even shorter. I assume the alternative has been explained to you? What you can expect if you attempt to confuse and muddy the water?" The King was enjoying this drama which Maitland had so thoughtfully arranged, but even he wished to hear the finale. "Delay any longer, my fellow, and I will become weak with hunger.

Press on, there's a good man."

"Our grateful thanks, your Majesty. I have indeed explained to Mister Wood the consequences, Sire." Maitland, knew Wood to be a spineless fool, but he had to get him through this period otherwise everything might collapse around them. The man wasn't blameless. In fact, he was as guilty as many, but he had been promised a pardon in exchange for his testimony. Fear, though, might still destroy him as easily as his lies had almost destroyed Miss Scott.

"With your permission, Sire, might I aid Mister Wood? I fear your presence has overwhelmed him, and I might be able to offer him some moral support."

"If you must, personally, from what I have heard, the man needs horsewhipping, but…very well, proceed." It made a strange picture, the elegant soldier and the defeated merchant. But as he took his position alongside Josiah Wood, the colonel whispered….,

"You useless piece of horse shit, speak, or by God, I will personally hang you for your part in this tragedy. You have your words; read them, and make it sincere."

Josiah winced at the shame of what he was forced to do but Maitland's anger was loathsome to behold. He had witnessed it in his home and had no desire to repeat the experience here. With the town watching him, Josiah knew it was not the time to test his threats. Clasping his speech in his quivering hand, he began to read…

"On behalf of what remains of my family, I offer my sister-in-law, Miss Abigail Scott, our abject apologies for the way she has been treated. Our conduct was unbecoming and uncalled for, she should not have been treated thus. In our defence, I have to state that we were duped and misled by both Reverend Bayles and Mister Pawell, the family solicitor."

"Lies!" Pawell the solicitor shouted. "I did nothing of the sort. I simply complied with a client's wishes; no more, no less. What the Wood family did had nothing to do with me. In fact, if he remembers, I urged them to act with a modicum of restraint which they chose to ignore."

"Who the devil are you sir, and who gave you permission to speak? You will remain silent as will anyone else so inclined to interrupt."

"That is Mister Pawell sire the Wood family solicitor." Maitland added helpfully.

"Pawell! I detest your name, as I detest your profession sir. Thieves and liars sir that is what lawyers are. Best advice I ever received was to expel every last one of your profession. From what I hear of you, sir, I have a mind to start with you…I dislike the sight of you… no doubt you are like those who thieve off of my people in London. There, I am hamstrung and can say nothing, but here, I am not so constrained. You are toads, sir, toads who willingly agree to anything if the price is right. Morals and the right of law mean nothing to your kind. My hard pressed people place their trust in your profession, yet you scheme, sir, scheme to feather your own nest, while your client goes to the wall. Now silence, sir, or I will have you imprisoned as well. Continue, Maitland."

"My thanks Sire. Continue Mister Wood." Haltingly, Josiah continued his speech.

"Sire, as the last of my family, I stand before you and beg forgiveness. I owe Miss Abigail more than I can ever repay. My father's....indulgencies were common knowledge to us, yet we remained silent. We witnessed what he did, but chose not to speak out. Not through loyalty, but through fear of what he might do. I fear, Sire, Miss Abigail was not the first to suffer at his hands. His excesses occurred more often than anyone knew, yet we said nothing. Likewise, we allowed Reverend Bayles to control and manipulate us. He was a demon Sire, a parasite, he deceived us and we believed all he said. More unfortunately we did not have the desire, or the strength to stand against him. Oh I know there are some who will scoff, but that man had desires which were unnatural. Desires which were allowed to go unheeded by the situation he and others made for themselves. As for what occurred after my father's demise...that unfortunate situation occurred because of a badly written and executed will. My brother, Nathaniel, was the legal inheritor and despite his unfortunate absence, his wife should have taken his position. The good of the business should have been taken into consideration. Perhaps, if we had listened to Mistress Abigail instead of outside influences, this unfortunate situation could have been avoided. Once again, I apologise for whatever inconveniences you suffered. I cannot conceive what you went through. Though we, too, have suffered, my family has been decimated, death's dark shadow has visited us and we were found wanting. Maybe if we had been more Christian, if I had not been so stubborn, my younger brother might have survived to stand here today with me. If such events had occurred, perhaps the man who schemed to relieve us of all we owned, would not have so nearly succeeded. I plead to you Abigail, forgive a stupid and ignorant fool, come home, join with us to re-build, not only our family, but also the business. With your assistance, we might revive our ailing fortunes, and make the firm into what Nathaniel would have wanted."

Cuffing a tear away, Josiah faltered, his words though were profound and made those present pause to reflect on what they had allowed to occur. Some saw him as a cad and a dunderhead, while others realised just how close the town had come to ruination by those who desired wealth and influence at the expense of others. Men, who had sat in Pettits, agreeing to march on the warehouses, huffed and puffed, Josiah had not named his nemesis, but those who had heard his rhetoric, knew who Wood refereed to. Only one voice rose in sympathy, and she rushed forward to clasp him tightly with an outward show of affection.

"Oh, Josiah, that is all I ever wanted. My love for Nathaniel was so great, but he died and then I was alone with…well, you know. Given time, our differences can heal. However, despite your apology being greatly accepted, it is time for everyone to be honest with each other, which is why Josiah, I must make my own confession. With your permission Sire?"

The King nodded, amazed by her strength and determination. This had to be done, it was what he had discussed, within his carriage, with his two advisers. He knew, this would not be easy, but she had to complete what she had started.

"Thank you, Sire. I came to Stormouth under the guise of a woman seeking aspects to paint. This was a fabrication, a ruse to get close to your family Josiah. I was never the innocent, most perceived me to be, I had ulterior motives, a task to perform and would have done so without hesitation had it not been for your brother Nathaniel. My arrival was at the behest of my father, but those orders came from…another, a man we must all obey," She paused as a mumble of aggrieved voices filled the room.

"Silence!" Maitland commanded. "Let her continue!"

"Thank you, Colonel. My task was to get close to the Wood family. To spy upon them, in particular Joseph Wood, and discover the premise of their wealth. Few knew of my task, my father was one, but he was denied access to the town by the heavy snow that cut Stormouth off for so long. He though took his orders from another, a man of whom I am not at liberty to reveal. But his name made refusal almost…almost, undeniable. I convinced them I could achieve what others could not, and so, I was allowed to remain." None save the General who stood close to the King, one of those from his carriage, saw the way the King smiled at her words. She was a credit to her father and her sovereign.

"I fail to understand. Why did men presume to do such a thing, why indeed did you think us capable of such deception?" Josiah asked, perplexed as to what Abigail hoped to achieve, she was supposed to be compliant, and not have an agenda of her own. This was not what Maitland had told him.

"That is easily explained, Josiah… the reason for my arrival was to discover why, despite an increase in trade, revenue had fallen so dramatically. The treasury demanded answers but your father saw through those sent before me which was why we were tasked to discover the reason."

"Why what connection are you to the Government?" Josiah demanded.

"My father, Josiah is a senior Comptroller of Customs. He and I have worked together before, it was he who devised this subterfuge. He felt that I, as an innocent, would be able to infiltrate your family and learn your secrets, without you realising my intentions."

"His plan was successful. I never suspected," Josiah conceded.

"Joseph Wood doing something amiss; there's a surprise," Columbine uttered a little too loudly, only to be nudged into silence by the mayor, who like everyone, wanted to hear every word that was said.

"I know that now, but before, I assumed you were all involved including Nathaniel. It soon became obvious that Joseph, and 'The Chamberlin' had been close, and that your father continued, to accept smuggled goods long after Pope had ended 'The Chamberlin's' rule. Your father was a cheat, and a thief. He embezzled thousands of pounds from the revenue, siphoned off his share of the profits long before he sent what was owed to London. For some time, the thought in London, was that your father was in fact 'The Chamberlin'. Obviously due to that man's demise, that assumption was proven wrong, but that was the idea for some time. As for me, well, my problems deepened when I fell in love with Nathaniel. Our marriage wasn't supposed to happen, but my father and…his confidant, agreed reluctantly. It was supposed to be a convenience, a simple expedience to unravel Joseph's financial affairs, and gather the evidence we needed to expose him."

"I never knew," Josiah said sadly. Maitland had told him some of what she spoke of, but had left out most of the personal detail. Immunity from the law was Josiah's escape route, so long as Maitland had names to pursue. It was a route which Josiah had grasped eagerly. Now, with Abigail between him and his wife, he felt at peace. Clasping their hands in a show of affection, Josiah looked for Sarah. Reluctantly the erstwhile sister joined them, only now was the realisation of what she had been involved with beginning to make sense. Shame made her remain silent, to listen along with everyone else, to Abigail's final condemnation of those who had harmed her.

"Sire I fell foul of two men. Men whom I have since discovered were to blame for most of the ills of this place. During my time of …vexation, while incarcerated in that foulest of places. I came to despise these men, and considered the means of my revenge. I rehearsed the words I would use when at last I would face my accusers. That scorn is burnt into my brain which is why Colonel, I ask that Reverend Bayles should be summoned to appear before us?"

"I only wish I could, ma'am, but as I told His Majesty, the blaggard's run, aint been seen for some time. Absconded I fear, before his crimes were discovered.

"Gone, me dear, flown like the Raven he were," Mr Johnson, the Mayor, added helpfully.

"It would appear he has indeed gone to ground, but I have issued orders that he should be found, brought before us to answer for his misdeeds. There is no place in this fair land for priests who take the Lord's name in vain. We shall do all that is possible to flush this laggard out and bring him to justice."

Those that knew what had happened to the priest remained silent. To do what was asked, would need the powers of reincarnation, therefore; Bayles would remain forever in purgatory. Maitland had already issued that order but nodded to Wright, who he saw appeared a little calmer now the events were going as predicted.

"As you command Sire. Word has been sent to every Port within a day's ride, but we will extend the search immieditatly."

"Flush the beggar out Maitland, I desire to hear what he has to say."

"If I may be so bold, Sire," Abigail asked. "As the priest is absent and may remain so for some time, might we interview the last of your criminally minded subjects?"

Abigail had no wish for the moment to wither and die while they waited for Bayles to be found. Too many people might lose their nerves.

"You may, my dear, you may. Told you I enjoyed fireworks, Cobb, did I not?"

"Indeed you did, Sire." Sir Stanley had so far remained silent, listening and holding his wife's hand tightly ever since Fitzwilliam had been removed. "A most enjoyable occasion, I am sure."

"Aye, birthdays are meant to be enjoyable. Could I trouble you for a further dish of Syllabub, Cobb? Maitland is making such a meal of this I feel dashed peckish. Miss Scott, please continue if you feel able after your brief confinement." The King loved any sort of play and this was one of the rarest he'd ever witnessed, especially as he knew more than some of the leading characters.

"My thanks, Sire, but I am quite well. May I request that my father brings the latest piece of evidence close?"

"Of course…Scott, damn your hide…Scott! Come close, do yah hear me, man?" The King could sound annoyed whenever the mood took him, but this time he spoke with a smile. "Aah, there you both are." An elderly man

Approached, he carried a bundle which the King beckoned to be given. "Normally I do not like such things, but Miss Scott has asked us to become this little thing's Godfather. So, we now introduce Master Nathaniel, Augustus, Adam, Josiah, George, Wood. My Godson."

The King held the child aloft as if presenting an heir to the masses. The child cried and he smiled before handing it back to its grandfather. Then he turned and demanded.

"Fractious little thing aint he? However, there be someone in this room who wished harm on this innocent child. Someone, who allowed my Godchild to be born into the world in deprivation, but who would have been far happier if he had died, as lived. I demand that person comes before me to answer for their cruelty. The rogue is hereabouts, his name, Benjamin Turnbottle! A knave I wish to see immediately! Where are you, you scurrilous dog?" No one spoke and the King grew angrier. "Must we send the army to retrieve you, Turnbottle? We know you are here, we have been informed thus...Aah, there you are. I spy you, you sniveling toad...come forward and explain yourself. Miss...my apologies, Mrs Wood, pray continue."

Turnbottle knew he was finished. A soldier stood nearby, while the two women stopped any escape, he was forced to acknowledge a Kings command Stepping forward he became the center of attention, the focus for quizzical examination by those who, only earlier today, he had deemed his friends and by a woman he had assumed, dead

"Good day, Mister Turnbottle. You appear confused; so unlike you, usually you know precisely what you are about."

Abigail had often contemplated if she would be able to confront either of them? Both Bayles and this one had treated her vilely, but now she knew, and she felt enlightened.

"I believed in you," she said quietly, "placed my life in your hands and did all you asked, yet, you deceived me. You, contrived, pretended and connived your way into my life. You pretended to assist, lied to my friends and placed me in a hovel which you said would be safe. Safe from whom sir? Certainly not from you, or the rats that inhabited that place, both human and otherwise. You spoke of your plans to reinstate me to my station and I believed you sir, believed every word, even when you appeared sick and unwell. I assume that was another ruse to lure me into your lies even further and garner my sympathies? I suspect that is the case, as I suspect your interest in me went no further than what I meant to you, and what I could give you. You desired the knowledge I possessed about the family, nothing more. I realised, perhaps too late, that once you had gained what you desired I would be discarded, as have so many others, who fell under your spell. What of your plan, sir, your grand scheme, was that a lie also, or did it truly exist? My suspicion is that, was your only truth you really did wish to build your utopia, but to do so you needed inside knowledge of the family. What then? Ruin the family and place yourself at the head of the merchants and the port? With such power you would have been no better than Joseph. You see sir ultimate power corrupts, and you have become corrupted. You desired the power he once possessed, you wanted to Lord it sir, over everyone, to control every aspect of life hereabouts. You would have become no better than Joseph for he too commanded wages, prices, who worked, who didn't, who lived, and who died. My suspicion is that it was you, sir, who arranged every terrible event that occurred in this town after Joseph Wood died. I also accuse you Mister Turnbottle of planning and arranging the death of Adam Wood. I also accuse you of endangering my own life, and that of my son. I condemn you, and demand that you answer such charges in a court of Law."

Not that long ago, she had lain dying, with, but a foul hag named Ma Epps to administer to her. Then, she had cared for nothing, except release from her pain. She had been so close Nathaniel had come to her and she had reached out to her dead husband. Fortunately, with God's Grace, she had survived. Removed from that hovel, then nursed by her two friends, she had remained in hiding until her father had arrived to assist her. How he knew what had happened, and where she was, remained a mystery which he refused to divulge. All he would say was that a young ensign had been involved somehow. She no longer feared death, or any man, since giving birth to her son he was her priority. Every waking moment was spent, determining and securing his future, which, with the King's patronage looked very secure. Her adversary looked sallow and beaten, she paused in her tirade to give him time to refute her claims. He was finished, but his rebuttal was vicious.

"Stupidity, madam! You cannot prove any of what you say. Look at me I am respected, wealthy, well known for my generosity to the poor. My God, Sire, Mrs Wood is addled, quite addled. She speaks eloquently, but has no hard evidence, simply accusations and insinuations. Certainly, she has not enough to garner a conviction in any court. Most of her accusations could be denied and countered by any reputable barrister. I can, Sire, call numerous witnesses who will contradict these claims. By God, I placed myself in harm's way simply to locate and find Mrs Wood; ask my housekeeper. It was to her that I sought advice that very first day. I mean, do I appear to be the sort of man who could manipulate so effectively as Mrs Wood states? No, I would not. I plead to you all, my contemporaries, and ask, if any among you believe such lies? Look at me. How could I devise such a perplexing plan and carry it out without being discovered?"

Turnbottle spoke well, and many were convinced, until a damaging accusation came from an unexpected quarter.

"I believe it, and will speak against you, if asked," Columbine stated flatly. "I will inform any authority, which seeks confirmation, that it was you that wished us, the other merchants, to move against the Wood family. I will also instruct John Mickelwhite to speak out. It was from him that you gained much of your information, I assume?"

"Columbine, we are friends, how could you?" Turnbottle asked.

"Easy. I dislike you, always have. You are a dangerous man who does nothing unless it assists you alone. Ask any of the other merchants, they will state the same. Joseph Wood might have been difficult to work with, but we knew where we stood with him. There were never any false statements from him."

"It would seem, sir, you have been cast adrift, hoisted by your own perturb." the King stated, adding simply. "Seems we have another for the Courts to deal with, arrest him, Maitland."

Turnbottle was an intelligent man, knew about the law and such forth. He realised that even with Columbine's accusation, and the bitch's so called evidence, a Court would struggle to prove his guilt beyond reasonable doubt. He would possibly escape imprisonment, but his time in the town had come to an end. Guilty or innocent, no one would do business with him anymore. Trade was his lifeblood, without it, or the trust of the merchants; he would be forced to move. More importantly, he questioned whether he would have the stomach to begin again. More likely, he would face a life of exile. Perhaps he would move to Bath, to spend the remainder of his days taking tea, and enjoying the waters there, or the outer reaches of Yorkshire.

"Madam, one question before I am removed," he asked. "The doctor assured me you were dead, as was a girl child. How…?"

"A golden Guinea, Mister Turnbottle. Yours, I believe, given to Mary-Ann that first night we met. That, was the token of your downfall, along with the conscience of a man who was asked to bend the rules a little."

"I fail to comprehend, it would take more than that to force him to lie."

"How little you understand the people of this town, allow me to explain. I was, at the time Knuckleheaded, to use the common expression from the fumes of the herbs administered. But Maggie explained what occurred, fate and her intelligence aided her, and myself. What you witnessed unfortunately was a blood soaked bed, but the body within was poor Ma Epps. She expired from nothing more sinister than old age, but in death she saved two lives. I knew little of the birth, the herbs worked their magic. After the good doctor resolved my severe loss of blood, my friends removed me and placed Ma's body in the bed. That was what they would have showed you thankfully; you stood no closer than the doorway."

"What of the name? I was told it was Alice?"

"An error on Ma's part. During my illusions, I, not only saw and spoke to my dead husband, but also to a childhood friend named Alice. The angel of death was close, but I escaped his clutches. Anyway, after I gave birth to a son, well, the name proved an unusual choice but it did lay a false trail for some time."

"I congratulate you on your deviousness. But the doctor…how was he persuaded to lie so convincingly? He and I have known each other for a long time."

"There you chose well, sir. Unknowingly, you commanded a man, known to Mistress Barker…professionally, to attend me. He kept Maggie's girls healthy for a small remuneration. You can imagine his surprise, when he arrived at the dwellings and saw her in attendance. Thereafter, it was just a question of persuading him that it would be better to do as Maggie asked, than for his name and habits to be made known around town. You see, my friend, you are not the only one who knows which strings to pull, and when."

Turnbottle remained silent, he had come so close but his time was almost done. His lies had been revealed, and the town gasped in shock at what he had done. He knew he would never see Stormouth again, yet the town had one last surprise for Benjamin Turnbottle. Forced under escort from the room, he was halted at the door by a sergeant. A man, dressed in Maitland's regimental uniform, who had stood patiently all evening until now. Viciously he struck out, the merchant fell to the ground; blood poured from his broken nose and cut lip. He cursed, expecting help from his guard, but no such assistance was offered. Instead, the soldier sat astride him, grabbed his throat with unexpected violence, and stared into his face. He was dark skinned, and bearded, he was worn and tired, but the eyes belied the truth.

"You bastard! I should have finished you years ago!" The sergeant spat the words with venom in his tone, while Turnbottle squealed in fear. Murder might have occurred had it not been for a King who demanded the assault ceased. Anger, though, made the soldier strike the merchant one last time. Turnbottle screamed in such a way the whole room heard his anger.

"You're dead, Wood! Everyone knows that! How are you here now?"

Nathaniel ignored the whimpering merchant. Instead he had eyes for only one. He looked for his wife; she saw him, and with tears in her eyes, and a smile on her lips, she rushed to his side. The King watched a tearful reunion, waited while they rediscovered a lost love. Then, when the moment was right, he asked Mrs Abigail Wood,

"Are we concluded, my dear?"

"Oh yes, Sire, and may I say how much I enjoyed your birthday fireworks."

FINALE

"In this world nothing can be said to be certain, except Death and Taxes."
Benjamin Franklin 1706 - 1790

For the moment Death's thirst for disciples was slacked, revenge had been wrought, and Death was satisfied. But for years to come, mothers would speak to fractious children, of the night, the devil had walked the town.

For those involved, their lives would never be the same again. As Turnbottle predicted, he never saw the town again. Convicted by a jury, he was sentenced to transportation to Australia for his part in the misfortunes inflicted upon the Wood family. He was never implicated in Adam's death, but many would remain convinced of his guilt. The merchant's descendants, if indeed he had any, would live with his shame, or attempt to regain what had been lost. Time would tell as to what would happen there.

As for Edward Bayles, priest, and despicable human being, his fate was decided that night in the blacksmith's shop. Men had meted out summary justice, dealt with a vile beast in secret. Dressed in the stolen uniform, Bayles Had been taken to the harbour and set adrift in a small burning boat. It had been while he was being prepared that Mary-Ann had so nearly discovered them at the Blacksmiths shop but she had never known how close she had come to murder. Bayles was supposed to have been discover further down the coast burnt beyond recognition, he would have been buried in an unmarked grave where he could rot for eternity, unknown and forgotten. Fate, though, had another end in store for him. His boat did not burn; it smoldered and was carried by the tide, out to sea. Many witnessed his passing, including sailors aboard the 'Kentsman' but did nothing to halt his final voyage. Lost in the vastness of the ocean the priest's, last parishioners, were the birds of the sky that feasted upon his hated flesh, and gnawed at his heartless body. By the time the boat rotted and flooded, there was nothing much left for the fish of the deep to feed on. His disjointed bones fell to the ocean floor to lie forever, testament to his evilness.

Man isn't born evil, or good, both lie within, waiting to discover which overpowers the other. The dominant one comes to the fore, when time and circumstances present themselves. Edward Bayles was himself a victim. He had learnt evil, prospered on it, and had died because of it. His killers had knowingly rid the world of a man who knew how to exploit the evil that existed within the world. As Bayles's executioner, Turnbottle felt no shame in ridding the world of such malevolence. No one would mourn the priest's death; it was a blessing to those that had known him.

Stormouth had rid itself of two villains, but there were more to be punished. Sir Percival Fitzwilliam, was quietly disposed of. The King arranged for his indictment to be heard before Sir Walter Howard, a more than willing judge. A man who, through family ties, knew of Sir Percival's dalliances and was more than willing to find the man guilty as charged. Stripped of his title Fitzwilliam, was sent abroad to complete his punishment. The last anyone heard, he was living on some distant island, destined to remember every woman he had defiled, and every husband he had cuckolded.

As for his regiment, their records were removed from the army list and forgotten. The men, as promised, were scattered to the four corners of King George's domain. However, the King punished only the wrong doer, and Fitzwilliam's men were the unfortunate casualties of war. While their menfolk were sent abroad, King George arranged for each man's wife or family to either receive a small pension, sufficient to keep the bailiff from the door, or join the husbands abroad. Few did, choosing instead to remarry and remain on the estates under the auspices of the new owner

Sir Stanley and Lady Cobb, continued to live in Stormouth, but never again would they hold sway over the town. King George made it known that he desired a new sitting member of Parliament, and the Government arranged that the rotten borough of Stormouth elected another at the next elections. With few voters, sufficient money was paid to entice another candidate, and Sir Stanley was sidelined for his part in this sorry affair. The Cobbs association with the town was waning, and very soon another family would buy their home, take over their position, and start again.

During the year 1773, almost everyone in Stormouth paid a terrible price. Though some, even those who through no fault of their own suffered heinously, did manage to rebuild their shattered lives. Bayles's housekeeper Ruby, was one such winner. Having given evidence at the trial in the smithy, she left England soon after. Turnbottle, paid her fare to Canada, where she was supposed to remain. That should have been the last they heard of her, but fate once again lent a hand in the affairs of the town. Sixteen years later, when many of those who had been involved in that year had died, Ida Furnell, aged and withered, still collected her titbits of gossip. She tended the graves of those who had been alive at the time, and on one such occasion she spied a familiar face. A woman, in the company of a young man, wept beside a headstone. Both were vaguely familiar, but by the time Ida had hobbled off to get the rector, both had disappeared like ghosts.

"Whom did you see?" The new cleric had asked but Ida stayed silent, not through respect but fear for the youth resembled a sinister presence from her past. A dark swarthy man with a prominent nose who had disappeared the night a King came to town. The 'Raven' was dead, so whom had she witnessed with the woman? That was what she feared to ask.

Later that month, a petition was presented to the town Jurats asking that a grave be opened and a body removed to be interned separately. The plaintiff, was one Ruby McAllister of Philadelphia, the body, that of her father buried without due reverence in a shared grave. Her wealth overcame any difficulties, and eventually a new grave was prepared.

As for Abigail Wood, her surprise was measured only by her joy at seeing her husband returned to her. His story was full of luck, hardship, and finally, joy as hers had been. His ship, wrecked in a storm, Nathaniel had clung to life by his fingertips. Close to death, only the good fortune of being rescued by a passing whaler had spared him. Forced to remain with them, until they reached a safe harbour. There he had eventually found a willing captain who offered him passage home. Fate, or a guardian angel, was watching over him, for as they passed Cornwall, his ship was approached by a naval frigate. Why they were stopped was never explained, but during a conversation between the naval captain and the Merchantmen's master, Nathaniel's name and story was mentioned. Before they were in sight of Portsmouth his name was in London. By the time his ship docked his name had reached the ear of the King, and a young ensign named Mathews had been dispatched with instructions to bring him to Court with all haste. Warned of what to expect, it had been Nathaniel who had devised his means of disclosure. The punch he had landed had been a release after so much pain, and Turnbottle did deserve a little physical discomfort.

So, poor little Stormouth returned to near normality. Death had visited, but most had survived its visitation. The winged angel had claimed enough victims from this town. It left on a pale horse, to seek others, to slake its thirst. Stormouth would live on, and as for Abigail well… her story continues, would it be right to say anymore?

THE END

Testimonials

K.Meador USA An intricately woven tale of intrigue and suspense, beautifully written

A Stanmore England. This is a real page turner. Loved it from start to finish

Sykehouse Oracle England if there were any justice this would be a best seller and deservedly so.

Lynn D Canada. Best debut novel I have read. Loved it from when that poor boy died to the delightful end.

Ann C Australia. The author delights in detail, describing both characters and settings with immense clarity.

Chris B England. Expectation is coupled with prolonged interest, anger, hatred, admiration, agony, sorrow and tears. In fact every emotion is examined and wrenched asunder, bring on the buckets.

Kangaranger, Australia. Where the hell has this bloke been? More importantly why isn't he with a publishing house?

Dollarman USA Inspirational, one of the best new books I have read. Well done

Just a few of the many genuine comments we have received. None were solicited though all (even the bad ones, which are few) were much appreciated.

Other Books
David T Procter
Will be bringing to you in the future

Forgotten Souls- A Jim Carter story

Dresden Green - A Jim Carter story

.The Smugglers Song - The Prequel to Dead Men Lie

The Kentsman - A continuation of the Stormouth story

The Devils Kiss - The penultimate Stormouth story

The Ties That Bind - The conclusion of the town's story

Mum There's a Red Indian in the Garden - A family history